The Beach Boys
of Sunset Beach

by

Jacqueline DeGroot

Other books by Jacqueline DeGroot

Thank you to my wonderful proofers who gave their time so generously for such a long book. Being shut in during the CO-VID 19 crisis does not mean you have time on your hands. I have been busier caring for my four-year-old grandson now that he has no pre-school to attend. A survey of most of my friends shows being at home means more housework, more cooking, more shopping, and more ideas for home improvement to talk the husband into. So I truly appreciate the week they all gave me to make sure I wasn't driving a train off the bridge. Especially as it was exceptionally fine weather that week, and they had just recently re-opened our beach.

Shaw Berke
Ray Cullis
Bill DeGroot
Peggy Grich
Sandy Payne
Sandy Raymond

The Kindred Spirit Mailbox

The weathered "post office" by the sea has been operating for almost forty years now. What was started on a fragile sand spit near Tubbs Inlet, between Sunset Beach and Ocean Isle Beach, is now an established landmark that thousands of nature lovers visit annually on Bird Island. Hundreds of photographers and artists have trudged to the west end of Sunset Beach—to the nature preserve of Bird Island, and the mysterious mailbox tucked high into a sand dune. And many a beach walker has rested on the roughhewn driftwood bench that invites you to sit and slow down for a while. Yours truly has even penned a romantic murder mystery involving the Kindred Spirit Mailbox.

Before a sand-shifting storm in late 1997 filled in Mad Inlet near Little River Inlet, at Sunset Beach, caution was needed when venturing to the part of Bird Island that resides in South Carolina. Beachcombers have been stranded by the high tide because they were drawn to the Mailbox and the messages left inside, or were spurred on to leave an immortal message of their own. The inlet is no more, so you can walk to the Mailbox at any time. Watch the tides though; it's a brutal walk at high tide—a most pleasurable one at low or mid-tide.

Notebooks, pens and pencils are kept in the mailbox, replenished by a team of secret helpers, so that visitors are able to leave personal messages while they sit and enjoy the sights and sounds of the waves crashing on the shore. It is an unlikely post box, but over the years the exchange of thoughts and ideas has filled thousands of notebooks.

The messages often express the writer's utter contentment with the paradise found there, with the serene beauty of the place, and with the unspoiled wilderness they can count on finding, year after year. Others delve deep into feelings, sharing emotions that run from overwhelming grief to young, exuberant love. It is a favorite place for men to kneel and present their sweethearts with rings. It is a cathartic place to search your soul and purge your thoughts, or gather them together.

Claudia Sailor, from Hope Mills, North Carolina erected the mailbox in the sand at the edge of the ocean after seeing what she called a mirage. She didn't know the purpose of the recurring vision at the time, but many years later when petitions in the form of signed messages left in the notebooks were pivotal in saving Bird Island from development, and turning it into the coastal reserve that it is today, she finally got her answer. Over the years, the mailbox and its upkeep have been credited to Frank Nesmith. A long time local and the man who helped Claudia shore up the first Kindred Spirit Mailbox in 1981, Frank became her close friend and confidant. Several years later he helped move the mailbox to Bird Island to the North Carolina site. Soon after, he and Claudia ended their relationship, as Frank did not want to start another family. Claudia was younger and wanted children. She married a lawyer who worked for the Attorney General in Raleigh. Sadly, her husband died of a heart attack only a year after they were married. She lived the life of a grieving widow with her kindergarten students becoming her children, and in lonely moments, she read the Kindred Spirit notebooks graciously sent to her by Frank.

Claudia had only visited Sunset Beach, whereas Frank Nesmith has been a permanent resident since 1975. He's been active in the community and devoted to preserving the marshes and the coastline that he walked daily until just a few years ago. Frank, along with a handful of volunteers, has collected and replenished the journals for almost forty years. In 2016 Frank received the Order of the Long Leaf Pine, the Governor's highest honor, for his hard work and dedication to helping preserve Bird Island and making it the sanctuary and coastal preserve that it is today.

Claudia *was* the "Kindred Spirit," the mysterious person who put up the mailbox by the sea. Frank faithfully collected the notebooks and sent them to her, treasures, which she lovingly read and saved. Originally, the mailbox contained notepaper and stamped envelopes that she asked visitors to the mailbox to mail to a Shallotte, North Carolina post office box. She collected them on weekends when she came to the beach to visit Frank. Claudia felt that the anonymity going both ways made the Kindred Spirit universal and transcendent, and that it lent to its mystical otherworldly quality. Few people knew the true identity of the Kindred Spirit.

When Claudia died suddenly in January of 2013, the free-spirited kindergarten teacher left behind a legacy that continues to roll on just as the waves continue to roll in. Frank Nesmith is in his 90s, but he and his family diligently continue to keep the mailbox in the sand up and running. Claudia's mirage is now a famous landmark that many return to and many more discover every year.

People have asked what has become of the notebooks that have been collected over the years. Several have expressed the desire to read a book with a collection of the poignant notes and ramblings. I can tell you that, having read through many of the notebooks, it would be a daunting task to catalogue even a small percentage of the messages. Many different hands write them, and they are written in a vast array of languages. Some are barely legible. And of course, there is no continuity as each missive is either a letter of gratitude, a plea of surrender, a heartfelt prayer, a poem of love, thoughts of desolation, a tribute to a loved one, plaguing inner thoughts, or full blown stories that span page after page after page . . .

How do you get to the Kindred Spirit Mailbox? Due to the accreting nature of the beach and frequent storms, the mailbox is now located in the dunes about a mile and a quarter west of the last Sunset Beach public beach access at 40th Street. There are two benches, and sometimes an American flag on a pole is in evidence. Things are constantly changing at the beach, so the flagpole, the benches, or even the mailbox could be a victim of the next hurricane or washout. It is about an hour's walk from the pier. So put on your Nikes, grab a bottle of water and some sunscreen, and *Just do it!* You won't regret it.

The following book is my best attempt to write a few stories from letters left in the Kindred Spirit Mailbox.

Jacqueline DeGroot

The Beach Boys of Sunset Beach

A Kindred Spirit Mailbox Legacy Story

The Cockpit residents and the women
who capture their hearts:

Chaz & Mags
Brent & Alyssa
Cam & Tamara
Dev & Gentry
Palo & Trixie
Kyle & Amy
Sean & Sandy
Rutger & Pauline
Alex & Emma
Deke & Shaw
Ryder & Kara

Chapter 1—Chaz
First to Arrive

The beach house known as
The Cockpit—East End
Sunset Beach, North Carolina
July 2019

Chaz saw her the first day he arrived at the beach, within the first hour, to be precise. He was the first of his group to arrive at the co-op beach house he owned with ten of his friends. He had a quick trip, having commandeered his partner Rick's Cessna rather than drive from Greensboro. He picked up his Jeep at the Ocean Isle Beach Airport storage lot and had a short drive to the house. Seemed fair, Rick, passing over the keys to his ratty old sixties-era plane, as he had made off with Chaz's five-week-old bass boat for three days without even telling him.

It was a great swap though—Chaz managed to get to *The Cockpit* before anyone else, despite having left hours later than everyone else. *And* he would have a freezer full of striped bass and white perch at his disposal when he got back home, courtesy of Rick.

As a bonus, he would also have a full report on how his new boat performed by someone who'd worked the NASCAR circuit to pay his way through school. Rick knew engines—car, boat, or plane—and he knew how to get peak performance by tweaking something or other, while crooning Do Wop to it.

Chaz was unpacking his much-maligned leather duffle when he spotted her out of the floor-to-ceiling window. He was on the top floor of the beach house, in one of the oceanfront bedrooms with a full bath, that he'd taken as a boon for being the first one to arrive.

The beauty's fluff of sunny blonde hair ruffling in the breeze caught his attention and made him turn back to the window in mid-step. His eyes dropped to the sweet curve of her denim-clad ass, then continued down to her shapely tanned legs. Roving up again, he noted the bare expanse of skin from just above her hips to the lime green bow tied between her shoulder blades, and ending at the sun-kissed nape of her neck. Gorgeous tan, he thought, like those caramel chews he loved to suck on. Mmmm . . . that neck. Yes, very suckable. Very lickable. Very kissable. He felt the welcoming flutter of arousal zing through his groin.

There was something earthy about a woman in a tiny string bikini top wearing skimpy cutoffs. It screamed summer and reminded him of pubescent nights spent at the carnival walking behind a gaggle of girls flaunting themselves in barely-there shorts and tight, nearly see-through tank tops. This was no girl though, this was a woman. She walked with a purpose, her arms swinging by her sides, the bright green triangles bouncing slightly and drawing his eyes to her chest when she turned back to kick off her sandals at the access. He stood at the window and watched her, mesmerized. With one hand tucked into the pocket of his own shorts, he couldn't help but notice *Old Faithful* jumping to attention and grazing the side of his thumb. *Down boy, we'll take care of you later—first lunch, then a reunion with the guys, then off to Myrtle Beach and all it has to offer.*

He stood at the window, watching the little vixen's hips sway as she walked down the beach access then turned right and headed west. He watched until she was a tiny speck of green and denim against the mottled tan of the sand. He wished he could have seen her face, but by the time he had spotted her, she had been nearly in profile to him, wearing huge Jackie-O styled sunglasses. In any case, his babe radar had opted to forego the face and had zeroed in on the body instead.

Shallow man, he thought. He turned to finish piling his clothes on the shelves in the eighteenth-century Scandinavian armoire. He'd designed and built the matching bedroom furniture around the piece as his contribution to the house five years ago when he and his buddies bought the lot and constructed the beach house.

He smiled at his self-deprecating thought. Yes, shallow indeed. And he wasn't going to apologize for it. He had two weeks to indulge himself. Two weeks of wine, women and song, as the saying went, and he meant to use every single one of them to further his cause. Which would be to wipe his mind of the concerns that had plagued him the last two years. He had finally got his business off the ground, dealt with settling his father into an assisted living community, and repeatedly dodged the last woman he'd dated, who couldn't seem to accept that he didn't want to see her anymore and was now quasi-stalking him.

What kind of woman bought a wedding gown and put it in a man's closet after their fourth date? He'd finally had to move into his office, shut down his Facebook account, and get a new phone to get away from her. Which reminded him, where was his new cell phone? Brent would be calling soon and he didn't want to miss his call in case he needed a ride from the Myrtle Beach Airport.

Not spotting his phone on the dresser or on one of the night stands, he left the bedroom and ran down the steps to the foyer where he'd piled the rest of his things: a beach tote, a hanging bag, a mini soft cooler, and his electronics carrier, which contained his iPod, MacBook, Kindle Fire, and hopefully, the missing iPhone.

He dug into the side pocket and with a satisfied sigh, pulled it out. He dug deeper and found the book he'd bought to accompany it, *iPhone for Dummies*. Not for the first time, he wondered if he shouldn't have stuck with his old Blackberry and just changed the number. He'd need a week to figure out how to use this little marvel. Good thing his vacation coincided with him purchasing it yesterday.

He took the phone, the book, and the cooler into the

kitchen where he emptied out a six-pack of Coors, a green smoothie bottle—his last in a detox regimen as a prelude to two weeks of mindless eating and drinking—and a collection of yogurt containers he'd brought from home. No doubt he and his buddies would fill the two refrigerators and two freezers with all manner of unwholesomeness as soon as everyone arrived and took their turn grazing the aisles at the local Food Lion.

For now, he enjoyed the starkness of the kitchen— the vast expanse of onyx and lapis granite countertops set off by light maple custom cabinets. With the influx of his highly acquisitive friends, every counter would soon be cluttered with Keurig and Espresso machines, donut makers, waffle irons, juicers, all manner of flavored coffee pods and k-cups, pretzel bags, microwave popcorn boxes, cans of nuts, boxes of cookies and crackers, and every variety of bread, bagels and chips imaginable. He'd heard Kyle was making his own beer and wine these days, so who knew what paraphernalia that entailed.

Chaz's near obsessive desire for simplicity had been the catalyst for his latest business venture, Gnome Homes. He and his partner, Rick, designed and built impossibly small houses where efficiency of space was crucial—where every board, every plank, every panel had to carve out a niche and every space had to have a dual purpose. On the market they were known as tiny homes, and they were becoming very popular across the country as baby boomers simplified their lives and opted for a cottage lifestyle. Their company was one of the first to customize with renewable materials so they were on the fast track, getting national awards for their designs and for balancing ecological concerns with energy savings.

They built houses that ranged from 600 square-feet to 1,200 square-feet, where every inch was trimmed, reevaluated and redrawn until it met his criteria . . . nothing wasted, nothing extraneous, nothing that one could live without. Whether a bungalow, a cottage, a rustic barn, a tree house, or a bunker on the side of a hill, if his company made it, you could be assured you got the most useable inch for each area of living space. It was, after all, how he'd lived his whole life.

He'd always been on the go, even as a little kid, living the minimalist lifestyle, picking up and running from one place to another as he'd followed his dad from one job site to the next, leaving things behind because they'd had to. They often had no way to take them, and no place to take them to.

When he'd made it to college, dorm life had reinforced this pattern of living. Having an 8 x 10-foot space for a bed, desk, dresser, hamper, banker's lamp, and a GT Xpress Meal Maker honed his efficiency skills. Studying wooden jigsaw toys taught him how to create templates to make interlocking furniture pieces with dual purposes, while saving space and making things stronger.

Architectural and Engineering classes taught him which materials he could count on for stress, load bearing, wearablity, and longevity. Forestry classes taught him even more. What rotted and where, what didn't and why. His focus on sustainability and treating the environment as his ever-present benefactor was utmost in his mind whenever he started a new project. To say he loved his work was an understatement. His work was what gave him purpose, what challenged him and drove him. He could not imagine ever doing anything more important, more vital, or more useful for the planet.

He poured a glass of ice water via the door of the huge four-door Profile refrigerator freezer and went out onto the back deck. Selecting a chaise from the group of mesh loungers, covered with pillows and pads in a busy purple and orange paisley print—those clearly must've been Cam's idea—he dragged it over to the west corner so he'd have a view of the sexy blonde should she be returning this way. Opening the *Dummies* book he began to read about the features and functions of his new iPhone.

An hour later, the bright green bikini top drew his eye away from his phone. Programing in new business contacts could wait. He shoved the phone in his pocket and watched as the lady in question came into focus. Several hundred feet away, he knew within a matter of seconds that her gait had changed. She wasn't strolling anymore with a saucy sway of her hips. There was no perky bounce in her step. Her soft looking fluff of blonde hair was now damp and stuck to her neck. She looked as if she was trudging through a quagmire. The carefree swing of her arms was gone now; they were limp and lifeless by her side. Had he been a betting man, he would have wagered she wouldn't make it back before tumbling face down into the sand,

He narrowed his eyes and tried to see her face, but she wasn't holding her chin up. She was staring at her feet as she plowed ahead, seemingly mindless of her surroundings and concerned solely with achieving her target. Then she changed her trajectory. She left the water's edge and was angled toward the dunes, making a beeline for the beach access next to *The Cockpit.*

As the woman struggled in the soft sand near the tideline, she weaved. In the same instant he stood to go down to her, he saw her lift her hand and wave to someone in the house next door. From the angle of her uplifted face, that someone was high up, on a higher level than he was—likely on a widow's walk. He'd noticed earlier that one was hidden by a panel of latticework and bougainvillea blooms. People often screened off areas for nude sunbathing and he'd wondered if that was the case next door. Only the helicopters and drones knew for sure.

He heard a string of ludicrous nonsensical curse words, "Daggit nabshat, umhat a waba," then the hurried scrape of a heavy wooden chair. Urgent footfalls of someone in flip-flops running down three flights of wooden stairs followed. The echoing staccato of the panicked steps had him standing and primed to run down and jump the balustrade of his own terrace, when he saw a tall brunette with a long ponytail leap the hedge bordering the patio of the house next door. She landed upright on the access walkway, bypassing the three steps leading up to it. It was an impressive high jump to say the least.

Arms pumping, she ran down the walkway, ignoring the people who moved aside to let her by. He could see that she had a water bottle in one hand and a cell phone in the other. When she made it to the blonde's side, in the sand shy of her reaching the walkway, they both fell to their knees. The brunette gripped the blonde's face in both hands, her gaze intent. She waved her away and reached for the water bottle that had fallen to the sand.

Chaz watched as she drank from the bottle and the other woman used her gauzy shirt to swipe at the blonde's glistening face. Then the brunette began rubbing the blonde's arms and they put their foreheads together, huddled in the sand.

Hmmm, clearly something going on there. Too intimate a gesture for casual friends. It figured. Two hotties next door and they were lesbian. He wished he had brought the binoculars out to the terrace. He still hadn't seen much of the blonde's face, even though her sunglasses had been pushed off then dropped into her lap by the brunette.

He could see them nodding and talking, and then after a minute they stood, the brunette helping the blonde to her feet. The blonde moved away when the brunette put her arm around her shoulders. He heard a distinct, "No!" to the support offered. Maybe because she realized how harsh she sounded, the blonde reached down and clasped the brunette's hand in hers. They walked the few remaining steps in the sand, and then stepped onto the wooden walkway. With each step closer to the houses that were lined up facing the ocean just past the dunes, their faces came into better focus. When they were twenty feet away the blonde looked up, threw her head back and laughed at something the brunette had said. Chaz had his first full-on view of the blonde's smiling face and the smooth curve of her neck, arched in ecstasy. His knees nearly buckled.

His personal *love map*—the sexual preferences for turn

ons and turn offs that determined what he was attracted to—was admittedly complex at this stage in his life, but he felt it was finally perfected now that he was approaching his mid-thirties.

The list of feminine characteristics he had initially preferred, based on his early experiences and genetic makeup—raging hormones aside—had taken shape when puberty rushed in: brunette, slim, pretty wide eyes, nice teeth and good skin. Wafting a little during the middle-school years, it allowed for any girl who smiled back and appeared to wear a bra. Sadly, his list had shrunk even more during his late teens . . . the smile was no longer necessary, and neither was the bra.

Into manhood, his list had been revised many times. While in high school his peers had helped influence his predilections, but his own attractiveness soon became the major factor in determining his success. While he had been building his lists, so had the girls, and theirs demanded social prominence, athletic prowess, and swoon-worthy cars. He had none of those attributes. He lived in the cheapest apartments his father could find, had no money for gas nonetheless a car, and was never in one school long enough to do summer training, enter tryouts, or earn a position on any team.

But as a graduating senior, his choices soon became unlimited as his height soared, his jaw squared off, and the college scholarships rolled in. He was his own man now. He didn't have to pick up and follow his father anymore. A part time job yielded a lumbering Oldsmobile with a back seat larger than any bed he'd ever slept in. He christened the striped tan and white vinyl seat twice the first night he had the car, with two dates back-to-back—a cheerleader who had never given him the time of day, and a waitress at the diner where he'd stopped to have some pie before going home to pack for college.

During his early twenties he was totally unprincipled and relished the vast variety of companionship that was offered at each bustling college campus he visited. Whatever *Playboy* was selling, he was buying. A few of the women he had dated had even made the college issue for the school he attended. He had relished the idea that his choices were validated by the premier men's magazine, and had enjoyed parading his not-so-modest conquests at a multitude of decadent parties. Then, at a friend's wedding, he'd met Julia and she'd revised his standards overnight. The idea of refinement and class suddenly had merit. He was smitten, and the happy couple was together for two years. Then, through his own boneheaded stupidity, he caused their devastating breakup. After that, he swore off women until finally, a year later, he rejoined the hunt.

He was very discriminating after the loss of Julia. Once attracted to women with long hair, large breasts, bubble butts and long, limber legs, now they had to have class, and care about causes. They had to own cashmere sweater sets and wear real pearls. But try as he might, he couldn't duplicate what he'd had with Julia.

His next phase was demure trendsetters and phony sophisticates, finally going international. He discovered he had a penchant for hot-blooded Latinos and savvy Asians.

He'd been dating a diverse sampling of jetsetters from the professional pool of sales reps he'd met during tiny house conferences when he'd met Lisa, the stalker who'd come on to him while he'd been preparing for a triathlon. He'd never dated an athlete and had been amazed by her stamina. It should have been a hint of what was to come. Like a pit bull, she hadn't wanted to let loose of her prize when he'd wanted to move on. He planned to go back to square one after this vacation: brunette, slim, pretty wide eyes, nice teeth and good skin.

But unbeknownst to him, his love map was once again being redrawn. As he stood watching the two women make their way up the long wooden walkway, laughing and bumping hips, he felt the universe shift.

As early as this morning, if you'd asked him his sexual preferences for a possible mate—for he was beginning to have thoughts of settling down and doing the family thing—he would have said dark and sultry. With hair long enough to wrap around his fist so he could gently tug her head where he wanted to place her mouth. She should be cultured, but with a fun side. With sleek long thighs strong enough to hike mountains, straddle horses, and him—so she'd be able to ride him late into the night. And a sweet side, one that would bend to a child's level to wipe away tears and ruffle unruly curls.

But now, now his body and mind were acting in accord, processing and selecting every facet of this nearly collapsing woman and fitting her as his ideal. Soft, short, flyaway, golden blonde hair; expressive, flared light brown eyebrows, arching like perfectly sculptured wings over brilliant green eyes; a heart-shaped face set off by a pixie nose and lips so full, so rosy pink they mimicked the lustrous lining of a conch shell. Yet somehow frail—petite and small—calling for something primal in him to protect her.

This was not a woman he wanted on top—at least not initially. This was a woman he wanted to dominate and own, one he wanted to claim and keep. He wanted to take her from above and command that she be his, only his. And he knew this so viscerally that it accelerated his heart and made him lightheaded. He had never been possessive of a woman. Hell, one of his favorite kinks had been to share them.

He blinked as the women passed under the shadow of a latticed arbor, and then he heard them making their way up the stairs and into the beach house beside his. Then he heard her laugh. Holy Mother of God. He actually placed his open palm over his heart and held it there. Jesus! Now what, he wondered as he stared out toward the sea, blinking in the brilliant afternoon sunlight. With one look, his love map had been destroyed. Decimated. He knew if he didn't have this woman, no other woman would do. His map . . . a world atlas if he was honest . . . had led him here, to *her*. Now what?

His cell phone rang just then and he reached down to

inch it out of his jean's pocket. He looked down at the display, saw it was Brent and smiled. "Hey Bro, been waitin' for your call. You need a ride or are you on your way?"

"Got a rental car after realizing there's no place in your ratty old Jeep to put my golf clubs. I just got a brand new set in a real nice leather bag, so I sure as hell don't want to put them in that leaky ragtop where only one door locks."

"Aw, *Busty's* been good to us. Trusty . . . reliable."

"You mean rusty and undependable. By the way, did you ever get those brakes fixed?"

"Yes, and it was inspected the last time I was here, if that makes you feel any better. And you know as well as I do that a good coat of rust is the best protection from the elements here."

"Says the man who builds his famous little houses with indestructible Japanese Shou Sugi burnt wood."

"Checking out my website, huh? Wish I could make a car out of it. You can't hurt that stuff. So where are you?"

"Driving on Route 9, just coming off 31."

"Good. I hear a few of the others pulling up out front. God, it's going to be just like old times in the dorm."

"Yeech, I hope not. Those bathrooms were smarmy and not a one of us changed our sheets unless a girl insisted on it."

"We're grown men now. We know how to use Clorox and Tide. Plus, we can afford to buy cleaning supplies and fresh linens now. They were luxuries back then."

"You got that right. We knew what a plunger was but not a bowl brush. Can't wait to hear all about your business, Bro. Heard you're going gangbusters with it and knockin' down awards left and right. See you in fifteen. Hey, save me a good room, will ya?"

"When you designed this house, you said all the rooms would be good."

"Yeah. By good, I meant soundproofed against Cam's snoring."

"Cam says he doesn't snore anymore. Says he had his

deviated septum worked on last year."

Brent laughed. "As if that's the only thing deviated about him. His surgeon should have done a BOGO on him. Seriously, I want the nautical room. Go throw a suitcase on the bed and lock the door from the inside, I'll pick the lock when I get there."

"Roger that. Hey . . . I really appreciate you dropping everything and coming this year." Last year Brent had been in the middle of a huge construction project and couldn't get away. This year he'd planned his latest job around this trip.

"Wouldn't have missed it. Hard to believe it's been ten years, huh?"

"Yeah. Seems like just yesterday we were tossing our hats in the air."

"And tossing our cookies over the balcony," Brent said with a loud guffaw. "Speaking of which, should I stop for some Petrone?"

"Ugh, don't remind me. I'm never doing tequila shots again." Chaz's hand went to his stomach in a reflex gesture at the memory of a night he'd give his first million to forget.

Brent laughed, "We'll see," he said, and then disconnected.

Chaz sat on the edge of his bed and rubbed at a spot on his chest that still ached from the memory. *No we wouldn't see.* He might drink a glass of wine occasionally, and take a sip of champagne at a toast for a friend's wedding, down a few light beers, but never hard liquor—never again. Though Brent had been there that night, even he didn't know how devastating that night had been for him. He'd almost lost his life that night. He *had* lost his girlfriend. One he'd been crazy about during his junior and senior year at Stanford.

He got up to get his empty duffle and walked down the hall to toss it on the bed in the blue nautical room. He pushed in the button on the levered door handle and pulled the door shut just as the rest of the guys began tromping up the stairs.

He leaned over the companionway and called down to

them. "'Bout time you got here. I've already been to the grocery store, rented the canopy, checked the grill, unpacked, and set the thermostats."

"Aren't you the good doobie," Dev called up at him. "Did you perchance scope out the curvy little hotbox watering the plants on the front porch next door? She is one sweet Carolina girl in those cute little boy shorts with that Pelican baseball cap on her sassy blonde head."

Heat as fast as a lightning bolt infused him. "Yeah, I spotted her." He didn't know why he said the next part, it just spilled out, "And because I spotted her first, I got dibs. Those are the rules, Bro. I've been watching her since I spotted her on the beach."

Dev gave him a narrow-eyed look.

Palo, tromping up the stairs after Dev, saw the conflict coming from two men who always seemed to love antagonizing each other, and jumped in. Jostling Dev's shoulder in comrade fashion, he murmured in his thick Italian accent, "There appears to be a consolation prize that's just as pretty, and since brunettes are usually drawn like a magnet to your dark good looks, I doubt you're going to have to work at it overmuch."

Dev looked over at Palo and smiled. "Yeah, they are drawn to me, aren't they?" He boyishly scrunched his nose up at Chaz, then flipped him the bird. "Hundred bucks says I get laid before you do."

Chaz laughed and the boom of it echoed down the staircase and throughout the central part of the house. "I'm looking for quality now, not quantity. And just because she's a looker doesn't mean I want to bed her. Maybe I just want to discuss books and movies." He didn't bother to mention that there seemed to be a distinct possibility that the blonde and the brunette next door might be a couple. And that considering his reaction to seeing her, the upshot of that being the case, it could mean unrequited adoration and a celibate future looming on his horizon.

13

"Ah, she's already shot you down," Dev said as he topped the landing.

"She has not. I haven't met her yet."

"You just said—"

"I said I *spotted* her."

"Oh, just *spotted* her. I'll give you twenty-four hours, after that, I'm moving in."

Like hell you are. "Fine. But then I just might take the brunette, too."

"Oooh," said Cam, from the bottom of the stairs, "Now that's the Chaz we all know and love—king of the double hitters. In your scouting out the lay of the land, did you spot any questionable young men? Make that questing young men."

"I don't have your gaydar Cam, so I really wouldn't know whether I spotted any like types. Last I heard, you were bringing someone to this shindig."

"Nah, he couldn't get out of a gig he was doing in Boston."

They all made it up the stairs, loaded down with a suitcase in each hand and laptop cases slung over their shoulders. Then they began fanning out in search of bedrooms to quarter themselves in. Chaz stood on the landing and watched them each try the door to the locked bedroom, shake their head, and move on.

King of the double hitters. He hadn't heard that in years. But he couldn't deny what had once been true. Often he hadn't been satisfied with one. And neither had Brent. It was one reason they were still so close. You didn't tussle the sheets together with one woman between you and not learn all there was to know about each other. But a lot had changed since college. A lot had changed since that night when he had tossed his hat, tossed his cookies—and due to a large quantity of tequila—irrevocably tossed aside the woman he had been in love with.

Chapter 2—Mags
The Horrible "C" word. No, not that one!

Margaret Ellen, or Mags, as her friends called her, was beginning to feel the effect of the late afternoon sun and the drag of the sand in her calf muscles. She should have remembered that high tide was moving in before she'd left base camp, the posh beach house her sister had bartered for her decorating skills in lieu of rent money so they could celebrate the results of her latest C.A.T. scan, at their favorite place—Sunset Beach.

Mags arms weren't swinging so enthusiastically now. In fact, she was beginning to have doubts about whether she was going to make it back from the Mailbox today without having to call for reinforcements. But really, how ridiculous would that be if her sister had to come get her with their tandem bike?

She patted the pocket that held her cell phone but didn't take it out. She was going to do this, and she was going to do this on her own, every single day they were here. You couldn't have something so life affirming as the miraculous disappearance of every single tumor, dissolving into oblivion, without being thankful and acknowledging the wonder of it all—*every* single day.

No doubt though, despite the gorgeous day, she *was* becoming weary of the walk. Four miles round trip was perhaps too much to tackle this first time out. Yet, she really shouldn't feel this tired; she'd taken a nice long nap after lunch. Still . . . Dr. Balfour had said she would have some lingering effects of the medicine in her system for quite some time. He had told her that a major plus would be that the residual amounts of the Sorafenib would continue to do its work, keeping any new tumors from forming—causing them to dissolve, shrink, soften . . . and then melt and disappear before they had a foothold. All good words for those nasty evil tumors.

Melt was the word she preferred to use. It had become her focus word. She had often sat staring, concentrating on her chest wall and willing those three small remaining tumors to completely dissolve. She had visualized them melting like M&Ms on a bed of freshly steamrolled asphalt—on an August day in Louisiana. Then she would grin as she imagined a summer downpour washing the remnants away—down the drain, deep into the earth. Away from any place a human could touch.

Over the last two years she had learned to use the power of her mind to go deep into her consciousness and envision things the way she wanted them to be instead of the way they were. Her positive thoughts to her negative disease kept her grounded and made her feel less helpless, less like a victim. As if she could have a hand in her recovery.

She had told herself all along that she *would* have a hand in her recovery. And ultimately, she had. She, along with her doctors, had charted a course, and now she was on the sunny side of the beastly mess. Her disease, hemangioendothelioma, known as E.H.E., had been vanquished—for now. She was in remission, although her particular type of cancer could be either waiting in the wings or gone forever. One never knew for sure. She sighed and blinked her eyes hard. She would live the rest of her life waiting to hear if her nemesis had deigned to reappear. It had been in her lungs this time, thirty nodules bilaterally—meaning in both lungs. But it could reappear anywhere, at anytime, or it could leave her alone to become a doddering centenarian.

When she was first diagnosed, there were too many tumors to just go in and get them out, but too few to make her systematic, meaning aware of them and suffering symptoms related to them. She'd been lucky in that aspect. They might not have found them for years if she'd been able to shake the bronchitis that had led to her having that fateful x-ray. Cancer. God, that had been one hell of a way to stop a life that was just showing a helluva lot of promise. She'd just tested for her C.P.A., signed a lease for an uptown office, and moved from her crappy old apartment into a really nice townhouse near the river. And, oh yeah, she'd just gotten engaged.

She'd heard about the stigma of cancer, but had never really thought about it until that day. But that Wednesday afternoon, her emotions ratcheted to the pinnacle, had been a defining moment. Her psyche had been shaken. Her core shifted as if a battering ram had run through her. Within moments, her belief in herself as someone above the cut and working toward the top echelon in her little circle of humanity, had suddenly been shifted. It was almost as if someone had stamped a big REJECT sticker on her forehead. She was defective now, someone to be culled away from the rest of the bright performers and sent away to either be discarded, or put back together in the proper, acceptable manner.

That evening, it hadn't helped her essence of spirit to learn her fiancé now felt her unworthy to wear his ring, that he refused to be there to share this battle with her. He had no problem telling her that he found her lacking now. She no longer fit the role of the perfect society bride he'd had in mind. She was flawed. And he was having no part of that.

But Mags was a fighter. She determined that after all her hard work this was not going to take her out of the game. And she was not going to spend a moment suffering heartache over a man who had turned out to be unworthy. She was glad she'd found out now, that "'til death do us part" did not apply to him.

She treated the news of her illness as if it was a test of some sort, one that required rigid course work much like the classes she had taken in her final year of postgraduate school. The ones that had kept her up late at night and at home on weekends, her nose against the screen of her laptop, her fingers paging through text books that had cost almost as much as her rent.

In the end, the only things she'd lost were her modesty— as it seemed every doctor she saw was focused entirely on her chest, though mostly through scans—and her scumbag fiancé.

He too had been interested in her chest, but certainly not if there was going to be any cutting going on. In fact, he had made it clear that he wasn't going to be onboard for nausea, fatigue, weight issues, or hair loss either.

He'd called and left a message on her answering machine the next afternoon when he knew she'd be at work, so he wouldn't have to talk to her. He'd asked for his ring to be sent back, saying it had cost him three months' income.

Her sister, in high dudgeon, had already taken the ring back to the jeweler and sold it. She had said, "Bloody hell, it might be three months' income to him, but it's nine mortgage payments to you. Let that bastard sue you. When you show up in court bone thin with a bald head, let's see who the judge favors."

She adored her sister, always had. Kara had read reams of material on her disease, taken her to every doctor's appointment, held her hair back from her face over every open toilet, until there was no hair, and made sure her life ran as smooth as it could while she was treated with powerful drugs that left her dizzy and frail. Now that she was recovered, she owed it to Kara to rebound and make her proud.

She saw Kara running toward her now, phone in hand, never hesitant to call for help for her. Seeing the worried look on her face, she forced herself to smile and make it up the beach and into her waiting arms. Yes, she was tired, she had walked way more than she should have. But with Kara's help, she was alive, and she was back. Life was good—so very good.

Chapter 3—Chaz
The Gang's all Here

Brent parked on a spur at the end of the curved driveway fifteen minutes later, and it was chaos as everyone unpacked, carted groceries, and found refrigerator space to cool down the beer or wine nearly everyone had stopped to buy.

Chaz went from room to room saying hi, offering to help out, and getting caught up with his friends from college, who were now his partners in this ginormous beach house. Massive to him, as nearly all the tiny houses he'd built could fit inside this one. His homes averaged 500-800 square feet, whereas this one was closer to 9,000.

Since there were ten partners they had opted not to rent the house out once it was built. Sean and Cam lived close enough to check up on it, and all of them found time to use it at least two or three times a year. Palo liked to bring his family here from Italy for Christmas every other year, and Dev usually hosted a come-if-you're–in-the-neighborhood Thanksgiving dinner for business associates and friends.

None of them needed the extra money or the headaches that came from renting a luxury home to vacationers, so the beautiful, fully appointed beach house stood at the ready should anyone need a break from their fast-paced lives. At a cost of 1.8 million, not including the oceanfront lot, there was a sizeable mortgage payment despite everyone initially ponying up fifty grand. However, split ten ways it wasn't a problem for any one of them.

Brent, as a highly successful architect based out of New York City, had been begging for a place to invest a large chunk of money for tax purposes.

Cam, the closest one and therefore the one with the most opportunity to use the beach house, had been thrilled with the idea. He worked as a producer in Wilmington for the various movies and shows being filmed there.

Kyle, a fabulous chef and restaurateur, who was making mega bucks from his cookbooks, products, and cable shows, was only too happy to have a free hand on designing the kitchen and dining areas.

Sean, the quiet, studious one who was Cam's best friend—but not that kind of friend—was an attorney in Wilmington who represented the agencies that enforced environmental issues. He had secured their loan and oversaw all the paperwork at settlement.

Palo owned a tour company and traveled around the southern United States promoting private tours to Italy, Greece, and Switzerland. He brought back the beautiful Tuscan planters that now held rosemary bushes that sent out a most delightful fragrance whenever someone brushed by them. He told anyone who asked about his college days that he chose Stanford for the city it was in—Palo Alto, rejecting all the other schools he'd received scholarship offers from.

Dev was an arms dealer—a legitimate one—specializing in adapting weapons for military use and training as well as outfitting the United States Army and Navy with the latest technology in sniper rifles, explosives, and GPS systems—the majority of them manufactured at his family's two-hundred-year old weapons plant in Kentucky.

Rutger was a sports enthusiast, and thanks to several lucrative sponsorships and patents, he was independent of work now and spent most of his time running marathons and supporting charity events.

Alex was a contract attorney in L.A. who had twin baby daughters. His wife had died from complications shortly after the babies were delivered. They had lived at Wrightsville Beach at the time, and he had worked in Wilmington, but then he moved to L.A., taking the babies with him the week after they were born. He hadn't made it to the beach house last year, or the year before. In May, he had emailed he'd be coming, only for a few days, but he hadn't confirmed and no one had heard from him since.

Deke had inherited his family's pharmaceutical manufacturing businesses and over the last few years was revamping factories and branching out. As far as they knew, he was still deciding about coming.

And then there was Chaz, the builder extraordinaire, who could design and build anything from a world class hotel or skyscraper, to an expansion bridge, or a hydroelectric dam, but chose to make tiny houses instead.

Chaz was delighted that so many of his friends made it this time. They hardly ever got them all. But Alex and Deke still had plenty of time to get here if their schedules allowed. Although Deke said he'd come this year, he had recently lost his wife. She had been in a coma for two years, so they weren't sure if he would make it or not, and no one wanted to be the one to call and check.

It was a rare thing to get them all in one place these days, when ten years ago, they would have been constantly together, living, studying, and partying in the same dorm—often in the same room. The gathering room in the frat house had become their first "cockpit." They had all missed the camaraderie and vowed to spend at least two weeks together every year when they agreed to build this house together. So far, they averaged eight attendees out of the ten partners.

The idea for the beach house at Sunset Beach had been Brent's. He had created the dream for them with pictures and blueprints, and a portfolio of swatches. And, one-by-one, they'd all anteed in and bought the lot, then construction began. Ten months later, they celebrated by signing their names in concrete on the pad in front of the outside bar.

Brent ducked his head into Chaz's room. "Cam's about to put the steaks on the grill, and I just made a batch of Sweet

Southern Tea. You wanna join me on the veranda to help shuck some corn? Rutger stopped and picked up some heirloom tomatoes and Silver Queen corn on the way here."

"Sure, be right there. I can't seem to find my Kindle charger. I could have sworn I put it on the nightstand when I got here."

"No problem. I brought mine. I'll go get it."

"Thanks." Chaz opened and closed all the drawers again, re-checked the bags he had shoved into the walk-in closet, and went through his electronics bag for the fourth time. *Where had he put it? He could have sworn he'd coiled it and put it on the nightstand. How could it have just walked away?*

"Here ya go. But I'm pretty sure you're not going to have time to read anything tonight. Dev has some big plans: PGA Tour Superstore, Dick's, Bass Pro, Greg Norman's, and that new topless bar down on Seaboard."

"What? No Dollhouse? That's been a first night tradition for years."

"Believe it or not, I think it got shut down. Dev says his cousin came here last month and was raving about this new place, says the girls have costumes in all manner of kink: leather, satin, lace, schoolgirl, librarian, says they even have a nun. I think he's hoping for a girl in camouflage. Should be hilarious."

"Okay, I'll go, but I'm driving Busty. It's been a long day and I'm not into the late night partying like I used to be. Maybe it's having to get up so early to meet all my subs on the sites, or maybe all the random hookups are just getting old . . . you know?"

"Uh oh . . ."

"What do you mean, uh oh?" Chaz asked as they made their way down the stairs.

"When a man wants to leave a tittie bar before the sun comes up, it can only mean one of two things."

"Oh yeah? And what's that?" Sean asked as they stepped into the kitchen, having overheard most of the conversation.

"They've lost their eyesight . . ." Brent began.

"Or . . ." Kyle prompted.

"They're on the prowl for a mate," added Brent.

"What?" Chaz said with a skeptical look on his face.

"Don't you read Tucker Max? He spells it all out."

"Well, he's got it all wrong. My eyesight is perfect and I am not seeking a mate. I am perfectly fine with my dating life, thank you very much . . . except for that latest stalker. I'm hoping that by the time I get back home, she'll have latched onto someone else."

"Wow, you have a stalker?" asked Cam, his eyes wide. It was hard to tell if he was terrified or impressed.

"Sort of. No dead bunny so far, but loud confrontations in restaurants, grocery stores, elevators, parking lots . . . she even showed up at a job site, hardhat and all, just to remind me of all I was giving up. "

"Come out and help me with the steaks, forget about shucking corn, I want to hear *all* about this," Cam said.

Brent handed Chaz a drink. "My specialty. And take my advice, just drink one."

Chaz walked out onto the veranda with Cam and while Cam seasoned the steaks, Chaz removed the grill from its recessed niche and lit it.

As he listened to Cam run on and on about a stalker he'd heard of that had been harassing a woman for five years, he looked out at the ocean, then at the house next door.

The pretty blonde was reclining on a slatted wooden lounge chair on the lawn reading a book. She had angled her chair to face the setting sun and she was facing him as well, albeit two floors below. He could see her slim, tanned legs sliding against each other as she read. It was sensual as all get out. He wondered what she was reading. One of those *Shades of Gray* or *Widows of Sea Trail* things probably. The women he knew liked to read that kind of stuff when they were on vacation. Beach reads, they called them. He often suggested a trip to the local bookstore on day one of a holiday break; he was all for anything that primed the pump.

He walked over to the alcove where he had been working earlier and grabbed the binoculars he'd put there.

"And as I was saying, she tried it all, the police, an attorney, even hired a private detective. She moved twice for God's sake."

"Mmm hmm," Chaz said as he lifted the binoculars to his eyes and focused the lens on the red and black cover of the book she was reading. *Me Before You*. Oh yeah, that title definitely smacked of some smutty porn. He smiled at his superior knowledge of women.

He'd go with the guys and check out the latest golf gear at The PGA Store, look at the boating equipment at the Bass Pro Shop, buy a new racquetball paddle at Dick's, and have a ridiculously expensive dessert at Greg Norman's, before checking out this new bar Dev was raving about. Then he'd make his excuses, come back to the beach house and download *Me Before You* on his Kindle. He'd see what the pretty little filly next door was filling her head with. And he'd be armed with valuable insights into her predilections.

He removed the binoculars and let his eyes linger on her tanned feet, shapely legs, toned thighs, nipped in waist, and the cleavage that was getting full sun, it glimmered as if coated with something greasy, no doubt sunscreen. He couldn't see her face beneath her visor, but her profile was angled toward him. She wasn't as stunning as some of the women he'd dated, with their high-defined cheekbones, sculpted brows, and sensuously made up pouts, but she was cute—fresh looking and sweet, despite being filled out in the chest area like a wholesome tavern girl. Yes, sweet, she looked adorably sweet, in a down-to-earth kind of way.

Always the ones, he thought, smiling, and lifting his glass from a side table. It was always the ones who appeared innocent who were hot to trot and craving a little naughtiness between the sheets, just when you were expecting to have to bring out your full seduction arsenal.

"You're not listening to a thing I've been saying," Cam said.

"I am too," he said. But he hadn't heard a word.

"Then you think it's okay for a man to chase a purple gazelle up a tree and feed it spicy green Doritos?"

"Is that what you said?"

"Word for word."

"Then you're right. I wasn't listening." He laughed and put the drink to his lips, took a big sip and spluttered. With a grimace he managed to gasp, "Jesus, what's in this?"

"Brent's cocktail du jour, Sunset Beach Sweet Tea. A shot and a half of Southern Comfort, Peach Liqueur, Captain Morgan's Spiced Rum, Peach Schnapps, Vodka, and then just to have truth in advertising, a shot of sweet tea he got at the Hardee's on 904. Swears it's the best around."

"God, one of these will knock you on your keister. You want mine? I'm not drinking this, no way." He handed it off to Cam.

"Who's the D.D. tonight?" Chaz asked as he watched Cam add the drink to his big thermal sipper with the metal straw.

"Rutger. He's training for an Ironman competition."

"Hmmm."

"You're looking at her again and not listening."

"You said Rutger is training for an Ironman."

"Doesn't that sound odd to you?"

"No."

"You didn't notice he's in a walking boot?"

"Shit. I didn't. He was sitting on his bed when I saw him. What happened?"

"He chased a purple gazelle up a tree and fed it spicy green Doritos. It pushed him out."

Chaz laughed loud and hearty. "You're an idiot, you know that?"

"But I'm a lovable idiot."

"You are that. Don't overcook my steak. I like it rare."

"I remember. Just seared on each side. Got it. Yours'll be the last on. How 'bout making sure the table's set?"

After checking the table, Chaz went inside to grab the lazy Susan tray that held the vast array of condiments. Ten men—ten ways of preparing steak. He smiled. Ten men . . . ten totally different lifestyles, careers, personalities, and lusts for living.

He placed the big wooden server in the center of the table and looked over his shoulder at the patio below. His own lusts were peaking just knowing that the woman on the lounger was reading about the order of orgasms.

Chapter 4—Chaz
Chow Time

They managed to get everyone seated at the double-sized masonry picnic table that Chaz and Kyle had custom ordered as a house-warming gift. They'd had it delivered when they all came to stay for two weeks, right after the walk through and closing. The two had tiled it over and glazed it themselves, using blue and yellow sunflower patterned pieces from Tuscany that Kyle had leftover from one of the restaurants he'd renovated. It was a one-of-a-kind table with a center starburst of a mosaic patterned after their alma mater—the dark green tree representing Palo Alto, superimposed over the cardinal colored S, representing Stanford.

As they dined on perfectly turned steaks, platters of sliced tomatoes with fresh basil and mozzarella, fresh buttered corn on the cob, and a giant-sized bag of Tater Tots someone found in the storage room freezer, they caught each other up on their day-to-day lives.

Rutger was indeed competing for the Ironman in Florida in a few weeks, so his food regimen had been shifted to the Paleo diet. He ate two steaks and what would have been equivalent to two whole tomatoes after scraping off the cheese and pushing the tomato seeds to the side of his plate. "I have a partner I'm training with and there's a group of us who meet once a week to plan out the trip, and to keep everyone pumped. Other than work, that's all I've got going on right now. That and this stupid foot. Can't wait to get this thing off. "

"What d'ya do to it?" Kyle asked through a mouth he was filling with steak.

"Something with the outside tendon. Turned my ankle on a curb and thought I had just bruised it really bad. I'd actually done a lot worse."

"So it's going to be all right?" Chaz asked.

"Oh yeah. This isn't going to keep me down. Should be able to take it off by the time I get back. Sucks that I can't run on the beach though."

"And how is work?" Brent asked.

"Gangbusters. Got a few more kiosks going up in malls in Georgia, and we're setting up to headline at the convention centers in six states next month. People seem to like the new designs of the iPad covers and we're having a hard time keeping iPhone cases and ear pods on the shelves in some locations, so it's all good. I bought out one of the last two investors six months ago so he could pay his ex-wife an alimony settlement. I only have one partner now, and he pretty much let's me run the whole show. It's all pretty sweet right now. I've got good health, good wealth, and good friends." He raised his water glass and everyone else raised their drink glasses in response.

"How about you Cam, how's it going in movie wonderland?"

"Wilmington is the place to be right now. Lots going on. Had a set-down with Travolta two weeks ago, he's about ready to sign on for two new movies . . .."

The back and forth banter continued between hearty bites and long slugs of beer as eight happy, randy guys one-upped each other, commiserated, and planned beach parties and dalliances.

Chaz watched it all as he took bites of his perfectly grilled porterhouse, giving Cam a high-five with his fork for his culinary effort. It was great to be here with his friends at the house they all had a hand in building, designing and financing. They were a family of sorts, a brotherhood to be sure, especially for him, as he'd had no brothers and hardly a friend until high school. His father was gone now, and his mother was never really in the picture, so he couldn't help but cleave to the only semblance of family life he'd ever had. Even if every principle person in it had been either deranged, drunk on his ass, in the throes of lust driven debauchery, or stoned. But they had been his and he theirs. They were all calmer now, settled into careers and successful in their own fields. Although most would tell you they were happy, he knew they truly weren't. They were all on the prowl for mates, every last one of them. He could see it in their posturing, their far off gazes over the dunes, their talk of women, decidedly in a more respectful way. It was mating season, for all of them. Except for Alex, who had already won his lady fair and then tragically lost her. And Deke, who had shared the same fate.

After this afternoon, he felt as if he might be first at bat. His body and inner spirit had never responded to a woman as it had today. On first sight. And of course, dreamer that he was, he convinced himself it was love. That she was his soul mate. That he might have found the woman who could complete him in ways no other person on earth would. He just had to meet her and then convince her that she felt the same way about him, all within two weeks. Unless of course, she was gay, then he had a lot more convincing on his plate than he could manage in two weeks.

When everyone stood to clear the dishes, he took the long way around to go back inside the house. He looked down at the yard next door. The blonde had the book she was reading raised high in the air, shielding her face from the lowering sun, now angled into her face. She was curled on her side and the way her plaid shirt was gaping allowed him to see the stunning swells of her upper breasts. Her legs were restless in her short ratty cutoffs and he could only imagine what she must be reading to make her rub them against each other in such a sensual way. She turned just then and saw him looking down at her. He winked. And then Brent bumped his elbow and the plate in his hand almost shot out like a Frisbee, only a quick grab kept it from toppling from his hand and ending up in the yard below

"You idiot," Chaz grumbled as he turned to face him.

Brent laughed. "Lovely to see your eyes all glazed over

like that. When you gonna make your move? Think she might be a candidate for a ménage?"

Chaz felt a charge go through him, it was one part simmering anger, one part irrational fury, and two parts jealously and abject possessiveness, all of which did not make sense as he didn't even know the woman's name. "Don't worry about my timing you sleaze bag, and I'm not doing anymore threesomes, you know that. They're history."

"Because of Julia," Brent murmured.

"Yeah. She didn't deserve that."

"She asked for it Chaz, she asked us both for it," he said defensively.

"Yeah well, she was drunk and we took advantage. She didn't really know what she was asking for."

"She was one of our best."

"Yeah well, when the sun came up, turned out she was one of my worst," Chaz said as he elbowed Brent out of the way and went into the house.

It had been a sore spot between them for ten years. Brent had never been contrite. It hadn't cost him a thing and he'd always thought Julia was all-wrong for Chaz anyway. After the breakup, they'd managed to stay friends because they were roommates and neither had the money to go out on their own. But their sex lives were separate and distinct now. A mark of maturity for two men who had decided early on that no woman would come between them, that their friendship was for life, whereas the women were not. Brent had not known that Chaz had been considering asking Julia to marry him. There had never been a point in telling him that he already had and that she had been wearing his ring when they both took her.

He often wondered about Julia. What she was doing now. Whether she had married. Whether she had regretted leaving him. Whether she had forgiven him for being such an ass in allowing another man have her.

After rinsing his dishes and placing them in one of the

open dishwashers, he walked back out to lean on the rail and look down at the woman wiggling her body off the lounger as a call came from inside the house next door. "Mags! Dinner! Last time I'm calling."

"Coming!"

Her voice was dulcet. *As sweet as her expressions, as honeyed as the tan on her body, as soft as the breeze bringing in the tide.* He sighed. Dear God, he was making up poetry now. He was a goner. He couldn't waste any more time. Tomorrow he needed to meet this woman. Who, no doubt, would own his dreams tonight.

Chapter 5—Mags
Life's a Beach

Was there anything better than a good book, a glass of wine, and a fine ocean breeze? Mags put down her book, arched her back, turned her neck, and stretched lazily in the creaky old lounger. She sighed and dreamily closed her eyes. If she hadn't closed her eyes just then, she'd have seen the man two floors above staring down at her with a hunger in his eyes that would have slayed a lesser woman.

She was so in tune with her body now after all she'd been through, that she truly appreciated the times when everything felt perfect. Tonight was one of those times. Nothing hurt. When at times everything had hurt, even her hair—which hadn't even been there at the time as it had all fallen out.

She rubbed her legs together, enjoying the slick feel of the lotion she'd applied after waxing them this afternoon. It had taken a long time for the hair on her legs to grow back after the chemo treatments, and one wouldn't have thought she'd have reveled at the sight of the short uneven dark stubble when it reappeared, but it meant so much more now. It was one more milestone toward normalcy. She'd let it grow for weeks before finally using the wax strips she'd brought with her. Not that anyone would be feeling her legs anytime soon. She wasn't ready for that. But as she ran a shin over a calf muscle, she purred and couldn't help smiling. She was going to be okay.

The smell of charbroiling steaks wafted down to her. Her tummy growled, reminding her that she hadn't eaten anything but a bowl of fruit since returning from her walk. She stretched and felt her book fall off the lounger to the small patch of grass that served as the back yard. She opened her eyes and blinked, taking in the setting sun priming itself to sink behind the houses.

She heard voices, male voices, overlapping and talking

all at once. Laughter and loud snorts, a congratulatory whoop, a series of handclaps. It did her heart good to hear people having fun, and the good-natured arguing and snippets of banter passed through her sleepy head: "You should talk, Bro." "Never in a million years." "I swear, I couldn't have imagined so many people." "And there we were, stuck on the highway, when who should come along . . ." "So I made this huge dessert, took me all day and they dropped it," "Chaz, put the binoculars down, you're creeping me out Stalker Boy," "Shut up Dev."

When she finally opened her eyes and got them into focus, she found herself staring up at a man who was leaning over a railing and smiling down at her. She was instantly aware of how her legs were shifting on the lounger and she stilled them. He winked and her eyebrows went up in surprise. He grabbed for something, gave a small wave, turned, and walked away from the rail. As he unfolded and stood to his full height, she saw that he was tall, very tall, with lots of dark hair that lifted in the evening breeze. He was dressed beach casual in a blue chambray shirt, open at the collar. But it was his eyes that drew her. And the sexiest wink she'd ever been on the receiving end of. She closed her eyes and dozed again.

A few minutes later when she opened her eyes, she could see a lot of men standing on the upper deck, all with dishes in their hands walking through the open sliding door and entering the house. The dark haired man in the blue shirt was nowhere in sight. She wrapped her hands up over her head, attaching them to the edges of the lounger, and stretched again. She heard her sister call to her. She even heard herself answer her. But it felt too good to go in yet. She closed her eyes and listened. A few minutes later she heard several cars start up and then men calling out things, back and forth somewhere far behind her. She strained to hear, but wasn't able to make out what was being said. A final door closed on the backside of the house, and a truck engine roared to life. Then there was the eerie silence of a house that had just emptied out.

She ran her legs over each other again like a grasshopper calling for a mate, and she smiled. A man had winked at her. A very handsome man at that. Her reaction to his smile and wink was the first sign that she was ready to be welcomed back into the world of womanhood. She might even like to smile and wink at a man, now that she had her life back and she wasn't afraid of losing it anymore. She might even want to flirt and dance and be a carefree woman again. Especially with a man as good looking as the one who winked at her.

She watched as the sun went lower in the sky, the surrounding area becoming a palette of a thousand colors, then lighting the barest edge before closing down the show for the night. She sighed and smiled when she heard her phone ring. She turned to look over her shoulder at her sister, who was standing on the second deck of the beach house with her cell phone to her ear.

She picked up her own phone from the side table, slid her finger along the screen and accepted the call, then said, "You've reached Paradise, how may I help you?"

"You can get your butt up here, dinner's ready. Manhattan Deli Pasta Salad, homemade applesauce and chicken done right."

"I want a steak," Mags mewled as she turned and shielded her eyes so she could face her sister.

"Really? You haven't had red meat in months."

"Can we have rib-eyes tomorrow? And a baked potato?"

"Wow, really? Sure. I'd love that."

"Maybe grill some corn on the cob?"

Kara snapped her phone closed and called down, "Geez. What's gotten into you? For months you've insisted on eating healthy." She crossed her arms along the rail and smiled down at her older sister who had finally gotten up and was now dragging her lounger up the tiny lawn. Her beach bag was hefted high on her shoulder bumping her hip with each tug.

"Want to be naughty, do wicked things," she said with a laugh.

"And you decided eating red meat is wicked?"

"Well . . . I'll start with that and see where it goes." She chuckled again, then gasped to catch her breath.

"I knew when you were waxing that you were on your way back. No one puts up with that kind of pain unless they're getting ready for some action."

"No, no action. But I might want to dance on the beach under a full moon this Sunday night, just you and me, like we used to when we were kids."

"To Santana?"

"Yeah! That's the ticket."

"I'll download some songs to my phone. Hey, you need some help? You're huffin' and puffin'."

"Nah, this dang chair is heavier than I thought. Musta been made in the 40s. I'll put it away and be right up."

"Just leave it there. I'll get it. The wine is breathing."

"That's creepy. Tell it to stop."

Mags folded the old timey wooden lounge chair, stowed it in the storage room under the house, and hung her towel on a clothesline that ran from the steps to a rafter, then made the trek up two flights of stairs. She was winded, but in a good way. Her lungs didn't burn, they filled easily and she expelled fully. Nothing was wrong except that their landlord hadn't heard of aluminum lawn furniture.

It had been a bout of bronchitis that had sent her to her doctor's office, where a chest x-ray had revealed her real problem. Ever since, just to be defiant, she often over expended her breathing, making sure everything was okay in that arena. She hadn't experienced any tightening in her chest once the antibiotics had done their job and cleared out the infection. And if she hadn't seen the x-rays and scans in the weeks following, she would never have believed she had so many tumors growing in her lungs. She drew in another deep breath, this one tinged with brine, hot sand, and a whiff from her sweat-laden suntan slicked skin—all reminiscent of wonderful beach smells from summers past.

As she finished her climb upward, she looked over at the house next door. She could see flashes of furnishings through some of the windows on the side facing theirs. Each room that faced the ocean had its own deck with sitting areas done up with either heavy rattan furniture or massive wooden Adirondack chairs fitted with colorful cushions. Complimenting loungers and side tables were scattered about, inviting one to settle with a drink and stare out to the sea.

Everything about the beach house next door screamed class; it was huge, with clean lines, freshly decorated in trendy colors and impeccably styled with every surface as pristine as if it had just been power washed—sitting at the ready, the windows gleaming in the waning sunlight, waiting for someone to come to the beach and occupy it. It was obvious that there was a lot of money tied up in that house. She'd been admiring it earlier, envying the people who could afford such a big slice of paradise and not even be here to enjoy it. It had been quiet and empty then, and she'd thought it such a waste. It did her heart good to know there were people in it now. People having fun. Very rich people, apparently.

She shook her head and admonished herself. She, of all people, had so much to be thankful for. Yes, the house next door was nice, very nice, but so was this one. It had the same view; the same beach to relax on, and the same sun that was now settling on the horizon. The same one that had been gently bronzing her skin all afternoon—it was one and the same. She remembered her mother always saying less was more. And her father, bless him, always telling his girls to simplify their lives and find more time for family. It took her cancer to rear its ugly head for them all to finally do that.

She reached into the recesses of her brain and brought forth one of the gazillion pieces of trivia from her treasure trove of mindboggling facts that never failed to put things in perspective for her: *an eight-ounce glass of water has more atoms in it than there are eight–ounce glasses of water in all the oceans of the world.* The vast sea right in front of her had her marveling and trying to comprehend such a profound statement. The one that followed almost always shut her mind down with its associations: *there are more stars in the universe than all the grains of sand found on all the beaches on earth.*

On the landing, she stopped to look out at the churning sea. We are so small and so insignificant in comparison, she mused. Except to our God. To Him we are everything. She reminded herself that she needed to be thankful for all she had right now, for all the prayers that had gone out on her behalf. She had a great job that she loved, a nice home, good friends, wonderful parents, and a devoted sister who had dropped everything to help make her well. Last month Kara had bartered her talents for this beach house so they could celebrate her recovery, and today, her sister had spent the afternoon making her favorite pasta salad, even though now all she really wanted was a nice juicy steak.

Tomorrow. Tomorrow they would have steak. And tomorrow she would fantasize about the handsome man who had winked at her and made her think falling in love and feeling like a woman again could be in her future.

Chapter 6—Chaz
Boys' Night Out on the Town

Chaz sat at the bar with Rutger, both nursing glasses of tonic water with lime slices and watching their buddies make fools of themselves over topless and semi-bottomless dancing girls. They did indeed have a wide variety of offerings, from harem girls to cowgirls, cheerleaders to nurses, dominatrix to schoolgirls in uniform. But none appealed to either man. Rutger was in training and he would not allow his edge to be diminished in any way. Not until after the Ironman. Chaz, well Chaz was thinking of only one thing now. Getting back to the beach house and downloading *Me Before You*, so he could give a book report to the blonde beach bunny next door when he saw her on the beach tomorrow.

"Look at Dev!" Rutger said pointing. "He's got that girl's hair stuck in his zipper. Wow, is that going to hurt, pulling that out."

Chaz followed Rutger's pointing finger and saw the kneeling woman trying to get her hair loose. Dev was trying his best to help, but the zipper wouldn't budge.

"Uh oh. One of the bouncers is going over."

"He looks like he's going to tear Dev out of his pants."

"Here take this," Rutger said, and slapped a Swiss Army knife in Chaz's hand.

"What am I supposed to do with this?"

"Cut her hair way from the zipper before Dev gets his face pummeled. With this walking boot, I can't get there fast enough. Go!"

Chaz did as he was told, getting to Dev before the bouncer could and opening the knife.

"What do you plan on doing with that?" Dev asked, his eyes huge as he focused on the shining blade.

"What do you think asshole?" Chaz said as he grabbed

the girl's hair just above where it was tangled in Dev's zipper, and with one quick jerk of the knife freed her. "Now let's get the hell out of here before that bruiser gets reinforcements."

Dev shot up out of the chair, shoved some bills at the girl, and while tugging frantically at his zipper, made his way out the door.

It was just after midnight and Chaz was ready to go back to the beach house. He had only one taker as the rest wanted to continue on to the next stop. So Sean and Chaz drove the long way back, staying on Business 17 and enjoying the sights along the main drag. They talked about Sean's job and how stressful it was getting to be, how he wished he'd never made partner and had just stayed in his small little office grinding out the paperwork instead of having to do corporate litigation for people too rich to care about anyone but themselves. And they talked about their dreams for the life they wanted to come home to every night, one that would make them feel as if they mattered.

The Jeep bumped along the roads through Calabash and along Beach Drive, and then up Shoreline until they got to Sunset Boulevard where they turned left to get to the roundabout that led to the bridge. Riding the crest to the top of the bridge, they looked at each other and smiled. Chaz said, "Troubles aside, how cool is this? Look where we are. Look where we live!"

Ten years ago, both had to scrimp and save, and deliver pizzas on the weekends to pay for used textbooks.

At the top of the bridge they lifted their arms up to the night sky and hollered, "We own this! We got a piece of this! Wahoo!"

They laughed all the way down to the bottom of the bridge, and were still chuckling when they pulled up in front of *The Cockpit*. Chaz stopped at the bottom of the drive to drink in the sight of the impressive beach house. They both emitted a huge sigh of reverence. Then they elbowed each other at their childishness, slapped their hands on the roll bar and pulled themselves up to take it all in, like a ship's captain at the wheel.

Standing on the floorboard, they reached high with both hands and stretched their fingertips out to the moon, not quite full yet. They knew they had already touched it. Knew how blessed they were.

Chaz retook his seat and parked the Jeep, then helped Sean up the steps as he said he was beginning to feel the effects of the last few drinks. Chaz could just see him taking a tumble and cracking his head open on the pavers, so he held him tight to his side and watched each placement of Sean's Ferragamo loafers before going up to the next step.

Chaz laughed at Sean when they got inside and saw that he had his shirttails out and one of his suspenders unclipped. "Never seen you mussed man. One day, when we get that dream life come true, promise me you'll stop wearing a coat and tie everywhere. You planning on swimming like that tomorrow?"

"No, I packed swim trunks."

"Bet they're pinstriped."

"No. At least I don't think so. I asked my secretary to buy some for me. I didn't have time to go shopping."

"God, wouldn't it be funny if she bought you a Speedo!"

They both laughed hilariously while Chaz got Sean up to his room, got him undressed and into bed.

Then Chaz went to the bar off the kitchen, opened a bottle of the red Kyle had been bragging about and went upstairs to find his Kindle so he could download and read the naughty book the pretty neighbor lady was reading. He used the cord Brent had loaned him, and again, he wondered where his own charger cord had gone.

Chapter 7—Chaz & Mags
The Meet and Greet

Breakfast was not a family affair the next morning. Most of the guys didn't even get in until 4 a.m. and one was still unaccounted for. Apparently, Cam had disappeared to go to the men's room at one of the tittie bars and hadn't been seen since. Brent had received a text shortly after three that they were to go home without him, that he'd see them at the beach house later. Everyone assumed he had grown bored with naked women and had set out to find a naked man.

Despite being up until 3:30 reading, Chaz was still the first one up. A Bloody Mary seemed called for since it was the first full day of vacation and he didn't have to go anywhere. He was sipping it on the veranda when he spotted his sexy little blonde making her way to the water's edge, a travel coffee mug in one hand, a beach chair on a strap on her shoulder, and the telltale red covered book in her other hand. He smiled. He'd already finished it, whereas apparently, she had not.

He put on his bathing suit, made a fresh drink for courage, grabbed a towel and went down to the beach.

He walked by her, and then turned as if recognizing something, and said, "Is that *Me Before You?*"

Startled, she looked up from her beach chair. Then smiled. "Yes, yes it is. Have you read it?"

"I have. It's a great book. Where are you at in it, I don't want to spoil anything for you."

"They're on vacation at that wonderful beach she found."

"Oh yes, Mauritius. Lovely place. When I flew into Sir Seewoosagur Ramgoolam International Airport I knew I had entered a whole new world. It was a delightful vacation."

It hadn't actually been a vacation. He'd gone there to arrange for a special type of wood for a showpiece outdoor bar he'd designed for a crazy eccentric widow who was building a beachfront villa in Boca Raton, one who had more money than sense.

"Wow, you've actually been there. The way Clark describes it, it's a place I would love to go to someday."

"You know when I first heard about this book, from the title I thought it was something like Fifty Shades, you know, me . . . before you . . ."

She laughed. "Well, I can see how that might occur to someone . . . a selfish someone . . . .me . . . before you." She laughed again and this time he laughed with her.

"It's an expected statement coming from a woman— from a man, well that would be extremely ungallant of him." He shot her his best smile.

"Jo Jo Moyes is most definitely a woman, I read her bio online. While I haven't finished the book, I'm far enough in to it to safely say it's definitely not erotica."

"No. But it sure is a damn good book. Aren't you staying in *The Big Blue Crab*?"

"Yes. And you're in *The Cockpit* right?"

"Yes. I own it with several friends."

"Are you all pilots?"

"Mmmm no. Two of us fly, but none of us are professional pilots."

"So why the . . . oh . . ."

He grinned at her. "Yes, we all have that in common. That part of the male anatomy."

She blushed from her neck up to her ears.

"I'm Chaz Russell." He reached down with his hand. We're here for two weeks. There will be eight to ten of us, from all over the country. We went to school together—Stanford."

"Margaret Collins. Everyone calls me Mags. My sister Kara and I rented the beach house next door for a month, or rather she did. Actually, she bartered for it."

Her sister. So . . . not gay. Or at least not necessarily.

"Bartered huh? That's unusual. What did she use in exchange?" He looked up as a woman approached. The brunette. Her ponytail swinging furiously as she walked, her legs churning up the sand as if marching to the sea. Mags turned to see who he was looking at.

"Oh, here's Kara now. Kara, this is one of our neighbors, Chaz Russell."

"Hi," she mumbled in his direction, her arrogant manner more than apparent. She ignored him and bent down before Mags. "You didn't take your multivitamin, so I thought I'd bring it down to you."

"Kara, you didn't have to do that. "

"*Yes,* I did."

"*No,* you didn't. I'd have gotten it later, it's not that important."

Hmmm, were they really arguing about a multivitamin? Why was that so timely? Why couldn't it have waited? Odd, very odd. Unless Kara was the opposite of a wingman.

"Chaz has read *Me Before You,*" she said to Kara. "After I finish it we're going to talk about it, right?" She nodded at him as she addressed her question toward him.

"Sure. We can do that."

"I'll make short work of it then, maybe by tomorrow."

"I look forward to it." Sensing he wasn't wanted, at least not by Kara, he waved and left to find a spot in the sand to place his towel. And there he sat, propped up on his arms, his legs stretched out in front of him, sipping his Bloody Mary, and staring out at the ocean foaming the beach, and wondering what Kara's role was and why she was so protective of her sister.

Chapter 8—Emma
Flash Forward to a Flash Back

Whump . . . whump . . . whump . . . whump . . . whump . . . whump. She ran at the water's edge, listening to her Nike-clad feet land before pushing off from the sand with each footfall. Feeling the rising sun warm her back through her cropped t-shirt, and the cool breeze lifting her ponytail, she pushed on. She was desperate to get there. Out of all the "emergency" trips she'd made to The Mailbox over the years, this one was the most desperate.

Her sneakers continued to pound the sand and imprint a distinctive toe divot; a leftover from the long loping gait she'd developed doing cross-country in college. Despite telling herself she wouldn't cry anymore, tears drenched her face. The sheen of her perspiration mixed with her salty tears stung her eyes, so she lifted the edge of her t-shirt and lowered her face to dab at it. When she looked up again and got her bearings, she saw the American flag, far off in the distance, waving in the breeze.

It had always been a welcoming sight, that majestic flag wavering in the wind, high above the dunes, but today it meant more. It meant sanctuary—a place to collapse—a refuge to empty her heart and to confess her deceitful deception. She pumped her arms and spurred herself on, eating up the last several hundred yards even faster. She hated running now, but she had to get to The Mailbox.

Her eyes fixed on the outcropping along the erratic dune line, she arrived at her destination, winded but relieved. She fell in a heap at the base of the rustic mailbox, tucked into a dune that was now inundated with the morning sunshine. The force of the breeze at the water's edge didn't reach far into this recessed niche, so she quickly felt the hike in temperature. The air was already stifling on this hot July morning. The heat waves rose from the baking sand, hinting at the extreme temperatures to come.

Emma sat with her knees tucked under her, her arms gripping the battered pole the mailbox was mounted on. Sand stuck to the sweat on her legs and collected under her manicured fingernails as she smoothed the sand at the base of the weather-beaten wood. She felt her desperation ebb and wane with the tide moving along the shoreline and dug her fingers into the crevices notched into the pole while trying to catch her breath.

She knew that this was the original pole, hewn from driftwood and dragged down to the beach almost forty years ago by a young woman and her friend named Frank. The woman had not been that much older than she was now. That woman, who had looked liked a young version of Ava Gardner was Claudia Sailor, and she had been full of life, excited about her promising future as a kindergarten teacher. Not so Emma. Not anymore. Instead, she was filled with fear about what lie ahead for her. At that moment, she didn't see how her future could look worse.

As she knelt and clung to the pole with both hands, she gave in to the sobs, her chest heaving from the effort. The words she had repeated to herself for two days choked out of her parched throat, "What have I done?" she cried out.

Not caring that the wind was taking her words, she sniffed back the tears that were making her nose run, and threw her head back to look toward heaven for help. The clear blue sky attested to the fact that while she was full-out grieving, the rest of the world was being treated to a near perfect summer day.

She gave in and collapsed, burying her head in her hands and letting her tears overflow her arms to drip onto the sand. When the wind shifted with the tide and she still continued to sob about how she'd ruined everything, she heard voices.

She lifted her head and wiped her face with the sweat-soaked t-shirt she had taken off. She heard the voices again— soft, low voices getting louder with each step closer . . . female voices, lilting with laughter.

She pulled herself up, locking her elbows to support her. She had to remember that this was not *her* Mailbox, it was everyone's . . . and more visitors were coming.

Saying a prayer to the Lord to please help her do this, because she couldn't stand the pain any longer, she reached for the handle to open up The Mailbox.

Exhausted, her body depleted by the hard run after her overnight flight from L.A.—followed by the worst crying jag of her life—she barely had the strength to pull open the door. Taking a cleansing breath that ended in a hiccup, she took out a notebook that appeared to have only a few pages of writing in it and fished inside the mailbox for a pen. She checked to make sure the ink wasn't dried out by making a few lines on the cover.

She thought about sitting on the bench but decided against it. She sniffed with disdain at the thought of visitors on vacation, tourists having a good time, carefree people doing their ritual walk to Bird Island, being in "her space" and being cheerful. How she envied them. Every year, traipsing down to The Mailbox to write in the journals about how beautiful the beach was, how perfect things were here on this coast, and how much fun they were having on their vacations at Sunset Beach. She had no patience for people who were happy right now. She was in so much emotional pain that she was sure she couldn't stand to see smiling, cheerful faces. Nor could she stand to have people see her . . . sense their pity, or worse, offer to help. There was no help for this.

She brushed sand from her arms and looked down in time to see a crab scurry off into a hole two feet away. She sighed and pushed off, forcing one foot in front of the other through the clumps of sand. She dodged the newcomers trudging up the small rise, and made her way to the water's edge, then reached for the hydro flask on her hip. The water was still cool, despite the ice having melted long ago. She took a few long, reviving sips and recapped it.

She faced the ocean and walked with heavy labored steps to an area with firm packed sand where the waves were gently skimming the shore. She watched the steady, unending undulations come and go, curl and uncurl while displacing pieces of shell and sand. She was dying inside, but did the world notice? No, not here. The waves continued as if nothing had happened. They went in and out as they always did, never tiring, never giving up. Orchestrated from the beginning of time to repeat the cycle into infinity with no mind to the woman at the edge, dying on the inside from a pain so sharp it threatened to eviscerate her.

She plopped down, her long legs folding Indian style in front of her as her butt hit the damp sand. Vaguely recalling her yoga instructor's words to "Find your sit bones and mind your posture and you can sit for hours," she settled into the sand.

She threw her shoulders back and breathed deeply. She stared out at the sun as it continued on its inevitable arc high across the sky. It hurt a little because it was so bright. Of course, she had forgotten her sunglasses. Another pang lined up to join the rest when she remembered where the sunglasses were—in a case over the visor in Alex's Lexus, back in L.A.

She deserved the burn of the sun on her retinas. It would be her punishment—one of them anyway. The big yellow sun, reaching high into the sky, didn't seem to care that she was lost. That she hurt. That she needed to scream from the stupid, stupid thing she had done. When she closed her eyes she could still see the sun through her lids, forcing more tears to gather in her eyes and cascade down her face. Stupid to go blind though, she thought, lowering her head. She would need her vision to write this mournful tale of woe.

She stuck the end of the ballpoint pen into her mouth and clicked it open and closed against her teeth. Then remembering that it wasn't her pen, and could contain a mishmash of germs, she pulled it out and chewed on her lip instead. There was nothing left but "the tellin'," she told herself. When they found her dried out corpse here in the sand they would want to know why. And maybe "the tellin' " would help. After all, thousands had come here before her to pour out their hearts into these journals by the sea at the Kindred Spirit Mailbox. Many had shared their sorrows with the universe. Now it was her turn. She gave a derisive snort.

Her tragic drama would rival Ana Karenina's, if there had been a kindred spirit post box for her to put her story in, back there in sub-arctic Russia. As Emma shifted the sand around her to conform to the shape of her bottom again, she thought of Ana. They shared the same stupid gene. Neither had seen disaster of this magnitude on the horizon, but even if they had, they had been helpless to save themselves.

Emma sighed deeply. She had ventured to The Mailbox many times, pen in hand, to write her thoughts du jour, never afraid to expose her fears, share her worries, or express her appreciation—because she believed in the Kindred Spirit. God was here, because, of course, He was everywhere.

But here, she knew how to talk to Him. It was easier here to confess, to beg forgiveness . . . to pray and plead for understanding. Because this was her church. And she had to do this. She had to find a way to move on. Because if things didn't get better, she could not continue like this. She couldn't live like this. She simply could not stand this kind of pain going forward.

The hot licking flame that wrenched her gut and ate at her from the inside, never abated. It only grew and devoured. It would be the end of her. But she was strong. She would do this. She clicked the pen a final time and opened the journal to the first blank page. Over the course of a week, she told her story.

Chapter 9—Emma
Telling Her Story to the Kindred Spirit

July 19, 2019

Dear Kindred Spirit,

I hurt. But I should hurt. I did an awful thing. So bad I doubt I can write about it. But I will try because I don't know what else to do. Here goes:

The beginning of summer I lost my job. I am an actress. I also do some modeling, mostly lingerie and swimsuits for Macy's and J.C. Penney—scanty stuff, but not naked, never naked. I have the body now, and it's good money. In a few years . . . well, younger bodies will prevail.

I trained as a singer through high school and college, took piano lessons after school for seven years, and went to gymnastics camp during the summers, but I've been a dancer all my life. I have won many dance trophies. When I went to New York City I thought I had a shot at being a Rockette. But the job I managed to land my first week in New York was on a soap opera. I became *Jenna* on the highest rated daytime soap.

In time it suited me, and I came to love my job. But after two years the scriptwriters decided to have me drive a car off a cliff and kill myself. It seems my cheating husband decided he wanted a divorce, and because *Jenna,* stupid, beautiful, fun-loving wuss that she was, couldn't deal with the shame of it all, she ended her life instead of fighting back. So not me. I don't usually give up easily.

I had a nice funeral though. The studio went all out to send me off into unemployment actors' hell. My agent said not to worry; I had potential, and good references. She'd find something. She didn't.

The last day on the set I actually begged them not to "kill" me. To just let me languish in a hospital bed or something, but the actor who was playing my husband had a new girlfriend with a freakishly large rack who needed a job, and he thought mine (her job as his new wife), would be perfect for her. He was the producer's son, so . . ..

A month after *Jenna* drove her Porsche off a cliff and had a very fine wake, I had to break my lease, say goodbye to all my friends, and start daily conversations with my agent again. After many fruitless weeks of traipsing all over New York City to nerve-wracking auditions, I went home to my family.

Home is Shallotte, North Carolina, where I have a huge family with lots of sisters and brothers and a gaggle of cousins, and where almost everyone is a friend, a neighbor, a former schoolmate, or related to me in one way or another.

My parents own a rambling rambler and that's no exaggeration. It was my grandpa's pa's house. So it's pretty old and has been added onto for many years. The main part, the original house, is part flagstone and fieldstone. There is a wing off on the east side that is red brick, then a more modern stucco wing is attached to that, with indoor bathrooms. On the west side there's a big ol' gray brick garage that is still part cinderblock with barn-type doors facing the front. Then the newest part, a long cedar shake addition, with a Hardi-plank half wall for the last twelve feet, was tacked on. It became my bedroom when I turned thirteen. And actually, it still is.

The whole house with all its add-ons is over a hundred-feet-long. So imagine the claptrap eclectic-ness of it all as it faces the road. Especially when there's a lit Christmas tree in the bay window of the red section, lights all over the roof of the fieldstone part, and a blinking Santa and all eight reindeer on the roof. Well, it's kinda weird . . . but it's home. And it's paid for. So Momma and Papa get to go to Vegas and Branson whenever they want. That's where they were when I came home and dumped all my New York belongings in my bedroom and loaded the rest of my crap into the garage.

Across the street is the house my Aunt Darlene and Uncle Jerry live in. Uncle Jerry inherited the barns and fields, while his sister Anna, who is my mom, got the farmhouse and the orchards and gardens behind it. In the early days, Daddy and Momma took care of the orchards and sold produce to the local markets and in the summer—in a lean-to on the highway—while Uncle Jerry did some plumbing work and sold off pieces of the farm.

In the 1990s, Uncle Jerry used money he got from selling a large parcel of land to buy a boat, which he claimed he went fishin' in every day. But one day, he kinda got caught hauling in some bales of marijuana and that ended his boatin' days. Even after making some deals and payin' some pretty hefty lawyer fees, he still had a lot of money left 'cause apparently he'd been "deep sea fishin'" without catchin' hardly any fish for a very long time. And he'd invested his ill-gotten gains wisely, buying commercial land when it was cheap, and doing business with a big brokerage company out west. Anyway, he's what they call "well fixed" now. He doesn't have to work anymore. But he likes going around visitin' old friends in his latest Cadillac and pullin' out a big ol' wad of cash when he buys their dinner or their drinks, or just havin' a big ol' cigar at the Bricklanding Golf and Country Club. It's like he needs to keep remindin' people that he's well fixed. But I never knew how well fixed he was until he offered me a job.

Emma paused in her writing; her pen was beginning to skip. She walked back to the mailbox to get another one and was distracted by a sea gull that landed on top of the mailbox. She watched it for a minute, almost eyeball to eyeball with it before it cawed a warning, then lifted into the air and crapped right on her shoe. She had to laugh out loud. It was the perfect symbol for her life right now—crappy. She opened the mailbox, got a fresh pen and went back to her writing.

I had just finished unpacking and was putting the last of my empty suitcases on a rack in the garage when the house phone rang. I picked it up in the guest bedroom. It was my Aunt Darlene. She doesn't miss a thing. She probably saw me pulling into the driveway at four a.m. this morning. In her syrup-sweet voice, she said, "Bein's as your momma and daddy are away, how would you like to come over for suppa? We'd love to see you!" She was making chicken bog and there'd be plenty, and peach cobbler for dessert.

I hadn't had a chance to check out the refrigerator or the freezer, but I knew I'd find plenty of food there—if I had a mind to cook it. But after the long drive from New York and all the unpacking, I was up for a home-cooked meal, and chicken bog was one of my favorites. "When should I come over?" I asked.

"Well, honey, you know you're welcome anytime. You just show up when you're ready. We can serve the bog anytime."

"Okay, I'll be over in about an hour."

"That'd be just fine." Her voice was southern sweet, the kind that made you wonder if she was really a Yankee putting it on a little too thick, but she wasn't. I'd scared her one time with a toad in my apron pocket when I'd been finger painting with my cousins. She'd screamed like Fay Wray caught up in King Kong's hand, her open palm patting her ample chest until she calmed. Then, like an aging, Brillo-haired Scarlet O'Hara, she cried out, "Lawdy child! You scared me six ways from Sunday. Now why'd you go an' paint him bah-lue anyway? You take him ta the creek, right this very minute and wash that paint off him, ya hear?" The southern drawl was so imbedded in her speech as she wheezed to catch her breath I never doubted her again.

Chapter 10—Emma's Journal Entry
Aunt Darlene's Chicken Bog and Uncle Jerry's Mission

As I recollect, this is how the evening went an hour later when I strolled into the living room to see my Uncle Jerry in his big-man sized recliner, in front of the big-screen TV, cheering on Kyle Busch.

"Well hi, sweet thing! I didn't think I'd see you again 'til Christmastime. You're lookin' fine though. Real fine."

"Thanks, Uncle Jerry. I got fired off my show. I'm sure Momma told you."

"Oh yeah, she did mention something about *Jenna* havin' some sort of ac-ci-dent. But I didn't think it was permanent. In those shows, even if you die, they keep bringing you back as someone else, or a ghost of your former self. Or else somebody keeps dreamin' 'bout you, an' you get re-in-car-nated."

"Well, not this time. I have to find another job and my agent says New York isn't where it's at right now. She wants me to go to L.A. Not sure what I should do. So I came home to think about it. "

"Hmm. Los Angeles. You don't say . . ."
"Dinner!" called Aunt Darlene, and from all over the house people came running from closed doors. Opening them then slamming them and calling out for their kids to follow. Were all these people out and about when Aunt Darlene had been pickin' the chicken off the bones, slicing the peaches, and setting the table, I wondered. But I hadn't been any better. I'd shown up just

in time to eat, just like they had. Poor Aunt Darlene, everyone took advantage of her—always had, always will. She more than allowed it though, she expected it.

I took the guest seat next to my aunt while all my cousins and their offspring tumbled into their usual places. When the last chair was scraped up to the table there were twelve of us, with the baby girl on Melissa's lap.

My aunt's face was flushed, sweat beaded her brow, and there was a fresh burn on the outside of her arm. To cook for this crew had to be a fulltime job. Maybe my uncle was "well fixed" but clearly his wife was not. I felt sorry for her and made a mental note to get up and do the dishes when the meal was over, even if I had to do them all myself. Which was likely.

My Uncle Jerry and his wife Darlene had two boys, Danny and Robbie, and twin girls a little older than me—Melissa and Mallory. They weren't identical; in fact they were so different no one ever believed they were really twins.

Danny and Robbie helped out on the farm, but mostly they collected junk and sold it at an auction house they had in town. Melissa, the oldest twin, went to East Carolina but dropped out to become a girl's basketball coach for the middle school. She married the divorced father of one of her students and became the stepmother to three boys, ages 5 to 9. A year later she had a baby boy and just recently a baby girl. The boy was now two and the girl just a few months old. Mallory went to Campbell University where she met a law student. Together, they went to Chapel Hill, and while he got his doctorate she worked on getting her master's degree.

Now here's where everything gets hinky. And how I got my next gig.

As the big bowl of chicken bog was handed down the table my uncle said, "So Emma, you serious about headin' out west?"

I scooped a healthy portion onto my plate. I was famished, and the delicious aroma of the yellow rice and the stewed chicken had me salivating. Plus, you never knew what would be left if you planned on a second pass. "I suppose so. I need a job, and according to my agent, L.A. is where it's at."

"L.A. is also where the twins are. Or right near. Maybe you can see them?"

Everyone who was chewing stopped. Everyone who was scraping a mouthful together on daisy encircled stoneware plates stopped. Everyone who was mumbling through an argument or correcting a kid's manners stopped. In other words, the room went silent.

The twin babies. I took a deep breath and held it. No one ever talked about the twin babies. I forced myself to look up from my plate and meet Uncle Jerry's eyes. They were hard and flinty with blood-shot whites as he squinted over at me, the craggy silver lines of his crow's feet prominent in his otherwise leathery tanned face.

"I didn't think we were allowed," I ventured, swallowing prematurely and almost choking on a piece of chicken. From the look on his face, I would say there was murder in his eyes, but I really am not sure if I know what that looks like. But that's what I thought it would look like if I ever saw it.

"We're not."

His eyes drifted down the table to each member of the family, all were sitting at attention, eyes riveted on him, mouths agape. No one dared to question him, not even me.

"Let's talk after dinner."

I nodded and bent my head back to my plate. I lifted a mouthful of bog to my mouth without raising my head, careful this time to chew it well.

Uncle Jerry took a roll from the basket on the table and tore it in two. It was the signal the rest were waiting for. They all resumed eating. The sounds of utensils on crockery, glasses being hoisted and ice clinking in them, and people chewing and smacking their lips continued. Inwardly I sighed. And remembered . . . the most horrible time in my aunt and uncle's lives. My parents' and mine, too.

My cousin Mallory—Uncle Jerry and Aunt Darlene's pride and joy—had been the first person in the family to graduate from college. She had attended Campbell University in Buies Creek, North Carolina where she met the love of her life, Alexander, a law student who finished getting his Juris Doctorate the year she graduated with a Masters in Education from UNC at Chapel Hill.

They married in a lavish *Southern Living*-styled ceremony worthy of the Charleston setting my uncle had chosen. I hadn't been able to attend the wedding due to my shooting schedule, but it's all I heard about every time I came home. Uncle Jerry had spared no expense. Everything had been grand and southern, and "trees elegant" as my mom told me, adding that the bride had been just as beautiful as the one in *Steel Magnolia*. The happy couple moved into a house near Wilmington and two years later Mallory was pregnant with twins.

Then, on an early February morning, I got the call that Mallory had given birth to twins girls and that things had not gone well after the delivery. Mallory died on the operating table less than an hour after the twins had been born. She had held Molly for a few minutes, but had never held Mandy. My mom cried so much that day that she couldn't get rid of the hiccups for days.

I hadn't been able to make the funeral as *Jenna* was getting married that day. But honestly, I don't think I could have stood seeing my aunt and uncle so devastated—or my own parents. Everyone was destroyed by this. Melissa had even tried to kill herself with a razor blade to her wrists, but she'd cut in the wrong direction and hadn't pressed deep enough, so just made a royal mess of the bathroom.

I had never met Alexander, but back in New York, I prayed for him and his girls every night before I fell into bed, exhausted from a day on the drama-crazed set that was my life now.

The light of Uncle Jerry and Aunt Darlene's life was snuffed out the day Mallory died. Any chance of a spark for their future happiness was eliminated when Mallory's husband hired a private ambulance and took the babies from the hospital that very day, not disclosing where he'd taken them. It was eventually discovered that Alex had moved the babies to another hospital, then a week later, he had moved himself and the girls to the west coast without a word to anybody.

The ensuing weeks and months were full of phone calls about news of legal maneuvers to try to get the grandchildren back or to at least to be granted visitation privileges. All were to no avail.

Alex, as the only parent, had sole custody, and he denied any member of Mallory's family access to the twins. To make matters worse, he refused the delivery of the gifts they sent, advising them that any future shipments would not be returned, but destroyed.

Uncle Jerry and Aunt Darlene had only seen the babies through the nursery window moments after they had been delivered. Then after Mallory died, fully expecting to either take them home as their own—or to at least help Alex with their care while he was working—they were shocked to learn he'd taken them out of the hospital.

Prior to the birth, they had gotten in touch with an agent in Wilmington to help them find a home nearby so they could help raise the little girls, now they wouldn't even get to see them.

There was a pall over both my parent's house and Uncle Jerry and Aunt Darlene's household. I felt it the few times I made it home. There were no birthday, anniversary, Easter, Thanksgiving, or Christmas celebrations that year.

To date they hadn't touched either baby. They didn't even have a picture of them. Alex had been present at Mallory's funeral, coming in after everyone was seated, and then afterward being shielded by his family and the funeral home employees on the way out. He had not bothered to attend the reception or to provide pictures for the memory board despite many calls requesting them.

I sat there listening to the sounds of everyone eating. I was unable to eat. The last bite I'd had, had taken four swallows to get down. I memorized the number of petals on each daisy surrounding the pile of rice on my plate. I recalled the one picture I had seen of Alex, the one that had been framed on the mantle after he had kissed his new bride, my amazingly sweet cousin, Mallory, at the altar.

He'd looked over just as the photographer had set up his shot, his fingers still curled under Mallory's chin, and Alex's piercing grey-blue eyes and hard-set jaw had captured his displeasure at the intrusion. It was a powerful picture conveying both possession and protection of a beautiful bride by her arrogant groom. It spoke volumes that she was looking adoringly at him while he was slaying the photographer with his eyes over the interruption of his kiss. Alex's dominance to Mallory's acquiescent nature was apparent, and I always wondered why Aunt Darlene chose it as her favorite. Maybe it was because it was so romantic. I always thought it was sexy as all get out.

I still saw those same penetrating eyes even though I knew he'd been cut out of the picture and his image burned in an ashtray over two years ago. Still, I shivered in my chair. I knew he'd be a formidable man, not one to trifle with. Not one to annoy or come up against. The thought of approaching this man out of the blue—a complete stranger to me in every way—and asking him if I could see my second cousins, terrified me.

I did the dishes as I promised myself I would; not at all surprised that no one offered to help. I was surprised that Aunt Darlene had disappeared though—until I heard my aunt and uncle arguing, just out of earshot, on the back patio. Out of earshot for most people, but not for me. My ears were tuned to the whispered cues on the set. I turned off the water I was using to rinse the dishes and tiptoed to the screen door.

"Don't do this," Aunt Darlene hissed.
"Why? We have a right, you know. She was our daughter!"
Uncle Jerry was hissing too, but his voice carried a lot more menace. He was angry. His voice was the raspy jeer of a straining locomotive while his snarl was that of an enraged ogre. Through the screen, against the porch light, he looked green and ugly. Motley in his anger, he bent down and got in his wife's face,

"Stay out of this, you hear!" The venom in his voice made me step back.

I went back to the kitchen, anxious to finish up and get home before they came back inside.

No such luck. I heard the sliding door click closed at the same time my aunt was making her way down the hall toward the bedrooms. It seemed every single family member had deserted me. The bog had been good. What I'd managed to eat of it before things had gotten tense, but clearly not worth this.

I was drying my hands on the dishtowel when Uncle Jerry came into the kitchen. He was no longer ominous looking. He just looked sad, very sad.

"Thanks for dinner. It was great. I'd better go now, I'm expecting a call from my agent." I hated lying, but if there was ever a moment that called for one, this was it. I folded the towel over the oven door handle where my aunt usually kept it.

"Emma, how much did you make a year working for that show in the city?"

"Mmmm." No sense lying, I thought. We had the same tax accountant. "One hundred thirty-six thousand last year, plus benefits."

"I'll pay you a hundred and fifty thousand if you go to California and get me some pictures of my grandbabies, let me know how they're doing, and maybe get me a video."

"Wha . . . What?"

The amount staggered me.

"Even as beautiful as you are, I figure it'll take you a month or better to get to know Alex well enough that he lets you into his home. Another month or more before he gives you access to his girls. When he does, get me a couple of photos, maybe a video or two, and let me know how they're doing."

"That's all? Some pictures, a video and a report? And you'll pay me a hundred and fifty grand?"

"There's no one else who can do it. No one else who would."

He looked so dejected. So lost. A man with nothing to look forward to but a smiling visage from the offspring of his cherished Mallory. He had adored her. I knew that. It had been in an open way parents weren't supposed to project. Favoritism for the one who was the most beautiful, the most promising, the one everyone liked and admired the most.

"She was special, you know?"

Yeah, I knew. She was the adorable one. The nice one. The one you could always count on. "Yeah," I said, my own voice sad with tears I had yet to shed in grief over her passing. "She used to help me with my homework. Once she even cancelled a date to help me study for an exam."

"Wish that date had been one with Alexander," he mumbled.

"What?" I asked, though I was sure I had heard him clearly.

"I can't help but think if she hadn't met him she'd still be alive," he said.

"Yeah, but would she have been happy? I talked to her several times and she was clearly in love with him and so happy about the babies she was carrying."

"Well . . . that's why I want you to check on things. It's not right when a man just up and goes, takes his wife's kids and disappears." His face was sullen, no longer angry, seeming to be placidly resigned to the events that had come about.

"They are his kids too, you know."

"Yeah, but don't you think we should make sure he's doing right by them? We have to check on them for Mallory's sake. Do this for Mallory."

It was a lot of money to waggle in front of an unemployed woman. I didn't have to take my clothes off, rob a bank, or write a bestseller. And I was likely going out to California anyway.

"Just think of it as another acting part. Meet the man, woo him a bit and get to see the girls. Easy Peasy. I'll even pay your airfare . . . and give you half up front."

"I feel like a whore with you as my pimp."
"You don't have to sleep with him! God, I'd prefer you didn't. You're too good for him. My Mallory was too good for him, too."

"Do you really believe that?"

"Well, what kind of man does what he's done?" Anger flared in his face.

"Maybe he had his reasons . . ."

In degrees, the red face glaring at me turned purple.

I drew in my breath and searched my mind for some kind of damage control. "Or maybe not. Maybe he had to move for his job."

"With no notice? No how-do-you-do? No by-your-leave? I don't think so. He's just one mean son-of-a-bitch. And I want to be sure he's treating the girls right. You in or out?"

"Uh. Sure. I'll go to California and see if I can find him. If I can, I'll try to get chummy so I can see the girls. Then I'm done, right?"

"That's all I want. A few pictures of Molly and Mandy and your assurance that they're all right. I paid an investigator a few months back to find some dirt on him, but he says he's squeaky clean, that there's nothin' I can use to challenge his custody of the girls. Says he goes to work, shops, runs, and ballroom dances at a la-de-da studio just like he used to with Mallory. I got no other way, Emma."

"Okay," I sighed. "I guess I can do it. It's not much of a part, but at least I get to keep my hand in," I said as a joke.

"You're going to have to class up some. Mallory was pretty classy."

I didn't take offense. Mallory was the epitome of class. I knew that. "Hey, I can do elegant. I can talk ballet and symphony; even play some Bach on the piano. And I sure as hell can dance. I've been winning competitions since I was six."

"And lose the southern accent. I imagine he'll be pretty steeled against that. And if he finds out who you are, that'll be the end of it."

I had taken voice lessons and been coached in all manner of speaking styles. I could do Bryn Mawr to Mary Poppins and every Disney character in between. "Don't worra, I'm a New Yaawker now. Or maybe I'll be from Bahstan . . . that'd be a hoot!"

"Don't overplay it, Drama Queen," he said as he clasped me around the shoulders. He looked down at my upturned face and smiled.

Drama Queen, that had been his nickname for me, and had been since I'd played Kate in *The Taming of the Shrew* in high school.

I smiled back at him. "Don't worry Uncle Jerry, I won't ham it up. I know how to go about doing this."

"I know you do. You have an advantage, knowing him without him knowing anything about you."

"I've never meet him, but how can you be sure he's never seen a picture of me?"

"Well, you'll know in the first minute now, won'tcha?"

"Yeah. I suppose so."

"C'mon, I got cash in my office."

"Seventy-five thousand?" My eyes widened with incredulity.

His chin ducked and one of his bushy gray brows rose to his hairline as he looked at me with a squinty-eyed glare. "You know how I feel about the banks. Keep serious money in stocks, anything you can deduct, use a credit card; keep enough in the checking account to impress creditors, and keep an emergency stash in the safe. This is an emergency. I want to see my grandbabies before I die."

I didn't mention the fact that he had several running around the house all the time that he hardly paid any attention to. But then as he'd said, Mallory was special. And because of that, so were her children.

He took several bundles out of the eight-foot tall Briggs & Stratton gun safe and handed them to me. "Get me some pictures, and I'll get you the rest."

As soon as I had the money in my hand I felt dirty. Tainted in a way I couldn't explain. It was not a good feeling. I should have hopscotched across the street home, but instead I stared down at my hands and dragged my feet. I'd never had a part I'd been this lukewarm about before—not even the one I'd done for the Tampax commercial.

Chapter 11—Emma's Journal Entry
Second Thoughts

Over the next few days I vacillated, wallowing between self-derision for accepting my new part, and elation for having such a hefty checkbook balance. I had never had this much money at one time. Once, I'd had a tax return for $6,300. But by the time the check came through, I needed it to pay for my modeling portfolio and summer acting classes.

Uncle Jerry booked a flight for me using his charge card and got me upgraded to business class for the following Tuesday. So I had time to go online and make some plans, check out places to live, rent a car and familiarize myself with the area a bit.

Alex lived in the Woodland Hills area so it made sense to settle somewhere close for a while. I found two places in Encino and arranged to see them on Wednesday. Then I called my agent to let her know I was taking her advice, and arranged to get handed off to one of her cohorts in L.A. to see if there were any opportunities for me there. I decided I would take just what I needed—my laptop, phone, and cosmetics—I'd shop for clothes, shoes, and toiletries when I got there. I knew the styles were different in California, and I didn't want to lug a lot of stuff around if I didn't need to. And since I had money in the bank, I didn't need to.

Two days before my flight, I got really antsy and had second thoughts about this "acting job" I had accepted. It just didn't seem right. No one except Uncle Jerry, and maybe Aunt Darlene and I, knew anything about the deal he and I had made, and I was sure he meant to keep it that way. But still . . . I had to talk to someone.

I called Mom and we talked about Branson, my going out west to check things out, and Aunt Darlene's Chicken Bog dinner.

"The family just doesn't seem the same," I said. "Everyone is still so sad."

"I know, baby. I know. It is the saddest thing. And then to lose the babies too . . . it hurts like a house a fire."

"Did you know Alex at all?"

"No, not really. I met him a few times before the wedding and then I sat by his folks at the reception."

"Oh? Where are they from?" I asked.

"Washington state, I think, or was it Oregon? Someplace out west. They used to grow blackberries. And she was a music teacher."

"Were they nice?"

"Yeah. Why you asking?" Her mom, always intuitive, was picking up on my nervous vibe. I had to focus, get back to my aunt and uncle's grief.

"I don't know. It just seems so strange. Her dying and him taking the babies all that way."
"Yeah. It was the hardest thing I've ever seen Jerry and Darlene go through. Gosh, to see what they wrote in the journal at The Mailbox, it just broke my heart."

"Journal? You mean down at *The* Mailbox?" I hadn't heard anything about that, but I knew the Kindred Spirit Mailbox well.

"Yeah. A year to the day after she died the whole family trekked down there to The Mailbox and each one wrote in a journal. Heart wrenching it was. Geez, the things they wrote. I wrote something, too. The pages were pretty tear-stained by the time it was my turn. Then Jerry had to practically carry Darlene back, she was so broke up she could hardly stand. I think a year later, the shock was worn off and now you know it's real. That it weren't no bad dream. That she really is never coming back."

"What did you write?" I asked, curious how Mom was dealing with the loss of her beloved niece, and trying to take her away from her brother and sister-in-law's grief.

"Oh, about how I missed her, especially at Christmas. You know how she always made those little minced meat pies with the drizzled icing and how she took such care to wrap each present special with each person in mind. I told her how I kept her wedding picture in my underwear drawer so I could see it each day when I was getting dressed. You know, Jerry and Darlene put all her stuff away, said no one could have a picture out, it was too hard for them to see anything like that. And I told her I prayed for her babies."

"Mom, what would you do if it were me, and somebody else was raising your grandkids that far away from you?"

"I don't know what I'd do, honey. There was many a time I envied Darlene her looks, her fancy house and cars, and her big fat purse because of all Jerry's 'adventures and exploits.' But that day Mallory left us, I stopped envying her anything. I know she'd give it all up for a day with her daughter and her babies. So I'm the lucky one. You're all I got, and one day when you have a baby, well . . . you know . . . I sure don't want anything to happen like this."

"Yeah."

"You need to get out of this funk before you go to California. Girl, this is no time to be gettin' yourself down." Mom was always the best cheerleader, brushing off the sadness and looking for the silver lining behind the clouds.

"I know. Hey, do you think that journal they all wrote in might have been one of the journals that went to UNCW?"

"I don't see why not. I think that's where all the Kindred Spirit notebooks go now—The Randall Library there in the Archive Section."

"Hmmm. Next time I go to Wilmington, I may check it out," I said, thoughtfully, wondering if I'd have time to do it before I left for L.A.

"Might be a thing to do next year on the anniversary. Although I think Jerry and Darlene don't need no remindin' now."

"No, I don't suppose they do."

"Well, your dad is calling me, the show is getting ready to start and he's got our drinks at the table. Hey, I won a hundert dollars at the slots today, ain't that a hoot? I'm havin' so much fun here. You take good care of yourself out there in Hollywood now, ya hear?"
"Mom, I'm not going to Hollywood."
"Well, how do you know? Good as you are you'll get there."

"Thanks, Mom. You and Dad have a good time and I'll call you when I get to California."

"Okay, Baby. Kissy kissy. I love you!"

"Kissy, kissy, Mom. Love you too."

I pressed the button to disconnect and while I still had the phone in my hand I Googled the Randall Library. I was connected to the Special Collections Department and spoke to Rebecca. She was so enthusiastic about my inquiry that I made an appointment for the next day. She said that since I knew the exact date of the entries, they'd probably have no trouble finding them.

That night, restless but not yet sleepy, I rummaged around in my mother's underwear drawer until I found the wedding picture Mom had ordered from the photographer's proofs. As I held the silver filigreed frame up to the light, I stared down at the happy couple. I'd forgotten how lovely Mallory had been. Auburn tresses that were piled high with pearl studded combs sweeping her hair off to one side. High cheekbones that were lifted into a wide smile graced a face that had creamy white skin enhanced with blushing pink cheeks. Her lips were full and inviting as she looked up to her husband who was lowering his face to hers. His dark features were prominent in his tanned face. Dark, almost black hair, brushed conservatively back, expressive winged eyebrows that slanted as his eyes softened for his bride, lips open to capture hers. It was an unusual shot for a wedding album. It was as if they were suspended in time waiting for that kiss. And now they were, I thought. For all eternity, waiting for their lips to connect again. It was unbearably sad.

I stared at Alex in the picture, trying to picture him straight on instead of in profile. He was clean-shaven but you could see the hint of his heavy beard beneath his skin alongside his jawline. It was a firm, angular jaw of some consequence on his striking face. It gave him a serious no-nonsense appeal. I didn't know the percentages for the right proportions of facial things, but his nose, mouth, cheekbones, and brows were just right—substantial, strong, and from this angle, rough hewn just a tiny bit. This was a man to be reckoned with. I wasn't surprised Alex had bested her uncle in all of his legal challenges. He seemed formidable.

I was about to put the picture back in the drawer when I noticed the earrings Mallory had been wearing. They were huge pearls with diamonds in half moons surrounding them. I had to smile. They were my mother's earrings, ones she probably had with her in Branson right now. I remembered how thrilled Mom had been that Mallory wanted to wear them as the "something borrowed." Uncle Jerry had a fit, as he had wanted to buy her something of her own. But Mallory would have no part of it; she wanted to honor her aunt by wearing her most treasured pieces of jewelry. I decided right then that if I ever got married that I wanted to be married with those earrings, too.

Looking at Mallory's ears made me focus on Alex's. They were very fine ears. Just the right size with small lobes, ears you could whisper into and have your lips graze while telling secrets. Geez, where had that come from?

I shoved the picture face down on top of mother's granny panties. Then pulled it back out to scrutinize his nose. I would need to recognize him after all. Nice, long, straight nose. From this angle never broken. A nice nose to run alongside one's neck, to nudge a strand of hair out of the way . . . what the hell?

The picture went back into the drawer and I slammed it shut. Two years without a steady boyfriend, other than the role-playing of *Jenna's* husband, that's what the hell. Well, maybe California would be promising in that arena. All the men I had dated in New York City felt they were entitled to a woman's body on the first date. I didn't like that. I wanted to know the men I slept with. I wanted to know there was more than sex as the goal for a date. But relationships in a city where any guy can get lucky at almost anytime were a stretch for most girls. Which was precisely why I was getting infatuated with a picture, for cryin' out loud. But I acknowledged that it didn't hurt for me to see him in a romantic way, as I was supposed to "woo" him as my uncle had said. I supposed in today's jargon that would mean seduce, or bed, or that other word New Yorkers were always using.

I took the picture out two more times before I went to bed, but after that it didn't matter as I had memorized every pixel on his face. I tossed and turned that night, alternately seeing Alex as a mean old ogre who collected children to make his shoes, and wedding-picture Alex who looked like he wanted to kiss a woman more than he wanted to breathe.

Chapter 12—Emma's Journal Entry
Randall Library

I pulled into the parking lot for The Randall Library just before three. Thankfully, it was summer break and most of the full time students had left for the day so there was ample parking. I had dressed for the occasion, as I was now in my dress-to-impress and any man-could-be-the ONE mode. Last night had been hard on me. I was twitchy for something, or someone . . . that photo had really affected me.

I walked around the front, up the concrete steps, into the anteroom and then up the stairs, all the way toward the back, as instructed. I came to the wooden doors with the Special Collections sign, rang the bell and stood, swinging my Coach purse behind me while I waited. It had been my one extravagant purchase on the day I had signed my acting contract for the soap. So I was already out of style, but I really loved that purse.

It wasn't long before a young woman came hurrying up to the doors and opened them. We introduced ourselves and I was ushered inside. Rebecca told me she had just replaced Jerry Parnell, who had been the director of the department where the Kindred Spirit journals were archived. But she assured me she was up to speed on the collection and led me through a warren of shelves, then pointed to a box on a shelf. Each box had a metal frame on the front with a card showing the months and years catalogued inside.
"This is where I found the journal with the date you selected." She pulled the box out and took off the cover. "I left it on top." She removed several other notebooks from the box and fanned through a stack she placed to the side.

"Notice that the cover of this notebook is different from those of the same time frame. Of course they are all different, as many volunteers provide them. But this one, with its deco floral print and shiny silver foil embellishments is unique. There isn't another one like it in the collection. And as the writing starts on the inside cover and continues with no interruption for the first twenty or so pages, it means that they probably brought this notebook with them. No doubt to make sure they had plenty of blank pages to write on. A lot of people bring their own notebooks. Some write in them before they take them down to The Mailbox and leave them there. Not everyone is physically able to get to The Mailbox, so other people often take their messages and leave them there for them." She showed me some small notebooks and personal journals, some with hard covers, some with spirals on the top rather than the typical side spirals. Even one with a leather-tooled cover and a trailing ribbon bookmark. All were unique in cover design and size.

She carefully loaded the journals back into the box and she told me, "I took the liberty of setting up a table for you so you could look through the journal and take some notes if you'd like. And iPhone pictures are allowed, but only with the flash off."

"That's wonderful! I am so pleased you found it."

"It's quite a story there. I am sorry for your loss as I understand from our conversation that Mallory was your cousin."

"Yes. We were close growing up, but I hadn't seen her much over the last few years. Still, I wanted to see what everyone wrote on the anniversary of her death. I wasn't able to attend the funeral or the first year memorial."

"I see. Well, I'll leave you to it. You brought some tissues, I hope?"

I smiled at her and waved my purse, "Yes, I'm prepared for the deluge." *But I wasn't. Nowhere near.*

KINDRED SPIRIT MAILBOX JOURNAL MESSAGES

(These are real messages from K.S. journals, the names changed and with slight editing)

I sat and turned on the table light Rebecca had thoughtfully provided, and then I took a deep breath and opened the journal.

On the inside cover was a handwritten dedication to Mallory using her first, middle and maiden last name. I thought it interesting that the writer didn't include her married name. Then the dates of her birth. born in March of 1989, died in April of 2017. Just 28.

Under it was a poem called *I Am Not Gone*—Injete Chesoni

I am not gone
I remain beside you
Just in a different form
Look for me in your heart
And there you will find me
in our love which forever lives on
In those moments when you feel alone
Look for me in your thoughts
And there you will find me
In sweet memories that burn strong
Every time a tear forms
in your beautiful eyes
Look up to the heavens
And there you will see me
Smiling down from God's glorious skies

Butterfly stickers surrounded the poem. There was a note at the bottom:

Mallory didn't just care about her friends and loved ones. She had a burning passion that was honest and true from her heart.

On the next page was a long message from her twin sister, Melissa, in her beautiful cursive writing, written with a fine point Sharpie. There was one butterfly sticker at the top by Mallory's name:

Mallory,

I wish that you were here. I wish that this walk that I'm taking today was with you and not because you left us. Just a year ago we were sitting in the backyard talking for what seemed like hours about our summer plans, about old and new relationships, life, and family.

The day we lost you, my life forever changed. I lost my best friend, one of the only people who knew everything about me. I lost my sister a year ago today.

The only comfort and joy I can find is when memories show up. Our days in dance class, summer beach trips, skipping school. Our 16th birthdays when our parents took us out dancing and we felt so grown up. Memories of our phone calls, friend's parties, going out to dinner, and venting about our day.

You were the most amazing person. You had this inner light that drew people. You were an amazing daughter, sister, and best friend. You always gave more than you ever took and shared unconditional love with each person that came into your life.

I would do anything to go back to that last night together when we sat in the backyard. I would ask you to stay longer. I can still see you picking clovers. This will always be my bittersweet memory of you, the last time I saw you.
You will always be loved; your memory will always live on with your two beautiful little girls. I love and miss you Mal.

Mel

I grabbed a tissue from the box and blotted under my eyes. This was harder than I thought.

The next page was signed Mama & Daddy. I knew this one was going to be worse:

Mallie,

There is not much your Dad and I can write to you in here that we have not already said to you in our hearts and minds. There is not a minute of the day that we don't miss you and wish we could do something to bring you back. We know that will never be, so we go on completing the things we know you would want us to. I'm sure your girls miss you. I hope their father is keeping your memory alive for them everyday. We wait for that precious day when we will be with you again. You are forever our Pooh Bear. We love you forever—Mama & Daddy

Next came Robbie's Letter:

My Dearest Mal,

One year down, I'll carry you with me always! No one's forgotten you. We all still love you and miss you immensely. Still kind of hard to believe you're gone. I love you Mal—with all my heart and soul!

Rob

A note from cousin Sue,

To see all of your loved ones today has been a blessing. Love and miss you. Sue

Some scribbles I can only imagine are from someone's toddler, then a note from Lisa, one of Mallory's friends:

Mallory,

It's been a year and a week ago that you came to visit me that one last time. I was 11 weeks pregnant with Ally and you and I made plans to go out to eat on the day you passed. I really wish we had gone out to eat like we planned, so we could have caught up since we hadn't talked for a while, like we had done from time to time. I would have told you about the big thing that had happened to me that changed my life. Maybe it would have changed yours too. I love you Mallory. I can't believe you're

gone. I miss you.
Love, Lisa, Jay, and Ally

Several hearts were hand drawn with xxoo following.

Then another note from Melissa:

Mallory—

It's hard to believe it's been a year since you were ripped away from us. I'll bet your babies are getting so big. It's just sad to know that bastard has anything to do with them. As you probably already know, I'm pregnant! Due on Daddy's birthday. You really should have given me a girl. I miss you dearly. Visit me in my dreams and watch over our babies. Aunt Carol sends her love, she's sick with a rotten gallbladder. I will always [underlined three times] *love you! Mel*

Taped to the bottom of the page was a small envelope. I gently pulled the taped edge away from the page so I could open the envelope. Inside were four sonogram images that were dated that very same day. They appeared to be the original pictures, shiny, postcard-sized, and on Kodak Xtralife Paper. On one there was the typed word BOY and a printed arrow pointed toward what I assumed must have been the baby's penis. Printed at the top were the words: Brunswick Women's Clinic, the date, and Melissa's full name.

I'd seen that little boy at dinner just a few days ago. He was, what, two now? It was an eerie feeling. And incredibly sad.

Danny's letter was next and his scribble was very hard to read, I had to read passages over and over again to figure out words. It didn't help that he'd used some kind of pen that had ink that ran, and either he'd been crying or there had been some raindrops while he was writing. And it was long; he filled the whole page, finishing with his name tucked sideways into the bottom corner.

Hey baby girl,

I don't even know where to begin . . . being here all I can think about is you being here and what you must have been thinking and feeling. It's peaceful to be here today because I know this must have been a peaceful place for you. I am at a loss for words because there is so much I wanted to say to you, if I had only known. I wish I could have been there for you, and it will always be my biggest regret. Losing you taught me to value friendship and to always be honest with the people who mean the most to me. I know I can't get the time back with you but I know I never want to have that same regret again. You are and always have been my sister, as much as we butted heads, I never stopped loving you deeply and I hope you know I loved you in our family. I'm sorry for hurting you and if I contributed to any of your pain. I miss you more than I can explain. This wasn't how it was supposed to be. We were supposed to have our whole lives together and it absolutely kills me inside that we won't. I think of you everyday, but honestly I just have to deny it most of the time because it's still just too hard. I try to think of all the good times when I'm sad and hope that the memories you ___ (can't get this word, maybe carry?*) with you are the best ones. Starting in 3rd grade on the playground helping you do backbends, and then our middle school days. And then all our silly times, and how grown up we thought we were. Then high school dance clubs, crazy times, and then how you were such an essential part of my adult life. You were such a blessing. I love you forever, Mal.*
Love Danny

Then my Mom's letter,

Oh my sweet Mallie, I sure do miss you. Christmas just isn't the same without you. You always made those little minced meat pies I love. And my, how you could wrap a present, real special like. And always the most thoughtful gift because you knew something about each person and decorated it just so. I keep your wedding picture in my underwear drawer so I can see it each morning when I get dressed. Your momma and poppa can't stand to see any reminders right now, they are grieving so bad. I want you to know that I pray for your babies every single night and I hope I get to see your little girls one day. Mallie, you are so missed.

Aunt Anna

Below my father wrote:

Oh, Mallie girl. Miss you. Miss your pretty smile. I remember you sitting on the stoop and telling knock-knock jokes to me and laughing yourself silly. I miss that little girl. Jesus, I do.

Uncle John

There was one letter signed with just a big heart:

Dear Mallory,

We are all here, your sorority sisters, your sisters of the heart. We are here to remember you as we walk on this lovely beach that was your favorite place to be. You always said it brought you peace to be here and we can see why. It's been a long year without you. Even though you are not physically with us, your presence remains in our hearts. We love you dearly and ask in Jesus name that he watch over your babies and your parents. Seeing the pain they are going through breaks our hearts. They love you so much, as do we all.

We're not going to say goodbye, but will continue to visit you here when we can. We will see your beautiful smile in each sunrise and in each sunset.

Love you Mallory, and thank you for being my first friend when I knew no one my first day at college.

And the last one:

Dear Mallory's Family:

I am truly sorry about your loss. Though I have never experienced a loss personally, from time to time I think about the day when my mom will pass away, and it rips me into pieces. But coming here to the Kindred Spirit for the first time and reading the love poured into this notebook for Mallory gives me courage. Your thoughts and memories keep her alive. I hope that each day is easier and easier. Many blessings to you all. Rest in peace Mallory.

Danielle

Of course I was blubbering big time, using a fistful of Kleenex to swipe at both my nose and my eyes.

I flipped through the rest of the notebook, noticing someone had punched a message out in Braille and idly wondering what it said.

There were several letters left to Mallory and her family penned on subsequent days, all sweet and loving. There were several anonymous letters, one pretty bitter about the father who had taken the girls away from their family. One wished a blessing of the day to Mallory's family. A graduate of UNC who wrote she wished she had known Mallory, and a letter written in Spanish. I knew enough to figure out that the woman had just lost her 13-day-old baby and wished she had died instead, as Mallory had. After that the letters had nothing to do with Mallory and everything to do with the beach, the Kindred Spirit, and everyone's very personal stories.

I closed the notebook, wiped my face with a fresh tissue and stood up. Rebecca saw me through a glass window and came from the office she'd been working in.

"Finished?"

"Mmm, yeah."

"Pretty sad stuff, huh?"

"Yeah, it really is. But I'm glad I could read what my family had written. I wish I had been able to be there that day."

"You can go back and write something now . . ."

I looked at her with questioning eyes.

"The Kindred Spirit is everywhere. I'm sure she wouldn't mind you inserting a special note to Mallory."

"Thanks. But I don't know what I'd say." Especially as I was planning to fly across the country to find Mallory's husband and demand that he let my family see Mallory's girls. Or seduce him until he allowed me to.

She touched my sleeve. "It's hard, I know."

I put my hand over hers. "Thank you. Thank you for finding the journal and for being so gracious."

"You're welcome. Come back any time."

"Thanks."

Finding my way through the warren of halls and shelves of books took longer going out. I was so heart-sore and lost in my thoughts. And maybe a little more determined than I had been before about helping Uncle Jerry and Aunt Darlene. Maybe I *could* get a few videos of the babies on my phone.

Chapter 13—Emma
Winging My Way to California

I packed my suitcase and put my laptop in its travel sleeve, and was ready the next morning when Uncle Jerry drove me to Wilmington for my flight.

When he dropped me off at I.L.M., he pressed a piece of paper into my hand. It had Alex's address on it and the name of the dance studio he frequented—L.A Ballroom Dance Studio in Sherman Oaks. Underlined was Wednesdays 7 to 9. I didn't recognize the handwriting. I looked into my uncle's face and he saw the question there.

"It's from the investigator I hired. Best way to meet Alex might be at those dance sessions. You're not likely to run into him anyplace else. You keep in touch, ya hear? I want progress reports. Don't leave me hangin'." He raised both brows at me, widened his eyes and jerked his head at me. It was as if he was drilling in the dictum. But I clearly saw the threat there if I didn't comply.

I arrived at L.A.X. that afternoon and picked up the rental car I'd reserved, a gold Solara, so I could drop the top and enjoy the California sunshine. I thought about buying a car, but without the guarantee of a job it seemed foolhardy. What if the show in New York called and wanted *Jenna* to have a long-lost twin sister show up to wreck havoc on somebody's relationship? Or a ghost sequence in somebody's head? Hey, it could happen.

A car here would be a liability. I'd wait until I got a job. For now, renting a nice convertible would solidify the image I wanted to convey for my role with Alex—nice, polite, sassy, classy "Emily." It was close enough to my real name that I'd answer to it, but not so close as to pinpoint me as Mallory's cousin—should he even know my name. But if he didn't recognize me, and there was no reason he should, I'd stick with Emma.

I drove to the Extended Stay America motel in Woodland Hills where I'd already booked a room. It hadn't had the best ratings or reviews, but it was close to where I needed to be and it was cheap at $130 a night. Tomorrow I'd check out a few apartments in Encino. The day after, I would go to the agency and meet my new agent. Maybe drive around and find the house where Alex lived with his girls.

With the time difference, it was well past the dinner hour for me, and I wanted to get checked in, grab a bite to eat somewhere and crash early. It had been a long flight with delays getting airborne and a chatty young mother with a whiny toddler sitting beside me. Plus, I was starting to get scared. I doubted whether I could pull this off. And wondered what I had gotten myself into. Alex was an attorney, and apparently a really good one. Was what I was planning on doing illegal in some way? What kind of trouble was I making for myself by trying to help out my family?

Chapter 14—Emma
Shopping!

I decided staying as close to the truth as possible was going to be my saving grace. When I met Alex at the dance studio, there would be no pretense. I was a professional dancer, keeping my skills sharp while going on calls, auditioning for whatever roles my agent thought suited me. I had been weaned on musicals, so it made sense to find a good dance studio and capitalize on that—it gave me more options, more roles to apply for. I'd have been perfect for a role in *La La Land* if I'd only been here a few years earlier.

I found a furnished studio apartment in Encino that would work for me, and met with an agent who truly didn't seem to like me being handed off to her. But then once we got talking and she'd taken the time to look at my headshots and resume she warmed up to me. We talked for half an hour and I left her my cell number. She said she'd get back to me. I wasn't optimistic though.

Next was a little shopping at the Sherman Oaks Galleria in preparation for my debut at the L.A. Ballroom Dance Studio next Wednesday night.

As I strolled around the mall, I noticed a lot of men walking around with children. So far none had two girls with them and none looked like Alex. And surprisingly, few were accompanied by an adult female. It led me to believe what I'd been told over the years, that L.A. was a city of single parents. I wondered if that were true, or if these men were just helping out wives who had their own busy schedules. Then I'd see two males strollering or walking a child and I'd remember that southern California was definitely a place where gender roles weren't as entrenched as they were in the south.

I went to Tuso, an amazing clothing store, and bought

some colorful printed cotton blouses and three amazing pairs of skinny stretch jeans that fit as if they were made for me—comfortable, yet sexy in the bum area and the exact perfect length for heels or sandals.

Then it was off to DSW for shoes, a conditioning treatment and blowout at Paul Mitchell, lunch at P.F. Chang China Bistro, and a carryout salad from Salad Farm for dinner later at the apartment.

The next day, in Nordstrom's, I found a gorgeous Joan Vass asymmetric heather grey spandex pants suit, two Kay Unger elastane dresses that would be perfect for dance classes, and a Johnny Was rayon and silk embroidered blouse that would go with anything I had. But I fell in love with the perfect pair of white capris that would work too, so I grabbed them off a rack on the way to the register.

After offloading my bounty in the car, I went back for a Carmen Marc Valvo dress that was black and gold metallic with a thin leather belt, a zigzag striped Missoni coral and grey poncho, and a slate blue lambskin jacket. All items I had debated because, although I loved them, I could not justify the price. Somehow on the way to the car and back, I had.

Almost out the door, I found the perfect dress for the night I would meet Alex. Knowing the dress had to be both memorable and sexy I couldn't believe my luck when I spotted it from the top of the escalator while I was on my way down. And as a bonus, it was my size. If it hadn't been, I would have had it altered, or I would have dieted or binged until it fit.

It was a cross between Marilyn Monroe's white dress in *The Seven Year Itch*, the one where she stood over the grate and let the draft lift it, and Julia Robert's dress in *Pretty Woman*, the brown and white polka dot one she wore at the polo match. This one showed cleavage, a nipped in waist, and lots of leg. I walked all over the shoe department looking for a pair of heels I could dance in that were the exact shade of brown I needed. Finally, I went back to my apartment and ordered them online, paying for expedited shipping.

Over the weekend, and during the first part of the following week, I kept busy taking a spin class, two yoga classes, a pole dancing class and a suspension wrap/aerial scarf class. I stocked my meager fridge with healthy protein bowls and cartons of chopped veggies to snack on. I checked in with Uncle Jerry and Mom, being a bit more optimistic about my new agent than I had a right to be. And I did more shopping. Chico's this time for more pants, more tunics, a few sweaters, and a drop dead gorgeous velvet-tasseled floral burnout kimono that went with pale blue leggings and a textured tank.

Wednesday afternoon I had my hair and nails done, and although I was pretty sure I wouldn't need it that night, I had my legs and certain other areas waxed. I just felt better when things were tidied.

When seven o'clock rolled around I was at the studio meeting one of the instructors and warming up. She admired my dress, marveling at how well the shoes matched and I could see she was genuinely impressed with how well I moved in it. Alex didn't show. But I didn't let it daunt me. I figured he probably wasn't able to come every week. Although I did wonder what had kept him away.

Chapter 15—Alex
A Hellish Day

Unbeknownst to anyone, Alex had finished the final negotiations on the settlement with the insurance company that handled Mallory's doctor's malpractice insurance. The insurance company had initially, in good faith, given Alex a check for two million dollars to relocate, set up house, outfit a nursery, and hire a nanny. He let it be known in writing at the time he accepted the check that he appreciated the gesture but the amount he was given was not going to compensate for Mallory's death. That he'd be coming back for more. And he did.

He spent two years preparing his case, projecting Mallory's income as a top level academic in a college environment proving she had plans to continue her education to attain her PhD while teaching, as soon as the girls started school. Several entries in daily journals that she had prodigiously kept, showed she had planned everything out, going so far as to select the professors she had already contacted.

Through correspondence with her professors and many colleagues, he showed her fervent desire to become a published author in the field of education, not only outlining her capabilities, but following up with her innovative ideas that leading writers in education and child development said had merit and would no doubt earn her publishing contracts.

He showed them her manuscripts in process and even a letter from a leading textbook publisher offering a sight-unseen contract on one of the books in progress.

When he was done collecting and collating Mallory's career prospects and providing certain proof that Mallory would have had a highly successful career as an educator at a top-notch university—quite likely advancing to the administrative level. And that she would undoubtedly have become an expert in her field of childhood development. Leading to book sales and lecturing fees on top of tenured salaries, he closed his case and asked for thirty-five million.

The session in front of the judge had gone well into the afternoon, with him providing so many detailed affidavits from so many people that they hadn't settled things until well after five o'clock. And by then he had been exhausted, the stress of the case taking its toll. Not only because of the constant reminder of Mallory and all they'd lost, and the wind down of so much work, but also the knowledge that Mallory would truly have made a difference if she'd been allowed to achieve her dreams.

The judge deliberated at the bench, reexamining documents and asking questions of both parties. Alex told himself that no matter what happened, he had to be content knowing he had done his best by Mallory. He had shown the world that her life would have been a worthy one.

In the end, the judge agreed—a very worthy one. He awarded 18 million to Mallory's daughters, five hundred thousand a year for each girl's life up to the age of 18, and another five million for Alex for loss of his wife and life partner, allowing for compensation to provide for his children's needs by his own income. Without a doubt, trying this case in a Los Angeles courtroom had netted a lot more than one in Wilmington would have, he thought as he nodded his acceptance and fought to keep his eyes from going wide with shock. He had won. Mallory would have been proud of him.

Alex sighed, gathered his papers, clipped the latches on his briefcase closed, and thanked the court workers for staying late.

God, what a day. He rotated his head back and forth, trying to get the kinks out. On the way to his car, he rubbed the back of his neck to loosen the tightened muscles. If there was ever a night he needed time in the gym or the relaxation of ballroom dancing this was it. But he was too wasted to do more than get in his car and drive home. His parents had the girls tonight so he didn't have to worry about getting them bathed, read to, and tucked in. He smiled. His little heiresses, as it turned out, due to events of the day. Thank God it was over with no chance of an appeal. He had been working on the case, non-stop, in a corner of his mind for over two years.

On the drive home he called his parents and told them the good news. They were delighted with the outcome. Knowing how hard he had worked to make all this happen, they were not only relieved, but bursting with pride. His mom invited him to come by for a late dinner.

"I think I'll just call it a night. Grab one of the Nourish salads or a frozen grain bowl."

"Okay, don't worry about us. We're having fun playing with Jell-O cubes."

"Okay, Mom. Thanks."

He hung up and settled in for the drive. But after a few minutes, he just didn't feel like going straight home. He looked at the clock on the dashboard. Six thirty-five. He could still make the dance class; get there at about 7:15. No one ever seemed to mind when he was late. Besides, he really needed the workout for his neck and shoulders if nothing else. And he was too keyed up to sit still. He was lonely in a way he hadn't been before. It was as if settling this case attached permanence to Mallory being gone from his life. There need not be any more daily reminders in the way of work. Her death had been vindicated by compensation for him and his girls. Not that he wouldn't have traded every single penny just to have her back.

Dancing relaxed his tense muscles like nothing else. Running kept them toned, lifting weights kept them strong, but dancing kept them limber and relaxed. Plus it was enormous fun. The only fun he really allowed himself to have anymore. And it was a way he could celebrate his stunning victory. He hoped for a dance that was fast and spirited.

When the exit to the studio came up, he took it. Within minutes he was parked and out of the car, his dance bag with his towel and shoes inside slung over his shoulder. It was hot. He should have taken off his suit jacket and left it in the car. No matter, he'd take it off once inside.

Chapter 16—Emma
Dance with Me

I was twirling with one of the dance instructors, doing a very structured waltz when I saw him.

He had just stepped through the glass doors and into the studio, dressed in dark business attire, looking like he'd just walked off the page of an Armani ad. On closer inspection, I could see that his white shirt was rumpled. He held a gym bag in his hand. I knew it was him right away, and I couldn't stop staring. Oh, that hair, so vibrant and black—in waves fanning back from the widow's peak, slightly off center. There was the barest graying at his temples. That was something new. I hadn't seen that in any of the pictures.

He scanned the room for the instructor and waved a hand with a wry expression on his face as if acknowledging his tardiness. He looked tired. Our eyes met.

I don't want to sound corny here, but it was the quintessential eyes meeting across the room scenario. I swear if I didn't know better, we were reliving the scene in Toy Story 3 where Ken and Barbie meet in the Day Care Center. As they saw each other for the first time, the music for *Dream Weaver* started and the air between them sizzled and snapped. They were mesmerized. Just as Alex and I were now.

Alex seemed to perk up, some weariness leaving his shoulders, and his blue-grey eyes brightening. He smiled at me. And had I not been such a consummate dancer, I know I would have faltered. As it was, I thought I might have stepped on my partner's toe.

Should I smile back? I didn't know. But I was supposed to be seducing him, right? That would require a smile, so I flashed my brightest grin back at him before my partner spun me away.

I don't know how I managed to finish the dance. I must

have gone on autopilot. I have no recollection of how I got back to my starting place. I only know that the dance instructor, who had offered to be my partner in lieu of anyone else being available, stepped away to greet the newcomer.

"Alex! Glad you could make it. Change your shoes and take over for me here. We have a new student—Emma."

Alex, now settling on a bench on the side of the room and removing his shoes, lifted a hand and waved toward me. The instructor moved away and went back to the front of the room to program the music for the next dance.

"Let's do a nice invigorating Argentine tango, shall we?" he said as Alex walked across the wood floor to join me.

Alex took my hand and I felt a slight tremor go up my arm. His eyes never leaving mine, he verified my name, "Emma?"

"Yes." He didn't seem to place me as someone he should know, so I went with my real name.

"I'm Alex. Pleased to meet you. You up for a energetic tango?" he asked with a smile.

"Sure. Bring it on."

His smile widened and music for *El Tango Rojo* came on.

While the instructor called out the moves to the less experienced in our group, Alex and I moved across the vast dance floor, taking all the space we needed to do a traditionally choreographed tango. I was surprised that Alex was so good, and after a few steps I'm sure he felt the same way about me. So we did what two experienced tango dancers always did, we vamped up and had fun with it.

I could not keep my eyes from focusing on his face, learning the lines of that firm jaw and wanting to run my hand over the five o'clock shadow that outlined it so well. His brows were well defined and almost severe looking, but the light slate blue of his eyes softened the effect, making him drop dead gorgeous.

Once again, thank you, autopilot. Because all I could

concentrate on was his firm hand on my hip and his other hand in mine. And of course, his face towering above me, looking into mine before and after each series of complex steps.

"You're good," he said, after one intricate turn.

"You too." It was too energetic a dance to talk much.

As we continued the steps I watched every nuance of his face. I watched it soften as he led us through our relaxed paces, harden and hold for the dramatic male parts designed to show his dominance over his female partner, then his lips smile when I surprised him with expert nuances.

When the dance ended and he held me in a full dip position, his eyes met mine and I thought I saw wonder there. Wonder and interest.

When the last bars of the music ended, he pulled me back up, but didn't release my hand. Instead, he squeezed it lightly. "Excellent dance. You're terrific."

I smiled and thanked him as the instructor called out. "Alex, you lucky dog, you're dancing with a pro there. Emma's just moved from New York. She's danced off Broadway!"

He looked down at me and grinned, "Really? That's wonderful. What are you doing *here*?"

"Just keeping my hand in. I'm actually more into acting these days, but you never know . . . gotta keep all your skills sharp."

He laughed. "Well I am very pleased to be able to assist you in that endeavor. And to think I almost didn't make it tonight. I'm glad I did though."

I felt myself redden, my typical roots of hairline to full on chest blush. I saw that he noticed. The dress, which I knew was pretty amazing in and of itself, had a big plus for me—it showed off my cleavage. And he was taking it all in.

The music started for a Quick Step number that I adored. I raised my eyebrow in question and added the impish smile that my father always said got me into trouble.

He took both my hands. "Here we go!"

He was a very good dancer, with great technical skills, and a genuine love for the way the rhythm of the music moved the body. He extended every movement, added the polished flourishes to make the dance his own story. It was obvious he had been taking lessons for some time. He was surefooted and knew the steps, smoothly going from one phase to the next with no time lost for memory to catch up. I had to admit we made a good team. The love of music and the passion for the dance thrummed through our bodies as we moved across the dance floor, our fingers connecting and our eyes glancing off each others as we spun, flew away, and then came back to reconnect.

We danced a rhumba next where I got to shake my hips at him and he got to show me his truly nice bum. And wherever he touched me, his fingers seemed to draw me out, enflame my skin, and cause my smile to linger. This man was affecting me in pleasant ways; causing me to tingle all over, and have a woozy head from the high I was on. He was a charmer on the dance floor. Gracious, polite, and one hundred percent sure of himself.

He was courteous during the breaks too. "Do you need to sit this one out?" "Would you like to get some water?" "How are your feet doing in those killer heels?"

A slow dance was next and he offered me the chance to opt out. It would require us to be hip-to-hip, cheek-to-cheek, and intimate in the places between.

But I smiled big and bright and offered my hand. I wasn't going to miss the chance to get up close to this man. For our bodies to mesh full on. To have his heart beat against mine. And while he held me and we slowly drifted across the floor, I remembered Mallory. I could certainly see why she would have been so taken with this man. Places that hadn't warmed up in me for a long time were starting to come alive and generate heat. I felt myself swaying for more contact. I had to hold myself back to keep from giving him the wrong idea. Or was it the right idea? I was a bit confused right now and decided to pull back a little. Attraction was one thing, sending the message that I was easy and on the slutty side was not.

"You okay?"

"Mmm, yeah. Just trying to keep from combusting." No sense in denying the remarkable chemistry we had.

He laughed. "I know what you mean. I enjoy dancing with you. You're fun to dance with."

"Thank you. You aren't so hateful yourself."

He laughed again.

"You here in L.A. by yourself?" There, he laid it out.

"Yes. Had a pretty bad break up before leaving New York. Being on my own is doing me a lot of good."

He sighed. "Hmmm. That does help initially. I've been on my own for quite a while too. But I no longer feel as if it's doing me a lot of good. Although I am getting a lot of work done."

"What do you do?"

"I'm an attorney. Contractual. Mostly in film and theater arts. Some literary. I manage a few musicians as well."

"I've known a few theatrical attorneys. Being on stage, there's always one or two hanging around representing the headliners. So you deal with agent contracts, publicity and media, and the occasional get out of jail card?"

He laughed. "I don't do the get out of jail card. Mostly literary rights, options, film agreements, contracts for sets, equipment, pay scale issues for stunt men, extras, models, that kind of thing."

"Sounds interesting. So you're on the production end. I'll bet you get to meet some fascinating people."

"Not as much as you'd think. They have business managers, and I have assistants who do most of the legwork. I prepare tedious amounts of paperwork on policies and procedures, negotiate contracts, and handle compliance issues when they come up. My staff tracks down the people involved, and they get all the paperwork signed so everyone's protected. I don't travel much anymore. I can't. I have two little girls at home."

"Oh. No momma?" I cringed to have to ask what I already knew. But it would have been expected for me to ask.

"No. My wife died over two years ago giving birth."

"Oh, I am so sorry." Again with the false words. I hated this. Of course I *was* sorry. More than he'd ever know.

"Yeah, it's been hard. But today's been a good day."

"Work went well?"

He nodded and shrugged as if work was of no consequence. "I met you."

His clarification left me speechless. And feeling a bit guilty. The music stopped and we stood staring at each other while listening to the rest of the class parting for the ten-minute break between the two-hour class.

"I have to say goodnight to the girls," he said as he pulled a phone from his pocket.

I nodded and went to the ladies room to touch up. Then I went to an open window that faced the street and watched as the cars below drove by.

"Have you had any luck finding work yet?" he asked from behind me.

"I just got here last week. I met with my new agent and she said she was sure she could find something for me."

"What are you interested in doing?"

"Mmmm, pretty much any kind of acting—stage, film, TV. I can sing and dance but I don't really want to travel with a troupe. I've done some modeling and a few commercials. I just finished a role for a soap. I got killed. Drove over a cliff in my Porsche."

He chuckled. "You're pretty good looking for a dead woman."

I looked over my shoulder and smiled at him. The music started up. A jitterbug this time.

He shrugged both shoulders as if to say you up for this? Jitterbugs kept you moving.

"Come on," I said, "let's show them how this is done."

We laughed more during that dance than I had during the past year. I can't remember ever having such a good time on a dance floor.

When it was time to leave, he asked if I was going to come back next week.

"Uh sure. Gotta keep my hand in. And it's good exercise." I hesitated before adding, "And I had fun with you."

"Good. I had fun with you, too. Then I'll see you next week." He squeezed my hand then turned left, picking his bag up from the bench on his way past. At the door he turned back and looked at me. He flashed a smile and winked. A Paul Newman smile, and I melted where I stood.

Chapter 17—Emma
The Perfect Dress

I spent the next week walking on clouds and planning my outfit for the next dance night. In between phone calls back home, a small progress report to Uncle Jerry—trying to tone down my enthusiasm for having met the handsome, sexy man who was stealing my every thought, and a shout out to Mom that I was okay and taking all the security cautions she ticked off each time I spoke with her, I ate healthy and exercised.

I spent time looking through the call out sheets for auditions, and stumbled onto an ad to read for Audible books. I had been gifted with several voices and had the ability to do a passable English accent so I went to the site, left a message and a demo. Then . . . I went shopping.

I didn't often vary too far from my healthy diet of mani-veggies—a phrase I coined for vegetables I lovingly garnished and "manicured,"—before popping into my mouth, fruit of all kinds, smoothies, salads, and roasted chicken. But today, I splurged and treated myself to a slice of cheese pizza at Pizza 90. Just one slice, but a big one, promising myself I'd have a grilled romaine salad for dinner.

Walking around to work off the delightfully greasy, thick-crusted pizza, I was leaning over the white industrial-styled railings on the upper level of the mall, admiring all the pretty display windows and watching couples pair up on the lower level. It was Saturday evening at this 24-hour mall, and tonight was date night. I was starting to feel a little lonely until my eyes spotted "the dress" on the rack by the front door of Tuso.

I pushed off the rail, found my way to the first floor and stopped in front of "my" dress. I lifted the hanger, held it up, turned it front to back, and felt the rows and rows of sweet, sexy lace. It was a charming apricot color, very feminine—innocent looking, yet very sexy. I could imagine the tiers lifting and shimmering as I danced in Alex's arms. I held my breath and checked the tag for first the size, then the price. Size 6, $149.

I was usually a size 7, but a six often worked. This one might, I mused, as I made my way to the dressing room. The body of the dress under the layers of lace was stretchy. I vowed that I would starve myself until it fit.

Ten minutes later I walked back through the mall to the parking area where my rental car was, holding a dress bag, hefted high, and smiling like I'd had pizza for lunch and still got into a size 6. And it looked dreamy on me. It was that perfect coral tone that matched my coloring. Really, one slide of the color wheel either way, and that shade just would not have worked for me. Blondes could not usually wear any shade of light orange. This sweet confection showcased my light tan and made my skin glow. I felt as if I had won the shopping lottery. Until I got back to the car and realized I didn't have any shoes I could dance in that would work with this dress.

I locked the dress in the trunk because I was sure that if any passing brunette who was a size 6 saw it, they'd steal it. It was that kind of dress.

An hour later, still at DSW, I was deciding whether to settle for a pair of tan patent leather heels, as there was no matching that color, or even finding a complimentary shade to go with that dress without dying a peau de soie pair to match, or going online to Nordstrom's, when the sales lady brought out a pair of clear acrylic Cinderella slippers and waved them under my nose. If I remember correctly, I followed her to the register and paid for them without even trying them on.

Chapter 18—Emma & Alex
Dirty Dancing

During their first night of dancing there were a hundred casual touches with each dance—his hand grasping hers, his long fingers gripping her waist, his hand holding her shoulder and sliding along her collarbone, his firm fingers at her hip, turning her. She hadn't known exactly when the casual touches had morphed into subtle caresses, but she imagined that it had to have been sometime during the second to the last dance—a sexy samba that had required a lot of hands on. His hands on her hips . . . his hands on her body, in places new acquaintances didn't usually allow contact.

The last dance of the night was one chosen from a grab bag. Each couple pulled a folded piece of paper from a canvas bag and on it was the dance they would perform for the others.

One couple drew a merengue, one a free-style, another a cha-cha, and one, a crazy Indian thing complete with tiny bells attached to the ends of their fingers. After each dance the instructor critiqued the couple on their technique.

Their paper, when Alex had unfolded it, had said to do a slow grind from the 50s era. When the music started they were both pleased it was a song they knew, Fats Domino's *Blueberry Hill.*

It turned out to be the sexiest dance of the night. With the center of their bodies pressed together as they swayed, it was very provocative. To finish off each lingering beat, they pretty much ended up grinding their pelvises together.

Toward the end of the song, Alex tossed his arm behind his back in the traditional American Bandstand manner, and swung it back and forth to propel them like a rudder, moving them across the dance floor. His other arm held her around her waist, cinched tightly to him. It was a possessive hold, one that conveyed ownership.

For the final bars, he bent his knees and jerked his pelvis up, lifting her to her toes and connecting them dead center to the area between their legs. The applause was thunderous. He continued to keep them tightly meshed, jerking her to him with each beat until the last note played.

The constant grinding of their inflamed cores had them both panting when Alex ended the dance and released her waist. He had a noticeable erection that he hid behind her back when he pulled her in front of him to listen to the instructor's commentary, and to watch for ways to improve their technique. They were praised for keeping their shoulders level as required while moving along in style, but they were admonished in a chiding way as they had both bent their knees multiple times to get the full effect of the "grind." Alex doing that lift and ragdoll hold, which wasn't exactly prescribed in the dance, earned them a shame-shame finger as well as a huge all-knowing smile.

Before separating, Alex bent and whispered in her ear, "If we'd done it any better, we would have burst into flames on the floor." He pointed to a spot a few feet away. "Right there," he said, "by all rights, there should be scorch marks."

She covered her mouth with her hand and laughed, whispering over her shoulder. "I think I might have the imprint of your zipper on my lower belly as well as my ass."

It was now their second night of dancing together and she was allowing full contact, touches that were casual, caressing . . . intimate. As far as she was concerned, if they weren't breaking the law, he could touch her anywhere he wanted, as every place he touched scorched with heat and begged for more.

Looking up into his gorgeous smiling face, she was amazed she was still on her feet. His eyes even caressed her—in swoon-worthy stares that felt as if they looked right into her soul—her deceitful little soul, she reminded herself. Then she sighed. Don't go there now she told herself. There would be plenty of time before next week's session for self-castigation.

"What's wrong?"

"Oh, nothing, just remembering how this dance ends."

"In a lift?"

"Yeah. I had pizza for lunch. Again."

He chuckled. "I don't think it's going to keep me from doing the lift. Keep your hands on my shoulders and I'll spin toward the center. You'll have no choice in the matter. And in that dress, you'll look spectacular."

When the music hit the crescendo, he lifted her easily by her waist. Her arms locked around his neck, and her hands gripped him tight as she spread her legs out and her dress flared around them while he spun her. When they settled into an arabesque in the center under the rotating mirror ball, she looked down at him as he gazed up. Their eyes met and held.

He whispered, "You are so beautiful."

She shuddered with desire. He grinned and slowly lowered her, letting each part of her body caress the corresponding part of his before setting her on her tiptoes.

Her theatrical background came alive as she kicked her leg up behind her. He took the cue and dragged her across the floor, her arms wrapped tightly around his neck, her toe lightly running along the smooth floor. They got to the edge of the dance floor amid loud shouts, whoops, and thunderous clapping.

Then the chant for them to kiss began. Mimicking the scene from *The Little Mermaid*, when Ariel and Eric were in the rowboat in the middle of the lake, and the frogs were chirping, and Sebastian called out, "Kiss the girl. Kiss the girl. G'won and kiss the girl."

And so he did. With one hand still on her lower back, Alex's other hand reached up and his palm held the side of her face while his lips took hers. It was the kind of first kiss every girl dreams of, filled with hunger and longing, and expertly accomplished as his lips moved over hers, tasting and savoring her petal softness.

It was not lost on her that this tall, powerful man, had succumbed to the will of so many others and gone against his, no doubt, private rules for public affection. But honestly, after that perfect dance where the two of them meshed as if born to dance with each other, there was no other culmination possible. Each move had been orchestrated as if designed by a divine choreographer. This kiss had been predestined—here, and now. She fell into the abyss of it, feeling the sheer magic of the moment carrying her away.

As his tongue swirled inside her mouth, commanding and taking, with the crowd around them watching their stunningly perfect kiss, he felt the power exchange, as old as time—the domination of a man taking a woman and magnificently claiming her with his kiss. It was heady. It was violent. And it was heaven. For her part, she succumbed and took what he offered—a dominant male commanding a woman to be submissive to him. An inevitable mating was now being thrown into the mix.

When the kiss ended and his lips lifted from hers, their eyes met. They both smiled. They knew this was the beginning of something special.

Clapping began all around them again, and as if a bell had rung signaling the end of class, everyone dispersed, leaving them center stage.

"That was really something. I felt as if I was the lead in a corny musical," he said, smiling down at her, still holding her in his arms. "And you were my fair lady," he added.

She looked around them at the people gathering their gear and leaving. "And we had six curtain calls and now the audience is finally leaving."

"Would you like to have a drink with me? There's a little tavern just a block from here."

"I would like that very much. Right now, a cool drink sounds wonderful."

He walked her to the bench where his dress shoes were and switched them out with his dance shoes. Then he took her by the hand and led her out the door.

"You dance as if you were born to it," he said as they walked to the little neighborhood bar.

"I've taken lessons all my life. If there was a day I didn't have some kind of dance class after school, I don't remember it. You're not too shabby yourself."

"My wife and I started taking ballroom classes early on in our marriage. It was a leftover from practicing for our wedding. It became our weekly date night. Every Thursday we went dancing and then had dinner at a Thai restaurant across the street."

"So now you dance on Wednesdays."

"It was the evening they had the style of dancing I liked best." He smiled, "And it was the night I had a babysitter."

Chapter 19—Emma & Alex
Three-Date Rule

It was noisy inside the tavern. A DJ in the corner was lining up pairs for Karaoke duets and, except for breaks between sets, it was too loud inside the little bar to be heard.

Alex ushered Emma to a tall pub table, the top of which was no larger than an album cover. Then went to the bar to get them each a glass of Pinot Grigio. When he returned with their drinks they clinked glasses and watched the performers make fools of themselves. Alex leaned in from time to time to make a comment close to her ear and Emma smiled and nodded as her body thrummed from the close contact. The vibration from his lips moving against her ear, jostling her dangling earring, and his warm breath caressing her whorls, made her lightheaded.

When the DJ took a break and the crowd settled down for a few minutes, Alex took Emma's fingers in his and said, "I enjoyed our kiss very much."

The low timbre of his voice and his hand clasping hers sent heat through her core and she felt herself blush. "Me too. It was a special moment, wasn't it?"

His hand released hers and he used the barest tips of his fingers to stroke the inside of her arm. "It was. But then I suspect every moment with you is special. You're so energetic, so lively, and so beautiful." His eyes met hers and held.

"Thank you. I just love to dance. And you're so easy to follow."

"My wife was not as confident on the dance floor as you are. She would occasionally forget the next step, and I often found myself lifting and carrying her through to the next one. You never seem to miss a beat."

"It's years and years of practice with different partners. You learn to gauge their patterns and adjust to their hold. The way you lead is confident and sure, it's a pleasure to dance with a man who has command of the dance."

She picked up her glass to sip some wine, but it was empty. He chuckled, picked his up and fed it to her instead. She took a tiny sip but then said, "I can't drink your wine."

He set the glass down and dipped his finger into it, then ran it across her bottom lip. "We'll share it," he whispered. Then leaned in to lick the moisture off.

She moaned as he pulled back to focus on her wet lips.

"Oh, the things I want to do with that mouth," he murmured. With his thumb, he pulled her lower lip down then leaned in to take it between his parted lips. It was his turn to moan.

Then the music started up again, blaring out into the busy tavern. Not heeding the call to commence dancing, he kissed his way to her ear. She shivered then groaned.

"C'mon, let's get out of here," he whispered. Then he stood, already knowing her answer. He threw a few bills on the table and offered her his hand, and together they left through the battered oak door.

He walked her around the corner, to the side of the building, and then leaned her against the siding. He pressed her flush against it his with body. She could feel his hard-on burgeoning between them. She looked up at his face and saw the surprise in his eyes as he realized there was a substantial bulge keeping them apart. "That hasn't happened to this extent in a long time."

"And why is that?" she asked, hating that she sounded coy, because she knew the reason. But she wanted to hear him say that he'd been abstaining, and that despite his grief for another woman—her beautiful, smart cousin—he still wanted her.

He shook his head. "My head just hasn't been into pleasure lately." He sighed. "I honestly didn't think the urge would come back after all this time." He grinned down at her. "I'm kind of pleased that it has."

"So you don't date?

"I don't," he stated.

She wriggled her hand between them and cupped him.

He groaned and pushed his erection into her palm. Several times. "I wonder what I should do about this. Be a shame to waste it. It might be the last one I get."

She smirked. "Well, that's a line I've not heard before. And I'd love to help you out. I mean, I'm really into you. But I have a firm three-date rule."

He pulled back and smiled. "That's a good rule. So, there's hope . . ."

She smiled up at him, "We could count last week as number one . . ."

He smiled back, "And tonight as number two?"

He couldn't keep the hopefulness from being apparent. Although his voice was deep, her fondling of him caused him to falter in his half-assed plea. It touched her. This man was so polite, so considerate. And it was obvious he hadn't brushed up on his dating skills since inviting his bride to the altar.

She nodded. "Could be. Got any plans for next week after class?"

He grinned. "I do now." And as he pushed back into her hand, he used his own hands to cup the sides of her face. He brought their faces close for an amazing kiss. He did things to her mouth, made her feel things that she'd never experienced to this extent. Trembles of pleasure coursed through her as his tongue seared her lips and meshed with hers as he explored her mouth. The intimacy was so tender, poignant, deeply touching. It was as if his tongue was loving her mouth—and taking life-giving succor from it.

He warmed her body from the inside out, teasing her with his tongue and drawing out long moans. His kisses were swoon worthy, heating her in places that she normally wasn't aware of, sending tendrils of flames igniting every cell, firing every electron.

When he ended the kiss she stood dazed.

He laughed at her transfixed state. "I'd better see you to your car so you can get home."

She came out of her stupor and dumbly nodded. Then took a step and stumbled. His hand reached out and he caught her by her elbow.

She looked down at her feet. "Oh these shoes, they are so beautiful. But torture to the feet. I should never have sat down."

He put his hand out, "Give them to me."

With the grace of a ballerina, she lifted one leg behind her and reached back to remove the shoe. He waggled his pointer finger and she hooked the strap of the shoe on it.

"Now the other," he commanded.

She obeyed as he held her steady, then she hooked the other shoe on his middle finger.

Then he bent and put one arm around her back, the other beneath her knees, and lifted her snug to his chest. She wrapped her arms around his neck and sighed. When had she ever felt this cherished?

She was amused by his formidable strength as he carried her so effortlessly, and charmed by the image they must have made as he carried her down the sidewalk, her glass slippers dangling from the hand hugging her knees.

He carried her two blocks to the dance studio's parking lot, both of them smiling the whole time. Then he gently set her on her feet by her driver's door. Theirs were the only cars left on the lot so he knew which one was hers.

"Nice wheels," he said. Using the security lighting she was able to punch in the code for the door. When the lock unclicked, he opened it for her, tossing her shoes onto the back passenger floor.

"It's a rental. I splurged a little for some fun in the sun."

He turned her in his arms and she thought he was going to kiss her again, but instead, with hands on her shoulders, he pressed her down onto the seat. Then he lowered himself into a squat and balanced on his toes. She recognized the yoga strength move he settled into, and she had to admire how strong he was as he as took her left foot into his hands and began massaging it.

The sound of her moan made his cock jerk. He smiled at his body's reaction. It had been so long since that part of him had jumped to the sounds of a woman's pleasure.

"Ohh, your hands are amazing. That feels so good."

"I can't wait to put them to use in other places," he murmured.

She couldn't help the shiver that zinged her core and heated her skin.

He finished with that foot, switched it with the other, and smiled at her delicious groans and moans as his fingers rubbed and kneaded the ball and heel, and then tugged on each toe. It was a wry smile and she knew in that moment that he had done this for Mallory. He knew what he was doing to her. Had probably perfected his technique on feet that had stood in fashionable high heels all day long, until Mallory had become pregnant.

He finished with a quick rubdown to both calves and watched as her face reflected the bliss. Her mind raced with guilt that finally blunted the pleasure, and had her opening fearful eyes to his. Though it was too dark for him to notice.

He stood and bent to give her a kiss on her check, his lips close to her ear while whispering, "Until next week."

He followed that with a quick kiss to her lips.

Then with both hands on her thighs, he turned her in her seat so that she faced forward, and closed the door. He waited until she was buckled in and driving off the lot before walking over to his Lexus SUV.

Chapter 20—Emma & Alex
Cupid, Hard at Work

And keeping to himself he plays the game
Without her love it always ends the same
While life goes on around him everywhere
He's playing solitaire
And solitaire's the only game in town

The music to *Solitaire*, written by Neil Sedaka, and performed by the Carpenters was being piped in over the sound system when Alex arrived at the dance studio the following Wednesday night. Eager to see each other, they were both early and were the first ones there.

Hearing the familiar song playing, Alex took Emma into his arms as soon as she crossed the dance floor to join him. He led her in a sultry slow dance while crooning the words to the song into her ear. When the song ended, both of his hands were on her hips and he pulled her in close.

He looked down at her, their eyes meeting. His lips bowed into a chagrinned smile, "I'm so glad I'm not going to be that lonely man tonight."

The smile she flashed him was dazzling. "Me too, no sad songs about being lonely for either of us tonight. I have to admit, I've thought of little else but you this week."

He nodded in agreement, "I thought tonight would never get here. I hope you don't think me presumptuous, but I reserved a suite at the Beverly Wilshire. We can get a drink at the hotel bar, and if you're hungry after class, we can order something to eat in the room."

He was watching her face for signs of unease at his suggestion. Her hazel eyes were wide with surprise so he added, "I hope you don't think it's too forward of me that I reserved a room."

"No, that's perfect. It's wonderful to know you've been anticipating our third date and what that means. I've been thinking a lot about us being together myself, but in all my imaginings, we were at my place."

"I wanted our first night together to be special."

"I've never been to The Regent Beverly Wilshire, but I've seen *Pretty Woman* a hundred times, so there's no way it won't be a special night for me."

"Well, I hope it will be special for other reasons," he said as he lifted her hand and kissed the back of it.

While they had been dancing, and talking, the rest of the class had filed in. Now the instructor was changing the piped in music to the class music and the small group took to the floor for their first set, a foxtrot.

After that was a spirited samba. Then a tango, and a free style they'd been working on followed.

An hour later, during a Viennese Waltz, he broke tradition and pulled her to him to murmur in her ear, his lips nipping the edge of her lobe to punctuate his last two words, "These classes always seemed too short—until tonight."

His arm came around her waist and pulled her in tighter. With their bodies aligned, and her breasts pressing into him, she could feel his arousal flaring below her belly. As he pressed his hand against her lower back to bring them even closer, she could feel the heat they were generating through their layers of clothing. The instructor shot them an "Ahem," and motioned their bodies apart with her waving arm. The hold in the waltz was supposed to be at arm's length.

He laughed, but complied.

Emma smiled up at him and said, "I thought about blowing off the class and just having you come to my apartment, but I didn't have your number."

"We'll have to remedy that," he said, as he spun her in huge circles around the floor. There were only six couples tonight so they had plenty of room to enjoy the romantic flourishes of the formal dance. "Let's do a low dramatic dip, shall we?"

"By all means," she said, and he turned her and spun her, and then dipped her over his arm in grand fashion.

They laughed at the over-the-top Hollywood-styled embellishment to the dance that was sure to annoy the instructor. Then there they were, him towering over her as she reclined confidently over his arm. Their eyes met with such heat, such passion, that it momentarily stunned them both. Lost in another world, they drank in each other's bright eyes, then moved to examine glistening faces with flushed cheeks and huge wide smiles. He focused intently on her soft beckoning lips. Her tongue slid out to roll in on itself and slick along her bottom lip and every muscle in his body tensed.

They stayed in hold long after the last beat, mesmerized by the moment. The instructor's clapping finally brought them out of their dazed stupor.

"That was amazing!" the instructor called out. "You two are simply breathtaking on the dance floor."

Alex whispered against her cheek so no one else could hear, "Something tells me, we're going to be breathtaking in bed as well."

A shiver of pleasure went through Emma's body as he slowly brought her upright. Her neck and chest were flushed, and she had hot quivers running through her body. She felt moisture pooling, her body readying itself to welcome him inside. She could not wait to be alone with him. Could not wait until they were naked and he was climbing over her . . . then entering her.

As soon as the dance session ended, Alex went to a bench and changed his shoes. Then he stood, took her hand in his, and led her out the door and into the fading twilight.

"I can stay the night, but I have to leave early in the morning." He gave her a pouty face. It was endearing that he was sad about it. "I have to relieve the babysitter who has an early morning class. But you can enjoy the hotel and sleep in. Breakfast will be delivered to the room when you wake up. Just ring the concierge. It's all been arranged."

He walked her through the parking lot. "Should we stop by your apartment so you can pack a bag? I arranged a car to drive you home in the morning, but you'll probably need a few things before you get back home tomorrow."

Her eyes went wide and her face lit up. She grinned, "I won't turn down a leisurely morning at the Beverly Wilshire. Oh my gosh, I wasn't expecting to stay over though. Maybe I will get up early, have breakfast, and go exploring before they kick me out."

He laughed and pulled her into his side as they walked over to her car and he murmured into her ear, "I was counting on leaving you limp and too exhausted to get up before noon. Don't fault my good intentions if you're not energetic in the morning." He ran his hand over her hip, possessively pulling her closer. "I'll follow you home so you can leave your car at your apartment."

"That would be great. I can pack a bag really fast. It won't take me five minutes to get ready."

Her excitement was palpable. He smiled his pleasure at her enthusiasm for his plans. He had vacillated, going back and forth each and every day this past week, before finally picking up the phone and calling the hotel.

"It's a plan then." He bent to brush a kiss alongside her cheek.

"An excellent plan," she affirmed, grinning wide, her face beaming her delight.

His nose nuzzled to her ear and he murmured, "Don't bother packing a nightgown. Once I get you naked, I'm going to keep you that way."

He felt her shiver and smiled into her hair, enjoying the subtle fruity mint essence of her shampoo.

He couldn't remember the last time he had been this excited, this happy . . . this alive.

Chapter 21—Alex & Emma
Hotel California

Eyes agog, Emma tried to take it all in. From the moment Alex made the turn and pulled under the *porte cochere* in front of the hotel, she had been swiveling her head absorbing it all.

He laughed. "Are you trying to place each scene with the setting in the movie?"

"Yes! I remember this driveway from one of the last scenes, when's she's in the limo and she's leaving him." She sang out in a strong clear voice, reminiscent of the tone of that sad scene, *"Lay a whisper on my pillow, leave the winter on the ground. I wake up lonely,* . . . " she sighed then mentally shook off the sadness of the song. "Oh, it's just so grand. Palatial! This must've cost you a fortune."

A man in uniform opened her door and she stepped out.

Alex smiled at her over the hood of his Lexus as he handed his keys to the valet and told him there were two bags in the back that needed to be brought to the room. Then he took her hand and led her up the steps. "It's worth the money just to see you so delighted and happy with it all."

At the entrance, she turned to face him, placing her hands on his chest and looking up into his face. "I'm going to be so delighted and happy with you, too," she said with a devilish wink and a huge grin. He beamed down at her. He loved that her smile was so gamine, yet so genuine. So sexy, yet not with the sophisticated air of the jaded women he was used to dealing with while drawing up their business contracts.

"You are," he promised, returning her wink with one so bold she was surprised her panties didn't drop to her ankles.

"And soon," she added, reaching up and working out the knot of his tie. She pulled it off, rolled it up and stuffed it into his pocket, patting it as if to say it was time to play.

He opened his collar, spread the plackets of his shirt, and placed her hand over his heart. He felt it speed up at her touch, felt his skin warm. He placed his hand over hers holding it there for a few seconds. It felt right, as if it should belong there. Then he lifted it and kissed each finger before gripping her hand in his and leading her into the hotel.

He allowed her several moments to turn in circles and gawk at the stately opulence and the well-heeled guests as he spoke with the concierge and requested the key to their room before dragging her into the elevator. She was saying, "Did you see that woman with her tiny little pink dog? And that dazzling diamond collar that matched hers? And that bellhop who was loading six guitar cases on a luggage rack?"

He pulled her in behind the closing doors, spun her around, and pressed her into the back wall of the elevator with his body flush to hers. His lips descended and he captured her lips with his, hushing her. All the way up to their floor he kissed her as if he would never get enough of her sweet taste, her soft lips, her delicious little sighs of pleasure . . .

The bell dinged and he dragged her out the door by a finger down the neck of her dress. By the time he got her down the hall and through the door of their room, while leaving a trail of wet kisses along her neck, he was panting and she was arching her head to give him better access. She was weak in the knees and clinging to him for support when his tongue outlined the spiral of her ear and threatened to send her in a heap to the plush carpet.

A bellhop was leaving, having placed the bags in the room and delivered a bottle of champagne placed in an ice bucket. "Are you ready for the champagne to be opened, sir?" he asked as he stood in the doorway.

"No," Alex said, "I'll open it later." He pulled a bill from his money clip and handed it to him, thanking him.

After Alex ushered her inside, and closed and locked the door, he took her by the shoulders and backed her up against it.

Then with a splayed hand on each side of her head, he leaned in and kissed her hard, claiming her mouth and tangling his tongue with hers until they were both senseless and grasping at each other's clothes. She was trying to pull off his suit coat to get to his chest; he was trying to get the zipper on the back of her dress undone so he could pull the sleeves of her dress down. When the dress was billowing in the front and the sleeves were down to her elbows, he reached inside and cupped her breasts through her lacy push-up bra.

"Your breasts are real," he said with whispered awe.

"Yes, they are real breasts."

"I mean, they're genuine."

Her lips bowed into a huge smile. "Yes, they are genuine—real, honest-to-God breasts."

"You know what I mean. They aren't fake. Any part of them." He reached behind her and unsnapped the clasp then reverently drew her breasts out from her barely there bra. He put his palm under one and hefted it in his hand. He looked down, his thumb running along the underside as if studying the texture, his fingers digging into the plumpness of the soft, smooth flesh he held in his hand. "No silicone."

She gasped at his touch. "You appear to be something of an expert on breasts." There was a questioning inflection at the end of her comment.

"When I was at Stanford, I dated quite a few up and coming models and actresses. Most had felt compelled to embellish what the Lord had given them. Sadly, most were comically overstated. They felt . . . stiff and hard. But yours, they're so soft and sweet," he ran a thumb back and forth along the underside, "and full . . . heavy in just the right way. "

"Given I live the life of a dancer, I often wish they were smaller."

"Oh, no no no," he said, as he handled both of her breasts as if newfound treasures. "These are perfect." He bent and took one peak into his mouth, ran his tongue around the tip and sucked.

Her head fell back and she moaned. Keened actually. The sound shrill and followed by a long hiss of undeniable gratification as pleasure coursed through her.

"Ah, that's what I wanted to hear." He set about making sure he heard more of the same, finally, pulling the dress off along with her bra, and taking both breasts more completely into his hands. As his mouth moved from one to the other, and he made murmuring sounds of appreciation, she arched her back so he could feed on her as he desired.

The sounds of his worshipful praise, as well as his expert touches and tugs, sent spirals of desire drumming down through her, wetting her panties. When his hand slid down her tummy and he found the band of her panties and slid inside, the flooding began in earnest.

His moan when he discovered her wet and needy, drowning his fingers in her hunger for him, sent heat flushing her face, her neck, her chest. Her blood heated and her heart pounded so hard she could hear it in her ears. When one lone finger entered her, her knees buckled and she collapsed into his cupped hand. He removed his finger, stripped off her panties and bent to pick her up.

"I think we'd better get you on the bed," he said, his voice husky. He carried her into the bedroom and placed her on the huge California king. His lips found hers as he followed her down. When he pulled away, he leaned to the side and watched his hand as it ran over her exposed body.

She saw him take in the trim little vee of light brown curls. Saw his eyes widen at the theatrically sparse mons she sported for practical purposes, and watched as his nose flared when he drew in her essence.

His large hand covered her in the most intimate caress as his long middle finger went back to where it had been, burrowed deep within her. "Now where were we?" he asked as he curled that finger and stroked into the wall of her vagina at the exact spot every cell in her body was screaming for it to be.

She groaned and arched into his hand.

"Ah yes, I remember," he said, then ducked his head and licked her clit.

She came off the bed to meet his mouth and he chuckled. "Like that, do you? Then you're going love this," he whispered. He stood, grabbed her ankles and pulled her to the bottom of the bed so that her bottom was on the edge. He knelt on the carpet and began feasting on her at the same time two long fingers did an intricate massage to the tight muscle trying to clamp onto them. Her cries to the ceiling, begging him not to stop, brought an onslaught of licking, tonguing and full out sucking on her clit until he felt her insides spasm around his fingers. She screamed his name before coating his lips and chin with the slickness that came with her orgasm.

"Oh, it's going to feel so good to have you milk my cock like you just milked my fingers. I can't wait to be inside you," he groaned, and added, "fucking you into that headboard."

He wiped his face on her belly as he worked his way up to her breasts. He pinched both nipples and delighted at her squeal, then tugged, making them hard again as he leaned over her and kissed her on the lips, letting his tongue slide in so she could savor the taste that coated it.

Her loud moan and arching back told him she liked what he was doing to her nipples, now points so hard and long he could scarcely believe they had been soft, silky crests when he'd first held her breasts in his hands. He gave them more of the torture they were begging for, twisting and tugging, pinching and lightly nipping. Loving her sobs and earnest hisses of ecstasy, he heard her surprising words of shame. They sent incredible jolts of pleasure straight to his cock.

That was something unexpected, he thought, with a wry grin to himself. Rarely did his own base sexuality surprise him, but he was both intrigued and delighted in her cries for more base treatment. His cock, behind the zipper of his trousers, strained for release. He felt the tip wetting the inside of his boxers.

"Yes, pinch harder. Ohhhh, it hurts soooo good. Yes! Oh, what an evil man you are to twist and tug on my tits so hard. Tell me how bad I am to want this!" she screamed.

Her words had him reaching down to adjust his cock. When he found that didn't suffice, he lowered the zipper and freed his straining erection. Then he obliged her. "You are so naughty. Letting me see these pretty tits of yours, allowing me to fill my hands with your sweet flesh. And to torture your long, hard nipples. You are gorgeous topless. You'd make a great stripper—showing your tits off, strutting like you know what the sight of them would do to lecherous men like me." He bent down and bit a nipple. "I love that you let me suck and bite on them like this, getting them so damn hard. And me too." He bent and bit the opposite nipple this time while twisting the other.

She cried out, "Alex I need you! Pleeeease."

He rubbed the tip of his penis up and down her slit, his moisture blending with hers. It felt amazing. "Is this what you want Emma? My cock inside you?"

"Yes! Yes, please Alex. Fuck me. Please," she whimpered. "Please, please, I need you," she continued to beg. She arched up and fumbled for the opening of his pants, tried to unfasten the only thing keeping his pants around his waist. She couldn't undo it with one hand, instead grazing his cock with her fingertips, making it jump to meet her hand and him to swear under his breath.

Hearing her beg while using his name made him harder than he ever remembered being. Looking down, he saw the blue veins bulging and the skin stretched thin to accommodate his widening girth and extended length. Having her touch him caused his cock to jerk again, demanding more of the same. Holding himself over her, he managed to undo his belt and the fastener above the zipper. Desperate, her hands joined his and within seconds she had pushed both his pants and his boxers down past his hips and over his ass. She gripped him in her hand, her thumb slicking the tip. He had to pant and take deep breaths to keep from spilling into her fist. She refused to release him when he covered her hand with his. He disciplined her. He reached between them and used the flat of his hand to smack her pussy.

She gasped and her eyes went wide with shock. She dropped her hand.

He chuckled at her reaction. He looked down into her face and admonished her, "You can play with my penis later, right now, I'm going to fuck you with it."

He gripped himself, rubbed the tip against her slick lips and positioned it at her opening, "Is this what you want?" he teased. His gorgeous smile beaming down at her told her she was going to get it and get it in every wicked way there was.

"Yes. I want that beautiful big cock inside me. Stop teasing me Alex. Give it to me!"

He loved hearing her so desperate to have him. She was perfect. Without knowing it, she said the things he needed to hear, things that made him so unbearably hard. He felt like the most wanted, most needed man in the universe. He reveled in it. Fucking loved it.

"You're going to get it and get it hard, that I promise you." He knelt on the bed and dug into his back pocket for his wallet. Removing a condom from an inside sleeve, he tore the wrapper with his teeth, then with the ease of never forgotten familiarity, rolled it down and pinched up the tip. Placing the crown of his penis at her opening again, he gave her a look with both brows raised that clearly asked permission. "Ready to feel me inside you?"

She nodded, "Please Alex," she closed her eyes and sighed, anticipating the pleasure. "Inside me now. Fill me with you."

She clamped her lips together as he shoved inside, sending her shoulders up the bed and her head into the pile of pillows. It was a rough, forceful entry, primal and exactly what they both needed. He possessed her, and the groan of satisfaction along with his head thrown back in ecstasy did amazing things for her ego. This man knew how to make a woman feel as if she was vital to him achieving pleasure, that she was the only person in the cosmos who could.

His head came forward and his eyes met hers. "You feel amazing."

She could feel him throbbing inside her. She closed her eyes and gave him a cat-ate-the-cream smile, clearly fine with the deep thrust that had sent her sliding across the sheets.

He wrapped his hands under her thighs, gripped her hips, and pulled her to him where they were connected. He began to move, relishing each sensation as if he hadn't done this in years, which truth be told, he hadn't. But his body certainly hadn't forgotten how.

He plowed into her with deep rutting thrusts that lifted her up against him then sent her toward the headboard and the protection of the nest of pillows. Over and over again, going faster and faster until he was grinding and hitting her just where she needed him, the upper ridge of his cock meshing and abrading her clit. Her long legs went around his waist and hooked behind his back to bring him even closer, tighter to that spot where she needed him, in her mindless, hip arching frenzy. He pressed tight to her clit with the root of his penis each time he impaled her, his vigorous drives and quick stabs forcefully pressing against her swollen vulva. His length inside her stretched the walls of her vagina, nudging the spot that craved friction and bringing her climax rushing over her like a wave cresting and exploding on the rocks.

She keened his name, grabbed his buttocks for all she was worth, and pulled him tight to her to still him. He held suspended in the moment, looking down at her. Her head was thrown back, her mouth open in a rictus of ecstasy, and her eyes scrunched closed to keep the world at bay. He felt her muscles spasm around him while she arched and went rigid. He rode out her orgasm letting her direct him, though honestly, she was gripping his buttocks so hard and holding him to her so forcefully he doubted he could have moved if he'd wanted to. He watched her contorted face as she shuddered against him and knew she was tumbling away into unimaginable delight.

He continued to observe her as she drew in a deep breath, her face relaxing, she went from what appeared to be a mindless ride of anguish, to a quiet surrender of bliss.

The grip of her nails in his butt cheeks loosened, her body collapsed under him and she opened her eyes to smile up at him. He leaned down and kissed her, his tongue claiming her mouth and his lips devouring hers and taking possession of her gloriously sated, sassy mouth.

Having lost all sense of restraint from watching her come, then feasting on her sexy as hell mouth, he abruptly pulled out. Using one hand to keep the condom in place, he lifted her and flipped her over. Pulling her hips up high so she was on all fours, he knelt behind her. Then entering her like a battering ram, he stroked fast and hard, pummeling, and sending her to her elbows. The sight of him entering her at that angle sent a low growl from his throat.

Gripping her hips in his large hands, he pulled her to him while he fucked her with dizzying speed until his body jerked and shuddered. He held her tightly against his groin as he emptied into her.

She felt his cock erratically pulsing as her vagina gripped him and saw through the mirror over the dresser on the opposite wall, that he had thrown back his head. Heard him release a groan that ended as a roar. She couldn't help in that moment to wonder where his thoughts were. When his mind left his body, was he with her, or was he with Mallory?

He had spilled everything he had saved for years into Emma, his head thrown back and his eyes closed. He had savored every surge of his body pulsing inside hers, and felt such a perfect wasting of tension leave his body, that tears released from his eyes. He was left with a giddy feeling of relief that he never wanted to go away. For the first time in a very long time, he felt one with the universe, and definitely one with this woman.

Finally spent and limp from his release, and the euphoria wavering afterward, he lightly swatted her right butt cheek, forcing her to flatten onto the bed. Then he fell on top of her, his elbows cradling some of his weight. He caged her in, kissing along her shoulders and neck.

After a few moments, he murmured, "You okay?"

"Never better. Did you just spank me?"

She could feel his chuckle reverberate through her. "And if I did?"

She lifted her head and looked over her shoulder at him, her brows raised. Then she gave him such a huge grin—one that conveyed that she might not mind more of that treatment—that he had to laugh out loud.

"You're going to be the death of me," he whispered into her ear.

"Ditto," she murmured into the pillow she had pulled to her to snuggle into.

A few seconds later he fell to the side taking her with him and holding her close, her back to his chest. One hand snaked around her waist; the other lightly caressed the underside of her breast. "You are amazing. There are no words," he said against her shoulder.

"Mmmm," she said on a long sigh.

His arm still around her waist, he pulled her tight to him and kissed along her neck. "Give me a few minutes and we'll get up and shower."

Her head whipped back, "We're done?"

To his great pleasure, she sounded miffed. He chuckled, "Not hardly."

He drew little circles on her hip with his fingertip. "My parents are taking the girls to a birthday celebration for my aunt on Saturday. Would you like to have dinner at my house?"

"Hmmm," she said as if thinking through a busy schedule. "I don't believe I have anywhere I have to be until next Wednesday, when I have a dance class with the sexiest dance partner you can possibly imagine."

"I can't imagine one any sexier than mine."

He moved his hand between them and when he slid himself out of her, he removed the condom. He rolled away to dispose of it, then slid off the bed. Reaching out he offered her his hand, "C'mon, before we both fall asleep, come shower with me."

She groaned but lifted her hand and put it in his. "Feels so good to just stay here."

"I promise you, it'll feel good in the shower, too."

"That's a guarantee?"

"Barrister's honor."

"Well, okay then."

He gave a tug and she followed. Once in the large ensuite, he set the water temperature for the walk-in shower and tugged her under the spray with him.

Using gel soap he lathered her from head to toe, learning her body and appreciating every inch. She paid back the favor, lingering on his hair and scalp. When they were both clean, he caged her against the tiled wall, rolled on the condom he'd slid on the tiled shelf, and lifted her onto his erection. "We'll go a little slower this time," he said.

"I have absolutely no complaints about last time," she said.

"Good, because customer service doesn't handle complaints about bad sex very well."

"What do they do about it?"

"They insist on more practice. You know, practice makes perfect."

"What happens if you start with perfect?"

He lifted her and then slowly brought her back down, kissing her breasts and stroking her ribcage, "Then we switch up and add variety."

"What kind of variety?" she asked, being sassy.

"Well, unless I misinterpreted your huge grin, we can do as the pirates say, 'The beatings will continue until morale improves.' Customer service wants everyone's complete satisfaction."

"Beatings? You want to do beatings?" she asked, a little unsure of where this might be leading.

He withdrew until he was nearly out of her, and then pushed into her again. "Nothing so brutal as beatings, but I can do a pretty devilish spanking now and again. If the lady so desires," he added. Then, as if not sure he should have broached the idea of any kind of kink, especially this particular one, he said, "It's not compulsory. Not like I'm the professor and you're the student who needs a better grade."

"Why does the thought of that turn me on?" She was clearly surprised at the idea. That was evident by the frown between her brows.

He had to laugh out loud at her expression. "You've never been spanked before?"

"Mmm . . . no. Not unless you include running through that fanny smackin' gauntlet my friends set up at my birthday party when I was eight."

"Ever been tied up?"

"Never."

"Blindfolded?"

"No. Except for that trust class in high school."

"Anal?"

"Once."

"Did you like it?"

She hesitated. "Maybe. Jury's still out on that one."

"No worries then . . . customer service has a lot of options for you. We aim to please."

"I hope they're not all on the agenda tonight?"

He laughed. Then sped up inside her, kissing the smooth

skin against her neck as he began fucking her in earnest.

"Not. Tonight," he panted. "This may be it for me. But . . . early morning might have its own pleasures in store for you."

"I'm not really a morning person," she panted back.

"Customer service doesn't usually have early morning hours. Usually. But we have to use the time we have . . . wisely," he grunted.

His hand on her jaw, he pulled her to face him, even though it meant a sluice of water running down her nose and chin. He captured her mouth with his and kissed her with languid strokes, murmuring, "I love your mouth, and God, what a sweet tongue."

He kissed her slowly, drinking her in, one slow sip at a time, then angled her face away from the waterfall and licked the remaining water off her lips. After a nip at the plump curve of her smooth bottom lip followed by a thorough tongue tangling, he set a new pace, one that built, adding layers of sensation on top of sensation as his fingers caressed every place he could reach.

Soon their cries of passion were echoing off the tiled walls. He lifted one of her legs over his hip, reached between them and just barely touched her clit with the back of his thumb. She came apart with him following mere seconds later.

When the water began to cool, they quickly rinsed off and he toweled her dry before carrying her back, wrapped in the towel, to the bed and tucked her in against him. He reached over and turned off the light, then whispered. "Customer Service will be sending a survey in the morning. If you can't answer every question positively, we want to know what we can do to improve our relations."

"Hmm. Sleep. We'll work on the survey in the morning."

"Good night, my beautiful dancing queen." He pulled her closer, his hairy legs nudging against her smooth waxed ones, his splayed hand on her taut belly holding her to him.

Dancing Queen. The name her uncle had for her. She didn't want him here in her head, not right now. Just the thought of him sullied this beautiful time with Alex, made her feel cheap. Used. Disloyal to the man snuggled in beside her. She forced the thought away. She didn't want anything to ruin the relationship she and Alex were developing.

Chapter 22—Emma & Alex
Feelings

"That was poorly done of me," Alex said with a look of chagrin as he stared down at the beautiful tousled-haired woman lying under him.

She stretched, forcing the twisted sheet covering her to expose her breasts. Then remembering she probably had unfavorable morning breath, she brought her hand down to cover her mouth.

He shifted off of her and stood, removing the used condom. She grabbed the sheet and pulled it up to cover her breasts then turned on her side to face him. "In what way was that poorly done?"

"You didn't come. Yet I came like a Texas oil well."

"I'm not a morning person. I can't get my head into sex at," she turned to look at the clock on the opposite nightstand, "five in the morning. But I'm more than amiable and willing to help you with your needs."

"Well, I appreciate you giving up a few minutes of sleep to service me and to let me use your wonderful depository," he said in a mock business tone as he ran a long finger down her nose before kissing the tip of it. "But I am more than willing to run the orgasm scoreboard up in your favor this weekend." He pulled up his pants and zipped them while she took a moment to admire his muscled chest and washboard abs before he slipped on his shirt. She knew he had to get home to relieve the nanny watching the girls, then shower and put on a fresh business suit before heading out again when his mom got there.

"If memory serves, it is in my favor at this precise moment."

He flashed her a satisfied grin, "You go off like a rocket with the right kind of provocation."

"Your fingers are magical and your tongue should be registered as a lethal weapon."

He laughed, throwing back his head and showcasing his shadowed jaw and neck. The man had dark, abundant hair in all the right places. He was so virile with his heavy beard and generous chest pelt that it made her mouth water.

"Should I send a car for you Saturday afternoon?"

"I can drive. I just need the address to put in the GPS."

He scribbled it on the pad by the phone then tore it off and handed it to her. "It's easy to find. I'll leave the gate open for you."

"What will we be doing? How should I dress?"

"We will be working on that orgasm tally. And the costume you're wearing now will be just fine."

She lifted the sheet and flashed him her body, "What, this old thing? And white is not really my color."

He shot her a grin as he put his wallet, handkerchief, phone, and keys into his pants and sport coat pockets. "The sheets on my bed are navy blue, you'll look stunning displayed on them."

"Displayed?"

"I have not had nearly enough time to ogle your killer body. You, on your back, with your knees bent and your thighs splayed at the end of the bed is going to be the image that gets me through the rest of this week."

He walked over to the bed and kissed her thoroughly, uncaring that neither had brushed their teeth. "Enjoy your breakfast."

"I'm going to enjoy exploring the hotel."

"Go to the spa and get a massage. Just charge it to the room. Everything's been taken care of."

He opened the door then turned back. "Just make sure it's a woman masseuse. The thought of another man's hands on you makes me think homicidal thoughts."

The door closed behind him and she groaned. How the

hell had she fallen for him so quickly?

This could not be good, these feelings she was having—for Mallory's husband, for the father of her parents' great nieces and her own second cousins, for pity's sake. For the man who did not know that their meeting had been no accident, that it had been orchestrated as a spying assignment.

Chapter 23—Emma
A Good Soak

Emma curled under the wonderfully soft duvet and fell back to sleep while reliving every sexy thing Alex did and said. When she woke up two hours later she was refreshed. And a bit lonely.

She stretched like the wonton, sexually satisfied woman that she was. Then typical to her, she bounced out of bed and started a bath in the opulent tub, reminiscent of the *Pretty Girl* tub, but not quite so big, or round. This was not the penthouse suite after all, she reminded herself. But it was still very impressive.

She knew Alex had money; that he'd come from money. And with a slight twinge of trepidation, she wondered for just a moment if this interlude had just been him having his one-night stand in a more lavish way than would typically be the custom for most men. Was last night his version of a Twilight Motel with a hot chick on the strip? She hoped not. She wouldn't be able to stand it if it was. But he had asked for more of the same, at his home, no less. She would have to be content with that.

Pouring in the scented bath salts, noting from the label that they were not merely Lavender or Eucalyptus, but Peach Mango infused with Persian Mint. Not just mint, mind you, but Persian Mint. Her mind flipped through long forgotten history lessons. Was there still a Persia? She didn't think so. Wasn't that modern day Iran now? So the mint came from . . . Iran? Even she, freethinker that she was didn't think she'd buy something touted as Iranian Mint. Well, that was marketing for you. Giving her mint that was from a dead and now war-torn civilization. But it sounded nice and smelled wonderful.

She stopped to wonder if she was marketing something bogus too. An out-on-her-luck actress, with notable dancing skills, selling the idea of an ingénue, to a man of the world, in need of companionship—and a budding physical relationship to handle all the awakening testosterone surging through his body. She was no ingénue, but she *was* down on her luck, *and* a consummate dancer, *and* she did aspire for something akin to companionship with a man who was kind and thoughtful . . . for a change. No, she wasn't bogus. She just hadn't been totally honest.

She stripped off the plush robe and stepped into the tub. Then had to do the compulsory submerge into the fluff of bubbles, kicking her feet and screaming, but not loudly, over how happy she was. And in this moment she was happy. Beyond happy. Filled with hope, and grand thoughts of a future with a man she was already half in love with. She felt she owned the universe.

No man had ever made her this happy—made her feel this special. She stayed in the bath until the water grew tepid and the mint, Persian or not, was hardly detectable.

She got dressed and packed her case, carefully wrapping the bottle of champagne they hadn't even opened inside her new jacket. She went down to the lobby and left her small case with the concierge. Then she went exploring. She found a breakfast bar and grabbed a latte and a warm chocolate croissant, browsed some shops, walked around the iconic pool where she was served a sparkling mimosa, and found her way to the spa for some pampering and a full body massage. Her body loose and her mind giddy from indulging so many deep-seated fantasies, she sat in one of the elegant sitting areas in the main lobby, people watching until it was time to meet her driver at the bottom of the steps to the impressive entrance.

Her head was in the clouds until she was dropped off at her apartment. Then reality set back in. She had three days until she would see Alex again. She had come to L.A. to find work. She needed to set her mind to doing that. She sat at her dinette table clicking though page after page of casting call notices. Then made a list of the ones that appealed to her, and that she thought she had a shot at, and planned out the rest of her week.

On Saturday morning she texted Alex that she wanted to make dinner for him that evening, and when he responded in favor of that, she went to the store. Then, like every besotted Disney princess, she sang corny theme songs while prepping the ingredients. By two o'clock she was on her way to his house using the built-in navigation system to guide her.

She was prepared for the gated entrance, but not for the seriously long drive leading up to the house. Everything she learned about him reinforced the idea that Alex was a very private person. And that he intended to keep his life and that of his girls isolated from the rest of the world. If he knew who she really was, he would not be happy having her here. It stung to realize how different their lives were. But she would show him, show him how much she truly cared for him, and that she wasn't interested in his wealth or disrupting the life he had with his daughters.

Chapter 24—Alex & Emma
Living the Fairy Tale

She followed the winding drive, trying to catch a glimpse of the house, but it was almost half a mile before the tall cedars gave way to a rolling stretch of lawn leading to a circular drive. The impressive house had even rows of trees with fruit heavy on the branches going up a hill as a backdrop to the scene. She felt as if she was an actor in a movie, driving up to a set. Well, she was an actor, but never on a set as grand as this.

The house was not so much a house as a compound, with each building having a distinct French flair to it, yet there were also Tudor touches. It was as if the builder wanted to downplay the impressive size by lending it quaint features like those of a rustic farmhouse, using both stucco and light-toned bricks along with fieldstone, and mullioned windows set off by cross-hatching with muted blue shutters. It was Old World eclectic in design, as if the owners weren't sure what European country their house should represent here in America. But the result was beautiful. Her family home was a mish-mash of architecture, too, but this was classy and elegant, whereas her family's house was kind of hillbilly.

There was a matching six-car garage angled and set apart to the left of the main house, and she could see two cars and a tractor in the open bays. Beyond, and to the side of the garage, was a stable. And while she couldn't see inside to see if there were any animals, she did see an orange cat scamper over bales of stacked hay, running to hide inside at the sound of her car on the drive.

To complete the setting around the main house and accompanying outbuildings, rows upon rows of orange, cherry, and apple trees provided shade to the magnificent rolling lawns. In the distance, the sun was beginning to drop behind the curved tile roof of the main house, casting everything golden. It looked like a fairytale house, and she adored it. It was perfect for two little princesses.

She was sorry she wasn't going to see them tonight. She was a little miffed at the notion that maybe he didn't think he knew her well enough to have them home and trust her around them yet. But then, their relationship was new, so it was probably wise not to expose the girls to someone they might get attached to. Or to set a bad example, given the immoral nature of a woman spending the night in their father's bedroom.

She had to accept, that from Alex's perspective, this was probably just a date. His night off from the girls so his parents could spoil them for a while, and his chance to be with a woman and do things people their age did to be social . . . and to scratch an itch.

She parked the car in the circular drive in front of the massive double arched entrance doors, inset with whimsical little latched doors. Such a cottage-down-the-lane feature that she had to smile. Adults and children of all heights had their own peephole. After she'd put the convertible top up and closed the door, she stood, taking it all in. Mallory would have loved this house. It was the fairytale.

She turned when she heard the sound of a rooster and laughed. At the same time, as she saw Alex come around the side of the house walking beside a horse—a golden blonde horse, with doe-like brown eyes and a beautiful coat of glossy brushed hair leading down to silky feathered hair covering its hooves. She was a regal mount and matched the splendor of the man leading her. Emma's heart almost stopped at the virile masculinity of the scene, seeing him there, tall and jean-clad, with dusty riding boots standing beside such a majestic animal. His hand was on the leather harness—close to the part that joined near the horse's ear—held with a causal familiarity that bespoke companionship. This was his horse. And the horse knew it well.

"Hi," he called as he lifted his hand to wave.

"Hey there," she waved back. "You have a friend, I see."

"This is Cinder," he said as he drew closer.

"Cinder? As in ashes?"

"As in Cinderella."

"Ah. The girls named her."

"It was either that or Minnie Mouse." He bent and kissed her lightly on the lips. "Hi," he whispered.

She smiled up at him. "Can I pet her?"

"Of course."

He watched as she stroked the horse's head between her chocolate brown eyes, then scratched behind her ears, and petted her long neck.

"You like horses."

"Yeah. I had one when I was a girl. Such a sweet thing. Lula Belle. Broke my heart when she died."

"What did she die from?"

"Equine Infectious Anemia. She was nearing twenty and got some kind of swamp bug. We couldn't get ahead of it and had to put her down. It was awful."

"They are susceptible to so many things," he commiserated.

"How long have you had her?"

"About four months. I was told the ponies needed company."

"The ponies?"

"Yeah. Each of my daughters has one."

"Dare I guess the ponies names?"

He laughed. "Do you watch the Disney Channel?"

"No. But I know little girls love Elsa and Anna."

"Well, one's a filly so that's Elsa, the other is not."

"Olaf?"

He laughed. "No Pascal."

"The lizard in Tangled?"

"My, you do know your Disney characters."

She blushed. "I know all the songs too."

"I know quite a few myself now," he said as his hand brushed the hair back from the side of her face and he bent to kiss her on the neck below her ear. "The Mickey Mouse Clubhouse song, Alena of Avalor's song, most of The Lion King's songs . . ." he kissed alongside her neck as he hummed "Can You Feel the Love Tonight," ending with his tongue circling her ear.

Cinder, not happy at not being the recipient of his full attention, nudged him away from her and they both laughed. "She's not happy sharing your affections," Emma said.

Alex smiled down at her, "Then I guess I'd better take her back to her stall. Walk with me, I'll show you around."

"Sure," she said with a huge grin. She wanted to know everything about him, see everything that meant something to him.

As he walked her past a grove of trees he said, "This is the orchard, or the beginning of it. There are three rows of orange trees, three rows of cherry trees, two rows of mangoes, two pears, two apples, one row of avocados, and five hedges of blackberries and blueberries. Beyond that are some fields with strawberries and string beans, cabbages and kale, and a whole mess of wildflowers. I put the girls in their wagon and take them to pick flowers for a big bouquet for their grandmother on special holidays."

He led her into the stable. There were eight stalls. She could see that most were empty. He led Cinder into a stall that had her name painted on a horseshoe hanging over the door, then he removed her harness, saddle, and blanket. Brushing her and spreading fresh hay about, he checked her water bucket and food bin before patting her on the rump. He closed the stall door and checked to make sure it was locked, then walked Emma over to see Elsa and Pascal, who were only interested in the apple slices he fed them.

"You take care of three horses, two young girls, orchards and gardens, and have your own legal firm?"

"I have a lot of help—my parents, a nanny, housekeeper,

gardener, someone who comes to take care of the horses twice a day, a paralegal, and three assistants. It is a lot of work, but I wanted the girls to grow up around nature, to learn to grow their own food, and to ride horses and climb trees. To always have a place where they could walk and play and pick flowers. They have a playground on the other side of the house and a pool with slides. I wanted them to have everything I could give them since they don't have their mother."

She sighed, "It's a beautiful place to raise kids."

"I couldn't believe my luck when my realtor called to say the perfect house just came on the market. She sent me pictures and I bought it within the hour. We were moved in within a week. That was just a few weeks after they were born. I love it here. It's close to the city, but far enough away to be peaceful and quiet."

She spun around and took it all in. "It is. It's perfect," she breathed.

He checked both of the ponies' stall doors, and walked over to where she stood looking out at the orchard. Dappled sunlight shone on her blonde hair giving it a burnished gold look and highlighting her perfect skin. He wrapped both arms around her waist, his chin resting on her shoulder to see her vantage point. She was watching a family of finches fly from branch to branch, chattering noisily about a rabbit disturbing their peace.

"You're perfect." He lifted her hair and kissed along the nape of her neck. "So beautiful, sexy . . . so sweet." His other hand slid under her sweater, found her left breast and cupped it. Then the edge of his thumb stroked her nipple through the lace of her bra. She moaned and he pressed his groin into her so she could feel how hard he was for her.

"I should show you the house. Before I end up taking you inside a barn."

"I like barns. They're earthy, and rustic, and—" she stopped talking and he stiffened when they both heard a motorized utility cart careen around the corner of a shed then pull up and stop short in front of the main barn door.

"That would be Clay, come to settle the horses in for the night."

"Well that puts a damper on doing naughty things up against a splintery stall door."

He laughed. "Let's go to the house. I've never counted how many doors there are, but I'm pretty sure none of them will leave splinters in your beautiful, smooth ass."

"I've got food in the car. We should get that out of the hot car first."

He took her hand in his and led her out of the barn, waving to the man who was climbing out of the little tractor with a utility body.

"I can't wait to see what you planned for dinner. I rarely get a home cooked meal. My parents are big fans of eating out, and are determined to expose the girls to many different cuisines. I mostly eat salads made from vegetables harvested from the gardens."

"It's one of my special dishes. I learned to make it while I was living in New York. It's called Slumgullion. It's easy and it makes a lot, and the leftovers are just as yummy."

They got the groceries from her car and carried them inside. While he took out the containers of chopped vegetables and put the package of meat in the refrigerator, she walked around the open great room that was part of the main living area of the house. The ultra modern kitchen was command central; everything else flowed seamlessly from the endless granite countertops and light maple cabinets to the muted birch flooring.

She stood in the middle of the family room area, her hands shoved into the back pockets of her black jeans, and her head tilted back staring up at the high ceiling. "Coffered ceilings, and window seats, you don't see those features anymore. This is gorgeous."

"Thank you. The special moldings and trim throughout the house is one of the reasons I fell in love with it."

"I can see why. It's a country house, but with a very well thought out floor plan and design. You can almost feel the love it took to build it."

He came up from behind her and turned her to face him. "That's exactly how I felt the first time I walked through the front door. It reminded me of the Blandings' house."

"*Mr. Blandings Builds His Dream House*. Yes, you're right. I can see it!"

He looked down at her delighted face and ran a finger along her jawline. "You are damned near perfect, you know that? Not many women of your generation have ever even heard of that movie."

"Well I do fancy myself to be an actor, and Cary Grant and Myrna Loy were some of the best there were."

He smiled, "Yeah, their comic timing was spot on. It's been years since I've seen it, but I still smile remembering how she connived him into going along with the project, each step of the way."

"We should watch it together."

"I'd like that. We can download it anytime, maybe even tonight. But first, I want to show you my bedroom." His voice was husky, deep with longing.

"Any particular reason?" she chided, playing the ingénue.

"I bought new bed linens. Wanted to see what you thought of them. See how you look displayed on them."

She reached up and caressed the back of his neck and brought his lips down to meet hers, "Lead the way."

Chapter 25—Emma & Alex
A Moment in Time

The kiss was everything a kiss should be—soft lips opening like delicate petals to receive a blessing of sustenance, tongues tentatively tasting and then voraciously devouring. His groan of pleasure and her moan begging for more had him bending and lifting her into his arms. He carried her to a hall off to the right that opened up into a huge master suite.

The style of the heavy French distressed pine furniture matched the house so perfectly that she knew he had to have bought the house furnished. The oversized iron canopy bed he placed her on was definitely custom-made. The silver patina of the antique frame dominated the room with its tall spires reaching toward the triple tray ceiling. There was a single wisp of white tulle draped over the scrollwork that came down to caress the intricate headboard. It was a massive bed. And when he placed her on it she felt the comforting firmness of a bed that could hold a set of twins jumping up and down on it, or two people having a vigorous romp before the sun came up, without anyone in the house hearing a single squeak.

He stood over her unbuttoning his shirt. She saw behind him to the custom cream-colored cabinet doors alongside one whole wall, joining a light sage painted wall at the corner. It was the European style to have custom cabinetry built into the walls for closet space instead of having walk-in closets, but she could see that this room had both, as well as a dressing room and an ensuite off the left, "Wow, this bedroom . . ."

"Yeah, I know. A lot of room for just one person. You're the first woman I've had in this room . . . on this bed."

"I'm thinking it's substantial enough to handle any workout you have planned," she said with a grin.

"Well right now, I want to take you nice and slow. Later

I'll bring out the whips and chains," he said with a grin. He climbed onto the bed and drew her sweater off, then undid the button on her jeans and pulled the zipper down.

He placed kisses along her belly, over her hip points and into the vee where her jeans were open and hinted at her navy blue boyshort panties.

As he knelt on the bed, nibbling on her, she reached her hand down to cup him. The twill of his pants was soft, but he was hard. As hard as the iron posts on his bed, she thought. It thrilled her to know how much he wanted her.

As the sun moved across the afternoon sky and the light lowered in the high transoms around the room, he pulled her jeans off, kissed her womanhood through her panties until they were damp from both his mouth and her moisture, and then he pulled them down and off.

He lifted the band of her bra up over her breasts so that they jutted out underneath. Her breasts compressed into hard mounds while her nipples sat high and prominent. "Oh, that's a look I like," he whispered.

He moved over her so that he could lick and suck on the marvelous mounds he'd uncovered. As his lips caressed every inch of skin, his tongue licked and his teeth nipped at the hard peaks. She crooned her pleasure and used her fingers to caress his chest, run her fingers through the dark curling hair covering his pecs, and to pluck at his nipples. Flat discs hardened to peaks and his moans joined hers.

She felt his hand skim down her side and his thumb slide along the crease below her pelvic bone. Then with his hand between her thighs, his thumb drifted between her silky smooth lips and into her opening. He thoroughly coated it with her wetness before using it to circle her nub at the uppermost part of her sex, until it was swollen twice the size and throbbing. She fumbled with his belt and managed to unbutton and unzip his pants. Then her hand found him, and like he had done to her, she ran her thumb over the tip to coat it then dragged it up and down the underside of his cock.

"I thought I was going to go slow. You're rapidly changing my mind," he huffed out.

"We can go slow once you're inside me," she pleaded.

"No we can't. I'm pretty sure of it. But let's see." He leaned up and reached over to the nightstand drawer and took out a condom. "Brand new box. Haven't had to buy these for years. There are so many kinds now. I stood there like an idiot trying to figure out which ones to get."

She smiled up at him as he slid it on. "Extra large, no glow in the dark, no flavors or weird ridges."

"You sound like quite the expert."

"Actually, no. I buy the novelty types for gag gifts. I don't believe I've ever bought any I've actually used. I think men should provide them, they know what they need."

"Well I got a box of 40, lubricated. That should get us through the weekend." His finger dipped inside her, going deep. He added another. "Doesn't appear as if I should have bothered with the lubricated ones, you're drenching my fingers."

He took them out and brought them to his nose, inhaled deeply, then licked them clean. She groaned.

"Let me just make sure."

He slid down her body and spread her legs as he fit his shoulders between them. His thumb caressed her folds, rubbing up and down. "You're glistening." He ran his tongue up through her slit. "Let's see if I can open the flood gates."

And he did. As she listened to him groan and felt every nerve respond to his delving and circling tongue, she let her head fall back and her eyes close. The bliss in that moment was overwhelming. She was no longer falling for this man. She had fallen, prostrate as she now lay, submitting in every way, she was his. Wanted to be his. She came like a train bursting through a snowdrift, pieces of her flying out everywhere. Her body pulsing and contracting and sending her over the edge into an oblivion that swirled and tumbled her until she came back to this age-old bed in this enchanting country house, and to this charming man who was now kissing along her thighs. For all time she wanted to be his.

When she saw his smiling, satisfied grin floating in a haze above her, she smiled back. A second later she felt him enter her, and from that moment on, she could safely say that the tempo he established was anything but slow. She had heard the expression "he took her" before, but it really hadn't signified anything to her. Alex took her. Took her to new heights, new depths, places she had never been. It was as if he took a special part of her, opened it up and let it bloom in his hand before giving it back for safekeeping. The orgasm she had while he was in her, releasing all manner of tension, angst, anxiety, distress, and fear, was unlike anything she dreamed possible. That one in body thing? Well they were. She was as much a part of him as he was of her for six glorious seconds.

Then the beautiful room floated back and his heavy weight denoted the body of a spent, virile male pinioning her to the bed. The slow tick of a clock off in the distance reminded her that this wasn't eternal, for her to make the most of her time with this man. This man she now loved.

"I'm starving," he murmured. "What did you say was for dinner?"

She laughed. "Slumgullion."

"Never heard of it."

"It's a humble beef and macaroni stew that had its origins during the great depression in Nebraska where they still had beef and produce, but little else. It's one of my favorites. I got the recipe from one of my theater friends. She used to bring it to work, heat it up in the microwave and drive us all crazy with the wonderful smells. I brought everything to make it and prepped what I could so it won't take long to make. Oh, and I made some garlic and herb bread to go with it."

"Sounds great. I'll help you, just tell me what to do."

They threw on their clothes, then he took her hand in his and led her down the hall to the great room and the expansive kitchen that was spectacular, yet homey.

Chapter 26—Emma & Alex
A Most Marvelous Dinner

Scattered on the counter were the contents of the two large canvas totes Alex had managed to unpack before being compelled to join Emma in the family room . . . leading him to take her into the bedroom.

On the countertop were the cans of tomato sauce and stewed tomatoes, containers of cut up vegetables, little baggies of spices, a box of macaroni, and a loaf of homemade bread wrapped in foil ready to be warmed in the oven. He retrieved the ground chuck from the refrigerator.

"Where's your suitcase?"

"I didn't think you'd want me to stay overnight."

He walked over to where she stood at the sink drying her hands. He lifted his hand to the side of her face, stroked her cheek with the tips of his fingers and met her eyes with a sincere gentle gaze. "Let me say this unequivocally, so we're not playing any games with each other. Anytime you can be here, I want you here. I would move you in right now, except my law degree precludes me from making you suffer cruel and unusual punishment by depriving you of sleep."

Then he leaned in and kissed her, brushing his lips so softly over hers that he left her lips tingling. She immediately desired more. More of him touching her.

"Good to know. I didn't think we'd come that far, so soon."

"If there's one thing I've learned over the past few years, it's that life is short, take time for the things that matter. You matter. I'm smitten. Totally mesmerized by you. And even though my practical side says don't put yourself out there again, my heart says follow this through, see the possibilities."

He ran his hand down her neck, used his thumb to lift her chin and looked her in the eyes, his expression serious. "Next time you come over, bring some clothes and whatnots, and leave them here so you can spend the night as your schedule allows."

" Okay," She whispered.

"Did you bring anything I can get from the car?"

"I keep a jump bag on the floor of the back seat, my 'whatnots' are in there," she said with an impish smile.

"Where are your keys, I'll get it."

"I didn't lock it," she shrugged. "You, know, what with the gate and then the long drive in, I didn't think I needed to."

"You don't," he said. He gave her a quick kiss and left to get her bag.

While he was out doing that, she familiarized herself with the kitchen. Checking out the slate-colored, state-of-the-art appliances, and ending with the Vulcan six-burner stove.

Alex brought in her Kate Spade satchel tote. "Where do you want this?"

"Mmm, guest room?"

"Guest room?" his asked, his eyebrows raised.

"Uh, yeah?"

"I meant did you need it here, right now, or should I put it in the bedroom. The room you'll be sleeping in is mine. You'll sleep with me."

"I just wasn't sure . . . what with the girls and all."

"They're too young to grasp anything odd about that. Besides, they're going to adore you." He hefted the bag, "So . . . my bedroom."

"Yeah. It's just makeup, my phone charger and my Kindle. Whether auditioning or acting, I need to touch-up my makeup all day long. But I'll bring some clothes next time if you're sure you want me to."

"I want you to."

He walked down the hall with the bag then returned to stand by her at the stove. All the lower cabinet doors were open.

"What can I do to help, you look puzzled."

"This kitchen is a dream. But I need you to show me

where you keep your pots and pans, I can't seem to find any."

He walked her over to a set of double doors and opened them wide.

"Oh my God," she said her hand over her mouth, "a butler's pantry," she whispered in awe.

Shelves at different heights lined three sides of a huge room, they were filled with platters, oversized ceramic bowls, stand mixers, blenders, and all manner of grocery staples. In the corner was a refrigerator freezer the exact duplicate of the one in the kitchen. The amount of storage boggled her mind.

Alex held his arm out indicating the two long shelves on the left of the entryway. They held top-line All-Clad professional pots and pans in every imaginable size, with their gleaming stainless steel lids atop each.

"I am humbled. I want to live in this room."

"Hmmm, so my bedroom doesn't hold its appeal anymore?"

She pointed to the low counter that doubled as a desk inside the pantry. "I could live in here. That granite countertop has possibilities for my carnal nature. It appears to be the perfect height for an afternoon tryst."

"I'll keep that in mind."

She grabbed a large pan and a medium-sized pot for the pasta. Shoving the pot into his chest she said, "Here, fill this halfway with water."

He saluted her, "Yes, Chef."

They worked side-by-side, sautéing the chopped green pepper and onions in oil, browning the beef, then adding the stewed tomatoes, tomato paste, and tomato sauce, and ketchup. Next Emma added the mushrooms, garlic, chili powder, water, salt, and pepper. She stirred it all with a big wooden spoon she found in a drawer dedicated to cooking spoons then turned the heat down to low. "It needs to simmer for a few minutes. How's that pasta coming?"

Alex looked at his watch, "Should be ready in

one minute."

"Where's that bag salad you said you had when we talked? I'll get that ready."

He pointed to the refrigerator in the pantry and she went to get it, returning with a bottle of Riesling she found as well. "Can we have this?" she asked holding it up.

"Of course. Help yourself to anything. I want you to be comfortable here."

"Oh, I am. My apartment is 700-square feet. I am very comfortable here." She made the salad while he opened the wine and poured two glasses.

The timer for the corkscrew macaroni went off.

"Dinner's almost ready. Can you check on the garlic herb bread?" Emma asked as she plucked a piece of the corkscrew macaroni from the pot of boiling water. She blew on it and then bit into it. "It's perfect. I'll drain it and add it to the pot for the last few minutes."

They sipped their wine while the Slumguillion sauce continued to meld with the macaroni, then Alex held Emma against the counter in front of the sink and kissed her until they were both panting and would have just as soon turned everything off and headed to the bedroom, except for Alex's stomach making churning noises, making them both laugh.

"Too busy feeding the animals to feed myself lunch today," he said with a lopsided grin.

Just then the timer Emma had set for the bread went off. "We're going to fix that right now."

Within minutes they were sitting at the counter with bowls of the steaming stew, slices of hearty herbed bread, a Caesar side salad, and glasses of the delicious Riesling.

"There's more wine in the wine cellar down the hall from the pantry. You have to punch in a passcode to get the door to open, it's the girl's birthday, then he rattled it off for her. But she'd already known it. And was not likely to ever forget it.

"I am majorly impressed."

"It came with the house, otherwise I'd have never indulged in one myself. But it did come in handy for keeping baby formula at the exact right temperature."

She laughed, "Oh that's funny."

"This is a-maz-ing," Alex said with a sigh. "I bet the girls would love this."

"Yeah, pretty spectacular for depression grub, huh?"

"Beats anything I've had lately. And this bread, it's great."

"A bread machine recipe I adapted as I have no bread machine here."

"So you like to cook?"

"Yeah. It de-stresses me."

"My wife liked to cook."

Emma froze, her spoon almost to her mouth. *Oh no, he was going to talk about Mallory. How was she going to listen to this and be able to eat?*

She had to say something, but what? Not to acknowledge she knew her now would be deceitful. To explain why she did, would end everything right here and now. She decided to shove the spoonful into her mouth and chew until it was mush, and then to swallow it slowly.

He didn't say anything more. But the tone had changed, they were both silent as they finished the last bit of the meal.

Alex, sipped on his wine while Emma cleared the dishes and put them in the dishwasher, then they both worked to fill storage containers and mark the leftovers for the refrigerator and freezer, as Emma swore the Slumgullion was even better on the second and third day.

While she was finishing up, rinsing out the sink and freshening the sponge before putting it in the holder, Alex came behind her and wrapped his arms around her waist. His lips close to her ear, he whispered, "Thank you, it's been ages since a woman cooked for me, well except for my mother. You can't know what that means to me."

She arched her neck, angling for his lips to linger. And

they did. He kissed alongside her neck, sucked on her ear lobe and breathed in her essence while his other hand held firm over her lower belly, holding her tightly to his burgeoning groin.

"Let's take a walk outside," he said, "the sight of the sun setting over the orchards is not to be missed."

Chapter 27—Alex & Emma
Rainbows and Sunsets

And he was right. Walking out to the perfectly aligned grove of trees, she saw them begin to be silhouetted under an orange, purple, and pink sky. It was surreal, watching day become night in small increments, their own slide show of nature being glorious.

"Oh Alex, this is amazing. I don't think I've ever seen a more beautiful sunset."

"Me, either," he said, but he was not looking at the setting sun. He was looking at her and watching the radiance in the sky shine on her face and brighten her eyes.

"I saw the sun set here the night I was called about the house coming on the market. After I toured the house, I came out here. It had rained before I got here and there was a double rainbow framing the house as I drove up the drive. It was as if Mallory was telling me that this was where she wanted her girls to grow up. I wrote a check that night. The house never made it to the MLS, or I'm pretty certain there would have been a bidding war."

Tears came to her eyes at the thought of heaven allowing Mallory to send a rainbow for her babies. She forestalled her sadness by exclaiming, "Wow! You owe your realtor, big time."

"I paid for her and her husband to go to Hawaii for their honeymoon last year. I know she saved me at least a hundred thousand dollars by bringing me out here that night."

"And look where you are, a little piece of heaven with ponies!"

He smiled with a wry grin, "Molly says she wants a pig for her birthday."

"When's her birthday, again?" she asked knowing full well when it was, and feeling a twinge of guilt at why that was.

Plus, now she knew it was the code for the wine cellar door as well.

"February 19th."

"Well, that's a way's off. Maybe she'll change her mind."

"Yeah, to a rhinoceros."

She laughed. "She sounds delightful."

"Do you like children?" It was a leading question and she knew it. Her answer would cement or undermine their relationship, as she knew the girls were number one in his life and always would be.

"I love children. But to be honest, the idea of having them scares me. I always thought adopting was a great idea. In fact, I almost did a year ago when one of my good friends got pregnant and wanted to end the pregnancy. I offered to take the baby rather than have her do that."

"What happened?"

"Her boyfriend turned into a knight on a white horse. Tiffany blue box in hand, he proposed. He wanted her and his kid. They are living the happily-ever-after life in Queens."

He smiled. "Great story."

She looked up at him and squeezed his hand. "I'm really sorry you didn't get yours."

He squeezed back. "It's a new story now. And maybe I will eventually."

He walked her over to a bench at the top of a slope that was angled in a way that guaranteed the best view of the orchard below and the sunset above.

She looked down and saw the etched bronze plaque.

Mallory, so we can share beautiful sunsets together. Alex

It was everything she could do to lock her knees and keep from falling onto the bench, blubbering like a baby. In that moment, she missed Mallory more than ever, and was a little afraid that her unshed tears of grief were going to swamp her. She was able to force her mind elsewhere to avoid the deluge, but still the slow cascade began any way.

The emotion she showed as tears streamed down her face touched Alex. Everything she did, said, or felt brought her closer to him. That she would cry over his dead wife humbled him. He couldn't think of any woman he knew who would be brought to tears by his feelings for his wife, and yet still willing to pursue something with him.

Reverently, she stroked the bench as she sat. "Oh, Alex. This is so touching. I love how much you loved her. I wish things had turned out differently." And she did. Despite knowing that this moment would never be happening. That the times she had spent in his arms would never have occurred. But she would gladly have given him back to Mallory if there were any way that God would have allowed it. She loved him that much.

It occurred to her then that, as a stranger to this story, she really should be asking more questions. And since she had been in New York at the time, she really didn't know the whole story. "How did this horrible thing happen?"

He sighed, and his detached attorney voice told the tale. He'd told it many times in depositions and in court, so that now he was able to step outside himself to tell it again. "Deep Vein Thrombosis, not diagnosed during the pregnancy despite Mallory having all the classic symptoms, was the start of her troubles. When an ultrasound confirmed the presence of a blood clot at her last doctor's appointment, she was treated with heparin to thin her blood and prevent further clotting. A foolhardy decision made by her doctor, as according to the readouts from the fetal monitor in her medical records, she was in labor at the time. Her labor pains were masked by the intense pain she was experiencing in her right calf muscle along with the severe swelling and pain she was experiencing in both legs. We were assured the heparin would reduce the swelling and tenderness in her calf. We were sent home, only to return in the middle of the night. She had shortness of breath, a rapid heartbeat, and bloodstained sputum. More heparin was administered. They were sure she had a clot making its way to her heart. Her doctor still hadn't noticed she was in labor. Then, right there in the emergency examination room, her water broke.

"Suddenly everyone was concerned about the excessive bleeding she could have during childbirth due to the heparin. The decision to continue to treat the clot or counteract the heparin was taken away when Molly made her appearance, followed by Mandy. They were trying to stay ahead of the bleeding when it was discovered Mallory had placenta accrete. The placenta was firmly attached to the uterine wall. Her doctor tried to remove it surgically and that didn't work. When the bleeding couldn't be controlled, it became necessary to remove her uterus.

"They consulted me as more surgeons were being suited up. I told them to save her life no matter what it took. They removed her uterus and four surgeons worked to tie off the blood vessels to stop the bleeding. She had lost so much blood they had to transfuse her several times. She was in shock by that time and the anesthesiologist who was bagging her to keep her breathing from being so erratic, was being spelled by the neonatal nurses. Mallory passed clots the size of apricots as she bled out. The team of surgeons tried frantically to stem the flow, cauterizing every blood vessel they could find in the pool of blood. The fresh blood they were putting into her was flowing out of her as fast as they could get it in. Then everything flat-lined when her heart gave out to a clot that made it through her lung. Within seconds she was gone. The twins were less than an hour old.

"Her doctor cried like the blubbering fool he was. He knew it was his fault. And after he took one look at the anger on my face, he knew his career was over.

"He never fought the malpractice suit. His insurance company offered to settle out of court the day I filed the papers. They knew I would be merciless. I told them I was going to take it to a jury.

"I had the babies transferred to another hospital that day. Then a week later, I packed up the babies and moved to California, away from meddling in-laws and too many bad memories to have to deal with.

"We needed a fresh start. Everything had to be new. I didn't want any part of my old life . . . except the babies. And they are everything to me. Without them I don't know what I would have done. It was because I had to focus on something that required every single waking thought, that I managed to survive."

He laughed. "The girls do that very well—extremely well. They saved my life.

"I had such guilt. Although I was thrilled from the moment Mallory told me she was pregnant, I was indifferent to the process. I think I only made it to two doctors' appointments, and I never read any of the booklets she was always leaving all over the house. I asked how she was doing all the time, and I rubbed her feet and massaged her lower back when she was sore, but I thought all this birthing stuff was woman's work

"I thought I was just supposed to pay the bills and hand out cigars. Now I wish I had vetted the doctor, maybe chosen a different hospital, and been with her every single minute she was in labor instead of off somewhere down the hall on my cell phone. I cared for the babies. I cared deeply. But I don't think Mallory ever really knew that."

She covered his hand with hers. Her tears for Mallory and all she'd gone through were running down her cheeks, dripping off her chin, creating wet spots on her new chinos. But she didn't care one whit about that. Her thoughts were full of anxiety. She hated this subterfuge and wanted to end it right now. But she didn't know how.

He wrapped his arm around her shoulders and drew her close. "Hey, I know it's a sad story, but we're beginning another one." He took a handkerchief out of his pocket and dabbed at her face. "I'd like to think that while we're sitting on Mallory's bench, watching a beautiful sunset, that she'd be happy for us."

The tears began in earnest then with her sobbing and blubbering into his handkerchief. Her heartache for the situation shoved to the back of her thoughts as her unshed grief for Mallory came to the forefront. Would Mallory be happy for them? Somehow, she doubted it.

Alex was shocked by how upset and sorrowful Emma was. Her empathy was on a scale unheard of for someone she hadn't even known. But he was glad for it. He loved that she cared. That she understood his grief and his loss. He felt they were building a good foundation with her understanding the life he'd had with Mallory. Because he was just beginning to realize that he wanted the same intimate, and loving relationship with Emma. They had the intimate part, and it was more than amazing, and he was pretty sure he was falling into a deep abyss and tumbling head over heels with the loving part.

When the silhouettes of the trees began to grow together into a cloaking dark shroud, and it sounded as if her crying jag was abating, he stood and lifted her into his arms and carried her inside.

Crossing the patio he noticed she was hiccupping. "I know a sure fire way to cure those hiccups." His grinning face looking down into hers made it clear what he meant by that.

She laughed and the sound made his heart leap.

"I've never heard of that cure. Does it work?"

"We'll have to see. I wouldn't suggest it to most of the people I hear hiccupping though."

Her delighted laugh as he carried her into his comfortable *Mr. Blandings dream house* left him with a feeling of contentment that was euphoric. He was enraptured with this woman, and it didn't scare him a bit.

Chapter 28—Emma & Alex
The Morning After

Emma and Alex sat at the hand-hewn round picnic table on the lower terrace eating spinach, mushroom, and feta cheese omelets along with some of the leftover herb bread Emma toasted. The setting provided a view of the recently added wooden playground and children's gym area, complete with swings and slides. It was clear to Emma that Alex planned to spoil his girls with toys and activities, like a good daddy should.

She knew that the twins were being brought back at 11. What she didn't know was if she was supposed to be here when that occurred. Was she supposed to go home now? Or was she supposed to stay and spend the day with Daddy and his girls? Her nieces. Alex, of course, was oblivious to her dilemma.

"The house doesn't have a water view, but I have a friend who has a beach house in Malibu, and I own a beach house in North Carolina for the times when I want to stare out at the ocean."

She forced herself not to react to that bit of news. Her mother had told her that he'd sold his house in Wrightsville Beach after moving to California. She had not known that he and Mallory had owned another beach house in North Carolina, too. "Oh, on which beach?"

"It's on Sunset Beach. It's not actually my house, I co-own it with nine other guys, all Stanford alum."

She knew that later it would matter how she responded to this. But she couldn't tell him she was from Shallotte; that would be too much of a coincidence. "I grew up in southeastern North Carolina, close to the coast so I'm familiar with Sunset Beach." She would not tell him that it was her favorite beach. "The last four years I lived in New York, so I made it a point to check out the Jersey coast. Their beaches are always crowded to the max, and nowhere near as nice as the Carolina beaches."

There was a slamming sound that reverberated both from inside the house, and around the corner of the house. Two more sounds came to them as faint clunks. Then another.

"I think I hear car doors. The girls must be home. They're early. I know you said you had to leave this afternoon, but I was hoping you would stay to meet them. Would you like to meet them?"

"I'd love to!"

She was glad for something to force a change of topic. She didn't want to lie to Alex, or to evade his questions, so it was better to divert to something not quite so revealing about her past. She was happy to have her dilemma resolved. And relieved that he *did* want her to meet his girls. She had almost forgotten they were the whole reason for her being there.

At the same time, she had to steady her nerves. She was going to meet her second cousins—Mallory's babies, her aunt and uncle's grandchildren. She closed her eyes to focus, much as she would before a major acting scene. She had to remember that these were Alex's children. They belonged to him. And that no matter what developed between them, he'd always love them first and foremost.

Chapter 29—Emma & Alex
Ponies and Princesses

It was chaos for a few minutes as the girls ran to their daddy, and he stooped to draw them into the circle of his arms. He lifted them together as he stood. He held them secure to his chest, looking from one to the other with sharp eyes trained on them, examining every minute detail to assure himself they were robust and thriving as he asked them questions. Did they have a good time? Were they good girls for grandma and grandpa? Did they eat breakfast? What were those new toys they held in their chubby little hands?

Alex introduced her to his parents who seemed genuinely pleased to meet her. His mother, a petite gray-haired lady, was elegant in a short stylish bob, wearing colorful capris Emma remembered seeing in a Chico's catalogue, with a sweater set to match. On her feet were serviceable retro Keds, which Emma knew were necessary to keep track of the two girls who were now running off to see their ponies. The dog that had come around the corner with them was running circles around them and chasing after them.

Alex's dad, dressed in shorts, a Polo shirt, and loafers without socks, waved at her as he ran past to keep up with the girls. "Pleased to meet you. Alex has told us a lot about you. Mostly that you're a good cook. And a great dancer. Hope you can run in those sandals."

Emma looked down at her woven leather slides. "Hmm. Probably not." She kicked them off. "But I grew up running barefoot in the grass, so unless you have cows leaving mud pies all over . . . " she followed as the group ran after one barking dog and two shrieking girls, who were clearly the light of everyone's lives.

The babies were adorable, beautiful cherubs with dark

brown curls, deep blue eyes, cute button noses, and sweet bow shaped lips. Her cousins were the epitome of healthy and happy, and just by being around them, they made others happy, too. She could see the love Alex had for them in his eyes and in the laughter that burst out of him as he tried to keep up with them.

She hung back for a few moments taking the scene in as each girl was strapped into a special saddle and each pony was led on a short rein around a small corral by an adoring grandparent. As she approached Alex, he reached out his hand to take hers. She felt such a peace envelope her as Alex gripped her hand and she watched the two giggling girls bounce happily on their little ponies.

"They are so sweet, such beautiful little girls," she whispered to him.

He squeezed her hand and then drew her in close. He settled her under his arm and she relaxed against him as they watched the doting grandparents parade them around the worn path in the small corral. She couldn't help thinking how her aunt and uncle would love to be a part of this. Her own mom and dad would adore these little girls.

"They are my life. My joy. My reason for carrying on." He looked over at her. "And now you, you add so much to that." He bent and kissed her on the nose.

The guilt that washed over her as she realized she was a dishonest interloper in his world, threatened to drop her to the ground. She actually slumped and might have fallen to the ground if he hadn't grabbed her by her hip and pulled her close.

"We're going to have to get you some sturdy shoes for this uneven terrain, maybe some serviceable mucking out boots." He laughed at the expression of disdain on her face. "Okay, maybe some riding boots."

Her eyes lit up, "Oh, those shiny tall dressage boots that make your legs look so long!"

He grinned at her, "I'm afraid they wouldn't be so shiny around here, he pointed to one of the ponies that was pawing the dirt and bringing up clouds of dust.

She frowned. "So more like Wellies," she said clearly disappointed about the suitable footwear needed around here.

"Tell me your size and I'll get you a pair."

"I can buy my own boots."

He leaned in and kissed her on the ear. "I insist. It will be nice to see them standing next to my boots in the tack room. Your size?"

"Eight, so I can wear thick socks with them."

Alex's father called out to them. "Mandy has a particular smell about her and your mom and I have a brunch date at the club. But don't worry, we'll drop Laddy-boy off at the house first so you won't have to worry about the dog."

Alex yelled over, "Well that's good, because Laddy-boy is *your* dog," he said good-naturedly. "Remember, I was not onboard with the girls having a dog this soon," he chided his dad, who just waved him off.

Alex released her hand, stepped aside, and went under the fence rail. "Okay, you're off duty. I got it from here." He undid the straps on Mandy's saddle and lifted her off. "Oh yes, she's got a ripeness to her all right."

He turned back to Emma, "Can you get Molly?"

Emma slipped under the rail, "Sure." My God, she was going to hold one of the babies!

Alex's mom helped unstrap Molly, then lifted the child and placed her in Emma's arms. "She's all yours now. It's been my experience that once one goes the other is not far behind."

Emma laughed as she hefted Molly and settled her on her hip. "Uh, thanks?"

Alex's mom laughed. "I'm Judy, by the way." She pointed at her husband, "That's Carl."

"Nice to meet you both."

"Have fun with the girls. We'll put the ponies up."

Alex and Emma walked to the house, each holding a squirming, bouncing baby.

"Are they always this happy?" Emma asked.

"Mostly. But they have their moments. Banshee screams when things don't go their way are not uncommon."

"Good to know."

"We'll go to the nursery to change them, then see if we can settle them down with some juice and cereal bars. You sure you don't mind staying and helping out?"

Emma grinned as Molly tugged on a hank of her long hair. "I don't mind a bit, but I'm probably going to have to put this up," she said as she gently eased the hair from Molly's tight grip.

"Yeah, Mom ended up cutting hers. And I notice she doesn't wear earrings much anymore."

"I can see why," Emma said as she fought to get another piece of her hair out of Molly's mouth.

The nursery was at the back of the house, at the end of a long hallway, opposite from the one that led to Alex's bedroom. And it was without a doubt, the cutest, most tasteful, and well-designed kids' room she'd ever seen. Although, to be honest, she hadn't seen that many. A few of her friends in New York had young children, and she used to babysit for makeup and dance costume money when she was in high school. While baby nurseries were not in her world, she knew this one was very special.

A second master bedroom had been converted to a make a double nursery with a kitchenette, play area, and sitting area. There were two power recliner gliders in what looked like kidskin gray leather with a low table between them that held books, binkies, a box of Kleenex, and an Amazon Echo. The chairs complimented the mint green walls and a birch forest animal mural covered one long wall.

A few feet away, two natural oak cribs with mobiles attached marked the sleeping area. Past that, were two matching changing tables. Between them was an adorable rattan clothesbasket in the shape of a giraffe. A diaper Genie painted like an owl was tucked into a corner. A couple of feet from the ceiling was a built-in painted shelf running the length of the wall that kept neatly labeled storage bins handy. Folded on one end of the high shelf were stacks of pastel colored animal quilts, Swiss dotted sheet sets, woven thermal receiving blankets, and an assortment of colorful bath towels. All manner of stuffed animals and dolls sat on dressers and shelves. In each crib stood a shaggy pony resembling the ponies now being put away in the barn.

A rattan day bed was tucked into a nook, under an arched window that held two tiers of ruffled white curtains and a dark gray shade to keep the bright sunlight out. A set of nesting toddler-sized tables and a set of matching chairs with two matching bookcases were off to one side. The bookcases were full of colorful books and puzzles; many showing signs of already being cherished favorites. On the floor were several geometric shaped rugs in muted gray tones, two imprinted with city scenes and country scenes joined by railroad tracks.

There were Disney-themed lamps on shelves, big quirky pillow poufs on the floor, and a large collection of toys in angled storage bins attached to a series of dowels. A set of wooden art easels sported paint-splattered smocks hanging from their A-frames, and chalkboards were attached to the walk-in closet doors that were filled with colorful chalk markings of indiscernible shapes. Assorted high-end bead mazes, stacked rings, block sets, and play tea sets sat on low shelves ready to be dragged to the floor and played with.

Emma had never seen a nursery so large, or so magical. It was well thought out, having an area to heat bottles and keep baby food, a bathroom to facilitate bathing and diaper changing, and a play area to keep one toddler busy while the other was being tended to. There was even a fabric-covered screen that could be set in place to partition off one part of the room from another in case one child was sick and prevented the other from sleeping.

Emma sat with Molly in her lap on one of the rocker

gliders. "Oh, this is nice," she murmured. "I could sit here and rock forever."

Alex laughed, "Well that's good to know, 'cause sometimes that's exactly how it feels, as if you're going to be rocking one or another until your arms fall off."

Emma leaned back and pulled Molly in close, laying her head on her shoulder. "I don't think I could get too much of this."

Alex was at one of the changing tables tending to Mandy. He looked over his shoulder at Emma, her arms wrapped around Molly, her eyes closed as she savored the soft weight of the baby she held in her arms. He knew how it felt to have his big heart beating against one of his toddler's smaller ones. The sight affected him in ways he didn't understand. Protective instincts leapt to the forefront at the same time genuine happiness surged through him at the sight of the woman he was falling in love with embracing and mothering his daughter.

Emma opened her eyes and met his. The smile she flashed him relieved any anxiety he was harboring. "I am feeling a distinctive rush of warmth between us."

Alex chuckled, "No need to worry, their diapers don't usually leak."

Then they heard Molly filling her diaper from the other end.

Alex, having just picked Mandy up, threw his head back and laughed.

Emma's face scrunched up and her eyes went wide as she held the toddler at arm's length while the expelling noise continued.

"My mom did warn you that whatever one does, the other usually copies . . ."

"Yeah, she did."

"Here, let's switch," he offered. "From the sound of that, it's going to be a challenge for a novice to change that one."

Emma stood and walked Molly to the changer. "No, no . . . I think I can manage. Just give me a minute to get used to the smell first. And to make sure she's finished."

Alex put Mandy in a blowup gym that served as a portable playpen and went to help out. But Emma didn't need any help. Without the slightest qualm, she cleaned the mess, wiped Molly's bottom and re-diapered her in record time.

"Wow that was fast," Alex commented after Emma had shouldered Molly and disposed of the diaper in the Genie.

"Had to be, I was holding my breath the entire time."

Alex laughed again. He wondered briefly how long it had been since he'd laughed so much.

"C'mon, let's get them a cereal bar and a fruit pouch, then with a little luck, they'll take a nap."

Emma followed him out of the room and down the hall to the kitchen. "Is it likely that they'll both go to sleep?"

"Nah, probably not. Mandy might, Molly is the stubborn one. You really have to wear her out."

"Great. And that's the one I've got." She lifted her high in the air as they approached the kitchen. "Let's show them how it's done, Molly." She spun her around and listened to her squeal before dropping her into her seat on the counter-mounted high chairs. "These baby seats are cool. I've never seen these before."

"They've been around Europe for a few years. People take their babies out to restaurants from an early age there, and these are portable so the babies have an instant highchair practically anywhere they go."

Emma stooped to read the name on the back of the fabric-covered seats that attached to the counter. "Inglesina."

"I like them so much that I've bought six of them. I leave these here, I travel with two in the Lexus, and I gave my parents a set."

"Well, they're pretty neat," she said as she watched him expertly open two Plum squeeze pouches that contained organic spinach, pear, and peas, fill sipper cups, and chop up strawberry banana cereal bars into manageable bite-sized pieces.

"Do they need that much fruit?" she asked.

"Trust me, they need a lot of fruit. A constipated baby is no fun."

"I thought they just drank apple juice."

"They do sometimes, but you have to watch the sugar. No way to make that potable without it having a lot of sugar. And sugar is the last thing you need these two to have too much of. Winds 'em up like you wouldn't believe."

"It's a whole new world."

"Tell me about it."

Chapter 30—Emma & Alex
Redneck Chandelier

After their lunch, the girls had playtime on the floor in the family room where Emma played patty cake with each girl, then peek-a-boo, then hide-and-seek behind the sectional sofa with all the pillows she'd tossed onto the floor.

"I can't believe you're not sleepy," Emma said to Molly.

"Told you. Getting them down for a nap is tough."

The girls had been fed, changed again, and given a half bottle of warm milk. Mandy had given a halfway yawn, but was stubbornly holding her own with her sister.

"I have an idea," Emma said as she stood, hands on hips surveying the room. I need some aluminum foil, some Scotch tape and a stepladder. You got those?"

"Oookaaay," Alex said, then left to get what she asked for from the kitchen, the utility room, and his office.

Returning with all three of the items, he sat on the floor with the girls watching as Emma tore off long sheets of foil, attached pieces of tape to the ends of each, and then placed the folding step ladder in the center of the low rough hewn coffee table that took up a fair portion of the room, in front of the sectionals.

"This looks pretty sturdy," she said, testing the stool before she gathered the foil strips. She taped each one to the inside of her arm, letting the long lengths drape down. Then she reached her other arm out to him, "Help me up, then hold the ladder for me, will ya?"

"I don't know what you're doing, but are you sure you don't want me to do it for you?"

"Nah, I got his. Just help me up."

He helped her onto the table, then up each rung of the ladder until she was standing on the fourth step and could reach her goal. He held her hips in his hands to steady her, and watched as she took each piece of foil and taped it to the topside of each of the five blades of the fan that hung over the center of the table. The coffered ceiling was high, but the fan was attached to the ceiling by a long pole. On her tiptoes on the fourth step, she only had to stretch a little to get each piece attached securely. As she stretched, her shirt gaped away from her body, exposing the taut skin from her trim waist to just under her bra. Alex reached up and caressed her smooth skin. She heard his groan of appreciation and felt her body tingle at his gentle embrace, but nonetheless, she swatted his hand. "Not now, that tickles. Do you want me to fall?"

"I'll catch you."

And she knew, without a doubt, that he would. When she was finished, he helped her off the ladder, then off the table.

"There," she said, standing next to him and looking up at the fan blades with the foil attached, surveying her work. "Perfect. Now, where's the fan remote?"

He took it off the magnetic clip attached to the wall switch and handed it her. She clicked the button to start the blades rotating. As they slowly turned, the foil strips made metallic crinkling sounds and flared out while the foil shimmered and reflected the sunlight coming into the room.

Then Emma clicked on the button that turned on the light in the center, a series of glass bulbs in a decorative flower petal design under each blade. Immediately a kaleidoscope of colors flashed off the foil. She turned the light on the lowest setting to mute the bright glinting colors reflecting off the foil.

She looked down at the girls and saw that they were gazing up, mesmerized by the spinning strips of foil and entranced by the noise of the foil rumpling. "Success!" she breathed out.

Putting down the remote, she picked up two oversized throw pillows from the pile on the floor and put them in opposite corners of the sectional.

"Hand me Mandy, would you?"

He obliged her by picking Mandy up off the floor and putting her in Emma's arms. Emma stretched and placed the entranced toddler in the corner and propped her up with the pillow so she could stare up at the spinning merry-go-round.

"Now Molly," Emma said with her arms outstretched for the next little cherub. She too, got placed in her own corner and was propped up with a pillow.

Emma stood back and theatrically wiped her hands together. "There. They'll be asleep in two or three minutes."

Alex stood, alternately looking at the fan, then down at each girl. Both Molly and Mandy could not take their eyes off the twirling silver banners as they slowly turned and spread out, the air currents keeping them softly rustling.

Mandy's eyes dropped, then closed. Half a minute later, so did Molly's.

"Wow," said Alex. "That's amazing. And very impressive."

"Works every time."

"Where did you learn such . . . skills?"

"I helped out in the daycare at my church every summer during vacation bible school. They had this clanking fan; it ticked with each revolution and it drove me crazy. So one day, I brought a can of spray lubricant in from home and stood on a table to see if I could silence the constant click, click, click. After I had sprayed the hell out of it, I turned to come down and one of the kids was handing me up the picture they had drawn. I asked the assistant for some tape to hang it. Then every kid wanted his or her picture hung from the fan. I added some crepe paper to make it look festive, and the next thing I knew all the kids were looking up, watching it go around and around. Within minutes they all had their heads on the table. The next day I added strips of foil for a tinkling sound. I call it the Red Neck Chandelier." She let out a long yawn, reaching up to cover it with her hand. "I think it has a universal effect."

"Well it's ingenious." He walked over to where she stood, smiling down at the sleeping girls.

Chapter 31—Emma & Alex
Stolen Moments

Since their first dance together, she'd intrigued him, brought him back to life in a way he never expected he could be again. She made him realize that he hadn't died with Mallory. As he watched her sleep on the long sofa between his two girls, he wanted her in a way that was beyond physical, although that was a very real way that he wanted her as well.

Viscerally, he wanted to breathe her in, absorb her essence, meld his mind with hers, and fuck the daylights out of her. He was a man who needed a woman for so much. And not just any woman, but this woman.

The twins were fine right now, tucked into the corners of the bolsters on the sectional sofa, propped and protected by pillows all around them. He knew they'd sleep for at least an hour, and if they didn't, they'd make it known that they were wake the second they were. "I think such a clever girl deserves a reward," he whispered.

He tossed the rest of the pillows on the floor in front of each girl, in case one or both should roll over and fall to the floor. Then he turned to Emma and lifted the tired beauty into his arms. She turned her face into his chest and sighed. It was such a lovely sound. To feel a woman who was so completely trusting in his arms sent pleasure pulsing through his veins. He had to have her, but it had to be gently, softly . . . tenderly. But most important, quietly.

The next room over was his study. It had a Murphy bed that was perennially out these days for the nanny to have a place to put her things. She typically emptied two or three carpetbags of stuff onto it when she arrived, packing it all up and taking it when she left.

He carried Emma to the bed, depositing her gently on the Glen plaid comforter. Her eyes were closed as she had fallen back to sleep, so he slid in beside her. He thought about letting her sleep. But then she moaned, turned into his chest, and placed her hand over his heart. Then her fingers began toying with his nipple.

He groaned. The little minx, he thought. He lightly kissed his way from the corner of her lips to her jaw, then down her neck. He'd show her not to tease him and expect nothing to come of it.

He lifted her shirt and kissed his way down her chest to her belly. Then he unbuttoned her jeans and slid her zipper down until he could pull them off. She moaned, but kept her eyes closed. He felt certain she was daydreaming. Maybe dreaming of a lover? Someone undressing her . . . to savor her?

With her jeans on the floor, he didn't hesitate. He put his hands around the front panel of her thong underwear, pulled it tight and with his thumbs inserted, tore the panel until he had a gapping opening, showcasing her sex. Then he slid between her legs and placed his mouth at her core, spreading her thighs as he dove in and took her with his mouth. Tenderly at first, listening to her soft sexy whimpers, then with concentrated attention and complete devotion to her clitoris, as she keened and came against his tongue.

When he looked up at her face and saw her head thrown back, her eyes still closed, but an undeniable expression of bliss on her face, he undid his own button and zipper and climbed up her body. Protection was the last thing on his mind as he entered her. He knew she was on the pill, that she was safe, and that he was safe. They'd had a talk about all that. And right now, he needed to feel her wrapped around him, gripping him, holding him close while he was inside her. He needed to feel the slick walls of her vagina clenching and milking him. And for a while she did, until his thrusts along with his thumb on her clit focused her again on her own pleasure.

When she arched up, cried out, and gasped his name, he let loose and every cell in his body thrummed its pleasure as he emptied what felt like his soul into her.

It would have been a gross understatement to say he was relaxed as he collapsed on top of her, taking her with him and rolling her into his side. He was at peace . . . with everything. In a way that he had never really been before. He knew in that moment that he loved this woman. Loved her with quiet surrender, not fighting it, but accepting the gift God had given him. Emma. Sweet, beautiful, funny Emma, who had managed to take a torn and broken man and make him whole again.

"Wow, I just had the most amazing dream . . ."

He chuckled. "Was I in it?"

"You were the leading player . . . and I was your *under*study. Get it? *Under* study.

"I got it. I used to hate studying. But I think it's going to be my new passion. You know, studying means training, learning, *examining*." He kissed the area beneath her ear, working his way to her lips. "And homework. Lots of *home*work."

"I think I might like the training part . . . Sir," she whispered into his ear.

He groaned.

"Let me revise that. The being trained part. "

He groaned even louder. "You're going to totally decimate me."

They both froze as they heard the sound of a baby wakening. A low wail. Then another joining in.

"Your decimation is going to have to wait," she sighed.

"As is your training . . ."

"Rain check?" she quipped as he got to his elbows, preparing to lift off of her.

"Definitely."

They adjusted their clothing and walked into the family room. The smell assaulted them before they got to the wide sectional.

"Are you sure you're not giving them too much fruit?"

He laughed.

"What goes in . . ." she murmured.

"It doesn't matter, Mom said she fed them scrambled eggs and cereal for breakfast. Whether it's formula, milk, eggs, cereal . . . this is how it all comes out at this age."

She scrunched up her nose. "How can something so noxious come out of two such beautiful little girls? Now boys, I'd understand."

"Hey," he said as he bent to pick up Molly and she bent to pick up Mandy.

"I'll help you change and feed them, then I have to go. I have a casting call tomorrow morning at eight. I need some beauty sleep."

He looked disappointed but he understood. She needed to get her career in L.A. off the ground so she would be committed to stay in California. "I understand. We'll all miss you, but I know you're itching to get back to work."

"Yes. I'm going to need money to replace those thongs you keep ripping off," she said with a huge grin.

"I'll set up a lingerie account. Because I intend to keep ripping them off."

"Good to know," she said as she carried Mandy back to the nursery with him following.

When the girls were settled, fed and the dinner dishes done, Emma grabbed her purse and jump bag, then kissed him on the cheek. He was sprawled on the floor with both girls climbing on top of him.

"Look at you. You've got girls climbing all over you."

"I wish you could stay and climb all over me . . ." he left the suggestion open.

"Me too, but I haven't even looked at the script I'm supposed to read."

"You will come back though?"

"Just try to keep me away."

He raised two fingers in the sign of a cross. "No way, I would never do that!"

The girls seemed distressed that she was leaving so she

played another round of patty cake, then gave them each a tiny stuffed penguin she had been carrying in her purse. "This one is Pen, and this one is Guin," she said, giving one to each girl. "They'll keep you company until I get back. You take care of your daddy, now. She gave each girl a kiss on the cheek, and kissed Alex on the mouth.

"You take care of you."

"See you Wednesday night?" he asked, trying to keep the longing out of his voice.

"Of course, it's date night!"

He smiled. He liked that she got that. They needed time together, on their own. He needed this relationship to blossom and grow. He needed her in his life. As she walked through the house to the front door, he wondered if he should tell her that he loved her.

But then he heard the front door latch click and realized she was gone and that he'd lost his chance. Molly put her hand on his face and pulled him back to look at her. Of the two she was the most insecure.

"She'll be back," he whispered.

Chapter 32—Emma
Mission Accomplished

When Emma got to her apartment she kicked off her shoes at the door and fixed herself a cup of Twinings Black English Breakfast Tea. During her early singing days on stage, she found a hot cup of tea not only settled her nerves but also cleared her throat of mucus, allowing her to hold high notes longer. Over the years she had tried all the designer teas, but her favorite was Twinings. Fancying herself to be somewhat of an English snob with regard to teatime, she stuck to tradition and always had a "biscuit," or cookie, if you will, with it. Today she reached for her cookie tin and chose an Oreo. Actually three.

Sitting in the rickety faux rattan swivel chair that came with the rental unit, she swung her legs over the side and picked up her phone from the side table. She had taken some pictures of the girls when she'd had the opportunity. One with them was a video when they were on their ponies being walked single file by their paternal grandparents, taken from the breakfast room window when Alex had been in the bathroom, and another of the girls playing on the floor of the nursery when Alex had gone to answer the phone. They weren't the best, but they would do, and they would settle her obligation to her uncle.

She added the caption: The girls are doing very well, they are little princesses, happy and healthy, and they even have their own ponies! On the second picture: Playing in the most amazing nursery ever. I changed Molly's diaper, and I can attest to the fact that both girls are eating just fine!

Then she shut down her phone, grabbed the script she was to read tomorrow morning and worked until eleven perfecting her lines and filling out character mannerisms she thought appropriate for the three roles she hoped to try out for. She had learned never to count on getting the lead and to study up on at least two minor roles. The leads always went to the women the director or producer was sleeping with.

Chapter 33—Emma & Alex
Getting Comfortable

"So how was your week? Did you get the part you auditioned for?" Alex asked, as he pulled her in close for their first dance of the night, a delightfully slow waltz so they could catch up on each other's lives.

"Too soon to know, it usually takes a week or better. But it wasn't a good sign that so many girls were called up on stage by their nicknames. The L.A. acting scene is full of established cliques, you really have to look or act quirky to stand out. Whereas I am . . ."

"You are merely beautiful, talented, and charming, with the voice of an angel."

"Thank you. But I was going to say, the girl next door or everybody's trusted friend. I need some quirk! You know, like Pauley Perrette."

"Who?"

"Abby Sciuto, the geeky forensic scientist on NCIS."

"Ah yes. Brilliant, but crazy as a loon Abby." He leaned back to look at her, "I don't think pigtails and a dog collar would be your best look. And just so you know, I am not all that fond of piercings and tattoos."

She laughed as he swirled her and led her around the dance floor. "Me neither. But don't worry, I hate needles."

"What else did you do?"

"I did some writing. I've been working on a treatment for a script I wrote."

"You'll have to let me look at it when you're done. I have some connections in the business."

"It's my first one, and even I know it's not that good. Maybe the next one. This one's just for practice."

"I have never met a modest writer. You are a highly

unusual person, Emma, you know that?"

"Well, I *am* modest about some things . . ."

"What *aren't* you modest about?" he asked. "C'mon, shock me," he teased.

She quirked one eyebrow and gave him a sexy grin. "Well, I took this dance course one time, 'How to Striptease for Money.'"

He jerked back and his own eyebrows rose in horror, "You stripped for money?"

She laughed at his reaction. "No. But I learned *how* to. It's really quite an art. You have to practice at home by hoola-hooping naked. I needed another dance class for my repertoire, and that one was actually a lot of fun."

"I'll bet . . . ." They were silent as he led her around the room, then just before the dance ended he asked, "Were there any men in the class?"

"No. It was just for women. And the door was kept locked until class was over. The artist who taught it was a much older lady, said she'd worked with Gypsy Rose Lee at one time."

"So do I get to see a demonstration?"

She winked at him. "Maybe. I'll have to round up some feather boas, a G-string, and some pasties."

"I'm getting a hard on. You're going to have to stand in front of me until the next set is called."

She laughed. She couldn't help it, she looked down. "Oh my."

"You *were* planning on coming home with me tonight, weren't you?"

"I'd better, or what you're sporting there is going to keep you up all night."

"I'd prefer you tend to it, rather than me."

She quirked a brow as if to say, what's in it for me?

"I have some brownies my mother baked fresh today on my kitchen counter . . . some Talenti Madagascan Vanilla Bean Gelato in the freezer, and a can of whipped cream in the fridge . . ."

"I like my brownies plain. But I think I can come up with another use for the whipped cream."

He groaned. "You're not helping the obvious and agonizing erection I'm trying to force down."

She laughed as a Quick Step was called. "You may want to sit this one out then as it's going to be bouncing all over the place."

He pulled her close, allowing her to feel how hard he was. "Maybe we should just leave now. Don't you feel a headache coming on?"

Five minutes later they were both on the highway, her following him in her car to his house where they would be alone all night, as his parents had the twins overnight on Wednesdays.

Chapter 34—Alex & Emma
96 Tears

He eased his car into the garage while she pulled into the circular drive in front of the house. They met at the front door where he used the keypad to open the door for them. The house was dark, the security lights with their eerie radiance leading the way inside. Once inside the foyer, their movement tripped the sensors and low lights came on in the main part of the house.

"Leave your stuff here," he said. "I'll come back for it later. I want to show you something."

She dropped her purse and overnight jump bag on the floor by the door and kicked off her heels.

He emptied his pockets on the table in the foyer, threw his suit coat over a newel, and lifted her into his arms and kissed her. "You haven't seen the upstairs yet."

"No, no I haven't," she murmured as she wrapped her arms around his neck and laid her head on his shoulder. He carried her up the stairs, stopping in front of a set of open French doors. Polished brass picture lights atop paintings along one wall lit the room. She recognized the style as impressionist, but none of the paintings looked familiar. In the center of the room was a black grand piano. The lid and the music rack were down. He carried her to it and placed her on top of the gleaming black surface.

"I have wanted to do this since I saw you turning in circles, trying to take it all in at the Wiltshire. You, on my piano, in nothing more than a black slip. Just like the scene in the movie you love so much. Me, getting to taste you and send you to another universe, with my tongue. Then fucking you into tomorrow."

"You know all my fantasies. It's not fair. I don't know any of yours."

"Yes, you do. It's the one where you kneel and say 'I need you inside me.'"

"Where?"

"I am happy with any orifice you offer."

"So who goes first?"

"Ladies first. Always."

"I'm not wearing a slip."

"I'm sure we'll be doing this particular scenario more than once."

He reached behind her and undid her hair so it flowed over her back and shoulders. The lights from the paintings across the room highlighted her hair. He ran his hands through it making it impossibly messy. Then he clapped. Once.

She startled and blinked at him in confusion.

"Gentlemen, will you excuse us please."

She smiled. He had stepped into the part of Edward Lewis, getting the attention of the men cleaning up the banquet hall.

He smiled back at her, and then reached behind her to pull the zipper of her dress down. When the capped sleeve sheath dress fell off her shoulders, he gently laid her back until her hair was spread out around her head, as glossy in the low light as the piano.

He unhooked the clasp of her bra and removed it. Then shuddered from the sheer pleasure of seeing her like this. He ran his hand down between her breasts, over her breasts, and then cupped her breasts. He pinched and tugged on her nipples, enjoying the sounds she made, delighting when they became low and whimpering.

His hand delved between her thighs, tugging at the center of her damp panties, hooking his longest finger inside one leg elastic and threading it through to the opposite one and pulling on the crotch until they were off her hips, then down and off her legs. He was delighted that he found her wet and ready. His middle finger entered her and she keened. He shoved two inside and she gasped. He worked them in and out and she pleaded. "Alex, Alex, please . . . please . . ."

"Please what?"

"Please . . ."

"Eat you, finger you, fuck you?"

"Yes!"

He laughed. "I'm not going to ask about the order."

He bent his head and kissed her on the little patch of hair she allowed to grow into a neat little triangle. Then he sucked on the tender skin around it, but not where she wanted him. No, it was too soon for that.

He tortured her with kisses, touches, licks and nipping bites while his fingers entered and retreated, and all the while he was playing a rendition of *96 Tears* with his opposite hand. Then he began fingering her clit with his right hand as if stroking keys in time with his left; he was playing the refrain on her needy, pulsing sex button instead of on the keyboard. Pressing, tapping, and flicking it in time with the song, he began crooning his own mishmash of the words to the song to accompany the keystrokes.

"I'm gonna get you there"

"We'll be together, for just a little while"

"And that'll slay you way down here"

"You're gonna cry 96 tears"

She was almost delirious with want when he finally gave in and latched onto her clit with his lips and sucked for the final refrain of the song.

She shattered against his lips, her legs trembling, her mind tumbling in the cosmos without a tether, as the pulsing nub went from a fully engorged orb the size of a marble to a shriveled pea. He looked up at her and smiled. Her eyes were closed to keep the bliss inside while her lips were in a rictus to stem the pull of the agony/ecstasy impasse that had caught her up and stopped her breathing. He'd heard her suck in her breath, now he was waiting for the return rush of it. It came as a deep sigh and then her eyes slowly opened. Tears dripped out of the corners of her eyes to wet the piano.

"Hey, I was just kidding about you crying 96 tears."

"I have never . . . that was . . . oh sweet heaven . . . . Mmmm." And her eyes closed again.

He laughed. "Hey Princess, wake up. Or I'm going to be pounding into an unconscious woman."

"Go ahead. I won't mind."

He tugged on her hips, sliding her across the piano top, mindful of the zipper on the back of her dress, until he had her on the keyboard amid a chatter of jarring off-key protests from the piano.

He forced her eyes to meet his while he undid his belt and the pants fastener, then lowered the zipper. There was no need to fish inside for his penis; it was hot and heavy in his hand straightaway, with its eagerness to be inside her.

He gripped her bottom and pulled her forward on the keyboard until she was angled so he could thrust inside. Then he did. They both groaned at the intimate connection. She slumped her head on his shoulder and he lifted it with his left hand to turn her to face him so he could kiss her.

The kiss was soft but desperate with want. Soon their tongues were tangling and vying for prominence. He began pumping into her with an urgency he hadn't had since his college days. A series of frantic deep thrusts sent the piano legs screeching on the polished floor and he pulled her in tighter. The bench was behind him so he lifted her from the keyboard and sat on it with her straddling his hips. Then he showed no mercy. He sucked her tits, gripped her ass, and drove up into her until he felt her trying to maneuver her hand between them. He let her, figuring that at this point, she knew what she needed more than he did. He was gone to the pleasure, and riding her for all he was worth. When she breathed out, "Now, now! Oh God, I'm coming." He stopped and held her to him. Then he felt his cock pumping independent of his wishes, sending hot ribbons of his semen up into her. This was sex unlike anything he'd ever experienced.

He was with her, feeling all she was feeling along with all he was feeling at the exact same moment. A moment suspended in time. And miraculously, he managed to stay seated on the bench with her in his arms, despite every muscle collapsing. He had the most primal feeling of exhilaration as if conquering demons, slaying dragons, and making this woman exquisitely happy were on an even par. And he had done it all on his treasured piano.

"I am falling for you so hard," he whispered, as if hearing the words out loud might have been too much for them both.

"Tumbling with you . . ." she gasped out, and then smiled down at him. "If you were Richard Gere and I was Julia Roberts and they were filming us, they would have had one hell of an X-rated movie in the can. I need some water. I am parched."

He lifted her up and separated them.

She grabbed for her panties knowing he wouldn't want to explain this to his housekeeper, or worse yet, his mother when she brought the babies back.

"Trying to mind the piano and the floor," she explained when he looked at her trying to get back into them. He zipped his pants and found his handkerchief in the pocket and handed it to her.

"We can take a shower after we get you something to drink."

"Okay, but I really can't leave the piano and bench this way . . . fingerprints . . . butt prints . . . DNA evidence . . ."

He laughed and took off his shirt. Then used it to shine the bench and piano lid and keys. "You're more like Abby Sciuto than you know."

Chapter 35—Alex & Emma
Every Man's Fantasy

After their shower, they lay facing each other, talking late into the night.

"So you play the piano," she stated.

"My mom was a music teacher. She played in church on Sundays and gave piano lessons on Saturdays. I had no choice in the matter. Now, I'm happy for all the time she spent teaching me."

"You play well," she said, running a finger down his nose.

"You can tell by one pop song?"

"I can tell by that amazing crescendo those wicked fingers knocked out."

He smiled. "I'll have to figure out what other songs are . . ." he searched for a word but couldn't come up with one.

"Diddlely?" she supplied.

He threw his head back and laughed. Then gathered her close.

"I think you just coined the perfect word for keyboard fingering."

When morning came, neither knew when they had dropped off to sleep. Or what they'd been talking about just prior to nodding off. But when Emma came back into the bedroom after starting the Keurig and getting herself a cup of coffee, she was shaking a can of whipped cream she'd found in the refrigerator. Alex quickly remembered their last conversation and pulled off the tie he had just put on.

"You calling in late?" Emma murmured as she put her coffee on the night table and climbed back into the bed, sitting back on her heels to face him. He had his jacket off now and was unbuttoning his shirt.

"Yup."

"Because I like whipped cream in my coffee?" she asked innocently.

He stopped unbuttoning and watched her as she lifted her mug and squirted a generous mound of whipped cream on top of her coffee. Then replacing the coffee on the night table, she tipped her head back and squirted whipped cream into her mouth. He watched as her tongue toyed with it, swirling it in her mouth and onto her lips before licking them clean and swallowing it all.

"How late can you be?" she asked.

"How late do you need me to be?" he croaked out.

She waggled her finger for him to come closer. When he came to the edge of the bed, she reached down and cupped his balls, then gripped his erection. "I think I can tame this penis in . . . five minutes."

He unbuckled his belt and dropped his pants. "Take ten."

Smiled up at him, "Yes, sir."

As he stood beside the bed watching her take him into her mouth, he told himself he was one lucky S.O.B. The woman cooked, she danced like a dream, she was beautiful, funny, great with kids, gave great head, and was a willing and adventurous partner in bed. He didn't care that she was unemployed. As far as he was concerned, she didn't have to work a day in her life. He had enough money and made enough money for all of them, Molly and Mandy, and any other kids they might have. Then her tongue did this rimming and fast licking thing around the head while she sucked and tugged, and fondled his balls, and he lost his train of thought.

He hadn't meant to come in her mouth, but then he hadn't meant not to either. He'd had a few seconds where he could have controlled the outcome, but she took them away from him and made him her slave for life in the process. Head thrown back to the ceiling he shouted a few choice cuss words, then let her have what she seemed to be craving.

When he came to his senses a hank of her hair was still fisted in his hand and she was on her knees beside the bed trying to catch her breath.

"Are you alright?" he asked with concern.

"I'm fine. I just need you to let go of my hair so I can get up."

He quickly opened his fingers and she pulled herself free.

"Oh God, I'm so sorry."

"It's okay. I'm fine, really," she said as she gathered her hair and pulled it into a high ponytail with the hair tie she had on her wrist. "I meant to put this on first."

"Did I hurt you?"

"No. I'm fine. Really. I just wasn't expecting . . ."

"Expecting what?" he asked in an anxious voice.

"A marriage proposal. Usually the *man* is on his knees for one of those."

His eyes went wide and he stepped back in shock. His mouth gaped.

She laughed. "Don't worry. I'm not going to hold you to it."

"I do remember thinking about it . . . before my brain shut down and my body took over."

"It was an intense moment, that's for sure."

"I think I was mulling it over. What did I say exactly?"

"Marry me. Marry me. Marry me. You actually screamed it. I wouldn't be surprised if your neighbors heard it."

"I don't have any neighbors that close. So?"

"So . . .?"

"What would have been your answer?"

"I think it's too soon. But in the throes of passion, I suppose my first thought would have been to say yes."

"Then I'll ask again when we're both in a rational state of mind."

"You do that," she said with a big grin. "Meanwhile, you have to get to work and I have to get to class."

"Class?"

"Yoga. I need to be flexible." She put her hands over her head and went into a full back bend, which she turned into a handstand before dropping one leg down to end up standing, all while wearing a camisole and boy shorts.

He groaned his appreciation of her athletic flexibility, while licentious thoughts bounced around in his head. He converted them to something proper to say, "The girls will love seeing you do that."

"Next time I'm here, we'll play outside and I'll dazzle them with my triple back flip. But right now I have to go or I'll be late for class. And that's just rude."

She took swigs of her coffee between brushing her teeth and gargling, and brushed her hair while dressing, then grabbed her purse and bag. Giving him a quick kiss, she thanked him for the "piano lesson," and after putting her coffee mug in the dishwasher, she ran for the door.

He stood staring as if a whirlwind had just gone through his house, taking something precious with it. Then he heard the front door click closed and he knew that it had.

Chapter 36—Alex & Emma
The Unfortunate Incident

The following Saturday afternoon, Emma put together puzzles, read books, made Mickey Mouse waffles, and changed each girl's diaper. It was a yucky rainy day. Alex had received a phone call that necessitated him getting a folder from his office. Emma had said, "No problem. I got this. Go get the folder you need, we're just going to watch Mickey Mouse Clubhouse and do some puzzles."

An hour and a half later when he still hadn't returned, she fed the girls food pouches, some juice, and some Cheerios. She changed more diapers. When she was sure both girls were neither hungry, thirsty, or wet, she propped them up in different corners of the sectional and put the Red Neck Chandelier on low. Within minutes they were both asleep.

She gave a huge sigh of relief, and then noticed Molly shiver. The child was near an air-conditioning vent, so she worried she might be getting cold.

She went to the nursery where she remembered there were stacks of baby quilts on the end of the high shelf. While stretching to tug one off the pile, it came lose and unfurled on the way down and knocked one of the baby monitors from the charging station to the floor. She heard a crack, then looked down at the floor. The monitor screen was in pieces, the back dislodged and the batteries rolling around on the floor. The screen was shattered. No way was it useable.

She had just finished unleashing a tirade of cuss words when the phone in her pocket rang. Pulling it out and looking at the screen, she sighed. Then decided to answer it, as she was alone right now.

"Hi Uncle Jerry. This isn't really a good time. Alex had to go into the office and I just got the girls to sleep, and while getting a blanket for Molly off a shelf, I managed to break one of the baby monitors."

"Hey, no worries, hon. Tell me the model number and I'll go to Wilmington today and get another one just like it and have it overnighted."

"You sure?"

"Of course. You know I'm always lookin' for ways to help my grand babies. I'll buy a new one and send it to you at Alex's address just like you was the one what bought it, 'kay?"

"That would be perfect. I know he won't want to be without it for long."

"No problem. Don't worry your pretty little head about it. I liked the pictures you sent. Maybe you could send a few more? Your aunt sits and stares at 'em all evening. It's a trial getting her to fix dinner these days, "I'll tell you that!"

"I'll take a few more now while Alex is out. Thank you for getting the monitor for me. I sure appreciate you doing this." She read him the model number from the other one in the charging stand. "I hope it's not too much money . . ."

"Not a problem, sweet cheeks, I got plenty."

She picked up the broken pieces from the busted screen and plastic casing along with the batteries and threw everything except the batteries into the trashcan. Then she took a quilted blanket for each girl and went to cover them. Using her phone, she took a few pictures of the sleeping babies and texted them to her uncle. She settled into what she was beginning to think of as her chair, a comfy oversized chair with a matching ottoman. It was roomy and supported a tired back just right. On the side table was the cup of tea she had reheated twice in the microwave but had yet to sip, and her Kindle.

She flipped on the table lamp. It was dark and gloomy due to the overcast sky and the steady rain. When she turned on the foil-embellished fan she hadn't bothered turning on the light. It was cozy here, she thought, as she stared out at the rain pelting the wall of windows. Despite having only been here a few times, she felt at home.

She was reading a book on her Kindle between sips of lukewarm tea, while listening to the noise of the fan blades and the soft breathing of the sleeping toddlers, when Alex pulled into the garage and walked through the house looking for them.

Finding them in the family room and noting that the girls were asleep, he bent and kissed Emma on the lips. "Sorry, it took longer than I thought to find the file. I had to call one of my assistants and wait for her to call back. Then there was a huge pileup on the freeway. The rain has made it madness out there. So glad I'm home," he said with a sigh and sank onto a chair opposite her. "They been good?"

"If you mean good as in ate, pooped, played, and then peed, yes. We checked all the boxes. Oh, and I broke one of the monitors getting blankets down off those very-high-for-a-woman shelves. So another one's been overnighted. You should have it tomorrow."

"You didn't have to do that."

"I did. I was clumsy. Next time I'll use the footstool in the corner. I actually didn't see it there until I was cleaning up the broken screen pieces. But don't worry, I fitted them back together to make sure I got all the pieces."

He looked over at her, giving her a broad smile. "You're amazing, you know that?"

"This was fun," she said. "I felt kind of . . . domestic."

"As in French maid?"

She laughed. "No. As in helpful and homey."

"Shame," he said as got up and ran a hand down her bare thigh on his way get the fan remote. "Kinda like the idea of a maid being punished for breaking something of the master's." He turned and waggled his brows at her as his finger tapped the remote button and the foil strips settled and stopped their soft crinkling.

She quirked one eyebrow back at him, "Why Master Alex, do you think I need a spanking?"

He smiled. "Yes, I do, as a matter of fact."

"Maybe tonight after the girls have gone to bed," she said.

"That's a long time to wait to reprimand you . . ."

She nodded at the girls, sleeping propped up in the corners. "Well, the Red Neck Chandelier does knock 'em out . . ."

"How about a little warm up in my office . . ."

"Don't you have some work to do?" she asked, pointedly staring at the file he'd tossed on the coffee table.

"There's nothing more important than keeping the help in line. The file can wait. Follow me Missy, a man has to discipline as he sees fit." He put out his hand. She put her Kindle aside, stood, and put her hand in his, followed him into his study, where he quietly closed the door.

He sat on an oversized ottoman and gestured to her. "Come over here."

She walked over and feigned a sullen look, her lips in a pout.

"Pull down your shorts and your panties, but don't take them off, just let them drop around your ankles."

With slow consideration, she shimmied her denim shorts down, taking her panties with them and pulling both down past her thighs, knees, and calves until they rested on her feet.

He hissed out a breath at her slow, deliberate reveal. He beckoned her to lie across his knees by crooking his finger. Then helped lower her onto his lap, facing her away from him.

He looked down at her perfectly toned ass, every smooth inch exposed to his heated gaze. He rubbed one cheek with his palm, warming it before smacking it hard. The sound reverberated through the room and she cried out. Mindful of the girls sleeping in the other room, he stifled the harsh sound with a hand over her mouth.

"You did a bad thing. You must be punished. I'm going to spank you five times. And it will hurt. But you must be quiet."

"Yes, Master,"

Her submitting words to him made him hard. Unbelievably hard. He was sure she had to feel the probing length of him against her belly.

He counted out each slap, watched as her white cheeks bloomed red and showed the outline of his hand—listened as she gasped from the sharp blows. Then he rubbed and kissed her heated ass to soothe it.

"I think you've been punished enough. Time for some pleasure." His fingers delved between her legs to find her drenched. Unbelievably wet.

He tugged her shorts and panties off then helped her to stand. He walked her over to his desk and gently bent her over it. Then he unzipped his trousers and placed the tip of his cock at her wet core. "Your pussy is soaking wet," he whispered, awed by the sight of her vagina glistening for him. "You like it when I spank you. You naughty girl."

He entered her slowly, staring down and watching as he took her. Then he gripped her hips and pulled her tightly to him with each thrust. He was ready to come in less than a minute. He fought to hold back as he reached under her, found her clit and flicked it back and forth with his thumb. Her panting sounds joined with his low groans. Her pleas not to stop urged him on until he felt her jerk against him. Her climax sent her into a frenzied succession of spasms. He pumped once, twice, and then on the third thrust, he emptied into her. Impaled as he was in her warm, wet heat, he collapsed on top of her. They stayed that way for several minutes, both bodies arched over his desk, trying to catch their breath.

She whispered, "That was . . . decadent."

"That was perfect," he groaned. "You are incredible."

He slid out of her as he stood, then tenderly rubbed her red ass. "So willing, so ready. So damned sexy."

"So tired."

He laughed and swatted her once more, this time lightly.

"C'mon," he said as he reached for some tissues from the box on the shelf above his desk and shared them with her. "Let's take a nap on the Murphy bed. If we hurry, maybe we can get half an hour in before they wake up."

He didn't bother with his clothes or hers, just pulled up his pants so he could walk, and led her over to the bed. He pulled back the comforter and eased her onto the sheets, then followed her down and pulled the cover over them. They collapsed into each other's arms and slept—for forty blissful minutes.

Chapter 37—Alex & Emma
Last Tango

Wednesday night's class was dedicated to Latin dances. Having received the heads up from the instructor in an email, Emma was wearing a tiered fringe dress in a vibrant blue and silver combination, stopping just above the knee. Her blue pumps with metallic chrome heels matched the dress perfectly. Alex, having come from the office, hadn't dressed for the theme, but he'd removed his tie and unbuttoned his shirt down several buttons to reveal his tanned neck and impressive upper chest area. He had also slicked his hair back giving him the look of an arrogant gigolo.

"Well . . . you look positively . . ." she said, searching for the word to describe how he was dressed.

"Yes," he prompted

"Cuban? 1950s era?"

"Ah, so not quite the flamenco dancer I was going for?"

"I could get my eyebrow pencil and fill in a thin mustache, that might help."

He laughed and waved her off. "No thanks."

The distinctive beat of *El Cantante* came through the speaker system just then, and as had been their custom every time the song came on, all of the students yelled out together, "Salsa!"

This particular rendition was eight minutes long so most couples were not in a huge hurry to get to the dance floor, but Alex and Emma, eager to find reasons to touch each other, were.

Alex had Emma spinning from his arms and reeling back into his clasping fingers with the fast-paced music the moment their shoes touched the polished floor. The fevered pitch of the song had Emma shimmying and shaking her hips, sending the fringe on her dress out in long lines around her body.

"You are the sexiest woman in the world," he whispered in her ear during one pass when he'd held her close for one long beat.

She threw her head back and laughed.

His heart bloomed. She was the most genuine, most playful, and living in-the-moment person he had ever met. And he wanted to keep her. He wanted her to be his forever.

When the song was over, they were both sweaty and smiling—and satisfied. In the way that a perfectly choreographed set left a dancer. The rest of the dances—a rumba, mambo, cha-cha, samba, merengue, tango, bomba, paso doble, and a very spirited jive, left them energized. But after the class was over, as they changed their shoes and walked out to their cars, they also felt drained, as if they'd had the workout of a triathlete.

"Man, I am bushed," Alex said.

Emma smiled up at him, "Yeah, I'm kind of wiped out myself."

"You want to call it a night?" he asked.

She stopped walking and turned to look up at him. "Is that what you want?"

"No. I want you to come home with me. But I understand if you're tired. I know you got up early for that commercial this morning."

"I am tired, but I would like to wind down with you. And I'm hungry. How about you?"

"Starved. I worked through lunch." He held his hand over his mid-section. "If the music hadn't been so loud, I'm sure you'd have heard it protesting."

She laughed. "Then let's silence that bad boy."

He took her hand in his, "Come home with me. Even if it's just for a quick dinner at the kitchen counter. I want to unwind my day with you, too. Then have you sleep in my arms."

"Sounds wonderful."

"I know I have pancake mix for the girls. I can make some pancakes and fry up some bacon."

"Hmm, breakfast for dinner . . . does that include mimosas?" she asked with an impish smile.

"I believe I can scare up a bottle of champagne. In fact, I think there are several bottles in the pool bar as well as a few in the wine cooler. Not sure about the orange juice though."

"I have no problem whatsoever drinking it straight."

"Last I looked, I had some Capri Sun Tropical Fruit juice pouches in the fridge," he offered.

"That'll work," she said with a chuckle as she used her key fob to unlock the car door.

Her opened it for her and she slid in.

"See you at home," he said as he bent to kiss her check.

"Yes, see you at . . . home." It was the first time she had referred to his house as home. She looked up into his face to see his reaction.

He was beaming.

Chapter 38—Alex & Emma
Three Little Words

By the time they got to the house, pancakes had lost their appeal so Emma worked some magic with a can of beans and a leftover pork roast.

After a light dinner of Great Northern beans done Tuscan Style and pork tenderloins fried in an easy aioli sauce, eaten at the breakfast counter, Emma was flipping through the latest copy of *Cosmopolitan* while Alex cleaned up. Her quick, standby meal, whenever she felt she was a little low on protein, hit the spot for both of them.

Tonight, after dancing and sweating so much, she thought they could both use the extra salt the pork dish provided. Being an actress meant paying attention to what you ate. It was a fine balance of mixing carbs in with fruit and dairy, being heavy on veggies and light on lean meats, and watching out for foods that were gassy.

She'd just turned the page to a swimsuit ad showing twenty somethings playing beach volleyball in skimpy bathing suits. None of which would keep her ample bosom from smacking her in the face with each vigorous jump. "What do you think is the sexiest look for a woman?

Dishtowel in hand, he tilted his head and thought for a moment. "A bath towel."

"A bath towel?" she chuckled. "I would have thought you say a string bikini or a negligee."

"Well . . . a towel wrapped around a woman is a good indicator that she's squeaky clean, and it's really easy to remove—one yank and she's naked. And likely her skin is already flushed to a delectable pink or peach shade from a hot shower or bath . . . . Mmmm. Oh, the possibilities that come to mind with a squeaky clean, warm and flushed woman."

She smiled and jumped up off the barstool. "I think I'm going to head to the shower."

She turned back at the entrance to the hallway leading to the master bedroom. "Thick bath towel, or thin skimpy threadbare one?"

"Depends on the surface I intend to take her on."

"Hmmm, bathroom counter?"

"So marble then?"

She nodded, tilting her head in the affirmative.

"Better go with a nice plush one. I would not want to cause any bruising to delicate, just scrubbed clean skin."

"Got it."

"Oh, and Emma?"

"Yes?"

"No bubble bath or after shower lotion. I want to taste *you*, not soap or an oily lotion."

After hearing her turn on the faucets, he went into the girls' master bath and stepped into the walk-in shower. After he was finished, he had time to get them each a flute of prosecco, light some fragrant candles in mirrored holders, and turn down the covers on the bed.

He was sitting propped up against the headboard when she came into the bedroom, wearing nothing but a thick sage-colored bath towel. The color enhanced the rosy tinge of her skin, and made a striking contrast for her low highlights blonde tresses, freshly blow-dried and falling in waves off her shoulders. But it was her eyes that drew him in, glinting in the low light of the room, bright and flashing with mischief, and so deep a blue he was dazzled by them.

Her smooth arms and legs had a nice rosy glow against the towel that covered only the under swells of her full breasts, her belly, hips, and womanhood, leaving the tops of her thighs bare and inviting.

"You are lovely," he murmured as he slid off the bed and went to her.

She was swept off her feet and carried back into the huge master bath that was still steamy from her bath.

Bundled in the towel, he placed her on the long vanity, then tugged the towel away from her body.

"Your skin is absolutely flawless," he breathed, captivated by every smooth, supple inch of her.

"I have a scar behind my knee and another inside my elbow from climbing trees."

"I'll kiss them first. Then you're going to new heights, my sweet Emma. I'm going to devour your body. Starting with those scars and working my way to those luscious lips. The nether ones . . ."

He kissed a small silver uneven line inside her elbow then a tiny white star on the back of her knee that wasn't tanned. Then he stood and thrust his fingers into her hair and lowered his mouth to hers and began a sometimes frantic and sometimes languid journey over her mouth, neck, shoulders, breasts, belly, and lower regions. Eventually kneeling to get her legs over his shoulders, where within moments, he had her gripping his head to her fully blossomed and drenched pussy. When she came, the sound of her cries echoed off the mirrored and tiled walls of the enormous bathroom.

When he had eased her back from the colorful realms where her orgasm had delightfully spun her, he kissed her lips and she tasted herself on his marauding tongue.

She was vaguely aware when he lowered her legs, then lifted her, wrapping them around his hips. Her eyes finally opened as he carried her to the bedroom then placed her on the bed, following her down and entering her in the same moment. His groan of approval, then deep inhale of satisfaction, gave her an immediate sense of everything being right with her world. As if for the first time in her entire life things were lined up as they should be, and the universe was giving her everything her heart had ever desired.

She was sublimely happy as she accepted his hard thrusts,

felt the heavy fullness of him inside her core, and reveled in the oneness of their intimate connection when he threw his head back with low growl accompanied by long hiss, gritted his teeth and emptied into her. She relaxed in the serenity of the moment as she held him to her and stroked her fingers along his shoulders and back.

This was true happiness, and she could hardly believe her good fortune. Until thoughts started crowding back in, reminding her that this good fortune had been contrived. Engineered in fact, in such a way that she now felt shame ebbing into the recesses of her mind and robbing her of her bliss.

He sighed, deeply content in the moment, and then her sigh followed. But her sigh was for a different reason. She had to come clean. She had to tell him who she was. Why she had come here. And knowing him now as she did, knowing how protective he was of his girls, she knew this was not going to go well.

When he leaned up, his body hovering over hers, his arms supporting him without even the slightest amount of strain, and smiled down at her, she knew now was not the time.

"I love you," he whispered. "I can hardly believe it's true, but I do. More than I would have ever believed possible." He effortlessly lowered himself until he could take her lips with his. And with a tenderness she'd not known before, he kissed her as if her lips were the softest of rose petals and that he needed to feel them rub against his or he'd perish.

Yeah, now was not the time.

Chapter 39—Alex & Emma
Even More Comfortable

They fell asleep in each other's arms. And groaned in unison when the alarm on Alex's iPhone went off at six a.m. He groped to put it on snooze.

"I do not want to get up," he murmured.

"Neither do I. In fact, I'm not sure I can. My body is like a limp noodle."

He turned her to face him. "I don't doubt it, you came completely undone last night. Three times."

"Are you bragging?"

"Yeah," he said with a grin. "I think I earned the right."

She smiled over at him and as she lifted a lock of hair off his forehead said, "Yeah, you did."

He ran a finger up and down her arm. "Do you think you could spend the weekend with me and the girls?" The want in his eyes was palpable.

"Yeah, I'd like that."

"We would too. Can you come out Friday night?"

"I have an afternoon meeting with my agent in the city, but after that I'm free."

"Good, we'll have dinner, maybe watch a movie . . . keep my winning streak going . . ."

"How could a girl turn that down?"

His face grew serious. "Do you like being here? With me and the girls I mean?"

"Yes. Yes, I do. They're amazing. And you . . . well . . ."

"And me?"

She knew he was fishing. He'd told her he loved her last night. She hadn't replied to that with a declaration of her own. She didn't think she should until she cleared the air, but she knew she loved him.

"You are the whole package, everything a young girl

dreams of. Quite the thing of adolescent fantasies, you are," she said as she ran a fingertip down his nose. "And I am falling for you, unbelievably fast." She ran her fingertip over his bottom lip. "We should talk, get to know each other better. The weekend would be a good time for some backstory on my part."

Alex's alarm went off again.

"This weekend, then. I get to learn about Cinderella's scars, pimples, and warts. I'll be home by four on Friday. It's a light day for me at work. Only two appointments." He threw off the covers. "But today is another matter, got 'em back-to-back until five, plus another for cocktails."

She admired his broad shoulders and toned ass as he walked to the bathroom. "I should be able to get here by five."

"Perfect. You don't need to get up if you don't have any place you have to be this morning. Sleep in and leave when you want. The front door can be set to lock automatically and the alarm will engage with the gate closing."

"I have a yoga class at ten, so maybe I will sleep a little bit more." She grabbed a handful of sheets and the edge of the comforter and flopped over to tunnel into the pillow."

"That's more like it. I like feeling as if I wore you out. If you jumped out of bed all vim and vigor, I'd feel as if I hadn't done my job very well."

"Trust me, you did your job *sublimely.*"

By the time he was out of the shower, shaved and dressed, she was sound asleep and looking like a mussed and tousled angel. Very lovely and very content. If he hadn't had an early appointment he'd see to it she stayed that way.

He couldn't believe he'd told her that he loved her last night. He had though. And he knew that he did. But it wasn't like him to put his cards on the table without knowing how the other player was setting up their hand. It bothered him that she hadn't professed her love to him. But he felt deep down that she felt the same way. Maybe it was too soon. He had just been so captivated by her, so absorbed in the moment and the magic of the night.

She'd said they needed to talk. He had Googled her of course, read her short bio, even went on Hulu to watch back episodes of the soap she'd starred on. And noted that if she couldn't get an acting part on her own, he could surely get her screenings with one of the many producers and directors he dealt with. He knew she was on edge, and worried about her career. She'd spent years perfecting her skills, now she wanted to reap the rewards for all her hard work. They would have time this weekend to really get to know each other, and for the girls to get to know her as well.

He admitted to himself that he was totally taken with her, smitten was the word that came to mind, but maybe thankful was more to the point. She had taken him from the depths of depression to the heights of euphoria in less than a month. Yet he was pretty sure his feelings for Mallory, though he loved her deeply, were never this . . . buoyant.

Because of Emma, he was coming to realize that he had been content with the sex life he and Mallory had. It had been satisfying and fulfilling. But sex with Emma was otherworldly. It was fun and creative, and nothing was off the table. She was every man's fantasy, yet he knew he should temper the emotional feelings he was developing for her, for things were moving fast with them. But at the same time, he wanted to be all in. He didn't want to miss a day in her company.

He smiled to himself. What would be the advice he'd give to one of his young clients, most of them rich actors, playwrights or singers? To slow down, live in the moment, but let there be many moments before there was a single decision that would take years to unravel.

He was looking forward to spending many breathtaking moments with Emma, starting with this upcoming weekend and continuing until hopefully, a decision would loom to secure their future. For now, he was content to be distracted by thoughts of her and her insatiable appetite for sex . . . with him.

Chapter 40—Alex & Emma
Secrets

Friday night was filled with games of peek-a-boo, hide-and-seek, playing with Duplo's, doing puzzles with animal sounds, running beads through expansive mazes, rearranging dollhouse furniture, and singing nursery rhymes that Emma was surprised she still remembered. *The Eensy Weensy Spider, Hush Little Baby, Do your Ears Hang Low*, and *Jesus Loves Me This I Know*, coming back to her as if she had sung them just yesterday.

Using the *I Can Draw Animals* book she had brought, they drew pigs, and bunnies, tigers, and elephants. None of which looked like the animal they were trying to depict. The girls watched *Elena of Avalor* in their high chairs while she and Alex fixed her special spaghetti sauce that was always a hit with the kids in her family.

After both girls ate the meaty spaghetti sauce and digitali pasta directly from the trays on the high chairs, they were taken to the bathtub where they played with bubbles and squeeze toys of every animal imaginable. Alex and Emma alternated between shifts of watching them in the tub and cleaning up the kitchen before drying them off, diapering them with overnight diapers and slipping them into footie pajamas.

A nighttime bottle was next as Alex and Emma took turns reading *Good Night Train, Good Night Moon*, and *The Story of Ping*.

Each with a girl in their lap, they were finally able to wind down their day. Alex told Emma about a new up-and-coming boys band he just signed as clients, and Emma told Alex about the job she had just finished, dubbing songs for a once talented singer who could no longer hit the high notes.

"Must be hard doing such wonderful work and not getting credit for it," he commented.

"No, not really. She paid her dues, she sang until her pipes got rusty. I feel like I'm giving her a chance to earn a few more paychecks. It's easy work. I love to sing. And it's not bad money."

"I can get you in touch with people who are going places."

"I don't want you to do that Alex. I don't want our relationship to be about what you can do for me. It's important that I do things for myself. If you miss a few rungs of the ladder on the way up, you've missed the journey."

"Mallory didn't want help either. She said she had to earn the privilege of getting through the system on her own. She had a reserved quality about her, always looking for the quid pro quo in any relationship. Can't say that I blame her though, her father abused her when she was young and it taught her that you paid the price to be the favorite."

Emma couldn't keep the shock from her voice, though she was still mindful of not waking the child in her arms. "What?"

"Yeah. When she was a young girl her father found ways to get her alone and forced her to service him."

Emma could hardly believe her ears. She almost blurted out, "Uncle Jerry?" But instead said. "Wow, that's unreal." Then she added, "How awful for her," as she knew she probably sounded cynical.

"Yeah. She didn't tell me until after we married. While we were dating, I had wondered why she was so hesitant when it came to oral sex with me, when other women her age were normally into it. It explained a lot. She said her dad was always insisting she accompany him when he went out on his boat, or to some old barn on his property."

Emma's blood ran cold. She knew her eyes had bugged wide and she had to coach herself not to react so blatantly. But she did remember her uncle taking Mallory out alone on his boat. And to his high-dollar barn where he kept his good truck and the antique tractor he was always working on. And what's worse, she did remember Mallory never wanting to go.

Her stomach plummeted and she almost missed what Alex was saying. "Yeah, I insisted she see a therapist for awhile but it really didn't help. She really didn't want to talk about it. She said she only told me so I'd know, that if we ever had kids to never leave them alone with him."

It was as if her body was chilling from the inside, icing and freezing her limbs, sending frozen tentacles growing toward her heart. Emma didn't know the skin on her body could pebble with gooseflesh so completely, but after hearing that, she knew the sensation of crawling flesh everywhere. Her uncle . . . Mallory . . . these sweet little girls . . .. Oh God, Melissa . . ..

As if he could read her mind, he said. "Mallory had a twin sister named Melissa. If Mallory attempted to refuse him he would tell her he'd go get her instead, so that's how he was able to keep her doing his bidding. People like him always have something to use as leverage. I wanted her to press charges. I wanted her to tell her mom. But she wouldn't. She said it would kill her mom. And it might just have. I don't know. But the morning after the girls were born, after I had lost Mallory, I knew I had to do something to protect them from that bastard. I never wanted him to ever even see them. So I moved the babies here where we could be with my parents."

Emma let out a long breath. "That's a lot to take in. Geez. I can't imagine." She truly did not know what to say, as she was still in shock.

"I've read up on it all. Abuse of all kinds. Not just sexual, but physical. I wanted to be alert to the signs, but it seems it's not something you can easily spot in others. People who abuse others are canny, manipulative, and they protect their secret well. It scares me to know that one or both of my girls could be subjected to any kind of violence or abuse."

"You'll have to prepare them in advance. Give them the skills to defend themselves."

"Yeah, and I'm going to. They'll have archery lessons, learn tomahawk throwing, go to karate classes, practice Crossfit, go to Ninja Turtle School."

She smiled. "Are you going to teach them Krav Maga before sending them to kindergarten?" She looked down to the sleeping bundle in her arms. "Or send them to a Black Ops military academy? This one looks more like the ballerina type to me."

He sighed. "I'm not sure any of that helps with an abuser. They develop a psychological advantage. And they are usually in a position of power over their victim." He looked down at the baby snuggled into his chest.

"The size difference at this age is overwhelming, they are helpless right now. And they will be unable to defend themselves for years to come. I know first hand how vulnerable they are, even from someone who loves them with all their heart."

He took a deep sigh as if searching for the words to unburden his own betrayal. "Mandy was screaming one night and nothing I could do would make her stop. It was loud, earsplitting. I checked everything. Tried everything to calm her. Her face became purple with rage. Because of what I could not imagine. I tried to figure out why. Did everything I could think of to quiet her. After awhile I got mad. I held her up and shook her. She stopped. But I'll never forget the look of fear that came over her face. I knew not to do that of course, it had just been a very bad reaction in a moment of panic."

"All parents have those moments . . . life is not like the TV ads."

"Still, I felt like the worst father."

"Understandable. But you've probably never done it again . . ."

"No, never. And I won't. I read about it. Extensively. I know what to do next time it happens."

"Which is?"

"After you've checked everything you can think of, leave

them in the crib to cry for a few minutes. Come back to check on them. Try to quiet them again. If all else fails, call the doctor."

"Sounds like a plan. Does putting them together help with something like that?"

"Sometimes. But I've discovered that it's more likely they're having a bit of temper because of something the other one did. Or not. I read that a disquieting restlessness can sometimes come over babies, that often has no cause whatsoever. The theory is that they get frustrated and that even they don't know why. You just have to give them time to cry it out. "

"I hear it gets worse when little girls start to dress themselves," she said with a huge smile.

"Sometimes I wonder how I'm going to manage them as they get older, but thankfully I have my parents, and my cousin who's their new nanny. Next year they'll go to pre-school, and then I'll have other parents to compare notes with."

"You should take them to church, they have wonderful nurseries in churches. They'll get a chance to play with other kids and socialize a bit first."

"After what happened to Mallory in her own home, I'm not sure I will ever be ready to leave them with strangers," he said, his voice somber.

"I used to help with vacation Bible school in my church. There are many volunteers overseeing everything, and everybody has to be vetted these days."

"Still, until they can talk, someone I trust will be with them at all times."

"That sounds reasonable." Reeling from all she learned about Mallory and Uncle Jerry, Emma needed a few minutes to herself. "Mine's sound asleep. I'm going to lie her down and get a shower if that's alright?"

"Of course. I'll finish up the kitchen. I think the floor could use a good mopping after their spaghetti dinner."

"They seemed to like it didn't they?" she whispered as she placed Molly in her crib and covered her legs with a thermal baby blanket.

"Yeah, it was great."

Emma nodded as she stood, then walked out of the room. She was remembering her Uncle Jerry at the stove, stirring his special sauce and saying his recipe was the best spaghetti sauce there ever was. Now she wasn't sure if she'd ever have the stomach to make it again.

Chapter 41—Alex & Emma
Come Together

"You seem quiet tonight," Alex murmured against the back of her neck as he nestled his legs behind hers in the big king-sized bed. She could smell the soap he'd used mingling with his aftershave; feel the brisk hairs on his legs rubbing alongside her smooth ones. She thought it was sweet that he took the time to shave at night. But tonight she didn't want his face between her legs. Or hers between his.

"Just tired is all."

"The girls are a bit wearing, especially after a full day of work."

It would have been the perfect time to tell him why she was so melancholy. To tell him that his dead wife was her dead cousin. That finding out that the girl she'd grown up with and admired so much had kept such a dreadful secret. That her scheming, conniving uncle had paid her to come here to spy on him and his girls. Her skin crawled at the thought of his perverse interest.

But he changed her mind with hands that caressed her belly and breasts, tugged on nipples with thumbs and forefingers, making them hard points and sending wild zinging sensations through her core. And emptying her mind of unsettling thoughts.

"You feel so good," he whispered as he took her ear lobe between his teeth then sucked on it. His fingers ran down her belly to the tiny patch of hair between her legs and found her growing nub and began circling it. He placed the tip of his penis at her opening and slid into her. His hand gripped her hip keeping her body snug to his as he gently thrust and retreated, drawing her deeper and deeper into an otherworldly transcendent serenity.

"I could do this forever, but my cock seems to think this is a race." He kissed the nape of her neck while his fingers expertly rolled and pressed on her swollen clit.

She moaned and moved with him, meeting his thrusts, "I think I'm going to beat you to the finish fine."

She reached behind her, slid her fingers between them and circled the root of his cock, gripping him and urging him to go faster. They both cried out, stilled for the briefest of seconds and came, him burying himself as deep as he could while holding her to him, her, using her hand between them to cup his balls.

"It was a tie," he breathed into her hair.

"It was . . ."

"Yes?" he prompted.

"Amazing, Awesome, Astonishing, Astounding . . ."

"All the A words then?"

"Not awful."

He laughed.

"I A-dore you."

I A-gape you."

He stilled. Then rolled her over and stared down into her face, a serious frown creasing his brow. "You love me?"

She smiled up at him, "Yes, I love you."

A wide grin replaced the frown and his eyes shone obsidian, reflecting the moonlight coming in from the high transoms.

"I can't believe it," he whispered.

"Why not?"

"I just didn't think . . . when you didn't say it before . . . I don't know, I just thought it was one-way."

She slid a finger down his nose, "Well it's not. I A-che for you."

"I will never get enough of you," he whispered, his voice raspy with emotion as he kissed her, his tongue going deep and making long languid circles with hers. Then they both stilled when the monitor crackled to life and a baby cried out.

"That's Mandy," Alex huffed out as he leveraged himself off of her.

"How can you tell?"

"Molly's too polite to interrupt a moment like this."

She laughed as he threw on pajamas bottoms.

"Let me know if I can help."

"I got this, go to sleep. My love," he added as he left the room and went down the hall.

Emma rolled over and stared at the ceiling, watching the fan high above make slow leisurely circles, and casting shadows on the walls. She turned her head and saw the moon through the skylight. It reminded her of all the nights she and Mallory had spent at the beach howling at the full moon.

Mallory. Mallory, who had made love with this man. Mallory, who had married this man. Mallory who had died having this man's children.

She'd tell him tomorrow. And tomorrow she was going to send Uncle Jerry back his money. Well, the part she hadn't already spent. But he'd get that back too. She'd see to it. She had some money hidden away for a rainy day. This qualified as a monsoon.

Chapter 42—Alex & Emma
Gainfully Employed

The next morning Emma made animal-shaped pancakes in ham cages. While she was cutting strips of ham to make a cage for Molly's tiger, Alex came up behind her and wrapped his arms around her waist. At the same time, he slipped her phone into the front pocket of her denim shorts.

"That was vibrating on the bathroom vanity the entire time I was showering. I managed to catch the name on the screen while I was stepping out. I think it was your agent. Must be important."

"Oh, sorry. I'll check it out as soon as I get this tiger and the last elephant done. This one's for you. Manly man appetite that you must have after last night." She looked over her shoulder and gave him a brilliant smile. He swatted her butt before going over to the girls sitting in their high chairs, and watching them chase pieces of pancakes around Elsa and Anna plates that were suctioned to the trays.

"How are my two little angels this morning? Is that a duck you've got there Mandy? May I have a bite?" He smiled as the little girl lifted her fork up to her daddy. "Suuure," she mouthed around a bite of ham.

"Oh, Daisy doodles," Emma breathed out in a long huff.

Alex looked up at her as she read a series of texts.

"Something wrong?"

"No. Something right actually, just at the wrong time. It was my agent. They need me to do a voice over for a cartoon show; one of the singers has tonsillitis."

"When?"

"I have to be there by eleven."

"Well go get ready. I've got this. Although I don't generally have this much mess to clean up from breakfast," he said with a nod at the countertop and stove littered with pieces of pancake, cutouts of ham, puddles of batter, and discarded halves of blueberries that she'd used for eyes.

"Being creative requires being messy," she said as she found her agent's contact number and touched the screen. She turned and walked down the hallway as the call connected and her agent came on the line.

"Yes, I can be there."

"No, I don't know where it is."

"Yes, if you could send the link that would be great."

"How long will they need me do you think?"

"Okay, I'll take a quick shower and be on my way. Thank you!"

"Yay!" she said to Alex as she turned back to him. "I've got my first voice over assignment."

"That's wonderful," he said with a genuine smile. "This could open some doors for you. That's big here."

"I know! I'm thrilled. But I've got to hurry," she said as she ran down the hall. "I don't want to be late."

"Any idea when you'll be home?" he called after her.

Home. She felt a quiver of pleasure go through her. He wanted her to go, but he also wanted her to come back to him, to *them*. *Here*.

"It's just some dialogue and a few songs, maybe four or five hours. Depends on how long it takes me to get the hang of it."

"You'll do great. And we'll be waiting here when you get back."

She pulled off her t-shirt and stripped off her shorts and underwear then stepped into the shower. She could not remember a time when she was happier. As she washed her hair, she ran through some scales and sang a few songs from *The Little Mermaid* to warm up. She recognized the name of the Disney show she'd be doing the voiceover for, but not the name of the princess she'd be playing. She would have to record the show for the girls so they could hear her playing the part.

Twenty minutes later she was on her way to the studio for a job most actresses worked years to get. She was on top of the world and could not wait to show the producers and sound techs what she had to offer.

Chapter 43—Alex & Emma
Animated Animation

When she pulled into the drive at eight o'clock, to see all the lights on in front of the house welcoming her, she grinned.

She'd had a wonderful day. The crew had been awesome, they had shown her the ropes, and they had been patient and kind. It had been fun. She had learned a lot, and had a new appreciation for what went on behind the scenes to produce a stellar animated cartoon.

She felt sure everyone liked her work. Several assistants had asked for her direct contact information. She felt reasonably sure she'd be invited back again.

The front door opened just as she closed her car door. He'd been watching for her. Her heart soared.

"Hey, there Princess."

She had texted him during a break that she was playing the part of a warrior princess, charged with saving her family from evil ninja-bots that were trying to destroy their kingdom.

He walked over to her and took her jump bag from her hand. "You must be tired."

"I am. But it's a good tired. Although my feet hurt."

"You don't get to sit to do all that voice stuff?"

"Oh, no. You need your diaphragm to expand to be able to speak up and sing with a full voice. You can't sit to do that. You're pretty much on your feet the whole time."

"Well, I happen to have some excellent foot rubbing skills."

"The girls asleep?"

"Just got them down. They asked about you all day. *Where's Emma? When's Emma coming back? I want her to make more animals in cages.*"

"Their vocabulary is really coming along. I'm surprised

how well I am able to understand them."

"My mom works with them on their diction."

"Hmm. Diction. Haven't heard that word since my old voice classes."

"Well, they certainly paid off today, huh?" he said with a grin as he led her into the house, obviously proud of her.

She smiled up at him, proud of herself, too. "Yeah. It was a great day."

"I kept dinner warm."

"Great! I am starved."

"Dinner and a foot rub coming up. You go get comfortable and I'll get it ready."

"You're too good to me."

"I may have ulterior motives in mind."

"I may be willing to entertain them."

He put her bag on the dresser and watched as she stepped out of her heels and took the clip out of her hair, letting it cascade down her back while she rubbed the crown of her head.

"You need a head rub too?"

"These clips are the best at holding my hair, but they dig into my scalp a bit. I'm good. Just tired. My whole body feels as if I've run a marathon."

"Get yourself comfortable in the family room, I'll get you some wine."

"That would be wonderful. Do we have any of that red left from the other night? It was really good."

"If we don't, I'll open another bottle. You just relax."

He left the room and she sighed. When had she ever had anyone take this kind of care of her? Certainly never as an adult. Alex was everything a man should be. Helpful, kind, caring, and with his five o'clock shadow and rumpled chambray shirt, touched here and there with smears of baby food and grass stains, he was devastatingly handsome. She couldn't wait to run her fingers through his hair and pull him down on top of her. Because, a day like this needed to be celebrated not only with good wine, but also with good sex.

He brought her a glass of the flavorful cabernet in a stemless wine glass. Then went back to the kitchen for a colorful pottery bowl that had a quilted bowl holder under it to keep the hot bowl from burning the hand that held it. Tilting her head in question, she looked at it, stirred it, lifted it to her nose, and sniffed. It was her go to dish—crispy fried rice noodles over vegetables and tofu covered in a sweet and sour sauce "Mee Grob? You gave the girls Mee Grob for dinner?"

He laughed, "Not hardly. They had chicken, mac and cheese, green beans, and applesauce. I ordered this for you when you texted you were on your way back. I knew it was one of your favorites.

"Yeah, but scallions and garlic? You're going to have some too, aren't you?"

"I got myself some Larb, so we'll be fine. Enjoy." He sat across from her while they ate and she told him all about her day in the sound studio, and he told her all about his day with the girls. "Molly disappeared for a few moments and had me panicked. She was playing hide-and-seek in the pantry. Scared the daylights out of me. I think she heard the panic in my voice, because she came out and said, "Here. Molly is here, Daddy." He bent his head forward so she could see the top of his head. "Do you see the new gray hairs?"

She laughed, "Oh yes, there are six new ones." She leaned forward and pulled out a piece of lime green string. "What's this?"

He took it from her and smiled. "Silly string. We decorated the playhouse windows."

"You're a good daddy."

"I try."

He took her empty bowl from her, "More?" he asked.

"No, that was perfect." She held up her almost empty wineglass. "Maybe a little more of this?"

He smiled and took it from her to refill it.

When he came back he handed it to her and then disappeared for a few minutes, returning with a basin of steaming water, a towel draped over an arm, and a tube of lotion sticking out of his shirt pocket.

Without saying a word, he knelt at her feet, and cupping her calves, eased them into the basin.

"Ooooh," she moaned.

With the lavender-scented soap in the basin, he tenderly washed her feet. Then gently dried them. Then repositioning them both so that they were facing each other on the sofa, he lavished her right foot with a soothing cream.

"Peppermint?" she asked, feeling the cooling, yet invigorating sensations spread over her foot.

"Mmmhmm," he murmured. "Wakes up the nerves, loosens the muscles." He used his thumb and fingers to expertly massage the ball of her foot, to press into her heel, to separate her toes.

"This is heaven. When do I get to do this to you?"

He laughed. "This is not a quid pro quo. This is my way of loving you."

She sighed and relaxed as he replaced that foot and picked up the other. "Okay, I'll take it. But you're gonna have to take what I dish out when we get to the bedroom."

He flashed a wicked smile. "You will get no protest from me, that I assure you."

Twenty minutes later, when he carried her to bed, she showed him her brand of massaging and lavishing a particular, achy, needy body part. And during the middle of the night, he woke her to reciprocate.

Chapter 44—Alex & Emma
Unraveling

Sunday morning brought sunshine through the high casement windows along with the crackling of two monitors followed by the soft cries of "Daaaaddy. Eeemmma."

"And so it begins," Alex muttered, as he pushed off the covers and grabbed for the shorts on the floor.

Emma groaned. "It can't be morning already?"

He bent and kissed her forehead. "Those two have an uncanny knack of following the sun. If its up, they're up."

She looked over at the clock, "It's just after six."

"I know. You go back to sleep."

"Okay." But she couldn't, especially after the girls climbed up on the bed and began poking their fingers in her face, whispering, "Emmmma, Emmma, Hey, it's morning time. Time to wake up."

A finger went in her ear. Two hands twisted her hair into a rope. One adventurous angel gently lifted an eyelid.

Alex came out of the bathroom and tried to shoo them away. "Let Emma sleep. She's tired." He took both girls by the hand despite their protests and led them out of the room, closing the door behind them.

But in the quiet of the room, she couldn't sleep. She felt left out, like she was missing something, some new sweet thing one of the girls would do or say, some tender thing Alex would do or say.

She threw off the covers, went to the bathroom to freshen up, and as she was brushing her teeth, decided to make her most comforting breakfast food.

Coming out of the bedroom and walking into the great room, already littered with toys that hadn't been there last night, she asked Alex, "Hey, you got any grits?"

"Uhhh, maybe. I don't do the shopping. I have a service do it. Let's see." He went to the pantry and lifted something from the highest shelf. "This it?"

"No, that's oatmeal. If you had any, they'd probably be in the freezer. That's the best place to keep them."

"Now that you mention it, I do remember seeing some on the freezer door. The one in the garage. I'll go get it."

When he came back and handed it to her she took the package from him and read the name on it. "Carolina Plantation. Where'd you get this, surely this didn't come from here? This is the king of grits, from Plumfield Plantation on the Pee Dee River, outside Charleston."

"Oh, if they're from Charleston, then they came in the move from Wilmington. I had a moving company pack up the house and they packed every single item including Dixie cups from the dispensers. Mallory would have bought them when we were there for our wedding. They're probably too old."

"Let's see. This is some primo stuff. If they've been refrigerated or kept frozen, they should be fine."

"I wouldn't know. Grits has never been my thing."

"We're about to change that," she said as she stood on her tiptoes to kiss him on the jaw. "Just let me see if they're any good. The date says they expire this December. And they're vacuum packed. And instant, which has a much longer shelf life."

"You sound like an expert on grits, but if you're at all concerned, I'll just run up to the store and buy some more."

"I am an expert on grits. I'm from the south. I know my grits. Let me check these first, I'll be able to tell if they're stale if the flavors have separated."

"I don't want you to take a chance that they're bad . . ."

"You do know they keep grain in silos for years, right? This stuff is gourmet and fresh batched. I'd be surprised if it's off."

She went to the stove, and using a back burner added the right amount of water with the grits to make four servings. Then she found some sausage in the freezer and defrosted it in the microwave before putting it in a frying pan and crumbling it as it cooked. Next she grated a brick of cheddar cheese, then got out some eggs and prepped them for scrambled eggs for the girls, and fried eggs for her and Alex.

When the timer went off, she dipped the wooden spoon into the pot of grits then ran a finger over the backside of the spoon and stuck her finger into her mouth. Alex sat at the counter, keeping an eye on the girls, but his brow lifted for her verdict.

"Perfect! These have wonderful flavor."

"If you say so. Still not convinced."

"You will be. Ten more minutes and breakfast will be ready."

When everything was brought to the table, Alex gathered the girls and got them into their high chairs.

"Now don't be upset if they don't eat them, they're pretty finicky when it comes to food," he warned.

"They have North Carolina roots, they'll like them."

He pulled out her chair for her then sat in his, "Okay, just don't want you to be disappointed."

"I won't be," she said as she prepared a plate for each girl.

Both girls stared at their bowls of mush, spoons at the ready but not eager to dig in.

Emma had learned that if Mandy tried something, Molly would. So using a tiny baby spoon she had found in a drawer, she scooped some up, blew on it, and put it on Mandy's lower lip. When Mandy opened her mouth to protest, Emma slid it inside.

They all watched as Mandy's tongue moved the pearly, cheesy, sausage mixture around inside her mouth. Then she swallowed. Then used her own spoon to scoop up more.

Emma didn't give Molly a chance to decline. She loaded

up the baby spoon again and fed it to Molly, who looked as if she was going to spit it out because of the texture, but didn't because of the taste. Soon they were both eating heartily.

"See?" Emma said with glee. "They like it!" She handed him a bowl with a spoon stuck inside, standing straight up.

"Looks like paste," he said with a wrinkled nose, "with clods of dirt in it."

"C'mon, be a big boy," she cooed. "The girls are eating it. Be a good example . . ."

He moved the spoon around in it, not at all eager to try it. But knowing how hard she'd worked on it, he reluctantly put the spoon to his mouth and inserted it. Then went back for a second taste. "It's not hateful." Then a third. "Okay, it's got merit. The texture's not as bad as I thought."

"It can be made creamier using milk instead of water, but I like the way the little pearls tickle my tongue."

"I'll give you something to tickle your tongue," he said with a grin.

She laughed and sat down to eat her breakfast. "Maybe later, when the girls take a nap."

"I thought we'd take them to the open-air farmer's market at the park this morning. We can stroller them around and get some fresh air while checking out the vendors," he said.

"That's sounds wonderful. I'd like that."

"Good, we can leave after we clean up from breakfast."

"Well, I cooked. So you get to clean the pot. That's the one bad thing about making grits. It's probably going to need a good soaking."

"Well, I have to say, they were worth it. They are delicious."

"Thank you," she beamed at him and dug into her own bowl of the steamy mess.

An hour later, they were taking turns pushing the double stroller and checking out the vendors when Emma noticed an odor coming from Mandy. "Her breakfast done pushed things through, I fear. Is there a place I can go to change her?"

He pointed at a gray bricked-in building. "The lady's room is on the other side. It should have a drop down table like the men's room does."

"Okay, be back in a few," she said as she slung the diaper bag over her shoulder and scooped up Mandy.

Ten minutes later, when she walked back with Mandy, she saw Alex talking to a tall brunette. The woman was animated, laughing and touching Alex's elbow then chucking Molly under her chin with a perfectly manicured hand. She recognized a woman flirting when she saw one, and she was surprised by how protective it made her feel. She decided she didn't like this woman even before she was introduced to her. What kind of a name was Dee Dee anyway? Who named their kid that?

Alex was saying, "Dee Dee's a personal shopper at Nordstrom's. When we first moved here she helped set up wardrobes for the girls. I had taken them from a hospital directly to the airport, so when we got to California, they literally, had nothing to wear. She was a lifesaver."

Emma smiled at *Dee Dee* then looked over at Alex. "Oh, I'm sure she was, that had to have been such a horrible time for you. Can you give me a hand getting Molly back in the stroller?" She moved between *Dee Dee* and Alex, and dumped Molly into his arms.

"Uh, sure."

"Oh man, was she ripe," Emma said. "Must've been all the carrots and peas from Friday night." She didn't know why it was important for this woman to know this wasn't a one-off date, but somehow it was. "There was poo on her jumper so I had to change her clothes. I'll soak it when we get *home*."

The woman got the message. "Well it was nice to see you, Alex. Please call me if I can help with outfitting the girls."

"My mom is really big into making most of their clothes now. It's a new hobby that has taken off big time with her. But I'll call you next time they need anything special or some new shoes."

Emma watched as the woman slipped her card into Alex's hand and said, "Call anytime." She turned back to Emma and said, "Emma, so nice to meet you," when it clearly was not.

"Nice lady," Emma said as *Dee Dee* walked off.

Alex laughed. "At least one of you was."

Emma gave him a crooked smile of chagrin. "I was bad, wasn't I?"

He tilted his head, "Mmmm, maybe."

"She was obviously flirting, in a very big way. Did you notice how she was touching you?"

"And you were having none of it," he chuckled. "You had your claws out."

"That was poorly done of me, I'm sorry."

"Don't be. It was kind of nice watching two women fight over me."

"We were not fighting. Posturing, maybe."

He wrapped his arm around her shoulders and pulled her close, nestled his nose into her hair. "You have nothing to worry about. You own my heart. I only have eyes for you."

She looked up at him. "Are you asking me to go steady?"

"I think I might be. Let's see if we can find a bauble you might like at one of the jewelry stands."

"Oooh, jewelry. Yes, please."

He chuckled. "Lead the way."

After much debate, she decided on a thin silver and gold ring with a simple design, two round wires had been woven together and then flattened. "It reminds me of the ocean," she said. "Waves churning and settling, up high and then down low . . . peaks and valleys." She reminded herself that she had something she had to tell him when the girls took their naps this afternoon. "Relationships are like that. They have their highs and lows."

"Well, we're riding a crest right now," he said as he pulled her in for a kiss. "And it feels wonderful. I like spending time with you, Emma. I like how easygoing you are with the girls, and how comfortable they are with you."

"They are very special little girls . . ." she said as her eyes spotted something up ahead. " . . . who would probably like to see a puppet show right now!"

She urged Alex, who was pushing the double stroller, toward a colorful tent with handmade finger puppets on stands, glove puppets piled high on tables, and colorfully painted wooden marionettes strung along wires attached to the sides of the tent. Within moments she was doing an impromptu show with the woman who had made them, to the delight of the girls and everyone passing by.

The two women, nodding to each other and speaking in the familiar language of the trade, put on two shows for the crowd. After which, everyone clapped, even Molly and Mandy. The woman made change for all the puppets she sold and thanked Emma profusely for her help. Then she gave Molly and Mandy two special handmade puppets she took from a little chest. "For you my dearies," she said as she bent to the girls sitting in the baby carriage, "for you and your very special mom who clearly loves to entertain children."

Emma started to correct her, but Alex stopped her by putting his hand in hers and saying, "It's okay, leave it. I don't mind the idea of that at all. Maybe one day, you will be."

Emma looked up at him, her eyes wide.

"Isn't that the way these things go?" He began chanting, "Alex and Emma sitting in a tree, K-I-S-S-I-N-G. First comes love, then comes marriage then comes baby in a baby carriage. We're just doing things a little out of order here."

She covered his hand with hers. "Alex, we need to talk."

He leaned back from her. "You're not already married

are you?"

"No, it's not that."

"Is there someone else back in New York?"

"No."

"Then we'll figure it all out in time. Meanwhile, I think we'd better get these two home, they've had enough sun and the angle of the sun is making the canopy useless. Plus it's naptime for these two."

Emma yawned as if on cue.

"Maybe all three of my girls need a nap."

"I don't sleep as well in your bed as I do in mine."

"Something wrong with my bed?" He jerked back at the affront.

"Yeah, there's usually someone horny in it."

He laughed and acceded, "There is indeed."

They walked back to Alex's Lexus SUV and loaded the girls into their car seats. The heavy breakfast, the warm sunny day, and the excitement of the puppet show took their toll. Both girls were asleep before they got out of the crowded parking lot.

Emma looked back at them, "They're asleep. What do we do now? Drive around until they wake up?"

"They'll probably go back to sleep if we get them home soon."

They had just gotten back and carried each child to their crib when the buzzer for the gate sounded. Alex walked to the panel where the closed circuit TV was. The window showed a police officer pulled up to the gate.

"Yes?" Alex called out.

"Officers Tate and Branham with Ventura County Juvenile Investigations Department with a warrant for Alexander Hale. Accompanying us is a D.S.S. officer. We have orders to place Molly and Mandy Hale under the protective custody of Ventura County."

"What?"

"Sir, are you Alexander Hale?"

"I am."

"Then we need to talk to you. Open the gates, please."

Alex pressed the button to allow the gates to open.

He looked at Emma and she looked back at him. Both had furrowed brows and looks of confusion on their faces.

"You know what this could be about?" he asked.

She shook her head. "No idea."

Alex pulled out his cell phone and pressed the button for his mother's cell phone. When she answered he started talking, his voice clipped and business-like. It was eerie how quickly he was able to detach himself from his emotions to deal with the problem. "Mom, I need you and Dad to come get the girls. Someone's pressing charges against me. Officers are here with an arrest warrant." There was silence for a few moments, then, "I don't know Mom, I'm waiting to see the arrest papers. Just come and bring your I.D.s and those custody papers I drew up."

The doorbell rang. "They're here at the door now, Mom." He pressed the button to end the call.

Alex went to the door and opened it. His hand went out for the papers as soon as the officers crossed the threshold.

He read quickly, flipping the stapled pages one over the other as he scanned them. "Physical abuse?" He flipped to the last page. "Gerald Mullins? What the hell! That bastard! What evidence do you have?"

"You'll have to ask the judge, sir. We only serve the warrant."

Alex looked over at Emma. She had gone white and had a hand clamped over her mouth.

"Emma? Emma, what's wrong? Emma . . .what do you know about this?"

"The new monitor," she whispered.

"What about it?" he barked.

"A few minutes after I broke it my uncle called. He

offered to get a new one and overnight it here for me."

He stood stark still; staring at her as he inhaled a long breath through his nose, remembering the conversation they'd had that night in the girl's room. "Is your uncle Gerald Mullins?"

"Yes," she whispered so low that he could hardly hear her. Yet watching her lips form the word and her head nod he heard the word as if she'd shouted it.

There was the space of a few moments where no one said a word.

The officers stood immobile, waiting and watching the tense interaction between the dumbfounded man and the speechless woman who was tearing up.

Alex stared at Emma as if seeing her for the first time. Taking in traits as if trying to match them up in his jumbled brain.

Emma stared back, her eyes welling with tears, her lips trembling, every muscle tightening for the blow to come.

"Pack your stuff and get out of here." His voice was quiet, yet so devastated that the pain of it penetrated before the meaning of his words hit her.

She touched the sleeve of his tropical print shirt. "Alex, it's not what you think."

He pulled his arm away and held up his hands. "No, don't talk to me. Just go." His face was stern, his eyes vacant.

"I didn't mean for this to happen. I was going to tell you. Please believe me. He asked me to come out here to see how his granddaughters were doing. Maybe get a few pictures. I swear that's all he asked me to do."

He turned and stared at her with menacing eyes. "You're Emma. Mallory's *cousin*. The New York *actress*. Get out. Now."

She tugged on Alex's arm, "Let me explain . . ."

He stepped away from her. "Do I have to have you escorted out?" He looked over at the officers standing by the door.

She turned pleading eyes to them.

They shifted their stance and waited. No words were

needed. They were inured to the haunted look in the woman's eyes. They'd seen this type of treachery and betrayal in families too many times to count.

When one officer shifted his hand to his holster, she understood. She had to go.

She turned and went into the bedroom for her jump bag and walked around the master bedroom shoving things into it. In the ensuite, she collected her toiletries by sweeping them all off the vanity and into the bag with her arm. While zipping the bag she saw her new ring. It had only been on her finger an hour at best. She slipped it off and left it on the counter by his razor.

She grabbed her purse from the dresser, went down the hall, and walked to the front door.

"Wait!" Alex barked.

She turned and watched as he went to an end table where the monitors they had just brought down and plugged in sat. He jerked the plugs from the wall and brought them over to where she stood by the door. Then he thumbed through the settings on the newest one, and turned the screen to face her. "Is this your uncle's cell number?"

She looked to where his finger was pointing. "Yes."

"Setting up a passcode, he was able to log on at any time to listen and view everything that happened in the nursery."

His eyes boring into hers told her that he was remembering the conversation they'd had about him shaking Molly.

Her eyes went wide with horror, and fear at the implications that confession could have for him and his daughters.

There were so many emotions crossing his face, but the one that registered the most was the hurt from betrayal in his eyes.

He dropped the monitors to the carpet then stomped on them shattering the screens. Then he pulled them up by the cords, wrapped the cords around the smashed mess and pushed them into her hand. "Give these to your uncle for me."

Then he turned to go down the hallway, calling after him, "Officers, please see that she leaves the premises."

Chapter 45—Emma
She's Come Undone

Emma drove to her apartment while shaking from huge wracking sobs. She had to fight to breathe. She battled with herself to stop crying. But it was futile trying to hold it in. She finally let everything tumble out. It was choking her with its intensity, welling out of her like a blubbering geyser. She couldn't find the tissues in her purse and used carryout napkins she found in the console of the rental. If she got pulled over now, the officer would not see a stunning model. He would see a haggard, defeated woman with a blotched up face and puffy make-up smeared into raccoon eyes, wiping her face with Taco Bell napkins. She was exhausted in every way a body could be.

When she was safely in her apartment, she began packing her things. Not caring much for the way they were going into her suitcase or the tote bags. Her heart reeled from sadness and anxious thoughts began to drown her with dread.

She had screwed up in a major way. And the worst part was she knew that there was no fix for this. None. What she had done could never be forgiven or forgotten. This shattering of her heart could never be undone. She knew in this moment that she would be like this forever—heartbroken and splintered for all time. The jagged edges of her heart were tearing at her each time she breathed and remembered the man she had betrayed.

She collapsed on the couch, trying to quietly sob in consideration of the neighbors, finally falling asleep at three in the morning.

The next day she went to the UPS store and shipped everything to her parent's house. Then she drove herself to the airport, turned in her rental car and boarded a flight home.

She cried all the way home, sniffling into one tissue after another while trying not to bother her seatmate, who was an

Asian man who didn't speak a word of English.

The next day, before the sun had come up, she ran to the Kindred Spirit Mailbox, and over the course of a week, she told her story.

She had used most of the notebook telling the story that now broke her heart. But once she had purged every last word, she was ready to move on. She had to find work. She had to find something to keep her busy, to give her a reason to get up in the mornings.

First thing on her list, was to pay back her Uncle Jerry so she'd never have to live with the knowledge that she'd taken money to ruin so many lives. Hers, for one. And, because she would have been a great wife to Alex, and a great mother to Molly and Mandy, theirs as well.

Back in L.A., Alex was likely still reeling from her betrayal, while callously putting things in place that would forbid her ever reentering his orbit. She was still reeling herself, in shock over what had happened. How quickly things had gone from blissful to chaotic.

What she had done as a favor had backfired. Yes, she had been an unwitting pawn in a scheme of someone else's making, but ultimately, she was the one who had betrayed Alex. She knew he saw it that way. She would never forget the look on his face when he had turned from the papers he was reading—a summons and a court order to prepare his children to be picked up by an officer of the court.

Alex had survived the devastation wrought by his wife's death two years ago when she died within the same hour she had delivered their twin daughters, a tragic death that was subsequently proven to have been avoidable.

Emma didn't think that what she had done could rival the pain of him losing his wife, but the desolation she'd seen in his eyes convinced her that maybe it had. Because of her, Alex had started to live again, tentatively beginning to fall in love and dream of a happy future. With that letter, she had crushed all hope for him. She had destroyed him.

My God, they had taken his children away. Quite possibly, they were able to live with their grandparents, but still. They were his reason for living. And she had helped them do it.

She gave in to the toxic flow of tears again, trying but not succeeding to purge her system of the deep regret that was poisoning her from the inside. There was no end to this; nothing would stem the memory of all she had lost. The malice of her actions replayed itself over and over again.

How could she have let him down like this? And what was worse, she had been only moments from telling him who she was, confessing her reason for being there, and begging his forgiveness for her duplicity, when the cops had shown up.

She was sitting on her bed in her parent's house, pondering what was next when she saw the picture of her beloved grandmother on her dresser. She looked at her lovely kind face. If only she were here now. She would know how to fix things. A memory came to mind. A day they had spent together . . . tromping through the woods.

She jumped up and grabbed the keys to her rental car.

Chapter 46—Emma
Grandma's Legacy

Emma drove to Crusoe Island in the Green Swamp, a tiny community that dated back to the 1600s. Portuguese pirates, French fugitives, Haitian refugees, marooned sailors, and battle-worn spies found their way here and hid from the life they'd left behind. For centuries the settlers prided themselves on their seclusion and anonymity, thriving and living off the land in an area the rest of the world didn't know existed.

Intermarrying, generation after generation of castaways sought sanctuary, fished, farmed, hunted, hewed dugouts, distilled their own liquor, and made their own laws.

Until Rand McNally maps and the advent of global positioning systems, the little peninsula where people didn't want to be found, had been a secret self-sustaining community.

Family on Emma's mother's side had roots in the hidden woodlands and wetlands. Hardworking and living a clean life, they spoke their own language, a patois that had a lazy, slurry singsong French quality to it. Living on land that was never sold, simply passed down to descendants with a glad-handed fare-thee-well, they made it themselves or done without.

At first, Emma was not sure she would be able to find her handed down parcel. There had never been a road to the place, just a beaten down path at the end of a dense thicket that opened up to a washboard lane. There, a tiny rustic cabin made from hand-hewn planks had stood, close to a boggy pond that was an offshoot of the Waccamaw River. Many years ago, all the hope and promise of the place had tumbled into itself, leaving only memories of endurance and persistence.

After a while, all remnants of the cottage had been carted off to be part of someone else's porch, barn, or outhouse. She wasn't exactly sure she was on "her" land or someone else's.

Things in the Green Swamp looked remarkably alike in that low country way swamps had of hosting all manner of vegetation, bugs, snakes, goats and deer, with the occasional bear and gator thrown in for excitement.

Her little piece of land wasn't so large that she had exhausted herself walking it, but walking *to* it had been a bit of a challenge. It had been years since she'd been here, and while it had been overgrown with weeds and brambles then, now it was like something out of a fairytale where she was the prince trying to get through the dense barrier of overgrowth that led to Sleeping Beauty.

Instead of thorns and vines with tendrils as thick as ropes, she had to break through stands of kudzu, part curtains of wisteria now devoid of their only saving grace—their lilac clusters, stomp over weeds with treacherous burrs, and gently push aside huge branches of Elderberry bushes that were brimming with berries so ripe they popped and exploded their purple juice into the air from the slightest touch.

Emma inspected a stump carefully before she plunked her butt on it. She certainly didn't need a swarm of wasps stinging her privates, or a nest of fire ants crawling around her ankles.

She was looking for buried treasure. Specifically, the old tin box she and her grandmother had buried here on her sixteenth birthday, three years before she passed away.

That morning, her father had given her an old jewel blue Dodge Coronet he'd purchased from a friend of a friend and spent weeks fixing up. That afternoon, her Grandma Hazel had insisted Emma take her for a drive in it. This drive, according to her grandma, would lead to a "tiny parcel of land where fairies and trolls frolicked in the sunshine while waiting for someone to visit."

Her grandma wouldn't say anything else, just held a biscuit tin and a trowel in her lap while she sat enjoying the breeze coming from the open windows and the sun, at the perfect angle, spilling on her face. Over the years since, she had learned that old people really loved having the sun shine on their faces.

During the thirty-minute drive she'd occasionally stuck her hand out and pointed with an arthritic finger to indicate a turn Emma needed to take. Her "Gram" gave a splendid smile when they parked beside a stand of trees. She stepped out, slammed her door and began walking. Emma had no choice but to follow.

After showing her the property lines and reminiscing about what had been where once-upon-a-time, they sat on a fallen log and her grandma opened the Royal Dansk cookie container. From her Gram's mysterious mien she was surprised that there were cookies inside. Emma took a few when they were offered then watched as her grandmother revealed papers hidden beneath the top layer of cookies. They ate the cookies and talked about the papers and what they meant, and then they found a suitable spot and buried the blue and gold Royal Dansk container.

It was many years later, and Emma was here alone now. And darned if she could find the spot where they'd buried that tin. She sat on the stump, elbow on her knee, her hand under her chin and surveyed the area, her head moving slowly like a jerky old irrigation sprinkler, scanning and stopping, mentally rejecting small segments of the panoramic view, then spraying a far-reaching jet out and moving on. When she saw it her head froze, her eyes stared into the distance, and then they teared up.

She heard her grandmother's voice as if she were sitting beside her on the stump. "There will be times when you will need a place to come to, a place that is all yours. No matter what this world dishes up for you, you will always have a place to come to that's all your own. If you need to get away, you can put up a tent and tell the world to leave you alone for a while. This land is yours to do what you want with. Build on it if you care to, or don't. Nobody else in the family knows about this place. Only you and I. T'warnt no one else I wanted to have it. Like I said before, it's a tiny parcel of land where fairies and trolls will frolic in the sunshine waiting for you to visit. And if you ever have a need, you'll know there's some ready cash to tide you over in that cookie tin."

She'd shown her the folded up deed, the legal papers transferring the land to Emma, and the envelope stuffed with hundred dollar bills. Then they'd finished eating the butter cookies, snapped the top back on, and buried the tin. Now, despite the altered terrain, she'd managed to find it among the rotting branches and overgrown brambles.

As tears coursed down her face, she stared at the creosote-coated railroad tie she and her grandmother had dragged over to mark the spot. She might not have spotted it as it was covered with pine needles and decaying leaves, but part of the spike that had been driven through the railroad tie was now exposed by a section of rotting wood, and it stood out as an anomaly where everything that met the eye was vegetation. She swiped at the tears on her cheeks, and bracing her hands on her jean-clad thighs, she stood.

She had been nineteen when her grandmother died, and a few weeks later she'd driven out and walked the land by herself, thinking about all the times she had spent with her Gram. She hadn't been here since, but now she knew what her grandmother had meant about needing a place to come to, a place where she could leave the world behind. If she'd thought to bring a tent, she might have actually set up camp and tried being holed up in the wilderness, allowing her soul to heal among the whispering pines.

But then she thought about the wildlife living out here, and what darkness would mean living all alone amid opossums and raccoons, hoot owls and hawks . . . and snakes. She shivered. No, this may be her land but she was not camping here without a Class A RV and a rifle or two.

She stood and walked over to the railroad tie. Put the heel of her hiking boot against the short side of it, looked up at the sun to find a southwest direction, and paced off sixteen steps—

as it had been her sixteenth birthday the day it was buried. She marked the spot using her heel to form an X. Then walked back to the place she where she had dropped her knapsack and camp shovel.

Minutes later she was on her knees unfolding and counting money. Twenty thousand dollars. Enough to allow her to give her uncle the rest of his money back, get back to New York to a friend's apartment, and tide her over until she found work again. She looked up through the clearing to the patch of Carolina blue sky. "Thank you, Grandma," she whispered. "Thank you so very much."

Chapter 47—Alex
Mel's Timely Package

Alex had taken a picture of Emma with one of the girls asleep on her chest. Both were lovely, so serene and peaceful in their slumber. It took his breath away every time he looked at it. He had taken it with his Nikon from the landing on the upper level. He had been above the sofa, looking down at them as they slept. He had just come out of his workout room, and was deeply moved by the contentment he saw on Emma's face and the safe haven Molly had found in her arms. He had taken the shot then sent it to his phone.

She'd been gone almost a week now. The pain of their parting was now obscuring his every thought. He could not get her out of his mind, could not purge his heart of her memory.

He started to push the icon that would delete the picture from his phone. But he couldn't do it. He had to have this, at least this.

One of his assistants knocked on his door, "This just came for you. Overnighted from North Carolina."

He looked up and felt his heart stutter back to life. Then he forced himself to calm down and breathe. It didn't matter that she had written him. She had betrayed him.

Still. He put his hand out for the envelope. Looked at the return address and his heart plummeted. It wasn't from her. It was from Mallory's sister, Melissa.

He held it in his hand for a minute debating whether he should just toss it in the trash as he had all the other correspondence from Mallory's family. But knowing there was a connection to Emma now, he had to satisfy his curiosity. At least make sure Emma was all right.

He pulled the tab and took out the single typed page and then all the pages that were printed out as screen shots.

Alex,

I found this in the Kindred Spirit Mailbox at Bird Island. I thought you might like to read it and see what the real Emma is like. Also, I make it my mission to thwart my father in any way I can, especially when it comes to little girls. I never want him to do to anyone what he did to my sister and me. I don't know if he meant to harm those babies of yours, but I'm glad you didn't take the chance. If you hadn't had that proof of Mallory's abuse, written in her own hand and witnessed, I want you to know, that I would have come forward to keep my father from taking your little girls away from you. But now I know that wasn't necessary, that my sister had the foresight to take care of her girls in the event of her death. I miss her very much. One day I would like to see her girls if you'll let me.

Emma's mom tried to get her to tell her what happened between you and Emma. But she has refused. But we do know what happened in the courtroom the morning after they took you to jail that night. Pa saw to that by getting a transcript. And then of course, the sheriff came looking for him after Mallory's letter was read, so now everyone knows. It was great you had those connections and wonderful that the judge deemed that while there had been abuse that it was understandable, especially after you had sought help to make sure it didn't happen again. I am so glad you resolved everything so fast.
Emma's spent every day running on the beach and every night crying herself to sleep. Aunt Anna is about to murder my pa. And my ma says she will be happy to load the gun for her. My husband says none of us, not me nor the kids, can be at Ma and Pa's anymore without him being there, so we've moved out. Ain't no one here happy, I can tell you that.

Emma is one of the finest people I know. She is always kind and gracious. If I could be anyone in the world I would want to be her. She is gentle and caring, and a really lovely lady. I know you believe she has done something wrong, but if she has, it is only because my father misled her. She is not a conniving person, she doesn't lie. Whatever she did, this was probably her first sin ever. You should forgive her. She has a heart of gold and wouldn't harm a flea. Seriously, I have seen her pick bugs up and carry them outside. Ones I would swat, squish, stomp on, or flush without a second thought. Whatever she did (and she simply is not telling, no matter how many times I ask), you should forgive her. I guarantee you it's not her fault. She doesn't have it in her heart to be evil in even the most minor way.

I know she loves you, she told me that. And I know she's dying on the inside, more each and every day. You should come get her.

Mel

Accompanying the typed page were printed photos of handwriting that was in a notebook. The first page was dated two days ago. It was fuzzy and hard to read.

Alex read what he could make out.

July 19, 2019

Dear Kindred Spirit,

I hurt. But I should hurt. I did an awful thing. So bad I doubt I can write about it. But I will try because I don't know what else to do. Here goes:

The beginning of summer I lost my job. I am an actress. I also do some modeling, mostly lingerie and swimsuits for Macy's and J.C. Penney—scanty stuff, but not naked, never naked. I have the body now, so it's good money, in a few years . . . well, younger bodies will prevail.

I trained as a singer through high school and college, took piano lessons after school for seven years, and went to gymnastics camp during the summers, but I've been a dancer all my life. I have won many dance trophies. So when I went to New York City I thought I had a shot at being a Rockette. But the job I managed to land my first week in New York was on a soap opera. I became Jenna on the highest rated daytime soap . . .

Alex sat back and stared at the raft of pages in his hand. It continued on for forty more pages, a mish mash of pictures of Emma's writing, taken as photos of notebook pages, and detailing Emma's time in New York, the loss of her job, and her return to North Carolina.

He came into the picture when her uncle proposed she go to L.A. and attempt to find the twins. Emma had written about talking to her mom about him and his parents, taking a drive to UNCW to read the journal entries left there by Mallory's family and friends on the anniversary of her death, ending with her taking snap shots of each page and including them. The pages had been hard to read, as they were black and white photocopies of the pictures she'd taken from the journals. But they had been hard to read for another reason. They had been so emotional and conveyed how much everyone had loved Mallory and missed her. The messages had not been flattering to him, not by a long shot.

He'd read how Emma had found a picture of him tucked into her mother's underwear drawer. Had been interested to see that she had been attracted to him even then. She wrote of packing for her trip, her excitement at arriving in L.A. and finding a place to live. She described in detail the things she bought in hopes of pleasing him, attracting him. And she had written of the times they had danced. The times they had . . . made love.

How she loved meeting his girls, playing with them and cooking for them. How she had thrilled to fit so seamlessly into the family she was falling in love with. The man she had already fallen in love with.

And she wrote about the betrayal. How the father of the cousin she had adored, who had ruined Mallory's life, had now ruined her life as well.

Alex realized that Mallory's father had ruined his life also, by taking Emma away from him. He decided in that moment that he wasn't going to accept that. That he wasn't going to give that sinful, evil man the satisfaction. He called his mother and arranged a flight leaving that evening.

Chapter 48—Alex
The Mailbox at the Heart of the Matter

Alex arrived at the beach house in Sunset Beach late the next afternoon, in a surly mood and muttering something about women being more trouble than they were worth. The only thing anyone was able to get out of him, while he methodically unpacked his bags and organized his things in drawers, was that the twins were with their grandparents and the new nanny, who was his second cousin . . . and that he needed a break from everything.

In what had turned out to be a genius move, Alex had arranged to have the spare French provincial bedroom set that had been his wife's before they married, moved into one of the beach house's upper bedrooms, before moving to California after Mallory died. He hadn't wanted to part with it in case one of the girls might want it later, and the beach house had needed multiple sets of bedroom furniture. As a bonus, the set being prissy, and white with shiny gold trim, no one ever chose to take that room unless they had to, not even Cam. Especially as it only had a full-sized bed, not even a queen, whereas most of the others were kings. Unless they had a full house of guests, his room was typically ready and waiting. Not that he'd been here much. But he had come here with Mallory a few times, once in September when she was early in her pregnancy, and they'd had the whole house to themselves. What a special time that had been.

Chaz tried to talk to him when he got back from golfing, but he was being closed-mouth about whatever was bothering him. He could tell that it was something serious though. Alex had never been the life of the party, but he wasn't usually subdued, or curt with his words, nor did he spend most of his time holding his hand across his forehead with his arm propped up, while staring down at the granite countertop.

Abruptly, Alex jumped up off the barstool and strode down the hall. He took the stairs two at a time to his room, where he stripped off his slacks and Polo shirt and donned a swimsuit and sleeveless tank. Then he retraced his steps and headed out to the beach. The last time they had seen him, they'd all been watching from the upper deck as he had paced back and forth at the water's edge, waving his hands in the air and talking to himself, clearly agitated about whatever was gnawing at him, and causing him to look like a spastic Mel Gibson in a *Lethal Weapon* scene.

He finally turned and faced east, ran the fingers of both hands through his hair as if knowing he had wildly disheveled it, and started off walking at a clipped pace, heading toward the pier and Bird Island. No one had seen him since.

Chapter 49—Cam
A Liberated Man

Cam smiled to himself as he drove his Miata down Route 17 heading back from Wilmington. It had been two days since he'd gone with the guys to that strip club in Myrtle Beach. He full out laughed. For years he'd thought he'd end up being gay. He was so convinced of it that he'd acted the part, trying to fit the role . . . just to be ready, when Mr. Right came along. He threw his head back and laughed again, the booming peal of it bouncing off the convertible roof.

He'd had gender issues all his life. And it was no wonder, with his mother dressing him in dresses until he was seven, and his father encouraging dance, gymnastic, and skating lessons as opposed to T-Ball or soccer. When puberty was considerably delayed for him, and befriending girls seemed to be way more trouble than they were worth, even he had to wonder which bathroom line to stand in.

At fifteen, puberty finally did descend on him, but alas, there was no attraction to the opposite sex, no desire to linger at the locker of a lip-glossed and heavily mascaraed Brittany Spears-wanna-be, no urges of any kind. And it had remained that way all through high school. Despite being exposed to beautiful girls in dance and drama classes, his libido was not involved— he'd often envisioned his sex drive, wherever it was hidden in his body, with a time lock on it. And for him, it just wasn't time. And maybe it never would be. But he never told a soul, never said a word to anyone. He didn't want to be the weird kid who never grew up. So he did what he always did in his improvisation classes. He pretended. He played the part.

Joining the fraternity at Stanford had changed things. In the co-ed dorm environment his friends pushed girls on him. If they'd known he was a virgin, they would most definitely have taken it upon themselves to fix that problem. So he did the only logical thing to make his sexuality a non-issue. He faked being gay.

A part of the stage world since he was six, he had no problem playing the part. He picked up the nuances easily enough—the looks and the lingo that was appropriate to each setting—the high drama and effusiveness of it all. He became so good at the demonstrative nature and the lavish way of dressing, that sometime during his senior year, he started believing it himself.

He'd become so entrenched in the role that it played out without him thinking much about it. Except that he never got that tingle, never got that jolt that sent heat coursing through his veins, never had the look that mesmerized, or the double take that slayed. Not once had he had the desire to kiss, caress, or fondle *anyone*, nonetheless squeeze the hundreds of male butts he pretended to admire in his varied attempts to convince the guys he hung out with that he was gay—while they were quite obviously not.

His frat brothers' appetites had astounded him as they plowed through hordes of women as if they were nothing more than mini-skirted, made-up, bustier-wearing gaggles of geese. He'd never make the grade, never stack up, and never have a friend if they knew he was a man without a gender.

It quickly became all-important that they never find out what he was, especially as he didn't even know what he was. His problem if he'd had to label it? Asexual. He had no sex. Well . . . he had all the necessary parts—male parts that is. And more than adequate in that department if research at the triple X stores accounted for much. But he had no sex drive, no sexual urges and no sex history to build on and build a reputation from. Not a prickle of attraction was to be had for either sex, despite being around some of the most beautiful people in Southern California. Having gorgeous women in his arms while choreographing countless erotic dances did nothing for him.

Falling into sweaty guys on basketball courts and on football fields did not send arousing pheromones his way either.

Alcohol didn't conjure up feelings of sexual prowess for either side, and pot only made him dopey and dependent on Dorito's. No subtle come-hither look or blatant display of nudity aroused him. Not in the least. Until he'd spotted Tamara.

That night, in Myrtle Beach, in the seedy, disgustingly lewd tittie bar, he came alive. Well . . . to be more accurate, his penis came to life—jerking and throbbing as it swelled against his zipper. He had an erection he hadn't forced to life for the first time, ever.

He had looked like every man in the bar, adjusting a prominence between his legs that to him was monumental. For once, he fit in. And it was ironic that he'd gotten the erection while simply walking around trying to find a man who might finally appeal to him. And really—where was he doing this? In a place showcasing women. So even if he had found that certain man, whoever he might be, he would have been here for the women.

He'd been sipping his Sea Breeze, wandering into the different rooms and trying to figure out the appeal this place held for guys, when he walked past a closed door and heard sobbing and a loud argument. At first, it sounded like some kind of boss maligning an employee. But the words he heard next stopped him just outside the door. "You either show your tits tonight or you're out! And that boyfriend of yours can cough up the money I paid him in advance for bringing you here. You got it? Tonight. The shirt comes off, or you're fired!"

"I just don't think I can do it, Mr. G. Please don't make me. Just let me dance. I'm a really good dancer, everybody says so." The woman was sobbing and sniffling while trying to get the words out.

"I don't care about that and neither do those men out there. They want to see you without your clothes on. And tonight you'd better show them your nipples. Tomorrow night, nipples and pubes, or you're history."

A long wail followed by hiccupping sobs came through the door. Then, "I d-d-d-on't t-t-t-hink I c-c-can d-d-d-ooo th-a-a-at!"

Well . . . oddly enough, that woke up something. The rebel that always wanted to defend, protect, and fight for the American way had a tiny fire building in his chest. And a warmth in the groin that grew. And grew. He remembered holding the drink aside and staring down as his trousers tented.

He got over his amazement just in time to move out of the way as the door opened and a fat bald man exited, slamming the door behind him. Cam had watched the man barrel down the hall, his fists pumping at his sides, his gate oddly bowlegged yet still allowing him to move fairly quickly.

Cam had turned back to face the closed door and listen to the low sobs coming from the other side. He was able to step out of the way, and pretend nonchalance, when another man entered the hall, this one tall and younger, but with a greasy appearance. As the man passed Cam on his way to the room, the smell of whiskey and tobacco assailed his nose. The apprentice Superman with the gloriously aroused manhood in his pants sensed a villain.

The drama was too intriguing to leave. He couldn't have walked away even if he'd wanted to, so aroused was he. Out of the corner of his eye, he watched the man enter the room and close the door. Cam sauntered closer and casually leaned against the wall, his ear close to the doorjamb.

"This is it Tammy, you don't perform tonight and you're outta here. And that means no dentist to pull that tooth. You might as well go back home 'cause I can't afford to keep you. If you want us to stay together, you got one option. Get out there and dance. And before the song ends, you better have that shirt off and those tits popped out of that bra. I mean it Tam, there's too many girls here that's willin'. I can't keep you with me if you aren't paying your share. It'll be easy to get another girl to take your place. We agreed, you know—you dance and I'll be your agent."

"Josh, really . . . I can't do this. I just can't!"

"You have to. C'mon, you're on in two minutes. You just get out there and you do it, ya hear? After the first time, it'll be easy. Isn't that what all the girls have been telling' ya? Bein' nekked in front of everyone is easy after the first time."

There was the sound of someone working the ancient doorknob trying to get out. Cam stepped to the other side of the hall, quickly spun back to face the door, crossed his feet at the ankles and pulled out his cell phone. He was fake-looking at the screen and making scrolling actions with his thumb when the dirtball got the door open and tugged the girl into the hall.

Cam looked up and met vivid green eyes pooling with tears in a face framed by a black velvet-covered headband. She had two thick blonde braided pigtails touching each shoulder. Her heavy stage make-up of drawn on lower lashes and rust-colored freckles spattering her small nose was glistening with tears. Her schoolgirl costume consisted of a tiny red plaid skirt, a baby doll-sized white shirt that was only capable of being buttoned below her white demi cup bra, and white knee-high tights that went to mid-thigh. From this close, it was obvious this uniform got a lot of wear. The tights had snags and runs, the pleats on the skirt had lost their razor crease, and the stretchy shirt had a noticeable tinge of yellow in the underarm areas.

In that split second, before the boyfriend pulled her forward, Cam felt his stomach drop and his knees fail him. And incongruously, heat zinged through his male parts. Heat had never zinged through there before, unless it had been caused it by his own hand. His balls had never felt so thick, so heavy.

He might have galvanized himself sooner were it not for the stars in his eyes and all his blood flowing south. As it was, he had to do a quick step just to keep them in sight as the man lead Tamara through a warren of hallways to the stage. Cam knew this world. Music was booming now, cuing her for her strip tease. He saw her boyfriend hiss something in her ear, swat her on the bottom, and push her up onto the stage.

An announcer's voice broke in with, "Gentleman, for your eyes only, our newest pupil, a schoolgirl, fresh from Missouri, Twisty Tamara!"

Tamara stumbled her way to the center pole then became one of the most graceful dancers he'd ever seen, and as a lead choreographer, he'd seen plenty of fabulous dancers.

She grabbed the pole, swung out, bowed her body and swayed. If lyrics could be put to her motions they'd win a Grammy. He had never seen a woman gyrate and shimmy against and around a pole in such a sexy manner. She used her legs to accentuate every pose so precisely that he instantly knew she'd trained as a ballerina. She went into a tap routine using the pole as one of the competing acoustics to her saddle oxford-styled tap shoes. It was perfection.

She ended the routine by doing a series of hip thrusting cha-chas to a deafening applause. But apparently she hadn't done the compulsory requirements, because her skanky boyfriend ran out on stage and ripped her shirt open to the final bada boom— bada boom—bada boom of the drums, yelling with each beat. "I. Told. You. To. Show. Your. Tits!"

After the shirt was dispatched by his rough hands tearing it off her, he grabbed the shoulder straps of her bra and jerked them down her arms exposing her to her waist.

While the crowd went berserk showing their appreciation and calling out all manner of vile chants about seeing more, she cried and grabbed for the shirt the man had recovered from the floor and was flaunting on a fingertip just out of her reach. She was trying to cover her tiny breasts with one hand while trying to get the shirt back with the other.

Cam galvanized. He whipped off his sport coat as he ran on stage. He had her tiny five-foot-two frame covered with his size 38 Long suit jacket before the boyfriend was even aware he was on stage. In one smooth motion, Cam had picked her up and carried her through the wings, as if it were his show and he was the leading man who owned the right to possess and carry the heroine away, cave man style. Cam was out the front door and hailing one of the waiting limos before the stupefied boyfriend could get his act together and give chase.

"There's an extra hundred in it for you if you can get us off the lot before her sleazebag boyfriend gets through that door!" he hollered to the driver leaning on the door of the first limo in line. Coincidentally, it was one of the two limos he had hired for their group.

The driver, recognizing him and spurred on by his words, pulled open the back door. Cam ducked in and slid across the leather seat with the young girl still in his arms. The driver slammed the door shut. Then he was behind the wheel and pulling out without hesitation into the late night traffic when the front door burst open and several men rushed out—the boyfriend, a bouncer, and the bald fat man, raising an angry fist in the air leading the pack.

Both Cam and the limo driver chuckled then actually guffawed. This was like a scene out of a movie, how could you not take a moment to enjoy it? Except Cam had a shirt getting rapidly soaked from the tears of a young woman who had just been humiliated by a man she had no doubt given her body and heart to.

Cam shifted her in his arms so he could uncover her face. Even though her makeup was horribly smeared and ruining his expensive shirt, he felt his first non-self-induced hard-on return when her soft lips curved into a tremulous smile of appreciation. "Thank you," she whispered.

As her small hand grazed the side of his face he felt his cock jump and harden like the nightstick he saw on the limo dashboard. He pushed the button to raise the screen.

Chapter 50—Cam
An Intervention

He sat up and got her comfortable after shielding them from the driver. Then he texted Sean that they needed to find alternate transportation back to the beach house, that he had taken one of their limos. After listening to Tamara cry, and watching the hard ridge grow and throb in his lap, he decided he wasn't going back to the beach house tonight.

"I'm not sure where I'm supposed to be taking you, but I don't imagine taking you home is a good idea if you're living with that self-serving moron. So tell me, is he really your boyfriend?"

She sniffed, wiped her nose with the handkerchief he'd given her, and looked doe-eyed over at him. She was in the corner now, her tiny feet drawn up, her arms locked around her knees, allowing her to keep her chest covered by the bulk of his jacket. "He was, until like twenty minutes ago. If I never see him again, I'll be totally fine with that."

"How long have you known him?"

"All my life. We grew up together and went to the same schools in Missouri. We didn't start dating until last year though. He never really paid any attention to me until I asked him to the Sadie Hawkins Day Dance during our senior year. We really hit it off though, and we've been together ever since. Last month he had this idea that we should move to Myrtle Beach, said he knew a few places where I could get work real easy. Good money, he said, couple hundred a day at least. He never told me I'd have to take my clothes off though."

"Did he find a job for himself, or was he only concerned with putting you to work?"

"He said he was making contacts for me. He was going to be my agent."

"Pimp is more like it," he muttered, turning his face to

the window to hide his disgust and to shake his head at the evil that was in people. "Let me guess: it was your savings that paid for getting you two here and setting you up?"

"Mmm, yup."

"Is there anything you need to get from wherever it is you're living? You don't even have a purse."

She toed off one of the beat up saddle shoes and put her sock-clad foot on the seat. He watched as she slid the sock down to her ankle and then worked it off her foot. And damned if he didn't feel a jolt of lust power through him at the sight of her small white foot being revealed. Gesu!

As a choreographer he saw gorgeous women bare their legs and feet all day long. The feet were usually a far cry from gorgeous—gnarly, red, and blistered from tight shoes, toe shoes, and balancing on five-inch spikes. Most days he was more interested in what type of shoe they were wearing rather than the foot that came out of them. It was one of the reasons why he initially thought he might be gay. But Tamara's pale, well-turned ankle and the dainty unblemished foot she was now unwrapping entranced him. Immensely.

She stuck her hand into the sock she'd just removed and brought out four things: a driver's license, a social security card, a hundred dollar bill, and a tiny photograph with what looked to be a phone number penciled on one edge.

"I have everything I need right here. Grammy said to call her if I needed bus fare back. I guess she knew things weren't going to work out the way Josh said."

"So you're going to go back to Missouri?"

"Yeah. Kinda have to. I don't want to have to strip to dance, that much I know."

"You had some pretty nice dance moves. I'm betting you've been taking classes for quite a while."

"Years of 'em. Ballet, tap, jazz, hip-hop, free-style, ballroom, even dance skating, roller and ice. My mama taught baton twirling and Grammy taught tap. Aunt Sadie had a dance school and I got all my classes free. When Josh said we'd go to Myrtle Beach, that he'd get me a job dancin', I thought he meant at someplace like The Palace or the Alabama Theater. He wouldn't even let me try out there, said they didn't pay enough."

She heaved out a big sigh. "I guess it's just as well. Grammy's going to need some help soon. She's getting pretty old."

"How about your mom? And you haven't said anything about a father."

"Mom died two years ago. Never knew daddy, he died broncin' a bull when I was just two months old."

"So you'd just be going back to Grammy?"

"She's a fine old lady. None finer. Told me over and over that Josh was dreaming too lofty for his britches."

"So would you like to dance if you could? I mean real dance—musicals, stage, full production gigs. Some skimpy costumes sometimes, but always covering the essentials."

"Oh yeah, sure! I love to dance. I was in Chorus Line and Oklahoma in high school, and did Hairspray at the community college last summer."

"Well, if you've got no place to go other than back home, why don't you give it one more go? I guarantee you that I can put you to work. My name is Cameron VanSant, I go by Cam. I'm a producer of sorts, specializing in choreographing films and stage productions." He handed her his card.

"I'm based out of Wilmington, so you'd have to live there. I can put you up for a while, at least until you get a few paychecks under your belt. I have an assistant who can help you with getting settled. She can take you shopping—get you some clothes, shoes, the necessary things you women need. And when the time comes, she can help you pick out an apartment. For right now, you can stay at my place. I'm not using it right now."

"I can't do that! I don't even know you. For all I know, you could be a high-class version of Josh."

He laughed at that, tossing his head back and enjoying

the first really good rumble in his chest in a long time. He brought out his iPhone and handed it to her. "Here, Google me. See what it says."

"I don't know how to use this."

He stared at her, his eyes almost crossing. "What? You don't know how to use a smartphone?"

"I've never had any kind of cell phone."

"Really? Where in Missouri did you say you were from?"

"Springfield. People have cell phones there. I just have never had that kind of money. Seemed like a waste. Everybody I knew, I saw nearly everyday."

He hooted at that. "You are a delight, Miss Tamara. Is that what they call you?"

"Most people just call me Tammy."

"Well, Tammy, this is who I am." He slid his fingers on the screen then handed her the phone and showed her how to scroll down the page. As she read her eyes widened. When she had finished reading the list of productions he was credited with, along with all the stars he had made famous, she faced him and whispered, "You're an angel."

"No, technically, that would be a backer. I rarely invest in the projects, although I do get a percentage in most of them. I produce, I direct the dancers, and I help with casting. Which is why I know I can get you a part—one that's perfect for you. But first we have to find you a place to live, get you settled, and make sure you're protected. Because that wanna-be-pimp of a boyfriend is sure to come looking for you. I want you safe and well away from him. Until you and Beth can find alternate housing, you can stay with me. And before you go off again, it's a huge converted loft. And I won't be there for the next two weeks so you'll have the place all to yourself."

There was silence as they stared at each other. Her, absorbing all he'd just said—him, examining every detail of her face and marveling over the fact that he had a raging desire to kiss each freckle, stroke each brow, and suck on that sweet, pouty lower lip. The noise of the tires shushing on the pavement was all that filled the back seat of the limo as it continued north on Route 17. He pressed the button on the intercom and asked the driver to head toward Wilmington, giving him the address for his Downtown apartment.

He had a hard on for a lovely young *woman*. Imagine that. His wide grin would have unnerved her if she'd seen it, but fortunately, she was replacing her sock and shoe and could not see how the sight of her doing such a mundane task was heating up his insides.

Chapter 51—Chaz, Mags, and Alex
A Promise of More

In the early evening, Chaz was leaning against the rail on the beach access walkway watching a family playing in the surf. Two young boys were vying for their father's attention as they showed off their prowess with skim boards. A toddler was attached to his mother's leg, giggling when she lifted her leg and gently dipped him into the water. Her hand was clasped around his crisscrossed jumper in the back to keep him safe. He smiled. If he ever had children, they would know they were safe—and loved. And that they had a home, a real home to grow up in.

"Hi."

He turned to the sound of Mags' voice, the sweet swell of her particular tonal vibration entering his ear, and sending pleasure waves throughout his body. Much like Victor, the RCA dog that had been attuned to his master's voice, he was attuned to hers.

"Please tell me you took your multivitamin, so I won't be shooed away again."

She laughed and he actually felt his cock twitch. When had *that* ever happened?

"I took today's and tomorrow's, so we're good until midnight tomorrow night."

"Good. Now where can we run away to?"

"Where would you want to run away to?" she asked with her arms splayed wide, indicating the undulating dunes, the pristine stretch of beach, and the waves tumbling to the shore.

"Good point. This *is* where everyone runs to when they want to get away from something."

"What is it you're running away from?" she asked.

"Work, although, that's not entirely true, as I managed to bring some with me."

"What is it you do?"

"I'm a custom home builder, a designer and an engineer of sorts. Right now I'm pursuing a new venture. I build tiny houses, all over the country."

"Oh, I've seen some of those online. They're adorable."

"I prefer practical and efficient to adorable, but yes, it's important that they have appeal, especially to women, who are generally the deciding factor in a home purchase."

"Hmm, well your vacation home seems to miss the mark, broadly. It doesn't seem so tiny to me," she said looking back on the beach house that many would call a mansion.

"Trust me, you get ten guys in there and it *is* tiny, and not at all adorable." He grinned over at her and saw her blush. Now that was adorable.

"Sean, one of the partners is an architect, he designed it."

"It's beautiful."

The moon was rising off to the left; the pale moonlight putting glints in her eyes and showcasing the satiny pink gloss on her lips. Now that was beautiful. "Thank you. We're all very proud of it."

"I came to tell you I finished the book."

"Oh, did you now? That's great. That means you must accompany me to dinner so we can discuss it."

"Like a book club?"

"Yes, a very exclusive book club."

"Just you and me?"

"Actually, it's me before you," he deadpanned.

They were both laughing hysterically when Kara walked up.

"Mags, dinner is ready. Steak and baked potatoes as requested."

"Okay, I'll be right there."

"Don't be long or your steak will be cold, I already took it off the grill."

"Okay. I'll be right along."

They both watched as Kara stomped down the boardwalk

on the way back to the house.

"Does she have a problem with me?"

"She has a problem with all men right now."

"Did she get dumped?" he asked.

"No, I did. I'd better go."

It took him a moment to absorb the shock. By then she had turned and was on her way back up the access. Who in their right mind would dump this woman? She was well on her way when he snapped out of it and called out, "Hey, what about dinner and our book club meeting tomorrow?"

She walked back. "We'll have to see . . . . Maybe we can meet here tomorrow night? Same time, same place?" she asked.

He nodded, and then took her hands in his. He almost leaned in to kiss her, but fearing her sister might be watching, didn't. Instead, he said, "I'll bring wine and something to nibble on. We'll have an impromptu meeting." He smiled and then winked.

She smiled back, her upturned lips displaying genuine delight, and it warmed him—actually sent trills though his body. What was he, a girl? What man flushed like this because a woman smiled at him?

He watched her walk up the access, cross the small lawn, and climb the stairwell into the house next to his. So close, yet so far.

He quirked his lips, zeroing in on his bedroom in the house to the left, then imaging which was hers in the house on the right. If they were on the same floor, he could reach her room in less than forty steps. His eyes were drawn to a flash of light in a glass panel on the lower level of her house.

He saw Kara standing to the side of a sliding glass door, watching him. As soon as Mags came into the room behind her, Kara jerked the slatted louvers closed.

He shook his head. What kind of drama was playing out here, he asked himself. God keep him from overprotective sisters, he thought as he put his hands in his pockets and walked up the boardwalk to *The Cockpit.*

Just before the access steps that led down to the pathway leading to the beach house, he turned and looked out to the beach. With relief he saw Alex in the distance, slowly ambling up the sand toward the access.

Whatever had happened during his walk, it had taken all the agitation out of his body. He looked relaxed. When he saw Chaz, he lifted an arm in salute. Chaz smiled. He was glad his friend had worked out whatever had been troubling him, and he was glad he hadn't had to go find him. Maybe he'd be ready to talk now. He'd give him time to settle in, have something to eat, then challenge him to a game of Foosball in the game room while downing a couple of beers. Although, by the look of him, Alex might need something stronger.

As soon as Chaz was inside, he went looking for Kyle, who was expounding on the virtues of a spiral slicer and making zucchini spaghetti while the most amazing smell came from a pot of marinara simmering on the Viking stove.

"Kyle, I need a bottle of your best wine and some snazzy appetizers for tomorrow night. What's it going to cost me?"

"Golf tomorrow morning and you gotta give me eight strokes."

"Eight? I've only played five times this year. Make it four."

"That's four times more than I've managed this year. Six would still be sticking it to me, but I'd consider it."

"Done. Make it two bottles though, I may have to give one to the zany sister as a bribe."

"So you've finally stopped spinning in circles and got yourself a date with the hottie next door?" Dev asked from behind the refrigerator door where he'd snagged a Corona.

"Yeah, and if I were you, I'd go check out her younger sister . . . she's pretty sweet herself, and if I'm not mistaken, she's just asking for a spanking, if you know what I mean."

"Really?" Dev asked, his eyes going hot, his face intense

at the thought of getting some kink while at the beach.

"Yeah, I think so. Definitely. I'd hit on that if I were you."

"Okay, I think I will."

Chaz had to fake a sneeze into his elbow to hide his laughter as Dev went back to the soccer game he'd been watching.

Chapter 52—Chaz & Cam
A Sex Education Tutorial

As Chaz grabbed the newel post to help hoist him up the last steps, he heaved out a big sigh. He'd backed away from what he was sure could have been their first kiss. He'd never failed to take a kiss that was being offered. Had never failed to get a first date kiss. Heck, thinking back on his track record, he'd never failed to get a hell of a lot more than just a kiss on most first dates. Mags was going to be a challenge, he thought, as he swung around to the top of the landing and ran right into Cam.

"Chaz, been looking for you everywhere, Man. Got a question for you." He followed Chaz into his bedroom and closed the door behind them.

Chaz turned and gave Cam a lopsided grin. "Cam, I don't swing that way. Besides, it's been a long day. I'm pretty much all in."

"I have a question and I don't have anyone else to ask. I need to know something."

Chaz dropped onto the bed and lifted one foot over his knee to take off his shoe. He sighed again. "What do you need to know?"

"I need to know how to have sex with a girl."

"You what?"

"I met this girl. I'm pretty gone on her. But I don't have any experience with this."

"You've never had sex with a girl before? Never? Not even before you found out you were gay?"

"Chaz, I hate to have to admit this, but I've never had sex with *anyone*."

"C'mon, you've had boyfriends, I know you have."

"No, Chaz, I haven't. I made it look that way. But I never really had a romantic boyfriend. I've never had sex with anyone, honest."

He took a few moments to process that. For years, he'd thought Cam was gay. "But now you've found a girl, and you want to have sex with her?"

"It's not so much that I want to, it's almost as if I have to. Every cell in my body tingles when I'm around her. My whole body is so tight and hard I feel like I'm going to explode out of my skin. I have to keep my hands in my pockets or hold them in my lap to keep from touching her. I'm going out of my mind. It's like I'm finally having the adolescence I was denied fifteen years ago. I'm horny. Finally. For the first time ever. And it's for a girl, a beautiful, sweet, funny girl."

Chaz fought from hooting with laughter. "You're kidding. I can't believe you're a virgin. After all that talk . . . all that posturing with all those gay guys."

"They were just friends. It was all talk. I was afraid to let you guys know. I thought you would make it your agenda to fix things if you thought I was, uh . . . unproven. So . . . I faked it."

"You were acting all this time? What fourteen years?"

Cam lowered his head, shook it side to side, and then with hands in his pockets, rocked back on his heels and gave a little chuckle. "Yeah. I was. Don't get mad. It was survival. You frat boys can be brutal. I didn't want to be initiated. I had no sexual urges back then. None. And what you guys were doing to girls . . . well, it seemed kind of depraved."

Chaz thought about that and had to concur. It was a co-ed free for all for everyone back then. He nodded and gestured with his hand for Cam to continue.

There were a few seconds of silence before he added, "When our friendship continued after college, I kept up the ruse. I didn't want to lose you guys. You're my best friends. And you never judged me."

Chaz closed his eyes and shook his head. One shoe dropped. Then the other. Then one sock, followed by the other, landed on the carpet.

"Well, you sure had me fooled. I would have sworn you

were playing for the other team."

"To be honest with you, until I met Tammy I thought that's the way things would go when it finally did happen for me. But really, I've never had the hots for anybody. Not once. Not until last Wednesday night. When I saw her it was like every nerve came alive. I was nervous, anxious, self-conscious, and giddy, all at once. And since then, every thought has been centered on her."

"Sounds like you're horny all right."

"Never really knew how that felt before. This arousal stuff is pretty powerful, kinda takes over everything."

"Yeah, it's a love-hate thing. Tonight I'm kinda hatin' it."

"I heard you met the girl next door."

"Yeah, didn't quite get off the ground though. Her sister keeps thwarting me."

He waved him off when he thought Cam was going to ask for details. "So what's your question?"

"Can you give me some tips? Tell me how to get started. I'm totally clueless about girls. I don't think I ever even kissed one, at least not in a way that mattered."

"Why me? Why not ask Sean? He's your best friend, surely you've been honest with him?"

Cam just shook his head.

"I can't believe this."

"I know. I'm kinda relieved if you want to know the truth. I hated faking that I was attracted to guys when I wasn't attracted to guys *or* girls."

"You know there are books on this kind of thing. You could start with "The Joy of Sex," just like the rest of us. And there's some great porn out there. I can give you a few titles. You can probably download them or find them in a sex shop in Myrtle Beach."

"No. I want it from the horse's mouth. From the legend, the man whose reputation for multiple orgasms is legendary and well documented."

Chaz sent Cam a condescending look, his facial lines tenting his eyebrows into a frown as he bent to pick up his socks. "I wish Ryder hadn't shared all that. It was supposed to be private, between me and him."

"He won't share the video. We've all asked."

Chaz grunted. "Because he knows what I'd do if he did. I only taped that to protect him. To show him she was the wrong woman for him. It was never meant to be shown to anybody."

"Yeah, but now it's going to keep him from losing a mega-huge lawsuit, so it's good that you did it."

"Not my finest hour. Who in their right mind would want something like that displayed?"

"I heard the camera stopped taping after two hours but that you were still going strong."

Chaz sneered over at Cam. "Don't go there."

"Back to the question at hand. Give me some tips. This is important to me and I have a lot of ground to make up for in a short amount of time. I don't have time to get the experience you have. And to be frank with you, I don't even want to be with another woman. Tammy's it for me. It's like I've been waiting for her all my life. And then suddenly, there she is. In a strip bar of all places."

"What?"

"Long story, and not a new one. Naïve country girl comes to the big city, lured by promises from a greedy boyfriend. He gets her an audition as a stripper. She tries to refuse. He forces her on stage. She can't make herself disrobe in front a bunch of men. The boyfriend rips her top off. Innocent, newly horny hero comes to the rescue. Sir Gallant takes her off in a limo while boyfriend, boss, and bouncer chase with raised fists. Our young hero squirrels damsel-in-distress away in his lair in Downtown Wilmington, gets her the acting job of her dreams, and leaves her in his capable assistant's hands so he can continue his vacation with his buddies. One of which he pleads with to give him a tutorial on the ways to please a woman, as he's totally clueless about how to make love to the woman he fell in love with at first sight. Sounds like a play—White Christmas, Cyrano de Bergerac, reverse Pygmalion, with a little Gypsy Rose Lee thrown in. I may have to produce this one day."

Cam sighed and gave Chaz his award-winning lopsided smile. Cam's face, while masculine and rough with stubble in all the right places, had a cherubic quality. And it usually got him his way.

"At least give me a starter lesson. I'm clueless here. I have no one else I can turn to. The guys would never let me hear the end of this. Especially if I asked for their play-by-play diagrams."

"So you're just going to tell them you're bi, and that you switched over in a Myrtle Beach strip club if this woman becomes an item?"

"If I have any say in it, this woman is going to become my wife. They'll all get behind me then." He smirked, "No pun intended."

Chaz snickered, acknowledging the humor in that.

"But right now, I need your help just to get her to girlfriend status. Will you please help me with that?"

Chaz let out a huge sigh. "Yeah." He dropped his trousers and grabbed a pair of sweat pants from the chair. "But I gotta have a quick run first. I have my own horniness to work off."

"Well if that works, let me go with you."

"It doesn't always work, but it sure does help sometimes. Grab your Nikes. And I'm not holding back, you're going to have to keep up."

"I may not have the sex moves you have, but I know how to run."

"Good, I'm running to the jetty. We'll walk and talk on the way back."

"Deal. Let me change. I'll meet you on the lower terrace."

The door opened and Cam left. Chaz dug through a drawer and found a t-shirt that would wick away moisture and pulled it over his head. Then he squirted on some bug spray, just in case there was no breeze and it was one of those rare nights when the bugs came out in droves. He grabbed a water bottle from the upstairs fridge in the game room and ran down the stairs.

They ran all out, all the way to the jetty. Then after making the turn at the hulking scarp of rocks, they huffed and puffed until they could talk. It was dark, but there was enough light from the moon to limn them in silver as they shuffle-jogged in the sand, trying to cool down.

Chaz talked, Cam listened. And wished he'd had a notepad and a pen. He thought about snagging a sheet of paper from one of the Kindred Spirit journals when they strode by the Mailbox, but knew he couldn't write at the pace Chaz had set for the walk back.

"The secret is to listen. Start with little touches: a hand to her lower back when you're walking her through a door, a gentle caress down her cheek when you tuck a piece of hair behind her ear, a casual glance off the side of her breast whenever you can manage it and it doesn't appear contrived. If you're driving somewhere, when you're holding the gearshift, stroke a finger down her thigh. If you're standing in an elevator, face her and use your finger to trace a wing of her eyebrow as if smoothing it over. Look into her eyes and concentrate only on her, nothing else. Then do nothing but talk for a while. Pay attention to everything she says, you may be able to use some of it later.

"When you go to kiss her, make it spontaneous. Catch her by surprise. And never wait until the date is over, it's too obvious then and oftentimes there isn't always a perfect moment at the end of a date, so all you get is a quick peck. Find secluded places to trap her so you can give her a slow and languorous kiss. Lips only at first, and take your time, keep it slow and unhurried, you're going for a dreamy swoon here. If she acts like she's into you, do it again. This time longer, and take the kiss deeper, pretend you're sucking on the most delicious strawberry, lightly suck on her bottom lip, try to take one of her lips inside yours. Lightly graze it with your teeth. Run your tongue alongside the smooth inner recesses of her mouth, duel with her tongue—invite her to chase your tongue back inside your mouth. Make throaty noises when she does that, reward her with moans and groans that let her know she's turning you on, making you want her.

"When you can finagle a place to be alone with her, go for the sweet spots . . . the sides of her neck, behind her ear, in her ear, but don't bathe it with slobber, or huff into it. Breathe into it as if she's taken your breath away just by being there in your arms. Work her clothing loose. But don't take anything off. That's an instant stopper. When she's ready, she'll give you a sign that she wants something off, lowered, or she'll just yank it out of the way for you. This is a time to pay attention to every sound she makes, watch every nuance in her face, meet her eyes directly with yours, give her the hint of a smile, but never, ever grin—it shows too much confidence and says gotcha. No woman wants to be thought of as easy, especially the really easy ones. They're very sensitive to the fact that they're a little on the slutty side.

"Figure out what she likes, the kind of touches she needs. First time out, I go with gentle, light touches . . . fingers tracing and caressing her skin as soft as lambskin on velvet. Don't hurry. This is the biggest mistake you can make. Take your time. Savor each new area you uncover as you slide your hand into her clothing. Kiss every exposed inch of flesh you can, exposing more as you move lower. Usually, the progression is from lips, to the jaw, to the area around the ear, then down the neck to the shoulder, baring as much skin as you dare as you kiss and suck, and lick. See what she likes, listen to what makes her moan and then do that again. If she stiffens, stop what ever it was you were doing and try something else. Tell her how nice she feels, how beautiful you think she is, how you've wanted to have her in your arms like this.

"If you can bare her breasts, you're usually home free. If she balks, it may be too soon, or because she doesn't like her breasts. She either thinks they're too small, or too big—which is not possible by the way—misshapen, mismatched, or some other apprehensive or ludicrous thought. If that's the case, fondle her through her bra. Suck and gently bite her nipples through the lace. If you get great success with that try to peel the cups back instead of removing the bra. If that works, kiss and caress the whole breast, ignoring the nipple. If you're doing it right, she'll soon be pleading for you to latch on. At this point, there's no harm in making her beg, so tease her as long as you can. Once you give in and start suckling her, you can usually start adjusting the rest of her clothing to make some progress where it counts. Pay attention to her sounds, she may want things more intense, ask you to suck harder. If that's the case, try biting around her areola a little. Then zero in on the nipple. Nibbling bites mind you, you don't want to hurt her.

"While you're paying attention to those breasts, look up and meet her eyes every so often. Smile, wink, let her see your tongue swirling over her breasts as if you can't get enough of tasting her. Shape her tits with your hands as you work your lips and tongue over her. Tell her you love her tits; women love it when you talk dirty. Try a little pinch around the underside and see how she reacts. If she yelps, back off. If she groans, give her more. And be prepared, you probably have a screamer on your hands.

"Meanwhile, you're working your way south. Figure out your game plan ahead of time. While you're dining or driving take a good look at what she's wearing. Plan the best way in. The target is between her legs. You have to plan your campaign to get there with the least amount of resistance.

"If she's wearing a dress, go up from the bottom, caress her calves, the backs of her knees, stroke along her inner thighs. This is generally not an area to pinch, it's a linear area to keep stroking, tracing, and drawing circles on. Write your name, they love that. Go higher and higher until you can get your fingers into her panties. Make sure your hands are clean, really clean. No grime, no residue from oily lotions, no spices left over from food, especially salt—it sucks up their moisture. I imagine curry or paprika wouldn't fare very well down there either.

Take it slow until you know for sure this is something she wants. It gives you time to back yourself off if you have to, if you're getting too close to losing it, and it gives her a chance to either get wet and ready, or scared and frightened. If she's not wet, you have no option; you have to get her that way. Go back to kissing her mouth, and do it thoroughly. There's no time limit here. She has to feel special, beautiful, and desperately wanted. Which by this time, it's usually not a problem convincing her that you want her, as you're painfully hard. If she's the playful type or you're sure she's ready and willing, you can involve her in the foreplay by putting her hand on your crotch and letting her play. If her hand just lies there unmoving, you may have a problem. Go back to kissing and do some heavy petting on those tits.

"If she's wearing pants, she'll be less accessible, and she may have planned things that way, so go slowly and never tug. Get her out of her pants by slowly shimmying them down, moving from one side to the other, making it go smoothly so she won't feel the harsh drag of her pants, leaving her more and more exposed. This is a good time to mention the temperature for lovemaking. If it's too cold, things don't progress well, if it's too hot, she's going to worry about being sweaty, maybe even smelling. Women are extremely sensitive to how they smell. It's always a good thing to reassure them that they smell wonderful— fresh and flowery, spicy and exotic. I should mention here, that if there *is* an unpleasant smell that repels in any way, back off and get out. You do not want to go there. Unless you've both just come back from a long run," he waved his hand in front of himself, indicating their present condition, "there should be nothing foul smelling—musky, yes, rank and rotten, no. Don't go there, not even with a condom. Find a polite way to say good-bye. Fake hiccups or something. No one can make love with the hiccups."

"That's not going to be a problem. I'm sure Tammy is fresh and pure and clean."

"Well okay then . . . get on with it. Situate yourself between her legs and get yourself comfortable—you're going to be there for a while. Now imagine you're eating a mango. You'll need to split her labial lips open if they are not wide, wet, and welcoming.

Chaz used his hands, cupped and held together, then opening them slowly to show him. "As she gets aroused, it's like a beautiful flower blooming and opening up. Hopefully, she's also getting wet, or you'll have to use your tongue to get her that way."

With his hands still parted he said, "Her clitoris is at the top of her slit, at the 12 o'clock position. Sometimes it's hard to locate. It's a tiny little nub kinda hidden under a flap of skin. But you don't go there right away; you have to work your way there. The slower the better, unless she tells you otherwise. Once you get there, that's your focus.

"You kiss it, lick it, gently suck on it and basically toy with it any creative way you can, until she comes. Could be one minute or ten. If it's longer than that, ask her what she needs you to do for her. If you manage to get her to come, with either a combination of your fingers, your lips, or your tongue, she'll generally let you find your release by allowing you to put your penis in her mouth or in her pussy. If it's in her pussy, use a condom. Always. Until you're married or at least living together and totally exclusive.

"So . . . on to penetration. Your penis in her vagina. That is the ultimate goal here. That is, unless you prefer things to go along the oral vein."

"This is beginning to sound like a lot of work. Isn't this

supposed to be fun?" Cam asked.

Chaz laughed. "Trust me. Once you get full access, it will be fun. A lot of fucking fun."

"Okay, continue."

"Where were we? Oh yes, penetration . . . once you get to your final destination."

"You make this sound like a battle."

"It is. It truly is. It's her will against yours. Your strategy outmaneuvering hers—with the ultimate goal of your weapon discharging inside her. It's sort of like a chess game, only with climactic results." He chuckled at the pun.

"Back to penetration. I assume you know your anatomy."

He stopped and picked up a broken shell, then stooped and drew an elliptical shape. Along the sides of the elongated shape he fanned in curving lines. "A pussy has inner and outer lips, like these. The entrance to the vagina is toward the bottom, yet the target for pleasure is the clitoris, which is at the top, hidden under a fold. You have to use the root of your penis and your groin to find ways to press against it during intercourse, gradually easing it out from its hiding place. Sometimes you can use your fingers as well. Get close, but do not engage it directly until it's prominent. Sometimes you can see it throbbing as it fills with blood, if you just barely graze it, she'll probably jerk. That's a good sign.

"You need the lightest touch here, you want her writhing. Begging for more. Circle and flick, keeping your finger moist by dipping it into her opening to wet it. Work it slow, build the sensations, heighten the pleasure. Delayed gratification . . . that's the key. Make her want it—desperately. She needs to climb the walls, she's so frustrated.

"When you get really good at this, you can get her started, tease her a little, then come back to it later—hours, even days later. All that frustration makes for one hell of an explosion, but you've got to be really good at it—and exclusive. It won't work if she can rub on someone else in the meantime. I used to love getting a woman hot in the car on the way to the airport, then kissing her goodbye at the gate. When I returned a few days later, she would literally sit in my lap in the parking lot and get off by rubbing against my zipper. But those are lessons for later.

"For the first few times, take it slow. Circle the tip of your finger around her inner lips, dip inside at her opening, drag your finger back up, circle her clit and then give it a tiny flick. Then repeat, repeat, repeat. If she's really wet, insert a finger and work it. If she's sloppy wet, you can use two, even three fingers to get her off. If she's not, you're going to have to get your head between her legs and make her wet. For this you're going to have to watch a video my friend. There are all kinds of flickers and lickers, thrusters and lappers. I'm partial to nibbling, using my teeth to graze her . . . and sucking—worrying that little nub between my lips and tongue while drawing on it, wrapping my lips around it and sucking it in, easy and then hard, building her slowly until I can reach up and tap, tap, tap directly on her clit with my finger while she blows. My only advice here is: If she says don't stop, I don't care if your jaw feels like it's gonna drop off, don't stop. Once she comes, it'll be your turn. Then you can suit up and fuck her. And trust me, once you're inside her, you'll know exactly what you need to do to make her come again. Just hold back until you're sure she's satisfied. Once you come, you're not going to be good for much of anything for a while."

"So much to know," Cam said, his face meeting Chaz's in the meager light of the moon bouncing off the waves as they knelt in the sand looking at Chaz' drawing of the female genitalia.

Chaz dropped the broken shell and stood. "You'll learn it. That's the fun part, finding out what works. Watching your girl go through the roof when everything fires up and connects. It's like watching a rocket going off. And if you're in her, it's even better, enough to send you sky-high along with her. Think of foreplay as lighting a fuse. Once you get her sparked up, you have to find ways to keep that fuse burning until you get to the explosion. If you light the fuse and get to the explosion too fast, it's kind of like setting off a dud. But the great thing about sex, is that you can start all over again using what you've learned to make it better the next time."

"How long before I get as good as you?"

Chaz laughed. "I've got some moves, and I've perfected some techniques. But if you've got the right woman, it doesn't matter. It's magical from the very first time. Everybody's got game if you're in love. So don't worry, if you're in love as you say, you'll figure it out in spectacular ways soon enough. That's the end of today's lesson. When you've become proficient in all this, I'll teach you about the elusive G-spot. Now . . . if you'll excuse me," he said as he whipped off his shirt and stripped down to his running shorts, "all this talk about sex hasn't calmed my libido any. I need a good swim. A few laps in the ocean should help me sleep tonight."

"It's dark out there, what about the undertow?"

"I've done the Ironman twice. I know what to do. I'll be fine. You go on in and get on your computer. Google vulva and see what you get. Get yourself familiar with all the wonderful little girlie parts that await."

He tossed his shirt on the sand and ran into the water. When he was in deep enough to dive, he dove and went under. When he surfaced, he did laps, counting slowly to a hundred before turning and repeating the count, until he had crossed in front of *The Cockpit* twenty times.

On the widow's watch on the house next to *The Cockpit*, a woman, wrapped in a lavender cashmere pashmina against the cool breeze, sat and stared, following the movement of his arms as he stroked and crossed the dark sea. Back and forth he went, in languorous strokes as she thought about the kiss that almost was.

When he surfaced and his chest came into view she sighed, when he walked up the beach, his board shorts hanging low on his hips, she moaned. God Almighty, he was gorgeous. From the dark hair he pushed back from his forehead with long fingers to his broad chest matted with a thick patch of hair, to those slim hips and muscled legs, he was one splendid specimen. And for the first time since that awful day in the doctor's office two years ago, she wanted to be with a man. That man, that hunky, hungry-eyed man who was walking up the beach, grabbing his shirt from the sand and now focusing his eyes on the lone woman sitting high above him.

Neither the four-mile run, nor the twenty-minute swim, did anything to diminish his desire. He wanted the woman whose eyes met this. He wanted to light her fuse and watch her burn as she exploded in his arms.

But like any good field marshal, he was going to bide his time and wait for the right moment to wage his campaign. As he'd told Cam, sex was a game, like chess. And when it equated to sex, he was a Grand Master.

"Good night, Mags," he called up to her with a wave before entering *The Cockpit* from the terrace level. He didn't wait for her reply, just flipped off the outside lights and made his way to the outside shower to wash his feet and then to the elevator. No sense tracking sand and salt water through the house, he thought as he used his shirt as a towel to dry off his feet on the way up.

When he passed Cam's door he saw him staring avidly at his computer screen. He was sucking on a mango and running his tongue over the flesh of the fruit. Chaz almost lost it there in the hallway. He bit his tongue and managed to just smile as he pushed open his own door and then closed it behind him. He'd have to remember to give him some book titles and film titles in the morning. But for now, he was going to take a shower and try not to think of the woman sitting next door, who he'd pictured in his mind as the lead player in each scenario he'd recited in his game plan to Cam. Hopefully, he'd done a decent job coaching Cam on how to delight a woman. Now, if he could just stop thinking about all the ways he wanted to give Mags her ultimate pleasure.

Chaz took a long shower then threw on a pair of shorts and a t-shirt and went downstairs to have dinner with his friends. The smell of a delicious spaghetti sauce tickled his nose while he was on the stairs. He was starving. For both food, and Mags. Patience, he told himself. This was not a relationship he wanted to rush.

Chapter 53—Mags
Hot and Bothered

Mags sat in the wooden chair, hunched against the breeze whipping the air since she was so high up. With nothing to stop it, the wind pulled at her wrap, threatening to undo it where she'd tucked it under her. Her hair fluttered around her face as it lashed back and forth against her temples. She was glad it was in a bun right now; otherwise, she knew it would sting as strands slapped her cheeks. It had been shoulder length when she started losing it. Her goal was to see it that length again.

It was late, close to eleven. She had gone inside for a while, but was compelled to come back up here. She was restless. Itchy, in a way she hadn't been for a very long time. She thought Chaz was going to kiss her this evening. But for some reason, he'd pulled away. She wished he had kissed her. She had really wanted him to.

She saw two men walking side by side along the shore. One she recognized by the uptick in her heartbeat. The other, she had seen arrive at the beach house next door in a Lexus sedan earlier that day. Must be another one of Chaz's partners, she mused. All of them seemed young, handsome and privileged somehow. But it figured, the inhabitants of the luxurious beach house had to have been successful to have even bought the lot, nonetheless to have built such a posh place. From certain angles, she could see the edges of an aquamarine lap pool through a set of sliding glass doors. What must it be like to wake to such extravagance?

Chapter 54—Alex
Time with Friends

Alex stopped at the outside shower to rinse his legs and feet, then climbed the steps to the beach house, using the masonry rail for support. His legs felt like jelly. He didn't know how many miles he'd walked, but his Fit-Bit had vibrated announcing the completion of 10,000 steps over an hour ago. Considering he'd spent the majority of the day at the airport in L.A. and then on the plane here, that was a fair amount of walking in a short period of time. But he knew the long walk on the hard packed sand hadn't caused the weakness in his legs. Most likely they were sore from the hour sitting Indian style by the Kindred Spirit Mailbox, reading the long entries Emma had written. He rubbed his chest. His heart was sore, too.

He slid open the door that led into the open kitchen area, and everyone who was sitting at the counter, cooking at the stove, and even Dev, who had his head bent perusing the offerings in the fridge, turned to stare at him.

He met each man's eyes with his own as his neck turned, taking a slow panoramic assessment around the room. He paused to acknowledge each man with a nod, a smile, or a quirked eyebrow before stopping at Kyle's face and letting his eyes drop to his hand and what he was stirring on the stove.

Kyle answered his unasked question, "Amatriciana sauce."

Alex nodded his approval.

Dev walked over and handed Alex the cold bottle of Corona he'd just opened.

Wrapping his fingers around it he lifted it in salute. After taking a long swig, he placed the bottle against his forehead. "Thanks. Sorry, I've been such a prick. Let me get a shower and I'll join you."

He took the beer with him up to his room. Once there, he walked into the ensuite, dropped his trunks on the tiled floor and entered the walled shower. Placing his beer on the soap ledge, he leaned his hand against the tiles, ducked his head and turned on the cold spray. He stayed like that, bent as if in defeat, letting the water cascade off his head and neck until he felt his head ache from the cold. Then he adjusted the spray, reached for the soap and began to wash. Midway, he reached for the beer and downed the rest of it.

He felt like a shit. He'd treated Emma badly. So very badly. He hadn't even let her tell her side of it. With a life so full of drama and every single thing causing so much angst, he'd forgotten there were innocents in this mess that had turned into his life.

How to fix it? How was he to get happy again? God, it had been so long since things had been good. And he was so tired of the sadness. The loneliness. The what-if thoughts that never seemed to stop running in a loop through his head.

While he toweled off and dressed, he realized things were never going to change if all he thought about was trying to get back to his old life. He had to let it go. Let Mallory go. They were over. As short and sweet as it had been, it had been temporary. And the only good things left from it were Molly and Mandy. And they deserved more than a father who was miserable and bitter, who always had a touch of melancholy, even on the best days. Emma had cracked a fissure in his heart and worked her way inside, and things had been getting better. So much better. But he'd let his hatred for his wife's father get the best of him, and by association, he'd accused an innocent girl of unspeakable treachery. And he'd destroyed them both.

After he pulled on shorts, then a Cubaberra shirt, fresh from the package he'd left in the dresser drawer the last time he was here, he stopped and stared at himself in the mirror over the white and gold dresser. The man looking back at him looked haggard. No wonder the flight attendants had left him alone, when they usually doted on him.

He reached for his comb and then leaned in to face himself eye-to-eye. "Well it ends here. I don't know if I can fix this. But I sure as hell have to try."

He ran the comb though his hair, slapped on some aftershave lotion even though he hadn't shaved, and went down to have pasta with his friends.

Chapter 55—Alex & Chaz
A Much-needed Tête-à-tête

How had his life turned into such a morass? He'd always thought of himself as a geeky nerd, except that according to a lot of women, he didn't look like a nerd, he looked like, what was it that one woman had called him? Oh yeah, Mr. Adonis. One day he'd looked up the word nerd and he'd discovered he really wasn't that much of one after all.

The definition of nerd was a foolish or contemptible person who lacks social skills or is boringly studious, or a single-minded expert in a particular technical field. Okay, maybe the last part applied. And a little bit of the first. He only liked social interaction that was pleasant. No loud arguments, no drama, no up-in-your-face theatrics when things didn't go as planned. No petty, conniving women, just the sweet debutante type with proper manners.

In fact, he was so anti-conflict that he had chosen his career with that in mind. No criminal law career for him. He did not need angst, publicity, or any kind of association with someone who already had conflict of one sort or another to deal with. No litigation, no lengthy trials that went on for years. No arbitration for class action suits. So he became an entertainment lawyer, specializing in musicians, TV, and Film, or what his wife had called a celebrity lawyer. He never had to sit before a judge as almost all his cases were settled in conference rooms. But mostly, it involved writing contracts, renewals, and negotiations. He had started his career in Wilmington, and done well. But Los Angeles was a whole other world, one that thankfully, his many paralegals buffered him from.

So how had he ended up with this much drama in his life? That was the first question he posed to Chaz as they sat in the game room after dinner.

"So how did all this happen to me? I had a life planned out. Law courses, business courses, accounting courses, all equaling boring corporate attorney. Cut and dried. No surprises."

"Life has surprises. Plenty of them," Chaz murmured as he sipped his wine.

"But it wasn't supposed to be that way, not for me. And it sure wasn't supposed to include tragic things. Has yours?"

Chaz lifted a brow as a reminder, "Our graduation night . . ."

"Oh yeah, The Great Graduation Debacle. I keep forgetting about that. You never were able to put things back together with her, were you?"

"Nope. My mistake made things just about as irrevocable as your wife dying."

Anger flared in Alex's face, he turned with his fist balled up on the arm of the recliner, "How can you say that? She died! That's pretty damned final."

"Julia said we wouldn't get back together if I was the last man on earth. I figure that's a lot of people dying just for me to see if she meant it. That's about as final as it gets."

Alex backed down, then got up and took a seat at the chess table.

"Let's play chess. As I recall you're a Foosball fanatic, and too good at it. Chess is more my style."

"You always were the geeky, brainy sort."

"The traits of a masterful conqueror," he taunted.

"Hmm, we'll see." Chaz took a seat opposite him and they both started putting the pieces back to the proper starting positions.

"So, still flying solo?" Alex asked.

Chaz knew Alex was asking about sex, and not planes. "Yes. I grew up."

"Brent hasn't, I take it?"

"I wouldn't know, but I doubt it."

"I would think it would be hard to break from that lifestyle."

Chaz lifted his head and shrugged his shoulders. "Julia had six orgasms that night. It was hard for me to see what she was complaining about at the time."

"They weren't all from you."

"I understand that now. Enough about me. What's going on with you? We weren't expecting you to make it this time," Chaz said as he brought a pawn forward.

"Things are all screwed up right now."

"At work?"

"No, that part of my life is pretty consistent. Contractual law and the movie and music business keep me busy. And now that everyone is writing a book, there's the literary aspect with copyrights and options added into the mix. I could handle bringing on another intern or paralegal if I could just find the time to interview some prospects."

"So, it's something with the girls?"

"No, they're doing great. My parents are so good with them. And the girls have made their lives so fulfilling. It's like they're both twenty years younger. It's a joy to watch. And it was a stroke of genius on my mom's part to suggest my second cousin for their new nanny when my last one turned out to be unreliable."

"So this all screwed up part, if it's not financial, and it's not about the twins, is there a woman involved?"

"Mmm hmmm," Alex said as he used his bishop to take Chaz's pawn.

"I figured as much. You've got that distracted look of a man at a crossroads."

"Yeah. That's a pretty good way of explaining it. I am definitely in the desert at a four-way intersection trying to figure out why my car is spinning like crazy trying to figure out the road I'm supposed to be on."

"Which one do you want to be on?"

Alex huffed. "Now there's the 64-million dollar question."

"So you came here to figure it out?"

"I don't know why I came here. It was like a magnet drew me all the way across the country and plopped me down here."

"So what's the screwed up part?"

"I thought she had betrayed me, but now it seems she might not have, at least not intentionally."

Chaz captured Alex's knight, replacing it with his rook. Tell me about her. How'd you meet?"

"Her name is Emma. And we met ballroom dancing."

"Ballroom dancing? You?"

"Yeah, before she got pregnant, when we lived in Wilmington, Mallory and I started taking lessons. Once a week we had a date night, and after dinner downtown, we went to this dance place on Oleander Drive. We got pretty good at it and had some great times learning to waltz, tango, rhumba, the quick step, all that stuff you see on TV nowadays. It was fun. And a great way for us to connect in the middle of the week when we were both so busy. I looked forward to it every week. But then she got pregnant and we didn't go as often. Toward the end she was so tired, I couldn't even get her out for dinner, nonetheless dancing. And then I lost her."

"I'll never forget when I got that call from Sean. It broke my heart," Chaz said.

"Yeah. Mine too."

"She was a sweet lady. I can't imagine her doing the rhumba though."

Alex laughed. "Well it wasn't her favorite. She liked the more elegant dances, especially the waltz."

"So back to how you met this girl . . ."

"After I got settled into the new job, the new house, and the exhausting life of being a single father, my parents insisted I take one night a week off to go to a movie, eat dinner out, or go to a club. They thought I needed to get back into the world and start dating. I wasn't keen on it, but they were pretty insistent.

I'd driven by this dance place a few times and one night I pulled up and went in. The instructor paired me up with some experienced dancers and it all came back. And I loved the music. It innervated me. It was fun to dance and be carefree, if only for an hour or two.

"So I kept going. And one week this beautiful woman with the most amazing legs showed up. I didn't know it at the time, but she was a professional dancer trying to keep her hand in and get some exercise while trying to find work. She'd just moved from New York City after losing her job on a soap opera. She became my partner. And we were like something out of Hollywood. We meshed; dancing with her was like being on a cloud. All the steps I thought I'd forgotten came back, I had renewed energy. She was the belle of the ballroom and I was under her spell."

"So this was Emma?"

"Yes." He sat back and steepled his fingers, closed his eyes, and sighed. "I looked forward to having her in my arms each week more than anything. Wednesday nights became sacrosanct. I lived to have my hands on her waist, her hips, around her shoulders, to grip her fingers and pull her into my chest. Then one night at the end of a particularly sensual dance, after the lift, I pulled her in close and kissed her. It was a magical moment. When people use the expression *the earth stood still*, well it sure did for me that night."

Chaz got up and walked to the small mini-bar and fixed Alex a martini, then poured it into a Solo cup. He fixed himself a wine spritzer. Walking over to Alex he handed him the martini, "Let's take a walk on the beach, you're so not into this game."

On the way down the access, Chaz resumed the conversation. "So you became a couple?"

"Well, not right away. We made out in an alley outside a tavern that night like eager teenagers and I asked her to come back to my house, but she had an early call the next morning, auditioning for some sitcom, along with a three-date rule she wouldn't budge from. We figured we were one date shy. We both had busy schedules, so it wasn't until the next dance night before we had a chance to see each other again. We made plans ahead of time to sleep together after class.

"We had an amazing night and phenomenal sex at The Wiltshire. I didn't want to leave her the next morning, but I had meetings I had to attend. I had the girls on weekends and even though I'd told her about Mallory and the girls, I was hesitant to invite her to the house. But when we met again on dance night, I began to tell her about my life. We talked late into the night and she said she'd love to see the babies. She offered to bring over the stuff to fix dinner.

"She was a natural with the girls, they took to her and she to them. She even gave them both their baths that night. Read to them, sang them to sleep and kissed their cheeks. It was an amazing thing to see, this sexy woman who was mothering my children as if they were hers, as if she loved them at first sight. I was a goner long before she led me into my bedroom and took off her clothes for me. Chaz, I have seen some beautiful women in my time, but this woman, God she is gorgeous. Big high breasts with perky rose tinged nipples, a tiny waist, long sleek thighs, a trimmed blonde pussy, hell even her feet were lovely. And her skin was so soft and perfect, as she stood there and blushed while my eyes took everything in.

"We made love three times that night and I came like a train going over a cliff each time. It was the most incredible sex I'd ever had. She was perfect in every way. I woke with her in my arms the next morning and thought maybe my life was going to turn out okay after all."

Alex took a long sip of his drink. "We had a few weeks of bliss, getting to know each other and her bonding with the girls. Then I got served. Out of the blue, I was charged with child abuse. The claimant was my former father-in-law. I read the writ and saw the charge. And I knew Emma had betrayed me. She was the only one who knew about the night I got frustrated with one of the babies, who would not stop crying, and that I had shaken her. I had been immediately horrified at my actions and had held Mandy tight to my chest and cried along with her. I knew I'd never do it again, and I haven't.

"I don't know why, but one night I confessed what I had done to Emma. She had been sympathetic and understanding and she had assured me that my having felt so badly about it ensured that I would never do it again. And she was right. The guilt drove me crazy and for days I watched Mandy like a hawk for any signs I could have hurt her. But she was fine. And it was forgotten until officers came to arrest me and I read the summons to court.

"The deputies that delivered it said they were sending a child custody advocate to pick up the girls, and that I should get any things they would need together. Emma was there at the door with me when I got the notice. I remember staring at it, dumbfounded as it all came back to me, the conversation we'd had in the nursery one night while we were each rocking one of the babies to sleep.

"I didn't handle it well. I told her to get out, to never come back. She pleaded with me to listen, that she could explain. But I wouldn't give her a chance. I was having none of it. I told her to get her things and go, and then I charged the deputies to remove her from my property. Where she went, I don't know. In that moment, I didn't care.

"I made a few phone calls and was able to get my parents vetted as guardians. They came over, got the girls and took them to their house. I was taken to jail, and because of my connections and clear record, I was booked and released.

"The next morning I hired an attorney dealing in custody matters. He was able to get me in front of a judge that afternoon, and after hearing my story the judge said, 'We all have these lapses of judgment. Yes, it was something that should not have happened. However, I am more concerned with chronic cases. You seem sufficiently contrite, and have brought in the necessary support people you need to help out and to assure that nothing like this ever happens again. Your attorney says you sought help immediately and that you've read up on how to manage similar situations in the future, should they arise. I've read your deceased wife's testimony against her father, detailing his sexual abuse of her as a child, providing motivation and possible reasons for the charges and the malice he has against you. I commend you for the lengths you've gone to, to keep your daughters out of harm's way. It's not easy what you are doing. Single fathers of one baby have it hard enough and you have two, so you are learning as you go. I see you took a childcare class at the hospital a week after this event happened?'"

"I told him, 'Yes sir. I felt I needed to learn some coping mechanisms and to find out what mothers do in these situations.'"

"He asked me, 'Did you get the answers you were seeking?'"

"And I answered, 'Yes. Now I know how to manage all the different types of temper tantrums girls have.' He smiled and said, 'Then you're way ahead of the rest of us.' He dismissed the case and wished me luck.

"So I got the girls back and everything was fine—except that it wasn't. I have been miserable. After it was all over, I wished I had at least let Emma tell her side. I could see then that there must have been an explanation since it was so out of character for her to do what I thought she had done. And for what purpose? How did having my children taken from me benefit her? I had let my anger override everything. And I had been unfair. My heart was shattered and I missed her. Down to my soul.

"Then I received a letter from Mallory's sister Melissa, telling me about Emma, how kind she was, and berating her father who had also abused her. She took pictures of journal entries Emma had written in a notebook and left in the Mailbox down at Bird Island. Some were too blurry to read. Today, I walked down there and read the forty pages she had written and left in the Kindred Spirit Mailbox."

"Wow."

"Yeah." He made an exploding gesture with his fingers, "Wow. I can't help but think that there's something mystical afoot. Emma couldn't possibly have known I was going to be here this week to read it. I didn't even know it 'til yesterday, and I didn't tell anyone but my folks and you guys."

"So what did the messages in the notebook say?"

"A lot. Turns out she's Mallory's cousin. Her Uncle Jerry was Mallory's father."

"Didn't you tell me that he had sexually abused Mallory as a child and that was one of the reasons why you were moving to California, to make sure he'd never have access to his granddaughters?"

"Yeah. You're one of the few people I told about that. It was right after Mallory died and I had to make some big decisions."

"Sounds like you made the right ones."

"Yeah, with pretty much everything, except this latest one with regard to Emma."

"Go on," Chaz said, encouraging Alex by rotating his hand in circles, "What else did the messages say?"

"So Emma loses her job in New York and moves back home to Shallotte, to a house which is coincidentally right across the street from her Uncle Jerry and Aunt Darlene's house, Mallory's parents house. They invite her over for dinner and Uncle Jerry starts scheming. He wants the girls back here but he doesn't tell Emma any of this. He offers to give her some money to tide her over and to get her to L.A. where she's been told there are more opportunities for her and an agent waiting to take her on. All she has to do is arrange to meet me and get a few pictures of the twins for him. That's it. That's what he tells her. But that isn't it. He's more devious than that, but she doesn't know any of that.

"So she flies to L.A. and she tracks me down using

information he provided that he got from a private investigator. We meet, we dance, we date, and she begins to stay over on weekends. I assume Uncle Jerry got the pictures he wanted at some point.

"Then one Saturday morning when I had to go into work to get a file and she's alone with the girls, she knocks over the baby monitor that's in the nursery, the one for Molly's crib. It shatters and breaks. Uncle Jerry happens to call when she's upset that she broke the monitor and she's picking up the broken pieces. He tells her not to worry, he'll overnight her a new one. No problem. He asks her the brand name and model so he can get the same one. She thanks him and forgets about it. It arrives by courier Sunday afternoon while I'm at the grocery store, and she installs it. She doesn't know that her uncle has programmed it to allow him to use the monitor to see Molly and to hear anything going on in the nursery through an app on his phone. A few nights later, we're both in the nursery rocking the girls and that's the night I tell her about the awful time I flew off the handle and shook Mandy. He hears what I say. He calls the Ventura County D.A. Charges are filed. I get served. I kick Emma out. She packs up and moves back home where she discovers her Uncle Jerry's true colors. She knows he threw her under the bus by sending that monitor, pre-programmed for him, so he could spy on the girls.

"She goes for a walk on the beach, and decides to purge her soul on paper, and low and behold her other cousin, Mallory's sister, sees it and writes me. Mind you, since Mallory died, I have returned every single thing anyone in that family has ever sent me. Yet she sends me a letter anyway. I went to the Mailbox today and read what Emma wrote. Now, you tell me, am I being manipulated? Again?"

"What made you go to the Mailbox today?"

"I had heard about it when I lived here before. You guys have all talked about it. But I'd never gone down there. Melissa mentioned it in her letter to me."

"So, you didn't plan to go to read the pages you couldn't decipher?"

"No, I didn't need to, I had the jist."

"So the idea to go, just popped into your head?"

"Yeah, I guess. I was pacing on the beach and all of a sudden I just started walking in that direction."

"Then you're not being manipulated, you're being led."

"What's the difference?"

"You were meant to come here and find Emma's letter. This time of the year, the journals get switched out several times a week. We're in high season. She wrote a lot. The notebook she wrote in is probably full. It's a miracle it's still in the Mailbox, unless it's one of the seeds."

"Seeds?"

"People don't just come to write in the notebooks, they also come to read the notebooks. The volunteers always leave a seed notebook or two for people to read, but then they eventually get collected too."

"You know a lot of odd things."

"I know you're supposed to go find her and try to fix things."

"You think so?"

"Don't you?"

There was silence. They could both hear the waves washing up on the shore.

Chaz drained the rest of his drink. "She didn't do anything wrong. Other than arrange to meet you. And once she found out about her Uncle's abuse of Mallory, she didn't want to have anything to do with him, right?"

"Melissa's letter said no one wanted to have anything to do with him any more."

"Well that's pretty admirable, don't you think?"

"Yeah. I suppose it is."

"Don't you want her back?"

"Hell yeah, I do."

"Then what are you waiting for?"

"I don't know where she is. The letter said she was going back to New York."

"When did she write the letter? Most people date those messages, if not, you can usually tell by the dates of the other messages around it."

"She starting writing it last week; finished it a few days ago. Melissa took pictures of the pages and overnighted them. I got them yesterday. "

"Well, you know where she lives. Just go there."

"What if she's not there?"

"Then go to New York."

"You make it sound so easy."

"Do you love her?"

"Yes."

"Then go find her."

"What if she won't forgive me?"

"What if she will?"

Chapter 56—Alex
The Chase is On

Alex left the house at noon the next day and drove his rental Lexus to the house that he remembered his former in-laws living in. When he saw it, his eyes tracked left to find the house that was directly across the street. He didn't know what kind of car Emma drove as she'd had a rental in L.A., so he wasn't sure if she was there or not. But he suspected she wasn't when all he saw was a big black Ford pickup truck and a ten-year-old Buick four-door sedan sitting at the top of the driveway under a double carport. If he had to peg Emma's style of car, he figured it would lean more toward something sporty, probably blue. She'd driven a convertible sports car in L.A. and seemed to enjoy driving with the top down.

He parked behind the sedan, just past the turn in, and walked up the drive, taking in the gourds on high hangers bouncing in the wind, the tall sunflowers swaying toward the sun, and the chickens scattering at his feet as he walked up the gravel drive. On the pale yellow painted door hung a dried up wreath of dusty pink tea roses. It was hanging askew; he righted it before he knocked on the solid wooden space beside it. There didn't appear to be a bell anywhere. He waited. He waited some more. That's when he saw the big black cast iron bell with matching clapper mounted on a stand close to the end of the porch. Was he supposed to ring that?

Sweat pooled in the center of his back, soaking his shirt, and he had to firm his jaw to keep from convulsively swallowing. What if she refused to see him?

Through the glass side panel of the door he saw an older woman shuffling forward, tilting her head this way and that, as if trying to make out who was at her door in the early afternoon on a hot summer day.

It was clear she hadn't figured it out when she pulled the door wide and blinked several times at the sunshine pouring in behind him. She put her hand over her eyes to shield them from the bright light and said, "How may I help—Alex! Is that you? It is you! Did you bring the babies?" Her manner had gone from mild annoyance at the interruption in her day, to jubilation that she might be able to see her dead niece's twin baby girls.

"Hello, Miss Anna. No, I didn't bring the babies. They're back in California with my parents. Is Emma home?"

"Emma? No, no she's not." She frowned, scrunching up her eyes and giving him a questioning look. Maybe Emma hadn't mentioned seeing him while she was in L.A. and she was wondering why in the world he'd be calling on her. Or she *had* told her and she was thinking him daft for daring to be here.

"Oh, do you know when she'll be back?"

"Did'nya you hear?" She clasped both hands to the area above her ample bosom and sighed. "They're considering bringing her character back as a long-lost missin' twin sister. She's done gone to meet with the writers. She left for New York 'bout eleven, but then she got a flat tire out on 17. Had to wait for a tow, so she's just now getting to the Ford dealership. I think they're seein' if they can plug the tire for now. Ya might be able to catch her. I jus' got off the phone with her. I can call her back if ya like, tell her to wait on ya."

"No, that's all right, I'll run over there right now. It's only five minutes from here. So that I don't miss her, what kind of car is she driving?"

"She got herself a fancy baby blue Mustang convertible from the rental car company this morning. She said seein's as it was a right nice day, she wanted to work on her tan on the way up there."

He smiled. A baby blue sports car suited her and he'd known that it would. He turned to go.

"Alex?"

He turned back to her, "Yeah?"

"My sister-in-law, Mallory's mama, told me that early this morning Emma came over and gave my good-for-nothing brother an envelope full of cash. Told him it was all there, every penny, and then she kissed her Aunt Darlene good-bye. Told her she was going to give New York another try."

Somehow, he'd known she would give the money back. There was a lot more to this Kindred Spirit stuff than he realized. It was in that moment that he truly believed that he was being led to her by some supernatural power. Now, if he could only catch up to her without having to chase her up I-95 with a state trooper on his ass.

When he got to the Ford dealership, he was told she'd just left, but that she had talked about getting a sweet tea for the road at the 211 Hardee's. He drove onto the Hardee's parking lot just in time to see her shoot through the intersection at the light putting her back on Route 17 heading north. He drove around the lot, having to courteously stop for two groups of seniors, then drove out the exit. He had to wait for the left turn light at one of the busiest intersections in the county. He felt his agitation heightening, making his fingers tap on the steering wheel and his foot twitch to connect to the accelerator in a risky manner. He had to tamp down his anxiety. Yes, he had lost site of her, but he was fairly certain he could catch up. From here, there was really only one way to drive to New York City—17 to 40 to 95.

The light turned for him and he took up the chase. He saw flashes of her car up ahead a few times, but because of summer traffic he could not catch up to her. A combination of sheriff's cars, red lights, and Emma driving well over the speed limit, had him losing ground instead of making it up. He didn't see her for a while, but figured if she was familiar with the area, she'd be taking the new I-40 Bypass, so he took it. Several minutes later, he saw her ahead of him as the road curved to the left on one of the long bridges that spanned the marshes on the outer fringe of

Wilmington. He could just barely make out her blonde ponytail flapping in the breeze.

He wondered if she was still grieving him as she had been when she wrote in the notebook, or if she was beginning to get over him now. Maybe she wasn't even thinking of him anymore. Maybe all her thoughts were on New York now, and her friends waiting for her there. Her mom had indicated that she'd pretty much fled to the city on hearing the news of a possible return to the show, as if it had been the best news ever.

The thought that Emma might have processed a single iota of the love she'd had for him out of her heart, filled him with dread. He hated more than ever that he had wounded her spirit so badly. Her nature had been one of compassion and caring right from the start. He should have known that down to his bones. But to stop his self-castigation, he rationalized that she was an actress, after all. And likely a pretty good one. But Melissa's letter had confirmed his initial feelings. Emma was the real deal.

He calmed the ache in his heart by reminding himself that he'd never have made it in the world of show biz as a legal advisor, therapist, and confidant for actors and singers if he'd been bad at summing people up. Of course, she was thinking of him. On Route 40, he thought he saw a glimmer of baby blue and pressed down on the accelerator with a heavy foot. His heart sank as he drew up to a Toyota Solara in the wrong shade of blue.

At this rate, he might not catch up to her until the 795 Bypass at Faison, if she even decided to take it. He remembered that most people often missed the exit for it wasn't well marked. He thought about calling her cell phone, and then remembered he'd deleted her contact from his phone in a moment of anger.

Chapter 57—Alex
Caught Up

It was a stroke of luck, or maybe serendipity having its way, when driving through the intersection where the Kangaroo gas station and the McDonald's near Goldsboro, Alex looked to the left and saw Emma's car. It was parked close to the road, facing forward, so that as he drove by, he could see the Enterprise tag on the front.

He made a U-turn at the next intersection. His heart was racing. He'd caught up with her! And just in time, as he really needed to relieve himself.

Realizing he could easily lose her again while in the restroom, he parked his car directly behind hers blocking her in. After spotting her at a table in the center of the restaurant, facing away from the side entrance he came in through, he took a right into the hallway that led to the men's room.

It looked as if his grand gesture was going to take place at a McDonald's. So be it. He wasn't going to put off telling her how he felt about her because the meal came in wrappers instead of on fine china plates, and one sipped through a straw while holding a paper cup instead of sipping from the rim of a fine crystal flute filled with champagne.

When he came out of the restroom minutes later, she was gone, her table vacant and cleaned off. In a panic, his eyes flew to the front window. He could barely make her out through the glare of the afternoon sun hitting it. But there she was, in the driver's seat, her head nodding, and one arm waving wildly as she sat talking on her phone.

He smiled. She was obviously perturbed at being blocked in. So the grand gesture? Not even in a restaurant, but on the parking lot.

He walked over to her car, approaching by the driver's

door and heard her talking.

"Some idiot blocked me in. Who does that? There are plenty of open parking spaces all over the place!"

He held back his snicker. She was angry all right.

"I don't know. It's a silver Lexus I think."

He tapped her on her shoulder.

She turned to face him and her eyes went wide.

"Yes, I am an idiot. An idiot for sending you away."

Her mouth hung open, the hand holding her phone went limp. She almost dropped it.

He reached over, took it from her hand and put it to his ear. "This is the idiot blocking her in. I've been following her for two hours trying to catch up with her to apologize and to ask her to marry me."

His eyes met hers and he quirked a brow in question. Both of her brows were raised and her eyes blinked with surprise. Her mouth snapped shut.

"Yes. That would be fine." He handed her back her phone. "The dispatcher would like to stay on the line for your answer."

His fingertips stroked her cheek. "I am truly sorry. That night was horrible and I didn't piece things together as I should have. Most importantly, I refused to listen to you. It wasn't until later that I remembered you had said you needed to talk to me about something, that very morning. That was what it was, right?"

She nodded, just slightly as she didn't want to disengage the hand now cupping the side of her face.

He brought his other hand up so that he was framing her face with both hands. He bent over the door to kiss her. The moment his lips touched hers he groaned, and without regard to the people standing in the parking lot or the dispatcher still on the line, he deepened the kiss. When at last he separated his lips from hers, he leaned his forehead against hers.

"Emma, will you marry me? Will you be my wife and Molly and Mandy's mother?"

Her eyes filled with tears as she looked up at him, met his eyes and whispered, "Yes."

He lifted her hand with the phone still in it. "Say it again, a little louder, for the nice lady waiting on the phone."

Emma turned her face to the phone and smiled as she said, "Yes. I said yes to the idiot."

They could hear applause and the clapping of many pairs of hands until Alex reached down and hit the red button to end the call.

Chapter 58—Alex & Emma
The Fairytale

They were sitting in her car, the top up now and the air conditioning running as they kissed, hugged and talked.

"We're going to have to learn each other all over again—at least from my perspective. You knew my wife years before I did. Hell, you grew up with her. And my daughters, they're your cousins." He stroked alongside her neck as they faced each other across the console, his eyes on her kiss-swollen lips.

"I know. I knew way more about you before we met; yet I really didn't know *you*. I only knew what others had told me. But I knew you had to be special because Mallory was so special, and I loved her so much."

"And I knew *of* you, but little else really. I never would have put it together that you were Mallory's family."

"I'm sorry for the deception. My uncle misled me. I can't believe how easily he duped me. Can we start fresh?" she asked.

"Yes. Except for the dancing and the sex part. I think we've got that down pat."

"I'm so sorry for what my uncle put you through. I see him in a whole new light now. I always knew he was a bit on the shady side, but I never thought he'd do something so despicable. And what he did to Mallory . . . why didn't she tell someone? He's an evil, evil man, and I told my parents I don't want to have anything to do with him ever again."

"Well I can tell you one thing, he's not invited to our wedding."

She sighed. "I didn't even make it to your last one."

He chucked her under her chin. "Well, you'd better make it to this next one."

They were quiet for several moments, each lost in their thoughts. Then he sighed deeply. "After all we'd been through, did you actually think that I would let you go? I told you I loved you."

"Well, you sent me away. Made the policemen see to it I left."

"I was distraught. Not thinking things through. You should have just gone back to your apartment and waited. I would have come for you. It took a while to sort everything out. But then, once I had, I knew I still loved you. And after seeing you with the girls, I knew in my heart that you would never have had a part in hurting them."

"No. Never," she breathed.

He kissed her, letting their lips linger. His fingers caressed the nape of her neck, stroked the vee at the front, and dipped down to her tight cleavage forced together by her push up bra.

"I saw a hotel a few miles back, a Sleep Inn, if I recall correctly. We have a lot to figure out . . . your job in New York, telling your parents about us, planning a wedding, relocating you to California . . ."

She kissed his jaw, moved up to his ear and lightly breathed into it before licking inside a whorl, "Let's put all that aside for right now and just go make love."

"Lead the way."

"You'll have to, you've still got me locked in."

He ran his hand over her thigh. "I plan on keeping you that way. Locked in with me."

He reached into his pocket. "I forgot something."

He took out the ring he had bought her at the open market, the one she placed on his bathroom vanity when she left. "I want to get you a huge diamond to go with this, but I love this ring on you, and what it means, so maybe this can be your wedding band and I'll have one made to match for mine by the same artist. Do you like that idea?"

"I love that idea." She watched while he slipped the ring back on her finger, this time on her left hand.

He murmured, "You said something about it reminding

you of all the highs and lows in relationships."

"Yeah, the waves rising and settling, going high and then dipping low . . . life's peaks and valleys."

"We'll have to remember that. Not every day is going to be like riding on a crest. But we'll have each other for the days that bring us low," he agreed.

"Yes," she kissed him hungrily. "We'll have each other, and our girls. I love you Alex, so much."

"I love you, Emma. I am so glad Melissa sent me that letter."

"Melissa? What letter?"

"She sent me a package containing photos of the journal pages you wrote in a notebook left at the Kindred Spirit Mailbox last week."

She touched his cheek. "Oh, Alex. You saw the worst of my feelings being poured out."

"No," he held her face between his hands and looked into her eyes. "I saw you Emma. The best of you. You as you truly are. Sweet . . . generous . . . kind . . . and loving. Always loving. Love me and let me love you, always."

There was a tap on the window. A man in a brown McDonald's shirt was standing there. Emma lowered her window.

"Are you guys going to block the parking lot all day? We're due for the dinner rush soon. People can get around but it's tight . . . ."

They both laughed. "No, no. We're leaving right now."

After a night at the Sleep Inn, they returned Alex's rental car and were going to continue the drive to New York where Alex was planned to negotiate Emma's contract for her if she decided to accept the part. He wanted to make sure it included a number of guaranteed episodes and flights back to L.A. every other weekend.

They were loading their stuff into the convertible when

Emma's cell phone rang. He could tell from her side of the conversation that it was her agent calling. A very excited agent, as he could hear most of her side of the conversation as well.

When Emma got off the phone she stared at him, her face flushed with happiness, her eyes bright, and she was sporting a beaming grin.

"Don't keep me in suspense . . ."

"Disney Junior wants me. I'm going to be a princess!"

He laughed and pulled her into his arms. "Lord, give me strength—three princesses in one house. How will I ever survive?"

He kissed her hard and fast and with such passion she felt lightheaded. Then just as fast and as hard, she pushed against his chest, "Hey, wait a minute! You didn't have anything to do with this did you?"

He grinned. "Keep you in L.A? Give you a well-paying job you'll love that you can only improve on over the years? Put a grin on your face as wide as the moon? If only I'd thought of it . . . I would have. But no, this was all on you. You did this all on your own, princess."

He gathered her up again, held her tight and spun her around. "I am so glad I don't have to give up my Wednesday night dance partner," he whispered in her ear.

"Ditto."

"Let's go to *The Cockpit* so I can show you off. We'll spend a few days with my friends and with your folks before we fly back home. There's a brand new pair of size eight Wellies in the tack room waiting to be broken in."

"Home. And new boots! I like the sound of that."

"Ditto."

He caressed the side of her face and gently kissed her lips, "You look pensive."

"Do you think Mallory would be pleased?"

"I know Mallory loved you. She often talked about how kind you were and how much fun you were to be with. She said you were the most graceful dancer she'd ever seen. And I agree with that."

"But raising her kids . . ."

"I think she'd be delighted that I found you."

"I found you . . .." she kissed alongside his jaw as she was in flats and it was the highest she could reach, "and my heart has been beating double time ever since."

"Well, it's good that it works both ways. Let's go to the beach and write about our happily-ever-after in that journal of yours."

They sealed the bargain with a kiss.

Chapter 59—Chaz
Pretty Girl Crying Ugly

Late the next morning Chaz listened as Mags clomped down the steps. In the two days they'd been here, he'd learned the distinctly different sounds his two young neighbors made when coming and going. Kara's flip-flops flapped, in a fatigued way. Mags sneakers or canvas boat shoes pounded, conveying exuberance. Nuances he doubted anyone would pick up on, unless they had a vested interest. Which he did—he silently worshipped Mags from afar, except she wasn't all that afar.

To secure a world-class evening picnic to impress her, he'd gotten up at a ridiculously early hour to play 18 holes of golf with Kyle and Sean. Cam was supposed to play as well, but he was M.I.A. again with the exception of some pretty weird texts he'd sent to both Sean and Chaz, and evidence he'd rifled through his drawers and suitcases during the middle of the night. Chaz was pretty sure the night flight was because Cam was ready to combust with horniness that was Tamara related.

Chaz leaned forward and watched as Mags came into view on the ground level. She jumped the low hedge leading to the access. His head lifted to the rail and his eyes focused solely on her as she set out for what appeared to be her daily walk to the jetty and back. Yesterday, he'd heard her call out to Kara at about the same time, "I'm going to the Jetty now! Be back soon!" And today he'd heard, "See ya later, Babe! I'm on Bird Island time!"

He was hidden from view, sitting in a lounger set several feet back from the masonry rail, scrolling through documents on his laptop. He was silent, content to watch her in secret as she made her jaunty way down the access, her tiny little butt swaying left and then right with each footfall. He was reminded of Trace Adkin's *Honky Tonk Badonkakdonk*. "Left, right, left, right, left . . . ." He had no choice but to smile as she continued on her way, carefree and happy as if every single thing in her life was perfect this morning. If her shimmying and saucily bouncing body was any indication of her mood, it was stupendous. His cock jumped, almost tipping the Mac Air off the perilous ledge, balanced between his bent knee and his lap.

She was a sweet thing in her lacy white cover-up and clogs, her tanned legs looking sleek and long under the impossibly short top that allowed her bikini-clad ass cheeks to peek out with each step. Today her bikini was lime green. Yesterday it had been bright orange. Her stride was easy and carefree as she swung her arms and tilted her head back and forth to the music coming from the iPhone that was clipped to an armband. He'd love to know the song that was playing, as apparently she was ically into it.

He watched until she cleared the access and was so far away, she looked like a cloud hovering above the sand. If clouds wore two bright aqua dots for feet.

"No, I do not believe this! This can't be happening! Shit! Shit! Shit!"

He slowly turned his head so he could place the voice that was raised, irate and desperate, coming from the house next door. If he wasn't mistaken, it was Mag's sister, Kara. And she wasn't happy with something. That was evident.

He waited a few more moments to hear if there'd be more of the same. Nothing, no more tirades. He went back to work, focusing on the spreadsheets on his laptop. He had two bids on tree houses to get out today, and if he got nothing else done, he had to get those emailed out by the end of the day.

Two minutes later he heard a woman crying. Instinctively, he looked in the direction Mags had taken. Nothing but sand, sea, and people walking dogs, even though it was way after eight and they weren't supposed to be on the beach with them. He turned his head to the left in time to hear a loud sob. Sighing, he put his laptop aside and stood—stretched. Who knew what waited, he'd better be ready. He walked over to the concrete rail and looked down, angling his head to focus on the small patio garden partially hidden from view between the two houses. No one was there.

Another sob pierced the late morning silence. Several more quickly followed. The distinct sound of a woman crying full on ensued a moment later. Not a sniff, sniff, boo-hoo handkerchief campaign, but a full on sob fest. There was no ignoring it. That would be rude and disrespectful. He hadn't been raised that way. Women were to be cherished, protected, and coddled if need be. His father had taught him that. He sighed again; this time expelling a long, slow breath that bespoke a resigned reluctance to get involved in whatever drama this woman next door was on a crying jag over.

He shook his head at his often-misguided sense of chivalry, as he backed away from the railing, and grudgingly made his way down to the lower level deck, and then from there to the stairs that lead to the patio at ground level. Wary of what he might find, he snuck around the hedge and then rolled his eyes in exasperation when he saw a disheveled looking Kara sitting on the bottom wooden step, hands over her face, tears streaming down her chin.

"Whoa! Whoa, what's up buttercup? Why the crocodile tears?" It's what he'd always imagined he'd say to a little sister, if he'd had one and came upon her crying her eyes out over some stupid little nonsensical thing. It seemed appropriate here. This woman was behaving like a child. *Who cried like this, unless in private?*

Kara's shoulders tensed and she sat back on the step as her hands flew from covering her eyes to covering her mouth. "Oh! I should have thought . . . how the sound would carry. I'm sorry, I'll go inside." She untangled legs that had been tucked under her and moved to stand up, but he was there before she could turn and hightail it up the steps.

"Wait!" He grabbed her by the elbow. "Talk to me. What's got you bawling like that? What's happened? Tell me."

Tears were loosed again as her eyes went wide and she shook her head. "No, no. I'll be all right."

"Tell me," he insisted, his tone brooking no argument.

She took a deep stuttering breath. "Just a little set back, it'll be all right."

"What will be all right?"

"The wall!" she practically wailed. Then hiccupped and whispered, "The stupid fucking wall."

He laughed. He had to. *The things he had imagined, and she was upset over a wall?*

He sat her back down. Patted her shoulder. "So tell me what this 'stupid fucking wall' did to make you cry like this?"

She sobbed, snuffled like a pig, and pulled her t-shirt up to mop her face and swipe at her nose. It was not at all ladylike, he saw she had a belly ring in her navel. A dangling Hello Kitty medallion was attached to it. It seemed a bit childish for a grown woman. She snorted and he almost laughed again, but instead, curled his bottom lip in and clamped his top lip over it to stifle the snicker that was ready to erupt.

"It's got mold!" Another wail. Another loud grunt followed with a sob chasing it. The t-shirt came up again and this time he saw a paint-flecked sports bra flattening her ample breasts. "Mold! Stupid, dumbass, scum-sucking, liver-licking mold!"

He dug his teeth into his lip to keep from bursting out laughing at her pitiful expression. *What could have happened to upset her like this? Liver-licking?*

"Okay . . . the wall has mold. Is that something to cry about? Why should you care? Just call the rental company and they'll send someone to fix it."

"Noooo! No, they woooon't! They won't," she sobbed again. "We're not renting from a rental company. I know the owner. And *she's* going to be *furious!*" She started to stand.

Chaz pushed her down by her shoulders again then sat beside her on the step. "Why don't you start from the beginning?

How did you discover this mold?"

She relayed her tale between intermittent sniffles, "When I pulled the wallpaper down."

"Pulled the wallpaper down? Aren't you going to get in trouble for that? Was it that bad that you couldn't live with it for a few weeks?"

"No. No. It's my job to take down the wallpaper. And then paint." She began sobbing full force again. "There's not going to be enough time! How am I going to do all this?" Her hands swiped at the tears still cascading off her chin.

"First tell me *why* you're doing it."

"Because I agreed to. The lady who owns this house said we could stay for free as long as I did some work for her. I'm a teacher at West Montgomery High School, she's . . . she's my boss, and she's the fucking principal!"

A loud moan escaped, followed by a hiccup that turned into a sob that erupted into a hideous grunt. Chaz had to turn his head and cough to disguise his laughter at how comically ridiculous she sounded. But this was no show; nothing was being put on here. No woman would dare fake this kind of invective. The tears were real; and no woman he knew would ever want a man to see her this way. Her once beautiful face was now red and splotchy, her cheeks shiny with tears, her nose running. It was comical, really. But somehow, he knew she'd slap him if he laughed at her distress. Hard.

"She said my sister and I could use her beach house if I did some minor remodeling for her. Said her bathroom walls needed updating. She said we could stay for free if I did all the work. All I had to do was buy the paint and supply the labor. I never once thought to ask how many bathrooms there were. I assumed there'd be two. There are four of them! And each one had wallpaper I had to scrape off. Look at my hands!"

He looked down at the cuts and scrapes, the raw knuckles, the chipped nail polish, the dried paint on her forearms, and the baby finger covered completely, top to bottom, with three different colored Band-Aids.

"Now this bathroom, finally the last one, has mold behind the paper! Black and green mold!"

"Well that's hardly unusual. There's a lot of humidity at the beach. It's really not that big a problem. Just call a plumber to see if there's a leak causing it, and once that's fixed, a sheetrock man can fix the wall."

"You don't understand! I barely have enough money for the last can of paint. I can't afford to hire *anyone!*"

"How about your sister, surely she can help with this."

"No! Absolutely not!"

Her vehemence was telling. But telling him what? If it concerned Mags, he had to know.

"Won't she help out if you ask?"

"Of course she would! But we are *not* going to tell her about this. I *promised* her a vacation. I insisted that *I* would pay for everything. And I *will*. Somehow."

"You don't make sense."

"Mags deserves this time at the beach—a few weeks when she doesn't have to worry about a blessed thing. It took forever to talk her into coming. I promised her I'd take care of *everything* and I will! After all she's been through, she deserves to have a carefree vacation and *I'm* giving it to her!"

"What exactly has she been through?" He knew about her being dumped. He'd like to know the story behind it.

The remembered promises of the last few months rang through Kara's head. "N-nothing. Just a lot of bullshit that's all. The point is, I am not going to bother her with this. I'll figure something out." She stood again.

He stood with her. "Show me what you're talking about. Maybe it's not as bad as you think."

"Trust me. It's bad."

She turned and began climbing the steps. He tagged after her. "So why is it you're out of money exactly?"

"Do you have any idea what they pay teachers? I can barely make ends meet during the school year. The summers without a paycheck only compound the problem."

"So why do this? Why tell your sister you'll pay for everything when you can't afford to?"

"Because . . . because I needed to do something for her. She's always done so much for me. She took care of me when we were younger. She saw me through college, paid a lot of my bills. It's my turn. I need to do something for her for a change. And she needed this trip. She really needed this."

"Why?" He was losing patience with her and it showed.

"I can't tell you. Please don't ask again. Her helping with this is not a part of this equation. Don't make me regret sharing this with you," she said and turned back to give him the stink-eye. "I mean it!"

He put his hands out as if to push away from her. "Okay, okay. I get it. This is all on you. Let me see if I can help."

They walked into the bathroom, him following behind her and noticing that she was wearing two different kinds of sneakers—one Converse, one Reebok; both stripped of their laces and covered with blue and green paint. She sat on the closed toilet seat, her elbows resting on her knees propping her chin while he walked to the wall over the sinks that had been exposed. It was covered with black, green, and in some places, red mold. He ran his hand over the surrounding edges of the wall as he looked around the room. She began deep breathing, trying to control her emotions. It was almost worse than the crying.

He stooped and checked under the cabinets, running his hands over the interior panels toward the back for signs of moisture. He closed the cabinet doors, stood, and picked up a scraper from the counter. With a deft hand, he removed a section of the wallpaper to the right of the largest mold cluster. It was as big as his splayed hand. Once that panel was removed, he saw the same thing, at almost the same height. A third section revealed an almost identical pattern of mold. The last piece he removed on that same wall revealed clean wallboard. He scraped off the second layer and then used the spray bottle on the counter to rewet the wall. He scraped until he had a large section of both the paper and the glue removed. The wall under the far right panel was clear.

Neither had spoken the whole time he'd been peeling and scraping. She'd managed her breathing and was now rocking back and forth on the toilet seat, her arms crossed over her chest as if bracing for the worst. He broke the silence with, "Was there a mirror here?"

"Yup. It's in one of the guest bedrooms, propped up against the wall."

"Did it cover most of this wall?"

"Mmm hmm. The whole area over the sinks plus some. It's pretty big. It was a bitch getting it down."

He looked around, studying the room. "Well, that's the problem then." He walked over to the connecting door that lead to a guest bedroom and shut the door. Then he walked back and closed the bathroom door that led to the hallway. On the way back into the room, he stopped at the combination bathtub and shower, pulled the shower curtain aside, and turned the water on full force, cranking the temperature to full hot. He tugged the shower curtain back in place, then reached in and lifted the toggle on the tub faucet. The water switched from a heavy stream running into the tub to a forceful spray coming from the showerhead.

"Hey, uh, should I be worried here?" It had just occurred to her how foolish it was to let a strange man into an empty house and then walk him upstairs and into a bathroom, no less. Now he had closed both doors and turned the shower on full blast. No way anyone would hear her if she started screaming.

"Relax. I'm not going to accost you. I want to show you something. Give it a few minutes for the steam to build."

She eyed him askance and he grinned. "If there'd ever been a time that I'd wanted you naked in the shower, watching you cry would have wiped all traces of lust from my mind, trust me on that."

She sighed. "I've never been a pretty crier."

He laughed. "I'll vouch for that."

After a few minutes, he walked over to the shower and turned the water off. Steam billowed around the room leaving a haze of humidity. He walked over to where she sat and pulled her up. "Put your hand on this wall," he said, leading her to a section of the wall where there was still a large piece of the shiny foil wallpaper left. He pressed her hand flat on the wall.

"See how moist that is?"

"Yeah. So?"

"So, every time someone takes a shower they probably close both doors. Since most people usually shower behind closed doors, they would logically close the one going back to their bedroom. The connecting door leading to the other guest room would likely already be closed.

"As steam built, condensation would have gathered behind the mirror and got trapped. Being an interior room, with no window, and most people not bothering to use the fan while showering, there would be no way for the paper to dry out. So the water sits on it, eventually soaking through the barrier to the glue, and mold finds a happy campground. Old wallpaper glue is food to fungus and mildew, so the mold continues to grow, and each successive shower compounds the problem by adding even more moisture and inviting more molds to the party. Until . . ." he gestured with one hand to the affected wall.

"Chances are this is the only place that has any mold. It's a simple matter to fix. We call a sheetrock man, he comes in, cuts out the bad places and installs new sheetrock where it's needed. You prime the wall with Kilz or some other mold resistance sealant, then paint. No big deal."

"It's a very big deal. I don't have the money for a sheetrock man. You're talking hundreds of dollars."

"Probably five or six hundred. With my connections,

maybe three-fifty plus $30 for the primer."

"Your connections aside, that's not going to work. I have $114 in cash, $165 in my checking account, and just enough credit on my charge card to get enough gas to get us home at the end of the week."

"I'll pay for it."

"I can't let you do that. No way."

"I want to help out. And I certainly don't want to hear you crying any more. It's worth it to me. I'm more than happy to pay to have the work done."

"No. I can't let you do that."

"Okay, how's this? I have a friend who owes me a favor. He's an expert at this kind of thing."

"He's local?"

"He'd love a weekend at the beach."

"And he'd do this for you? Drop everything and come to the beach?"

"Oh yeah. He'd do this and more. He owes me big time."

"And you wouldn't have to pay him?"

"Not a dime."

"How much would the materials be?"

"$114. Coincidentally, the exact amount you have in cash."

"Seriously. How much would the sheetrock and the primer cost?"

"Seriously? $100 for the sheetrock, including delivery— it should take two sheets at most—$50 for some tape and a little mud, and $15 for the primer. You only need to seal this wall so you can get by with a quart. So say, $165."

"Coincidentally, the exact amount I have in my checking account," she mimicked. "Are you're sure you don't mind doing this?"

"If it will make you stop crying, I definitely do not mind."

"Deal," she said and she thrust her hand out.

"Deal," he said, shaking it firmly.

"But you can't tell Mags that I was crying. Or that I roped you into doing this."

"You didn't. I offered. It's win-win. You get some help with this project so you can get your boss off your back, and I get to see my friend."

"So who is this friend and where is he?"

"His name is Ryder and he lives in Nashville."

"Nashville! Tennessee?"

"Is there another?"

"Yeah, there's a Nashville in North Carolina."

"Never knew that. But he's from Tennessee."

"That's ten hours away! He's not going to come here for this!"

"Oh yeah he will."

"What the hell kind of favor does he owe you for?"

"I slept with his fiancé."

"You what!"

"Long story. Suffice it to say that I kept him from making the biggest mistake of his life."

"One night, when we're celebrating me finishing up these friggin' bathrooms, you're going to have to tell me the whole story."

"Tell me why Mags deserves you bankrupting yourself for this vacation and I'll tell you now."

She shook her head. "No can do. Sisters stick together. It's her secret. If she wants you to know, she'll tell you.

"Suit yourself. I'll go make some calls."

"Wait. I'll go get you the money."

"I think I can trust you for it."

"You're not paying. I'll get you the money." The steel in her voice surprised him. He watched her as she opened the door and strode down the hall.

He smiled. He respected her. She had integrity. And she certainly cared about her big sister. It was nice. Both Kara and Mags were turning out to be the best part of this trip. They were genuine. Quirky, but real down to earth people. He felt as if he'd known them for more than just a few days.

Kara came back and shoved $114 in loose bills and change into his hands along with a check made out to cash for $51, then stood on tiptoes to kiss him on his cheek. "Thank you," she whispered.

"You're welcome."

"Don't forget our bargain. Mags can't know how upset I was."

"Well if you don't want her to know, you'd better go find an icepack. Your eyes are as red as cherries and your face is puffy as all get out."

"Thanks."

"Don't mention It.'

Chapter 60—Chaz
Calling in a Marker

Chaz made the final adjustments to the proposals for the two Treetop tiny homes and emailed them to his clients. Then he called Ryder to tell him he was calling in his marker for the huge favor he'd done for him the night before his wedding.

"I'll load up my truck and be there by morning. You got a room for me in that big mansion of yours or should I book a room at the inn?"

"Heck yeah, we've got plenty of room. Just pack a bag of clothes; we've got everything else. The guys'll be thrilled to see you."

"I could use a little down time. Gotta be back by Tuesday next though. Got a court date."

"Oh?"

"Yeah. Can you believe it? That bitch's parents are still trying to get me to pay for the wedding that didn't happen."

"I hate that you've got the evidence to prove you're the injured party."

"Courtesy of yours truly . . ." Ryder snickered.

"That was not part of the deal. I didn't agree to that video going public. Is that tape ever going to be destroyed as we agreed?" Chaz couldn't keep the heat out of his voice.

"Yeah yeah . . . as soon as I get all this legal wrangling over with. But I don't know why you'd be upset about it. It shows you to the best advantage. A lot of men would love to have a sex video showing them off to such a *large* advantage."

"I only agreed to taping it so you'd have irrefutable proof of her infidelity."

"Oh boy and do I ever. Did you have to make her come three times though? You made me look a tad bit bad in comparison, you know."

"You gave me a job to do, now you're dissing me for doing my best to see it done right?"

"You made me look bad bro, three fucking orgasms?"

"Well, to be technical, they weren't all from fucking."

Ryder laughed. "At least I know I hired the right man for the job. Can you believe it, she actually tried to get your number from me."

"She never even got my name before we went back to my hotel room."

"Yeah," Ryder said wistfully. "It's sad that I almost married her."

"Yeah. Sorry about that."

"Don't be. You did what was necessary. The right woman will come along. I truly believe that."

"Well do me a favor and get someone else to do the honor of proving her virtue next time."

"Look, you know I wouldn't have done it if it weren't for all the innuendos and snickers I got each time I came back to town. It was as if the line of men interested in bedding her graciously moved back to the wings and waited until it was time for me to leave town again. I could almost *feel* her being unfaithful while I was away."

"Don't beat yourself over the head about it. If she'd loved you, she wouldn't have entertained all those men. This is on her, not you."

"Yeah. Yeah. But gosh darn, Chaz. I was so ready to be married, to settle down and have a whole passel of kids."

"You saying I did too good a job? Maybe I shouldn't have tried so hard to steer her astray?"

"I heard the tape, Chaz. You didn't try all that hard. You said: 'I've got a suite at the Lincoln, I can be eating you out in ten minutes, and let me tell you, my tongue is as trained as they *come*. Which, coincidentally, will be the operating word of the night.'"

"You memorized that line?"

"Best one I've ever heard. And sadly, I can attest to the fact that it works."

"Sorry Bro. But you hired me for the job . . ."

"And you did it well, my friend. Now . . . for the payback. Tell me about this schoolteacher and how imperative it is that I not make her cry. Ever."

"She's pretty intense. Determined to get this done without telling her sister how much she's going into the hole for it. Haven't got them figured out yet, but it's pretty obvious they are devoted to each other. It's nice to see."

"Well, I'll be glad to help out. I'll be on the road in twenty. Make up a bed for me."

"Done. The door will be open. Top of the stairs, third door down. Hemingway Room. I'll put some Jack Black on the nightstand."

"I don't deserve a friend like you."

Chaz laughed. They had the strangest relationship. No one would ever believe the off-the-wall things they did for each other. If he'd had a brother, Ryder would have been perfect for the role.

Chapter 61—Kyle
Let the Games Begin

Kyle put the finishing touches on the last of the appetizers he made for Chaz. He'd had to take a drive to Boulineau's in Cherry Grove to get the beef for the filet mignon sandwiches. One couldn't find better shrimp for the mini-Thai skewers than those in the fresh case at Bill's Seafood though.

Chaz hadn't been able to provide any information as to what this date he was drooling over liked to eat, so he'd made eight different tasting selections—including tiny double-decker sandwiches made with braised beef, curried lobster, tamarind shrimp, rosemary chicken, sausage en croute, and roasted root vegetables with a garlic lentil paté, in the event she was vegan or vegetarian. If a man as virile and good-looking as Chaz couldn't get into a woman's panties with these, he thought as he packaged the bundles up, he needed to play for the other side.

He laughed out loud at the thought of Chaz and Cam as a couple while he deftly sorted the evening's samples of gastronomic seduction into an insulated cooler. He had made enough to fill a plate for himself, and those he hid in the convection oven. No one else knew how to use it, so he knew they'd be safe for an hour or more. There was a golf tournament on cable TV coming on in a few minutes. What better way to enjoy it than with a few ice-cold long necks and the first-class snacks he'd spent three hours whipping up after he'd beaten Chaz at golf this morning. Life was good.

The doorbell rang just as he tucked the last wrapped parcel into the soft cooler he'd bought at the Island Market for Chaz to use. Hearing no one on either level making a move to answer it, he ran down the stairs to answer the summons, stopping just short of the landing when he glanced through the etched side light and caught sight of the woman waiting on the other side of the door.

Whoa! Who was this pretty lady? She was wearing a skimpy white sundress tied to her shoulders with tiny strings. She had a nice tan and piles of auburn hair gathered into a high ponytail on top of her head. Her hands were behind her back as she sashayed back and forth, shifting her weight from one foot to the other, causing the puffed bell of her dress to swing and showcase her slim hips as she waited for someone to come to the door.

He envisioned her smiling shyly and presenting a bag of fragrant cinnamon crullers, a bottle of something pink and bubbly, or just a single perfect rose. He wondered which of the guys she was here to see. Which one of the lucky bastards playing cards in the game room was going to get her sweet offerings?

He opened the door with a big smile on his face. And ducked when he saw the gun, but not in time to avoid the blast from a water soaker set on automatic. A few seconds later, he heard the click of the trigger being released and the woman whispering, "Aw shit."

He mopped his face with the dishtowel he'd had tucked into the apron on his hip and cursed in four languages. The woman's startling blue eyes opened wide and she took two big steps backward. The look in her eyes as she backed away conveyed confusion. Then panic. She turned to run. But he was too quick for her. As she spun to the steps, he caught her by the elbow and hauled her into his wet chest. Water dripped from his hair to her cheek, then down her neck and into the vee of her cleavage. He looked down at her, following its path until it disappeared between the swells of exceptional breasts. He showed her his teeth as he growled, "What the hell lady?"

"I'm at the wrong house! I'm sorry! I'm sorry!"

"That's not going to cut it." He reached behind her where

she'd shoved the gun, jerked the soaker from her hand, aimed it at her breasts and pressed the automatic trigger.

He allowed the grin he'd answered the door with to return as she shrieked. He watched her breasts come into full view through the thin cotton of the camisole-styled top of her dress. She wasn't wearing a bra. A wet t-shirt couldn't have shown her off to better advantage.

"Nice," he murmured. "Very, very nice."

"Stop it you moron!"

"Not a chance." He emptied the gun onto her chest while she tried to get a grip on his arm and knock it away.

When it was empty, he released her and stood back to admire his handiwork.

"Look what you've done!" she cried out as she stood on the front portico, looking down at herself. Her skimpy dress clung to her in all the right places.

"How am I supposed to go back to the party like this?" she hissed. Hopping mad, eyes ablaze, and frenzied rage in her voice, she clenched her fists at her side and shook while she let out a scream of anguish. It caused her breasts to jiggle. His eyelids couldn't open wider. His famously expressive brows arched to meet the shock of hair on his forehead that was dripping water down his nose.

When she saw where he was staring, she clamped her mouth shut and shivered with rage. She tried to cover herself with her hands. "Ohhh, you, you . . . you oaf! Look at me!"

"Trust me I am."

"No! I mean, look, I'm soaked!" The venom in her voice directed to him was comical. She was what, all of five feet, he was six-eight.

"Yeah, I know the feeling." As if to emphasize it, he bent and shook his mop of wet hair at her. Heavy drops pelting her in the face.

"Stop it!" she yelled. She grabbed the towel from his hand and used it to blot her chest, sending her tits quivering all over again.

"You're killing me here," he said, his eyes never leaving the softly mounded flesh under the soaked cotton. By patting her chest with the towel, she had only emphasized the nipples, now peaked and straining against the material. He couldn't tell the color exactly, but certainly rosy or dusky pink, not brown.

"Ohhh!" she griped, her voice shrill, exasperation evident by the way she tossed the towel back at him. "Get a wife! I mean life!"

"I liked it better the first way. Are you available?"

She growled at him, grabbed her gun back and stomped down the stairs.

He stepped outside. "I don't know where you're heading, but every person you pass is going to get a really nice show. How 'bout you come inside and we dry you off?"

He watched as her head ducked down and she stared at the front of her dress. In the bright sunshine her whole front was see-through, all the way down to her waist and then some. He could make out her tiny panties, also white. And where they were wet, he could see an auburn shadow. The wet material was sucked in at the apex of her thighs.

She spun away and faced the street. Her back was just as lovely as the front, tanned and smooth all the way down to where her dress dipped in to just above her sweet little ass. The legs were killer too in high platform sandals. The sound of a car coming had her facing back to him, one hand shielding her breasts, the other using the bulk of the gun to try to hide what was behind the tiny scrap of cotton at her crotch.

"Yeah okay," she mumbled, "you got a blow dryer?"

"Several I'm sure. C'mon in and I'll get one."

"I don't even know you." Yet she stalked back up the steps and walked into the house under his welcoming arm, one hand and forearm covering her breasts. Well almost. Part of a nipple showed between her splayed fingers. He almost fell to his knees.

"Yet you tried to *off* me," he said.

"It was a game! I was given this address, 1250 right? And a task to complete by the game master; you're supposed to be someone in the wedding party."

He closed the door and led the way up the stairs to the second level. "Hmmm. Plausible. Numbers here on Main Street usually have an east and west designation. This is 1250 *East* Main. On a south-facing beach it can be confusing. Get up here and I'll introduce myself."

She dropped her water gun on the thatched welcome mat and stomped up the stairs.

When she got to the top he offered his hand. "Kyle Keir Merritt, World-renowned chef. Maybe you've dined in one of my restaurants? Bought one of my cookbooks?"

"Not going to work Kyle, not moving my hands."

"And you are?"

"Amy Anderson. Bridesmaid. Perpetual. I mean lately, it's like a freaking career."

He laughed. "I'm very familiar with weddings."

"Oh, get married a lot?" she asked as he led her over to the utility room and held the door open for her.

She dropped her arms to maneuver under him, as it didn't appear he was going to take his hand off the top of the door. From his vantage point, he was able to look down and see not only the outline of her full breasts, but her flat tummy, and the dress still clinging to her mound, now beginning to deepen the contrast of dark pubic hair to see-thru cotton. If he hadn't been leaning against the doorjamb he would have fallen to the floor. It took him a few seconds to recover.

"Er . . . no. But my career is helping people get married. I do at least one celebrity wedding a month—I do the food."

She turned back to him and hand patted the area below her throat, "God help you. You're a saint."

"Flash me those tits one more time and I'll prove you wrong."

Her hands flew to cup her breasts and she spun to face four laundry machines, two washers and two dryers.

"Geez, is this a hotel?"

"Nah, just a big house. Take off your dress and throw it in one of the dryers. There are bath sheets on a shelf in that cabinet. Help yourself to one to use to cover yourself while your dress dries. Or if you'd rather, there's a powder room right down there," he said as he pointed down a short hallway. "There are towels under the cabinet there too, help yourself. Or I'll go upstairs to get you a hair dryer if you'd rather. And uh . . . a robe."

"A robe would be swell," she said as she turned and opted for the powder room instead of the utility room to change in. She went down the hall, squeaking in her platform shoes and leaving a wet trail on the wood parquet floor.

He stared, mesmerized by her hips. She was shimmying, and using her hands to keep the wet dress from inching up and gathering between her ass cheeks. She was not successful. Both cheeks were defined as firm, round, and high. She reached behind her and pulled the material away from her skin, inadvertently showing him the backs of her thighs just below where they joined to her ass.

He shook his head and whispered, "Mercy."

She slammed the bathroom door.

He waited for it.

Chapter 62—Kyle
Gumdrop

"Yikes!" she screamed. "What the—"

"It's just a mural," he called out. "There's not really a leopard ready to pounce in there."

"We're even. My heart just did penance for soaking you." Then with a low voice full of awe, "Gosh, this is amazing. It's so real looking."

"Yeah, we get that all the time."

Dev leaned over the railing, one floor up, on the breezeway. Kyle could make out his raised brow and quirked lips. "Did I hear a female scream?"

Kyle put his hands on his hips and looked up at his friend. "Yeeesss. Yes, you did. Leo the leopard . . ."

"Ah." No explanation was needed. Every female, and some males too, got the shock of their lives on their way to peeing. Some never made it to the seat.

Chaz and Palo joined Dev on the landing, both coming from their rooms with wet hair and bath towels held up by a hand on their hip. A navy blue towel from the nautical bathroom hung low on Chaz' as it caught runnels of water that dripped from the dense mat of chest hair, while a Stewart plaid wrapped Palo's torso and clashed with the paisley one slung around his neck. He used the end of it to swipe at a line of shaving cream on his jaw.

Dev's quizzical expression intensified. "And?"

Kyle started up the stairs, "And she's using the jungle bathroom while I hunt down a blow dryer and robe."

"Sounds interesting. Who is she and what did you do, forget to lock the top on the blender again?"

"No. She's on a scavenger hunt of sorts. She came to the wrong house with a loaded water gun. I turned it back on her. You ought to see the dress she's wearing, it's plastered to her . . ." Kyle motioned with his hand waving across his chest.

"Boobs?"

"And butt. Pretty spectacular."

Just then the bathroom door on the ground floor opened and a voice called out, "Yo, Rambo! That robe? Naked and wet here. With the AC blowing like a turbine in here, I've got frozen gumdrops for nipples."

Kyle gasped, imagining the sight, while the three at the top moved to a better vantage point along the rail, and tried to angle their bodies to see the source of the voice and with any luck, those gumdrops.

"Chaz, toss my robe down, will ya? It's on the back of my bathroom door. Palo, can I use your blow dryer?" Both men sighed and turned back from the landing to do his bidding. Dev dropped a striped beach towel he'd been holding. "Here, we can't have frozen gumdrops now, can we?"

"Thanks," Kyle muttered as he caught first the towel, then the robe, and then the toiletry kit that held the blow dryer.

Kyle walked back to the bathroom that housed the little spitfire with the auburn hair—top and bottom. Amy was poking her damp head out the door opening. He could see she had one of the jungle print hand towels covering her chest. He tried to angle himself to see her reflection in the mirror but to no avail, she was hugging the door too close to the jamb. He got hard just thinking of the view he'd have if the angle were just right and she was bent over trying to keep her lower half out of sight.

"Here you go, Gumdrop. Towel, robe, blow dryer. Give me your dress and I'll throw it in the dryer. It'll be faster that way."

"Don't call me Gumdrop."

"After that comment, you have little chance of anybody in this house calling you anything but."

She tossed out the wad that was her dress. It landed with a splat on the wood floor. Kyle raised a brow at her insolence and bent to pick it up. The robe was snatched up and the door clicked shut. A few moments later it opened again with her cocooned in his plush bathrobe. The belt was double knotted. He knew then that he would never wash it again.

"What setting?" he asked, hefting the wet blob in his large hand.

She let out a long sigh. "I don't know your settings, let me do it."

He led her back to the kitchen the long way, trying to avoid her being under all his friends who were now clustered at the rails on the upper floors. They skirted the living room, the gathering area, and the formal dining area, then came back around to the kitchen through the other side. He led her past the center island to the area behind the triple-sized pantry

Along the way, she took in the high crowned ceilings, the Mediterranean archways, the tiled and inlaid wood floors and the massive furnishings. This was not a dainty beach cottage. And from the looks of it, a woman hadn't had a say in any of the furnishings. Everything was bold, stylized, serviceable, high tech and expensive. There was an oversized cream-colored leather sofa with four matching Stressless chairs, along with ottomans semi-circled around a huge flat screen TV that took up the center of one gigantic wall. In the middle of an open floor plan, the entertainment area dominated the first floor. From that grouping, you could look up and see doors to rooms on the next two levels that branched off in all directions. The house was spectacular, she thought, like walking into a *Southern Living* magazine. She wasn't paying attention and bumped into the back of Kyle. He had stopped, she had not, and now she was practically climbing his back at the abrupt halt as she stumbled into him.

"Whoa," Kyle said as he spun back to her. He had just tossed her dress in the laundry tub so his big hands were free to catch her under her arms. He used the momentum to continue the turn and lifted her like she was weightless onto the folding counter next to the ultra modern laundry machines. Her feet dangled over the edge and the robe opened to reveal bare legs and smooth inner thighs before she managed to pull her legs together and close the robe.

"You okay?" he asked.

Embarrassed to be caught unaware due to her ogling the house, she just nodded.

He picked up the wet dress up from the laundry tub, shook it and squeezed the excess water out, and then stepped in front of the washer and dropped it in. "Normal, Regular, Permanent Press, Delicates, Hand Washables, Super Wash," he read.

"We don't need to wash it."

"Oh." He took the dress out and stepped in front of the other machine. "Casual, Delicate, Quick Dry, Timed Dry, Bulky, Heavy Duty, Sanitize, Steam Refresh," he read.

"I don't know. It's new. Let me read the label." She reached for the dress, brushing her fingers against his. Warm, capable, nice long fingers, with a dusting of light hair on the knuckles, and immaculately clean nails, he had capable-looking hands. She could envision them kneading dough, among other things. She fumbled as she searched for the inseam label. "95% Polyester, 5% Spandex. Machine wash cold, Line Dry. Cool Iron."

"Hmm. Not supposed to have clothes drying over the balconies, but I'll chance the wrath of the powers that be if that's our only option."

She smiled. "I'm sure delicate will do just fine. Here, let me wring some more water out first so I won't have to be here all day." She wiggled her bottom trying to get to the edge of the countertop so she could hop down. He got there before she could. With his hands at her waist, he effortlessly lifted her to the floor, then stared down at her. Without her platform heels he was easily a foot and a half taller, making it hard to look into her eyes. He reached out and tilted her chin up, his hand cupping her cheek and jaw. He felt her whole body shudder. She swallowed. Audibly.

"If you had to be here all day, would that be so bad?" he asked just before his lips descended and captured hers. More like claimed. Possessed. Mated. His lips were soon busy doing all of those things.

"Ohhh, Gumdrop," he murmured as his tongue learned the slick softness on the inside seam of her lips, "I'm going to need to do this for a while."

Chapter 63—Kyle
Always a Bridesmaid

He'd kissed more than his fair share of women—on every continent. And he'd kissed them in a variety of ways—under exotic waterfalls, up against centuries-old wine casks in beautiful vineyards; on top of butcher blocks while slathering rich, creamy ganache over pouty lips, and once, in a moment of insanity, while skydiving in a blizzard in Switzerland. Until now, the kiss between bites of pomme frites drizzled with truffle oil and sprinkled with freshly grated Parmesan Reggiano cheese, and lips coated with a garlic-infused olive oil, had been his favorite. What an amazing kiss that had been. But then, after the fact, he thought he should credit the perfectly cooked fries for most of it.

But this kiss? He'd never kissed a woman like this. Like it was something celestial. Monumental. It was the lightning bolt of kisses despite being soft . . . slow . . . and tasting of . . . *what was that, grape bubble gum?* He had to smile between forays into her silky depths. Had she swallowed her gum just before he kissed her? He had never smiled mid-kiss. She read his thoughts. Her lips bowed into her own smile and he felt her tiny giggle bubble up and out. They shared the absurdity with foreheads touching, and then got right back to kissing, sharing the feast of dueling tongues and lingering lips.

Fearing separation, when he was nowhere near ready for that, he gripped the back of her neck and pulled her close, then anchored her to him by using his teeth to tug on her bottom lip to bring her even closer. Tonguing her with reckless abandon he followed the tang of grape. He heard her moan and felt her grip his shoulders, and immediately sensed her desire to climb up his body and wrap her quivering legs around his hips. He bent and wrapped his hand around the outside of her thigh to lift her. He needed to feel the heat of her core mated to his. Now.

Amy was a goner. It was as if kissing him was all that mattered in that moment. The rest of the universe be damned. His tongue made another lap, flicking on her smooth inner lip and then he used his teeth to suck her bottom lip into his mouth. It was as if he couldn't live another second without her taste as his possession. She had never been kissed with so much devotion, so much ardor, so much . . . *damn his tongue. It had talent. And he had a gift for possessive thrusts, parries, and flicks.* It had taken her a moment to register that he was actually tasting her, savoring the nuance of her mouth. The thrill that what he had found on her tongue pleased him, that it was enough so that he wanted a return pass before choosing to devour her, was heady. This was a swoon worthy kiss. She hadn't had all that many tongue on tongue kisses, but she knew there was never going to be one better than this one. Simply not possible.

She giggled when she remembered how she had just managed to swallow her gum before his mouth had descended and his tongue had swept inside. She felt his mouth smile against hers. He sighed deeply and pressed his forehead to hers, then bent and took her mouth again.

She moaned as she felt every part of him that touched her body harden. His already hard body became encased, as if he had suddenly been dipped in steel and was now wearing a suit of armor. She had never felt so overwhelmed by a man. His hand came down to grip the back of her thigh and lift it. With little effort he had his center pressed to hers. Holy cow.

He was sure he was harder than he had ever been. With her thigh raised he was nudging her core. A hand on her lower back brought her closer and splayed her hips even more. Where they were connected he could feel the flat of her stomach graze the thick head of his penis. The base was pressed to her pelvis. He groaned. He desperately needed more contact, of the lascivious type.

"You kiss . . . like nobody's business," she said, taking a deep steadying breath. "That was wild."

"I'd like another, if you don't mind." His hand cupped her cheek and he dipped his head to mesh their lips from a different angle. This time, he was the one who emitted a low, erotically charged moan. Soft nips ending the kiss made her gasp.

"I could do this all day and never tire of it," he whispered as he pressed his erection into her.

With a hand on his chest, she pushed away from him, "Wanna go to a wedding?"

If she had punched him with the hand she held to his chest he couldn't have been more surprised. He blinked and stared at her as he worked to regain his composure. She had the prettiest eyes, all blue and sparkling, he could almost see the madcap mischief they held inside. He grinned down at her, he couldn't help it. "Ours?" he managed to ask as he leaned in and kissed her on the nose, then on each eyelid, on her temple, working his way toward her ear.

"No silly. Jessie Mae's and Donnie Lee's."

"Will you be there and will there be cake?"

"I have to be there. I'm a bridesmaid. And unless I can come up with a date, Jessie Mae says she's got one lined up for me. I suspect it's her cousin Jedidiah; his wife ran away and left him last year. And yes, there will be several cakes, I know 'cause I made 'em."

"But you'd rather take *me* than end up with Jedidiah?" he asked, shifting her in his arms so he could kiss along her neck. "God, I love cake."

Her moan was equal parts wanton and regretful. "Yeah. No brainer there. You've got your own teeth, your own hair," she reached up and pulled on a hank of his chestnut mane, "and I imagine your own . . ." she gave a bump with her hip, thrusting her pelvis against his erection, " . . . unadorned male part."

He fought back a groan at the contact. Almost missing her run on rambling.

"Last date she fixed me up with had four teeth missing, wore a toupee that was taped on backward, and talked all night about the pump in his pocket that he guaranteed would pump him up to whatever size I would take delight in. Did I mention there will also be a groom's cake?"

With his hands on her shoulders, he held her away from him so he could get some relief and to see if she was making this up. When he saw that she wasn't he laughed out loud.

"Sweetheart, I can assure you I have teeth that can tear a filet mignon to shreds, hair that will withstand any amount of tugging in the moment of passion, and as for my male part," he hip bumped her back. "I've never had a complaint. Your satisfaction is guaranteed, no pump required."

"Words every woman wants to hear. But are they true?"

"I can provide references." He took her hand and placed it flat on his erection. "And hard proof."

"Yikes! I'm pretty sure I don't have the accommodations for that."

"Trust me, it's one size fits all. And after I lick and suck on you for a blissful eternity, we'll do just fine."

Her knees went weak and she had just about melted into his arms again when they were both startled by footsteps in the hall. Amy looked around Kyle's arm to see a tall, rakish man leaning on the doorframe with a raised brow and a huge knowing smile on his face.

"I hate to break this up Kyle, but it's . . . date time. You got the goods ready for me? I don't want to be late. I'm in agony trying to impress this woman."

"Yeah. I know the feeling," Kyle muttered, his reluctance to separate himself from Amy evident.

"I don't think you do, bro. Your girl's already got her hand on your dick, while I'm just hoping for a good night kiss. So a little help here if you don't mind?"

Kyle took a long steadying breath and pulled Amy's hand away from the bulge in his trousers. His cock was acting as a magnet, jumping and trying to draw the warmth of her hand back. He took a steadying breath and held her hand under his on his chest.

"It's all ready packed and in that carrier on the counter for you. And it's bullet proof. If you can't impress her with that, you need to date Cam," Kyle said, without taking his eyes off of Amy's.

"I owe you one. Sorry to interrupt. I'm Chaz by the way."

"Nice to meet you. Good luck on your date."

"Thanks Gumdrop."

When it was clear from the sounds that Chaz had grabbed the cooler and vacated the kitchen, Kyle placed Amy's hand back on his erection. "Now, about this wedding, that apparently, is not ours?"

"No. Not ours," she whispered. She tried to remove her hand but he held it firmly in place. "But they will have cake. And I'm all for finding out if you slow dance better than Jedidiah."

"A challenge I can rise to. Meanwhile, delicate?"

"Delicate?" she asked, confused.

"The cycle, for your dress."

"Ah yes. Delicate."

"And about the cakes . . . you said you made them?"

"Yes . . ."

"So as any good baker knows to do, you brought *extra* icing?"

"Sure. In a pastry bag . . . with a # 4 tip, ready and waiting to decorate . . . well, anything that needs touching up."

He groaned.

"I also have a #16 star tip I can switch out, to quickly cover any *large* surface that needs icing—" she wasn't able to finish.

He groaned as if in pain, pulled her hard against his chest and kissed her senseless.

When he lifted his face from hers, she looked up at him, her eyes dazed and unable to focus.

He stared down at her, taking in the sight of her. Wide eyes in a pixie face, she was a little sprite dwarfed by his huge robe. She amused him in so many ways.

"My dress?" she reminded him.

"Mmm, what about it?"

"We need to dry it . . ."

"Yes, yes we do," he said as he moved away and picked up the dress. He put it in the machine and set the control to Delicate, and turned the machine on. Then he took her hand and led her into the kitchen and over to the island counter to a bar stool. He lifted her onto it.

"Woman, I don't think I will ever walk into a laundry room again without going instantly hard. I'm sure that just seeing a box of *Tide* will trigger profound memories from this day forward."

"So," she whispered, fingering the lapel of his robe and brushing it against her smooth cheek. "Will you come?"

He grinned and his eyes crinkled at the corners, "Only after you do."

"I mean to the wedding," she huffed.

"Oh. Well, you said there'd be cake, right?"

"Yes," she said with a tiny, endearing smile. "There will be cake."

"And you'll be there . . . with icing at the ready?"

"Maybe . . . we'll have to see how it goes . . . food play is a pretty big commitment for a first date."

"Yeah, but this is a wedding. A first date that's a wedding counts for three, maybe four regular dates."

She laughed. "Come to the wedding, eat food you don't have to fix. Even if it's not up to your caliber," she said, waving her hand over her head and indicating the vast gourmet kitchen and the loaded shelves beyond the double pantry doors. "Dance with me, eat cake, and let's see what happens."

"Sounds like a plan. Except I don't have a suit or a sports coat here. I'll have to run over to Belks before they close."

She laughed. "This is a beach wedding. All you need is Dockers or linen shorts, loafers without socks, and a tropical Hawaiian shirt. You don't even have to tuck it in . . . " she reached down and ran her fingernail along his zipper, "or wear a belt."

He groaned again and pulled her close. "It's going to take some time for that dress to dry . . . "

"Yeah. So why don't you offer me a drink? We can get to know each other while my dress dries and I'll call my friend and let her know I haven't run off. She's already lost two bridesmaids, so she's a bit antsy."

"Sounds like a story I should've heard before agreeing to go to this wedding."

She smiled up at him, "Too late. You agreed. Now how about a cocktail? Any chance you can you make a Sunset Beach? I had one when I got here yesterday and instantly got addicted."

"Only the best you've ever had. I serve them at my restaurant in Charleston—calls for coconut rum, Chambord, orange, pineapple, and cranberry juice, grenadine, and shaved ice. I have a raspberry coulis on ice that I can float on top that will make it exceptional. You just sit there and watch while I perform my magic."

"I was kind of hoping you would save that for after the wedding," she whispered, using a put on Jessica Rabbit voice.

"Don't worry, there's no end to my magical abilities," Kyle said, hands on hips, in a voice so deep the image of Buzz Lightyear popped into her head. They both laughed at their comic mimicry as three masculine snorts sounded from the doorway. Both Amy and Kyle turned and looked at the source.

Kyle grinned, "Gumdrop, meet my ugly uncouth roommates . . . Dev, Palo, and Brent. Guys, this woman shot me when I opened the door. I had no choice; I had to turn the gun back on her. And then, I had to make her take off her wet dress. Now I'm going to force-feed her some drinks and have my way with her."

"No having your way with me before the wedding," she deadpanned.

"Wedding?" all the three men parroted.

"Yeah. On the beach. Tomorrow night. Neither of us can wait. I'm a sucker for romance, and apparently, he's a sucker for cake."

"Uh, wedding, Bro?" Dev asked as Kyle opened the Sub Zero and took out all the fruit juices, then walked over to the counter and plucked up the bottle of Captain Morgan's rum. He rummaged in the cabinet for tall tumblers as he nodded.

"Yeah, I'm gonna go to a wedding where I don't have to cook. Gonna dance with a beautiful bridesmaid, and beat up a guy named Jedidiah if he gets near my girl . . . or my cake."

"So you guys are going to have to fend for yourselves tomorrow night, I'll be eating out." He gave her a look and raised a brow that put special emphasis on that last statement. He thought it was sweet that she flushed from the neck up.

"No problem, Bud. We all know how to use the grill," Brent said as he watched Kyle dump stuff into the triple-sized commercial blender. He sized up Amy and winked at her, "I have to say, she looks a ton better in your robe than you do."

He extended his hand, "Nice to meet you, Gumdrop. Take care of our boy here, but no more gunfights, okay."

He looked over at Kyle, "And you, you work out your problems with your inside voice, no aggression. Okay kids? Play nice."

Dev brought the gun in from the front porch and began refilling it. "Think I can sneak up on Chaz and Mags with this?"

Amy laughed. "I don't think I'd advise it. He seemed pretty nervous about this date."

"Yeah. This'll be a great way to get over those first few awkward moments. Nothing says hero and protector more than a man willing to step in the way of a soaking stream of water."

"Don't do it," Kyle warned, his voice low. "I think Chaz is serious about this girl. And I don't want your ruining my appetizers."

"Why do you say that?" Brent asked.

"He spent the first night here staying up and reading a whole book just to impress her. Remember, he left the strip club early to come home to read? Who does that?"

"You know, we lost Cam that night too. Anybody heard from him today?" asked Brent.

"Yeah. He texted me. Some business in Wilmington came up. Said he'd be back in a day or two and not to drink all his Scotch."

The doorbell rang, then a man hollered as he stepped into the house. "Anybody home?"

"In here. That would be Ryder," Kyle said. "Another reason I think Chaz is serious about this woman. He had Ryder drive all the way from Nashville to fix some dry wall for this woman's sister. Two measly pieces of sheetrock. He could have had it delivered and done it himself in less than an hour, but no . . . extenuating circumstances he said. So instead, Ryder drives for ten hours. Somethin's up there." Palo nodded agreement and turned to Kyle. "When's the last time he asked you for your help with gastronomical warfare?"

"Mmmm. Never."

"So he must have a campaign going here. Just what are you making Kyle? You are using every ingredient in the house," said Palo.

"Sunset Beaches. For Amy. While her dress dries."

Palo laughed. "Sounds like you've got some kind of impressive campaign going on yourself."

Kyle blushed while Amy laughed. "Don't worry fellas. I don't impress easily. It's going to take more than a handsome man with a great smile and a few zing worthy kisses to take me down," she said as she sipped on the straw stuck in the orangey-pink drink Kyle handed her. "Mmmmm. Wow. Okay, count me impressed." To Kyle, she lifted and pointed to the dripping straw, "I wish my hair was longer so you could club me on the head and drag me to your cave by my ponytail."

He smiled over at her. "Your hair is long enough," he

said as he refilled her glass. The doorbell chimed again.

Palo went to answer it and came back with not only Ryder, but six other people.

"Some friends of yours Amy, wondering why it took so long for you to take down your target."

Behind Ryder were four women and two men, all carrying empty soakers. Amy jumped off the bar stool, clearly anxious at their arrival.

"Uh, hi guys. I got lost. Found the wrong house. Something about getting east and west confused. Mmmm this is Kyle, and Dev, and Palo. Dev's the one refilling my gun."

"What happened to your clothes?" one of the guys asked. "Weren't you wearing a dress?"

"It got wet. It's in the dryer. But it's probably dry by now, I'll go change."

"You guys want a drink? I just made a batch of Sunset Beaches," Kyle offered, raising a tumbler he'd just filled.

"No!" Amy said a bit too loud and forceful. "I mean, we can't. We have to go back to the party. Don't we Jedidiah?"

"Uh yeah," he said, clearly confused but obviously happy to go along with anything she said.

"I'll just be a minute. You guys wait outside."

"That's not necessary," Kyle began.

"Yeah, it is," Amy said, pointing her finger emphatically with it thrust toward the front door. "Out, I'll be there in a minute." There was no mistaking the tone or the commanding look in her eyes as she ordered her friends to wait out on the porch.

As soon as she was sure they were on their way to the door, albeit grumbling as they went, she spun and ran for the laundry room. Once there she slammed the door. You could hear the dryer door open and close. A minute later Amy came out with the robe over her arm. "Thanks for the loan of your robe. And the drink. It was great, the best . . . like you said, magical."

Kyle grabbed her by the forearms as she spun to leave,

"Wait, what's your hurry?"

"It's rude to duck out on the party. After all, I'm the one hosting it. You know, maid of honor duty 'n all. I should get back to my friends. And I feel bad that I didn't call them."

"We're still on for tomorrow? For the wedding, right?"

She hesitated, closed her eyes for a second as if contemplating whether this was a good idea or not, then as if deciding something monumental, she quickly nodded. "Yes. Come to the 40th Street Access at five, we've rented a bunch of bikes to use to get down to the Kindred Spirit Mailbox where the ceremony will take place. After the ceremony, we'll ride over to The Sunset Inn for the reception under the tent. If you get to the access by 4:45, we can ride down to the mailbox together."

"Sounds like fun. I'll see you at 4:45 on the beach side of the access so we can ride down together." He bent to kiss her, but she ducked under his arm.

"I'm sorry. I have to go."

She fled, crossing the ceramic tile at a double pace and closing the front door behind her before he could react and follow.

He turned from the doorway, which was as far as he'd gotten, and walked back into the kitchen as if caught in a daze. Palo, Brent, and Dev, still holding Amy's soaker, stood staring at him.

"Something's wrong there, Dude," Dev said.

"Yeah, she was some kind of spooked by her friends showing up," Brent added.

"Her friends seemed real happy they'd found her," offered Ryder.

"She was so totally different before they showed up. What's up with that?" Palo added.

"I don't know," Kyle said as he walked around the counter and began cleaning up. "I really don't know." His heart wasn't into bartending anymore. He made a motion to dump the contents of the blender into the sink but Palo jumped forward and stopped him. "Hey, hey! Just because Miss Perky Tits left, is no reason to deprive the rest of us."

Chapter 64—Chaz
The Book Club Meeting

Chaz had everything set up when Mags strolled down the boardwalk to join him. He'd even managed to provide the perfect backdrop, as the setting sun behind the houses lit up the sky in soft pastels. As a bonus, the moon, just beginning its climb over the ocean, reflected beams of light off the water. The access itself was too narrow to spread out on so he'd thrown a quilt on the sand a few yards from the steps. On it was the open food cooler, its contents arrayed in a semi-circle on the blanket by the time she stepped off the last step. He stood and cupped her elbow to guide her to her seat. Gracefully, she knelt, and then tucked her legs under her. He noticed she'd brought her book and he smiled. He'd almost forgotten that this was a meeting about the book. To him, it was so much more.

"Finished?" he asked, nodding at the book.

"Yes," she sighed. "I wasn't expecting that ending. I had a good cry when I turned the last page." She patted the cover and sighed again. Then smiled up at him.

"This is pretty impressive," she said indicating the hand-painted acrylic wine glasses and the fancy scalloped cake boards with doilies that each dish was presented on. Little cards accompanied each sampling, taped on with a formal description and a list of the ingredients. "Did you have this catered?"

"No, as I mentioned, one of my partners in the house is a chef. But he's really a lot more than that. He owns a few restaurants, has a slew of cookbooks published, and has his own cable cooking shows. You might have heard of him, Kyle Merritt."

"Oh my, yes I have. I tape his shows all week and then

watch them on the weekends. I can't believe I'm going to be eating food that Merritt the Master prepared."

"We just call him Kyle. He says all that master stuff the network dreamed up four years ago made people think he's into BDSM. He still gets some very strange fan mail from time to time. But, yes, he did prepare all this especially for you. Although, he reminded me many times that it would have been nice to know what you liked and didn't like. I hope there's something here you'll enjoy. He was afraid you might be vegetarian or vegan, so those two dishes over there fit the bill." He pointed at a pasta concoction and some fancy root vegetables that were beautifully garnished.

"It all looks so fabulous. I'm not at all particular, I like most things. I am into organics though, whenever I can find them. I think it's healthier."

"Yeah, that's what Kyle says too. I can attest that he went to several local farmers markets and two different butchers. He says the key to good food lies in the quality of the ingredients. I'd love to take you to one of his restaurants, he has one in Charleston . . . we could go one afternoon . . ."

"Oh, and I'd love to go. But we're leaving at the end of the week and Kara seems to be housebound with the decorating projects she's committed to. I'd hate to abandon her like that. She went to a lot of trouble to be able to spend her vacation with me."

He nodded. He'd pressed too soon. He should have waited to broach the possibility of another date after this one had gotten off the ground. He could smack himself for his stupidity. He reached over and handed her a plastic plate with an etched seashell border. "Help yourself to whatever appeals to you. Kyle apologizes for the not-so-fine china, but we always adhere to the no glass rule on the beach."

He pulled out a Gatorade bottle; it was filled with a dark maroon liquid. "He even decanted the wine into this. It's some of his best claret. He makes it himself without nitrates so I know it's organic."

"I feel very special," she said as she lifted the glass he had given her. "Lovely glasses."

"They're hand painted by a local artist, Amy Blake. We met her when she was painting the murals in the guest bathrooms. She does great work. We have a jungle powder room on the lower level that has a leopard stalking toward you on the backside of the door. It's so lifelike that it scares the bejesus out of a lot of people. They usually don't spend a lot of time in there," he said with a chuckle.

"I am amazed at how upscale this beach is now. When I was a kid we stayed here at a cottage that had pine paneling throughout, a window AC unit that never turned off, a percolator coffee pot, a hot plate, a toaster oven, and an outside shower."

"We have an outside shower."

She quirked a smile at him, "This outside shower was the *only* shower. You probably have two or three more in your house."

"Nine."

"Nine?" Her mouth fell open.

"Well, there are ten partners. We're rarely all here at one time, so usually we each have our own bathroom. A far cry from our dorm days when we were tripping over each other going in and out the bathroom door."

"Going to the beach is supposed to be like camping. Grilling out—"

"We have a grill, we grill out."

"Eating at picnic tables—"

"We have a picnic table. Kyle and I tiled it."

"Sitting around a campfire—"

"We have a fire pit. Two actually."

She sighed. "I guess what they say is true. You can't go back." She picked up her plate and delicately lifted a piece of the stacked beef filet into her mouth. "Mmmm."

"It's funny you should say that about not going back. I

just put a bid in on two treetop houses. Both owners have such fond memories of their childhood tree houses that they want to live in one now."

"I don't imagine those are going to consist of scrap wood dragged through the forest?" Her raised eyebrow drew attention to her perfectly sculpted brows and stunning sapphire blues eyes. He noticed she had drawn a tiny line on each lid at the edge of her lashes, and added a dusting of violet eye shadow. She was gorgeous.

He laughed and said, "Not unless you consider floating timber all the way down river from the forests of Borneo, transporting it by boat and truck, then lifting it by crane into the tree 'dragging it from the forest.'"

"And I imagine it's not free salvage."

"Certainly not, the checks I'll write for the wood alone will be in the tens of thousands."

"So not exactly the tree houses of their youth."

"It's improving on the idea."

She smiled. "I can see you love your work."

"I do. How about you?"

"I do most times. When I'm overwhelmed, it's not so much fun. There's always more to do than the time in which you have to do it."

"That's when you hire more people."

"Actually, I'm getting ready to do just that when I get back. I'm adding two assistants, both interns working on their certifications. I hope to have them trained and ready to dive into my piles of tax work before the end of the year. If all goes well, I might even be able to take another vacation next year."

"Same time, same place?" he asked before he popped a piece of shrimp into his mouth and then sipped his wine.

"I doubt it. Kara doesn't seem to be having the best time here. I hate that she promised so much redecorating work to the owner in exchange for the use of the beach house. And she refuses to let me help. If I had known that, I would have simply rented another beach house somewhere else."

"Hmmm. Then we would not have met. We would not be sitting here ready to begin our book club meeting."

She laughed. "No, I suppose not."

She nibbled on a slice of savory sausage wrapped in phyllo as she stared out at the ocean.

They were quiet for several minutes while they both ate bites of sandwiches and chunks of chicken and lobster, as they stared at the waves tumbling at the water's edge. She was the first to break the silence.

"So tell me your impressions of the book. Other than how unbelievably sad it all was."

He chewed thoughtfully, then finished what was in his wine glass before beginning, "They, like us, would not have met if the circumstances had been different. If he'd never had the accident, he'd never have met her, never have fallen in love with her, never been in a position to make her life so much better, and so much more meaningful."

"But if he hadn't had the accident, he might have married Alicia."

"She was shallow. She would not have been able to deal with the consequences of the 'til-death-do-us-part if anything bad had happened after the I do's."

Mags face paled; she shut her eyes and sunk her teeth into her bottom lip. A moment later she said, "Not many people are capable of that kind of devotion. What Will and Louisa had was a real and true love. I wish they had been granted some kind of miracle. They deserved a happily ever after."

"How about you? You don't seem to believe that you deserve that too."

"I've already had my miracle. It would be foolish for me to wish for another." She took a big gulp of her wine.

He tilted his head, leaned back on his elbows, and watched her. It was starting to get dark, but he was close enough to see both anger and sadness in her eyes. "What miracle did you have?"

She laughed and waved him off. "This book club meeting has gotten maudlin. Let's talk about the rest of your partners."

"Seriously, what was your miracle?"

She laughed again and turned from him, reaching to clean up the piles of napkins and plates. "I got a scholarship to Chapel Hill, graduated with honors, and got my CPA certification inside of two years."

"That's not your miracle."

"You don't think doing all that is miraculous?"

"For others maybe, but probably not for you. You seem more than capable of all that without a miracle."

"Well if you must know, my miracle is my sister. And here she comes now. Who the hell is that with her?"

Chaz looked up and saw Kara walking down the planks toward them. Ryder, in cowboy boots and grungy jeans, was walking behind Kara. His eyes were lasered on her swaying ass, his wide grin visible by the moonlight shining off his perfectly white teeth. If a man ever looked like a wolf in heat, he did.

"That's my friend Ryder. I called and asked him to come help Kara out with her little *decorating project*."

Mags looked over at Chaz, a confused look on her face as she tried to figure out when he had arranged that with Kara.

"She doesn't look very happy," Mags noted.

"Yeah, but he sure does," Chaz said with a chuckle.

Chapter 65—Ryder
Kara Loses a Bet

Kara walked passed Chaz and Mags sitting on the blanket as if wearing blinders. She didn't acknowledge them in any way. Her head held high, shoulders back; she walked with purpose as she strode down the beach to the water's edge. Anyone looking out a window and following her movements might have thought her march to the ocean reminiscent of Virginia Wolf's walk to her death, except the path she was blazing was a sand twister as she swung her arms furiously and stamped her feet in her paint-splattered clogs.

"Kara?" Mags called after her.

Ryder followed in her path, pulling up short when she stopped suddenly. He bent to whisper something in her ear and then patted her on her denim-clad butt. She wore frayed shorts and a ribbed tank top. The fluorescent paint flecks on her rubber shoes appeared as fireflies under her feet when she kicked off her shoes. She resumed her trudge to the sea.

"Ryder?" Chaz called out. The alarm he'd heard in Mags voice had turned his own judgmental. With one word he managed to accuse Ryder for Kara's anger.

Ryder laughed and turned back to the couple on the quilt. As he came alongside, he said, "Relax. She's just a sore loser. She bet me I couldn't hang a sheet of wallboard before her pizza got done cookin'. Told her I only needed ten minutes to do it. Well she did not believe me. Ended up betting me I couldn't."

"What did she bet?" Chaz said, getting to his feet and bringing Mags up with him.

"I believe her exact words were, 'If you can fix that hole before the timer goes off, I'll skinny dip in the ocean.'"

"Oh, she wouldn't . . ." Mags began.

"Ryder. Hell man, why'd you have to go and set her off?"

They all watched as Kara waded into the ocean. She was neck deep when a piece of denim waved in the air, followed by a slash of orange. She'd removed her shorts and tank top. Facing England, Kara dangled a bra and panties in her other hand. She looked as if she was reaching for the stars and offering her clothes in supplication. Her gay laughter boomed back at them.

Ryder stood staring, hands on hips, a big boyish grin blooming. "I didn't think she'd do it. Damn, boy shorts, exactly as I figured."

"Kara!" Mags called as a big wave crashed over Kara and she disappeared under it.

Ryder had shucked his boots and was running, arms and legs churning, before either of the two of them could react. The tide was up, so the beach was close, and the waves dynamic. As Mags and Chaz ran down to the water's edge they watched as Ryder ran into the ocean and dove into a curling wave.

Chaz had just kicked his shoes off and entered the water when he saw that Ryder had her in his arms. He was holding her to his chest, her legs wrapped around his waist, and although it was dark and they were silhouetted, he could tell she was naked; her white backside gleamed in the meager light. Kara was clutching Ryder around his neck, her head resting on his shoulder as if trying to catch her breath. Ryder lifted her higher into his arms, his forearms holding her up by her ass as waves lapped around them keeping her somewhat modest.

"She lost her clothes," Chaz said. "I'll get the quilt."

He ran back to retrieve their tablecloth and to shake the sand off as Ryder carried Kara tight to his chest through the rough incoming tide. As he came closer, he managed to whip off his t-shirt with one hand, and used it to cover her lower body as he waded ashore. He adjusted it around her hips when he stood her up at the water's edge.

Chaz brought the quilt and handed it to Mags. She took it from him and wrapped it over Kara's shoulders, crooning and admonishing her in soft tones. Once Kara was bundled in the blanket, Ryder bent and put his arms under her knees. He lifted her easily against his chest and carried her up the beach, over the access, and into the beach house.

Mags and Chaz stood watching for a moment, then they gathered up Kara's clogs, Ryder's boots, the book, the trash, and the picnic cooler.

Chaz looked down at Mags as she climbed up the access steps. He smiled at her worried expression. "All-in-all, I think their first date went rather well."

She laughed. "Probably better that ours, he didn't have to arrange a five-star dinner."

"Yeah, and he's already got his girl naked."

She gave him a sideways smile, then it slipped into a frown. "Chaz, this has been wonderful. I had a really good time. You're a lot of fun to talk to. Thank you."

She was calling an end to their date. It couldn't be more apparent that the book meeting was over. "Hey, the night is young. We can go for a drive or sit on my veranda and study the stars. Besides, if you go in now, you're probably going to catch them in an awkward moment."

"I know my sister. She's probably upset and scared. I'd better go to her."

"Ryder is with her. He'll take care of her. He won't let anything bad happen to her."

"Ryder . . . just who is he?"

"He's a very good friend of mine, an old college roommate. He came here for a visit and I asked him to pop in on Kara when he got here. I knew she had a problem she was working on that I thought he could help her with. He's a subcontractor, does framing and sheetrock work, along with running a ranch."

"What problem?"

"Musta been something involving sheetrock. You heard the bet."

She shook her head. "It's not like Kara to make a stupid

bet like that."

Chaz threw back his head and laughed. "Ryder brings out the raging bull in everybody. He likes to wave a red flag and rile people up. He must've egged her on; he does that. Annoys you until something snaps. Funniest man I know, though . . . it hides a heart he wears on his sleeve. He's a good guy, Mags. You don't need to worry. Spend a little more time with me?"

She wavered. "Let me check on her."

"Sure, if you have to."

"Come up with me, and if all is well, we'll scoop some ice cream and sit on the rocking chairs on the back deck."

"Sounds good."

He lifted the cooler over the low hedge, leaving it in his back yard, and followed her up the stairs to her place, taking the liberty to put his hand on the small of her back when they got to the top. It felt so right for it to be there. In his mind's eye he saw all the ways and times in the future that it would be there to guide and protect, and to show ownership as it touched ever so slightly to: a dark blue evening gown, a white lacy dress, a sheer black peignoir, the silk of a maternity top, the velour of a holiday robe . . . He took in deep breath. The images where overwhelming. Amazing. Perfect.

"You okay?"

"Mmm. Just looking ahead and figuring some things out."

"Good things I hope."

"Staggering."

"I hope you like birthday cake ice cream. I think that's all we have left. Kara ate the last of the butter pecan for breakfast."

He laughed. "It's freeing being at the beach, isn't it? No rules, no compunctions," he said as he held the screen door open for her.

Mags opened the door to the beach house and they went inside. It was dark in the living area but the hallway was lit. They stood listening as Ryder and Kara's laughter could be heard from down the hall. The steady drumming of water indicated that they were clearly sharing a shower. "Hmm. Apparently too freeing," she whispered.

"Maybe my veranda would be a better option."

"Yes, I suppose so."

"Grab the ice cream."

"Good idea."

Chapter 66—Ryder & Kara
Getting Naked in the Ocean is an Icebreaker

Ryder sat on the closed toilet lid as Kara raced around the bathroom pantomiming, "And then he turns the water on full force and here I am, alone in this bathroom with a man I just met . . . . Oh, damn, I just did it again, didn't I?"

They both started laughing and couldn't stop. They had come upstairs and into the beach house to get toweled off. Smells from the pizza, still in the warm oven, beckoned. But Ryder, due to past events where Chaz was concerned, was wary, and had questions about how she and Chaz had met. And Kara, in the delightful storytelling way she had, took and showed him—retelling every moment—from Chaz finding her crying on the steps, to him negotiating Ryder's fee for having him come to her rescue.

Seeing her now, while he was sitting on the closed toilet seat, laughing as she remembered how frightened she had become when Chaz had started closing all the doors, she looked genuine . . . and so very pretty. The kind of pretty you could kiss on and not worry about messing it all up. She didn't need makeup; her lips were the perfect shade, like the underside of a crimson rose, and her skin was flawless with its light tan and hints of sunburn showing through. And those lavender blue eyes, dewy and full of mischief, they followed his every move and captured things he knew others never saw.

Before he knew what was going to come out of his mouth, he heard himself say, "I'll help you prime the wall. After it dries we'll paint it and tomorrow we'll hang the mirror. You'll have this job done so you can enjoy the rest of your vacation."

"Thank you, that would be wonderful. Geez, to have this job finally done . . . what a load off my back that would be. But first, pizza! There's plenty to share, as my sister is on her *date* with Chaz."

"Which we probably ruined. Why didn't you tell me they were on the beach? It looked like we interrupted something special."

"Well, that's probably for the best. We're leaving in a few days, and the last thing my sister needs now is another man to let her down."

"There's a story there, but it doesn't sound like the stuff that aids digestion. What kind of pizza did you get at the store?"

"Store? It's not a frozen pizza. I made it. It's completely homemade. And if you're a meat lover, you're going to be happy."

He smiled, "I am already happy. Just seeing the relief on your face that this job is going to be done soon has cheered me I'm glad Chaz called me to come help."

She tucked an errant curl behind her ear and blushed, then flashed him that pixie smile he was coming to adore, "So am I." Then she stood and sashayed her little jean-clad butt into the kitchen.

Chapter 67—Chaz & Mags
Knocking Down Barriers

Chaz sat watching Mags eat her ice cream. Had anyone ever eaten that blue, green, and red sprinkled goop, with the rivers of blue icing running through it, so delicately? So sensuously? He watched as her lips pulled the sweet confection off the spoon, and let it linger on her tongue, before her throat worked to swallow it. Sometimes, she turned the spoon upside down and licked the creamy confection off. He watched with avid interest, as she thoughtfully appeared to be making love to the spoon.

She was lovely, truly lovely. His eyes lowered and he took in her long legs swinging over the side of the corner basket chair that was suspended from a beam.

"It's peaceful here," she commented.

"Yeah, this is the quiet hour. The time between dinner and late night reveling. Most of the tourists are on the mainland dining. Soon you'll hear the sounds of them tromping up the decks and settling in. The young ones will venture back out to the beach. The dunes here are so wide that you can't hear all that much unless people are yelling. But interestingly enough, on a quiet night with low surf, you can hear almost every word being spoken on those two accesses." He gestured with his hand to the long, deserted wooden pathways leading to the beach on either side of their houses.

"I'll have to remember that. "

"Why? Do you have horrible secrets?"

"No. Not really. My life's been pretty conventional. Accounting isn't usually a high drama profession."

"Why did you choose accounting?"

"I like numbers, computers, and being able to resolve things in black and white. And I like working alone, in my own space. The thought of being in an office with a boss looking over my shoulder never appealed to me."

"Yeah, I know what you mean. I kind of like running my own show too. And I like being able to set my own schedule."

"Tell me about these houses you're getting ready to build," she said, scraping her spoon around the bottom of the bowl before savoring the last spoonful.

He smiled and wished he could taste her blue tinged lips. He got up and grabbed his laptop from the table just inside the door and then pulled her up from the swinging chair. "Come sit on the lounger with me. I'll show you some pictures of the houses I've built and the plans I just sent off today."

They sat side-by-side, head-to-head, looking down at the screen as he scrolled through his files showing her pictures of the tiny but well-thought-out houses he'd built. She smelled of fragrant jasmine and cake icing, and he knew it was a smell he'd remember forever.

He let his fingers stroke along her arm where they were crossed over her knees as she bent forward to look at the screen. She uncrossed them and instead leaned her head on the arm farthest from him. He patted her knee once and she moved it away. At this rate, he thought, there was no way he was going to get a goodnight kiss on this first date. He blinked and had to acknowledge that of course, she didn't see it that way; to her, this meeting had been about a book, not about courting.

To him, it had been a first date. And he'd never gone without a goodnight kiss on a first date. Hell, he usually got a lot more than a kiss on a first date. But she didn't think this was a date. He knew that.

Ten minutes later, when she yawned and apologized for being so tired, he knew the evening was coming to an end for them.

"The mornings on the beach are precious to me. I am drawn to seeing the sunrise, so I'm not much for late nights. Thank you for the wonderful dinner, I had a good time."

"Me, too. Thank you for the ice cream."

They both stood. There didn't seem to be much to say. Yet their eyes spoke volumes. Things they wanted to say about the desire they felt, yearnings they both knew were too soon to act upon.

Chaz was pretty sure she wouldn't follow through on any urges she might have before she left to go home, unless he made it happen. But he sensed that she was like a wild horse, not wanting to be touched, fondled, caressed, or . . . ridden anytime soon. That she was skittish intrigued him. He wanted to know what had caused it. He wished he knew what these barriers she'd put between them consisted of. After dating and bedding scores of women, he felt as if he was a novice at seducing. She wasn't taking any lure he put in the water. But he wasn't about to give up.

"Any chance I could meet you for the sunrise tomorrow?"

"Hmmm. It's a private time for me. I meditate and pray and give thanks in my own little world. It's quiet time that I need to prepare for the day. I hope you understand."

He nodded, then took her hands in his. "I do. But make an exception. Just this once," he said with the same firmness he used with clients who wanted to renegotiate changes in house plans once the project was underway. "Let me share the beauty of the one thing we can truly count on in this chaotic world—the glorious rise of the sun over the water on this beautiful beach. I'll bring the finest Costa Rican coffee money can buy. And fresh cinnamon rolls."

She met his eyes, took in his sincerity. Felt the squeeze of his fingers against hers in a silent plea. "Okay. Beach chairs at dawn right there," she agreed, pointing at a spot off to the left.

"Thank you." He bent and kissed her on the cheek. She froze as if she hadn't wanted to allow him that liberty, but stayed still for seconds after as if savoring his touch.

He didn't linger, sensing her rebuff. "Tomorrow then. How do you take your coffee?"

"Black. And double icing on the cinnamon bun."

"You got it!" He walked her down to her yard then watched her climb the stairs and enter her house.

Climbing the steps back to his own place, he was buoyed. He'd arranged another date. He would get to see her first thing in the morning, fresh and dewy from her slumber, eyes soft and dreamy as they sat and watched the dawn perform its glorious show. Please God, don't let it rain in the morning, he begged as he retraced his steps and opened the door to the house. Kyle was in the kitchen juicing something in the blender.

"Hey, how would you feel about making some cinnamon buns for breakfast?"

"Sure. I've got the ingredients. I'll make some when I get up."

"Uh, what time might that be?"

"Probably ten-ish, why?"

"Hmm, that won't work. I need them ready around five-thirty."

"Then I suggest you go to Lowe's or Publix's and pick some up at the bakery."

Chaz looked at his Fitbit, checking the time. "Think they're open now?"

"I'm sure of it."

"She wants double icing . . ."

Kyle laughed. "You've got it bad."

"Yeah, I think I do."

"I'll whip some up tonight. They'll be in parchment paper on the counter with your name on them. You'll just have to warm them in the microwave for seven seconds. Seven seconds. Only seven. Got that?"

"Yeah. Seven. Got it . . . you sure you want to do this? I can just go buy some. Scrape the icing off one and put it on top of another . . ."

"It's worth it to see you this undone by a woman. Plus, I'm still on Milan time so I'll be up 'til two or three anyway. So . . . none of your legendary charms working on this one?"

"Well, not mine, but certainly yours. She likes good food—your food especially. She says she watches your show."

"Well then, you've got a shot as long as you stay on my good side."

Chaz made to bow, raising his right arm and circling it in deference from his forehead to his knees. "I am in your debt. Your wish is my command. Seriously," he said as he stood, "thank you. Let me know how I can repay you."

"Oh I will . . . I will. I store these things up. Meanwhile, drink some of this." He poured a thick pulp from the blender into six tall glasses and added champagne.

"What is it?"

"Kill-Devil Punch."

"Okay, what's *in* it?"

"Raspberries, pineapple juice, lime juice, club soda, superfine sugar, aged dark rum, and a bit of some decent bubbly," he said as he hoisted the champagne bottle. "It'll make your Johnson stand tall."

"It would be great if I needed to call it into service soon. But I don't think your cinnamon buns are going to be *that* good." He took a sip of the drink and nodded, "Although this might do it."

Kyle laughed and slid a tray of sandwiches he'd made toward Chaz. "You never know . . . I've been told I have nice buns. . . . And once, I had a woman promise me head for one of my croissants, but then they had Belgian chocolate and roasted hazelnuts inside, so you can't blame her. These sandwiches are leftover from dinner. You hungry?"

Chaz looked down at the works of art—towering piles of different kinds of double-deckers, each with its own distinctive bread, vegetable, meat, and defining sauce.

As Chaz wavered, Kyle ran through the options: "Charred Eggplant with spicy brie and caramelized onions on a brioche, BLT with roasted asparagus and jalapeno aioli on a ciabatta, curried chicken with baby spinach and fresh fennel with Greek yogurt and drizzled with honey on focaccia."

"They look amazing. But I'm sorry; I'm just not hungry. I filled up on the appetizers you made and then had a big bowl of ice cream. And now I'm drinking this awesome drink you just made. Don't you ever get tired of all the work this entails?" he asked, his hand encompassing the huge ceramic platters of demolished food, the array of appliances still plugged in and pulled from their custom cabinets or as Kyle referred to them "their garages," and the different drink offerings splattered along the counter.

"No, I love my work, but this is play. There are no cameras and no critics. *And*, it's Rutger's night to cleanup, so it's extra fun!"

"Well, we all appreciate your cooking. Always have. Even when you made Chicken Cordon Bleu on the Foreman Grill in the dorm, your cooking was primo."

Kyle laughed. "That's a cookbook I should do: *How to Feed Your Friends and Get a Degree using a Foreman's, a Rocket Pocket, a Waffle Iron, and a Hot Plate.*"

"If memory serves, you burnt out the hot plate the second semester."

Kyle laughed again, a loud boisterous guffaw. "Damned lasagna turned into soup! What a mess that was."

"It was still good, even spooned off the counter."

"Seems so long ago," he said wistfully, and it was the first time Chaz sensed Kyle's life wasn't as perfect as he made it out to be.

"Hey, let's go watch tennis with the rest of the guys," Kyle said, picking up the tray to take with them. "Somebody'll polish these off before the night is over."

"Sounds good. I've got to get up early, but I'm not ready to head up to bed just yet."

"Hey, whatcha drinkin' Chaz? Looks a bit girlie," Dev said as they walked into the TV room. Dev hoisted his Avery Rumpkin beer bottle against Chaz' fuchsia-colored highball glass as Chaz walked by him.

"Well, if you must know . . . Kyle says this punch will make my Johnson stand tall, so no, not so girlie," Chaz countered with a smile. Then he looked down at his crotch and laughed. Well, maybe I might need a little bit more."

As he sat down they all laughed.

Palo said, "I never did understand why they call the penis a Johnson."

"You know I never did either," said Sean, "but I sure as hell laugh every time I drive down here and see that sign for Seymour Johnson Air Force Base."

They all laughed again. "Yeah, can you imagine meeting a girl and telling her you're stationed at Seymour Johnson right out of the gate?" said Brent.

They all hooted at that.

"I hear that girls at bridal parties have a game where they write down as many slang names for penis as they can think of in one minute," Rutger said.

"What does the winner get?"

"Nothing. Just the shaft," Rutger adlibbed.

They all laughed uproariously at that.

"Well, I can think of a few," said Brent. "Cock, prick, dong, peter, woody."

Dev continued, "Manhood, road flare, dangle, snake, member,"

Kyle joined in, "Cannon, ramrod, baby maker, third leg, pecker, dick, rooster."

Chaz began where Kyle left off, "Wang, python, cobra, one-eyed monster, tool, joystick, gearshift, wand."

Sean joined the hilarity, "Sword, shaft, Cyclops, wiener, hard drive, boner."

"Lollipop, morning wood, cigar, pickle, pud, skin flute, sausage," this from Dev.

"Now you guys are stretching it," Palo said.

They all hooted again at the innuendo. Brent and Sean

were crying, tears running down their cheeks.

From, the doorway came the voice of Cam as he leaned against the curve of the arch, "Vlad the Impaler, magic bullet, Thor, Leviathan, Big Willie, Rodzilla, Jackhammer, stud, squirt, package, boner, knob, meat thermometer, dipstick, Bruce."

They all stopped and stared at Cam, "Bruce?"

"Well, that's what I call mine, Bruce the oil derrick."

They all hooted again.

"Wanker, pocket rocket, salami, Willy Wonka, Mount Joy, King Tut, Tally Wacker, the Hulk—" Chaz added.

"Schlong, Schwance, Thrill Drill, Shaftesbury, phallus, sex pistol, junk, Titanic, mongoose, Rumple Foreskin, Long Dong Silver, Lad," Dev said.

"Lad?" asked Kyle.

"As in, well here's Laddy Boy now . . ." Dev guffawed. "I hear that's what Alex named his new dog. Only he says it's not his dog, it's his parents. But it's really the twins'."

"Here Laddy Boy," Sean mimicked, patting his thigh. Then laughing hilariously.

"Isn't it called a Smackle? Or something like, that in Yiddish?" asked Palo.

"No, it's Schmeckle."

"Oh."

Ryder came into the room and saw everyone with tears running down their faces, "What are you doing and how long have you guys been doing it?"

"We're talking penis names. And you wouldn't believe how many there are," Sean said.

"Ah, the external male intromittent organ, consisting of root, shaft, foreskin, glans, and meatus. Fun little tool. Especially if you have a playmate to share it with."

The whole room howled.

"Enough of the penis talk, I think naming all the slang terms for tits might be more fun," said Kyle.

"Yeah!" several chorused.

"Count me out," said Chaz, "I have a date with destiny at sun up."

"Destiny? I thought her name was Mags?" said Dev.

"Very funny."

"Yeah, and I have to go make cinnamon buns for the occasion. With double icing. You owe me Charles James Russell," said Kyle. "Rutger, don't forget you have KP tonight. Might be a good time to get started before I make another big mess you'll be responsible for."

Rutger groaned, but stood up and followed him into the kitchen.

Chapter 68—Mags
Here Comes the Sun

What the hell was she doing? As if she didn't have enough trouble with Kara. She'd heard her and Ryder in the shower last night, so had Chaz. But now she says they were mistaken, that she was never naked in the shower with Ryder. That they were just laughing and talking, and then eating pizza afterward before he left to go back to *The Cockpit*.

But she did say she had left the door wide open for more time with him, hoping he'd come over today and after reattaching the mirror, maybe he'd ask her out. And just how was that going to help things? Dear God, he was from Tennessee, or was it Kentucky, she couldn't remember. They were from Raleigh. Kara didn't need a long distance relationship. But then she tilted her head and thought further. It wasn't often that she thought about her little sister as a grown woman with needs, but she had to accept that maybe her baby sis could use a hook-up. She certainly deserved it after all she'd done for her this year.

She herself had encouraged the hunky little house builder—when she absolutely, positively hadn't meant to. She could sense he was the kind of guy who liked to play around. Although he really had seemed sincere, and he did seem to have a real interest in her.

She had noticed him admiring her body in an approving way, more than once. But he did seem drawn to her thoughts, and he was always asking her provoking questions. And he was nice, really nice. Was that just his M.O.? Did he seduce by conversation and a pleasant manner, rather than subtle touches, or lingering gazes, bent on conveying fascination with her eyes? That was the way of things these days, wasn't it?

Jeremy had done that. Told her how pretty her eyes were—*like radial shards of lapis lazuli, perfectly aligned to draw him in.* And she fell for it. But for all his charm, in the end, he simply hadn't loved her as he'd said. Maybe with more time he would have. But on the day she had needed him to love her and to be supportive, he hadn't been.

She'd hardly gotten the words of her diagnosis out of her mouth, barely outlined the treatment program when he put his hands out and stopped her. He wasn't doing this, he told her. She thought he'd taken her hands in his to soften the blow, but he'd actually been trying to twist his engagement ring off her finger. Because she was sick, she wasn't enough for him. Marriage to her was off the table now. He wanted children. Healthy children. Not ones with genetic predispositions to a horrible disease. And he didn't want a wife without breasts, he'd said. He didn't think he could handle that. He'd not paid a whit of attention to the type of cancer she said she had. She had cancer of the blood, tumors confined to the lining of her lungs; she didn't have breast cancer.

One day she had been ready to get married, anxious, just as he had been, to start a family. And the next, a husband and children were no longer in her future. But her damned internal clock was still ticking like a metronome; she heard it when she woke in the morning, and when she was staring around her moonlit room at night. She was ready to hold a sweet little baby in her arms. From the moment she had become engaged to Jeremy, she'd had dreams that revolved around being either pregnant, or having just given birth to a beautiful squirming baby.

But all her dreams died that night. And despite the constant ticking of that clock in the back of her mind, reminding her of what she'd lost, she'd had to go it alone, seeking out treatment for her newly diagnosed disease, while working to keep herself and her new company afloat. It had been tough, and dealing with heartbreak hadn't helped. But having seen Jeremy in this new light, seeing how calloused and selfish he was, had opened her eyes to other things, and she'd known it had been a blessing to discover his true feelings before it had been too late. In the end, she hadn't missed Jeremy. Not for one single minute had she missed the man she had almost married. Once she'd known she'd beaten it and wasn't going to die, she had thanked God for her cancer.

But now . . . now it was time to move on. Time to get her life back and to plan a new future. This time with a man who wanted her, as she was, not for what she could give him.

"Hi!" Chaz said as he put down his chair and handed her two packages. "Hold these for a sec while I open my chair, will ya?"

She took the warm bundles and held one in each hand while he opened his chair and set it on the sand. His chair was the type that had a cooler that folded out on one side and a side table with a cup holder on the other. Out of the cooler he took two tall metal thermal containers, which he placed on the side table, and out of his jacket pockets he took two Styrofoam coffee cups and two plastic champagne flutes.

He took the packages back from her and added them to the table, then poured them each a cup of coffee. "Here ya go, freshly brewed Arabica coffee from Costa Rica," he said as he handed her one of the steaming cups. Then he unwrapped one of the bundles and handed it to her, the cinnamon bun gleaming in the semi-darkness, due to the stark white icing smoothed over the top. "And your double-iced cinnamon bun."

She laughed. "You are an exceptional concierge. What am I going to owe you for this personalized service?"

He smiled at her as he sat down and picked up his coffee. "I'm going to expect you to put out."

She coughed, and then laughed. "Really?" she challenged, as she lifted her cup to her lips for a sip.

"Hey, this is no different from a prime rib dinner. And given the particular chef involved, this would have been a lot more costly. Especially considering the delivery charge from Milan, had he still been there."

He unzipped the cooler and took out the premade mimosas and filled both flutes.

"Mmmm," she sighed. The coffee is excellent."

"Yes, you can see I'm going for quality here. Try the bun."

She pulled a piece away from the edge and popped it into her mouth. She sighed long and low. The sound of her pleasure zinged through him.

He handed her a flute and they toasted the day, raising their plastic glasses to the sliver of light just breaking the horizon.

Mags sipped from the flute, "Mmmm, this is amazing."

"Some secret ingredient Kyle won't tell about."

"I taste . . . lavender?"

"Yeah, maybe. You never know with him. He's always trying something off the wall."

"Well this is truly delicious," she said, taking another sip.

Chaz unwrapped his roll, pulled off the major part of the outer ring and tilted his head back to drop it into his mouth. His own sigh of appreciation hummed in the air as he savored the sweet confection. "Kyle definitely has the touch."

"I mean it, this is fabulous."

"Swoon worthy, yet?"

She smiled over at him. "Getting there. I can't wait 'til I work my way to the center, that's the best part."

"Hmmm," he said, "I was just thinking the same thing." He looked over at her, pointedly staring in her lap, then raised an eyebrow, and winked.

She put her coffee down on the side table and swatted his arm. "Behave."

They sat in silence, eating and sipping and looking out at the horizon where the sun was beginning to creep over the edge. Surrounded by muted pinks, purples and oranges was a glowing yellow orb, gently and slowly lifting.

"Here she comes, Her Majesty dressed in her finest," he said.

She nodded and mumbled around the bite in her mouth, "Mmm uh, so nice. This is so very nice. Everything is sooo good. Oh, that is glorious. I'm surprised it's not accompanied by the Hallelujah Chorus."

He pulled out his phone, found the app, downloaded the song, and hit the arrow to play it—all within fifteen seconds.

They both sat, staring at the enormous ball rising on the horizon, listening to the most celebratory song in all Christendom, and savoring a confection so perfect for the occasion.

He smiled over at her then took his thumb and wiped the icing from her bottom lip. Without hesitation, he stuck it in his mouth and sucked. "Mmm, yes. *Very* nice."

He saw her shiver and was pleased. She had finished her bun now so he took the wrapper from her hand and replaced it with his hand.

They sat alone in the sand, holding hands and watching the sun rise into the sky, until suddenly they weren't alone anymore. People with yapping dogs walked toward the sun, two men with tackle boxes and rods walked to the water's edge, and a group of women with yoga mats on their shoulders began setting up for class on the hard packed sand.

"And so, another day at the beach has begun," he murmured.

"There's something so special about being here, isn't there?" she said as she turned to face him, her smile beaming.

She looked radiant in the early glow of the dawn. And happy in a way he rarely saw in a woman. She was content in the moment. There was no manipulation for the future in her mien. She had a satisfied smile that melted his heart. He wanted her. For always. And he knew it just like he'd known the sun would come up.

His hand holding hers squeezed. "You have plans for the day?"

"My daily walk to the Mailbox, something Italian and fattening for lunch, and a nap."

"Sounds like a perfect day at the beach." He hesitated, and then took the plunge. "Mind if I join you in it?"

"For which part?"

"All of it." He focused his eyes on hers, his meaning clear.

She met his eyes, saw the desire there. "Even the nap?"

"*Especially* the nap."

He turned in his seat to fully face her. Still keeping their hands joined against her thigh, he wrapped his other hand around the side of her neck and pulled her to him. His lips took hers in a soft sensual kiss. As his thumb caressed her jaw, he eased his tongue between her lips and sought the under side of her bottom lip. Groaned when her tongue tangled with his to draw him in further.

His hand slid up and then behind her head to pull her closer, opening his mouth further and capturing her lips and tongue with his. While the sun rose high in the sky, he savored all the traces of cinnamon and icing, and her. He swallowed her moans and chuckled at her gasps as his mouth moved up the side of her jaw and his lips sucked on the area just behind her ear.

He whispered against her neck, "In an hour the beach house will be empty. The guys have charted a boat to go fishing. We'll have the place to ourselves until they get back late this afternoon. We can go exploring . . .," he said as his lips tugged on her ear lobe, his tongue circled inside her ear, and he kissed the vee at the base of her throat.

"You'll show me the house?" she gasped.

"Every single room," he murmured. His eyes meeting hers and conveying such want, such need, that she felt alive again. Like a woman, a woman with needs that rivaled his. She decided in that moment, that she would take this day at the beach as a woman coming back to life. She would revel in every single minute.

Next week she would be back home, getting back into her old life and planning a new future. Today? Today, she would have some fun.

Chapter 69—Chaz
A Play Date

When Chaz walked into the beach house to put his things away and to get his walking shoes, he was surprised to see Kyle was the only one not getting ready for the fishing trip.

"Aren't you going fishing?" he asked him as he emptied the cooler into the sink.

"Nah. I have to go into Shallotte to get a Hawaiian-type shirt for the wedding I'm going to tonight with Amy."

He quickly improvised. He wanted the house to himself until late this afternoon. "I'm going to Shallotte for lunch later. I can pick one up for you. Extra Large, right?"

"Yeah. You sure?"

"Hell yeah. I owe you. Besides, I need the place alone."

Kyle laughed. "Ahh, my cinnamon buns did the trick, huh?"

"I'm not sure what did it, actually. But they sure helped."

"Alright. I did want to go fishing." He reached into his pocket and pulled out a hundred dollar bill. "Get me a nice one, not too loud mind you."

"You got it. And thanks!"

"No problem."

Ten minutes later, he and Mags hooked up at the access and began their walk to the Mailbox. He took her hand and they made their way across the soft sand to the hard packed sand at the water's edge. They started walking west, going away from the sun. They dropped their hands when they got sweaty and both took sips from their water bottles while they kept a brisk pace.

After a few minutes of walking and people watching, he turned to her and asked, "So what were you thinking about this morning when you were sitting in your chair waiting for me?

You looked pretty deep in thought when I got there with the goodies."

She was quiet for a moment, her lips pursed as if wondering if she should tell him what she'd been thinking. "I was thinking about the past—and the future."

"The past meaning your breakup?"

"Yeah, but not so much that. Jeremy wasn't right for me. I see that now. We wanted the same things in life, but we didn't have the right kind of relationship to make it work."

"What kind is that?"

"The kind where two people love each other."

"You didn't love him, but you were going to marry him?" he seemed surprised at that.

"I didn't know I didn't love him until we broke up."

"Say again," he asked, clearly confused by the look on his face.

"Things changed very quickly as I had a lot going on at the time, but the one thing that was soon crystal clear after he broke up with me was that I did not miss him. Not one bit. What I did miss was the future we'd planned. I still do."

"What kind of future were you planning?"

"I wanted kids. And I didn't want to wait too much longer to have them. He wanted a wife, and kids, probably more than I did actually. We both wanted the whole deal, a house in the suburbs, green lawn with a climbing tree in the front and a swing on one in the back. Flower boxes . . . a vegetable garden . . . bird feeders," she said wistfully. "We were ready to be Harry and Harriet Homeowner, PTA members, and pillars of the community!"

She'd put a weird emphasis on *pillars of the community*. He felt as if she'd said it with false bravado, as if it truly could never have happened.

"What changed?"

She didn't say anything for a long time. Then she looked over at him, took his hand back in hers and said, "I don't want to talk about it. Not today. Today is for us. I want everything to be perfect today."

He brought her hand up to his lips and kissed it. "If I have a say in it, it will be."

They crossed under the pier and stopped for another sip of water, it was still early, but already a hot day.

When they got to the Mailbox, they both wrote something in the notebook and then sat on the bench watching the ocean waves roll over themselves in a timeless fashion. They laughed at the antics of the sandpipers and admired the regal way the gulls soared seemingly effortlessly against the blue sky. The pelicans dipped in unison from their perfect formations, and then returned to their places in line as if choreographed by Bob Fosse.

It was the most beautiful place in the world to be, at the most perfect time, with just the right person, Chaz thought.

His thoughts were mirrored by hers as she leaned up onto her tiptoes, as the bench was so high, and scooted herself over, until she was under the shelter of his outstretched arm. She kissed him on the cheek. "This is the most perfect beach day ever. Thank you."

"It's barely eight-thirty. I have lots more planned for you."

He took her in his arms and kissed her properly, hard and deep. Then he stood, put his arms under her knees, and picked her up into his arms, snuggling her to his chest.

Laughing, and telling him to put her down the whole time, he carried her down the beach and into the surf.

They romped in the breakers, splashing each other and then ventured further out to ride the waves in, letting the force of the incoming tide carry them back to the shore over and over again as if they were the only people in the universe.

When they were tired, they sat in the sand, their legs crossed in front of them with hers tucked between his, her back to his front, watching the ocean do its mesmerizing magic, making them forget everything except these moments when they were falling in love.

Chapter 70—Mags & Chaz
The Day is Young

The walk back from the Mailbox was not as tiring for Mags as it usually was. Chaz kept her entertained, making outrageous suppositions about the people who passed by them. Relating made up histories and scenarios that were so unbelievable and yet, oddly plausible in the way he filled in the details. And with the southern drawl he took on.

"That's Anna there," he'd say, pointing at a couple, "that's not her husband Joe though. He's back at their campground at the KOA, in their RV, shagging the pool monitor named Ruth again. Ruth's husband, Pete, well, he's at the doctor's office finding out he got gonorrhea from his secretary.

"You can just imagine the rockin' that's going on in that there Fleetwood Bounder. Joe and Ruth hurryin' to get to it before Pete gets back.

"And now Anna here, she's going to hook up with Jim the bartender, who she met last night while Joe was in the men's room sufferin' from the all-you-can-eat crab legs drowned in butter. Jim, the bartender, told Anna that he's got a brand new pick-up truck what needs breakin' in, if'n she knows what he means . . . and how could she not, as he'd said it with a wink."

Chaz turned halfway back and pointed, "See they're headin' to the pier parkin' lot right now, gonna crank up the A/C and check out those new leather seats with the all-the-way back recliners."

Mags laughed so hard she had to hold her side.

Chaz finished with, "The scene fades away and a narrator, very likely Denzel, says in his woebegone voice, 'At first ol' Joe only ailed from the crabs that he et at the all-you-can-eat buffet. Then Joe caught what Ruth had, and Anna caught what Joe had, and Jim caught what Anna had. It was not a fun time at the beach that summer.'

"Now over yonder is Gloria with her cousin Ned, they had a baby once, they sold it online as a food processor . . ."

"Stop! Stop," Mags pleaded with her hand on his arm. "I can't take anymore stories. My side hurts."

They were at their access before they knew it. He turned to her and kissed her on the cheek. "Mmmm, salty. I have to watch my sodium intake, so let's shower and regroup in half an hour. I thought I'd take you to lunch at the Wing & Fish Company in Shallotte. I have to run to Belk's to get a Hawaiian shirt for Kyle to wear to a wedding tonight. Payback for all the food he's been making me to win you over." He gave her a wink. "We can go together if you like. Or, there's some sandwiches Kyle put in the fridge and some hideously healthy kale chips he made. Then . . ."

"Then?" Mags prompted.

"We'll go looking for an RV to set to rockin'."

"No surprises like the ones Ruth and Pete were responsible for passing out?"

"I'm clean. I've had a stalker for six months. I haven't even been out in public except to work," he sighed.

She laughed. "Well, as a requirement for setting up my company and getting my own insurance, I've had to have a lot of tests this year, and a full workup just last month before they renewed it. And Jeremy's been out of the picture since November before last. I can probably get you some kind of report from my online portal if you'd like."

"Not necessary. I believe you."

"I probably shouldn't believe you. You are quite the storyteller."

He laughed. "I would never tell a lie," he said, crossing his chest. "Especially about something like that."

"I'm not on any kind of birth control though."

"That's not a problem, darned near every nightstand in that house has a box of condoms. I have the variety pack," he said wiggling his eyebrows.

She laughed. "I'm going to have to have a nap after lunch, I'm beat. And trust me, a tired Mags, you never want to meet."

"Good rhyme! I could use a nap, too. Someone had me up at the crack of dawn. I saw the dawn *arrive*."

She smiled up at him and he thought her the prettiest thing going with her flyaway blonde hair, golden tan, rosy cheeks, and shiny-from-sunscreen nose.

"We'll nap on the Baleares day bed on the top deck when we get back, it has a retractable canopy." He pressed a finger to her forearm and watched as the redness showed white against the area he'd pressed. "Looks as if you've had enough sun for one day. That way we'll still be able to enjoy the sea breeze."

"Sounds good. I'll go check on Kara."

"Ryder texted that he was taking her to lunch, then to Lowe's. Seems he's talked her into another do-it-yourself project. I think it's going to require a lot of banging. You may just want to spend the rest of the day with me."

"Okay, then. It's a plan. I'll just take a quick shower and come over."

He brushed a wisp of hair from her temple where it was billowing in the breeze and tucked it behind her ear, then caressed her cheek and kissed her lips. "Are we moving too fast for you?" he whispered.

"Uh, no. Maybe . . . I don't know."

He smiled, "Come over whenever you're ready, I'll leave the back door open. Let's start with lunch, then a nice nap. . . and see how it goes."

Chapter 71—Mags
A Hot Date

Just as Chaz had said, no one was home at the beach house she and Kara were staying in. It was eerily quiet with all the lights out and only the hum of the refrigerator to accompany her as she downed a bottle of water and stripped on her way to the shower. Her bathroom had been the first one stripped bare and redecorated, and each time she walked into it she marveled at her sister's talents.

The walls were a beautiful light blue that recalled the perfect summer sky. A mirror with a white lacquered frame hung over each sink and a large mason jar with white silk hydrangeas sat on the counter. Fresh new fluffy white towels hung on the towel rods and a pile of hand towels in contrasting shades of blue decorated the newly tiled counter. Where her sister had found the broken china shards in a thousand shades of blue she hadn't a clue, but what a stunning effect. And she had helped her sister clean the shower tiles and glass door from the soap film and the hard water hazing that had built up over the years.

It was a lovely room now; a far cry from what it had been when they had arrived. She was so proud of her sister's efforts to revamp it. She'd known she was a great teacher, but she'd had no idea she was talented in the fixing up department.

After she had stripped off her damp shorts, peeled off the underwear that was stuck to her skin, and bent to pull the sweaty tee shirt over her head, she struggled out of the sports bra, finally wrestling it off.

She stepped into the heavenly waterfall, letting it sluice over her body before applying L'Occitaine Citrus Verbena, her favorite sugar scrub, and vigorously cleansed her body. She shaved with meticulous care using the shower gel, though really, the chemo had made shaving or waxing almost unnecessary. Her pubes had finally returned just last month in surprisingly soft curls, now tinged with auburn highlights. So, while she was a pale blonde on the top she was now a chestnut brunette on the bottom.

She hoped Chaz would pay some attention to those springy new curls and the area they framed. It had been so long since a man had lingered there. It hadn't really been Jeremy's "thing," as he had often told her. So there'd had to be a tradeoff for the concession. And once she'd done her part and he was replete, he often found some reason to renege. He'd really been a lousy boyfriend. She wondered why she hadn't seen it before now. Was she so focused on the baby path that she had compromised and settled, rather than giving herself more time to find the right man?

She ran a razor over the tops of her thighs to define the edges, but it hadn't really been needed. Her new natural contour was providing a tidy trim job down there. Chemo had it benefits, she thought, as she ran a loofah over her skin and pumiced her feet. That hadn't been necessary either; walking on the sand had abraded the bottoms of her feet and made them nice and smooth. She ditched her shoes at the end of the access along with everyone else's unless she was going to the Mailbox. And often wondered at the novelty of a place you could leave high-end sandals and Crocs in the sand, and still have them be there when you returned for them.

As she toweled off she mused, just what did one wear to lunch followed by a nap, followed by hopefully, a "rockin'" good time. She opened drawers and pulled out the possible choices, deciding on a lace longline balconette bra in lilac and a matching lace cheeky panty that displayed half of her ass and dipped in a low, ribbon embroidered vee below her navel. It was nowhere near as revealing as a thong would be, but she hated those things. She didn't think it was sexy to expose that much.

Underwear had been her passion through college, and for every special occasion, when asked what she wanted as a gift, it was a gift card to either Victoria's Secret or her new favorite, ThirdLove. The company touted a perfect fit, and really cared about the comfort of its products. The cup, the tag, the underwire, the straps, and the fabric were all customized. They even took into consideration the shape of your breasts. Not all were round and perky. And comfort was key while sexy ruled. She had initially been skeptical because of the outrageous price, the balconette bra alone had been $84, but now she often forgot she was wearing a bra at all. It would be perfect for sleeping in, next to Chaz—perfect for Chaz to caress the breasts tucked inside.

She could not remember when she had been so excited about the prospect of having sex. She dug through her drawers and pulled out a soft over-sized raglan tee in pale green and a pair of skimpy white drawstring shorts. She didn't see any reason to put on makeup, her skin glowed from the sun and it would just end up all over his sheets. Lip-gloss was all that was called for and she hoped that it would soon be transferred to Chaz' lips. She took a minute to blow dry her hair and to use a round brush to give her hair a wispy perky look. Then she slipped into her toe-wrapped sandals. As she walked by her dresser, she spritzed on some 4711 Echt Kölnisch Wasser, and she was ready to go. She'd used the original citrusy eau de Cologne in the splash form since high school. She considered it her essence, but often thought herself a fool to think of it as only hers, as many people going back to the 1790s probably thought the very same thing. It was a fresh clean scent and many people often stopped to ask her what it was she was wearing. And it was cheap, ridiculously cheap.

She left a note for Kara saying she was having lunch with Chaz in Shallotte, and that they were going to Belk's afterward to pick up a shirt for one of his friends. She didn't mention the nap, or the romp they had planned upon awakening.

She grabbed her key, locked the door and ran down the steps before realizing he could hear her eagerness in the slap, slap, slap of her sandals on the decking. She really should be more demure. She smiled. Nah.

Chapter 72—Chaz & Mags
Foodies Delight

Chaz was standing on the deck with a drink in his hand watching her as she ran down one flight from her house then up two to his. He smiled. Good. She was excited. Just as he was.

When she came through the screen door he had to grip his glass to keep it from slipping from his hand. She was every man's dream. She looked dewy, soft, energized from the inside out. The girl next door, her eyes lit from within and her smile igniting the world around her. It certainly lit a fire in him. He felt his cock jerk. Warmth flooded his veins and his body steeled. He was on the verge of suggesting they forego lunch and just head upstairs when she sashayed over.

"Did you say there was a dine-in option for lunch?" She ran her hand up his arm, sending heat coursing through him.

"Yeeaah," he managed to gasp out. Then forced himself to regroup. "If you'd rather eat here, there's plenty of food that's ready to eat. Kyle's been on a nonstop cooking binge."

"So what culinary delights are on the menu?" She ran her hand up the front of his Cuban guayberra shirt. He stilled. If she touched his nipple he'd be done for. There would be no lunch. Maybe not even dinner. Nothing but him getting that damned shirt off.

He stilled her hand with his covering it and grinned down at her. Then he took her hand in his and walked her over to the commercial-sized refrigerator. He opened the top right door. "While they may be leftover they are indeed delights."

He took a huge tray out of the refrigerator and pointed at each saran-wrapped sandwich. All were fat and stubby from piled high ingredients. "You have your choice of: spicy pulled pork with a cilantro and cabbage slaw on a brioche, a turkey wrap with bacon and roasted corn and avocado aioli sauce, mushroom and grilled onion melt with rosemary and provolone on grilled sourdough."

He walked her over to the huge butler pantry and took out a big glass container and unclipped the locks around the sides. "And here, here we have Kyle's famous kale chips. These are made from a blend of paprika, cumin, garlic powder, Tellicherry black pepper, thyme, fresh minced parsley, and olive oil pressed just last week."

Mags followed him over to where he set the open container on the counter, and with pinched fingers plucked a chip up and popped it into her mouth. "Mmm, that's surprisingly good." She took another. "I am impressed. This is just regular ol' kale?"

"Mmhmm. Kyle calls it decorative kale. It's the stuff they use to put under other stuff so you don't see the plate. Although considering what some of the plates cost that he uses, I don't know why you'd hide them." He sampled one himself. Then leaned down to whisper in her ear. "Protection."

"From what?"

"Garlic. Now we can both have garlic breath, and we will only offend others."

She laughed and took another chip. "Seriously, this is good stuff. Is the recipe for these chips in his new cookbook?"

"I haven't a clue. But I don't think there is a particular recipe as each batch he's made has been different."

He walked over to a large glassed-in cabinet along the wall that went from floor to ceiling. With a grand gesture he opened both sides. "Voila! Wash and dry some kale, take your pick of these, add olive oil, and bake. That's the recipe."

She walked over, her eyes agog. Inside were beautiful ceramic containers, each swirled in a pattern in the traditional Italian colors of blue, white and yellow. Each container was four inches high and three inches around with a domed cap, and around each cap was an engraved gold tag that hung on a matching gold chain. She walked closer and read the labels: Anise, Cardamom, Fennel, Rosemary, Thyme, Garam masala,

Chinese five-spice, Saffron. You name the spice, and it was there. There were over a hundred little ceramic canisters. There were six types of curry, seven types of salt, nine types of pepper, and so many spices that she'd never even heard of.

"Wow."

"Yeah. It's amazing to watch him actually. He just grabs a handful of the containers, sprinkles some here and there, throws in a dollop of this or that, and it's fabulous food each and every time."

"I have never seen anything like this," she said. "I am awed by the variety of spices available at a beach house, a vacation home for gosh sakes."

"If he's going to make something, it's going to be first class all the way."

"Very impressive." She took another kale chip. "So what's in this batch again?"

"A blend of paprika, that means he uses a combination of these," he leaned in to the spice shelves, "there are five different types of paprika, cumin—I only see one of them, garlic powder—four kinds, Tellicherry black pepper, thyme, and fresh minced parsley. I think he says the fresh parsley takes some of the bitter edge off the kale."

"Well, I love these." She took another.

He went over to the counter and spun the sandwich tray that he'd placed on a wooden lazy Susan, "Take one."

She took the wrap that had turkey, bacon, and bib lettuce with an avocado and roasted corn aioli sauce. "If I lived with this man I would be fat."

"He goes through a lot of girlfriends. I never really thought about it, but that could be the reason," he joked.

He took the mushroom and grilled onion melt with rosemary and provolone on sourdough slices. They sat at the counter eating, her eyes taking in the fabulous kitchen, his eyes taking in the fabulous girl sitting beside him.

When they were done, he took a baking sheet out of the oven that had been put under the broiler then left to sit. Chaz had turned it on while they ate their sandwiches. "Kyle said if we had lunch here that we should end with these."

"What are they?" she asked looking at the cookie sheet he put on the granite countertop. It looked like a big pile of melted nachos.

"He calls it Bubble Cheese."

"Bubble Cheese?"

"Mmm hmm. It's cheese that bubbles, sometimes he even lets it brown. That's basically it. But he uses the most amazing cheeses. They come from all over the world. He has them flown in. The Solo di Bruna Parmesan Reggiano is probably my favorite. Although the English Farmhouse Cheddar is pretty remarkable too."

She picked at the pile with a fork, lifting here and there to get the idea of the melted goop that had browned and crisped with fragile little bubbles all over the top. "So he just slices cheese and melts it?"

"Until it bubbles under the broiler. It's really important that it bubbles a bit. And you can't use every cheese, this only works with some of them. Trust me, I tried. Fried Boursin was a disaster."

She laughed.

He picked up a piece of charred Emmenthaler, walked around the counter blowing it, then fed it to her.

"Oh my God!" she breathed. This is great."

"I know, and so easy huh?"

His fingers were at the right height to skim them along the sides of her thighs. So he did. And was delighted to see her shiver and flush from his touch.

He fed her bits of the fried cheese, and watched as her eyes closed and she took in deep breaths as she savored each one. This was a sensual woman, he thought, very much into enjoying life's guilty pleasures. He was hopeful that the afternoon would bring a different kind of pleasure for her to savor.

Chapter 73—Chaz & Mags
A Trip to Belks

Mags smiled up at Chaz, "Enough, if we eat any more cheese, we're going to be like an old married couple in bed fanning the covers."

"I can't believe you said that," he said as he barked out a laugh. He grabbed his water bottle and took a long swig. He picked up hers, nudged her with it and encouraged her to do the same.

"What? Hydrating?" she asked.

"Yeah, you're going to lose a lot of body fluids this afternoon."

"I can't believe you said *that*," she murmured, but put the bottle to her mouth and drank.

"Now, let's get that shirt for Kyle then come back for a nap," he said. "We might just be able to lie down after having eaten all this food by the time we get back."

Together they cleaned up the kitchen. Then Chaz grabbed the keys to the last car in the driveway, and they drove to Shallotte.

Chaz let Mags pick out the shirt for Kyle, and Mags picked out a cute sundress for Kara. "She's been doing so much for me, cooking, cleaning, laundry . . . she deserves a reward. Plus, she lost her favorite jean shorts to the sea. This will look stunning on her."

"Just why does she insist on doing it all? It's as if she thinks you need a vacation, but that she doesn't."

"We agreed not to talk about that today. Today is for fun, and relaxing, and . . ." she leaned up and kissed his cheek, then whispered in his ear, "a few naughty things thrown in."

"Well, I'm onboard for all of that. Let's go pay for these and go back to *The Cockpit*."

387

"There is definitely something perverse about me wanting to go back with you to a house called that."

"It was the only thing we could figure out that we all had in common. We're all so different, but we all have that particular part of the anatomy."

She shook her head. "If it was a house for ten women what would it be called then?"

He thought for a moment. "The Pussycat House?"

She threw her head back and laughed.

He fell for her in that moment. Hard. She was it for him. He'd never understood the expression head over heels in love before. But now he did. He was tumbling, falling and rolling—plummeting into the depths of an emotion so strong he was lightheaded from it. It was euphoria, an elation unlike anything he'd ever experienced. He was not only blissfully happy, excited, and energized in a whole new way; he was at complete peace with the thought of keeping her for all time, making her his in every way possible. And now, his desire to be with her in a physical way was usurping all other thoughts. He had to have her.

They paid for their purchases and drove back to Sunset Beach, holding hands across the console of Dev's customized Hummer H3 that he called The Beast.

Chapter 74—Chaz & Mags
Bliss

It should have been awkward, them arriving back at the empty beach house for the specific purpose of having sex. But it wasn't. They were laughing at the antics of a crazy woodpecker pecking at a flagpole on a house across the street.

"Crazy bird, he's not going to find any bugs in that pole," Mags said as Chaz was punching in the code for the front door.

"If he can even get his beak into it. That's some pretty solid metal. But I understand that if they like the sound they make, they'll keep coming back just to make it. We thought about putting up an American flag in the front courtyard of the circular drive. But it turns out there are a lot of rules about installing an American flag on a permanent pole. Did you know it has to be taken down at night unless the flag is lit anytime it's dark out? We were checking out solar lights when the guy across the street, a Vietnam vet, decided to install his. We thought two big flags on tall poles so close to each other would look rather odd, so we didn't do it. So now he has the noisy woodpecker."

"I have a neighbor at home that is wind chime crazy. She had six of them. I hated the noise they made. I finally had to talk to her about them—sweet old lady living all alone. It took me forever to build up the courage. Turns out her kids never knew what to give her for her birthdays, Mother's Days, Christmases . . . so they kept giving her wind chimes for her garden because once, she'd said she'd like to have one. Well, she was hard of hearing yet hardly ever wore her hearing aids, so she never even heard them! *I* was the only one hearing them. She took them down for me and we've been good friends ever since."

"That's a great story," Chaz said as they walked up the stairs to the main living area. He hung Dev's keys on the special key rack they'd had made for all their keys. Then turned to face her.

He took her face between his palms. "We're a great story," he murmured as he bent to kiss her. The kiss was full of longing, sweet yet fiery, his tongue breeching her lips and taking bold possession.

"I want you so badly," he whispered. His hands circled her waist then dropped to her buttocks and pulled her in close. His erection notched between her thighs and prodded.

"I can feel that you do."

"Any reservations?"

She smiled up at him. She was gone on this man. So totally gone. "None whatsoever."

He lifted her into his arms and carried her down the hall to his bedroom. He kissed her hard and fast as he placed her in the middle of his bed, then followed her down, after kicking off his shoes.

Then he slowly undressed her, removing her sandals, her white shorts and her sleeveless blouse, to reveal the sexiest lingerie he'd ever seen.

"You are a delightful confection, like soft spun lilac sugar. Cotton candy that I'm going to eat right up." He began kissing her through her bralette, covering every inch of the full cups, while ignoring the nipples that strained against the lace. She writhed on the duvet, finally grabbing his head and directing his mouth to a hard peak. He sucked through the material before he pulled one cup aside and took her nipple into his mouth. She moaned and the sound of her pleasure made his cock jump and grow even more than it already had. He reached down to unzip his fly to stem the discomfort.

The other breast received equal treatment before he unclipped the clasp and pulled the straps off her shoulders. He flung the bra to the floor.

"Look at how lovely you are." Then there was no more talking as his mouth stayed busy pleasuring her.

After lavishing her breasts and causing her to arch off the

bed he kissed down her torso and decided to torment her in other ways. He kissed between her legs where the lace of her crotch was soaked with her wetness. He murmured his approval and slid his fingers under the elastic until he was able to enter her and send his finger deep. Her hips lifted to meet it and she moaned, "Ohhhh, yes, yes."

Two fingers went inside her. She arched up to meet them.

He removed his fingers and slid her panties down her legs. Then he ducked his head and feasted. She was like a lit firecracker, gyrating and searching for his roaming tongue, trying to get it to touch her where she needed to feel it. He murmured against her, "Not yet." And spanked her lightly on the inside of her thigh when she refused to cooperate. "I am not ready to move on yet, behave."

His tongue swirled inside her, lapped up and down her sleek lips, then his lips kissed and sucked on her sweet flesh, tasting every part of her. Except the throbbing part she wanted him to taste . . . lick . . . suck.

"Chaz, please."

"What angel? Please what?"

"Please, here." Her hand came down and she used her middle finger to touch her swollen clit. "Here. Kiss me here, please."

He did. Tongued it. Then lightly sucked.

Her hips left the bed to grind against his mouth. She came with rough jerks, uncontrollable spasms, and a violent thrashing of her legs as he felt the throbbing nub pulse against his tongue.

Her loud, "Ah, ah, ahhhhhh!" filled the room, the sound music to his ears in the otherwise quiet house.

He allowed her to come down from her peak, settle her hips back onto the bed, before kissing lightly all over her, fondling with her sweet, curling, damp hairs, and licking the moisture off her thighs.

Then he stood to remove his clothes and took a condom from his pants pocket. He looked down at her sprawled on the covers. In his bed. Looking dreamily up at him.

She watched him roll the condom on.

He saw her chest heave at the pleasure the sight gave her. When he was fully sheathed he asked, "You ready for this?"

"Absolutely."

It was all he needed to hear. He covered her body with his. Allowed his cock to prod and poke, then laughed when she greedily grasped it and placed it where she wanted it and shoved it between her slippery lips.

He slid inside and took a few seconds to appreciate the joining of their bodies before moving. "I like this," he whispered against her neck. "I like this a lot."

"Me too," she agreed, looking up at him, one hand caressing his cheek

Then he started moving. Thrusting and grinding in rhythm with her as she used her hands clasped to his buttocks to guide him and urge him on. Her legs wrapped around his hips and pulled him even closer. Then she froze, dug her nails into the flesh of his cheeks and arched into him, holding him tight to her while another orgasm took her. He felt the pulse of it, the heat and shuddering response of her body eclipsing anything he'd ever felt before. It was as if an earthquake rumbled through her body, morphed into a volcano, and spewed like a geyser. He went with her, over the edge to his own oblivion, his heartbeat racing as his body released into hers, the very essence of his manhood claiming her.

Within seconds, he was collapsed on top of her, trying to catch his breath.

Her whispered, "Again please," made him chuckle.

He dropped to her side and pulled her in close, holding her tight to his chest.

"Definitely. Just give me time to regroup."

She stroked her fingers down his back, toying with his buttocks. "Not going anywhere."

A minute later she was asleep. He kissed her temple and joined her.

The sound of many feet clomping up the stairs woke them and Chaz jumped up to close the bedroom door and to remove and dispose of the condom. On the way back to her, he glanced at the clock, picked up his shorts, and fumbled in his pants pocket for another condom. It was almost four o'clock. They'd slept for two hours, him holding her with their legs entwined. Heaven. Pure heaven.

He slid back in beside her. Her eyes fluttered open. She too, looked at the clock on the nightstand. "I can't believe we slept away the afternoon."

He smiled. "Well, apparently we needed it."

"It was a nice nap."

"It was," he agreed.

"Well, I guess I'd better be going, Kara's going to be wondering what happened to me."

He kissed her shoulder. "Let her wonder." His hand cupped her breast, ran down her torso, and then up between her legs. His fingers stroked her, entered her, and quickly made her ready for him. Then he rolled over onto his back, taking her with him. He rolled on the condom he'd placed on the bed, and then easily lifted her onto him.

As she settled onto him, he stroked her breasts, pinched her nipples, and toyed with her clit. When the bed began to squeak with her exuberance he knew all his friends were listening. But he didn't care. Not one whit. He let her ride him to her pleasure and then grinned broadly when she found it, throwing her head back and moaning as she straddled him, then she let out one soft whimper after another and collapsed.

"You've ruined me," she whispered a few moments later.

"How did I ruin you?"

"You made me remember how good sex with a man can be. I'm an independent woman. I was thinking I might be able to forego men in my future. You've quashed that idea."

He turned to her and played with a curl of her hair. "Have I now?"

"Yes. I am totally ruined."

"When can I see you again, so I can do more of the same?"

"I'm not sure. Kara and I were going to go out for dinner tonight, but now that Ryder's in the picture, I don't really know what the plans are."

"Do they have to involve you?"

"That is a good question. Is this Ryder guy going to be trouble?"

"No. He's a good guy. He'd really like to settle down and have a whole passel of kids, but it just hasn't worked out for him."

"Well I hope this is just a quick fling for her, he lives too far from Raleigh."

"I live pretty far from Raleigh too, but I don't want this to be a quick fling."

She turned on her side and snuggled into him. "We're leaving in a few days. I've got a business to run and you've got a business to run. I don't see how this can work."

"We'll figure it out. This is too good to let go."

"It is, isn't it?" she agreed.

Just then her phone rang. "That'll be Kara."

"Why don't you see if she and Ryder want to go out to dinner with us? My treat."

"Okay, I'll ask. Do you mind if I take the call in your bathroom?"

He gave a flourish of his hand. "Help yourself. Me casa es su casa."

He watched as she slid out of bed, bent and grabbed her phone from the pocket of her shorts and dashed to the en suite as she swiped at the screen. What a fine ass, he thought. A delectably fine ass indeed.

Chapter 75—Chaz & Mags
Last Night at the Beach

When she came out of the bathroom she had a frown on her face.

"What's wrong?" he asked.

"She said she and Ryder need to finish their project tonight because we're going home tomorrow. I thought we were leaving the next day. She said originally we were, but the owner of the house, who's her boss, said she has a renter coming in the day after tomorrow. So, it turns out tomorrow is pack up and clean up day, then the drive home."

"Well, that is not the best news, but let's make the most of your last night. How about we grab some binoculars and go birding at the observation deck on Shoreline Drive, then continue on to Calabash . . . go to The Grapevine and have a nice, intimate dinner, just the two of us?"

"That sounds nice. I'd like that."

"Kyle's got that wedding tonight so we can use his car, or you can experience *Trusty Busty*, my open-air Jeep."

"Oh, it's all about the experience, let's do the Jeep. I'll go get a shower and put on a sun dress."

"I'll do the same, but chinos and a shirt for me instead. Hey, I have an idea . . . how about we shower here, together?"

She pushed against his chest as she walked by, then grabbed her clothes off the floor and began dressing. "Because I am hungry, and that will only delay dinner."

"Oh, I get it, stomach trumps spontaneous shower sex. I'll have to remember that."

She stood from pulling up her shorts. "Actually, it wouldn't normally. But I'm worried about Kara. How's she's going to deal with leaving Ryder tomorrow. She seems pretty gone on him."

"He's an easy guy to get to like. He's a genuine guy though, so I can't imagine he's stringing her along."

"It's not that. She just hasn't dated for a while. I think he's been good for her. But he lives too far away to be boyfriend material."

"You never know . . . she can teach anywhere, and he can build anywhere. Hell, I'd hire him and promise him the moon. But honestly, I'm not worried about them right now. I wonder about us . . . and our connection."

"I don't want to think about tomorrow today. Let's go watch some birds and fill our bellies with pasta."

"Good idea. I'll call and get reservations for six. I'll pull Busty over to your driveway at five-fifteen, that gives us plenty of time for bird watching on the way."

"It's a date."

He smiled back, then walked over and wrapped his arms around her and looked down into her face while caressing her cheek, her ear, her neck.

"Yes, yes it is. We've come a long way this week. You can actually say the word date now."

She smiled up at him. "Just remember, we're leaving tomorrow. Time for us both to get back to our jobs."

He sighed. "But we still have tonight. Let's make the most of it."

She nodded and then left his room. He heard her going through the house, saying hi to the guys who were returning from the fishing trip and unpacking coolers as she made her way through the house and out through the door on to the back deck.

He would have accompanied her on her walk of shame, except he hadn't bothered to dress, so focused was he on securing her for her last hours here at the beach.

Chapter 76—Chaz & Mags
Love Birds Bird Watching

They stood side-by-side leaning on the railing, binoculars propped on bent elbows as they stared out at one of the Twin Lakes, and called out names of birds they were identifying.

As an official stop on the North Carolina Birding Trail, the bird walk platform was a busy place. They had a dual head optical zoom binocular donated by Sunset Vision that could get viewers 20 times closer to the birds, but Chaz had always found that bringing their own, allowed for more time to relax and view the birds and alligators. When people were waiting, you felt guilty about lingering and watching the wood storks flock to the trees to roost for the night when sunset was settling in.

"I see a red headed woodpecker going at it on a dead tree over there on the right."

"Yeah. He really is. Grubby bird looking for grubs," Chaz murmured. "He should have a talk with Flagpole Woody. "Hey look to your right, there's a black-crowned night heron still as a statue stalking a frog. Watch it. Watch it. Yup. Got it. What a patient hunter."

"There are so many egrets. Never seen so many in one place," she whispered as she refocused her set of binoculars on one that just flew by.

"This is really the best time of day. They are feeding and arriving back home at the end of a day spent in the marshes."

"What a perfect place. Those houses across the way must cost a fortune."

"Some of the best real estate in the county, maybe even the country. I'm glad we built *The Cockpit* when we did."

"You should build a tree house here."

"The trees are not big and sturdy enough this close to the coast. The roots are not deep enough in most cases, unless you want a really tiny tree house."

"Actually, I'm not all that crazy about the idea. I can see the appeal for a vacation maybe, but not for day-to-day-living."

"I'm getting ready to build one with twenty cat walks. When it's finished, you should come see it."

"Where's it going to be?"

"Oregon."

"Yikes, that's a long way away."

"I know."

Nothing else was said as they each drew into their own world, watching Summer Tanagers, White Ibis, and Snowy Egrets hunt, fly in to roost, and settle in for the night.

"Our reservation is in ten minutes," Chaz murmured. "But if you want to stay, I'm sure I can change it."

"No. I'm hungry. I'm sure I could stay here and do this for hours. It's so peaceful. So beautiful."

"You're so beautiful."

She put her binoculars down and looked at him. Really looked at him. "You are amazing. So kind, so generous, so caring. Where've you been all my life?"

He took her hand in his. "Working my way here. To this moment."

She met his eyes. Drank him in. "I feel things I shouldn't feel."

"Who says you shouldn't feel them?"

"My heart," she whispered.

"Well, tell it to shut up," he murmured as he leaned in for a kiss. "Tell it to shut the hell up."

He took her lips with his and kissed her deeply, savoring the taste of her, the smell of her, the essence that was her. He wanted to keep her. He just hadn't figured out how to do that yet.

Chapter 77—Chas & Mags, Ryder & Kara
Dinner at Mac's Place

Mac, with his uncanny memory, recognized Chaz and flirted with Mags before ushering them to a corner table and arranging for their drinks. Tonight was going to be a celebratory time, so Chaz ordered a glass of champagne for the two of them.

They toasted the book, *Me Before You,* and unrequited love everywhere as they finally acknowledged theirs was not a one-sided love affair, that they were both in sync with their feelings.

"I don't want us to end," Chaz said, after they had ordered, and handed back the menus. "How can we do this?"

"Maybe you could fly into Raleigh one weekend a month . . ."

"Maybe. But I want more."

"More? How much more?"

"I don't know. I just want more. More of you." Her took one of her hands in both of his. "I am falling hard for you. I'm thinking long-term. Permanent long term."

"Permanent long-term," she repeated.

"Yeah. The ring, the walk down the aisle, the honeymoon in Mauritius . . ."

"You can't be serious."

"I believe I am." His eyes met hers. "I love you, Mags. I knew it from the moment I saw you on the beach that day, when you had trouble getting back from your walk to Bird Island."

"You saw all that?"

"I was ready to be Sir Galahad but your sister beat me to it. You two are very close."

"Yeah. We've always been there for each other."

Their plates were delivered.

"Mmm, this smells heavenly." She had ordered the Santa Fe Pasta.

He broke a piece of bread and dipped it in the olive oil with garlic and Mediterranean spices. He was nervous. He'd put it out there that he loved her. Her response hadn't been to acknowledge her reciprocal feelings.

"Are you looking forward to getting home?" he asked, trying to keep the conversation relevant.

She took a bite of her pasta. "Not really. I guess I've been away from it too long."

"Why is that?"

The waiter came back to ask how everything was.

Then Ryder and Kara came strolling up to their table. "We finished our project!" Kara announced.

"Great! Now will you tell me what it was?" Mags asked as she put her fork down beside her plate.

"We'll show you. Tonight. After dinner."

"You haven't eaten yet?"

"No, we wanted to get it done. And now it is."

Chaz looked up at Ryder, the question in his eyes.

"We're waiting for a table."

Chaz didn't hesitate. He pulled out a chair for Kara, then one for Ryder. "Here, join us. We invited you, after all."

"You're sure?" Ryder asked.

"Definitely," Chaz murmured, when it didn't seem all that definite, at all. But his innate politeness always came through.

The waiter came and took their drink and food order and Ryder and Kara regaled them about the bathroom renovation they'd done together. And the hilarious challenges they'd had with this new project while shopping at Home Depot.

"So, we get to see this mysterious project when we get back to the beach house?" Mags asked between bites of chicken and pasta.

"Yes. It's a gift for you," Kara whispered. "We made

something for you. We'll need Chaz and Ryder to lift it into your SUV."

"You sure it'll fit with all our stuff?"

"Yeah, Ryder already measured."

"Can't wait to see what this is," Mags murmured, giving off vibes that she had her doubts about whatever this project was, coming home with them.

Mags looked up and scanned Kara's face. "So it's just for me?"

"Yeah, it's for your new office."

"Aww, that's sweet. Where did you make this? I never heard any banging going on."

"We screwed," She looked over at Ryder and winked, "it . . . together."

Mags cleared her throat in a very practiced way, as if she had always warned Kara of her indiscretions in this manner.

"I know, I know. Oversharing."

Ryder reached out and covered her hand where it rested on the table. "It's okay. 'Cause it's gonna happen a lot more. I asked Kara to marry me."

The wine glass in Mags hand stopped on the way to her mouth. "What?"

Kara brought her other hand up from under the table. On her ring finger was a small brilliant cut diamond. "He took me to Tripp's and we picked it out this afternoon."

"Kara, this is pretty fast."

"I know I know. I knew you'd say that. But it's not like we're getting married tomorrow. I have to find a teaching job in Tennessee first before we can plan anything."

"You're moving?" That seemed more of a surprise than the fact that she was engaged to be married.

Sensing her agitation, Chaz, put his hand under the table and clasped the one resting on her thigh, and gently squeezed it.

"His job pays way more than mine and I kind of like the idea of a fresh start. And you know I pretty much hate the principal I'm working for now."

"Yeah, but you were about to reap some nice benefits from how beautiful you've made her beach house."

"That wouldn't have lasted more than a day or so. She's a mean woman. I know you don't want me to move away, but it's not like I'm going tomorrow. And Raleigh has an airport, and Nashville has an airport."

"And I have access to a plane," Chaz said, squeezing her hand again while raising his other one for the waiter who was passing by. "Can we get a bottle of champagne and four glasses, we're celebrating an engagement."

"Yes, sir! Wonderful news."

"Not so sure about that," Mags muttered.

"C'mon Mags, be happy for me, I'm in love!"

Mags looked over at her, took in her bright eyes, her glowing face, her wide grin, and she smiled. She supposed her wild child sister could have done worse. At least this guy had a job. And after all Kara had done for her these last two years, she deserved some happiness. She smiled and gestured to take her hand. "Let me see that ring."

After admiring it, she got up and walked around the table to give her sister a big hug. "I'm happy for you. Just sad you're going to be moving so far away."

"We both work so much that we hardly ever see each other, except for occasional weekends and holidays. And Ryder says you ain't seen Christmas done right until you've seen it in Nashville."

The waiter brought a stand that held a bucket with an opened bottle of champagne in it. Chaz did the honors of pouring and then toasting the happy couple. Then they finished their dinner, and over cheesecake argued over who was going to World Series.

When they got back to the girls' beach house, Ryder and Kara led them under the steps to an area back by the outdoor shower. Then Ryder pulled off a tarp covering something low and bulky, and Mags saw the beautiful glassed-in credenza. The low cabinet was several feet long with an open bookcase built into one end. The wood was fine-grained ebony, rubbed and finished to a soft satin finish. The knobs on the cabinets had a soft silver patina and were etched sand dollars.

"Oh, it's gorgeous," Mags breathed, as she walked over and smoothed a hand along the top. "Kara, how did you do this? This is amazing."

"Ryder showed me how. He makes furniture when he's not doing construction work."

She turned to Ryder. "Thank you. It is lovely."

"I figured you needed a place for all those accounting books you collected while getting your CPA. Now you can get them off the floor."

Mags laughed. "Yeah, that'll be nice. And a lot more professional looking for clients."

Ryder went over to his truck and got out two cloth furniture pads. "These will protect it until you get it home. Chaz, can you help me get it into Mags' truck?"

"Sure. You want to back her SUV up, or carry it around to the back?"

"It's pretty heavy, let's back it up."

Mags handed Ryder the keys and together he and Chaz put the back seat down and loaded the cabinet on its side into the back. Mags and Kara stood watching them, their arms around each other smiling.

"It's going to look so nice in your office."

"I know! Thank you Kara, and congratulations. Looks like you found a good one."

"He's the best. We really have a good time together. We laugh so much. I can't wait to be his wife."

"Well, I guess we'll be planning a wedding."

"Yeah. But not yet. I need to find a job first."

"I'm sure you'll find one. You're a great teacher."

"Yeah, but you-know-who has to write a good

recommendation."

"She will. Tell her your sister has connections that can get her audited."

Kara snorted with laughter.

After the cabinet was loaded, Ryder and Kara left for what would be their last walk on the beach together, as Ryder was leaving at dawn to get back for a job the following day.

Chaz walked Mags to her door. "Our dinner out got crashed."

She nodded, "And wow, what news. Tell me the truth Chaz, is he going to be good for her?"

She unlocked the door and he followed her inside.

"He will be a great husband and an even better father if they have kids. And the clan will love her."

"The clan?" she asked as she removed her sweater and put her purse on a side table.

"His family has lived in that area for two hundred years. His mom and dad are genuinely nice, helpful people. He won't tell her this, and nobody else will, but they have money. Lots of it. They come from hardworking, frugal people who have always worked for themselves. There's no telling how much money has been squirreled away and handed down over the generations. She won't have to work unless she wants to, and she won't want for anything. Except maybe for Ryder to stay home more often. He has a good business going, travels all over the country doing custom jobs. I use him myself, whenever he's available."

"Well, she seems to love him."

"You should know he was engaged before and that I am the reason it didn't work out."

"What?"

"I told your sister about it already. It's the reason he's here actually. He's been helping her with the chores the boss from *The Devil Wears Prada* lined up for her. As a favor to me, he drove out here to do some sheetrock work. I called in a ten-year-old-chit."

Just then, Kara burst through the door. "I'm sleeping in the big house tonight! It may be two or three weeks before we can see each other again. Gotta get some stuff."

"Oh, okay . . . I thought we could talk."

"We can talk tomorrow," she called out as she ran into the bathroom with her cosmetic bag. "We'll be in the car for three or four hours."

Chaz rubbed his fingers up and down the back of Mags' neck. "You could come to the 'big house' too. Or I could stay here?"

"She's tired, Chaz. She needs her rest," Kara called out. "Can't you tell by the blue shadows under her eyes? And tomorrow's going to be a long day for her."

Chaz took her shoulders and turned her to the light, looking down into her eyes. "She's right. You do look tired. "I'll come over in the morning and help you guys clean and pack up."

"You don't have to do that."

"I want to. And it'll be a way to spend more time with you before you head home. I know my way around a vacuum and a mop. I can do that while you gather your things and pack them up."

"Okay. I have a bunch of food I want to pack up and drop off for Second Helping."

"I can help with that too."

"Okay. I am a bit tired. I'll go read in bed for a bit."

He kissed her lightly on the lips. "Can I tuck you in?"

She laughed. "I'm not a child."

He gave her a wicked leer, "Oh, I definitely know that. How about I just undress you?"

"I know where that will lead . . ."

Kara walked between them to get to the door. "She's tired, Chaz."

He held his hands up. "Okay, okay. I'm going. But I really would like to know what this over protective sibling thing is all about."

"And I would like to know about this engagement you broke up that merited a favor from Ryder . . ." she smoothed his hair back from his forehead, loving the feel of the thick strands.

"Let's talk in the morning. I really am all in right now," she kissed him on the chin.

He kissed her on the lips, letting his lips mesh with hers before pulling back. "See you in the morning then, what time?"

"Nine-ish. I want to go to the Mailbox one last time first."

"See you then." He closed the door behind him, and then stared at his hand on the knob. Another night of him not knowing what was going on between Mags and her sister. He was beginning to have a suspicious feeling. Dread hinted at the edges of his consciousness. He was pretty sure he knew why. It terrified him not knowing everything that concerned Mags.

Chapter 78—Chaz & Mags
The Mailbox Shares a Secret

Early the next morning, Chaz watched Mags leave for The Mailbox. Heard her clomp down the steps, and then watched her walk across the access. She was going to leave without telling him what was going on. She was going to end this, and get back to her life. Without him. He knew it. Something was not going to allow her to take this happiness they had when they were together and run with it.

He finished his coffee, giving her a good head start, and then followed her from the street side so she wouldn't see him. He walked to the end of the road, where the last access was, where Bird Island loomed in the distance.

He walked down the 40th Street access, stopping to read the messages on the shell trees and then did push ups against the bench seat that had a clear view of the beach.

When he saw her pass by on her way back, he waited a few minutes until he could see that she was far enough away that she couldn't turn back and recognize him.

Then he walked down the rest of the access and took an angled path down the beach, heading directly to The Mailbox.

He got there and was thankfully alone, so he could rifle through the notebooks and find her entry. Realizing he had never seen her handwriting, he looked for the date. He knew he'd found it when he saw a letter in beautiful blue cursive. The precise handwriting suited the meticulous trait of an A personality. He took the notebook to the bench and read:

I came to Sunset Beach to get my bloom back. Somewhere between vomiting up my stomach contents four times a day, and hearing those wonderful words from Dr. Balfour that I was out of danger, I had lost my glow, my inner bloom. Strangers have told me, and my best friends have expounded on this over the years, that the thing that first drew them to me was my radiance – the light that came from within, from being content with my near-perfect life. My bright positive outlook was because things had always gone so well for me. And I knew it. I was thankful for it. I reveled in it and I made sure everyone around me shared in my joy. I loved my life. Until two years ago when things became far from perfect with three little words, "You have cancer."

So like an apple that needs to be shined against a flannel shirt, I came here to recapture my inner glow. I know what it is. I know where it comes from. It's just a little buried right now. I need to find it and let it shine as they say in the song, so others can see it, too. So they can know I'm all right now, that everyone's prayers have been answered.

But like a glowworm, I need a little re-charging. I am a cellphone on the last bar. Slowly this island has worked its magic on me. Soon, I will shine on, shine on, like a harvest moon up in the sky . . .

One of my nights here there was a Super Moon Party on the beach. I basked in the light of the moon while celebrating my victory, absorbing every ray. Tomorrow I will head home and I will glow, because I met a man who said I was beautiful, and showed me that life can be beautiful and fun again. I'll be back next year to see the sunrises and sunsets and to bask in the glow of moonlight on this beautiful beach. Mags

He ran back after reading her entry. Toward the end of the run, he angled across the soft sand. With a purposeful stride, he had one goal in mind. He saw her up ahead, leaving the beach and then climbing the access. His eyes followed her as she went up the steps and entered her house.

He ran up the steps. Knocking on her door, then walking right in, he had to step back. Though it was not yet close to ten, he was surprised to see several tote bags and a full set of luggage ready and waiting by the door, along with a box of food marked "Second Helping."

She was in the kitchen, standing by the fridge, chugging down a bottle of water. Her eyes met his and she choked. Then fought to keep the water from going everywhere. She lowered the bottle. Took in his sweat-coated face and limbs. It was obvious that he'd been running on the beach. She had a feeling that he'd discovered her secret.

"Were you trying to leave without seeing me?"

She sighed. "Kind of."

"I just came from The Mailbox. I read your letter. Why didn't you tell me?"

Tears filled her eyes as she stared up at him. "You thought I was perfect. Why would I want to change that?" she sobbed. Pulling a paper towel off the dispenser over the sink, she used it to swipe at her face. He handed her a handkerchief that he took from his front pocket.

He pulled her in close and kissed her under her ear. "I still think you're perfect. Just because you were sick doesn't change that."

"It sure did for the man I was engaged to."

"Is that why he broke it off?"

"Yes, said he couldn't deal with it all, especially if I lost my breasts. He'd never even paid any attention to the fact that I told him my cancer was in my lungs. Plus, he wanted children and he didn't want them to be genetically predisposed to cancer."

"I'm not him. I'll take you anyway I can get you. And any kids you'd like to give me."

"I'm in remission now, but what if it comes back?"

"Then the man who loves and adores you will take care of it."

"I don't think I can go through all that again."

"Yes, you can. And you will. I'll get you through it, because I don't ever want to lose you. I love you, and I'm confident that you love me."

There was silence as she painstakingly opened his handkerchief, then ungraciously blew her nose into it.

He chuckled. For a dainty woman she made a fair amount of noise.

"You'll have someone who loves you taking care of you if your cancer ever comes back."

A loud "Ahem!" came from the elevated walkway.

They both looked up to see Kara looking down at them and smirking. "She had someone who loved her taking care of her this time."

He smiled back up at her, "And I thank you for that with all my heart." He placed his hand over his heart, to drive the message home and to also take something out of his shirt pocket. He took Mags' hand in his and slipped the ring he'd taken from his pocket onto her ring finger. "But I've got this now, she's mine."

Mags looked down at the ring on her finger. It was a wide gold band with a huge heart-shaped diamond embedded in the center. She doubted she'd ever seen a thicker, heavier wedding band, yet it appeared stylishly feminine on her finger.

Then he pulled a box from a flapped pocket on his khaki shorts. He flicked the box open with his thumb to show a male version of the same band.

"I don't want anyone to have difficulty seeing these," he whispered. "Even from a distance. You belong to me now. And I will always be there for you, no matter what. You can count on it."

He took her face between his hands and kissed her hard. "I love you Mags, you will marry me, won't you?"

She smiled up at him. "Yes."

While she began crying again, Kara began clapping.

"Bravo Chaz. Well done," she called from above, her

own eyes tearing.

"He looked up at her and grinned. "I would have sworn you didn't like me."

She sassed him back. "I didn't."

"What changed?

"Ryder. And what you agreed to do for him. You kept him from marrying that scumbag."

"I have yet to hear this story . . .," Mags prompted.

"Uh, I'll embellish later. For now let's just say I proved her unworthy to marry my friend."

Kara called down. "And there's a video! He saved Ryder a lot of money too."

"That's not a given, the case is in its final appeal."

"Who's going to find in his favor with that proof?"

"Kara," he warned. "You are not going to see that tape and neither is Mags."

"Well . . . still it was a gallant thing to do. Under the circumstances," Kara called down, then turned and stalked off.

"What was this favor you did, or shouldn't I ask?"

He smiled down at her and ran a fingertip over her bottom lip."

"I'll give you a sample later, after I get you home."

"You're coming with us? I thought you were here for two weeks."

"I have several days left of my vacation, but I'd rather spend them with you than with nine sweaty, smelly guys. Plus, you'll need help getting that chest into your house. I'll come back here in a few days and fly Rick's plane back to Greensboro. Then I'll work on relocating my office so I can be closer to you. That okay?"

She wrapped her arms around his neck. "That's more than okay. It's perfect."

She looked down at the ring on her finger. "How did you ever manage to get these overnight?

"I built an anchor store for a jeweler in Greensboro a

few years back. He went to his store last night and picked out a set of wedding bands matching my description, then had them couriered here. They got here around two a.m."

"Wow, a little bit of trouble."

"I had a hunch you were going to run out on me. Not give us a chance. I had to show you that I'm in this. Whatever comes, I'll be by your side. Always."

He bent and kissed her, sealing the promise to always be there for her.

Chapter 79—Kyle & Amy
A Beach Wedding and Cake!

Kyle got to the beach access at the prescribed time and commandeered a bike for himself as well as one for Amy from the bike rental guy. And twice, while he was waiting for her, he had to give one of the wedding guests the stink eye as they circled, admiring them. As the first one there on the beach, he'd chosen two of the newer bikes that had been reserved for the wedding party. He figured, if you were the last one to a wedding, you deserved to ride the rusty bike with the creaky wheel.

Amy got a late start leaving for the 40th Street Access. She arrived huffing and holding her side as she hurried down the wooden decking, her bouquet gripped in her hand. Due to the heat and humidity, her pert, fluffy hairdo with the side swept bangs was no more, replaced by a messy bun and windblown bangs. One of the other bridesmaids said that it showed off her graceful neck. So that was a plus.

Kyle saw Amy's auburn hair, piled high, bobbing between the bridal party members before she came into view on the long boardwalk. He'd known it was her; that hair of hers was distinctive. It wasn't a color many women could wear. Yet it suited her perfectly.

When he saw the dress she wore, he appreciated the fact that she had forged ahead of the group, as now he had a truly lovely view to admire until she got to him. When she looked up and saw him waiting for her, she smiled and he couldn't help but place his hand over his heart. It was as if he was trying to keep it from lurching out of his chest, like it did in the old Pepe Le Pew cartoons.

She was lovely, fresh looking. And she seemed delighted to see him at the end of the wooden planking, standing there between two bikes daring anyone to try to run off with his steeds.

When she got closer, he frowned in concern. Why was she holding her side? She seemed out of breath. It was warm, and it was the longest beach access he'd ever seen. She'd probably been running for hours, doing all manner of things.

He stepped forward to meet her. "You okay?"

"Yeah. Sure. Just out of . . . breath. You?"

"I'm fine. Just getting worried. Thought I was being left at the altar, in a manner of speaking."

She smiled. "No. Just a myriad of problems."

"Why are you holding your side?"

She gave him a wry look. "Problem number one. My dress is a tad too small."

"Don't they do fittings for these kinds of affairs?"

"This isn't that kind of wedding. You go, pick out one of the reserved dresses and just show up in it."

"So you didn't try it on?"

"I did. I knew it was too small then, but the size 6 was cheaper than the size 8 as it had a lipstick stain on it." She lifted a gaudy rhinestone broach from the silky fabric. He figured it was about two inches up from where her nipple would be. Sure enough, under the pin was a mauve smear that clearly no amount of scrubbing had been able to remove.

"Figured I could get down to a six and make it work. They must've sized the dress wrong. Even losing eight pounds I couldn't get my breasts to cooperate and get down to a size 6."

"Thank God!" he said, clutching his chest as if acknowledging that she had just averted disaster.

Amy laughed and smacked him on his Hawaiian print sleeve. "C'mon, we'd better get down there, we're already late."

"I have your horse saddled and waiting," he said, indicating the woman's bike. "Almost had to do battle to keep it. I had no idea how popular baskets were for women's bikes."

"Thank you. The basket will be perfect for my bouquet."

He helped her onto the seat then helped her tuck portions of the dress out of harm's way. In the process, he ran his thumb alongside her knee and saw her shiver. What an excellent sign, he thought. Even unable to breathe, she's eager. "You didn't forget the surplus icing?" he asked, leaning in, by her ear.

"Under the tent in a cooler. Ready and waiting."

He felt a shiver of his own go through him as he imagined her licking—

"Hey! Who's he? What's he doing here?" a voice called out in their direction.

"I told you, Jedidiah, this is my date. Kyle, this is Jedidiah."

"Well, he's not in the wedding party. You're supposed to be with me."

"Only when we're standing up for Jessie Mae and Donnie Lee at the ceremony."

"And at the head table. And for posed pictures. And for dancing."

"There is no head table and you get one dance, that's it. And no pictures, period. I do not want to remember this dress. There goes the bride, we'd better hurry!" she called over to Kyle. He got on his bike and together they peddled the 1.4 miles south to the Kindred Spirit Mailbox on Bird Island.

On the way down, Amy explained that the couple had a South Carolina wedding permit, as The Mailbox was located just over the North Carolina line. The groom had proposed there and the bride, who had always wanted to be married on the beach, decided that The Mailbox was the perfect place for the wedding. Most of the guests were thinking otherwise.

By the time they all got down to the little encampment everyone was anxious for the ceremony to be over with. It was hot. There was no place to sit. Sand was getting in the women's shoes. And the men—never keen to be at a wedding in the first place—bemoaned the lack of a bar, and the groom not having the foresight to have thought of trolleying down a cooler of beer. Someone handed out bottles of cold water though, and each participant thankfully took theirs as they "parked" their bikes.

Amy handed Kyle one of the wedding favors, a wooden block that had been hand painted with the flowers chosen for the bride's bouquet with the bride and groom's names intertwined on a ribbon that wove around the stems. "I painted all of these, took me forever, every night for a month. Aren't they pretty?"

He looked down, "Yes. Very nice." He shoved it into his pants pocket. He had no idea what it was for, or what he was supposed to do with it.

"It's for your bike."

"My bike?"

"Yeah." She bent down and placed hers under her kickstand, giving him a view of her inner thigh that sent heat coursing below his waist. It was 82 degrees. He didn't need the erection or the heat right now. His addled brain said, "You bury it in the sand?"

"No, silly. You use it to disperse the weight to a bigger area so your bike stand doesn't sink into the sand and topple your bike over."

"Oh." He took it out of his pocket, looked at it again, and said, "Clever, very clever," before he placed it on the sand, set his bike stand atop it and let go. "That's amazing, Amy. You're beautiful *and* brilliant."

He looked around at all the parked bikes, each on its own round little flowered block. Thirty-some bikes. Simple thing really, she could have just handed out jar lids, they would have done the same exact thing. But she had stayed up every night for a month and hand painted each one for the wedding guests. *How had he ended up on a date with such a sweet young thing?*

He smiled at her, helped her shake out her dress, then took her hand and walked her over to Jedidiah. "Here, you may stand next to her. You may talk to her. But no touching. I'm going to be right over there, watching." Kyle pointed to a place not ten feet away. Then he bent, kissed Amy on the forehead, and winked at her before he went to stand by the only other man there who seemed to be on his own.

The ceremony went smoothly, until the groom dropped the ring in the sand. Amy came to the rescue with a piece of tulle she unwrapped from her bouquet and used as a makeshift sieve. *Resourceful. This woman was a wonder.*

They had to hang around the beach for photographs, then en masse they all made their way back to the access where some turned in their bikes. Kyle and Amy opted to keep theirs and rode them to The Sunset Inn, stopping twice to pet dogs. He soon learned that Amy couldn't stand to pass one by without saying hi and giving their snout and forehead a vigorous rub. "Dog is God backward, it's a good time to count your blessings," she said. *What a tender heart she had,* Kyle thought as one dog licked her chin joyfully while he got a two-handed scratch behind both ears.

It seemed Amy had a lot of official duties to perform when they arrived at the site, so they parted, and while he moseyed around sampling the big-box-bought hors d'oevres and watching the deejay set up, she got the toasts going. Kyle kept a roving eye on Amy as she moved through the crowd, letting Jedidiah know he was still on duty by looking pointedly at him and then refocusing on Amy.

A few times, while Amy was at his side introducing him, people broke in saying, "How are the—" or "What's happening with—" Each time Amy abruptly cut their words off by saying, "Just fine, everyone's just fine," followed by a steely, slit-eyed look that he supposed meant something to the recipients because each time, they got the message and slinked away.

It happened again when they were standing beside the cake table. Together, he and Amy had cut and plated all three tiers of both cakes. They had just put aside two plates for themselves when a big, well-perfumed woman with pink flamingos bouncing around the brim of her hat marched up to Amy. She reached out and gripped both of Amy's shoulders, pulled her into her ample chest and smothered her with a hug as she gushed, "Amy, Amy, Amy. I've been thinking about you so much lately, how have you managed with all the—"

"Esther Mae! I have been thinking about you, too!" Amy stepped back and took both of the lady's hands and quickly walked the woman away from him. As she took the woman away without even introducing him, he could hear Amy chattering and talking over the woman's words, "You don't need to worry about me, honey. I'm doin' jus' fine. Things could not be better. No indeed. And business simply could not *be* any better. I'm up to my elbows in batter nearly all the time."

He frowned. For the fourth or fifth time, he had the distinct feeling that Amy was hiding something from him. He couldn't be sure. But darned if she didn't stay glued to his side and determined to keep her friends and family from talking to him. Maybe he was imagining it or maybe she was just protecting him from being saddled with the more peculiar guests that seemed to attend most weddings. She certainly knew everyone there, and clearly everyone there knew her and cared about her. They all seemed to be concerned about her welfare, that's for sure, he thought, as he grabbed their cake plates and made for a secluded table in the back of the tent to wait for her return.

He watched her pat the woman on the shoulder, give her a quick squeezing hug, and grace her with a smile that was genuine. She looked up and scanned for him and when she saw him, beamed that same smile at him.

"Cake time!" she said as she slid into the seat beside him. "Time to see how all this hard work tastes."

He nodded over toward the cake table. "I don't think you have to worry. That old man is going back for his third piece."

She turned to see who he was talking about and nodded her assent as she laughed. "That's Grandpa Gary, he has an artificial leg and everyone says he stores food in it. He lives for buffets. And my cake," she added with a smile.

God, she was beautiful, so fresh, and so alive. He'd never met a woman who smiled so much and who seemed to enjoy everything and everyone.

"Mmm," she said as she drew her fork from her lips and savored her first bite. White icing dotted her bottom lip and her tongue darted out to smooth and then capture it. He moaned and she looked up at him. "Good?"

"Oh yeah," he murmured. "So good."

"Great. I love it when my cakes taste as good as they look."

I love it when a woman tastes as good as she looks, he thought. He smiled at her and fed her another huge bite. "So where did you stash the extra icing?"

"After I did the last touch up I put the rest in my room," she said, pointing with her fork to the inn behind them. "In the mini fridge."

"Hmmm. Sounds promising. Did you remember the star tip?"

"Of course. I can't do scallops, stripes or fluted edges without it."

"I can't wait to use it myself." He leaned forward and kissed her behind her ear. "I can't wait to fill you like a cannoli and then lick and suck everything out with my tongue." He felt her shiver and went instantly hard.

"Mmmm," she murmured. "Fill me. I like those words. But I may need something . . . a bit more substantial than icing."

"Honey, I've got something more substantial for you. Don't you worry."

She smiled and drew a finger across his bottom lip. "Finish your cake and then dance with me."

"I can't get on the dance floor just yet. Everyone will see how 'substantial' I am for you."

She laughed and put her hand under the table, ran it up his thigh and caressed him.

He groaned and gripped her hand. "I need to get you alone. Let's go to your room now."

She gave him a squeeze and jumped up as a group of

women approached their table. "It's time for the bride to toss the bouquet. They're going to leave to go on their honeymoon in a few minutes. I have to help clean up, and see to the last of the guests, then we have all night to . . ." she bent and swiped a dollop of icing from his plate and smeared it on the dimple in his chin. Then with her hand on his cheek, she ducked her head and licked it off. She finished her sentence, "play."

He cursed and grabbed her hand. He met her eyes as he turned it, laced his fingers with hers and kissed her palm. He ran a lingering tongue to her wrist.

"As soon as I can stand I'll help you clean up."

"You don't have to do that."

"I want to. And I want one dance. One nice slow dance when everybody's cleared out."

"You just want to rub up against my body," she teased.

"In the worst way."

"C'mon Amy, it's time to catch the bouquet!" the bride called over to her. Everyone's attention was on them, so Kyle retook his seat and waved her away.

"Go, but don't get hurt trying to catch that thing. I see a few heavy weights lined up and panting with hunger in their eyes."

She laughed, "The last thing I need is a reason to make another cake."

He watched her walk to the makeshift stage, following the sway of her hips, the short hem of her dress, and her beautiful legs in high heels taking her into the crowd until all he could see was her perky updo with the spikey auburn tufts lifting in the breeze. His lips itched to run up and down the silky length of her exposed neck. He promised himself that later, he would satisfy that itch. She was so damned sexy, so adorably lovely. She turned and smiled at him and the hair that framed her face along with her wispy bangs set off her dazzling blue eyes. She looked like an angel.

As the bouquet was thrown, she stepped back to let the others vie for it, but it sailed over all their heads and landed on her chest. Her hand moved up to clasp the bouquet against her breasts. Her head bent and she lifted the bouquet to her nose. Her eyes closed and her smile widened as she enjoyed the fragrance. He had never seen a woman take such pure delight in flowers before. As everyone clapped he heard a woman a few tables away say, "If anyone needs a husband, it's her."

He wondered what that meant as he stared at the woman who, in pure joy, breathed in the scent of the tiny tea roses again.

Chapter 80—Kyle & Amy
The Dress from Hell

Two hours later, Kyle and Amy placed the last tote box in the mother of the bride's SUV. Kyle had helped her clear the tables, stuff the tablecloths into laundry bags, dismantle the tables, fold and stack the chairs, pack up the food, which he was displeased to see that there was no cake remaining to be boxed, and then she oversaw the return of all the rental bikes.

He managed to have that slow dance he wanted, but just barely. The band was shutting down, playing one of their last songs, appropriately, a rowdy edition of Roy Clark's, *Thank God and Greyhound she's Gone*, when Kyle snuck the bandleader a fifty dollar bill along with a folded sheet of paper. Within moments the strains of "*Just the Two of Us*," were filling the empty wedding tent.

He pulled a tired, sweaty Amy into his arms and looked down into her face, her pained face.

"I have to get this dress off."

"My sentiments exactly."

"I mean like now."

"That's the best $50 I ever spent," he said with a chuckle as he nodded to the bead leader and flashed him an all-knowing grin.

"Unzip my dress," she hissed.

"Let's get to the room first," he murmured, his lips moving against her neck, his strong arm pulling her close to his chest while with the other he stroked her arm, teasing the spot inside her elbow.

"Unzip me now, or I will—" She passed out in his arms before she could finish her sentence.

"What the—" he said as he caught her and lowered her to the dance floor. He flipped her to her side and drew the long zipper down her back. She heaved out a long sigh of relief and collapsed onto her front.

"Jesus," he said as he knelt and ran his fingers over the deep ridges and depressions he found circling her from her shoulder blades to her hips. It was like she was one continuous spiral of welts.

Without a thought to the band still playing and the catering staff packing up, he flicked the closure on her strapless bra and released it.

"Oh my God, it feels wonderful to be able to breathe," she sighed. Several shuddering deep breaths later she blinked her eyes open and smiled up at him. "Thank you. I just couldn't suck it in any longer. I didn't even allow myself to eat, except for the cake I had with you. I was so afraid this dress was going to split down the seams."

"It might have been better if it had," he said shaking his head at her while he stood. Then, as if lifting a sack of grain, he lifted her up and hoisted her over his shoulder. Her dress had splayed enough to show all of her back and the beginning slope of her derriere as it lead down to the tiny pink scrap of her panties. He didn't care; he just wanted to get her comfortable. He soothed her backside and shielded it by rubbing her with his hand through the parted dress.

"You should be spanked for abusing your body like this," he said in a husky voice as he left the tent with her shoulder-length her hair now loose and flowing, shining like an auburn beacon in the darkening night, as he carried her up the steps and into the inn.

The strains of *Just the Two of Us* died out as he slid her room card into the lock and pushed open the door with his foot. "You owe me a dance," he murmured as he let her slide down his body just outside the bathroom door.

She smiled up at him, "Thank you for undressing me."

"No problem. Hold on a second," he said as he propped her against the long bathroom counter, "As soon as I get the tub filling, I'm going to finish the job. Then you're going to take a long, soothing bath."

He reached down and adjusted the taps then came back to her. "Why did you do this to yourself?" he asked as he reached for the elastic band now practically glued to her chest wall on the upper and lower swells her breasts. He had to peel it off her. He didn't know whether it had melted to her skin or just attached itself firmly from the constant, tight pressure. When he managed to get her unstuck, he pulled the bodice of the dress away revealing creamy white breasts between parallel lines of angry red train tracks. The long clefts in her skin circled her body from front to back, corresponding with the tight binding on the dress he bent to remove.

He knelt to unpeel the lower portion, having to deal with it sticking to her sweaty skin. When he had the dress at her feet, his arms encircled her. He placed his forehead on her belly. "Oh, look what you've done," he whispered. "I can't imagine how much this is hurting. Why did you do this?" He looked up at her, his face anguished.

"The dress was just too tight. I didn't know it would keep getting even tighter though," she said with a sad smile. "But I made it through the day!" she said as she brightened. "And I never have to wear that damned dress again."

He stood then and pushed her hair away from her face as he looked into her beautiful blue eyes. "I'm going to make sure of that."

He kissed her cheek, then bent and retrieved the dress. With hands used to kneading bread and ripping open huge bags of rice, he tore the dress in two.

He bent and gripped both sides on the hip of her tiny pink thong and tore it as well, dropping it to the floor before he scooped her up and gently lifted her into the tub.

At first, the hot water burned her abraded flesh, and she hissed. But as her body got used to the warm, soothing balm of the water, she sighed and sunk deeper into the tub, reclining against the back.

He towered above her, shaking his head. "You worked way too hard today. And in an iron maiden no less."

"Iron Maiden?"

"A conceptual torture device linked to the Middle Ages. A sort of casket with spikes to impale people inside, but there really was never such a thing. It's just a phrase that means something torturous. Even a size larger, that dress would still have been torture."

"Yes, I think so."

Chapter 81—Kyle & Amy
The Best Part of Cake is the Icing

Twenty minutes later, after she had bathed and soaked, and her skin had returned to somewhat normal, she got out of the tub and Kyle, hearing her, came to dry her off and carry her to the bed. He sat her on the end, her feet dangling.

There was a bottle of champagne in a bucket with two crystal flutes beside it. She wondered where that had come from. Certainly not from the wedding party, they were a beer-drinking crowd.

He answered her unasked question. "I had someone bring it from the beach house."

"Awww, that was sweet of you."

He handed her a flute filled with the sparkling gold liquid. "I think I've only had champagne twice in my life."

"We'll have to work on that."

"Mmmm, this is delicious. So light and bubbly."

"You're light and bubbly. Drink up." He bent to kiss her on the neck. He didn't mention that it was a $600 bottle of Taittingers. "You deserve it."

"I want to do wicked things to you," he whispered in her ear.

"Mmmm. I think I want that too."

"Are you protected?"

"No. I haven't had sex in a long, long time. Didn't feel the need to. Plus birth control is not in the budget right now."

"No problem. I've got it covered. And, I'll have it covered," he said with a chuckle. "But first . . ." he held up an icing bag. "Lie back and let me have my way with you."

"Are you really going to use that?"

He put his left hand on the top of the towel and pulled it down. With his right he dotted her nipples with the icing. Then knelt, and one after the other, he took each one into his mouth and sucked, laved them clean, and sucked some more.

The towel was pulled off completely, and she was gently lifted further up the bed, then her legs spread. The bag was hoisted in his right hand.

"You aren't really?" When she felt the tip touch her opening, she gasped, "No!"

He laughed and with a rough, gravely voice hissed, "Yes."

With a deft and expert hand, he squeezed the bag and filled her.

She came twice from his tongue attempting to clean her of any trace of icing. She called out his name, and sighed, then beckoned for him to get up onto the bed with her.

They kissed like teenagers, getting to know every nuance of each other's mouth. Kyle kissed alongside her jaw, down her neck and lavished her breasts until she begged him to get himself inside her. Now.

He stripped his clothes off, donned a condom and did her bidding. Three times that night, he did her bidding. He could not remember ever being with a woman so into sex—so into him. Around two a.m., he fell asleep still inside her, and he slept the sleep of the dead.

When he awoke, and didn't see her in bed, then saw that her suitcase on the rack was missing, he breathed out one word. "Fuck."

Because now he knew how it felt. He was usually the one who did the running out without leaving a note.

Chapter 82—Kyle & Amy
Ode to a Water Blaster

It took a private detective two days to find her using the meager information he had about her and her friends. But finally, at 11 a.m. he got a call with an address.

The house was small, but tidy. Two levels of slate siding, painted a soft buttercup yellow with delft blue shutters and an actual picket fence delineating the front and back yards from those of the neighbors', whose yards and homes were not so tidy.

When he knocked on the door, he didn't know what to expect. But it wasn't children—five of them. Guessing at their ages, they were from two to seven.

Amy showed up a minute later, standing behind the tallest boy and running her fingers lovingly through his short brown hair.

Her eyes wet wide, her mouth made an O. "Kyle, what are you doing here?"

"I've spent two days and a lot of money looking for you. Why don't you tell me why you left without saying good-bye?"

"Randy, can you take the others in the back yard while I talk to this man?"

The boy corralled the other kids, and took them through the house and out into the backyard. Kyle followed her inside and could just barely make out a rusty swing set through the back windows of the house from where he stood in the living room.

"I'm sorry. I rarely get a chance to get away. Some parishioners offered to watch the kids for the weekend of the wedding, so I parceled them out and decided I was going to enjoy myself and have sex with anybody who appealed to me. You appealed to me almost right away.

"But I know I can't have that kind of life anymore. I have to think of the kids."

"Are they yours?"

"They are now. They were my sister's. She and her husband died in a car crash almost two years ago, coming back from her postpartum appointment after having the twins. So they're mine now, all five. Randy, Joey, Winona, or as she prefers, Winnie. The twins are Jessie and Janie."

"Wow. No wonder you were so . . . determined . . . and pent up with a need for pleasure."

"Well, I didn't have the time for any building-up or bonding. And I knew whatever I had wouldn't be a lasting thing."

"Well there's the rub. I want more."

"You can't have more. I am stuck here and I am too busy trying to take care of kids and earn an income so we can get by."

"Can I come in? Can we at least talk?"

She stood aside and let him in. He followed her into the small kitchen. It was the only place that was cluttered. Pots and pans were in the sink and bowls of different colored icing were everywhere. In the center of the counter was a huge cake she was in the middle of decorating. "We'll have to talk while I work, I have to deliver this cake by 5 o'clock. It's for a 50th anniversary party tonight, and I'm not anywhere near done."

With his trained eye, he examined the cake. She had talent. She was good at this. But he knew from experience that a cake like this required more time than most professionals had. For someone with five kids to care for, it was unheard of to even attempt something this complicated.

"It's the hotel where they were married." It even had stained glass windows made of several colors of melted sugars swirled into patterns.

"In Chicago?"

"Yes.

"I know the one. This is very ambitious."

"I know."

"How can I help?"

"Are you serious?"

"Of course. Let me wash up and let's get this done and delivered."

They worked side-by-side for almost two hours, with interruptions for snacks, diaper changes, trips to the potty, and to kiss and mend an assortment of scraped knees and boo-boos to fingers.

By 4:30 the cake was loaded into Amy's Kia hatchback.

"There isn't enough room for all the kids to be in my vehicle at the same time, so Randy goes over to his friend Danny's house and his mother watches him until I get back."

"I can take him in my car. Then I can help you unload and mind the kids."

"That would be great." She heaved a sigh. "Just need to prep some of the icing in case I need to touch anything up."

Five minutes later they were driving in a two-car caravan through the small town of Fairmont, on their way to deliver the cake.

Kyle was able to talk to Randy and to discover how fatiguing and stressful it was to be the oldest child; responsible for things only adults should have to worry about. He was a great kid, but he was losing out on so much of his childhood right now. It broke Kyle's heart.

After the cake had been delivered and the check collected, they drove back to the house, where it was now time to get dinner on the table. Kyle whipped out his cell phone and had several pizzas and a big order of chicken wings delivered. From the reaction of the older kids, it was a luxury Amy couldn't afford.

Two hours later, the last kid was bathed, dressed for bed, had been read to, and tucked in with a kiss on the forehead. Amy looked as if she was ready to drop.

"C'mon," she whispered. "Let's go out on the porch so we can talk without waking them."

Kyle followed her out and then looked around at the screened-in porch. It was all of maybe 6 x 8, probably the smallest space he'd been confined to since he had been a kid being shuffled from continent to continent, city to city, apartment to apartment. And some of those apartments in London and Paris had been pretty damned small, he thought.

"I know, it's tiny. But it's a place where I find solace. I screened it in myself," she said with a beaming smile as she sat on one of two plastic Adirondack chairs, both with a colorful throw pillow. A twelve-inch section of a tree trunk served as a table between them. "The mosquitoes are vicious during the only time I can ever collapse out here—after all the kids are finally asleep for the night."

"You've really had a hard time of it, haven't you?"

"Not really. I love the kids, and they're good kids. But we do have our moments. Meltdowns are a daily thing with the twins right now, so that's a bit hard."

"I can't have kids. That's probably why I love kids so much," he blurted out.

"That's sad."

"You're the only one I've ever told that to who hasn't signed a non-disclosure agreement."

"How do you know this to be true?" She sipped the wine he'd poured for her, taking the smallest imaginable sips. And he knew why. At any moment, one of the kids could need her, and she'd want to be sober enough to deal with whatever the problem turned out to be.

"My parents traveled all over Europe, we were in a new place every other month or so. They were bilingual. Actually in their case, added together, multi-lingual. We traveled with the diplomatic corps, interpreting at functions. They also gave private language classes in the evenings to the staff and their families at the embassies. We were never in one place long, and so my immunizations got overlooked. I got a bad case of the mumps when I was seven. The doctors said I would most likely be sterile.

"I spent my twenties and thirties trying to prove them wrong. Mentally, I granted the first person I slept with who turned up pregnant the gift of matrimony. Naturally, I didn't tell them this, or they might have done the deed with someone else, as there were several women who desperately wanted to walk down the aisle with me during that time. But alas, there were no little sticks with blue lines in my future with any of them."

"You could have adopted."

"I could have. But to be honest, I never had a candidate I was all that into to raise a child with."

"That's sad."

He shrugged and sipped his wine. "Just the kind of crowd I ran with then. The women were not the maternal type. At least not at the stage of life that I found them appealing," he said with chagrin.

She laughed. "You liked them young and adventurous, yet you wanted them to be nurturing, and willing to alter their bodies forever for you?"

"You make it sound . . . despotic."

She smiled, "Wasn't it?"

He chuckled. "I suppose it was."

"Different times," she murmured.

"Yes. But you know what? I like this. You and me. We're both being brutally honest. Probably in a way I have never been with anyone else."

"I wonder why?" she didn't even try to hide the cynicism in her tone.

"You make me laugh. You make me wonder. You make me grateful, your life is so hard . . ."

"It is. But it has its rewards."

He took her hand in his as they watched an owl land on a branch and start its nighttime serenade for a mate. She had made a tiny garden just beyond the porch decorated with gnomes and a fairy cottage. Solar lights on the corners had come on giving the little fenced in patch an ethereal quality. The spindly tomato and herb plants cast ghostly shadows that flickered with the breeze.

"Should I get in my car and go back to the beach?" he asked, fishing for an invite to her bed.

"You are welcome to stay, and welcome in my bed. But if by some miracle I get pregnant . . . I have friends with shotguns. Men who love to hunt."

"I get the message. But if I were to get you pregnant . . . I would pay them off and offer you the moon."

"I have no use for the moon. I don't have a place big enough to keep it. But I wouldn't mind a repeat of our first date. I would like you to hold me and cherish me as you did that night. I find I need the touch of a man more than the plowing of a man."

He stood and took what remained of her drink from her hand. "I'm going to change that. Before the night is over, you will beg me to 'plow' you."

The owl hooted just then.

"He wants a mate," she said.

"So do I," he whispered.

And she knew by the look in his eyes that he thought he had found one.

"If you wake the babies . . ." she whispered, and he heard the threat in her voice as he led her inside.

Chapter 83—Kyle & Amy
Emulating a Water Cannon

He pulled her to him when they were standing in the kitchen. "Where is your bedroom?"

She pointed to the sofa in the living room. "You're looking at it."

"We're making some changes tomorrow. If there's anyone who needs a good night's sleep and a decent bed it's you. Does it open up?"

"No."

"I'm too tall for that sofa. Let's put the cushions on the floor." He took the cushions off the sofa and from both the matching chairs, making a grid of nine with one left over for the center.

"Those are not going to stay together," she murmured as she looked down at the floor.

"I know. We'll make do tonight, but tomorrow I'm getting us a bed."

"Tomorrow?" she whispered. "Us?"

"I'm in this, baby. So in this." They were standing by the kitchen counter that separated the two rooms. He boxed her in with his arms and kissed her. A deep, searching kiss, full of tongue and sensual lip action.

She moaned.

His hands gripped her bottom and pulled her into his groin so she could feel how hard he was for her.

She ground herself against him and his breath hitched.

"You feel amazing," he whispered against her neck.

"I want you inside me, and please, please, don't waste any time."

"I like taking my time and loving every inch of a woman."

"Don't. Please. Just. Do it."

"Okay," he breathed. He unzipped his pants, and hiked her skirt up. Then dragged her panties down until they hit the floor and she stepped out of them.

He lifted her onto the barstool after turning it around and pulled her to the edge. She spread her legs. "Now," she said. "I'm ready. So ready."

"What is the hurry?"

"Trust me," she whispered in his ear.

He rubbed the head of his penis against her, finding her wet and ready. He reached into his back pocket for a condom. She plucked it from his fingers and expertly rolled it on. She was so wet he had no trouble entering her. He actually had the weird sensation of being sucked in.

She wound her legs around his hips and settled herself in at the angle she needed both for her back against the chrome rail of the barstool, and for her ability to be able to receive his thrusts where she could direct them.

He moved inside her, thrusting and retreating, making the connection with her clit complete with each thrust, and using his thumb to stroke the growing nub as he departed her sweet haven.

"You feel so good," he murmured between nibbling kisses.

He felt her clit, ripe with want, vibrating with need under his thumb.

"Now, *plow* me," she said "and fast."

He wasn't going to argue with a woman who knew what she needed, so he did her bidding. Pelting her and shoving himself inside her so hard he had to repeatedly drag her ass from the back of the seat. She reached around him and grabbed his butt, pulling him tight and forcing him deeper. Then she threw her head back, moaned, and tumbled over a cliff, gripping him and milking him until he had no choice but to surrender and empty himself inside her with a roar that she quickly silenced with her hand, then mouth.

As they collapsed into each other, holding tight to one

another, they let their breaths mingle and their lips wander. Then they heard the faint cry of a baby down the hall.

"Hmm," he whispered. "That's the reason for the rushing."

"And the shushing. Yes. You can't take your time peeing, pooping, reading, or masturbating. You'll be interrupted every single time. It's like an unwritten rule."

"Duly noted. I will work on my orgasm targeting skills. See if I can get the deed done in under five minutes. Although that is in direct contrast to all my training heretofore."

"That's the spirit," she said as she lowered her legs and slid into a standing position. "Let me go see what baby Jessie needs."

"How can you tell it's Jessie and not Janie?"

"You get used to the nuances. Janie's is higher pitched."

"Ah," he said, as if storing that tidbit for later. He palmed her cheek and kissed her. "Let me get her."

"You sure? You could be rocking her for hours."

"I've dreamed of this for years. You go to sleep. Let me have some fun."

"By all means, have at it." She kissed him on his prickly jaw. "And thank you. I needed that."

"There is a lot more where that came from."

"Well, when you get her back to sleep, I'll be waiting on the new and improved floor."

"What if she's wet?"

"Then change her, everything you need is on the changer."

"What if she's hungry?"

"She won't be, she had a bottle not that long ago."

"What if she won't let me rock her?"

"Jessie will let anyone rock her. For hours. Your arms will go numb before she objects."

"Okay, then. I've got this."

And he did. An hour later when she got up to check on them, he was asleep in the rocking chair with Jessie curled into his arm like a football. She smiled and left them to their dreams and went back to finish one of hers.

In the morning, when Amy woke up, Kyle was half on their makeshift bed, half on the floor. His arm was slung around her waist, protective and comforting. She inched away and found her way to the bathroom. It was summertime, and no one had a particular time they had to get up, so she usually let the older kids sleep in. The twins' internal clocks were still guided by their tummies, and when one woke up hungry, the other did too. So after freshening up, she got their bottles ready.

She heard Kyle go into the bathroom, then come back to "make" the bed. Or in this case, "make the couch."

When she felt his hands wrap around her waist and his lips caress the side of her neck, her knees started to buckle. The things this man could do with his hands . . . his lips . . . and his cock. She got wet just thinking about it.

As if scenting her, he inhaled deeply. "You're aroused, aren't you?"

She reached a hand behind her and clasped him, "You're aroused, aren't you?" she mimicked.

He laughed. "Damn straight. I think I've sported a hard-on in some form or another since the moment you blasted me with that water gun."

She laughed. "That was funny. It was a novel way to meet someone, that's for sure."

"Divine providence," he whispered. "This was destiny. And now that I've found you, I'm never letting you go."

"Wait a cotton pickin' minute. I'm the one who found *you*."

"So you did. Finder's keepers. I'm all yours now."

She spun in his arms. "Seriously, what are you trying to tell me here?"

"I want us to be a couple. Well, actually a family. All of us."

"Just how's that going to work, you don't live here, you don't work here."

"I can live anywhere I want. And work wherever and whenever I choose."

"What about your restaurants, your shows?"

"I have great chefs managing my restaurants. And my show? I can tape from anywhere. I just need a state-of-the-art kitchen and my producers can line one up practically anywhere."

"And you want to stay here? With me? And the kids?"

"Yes." There was no hesitation. He wanted her. She could see it in his eyes.

"What if it doesn't work out? I mean the kids are noisy, aggravating at times, and are often the most selfish beasts on the planet."

"I'm the easiest person in the world to get along with, and I love to cook for a crowd. It's going to work out just fine."

"And if it doesn't?"

"We'll change up something. We'll make it work. Now that I've found you, I'm not giving you up. You are mine."

"What about Jedediah? He's going to be heartbroken."

He laughed. "If that's your reason for saying no, I'll bow out now and let him have you."

"Would you really?"

"No. You're mine. Everything else will work out as long as you agree to that." He grabbed her to him and kissed her hard and fast, his lips slanting over hers, his arms tightening around her and pulling her closer.

"You are mine. I'm keeping you Amy Anderson. Forever."

"Well, Kyle Keir Merritt. I'm going to let you keep me. For a little while. Because I think after a few months, you're going to get tired of this domestic bliss." She waved her hand in the direction of the bottles, nipples, and caps lined up to be washed, the piles of laundry clearly visible through the open door to the laundry room, the dining room filled with art projects, and the living room littered with toys.

"Forty years from now, you're still going to be waiting for me to leave."

"You're sure about this? You're going to take all this on for a little nookie with me?"

"I'm going take all this on for a *lot* of nookie with you."

She laughed. "Okay, then. I hear the monsters coming from their lairs. And they're going to be growling with hunger."

"I believe I can handle anything they have a hankering for."

"Well, breakfast is the easy part. If you can open a box of cereal and poor milk, you're in."

He grimaced, "No, no, no. Let's at least do some bacon, eggs and pancakes."

"I'm telling you, your cooking skills are not going to be appreciated by this motley group. Make it easy on yourself. Get out the Fruit Loops, Cheerios, Cocoa Puffs, Lucky Charms, and Boo Berry, then turn on some cartoons."

His eyes went wide. "Surely you jest. Oatmeal, Mueslix, or Granola at least."

"See, we are not compatible."

"Food-wise maybe not . . ." he kissed her until her eyes fluttered closed and she moaned, "but we've got physical compatibility down pat."

"Now where is your best skillet? I'm going to give them options. Wean them off all this sugar . . . get them eating something a little healthier."

She handed him a frying pan so old it had peeling Silverstone on the bottom and around the edges.

He looked at it, his face aghast, "On no, this not going to cut it. I draw the line at using inferior pots, pans, and cutlery."

He took out his cell phone and pressed a button. "Justin. I need you." He gave him the address. "Plan to stay in town a week. I'll need you to outfit a kitchen, order in some food, bring in some toys and some playground equipment, and a bed, we need a queen bed right away. I don't think a king will fit. Today if possible. Yes, and stop and get my stuff from *The Cockpit*, I'll be living in Fairmont." He looked over at her, her eyebrow was quirked in annoyance, "for the foreseeable future. Yes, see you this afternoon."

Her arms were crossed over her chest. "You are not going to just come in here and change everything."

"Not everything," he looked around, "this place has great bones. And I love all the new paint schemes. But the appliances do need some updating, and we've already agreed on the bed. And who doesn't like new playground equipment?"

Just then the three older children straggled in, two carrying a mewling baby in their arms.

"Playground equipment? We're getting a playground? Can it have a slide?" asked Randy.

"And a teeter totter?" asked Winnie

"And a jungle gym I can climb on?" shouted Joey.

Kyle took one of the babies from Joey. Amy took the other from Randy. She hissed at him, "We should talk about these things first."

"Okay, next time we will, I promise. Just as soon as I get a decent kitchen set up."

"I've committed to two cakes this week, so you can't touch my oven. I don't have time to learn how to use something new."

He lifted his brow, "Really, you want to keep that old oven?"

"I know how it works."

"Honey, I'll show you that the new ones work much better. You'll see. And I promise, I'll help you with all this. Your customers will be able to brag that Kyle Merritt helped bake their cakes. Let me lavish on you. Let me love you. You've had it so hard for two years. Please let me make things a little easier for you. If I had my way I'd move you into a mansion today, but I know that's not what you want. You want to raise those kids in the community they were born in, and so do I."

"Okay. But I want a full set of Kyle Merritt pots and pans if you're taking away my crappy Silverstone."

He hooted. "I'll add in the dinnerware and cutlery sets as well."

He pulled her to him and kissed her in full view of the kids. Then pulled away and looked down into her smiling face. "I love you, Amy. I don't know how it happened so fast. But I've never been so sure of anything in my life. You are it for me."

She kissed him back. "Jumping off a cliff here."

"Yeah?" he prompted.

"You're it for me, too."

Chapter 84—Deke & Shaw
Aerophobia

Shaw Marin sat in the molded plastic seat at the United Airlines gate waiting for everyone to board Flight 5809. She was at the Salt Lake City Airport, heading to LAX. Praying, as she listened to the rows being announced, and watching as people boarded. First the handicapped, and those with young children, then the elite business class, followed by the stragglers—those who rushed up to the yawning opening where the ramp was secured, anxious to board before the door to the jet way closed.

Two other women also sat looking expectantly at the uniformed ticket agent who was holding a microphone and counting ticket stubs. Then a phone rang and she picked it up, listening intently to the caller for several moments.

Shaw hated flying stand-by, but she had no choice. She couldn't afford the price of an airline ticket, and had to count on the connection to her sister for the friends and family benefit, allowing her to fly in an empty seat when a flight was not fully booked. But sometimes it took a whole day to get on a plane. A day wasted that she could be experiencing a break from a day of teaching kindergarteners and an evening of caregiving—a day of freedom to do whatever she wanted. Sometimes that meant going to a museum or an art gallery, taking in a movie, or simply sitting by a motel pool with a good book.

But since this was an evening flight and there were always people who couldn't get here on time due to traffic or job constraints, she felt confident of getting a seat.

However, this time, it appeared as if there were two other women vying for whatever empty seat there might be on this flight.

She looked at the women, both sitting in the scarred plastic seats with their legs crossed at the knee, one leg swinging erratically as if pumping to keep them inflated. Both looking tense, listening for the very same thing she was—their name to be called.

Flying standby was akin to winning the lottery. When you heard your name called, you knew your fortune had just changed. She wondered how impacted their lives would be if their names were not called. Would they miss that trip to a vacation spot and a rendezvous with an illicit lover, or be deprived of being present for the firstborn child of a brother or sister? Or would they just get back to school or to their jobs a day later than planned?

They were both Hispanic so that could be a plausible scenario, simply going back home to jobs or families. But she seriously doubted that their reason for flying into LAX and then driving to Mexico matched hers.

She jolted in her seat as the intercom crackled to life and the dulcet tones of the boarding agent cum flight attendant murmured, "Would Ms. Shaw Marin please come to the boarding gate."

Shaw jumped up from her seat and grabbed her backpack. Before she could get to the counter the message was repeated twice, each time in a more insistent voice. They were ready to close this flight. She met the eye of the agent and walked faster.

As she walked between the rows, she glanced at the other women. One had an unhappy resigned look as she blew out air over her top lip and sent her bangs aloft. It bespoke the attitude of one continually believing they were being overlooked. The other had a demoralized look as well, but judging by her designer jeans and chic gladiator-styled half-boots, her frown was more likely about being entitled and used to getting her way. Still, Shaw would have signed over her ticket to either one of them if getting on this plane weren't a matter of life or death. She hated being the cause of making anyone unhappy.

The attendant handed her a stub after tearing part of a ticket off, saying, "It's your lucky day, an executive can't make the flight so you get a business-class seat. Enjoy the flight." Her smile wasn't genuine, but then they never were anymore.

Shaw hitched her backpack high on her shoulder and hooked her thumb under the strap. With a smile that was genuine, she trotted down the gangway. She'd had more than her share of bad karma lately. It was about time things started to swing the other way. Geez, business class! She had never flown anything but coach before.

Once on the plane, she matched her ticket stub to the left window seat in the first row, as everyone on the plane looked up to see the newcomer, the person who had kept them from already being airborne. She slid into the far seat, noting the empty aisle seat beside her, wondering if one of those women still at the gate would soon be joining her.

She removed her light sweater and after rolling it up and placing it in her backpack, took her change purse from a zippered compartment. Then she stowed the bag as her carry on under her seat. She had learned never to travel with more than a small carry on. Having an extra set of clothes and her own toiletries just weren't worth the hassle. And it being late September, it was easy to layer clothing so the air conditioning of the terminal didn't chill her, and the stifling heat of the airplane pre-flight didn't overtax her Mitchum antiperspirant.

There were no seats in front of her, just a wide expanse of empty floor space, and then a wall niche with a curtained off section for garment bags and strollers on the left. Man, this was roomy. Though she was only five-foot six, she appreciated the extra room to stretch out as much as anybody. She fingered her tiny leather purse. She wanted to have her cocktail money handy. Flying unnerved her. A vodka tonic or a glass of wine always helped to ease the stress of knowing she was miles up in the air, tethered to absolutely nothing.

She was fidgeting with the zipper on the small change purse and wondering why the airline hadn't given the seat beside her to one of the women still waiting in the terminal, when she heard the restroom door on her left open and then click shut. She looked up in time to see a tall dark-haired man step into the aisle. His eyes met hers and she froze in her seat, her eyes widening the only exception to her perfectly still, arrested in motion, state. She instantly stopped fidgeting, stopped breathing, stopped all brain activity except the process that allowed her to read the blaring thought banner that was running through her head. *Sweet Lord, that man is hot!*

As he stared at her, she stared back. His deep blue eyes, azure gems set under dark slashing brows were clear, and so penetrating that she felt her throat go dry as he returned her assessment.

He sported a summer tan that emphasized his sharply defined features and had thick, luxurious black hair peppered with gray at the temples. With the barest hint of an evening shadow along his chiseled jawline, a regal nose, and full, sensuous lips, he was the embodiment of all things handsome. His impressive broad shoulders, set off by a camel-toned business suit fit his long lean body in a way that could only have been accomplished by being custom-made. He reminded her of an athlete. The kind that was required to travel in business attire rather than a jersey and jeans. A starched white dress shirt open at the throat and snug across his chest, hinted that there might be a virile pelt of hair on that muscular chest. His raised eyebrow and smirking upturned lips completed the image of a victor anticipating a welcoming homecoming from an adoring fan.

The instinct to size someone up in five seconds to decide whether you would or wouldn't do them, bounced at warp speed and ricocheted inside her brain. She had her answer in a nano-second. She would definitely do this man—if she wasn't married.

After a cursory nod, quite likely duplicating her sentiment, the man strode across the aisle and stopped at the empty seat beside her. Discovering that this man was going to be her seatmate, the person sitting next to her all the way to LAX, caused a delightful shiver to pass through her body. She was chilled and heated within the same second, causing a tremor to run through her and making the hand that was holding onto her purse jerk. In her nervous anxiety, she had worked the zipper loose. She felt something roll across her thumb and slide off her lap, careening off her knee before clattering to the floor. With an inward groan, she watched as her little bullet vibrator hit the floor and rolled toward the bulkhead in front of their seats.

With grace born of the very young and very athletic, the man stepped forward then easily stooped and then stood, having retrieved her fallen object before it finished rolling. Upon standing, he held it between his fingers and examined it.

She saw the curiosity in his expression, the lift of his brow and the quirk of his lips, and answered his unasked question, "It's my neck massager. I get tense when I fly."

He looked at her, both confident and amused, and cocked a disbelieving brow. Then he flashed a smile that the devil had to have gifted him with. "Are you sure? It looks very much like . . ."

"Like a very small neck massager," she finished, her tone emphatic even as her face flushed from complete embarrassment.

He stood above her, hesitated, and then returned to his seat, still examining the tiny silver bullet, turning it over between his long, well-manicured fingers. Pressing in on the rubber tip, he turned it on. Then he reached over and dropped it like a tiny little bomb into her lap. Right into the crease at the top of her skinny jeans and close to the exact area she had intended to use it on later this evening.

"I was sure it was something else," he said with a wide all-knowing smile showing off perfectly straight white teeth. "I apologize for my wayward thought. Enjoy it in good health." His smirk conveyed good-natured humor blended with subtle mockery as he settled into his seat and buckled his seatbelt.

She didn't believe he was sorry. Not for one single second. And as she picked the wayward sex toy up out of her lap, she decided she would not do him, married or not. No, never in a million years.

Hastily turning her little bullet off, she slid the vibrator back into her purse, feeling the eyes of the evil man mocking her as he looked over her shoulder. She fingered her cocktail money, sliding the bills between her fingers. She could not wait until the drink cart came her way. Realizing that she would be one of the first on the plane to be served due to her proximity to the galley cheered her immensely.

The cabin door was closed with a loud thump, and then audibly locked. Loud engines revved and within seconds the pilot began backing the plane away from the gate.

The next few minutes were devoted to everyone buckling their seat belts and settling in as the male flight attendant ran through the safety instructions. She always paid rapt attention to the flight attendant unlucky enough to get the honor of possibly saving lives. She felt following instructions was the least she could do for the free ride. Her sister had once told her that if one person paid attention, others around them would too. So, like the good kindergarten teacher she was, she did her part to make sure everyone would be prepared should the worst happen.

The plane taxied to the runway and they waited until the captain was given permission to take to the air. It was a tense and noisy time as they could feel a crosswind buffeting them the entire time.

Looking out her window, Shaw could see a windsock and several banners flapping wildly as trash skittered across an adjacent runway. Then the announcement came that it was their turn and they began bumping down the runway until finally, the huge plane lifted with a shaky jerk into the air.

Moments later, as they were climbing, they hit an air pocket and she felt a quick drop before they smoothed out and surged upward again. It happened several more times. They continued climbing as the plane shook and rattled as if threatening to come apart.

She could hear metal rattling in the galley. Sounds making her think doors were popping open. Eerie whistles of air escaping from somewhere and then the insistent flapping of paper made a strange cacophony mimicking her preschooler's attempts at mastering percussion instruments. One of the overheads several rows behind her crashed open and she heard the contents spill into the aisle with loud clattering sounds amid gasps and startled screams.

At the worst of the turbulence, she gasped and grabbed the armrest between her and her seatmate. Unfortunately, the man's arm was already reclining there and her fingers ended up gripping his hand instead of the armrest. Realizing what she had done, despite knowing she was curling her nails into the man's skin, she didn't remove her hand. It was an odd comfort to connect to someone—even though she did not like the man, handsome devil that he was—she needed to know that someone else was on this doomed plane with her. That somebody would be beside her when they crashed.

The plane managed to recover, rise higher into the sky and level out. Collectively, there was a long sigh. The man used his other hand to lift hers from his. Then, almost as an afterthought, he turned his hand over, placed his palm against hers, and gripped her hand firmly, entwining their fingers before placing his arm back on the armrest.

"Everything's going to be all right. There's no need to fear. We just drew the wrong runway for the weather we're having. It's all over now." His voice was soft and soothing, his thumb stroking alongside hers, reassuring.

It was the first time someone had cared to comfort her in a long time. She looked up at him and he smiled. Full lips framing beautiful teeth, and twinkling eyes conveyed his sincere concern. She closed her eyes, took in a deep breath, and when she opened them again, she managed to smile back. It didn't mean she wasn't independent if she accepted comfort from someone else, she told herself. It didn't mean she was a weak, helpless female because she was letting a total stranger hold her hand in such an intimate clasp.

She sat back, her head against the headrest and her eyes closed for several moments, her hand still in his, until she felt him separate from her. She disliked the separation and wanted him to reconnect their hands.

She felt something cold against her hand and her eyes opened to see an iced champagne flute hovering in the air by her hand and then her fingers being wrapped around the stem. Her heart fluttered. Moments later he filled the flute with a light golden liquid that shimmered in the evening light being filtered through the window beside her. Bubbles rose to the top of the crystal glass and burst with an effervescent fizz that she could hear in the intimate space between them and feel tingling on her hand.

"Bless you," she whispered, and gave him her very best, most genuine smile. The one she reserved for children, those little imps who had finally learned to pick up their toys and paint on the paper instead of on their desk.

Seeing him smile back, so fully that the corners of his eyes crinkled, warmed her in neglected places.

"I figured you could use something to take the edge off. I always do."

She took a gratifying sip, feeling the bubbles pop over her tongue. "Mmmm," she groaned. "This is delicious. Thank you." She looked over at him and saw his nostrils flare and heat light up his eyes . . . gorgeous sapphire and ice eyes that missed nothing.

"It's Gloria Ferrer, a decent brand and one of my favorites when flying." He lifted his own glass and toasted her, "To a smooth flight and a better landing than lifting."

"Yes," she murmured as she raised her glass and then took another fortifying sip. She handed him her folded cocktail money.

He waved it away. "This is business class, you don't pay for alcohol in business class."

"Really?" she asked, stunned that she hadn't known that.

But then why would she?

"Really. It's one of the perks. But it would have been my treat regardless."

"Thank you again. This is exactly what I needed. This is my first time flying anything but steerage. My sister works for this airline so I can fly for free, but it's always been stand-by, and never business class. At the gate I was told that an executive couldn't make the flight so I guess I got his seat."

"Yes. My business partner, in fact. He has the flu. Probably the first case of the season. We often make this flight together. This aisle and window seat are reserved for my company every third Thursday. "

"I'm sorry he's sick." She stared hard at her glass and then took another sip. "Well . . . maybe not. I really needed to make this flight." She shook herself from her reverie, then giggled and smiled over at him. "But I do hope he feels better soon."

He laughed and she was surprised by how good it made her feel to hear it. He was such a good-looking man. Broad sensuous lips bowed into a generous smile and when he threw back his head and laughed he was devastating—a pure pleasure to look at.

"So are you traveling for business or pleasure?' he asked.

She tilted her head and thought about that. After a few seconds she said, "Neither." She took another sip and thought some more. "I suppose you could say I am traveling out of necessity. Yes, that would be the word. Necessity," she stated, with a satisfied nod of her head.

"So, it is necessary for you go to LAX? But not for work, or to play?"

"Yes. I go from there to Mexico where I will buy drugs."

He choked on the sip he had been taking. Then shifted on his hip so he could pull a handkerchief from a pant pocket. He dabbed at his hand where he had sloshed some of his champagne.

She had the weird urge to lick it off his hand. To savor

his skin, or to prevent the waste of a very fine champagne? "Oh, not the illegal kind," she quickly added. "The pharmaceutical kind. I have a prescription, even though I have learned it is not necessary to have one there."

He pursed his lips in consternation. He had seen it many times. Knew that for a lot of people, traveling outside the country, whether it was to Canada or Mexico, or even China that it was the only way they could afford some of the more expensive drugs. His family was in the pharmaceutical manufacturing business, and he saw the long lines outside Mexican drug stores first hand—all the time.

His four-generation-owned pharmaceutical company had gone public ten years ago and now he served on the board of directors as the C.E.O. His expertise was in law as it pertained to disclaimers, product evaluations, testing and compliance. But lately, he had fallen into the mergers and acquisitions sector, which inevitably had led to production. He was flying home from one of their new factories and preparing to oversee and revamp a manufacturing facility they just took over. But he certainly wasn't going to tell this woman that.

People who couldn't afford the price of the drugs they needed only saw their need; they did not understand the costs involved in research and development of a new drug, nor the stringent procedures and additional costs needed to sell them in the Unites States after years of fighting for FDA approvals. Just preparing and distributing the pamphlets and paperwork that had to accompany each drug up for approval ran into the millions. And many new drugs didn't even make it through the trials. But people who needed the drugs only saw their side of the story. And of course, it *was* a lucrative business, even with all the regulations. It had to be, or no one would subject themselves to all the stress of documenting side effects, settling lawsuits, adhering to new directives on a daily basis, and dealing with all the controversy attached to producing life saving drugs. No doubt, this woman would see him as the enemy if she knew what he did for a living.

"So you don't have health insurance?"

"It is not me who needs the drugs. It is my husband. He was in a bad accident two years ago. He is on many drugs paid for by the insurance company of the man who hit him. But there is one drug they won't pay for and that's his insulin. He was diabetic before the accident so they will not pay for it. When he was working we could afford it, but now we cannot."

The flight attendant who was serving their dinner interrupted them. He asked for more champagne for them after pointing to her empty glass and getting her nod of approval for a refill.

"I want to hear more after dinner, that is, if you don't mind telling me."

" I don't want to burden you with my problems."

"It's no burden to listen. My name is Deke by the way, Deke Scotchkiss."

"Nice name. It evokes . . ."

"Yes?" he asked when she hesitated, one brow lifted in question. It was obvious he'd defended his name many times before and he smiled to share her amusement at his provocative moniker.

"Well, Deke is rather nice and manly, and your last name has two things that go well together . . ." she hesitated again before adding, "I imagine. I'm not really a scotch drinker."

"Ironically, neither am I."

"But I do like butterscotch. I'm Shaw, Shaw Marin. And about my situation, I've found that most people have their own weighty troubles dragging them down. You don't need to hear mine."

He snickered. "You don't know the half of it. But I still want to hear about you." He took her chin in his hand and turned her face toward his. "I am enjoying talking to you, Shaw." His eyes told her he was being truthful and it was as if his statement was a heartfelt plea to share more with him. He dragged his thumb lightly under her lower lip before dropping his hand.

She dropped her eyes, afraid he'd see the desire spiking through her. Wow, she thought as she smiled, and then took the glass of champagne he passed over to her.

"I am enjoying talking to you as well. I'm afraid you are loosening my tongue with this," she said as she held her glass up to him.

He clinked his refreshed glass with hers. "It sounds as if you could use a good ear, a soft shoulder, and someone to ply you with alcohol to make you forget your troubles for a little while."

Her smile dropped. "For a very little while I'm afraid. I must return Sunday morning. I have school and I have a job, and I have a husband who needs 'round the clock care."

"You will likely be in line all day tomorrow. You will exhaust yourself."

"It is not so bad. The people at the Pharmacia are very nice. And often there are many Americans I can talk to. Some I have met before."

He shook his head as he picked at the salad the attendant placed in front of him. It shouldn't be this way, he thought. People shouldn't have to work this hard to keep healthy. Still, he was part of the problem, not the solution.

"And I have a book I am enjoying, In fact, I have a monkey in the tree right now," she added.

"A monkey in the tree?" he questioned.

She laughed hilariously. The sound was one he instantly adored. He'd find a way to make her do it more, he promised himself.

"It's when you are reading a truly good book, and you get to the very best part. You want to read more, so you chase that monkey through the byzantine branches and limbs of a knotty, twisted up tree."

She giggled and he felt something kick in the area of his heart, as if just by the sound she had quickened him back to life.

"And then?" he asked.

"And then you get to the top and you have the most marvelous feeling before drifting slowly to the ground with a deep satisfied sigh."

"And then?" he asked again, a smile quirking his lips.

"And then you go back to the library and try to find another book that will do the same thing for you."

"Another book with a monkey in it?"

She laughed. "They all have monkeys if they are well written. They are, how do you say it, McGuffins?"

His smile grew broader. "Yes, McGuffins. Hitchcock's word for the Maltese Falcon, something one has to find, has to have."

"Yes, that is exactly it!" She seemed so happy that he got it, that he understood the meaning of something so important to her. And the thrill it gave him to see her like this had him wondering if she was going to end up being his McGuffin.

After the dinner trays had been collected and the empty splits of champagne removed, Shaw sat with her chin propped on her elbow on the armrest looking out the window and watching the sun as the plane chased it down over a cornfield.

Deke, just coming back from the restroom, was immobilized by the beauty of the woman silhouetted in the dying sunlight, an expression on her face so melancholy it broke his heart. Her gorgeous face had mesmerized him from the moment he had seen her. She had striking features, high cheekbones, a fine nose, and expressive elegantly shaped brows. But it was her dark blue eyes that had drawn him in. Full of sparks and limpid lights, he had stood stunned outside the restroom door, taking in her exotic good looks from that very first glance. She was obviously an American, but somewhere in her genes there was proof of an amorous Italian—one with a zeal for life. Something he had to acknowledge, he had lost. And was doubtful of ever finding again.

Bantering with her while he had held her bullet-styled

vibrator in the palm of his hand, his interest had been piqued. Now, even with her tormented mien, as she stared at the disappearing sun on the distant horizon, she was lovely. She was a sensual feast for the eyes that brought all of his senses to attention, especially the one that had been long neglected—that of touch.

His itch to feel a woman in his arms, to have his fingers caress soft smooth skin, to have his cock slide into a warm welcoming body as the sun came up, was often overwhelming. He watched as Shaw's thumb held her chin and her index finger stroked her full bottom lip. He groaned and shook his head. He wanted this woman. Wanted her eager and willing in his bed.

He had to smile and arch a brow at his wayward thought, as typically, he got what he wanted. A wave of sadness washed over him. Well, he used to, but no more. No, he never got what he wanted anymore. Still . . . he could enjoy time with this beautiful woman while it lasted, knowing her no-doubt lovely body would never grace the expensive designer sheets his wife had bought for them their last Christmas together.

"Dime for your thoughts?" he asked as he slid back into his seat. Her legs were crossed at the knee and she dangled a low-heeled sandal from her toes. Her pink perfect little toes. He was going to need some solo time in the shower when they landed at LAX and he arrived home. He loved women's feet. They were so sensuous, and he could draw out the most exquisite moans from rubbing them. Men who didn't start with the feet were denying themselves countless groans of pleasure.

She turned to him with a hint of a smile. "Dime?"

"Inflation."

"That would be overpaying on a grand scale."

"Have it your way," he said and he flipped a penny into her lap.

She picked it up and turned it over looking at the images on both sides. She rubbed her thumb over the profile of President Lincoln. "Did you know that Lincoln battled depression practically all of his life?"

"I had heard that. He'd had a lot of sadness in his life that he'd had to work through, pretty much on his own as his wife was even worse than he was in that department," he answered.

She nodded and said, "The night he died, along with a small knife and a five-dollar confederate bill, some letters and newspaper clippings were found in his pockets. Letters and news clippings that praised him for all the good he was doing and all the wonderful things he had accomplished. It was said that he kept them on him to encourage him whenever he was feeling desolate and despondent."

"Hmmm. So, where are your letters? That tiny little purse doesn't look as if it could hold your many accolades."

She threw her head back and laughed and he felt a zinging sensation deep in his chest. *My God she was stunning! And totally beguiling when she laughed.*

She smiled back at him but didn't answer the question he had paid her for or the one that had followed.

"Why so melancholy? I mean, I know you must have plenty of reasons to be sad, but why specifically right now?"

She looked over at him and then lowered her head as if drawing courage by looking at her hands now folded in her lap. "You comforted me. You can't know how much I miss that."

He turned in his seat to face her and with his fingers on her chin, tilted her head and turned it up so that she had to face him. His eyes met hers with such intensity it was as if heat waves were shimmering between them. "You can't know how much I want to comfort you more."

He didn't realize it until the words had left his mouth, but it was probably the sexiest come on line he'd ever uttered in his life. Only it wasn't a come on. It was a plea.

She sighed. "I was thinking about widows. How lucky they are in some aspects."

"You're going to need to elaborate on that thought," he said. "Most widows would not agree that they are the fortunate ones."

"Well, they are not half-widows now, are they?" she said bitterly.

He took both her hands in his. "Tell me. What's this all about?"

She sighed again, taking a deep breath in through her nose and then letting it out just as deeply. Yoga breaths, designed to calm her. He knew them well.

"Well, when your husband *dies*, people show up to help—chaplains, family members, coworkers and friends. They send flowers and food, they send cards and letters, and they come by to hug you and hold you in their arms. They sit with you for hours. They lean into you and cry with you. They wipe your cheeks and theirs. They tell you stories, recall memories that were never shared before. They take you out to dinner or to a movie. They comfort you. See that you are not lonely."

She took another deep breath and continued. "When your husband is very badly hurt, but by some miracle does not die, they don't do those things. It is a very different time. They may stop by the hospital and wait in the family lounge for a while to let you know that they came, but as they are not allowed into the ICU, where you spend all your time, they go home without giving you any comfort. Yes, they send cards. Some of them cute and funny when that is the absolute last thing you need. They know you are at the hospital all the time so they don't send flowers or food. They don't call. They don't want to intrude. When they do call, their words are stilted. No one knows what to say. Is he going to die? Is he going to make it? What will he be like if he survives this? And then when he does survive, there are congratulations and well wishes, but you're pretty much on your own now. You have survived the crisis. Your husband has lived!" She put too much emphasis on the word *lived*, and he saw where this was going. He absolutely knew where this was going.

"But really, the husband you loved is gone. All the good

parts are gone. Mostly bad parts remain. His personality has changed. He is not the man you said 'I do' to. He is a mean, angry stranger. Maybe they don't see it; as he is able to be civil with them, carry on short conversations, eat the applesauce cake and oatmeal cookies they brought. He says a few things to them that make him appear brave and accepting. But he is not. Not by a long shot.

"When they leave he is anything but accepting. He is angry, sad, accusing . . . bitter. I have lost the husband who was happy, fun to be with, sexy, comforting, strong and protective, witty and wild, able to lift me into his arms and make love to me, holding me against the foyer wall when he is so besotted with me that he can't make it to the bedroom. I have lost the man who sleeps with me, eats with me, goes shopping with me, takes hikes and watches brain-numbing TV with me. I am a widow. I have lost my husband. A new man is here pretending to be him, but he is not. No one knows that. No one but me. As my husband is still sitting in his easy chair, able to talk, able to take his pills with a swallow of vodka, watch TV with them, and then pass out after they leave. They are all happy he is still alive because they loved him so much. But if they spent more than twenty minutes with him, they would know that I am living with a stranger. I am a widow, as I have lost the husband I loved. But I don't let anybody know that. I am trying to honor the man I married, not the man I now live with."

He takes her hands in his and rubs her fingers. "Have you no one? No one who understands? No one to comfort you?"

"My sister. She is my rock. She understands. But she is sad, too. She adored Matt. Now she says she is coming to hate him for how unhappy he is making me, and for how much more work I have to do now to take care of him. We both agonize over how much our financial situation has changed. His workman's compensation helps, but there are so many more bills to pay now. She helps in many small ways, as she can; she gets me free airline tickets so I can go to Mexico for his insulin. But Matt wasn't on the job a full week, let alone the three months required for health care benefits, so we have no health insurance. I am a kindergarten teacher, I don't make much money. I received a scholarship to go back to school so I can get a better job, but even that costs money, as I have to buy books and gas to get there.

"My sister doesn't know that this quarterly trip to Mexico is a mini-vacation for me. She doesn't know that I will drink on the plane to numb the pain, watch an X-rated movie on the motel TV at night with a sex toy in my hand, sit by a crowded pool in the late afternoon reading a book, a pool that I would never go into as it is not sanitary, but I go there to allow strange men to appreciate me with their eyes, because I need to see the lust in their eyes to know that I am still desirable."

She saw his eyes go wide with shock, knew where his thoughts went, and touched his arm. "No, I would never let them approach me. Never." She shook her head and he watched as her curls tumbled off her shoulders. "I could not allow physical intimacies with others so casually. But I need to know that I am still pretty, still desirable. I always go back to my room alone and see to my needs in my own way. I am careful to make it known that their advances would not be appreciated.

"It is a special time for me when I come to L.A. I get to eat my favorite Mexican foods and drink some wine alone in my room, watching whatever movie I choose on TV for two whole nights.

"Then I return with Matt's drugs, kiss him on the forehead and tell him that I loathe this trip. When in reality, I look forward to it with every fiber in my being. I need this escape. If only for two days, I can pretend I am no longer a half-widow who no one cares to comfort because her husband did not die. He survived. But he survived as a different man. One I no longer love."

He looked into her watery eyes. He hated to see her holding back unshed tears. Tears that he knew needed to fall, to be allowed to course down her cheeks in order for her to be cleansed and renewed. He had lain in bed many a night doing just that until his pillow was soaked through.

He wanted to pull her into his arms and hold her. Give her the comfort she so badly needed. But would she allow him to?

He lifted the armrest between them, took a chance, and pulled her to him. Nestling her close, wrapping one arm around her trim waist and bringing her hip snug against his. He wrapped his other hand around her head and pressed her face into his neck. Then he cooed into her ear, "Let it go. Let all the sadness drain out. It's time you grieve the man you lost. I've got you."

Chapter 85—Deke & Shaw
Strangers on a Plane

After dinner, and her little tirade and crying jag, they sipped some peach brandy that Deke procured from a particularly friendly flight attendant, who seemed to know his tastes quite well. The attractive attendant smiled at Deke every time he beckoned, but never once did she acknowledge Shaw. Shaw thought it was because the flight attendant knew she was an interloper—that she didn't really belong in business-class.

Both Deke and Shaw declined coffee, as she needed to get some sleep so she could be up early to get to Tijuana in the morning, and he had an early morning meeting with contractors.

Deke wanted to hear more about her, her life before marrying, her life after, her family, and her dreams for the future. She finally relented and told him how she and Matthew had met when she was in college, how they got married on the beach, and how they loved to go camping or boating anytime they could cobble two days off together. She talked about her job as a kindergarten teacher, about her family in North Carolina, and how her life was now one tedious errand or chore after another until she fell into bed, just to wake up and begin the cycle all over again the next day. Then, because he insisted, she told him about the accident.

"Matt worked as a lineman for the electric company. He loved his work, especially when disaster struck and he could use his extensive training and remarkable climbing skills. He was always eager to go with the co-op teams whenever there was a neighboring county in trouble. His expertise was in repairing damage to the high power lines. So he was very much in demand whenever there were poles down due to wind or ice storms, tornadoes, flooding, or hurricanes.

"He was in a bucket fixing lights on a high-rise bridge when the driver of a tractor-trailer, who had fallen asleep at the wheel, ran into the utility truck that was anchoring Matt. On impact he was separated from the bucket and flew through the air and landed seventy feet away on the concrete embankment that bordered the oncoming ramp. He was unresponsive when they got to him. They did CPR until the EMTs arrived, and then he was airlifted to a trauma center. He had multiple cranial, rib, and spinal fractures. Thankfully his spinal cord was spared and it was intact. He was rushed into surgery for them to put a drain in place to help relieve the pressure in his skull. Over six months he saw 165 medical providers, including those on his trauma team, neurosurgeons, reconstructive plastic surgeons, psychologists, psychiatrists, speech therapists, physical therapists, primary care doctors, ear nose and throat doctors, cardiologists, radiologists, eye doctors, internists and even dentists. All the providers used some form of the word "miracle" during his visits. His main issues now, over two years later, are balance and coordination, really bad dizzy spells, a complete lack of taste and smell, vocal hoarseness, and debilitating pain. A mall walk in one door and out the other leaves him short of breath. Severe ARDS while he was hospitalized left him with infections that have yet to be resolved, and issues thought to be due to an ear infection are likely from more undiagnosed brain trauma.

"We were both pretty wiped out after several appointments daily for over a year. Matt is especially tired after PT, and he continues to be very immune-compromised. He's predisposed to having open wounds on his head and in his trachea and stomach, so we get a bit nervous being out and about, especially if someone nearby is coughing or sneezing, or a baby nearby has a runny nose. He is not able to eat normally, but he enjoys his morning protein-filled smoothies with vodka and we puree pretty much anything he wants to eat, except crackers, which he is able to break down with his saliva. He can't taste the salt though, so I have to limit him to six. We are awaiting a crucial MRI, where we will see if the broken vertebrae (c6 and c7) will require spine surgery, or if the significant pain Matt is experiencing is from herniated discs or other tissue injuries. If so, that will keep the C Collar in place much longer. He is currently in one and has been since the accident. Although I often come home and see that he has removed it and tossed it on the floor.

"As it stands now, the neurosurgeon has told us it will be at least three years before Matt is truly "out of danger." He will continue to have to be careful throughout his life, given the massive amount of brain injury, and the complex/compound fractures to his face and skull. His wish list when we ask for prayers is for his neck to heal and to avoid any future spine surgeries. And of course, he'd love to look handsome again, to be able to smell, and in turn, taste.

"He was quite the 'foodie' and loved trying new recipes, doing cook-offs, and searching out exotic foods whenever we traveled. He would like better balance, to stop tripping over his own feet, to be more coordinated, with a better equilibrium, and to have no more dizzy spells. He would like better pain management, to regain the feeling back in his legs. The neuropathy does not seem to have a cure. He would like better speech, and for the hoarseness to cease. It is not surprising that he has this though; given the time he spent on the ventilator and because of his tracheotomy. He hates living with Traumatic Brain Injury, mourns the loss of his career, is embarrassed by the way he can't remember his friends' names, and all the other daily challenges due to memory loss issues. He deals with confusion, frustration, depression, anger, and anxiety every day over all the abilities that he has lost. His mental health is far from good. He's a powder keg with a short fuse. Sometimes I'm afraid to be with him, although I suppose I could overpower him if I had to. Except he fights dirty and I can't bear to hurt a living thing.

"Next month he will start with another speech and language provider and someone who will work with him so he doesn't trip or fall every time he looks up or glances in a different direction. His full bilateral loss of smell and taste has made him ill several times because he has no way of knowing if something is tainted or has soured and gone bad. I have a fulltime job so I can't always be there to be his sniffer. I've started to just throw leftovers away, rather than try to remember when something was cooked and pureed.

"Then we have his diabetes, which has to be managed carefully, because he can't just grab some orange juice or a candy bar if his levels are low. And he often tends toward too many fruit smoothies because they are easy and "pretty," and he can disguise the alcohol in them. Then his sugar spikes.

"So you can see, he needs twenty-four hour care. I can leave him alone to run to the store or to take a quick walk, but longer than that and he's liable to fall down going to the bathroom or take one too many pain pills or drink too much beer or vodka, because despite having dizzy spells that he hates, he loves the dizziness he gets from drinking. His doctors would have a fit if they knew how attached he is to alcohol.

"I have to be honest, I'm scared he's going to hurt himself or kill himself almost every minute of the day. It would take nothing to make him hit his head on the commode or on a countertop on his way to the floor.

"I'm scared for our future. We used to be so happy. Now it's hard to make him smile, to give him a reason to want to go on. And I suspect his medicines are keeping him from wanting to be with me in a sexual manner. Not being together in a physical way is making us grow even farther apart. It is not a happy life we have anymore. And then there are the bills. And they are never-ending.

"Our attorneys say we must wait another year to sue for damages. They say all the things wrong with him must be discovered and that it generally takes three years to do that. Good God, if Matt discovers anything else wrong, he's liable to take all his pain meds while I am not looking.

"Some days I feel as if I am living in a nightmare that will never end. On other days, I see the end coming and it terrifies me. Meanwhile, I do what I can to keep a roof over our heads, and him on insulin."

She whispered as if to herself, "If he dies, it cannot be my fault. I could not live with that."

Deke sat with his fingers steepled, his typical posture when giving something his full attention. He let out a deep sigh as he admitted to himself that although he didn't know her very well; he believed her final whispered statement to be true.

She seemed like the type of woman who would be fully invested at the altar when the 'I dos' were being said. He hated that this was the life this beautiful woman now had to live. And he was shocked to learn that her life mirrored his in so many ways. He took her hand in his when she leaned her head back and closed her eyes. He was still holding it long after she nodded off.

He motioned to the flight attendant, who seemed miffed that he was holding this woman's hand. But he'd learned to ignore women who expected him to come on to them just because they thought themselves pretty. He asked for a bourbon on the rocks. They had forty-five minutes before landing but he was not capable of napping, despite the full day he'd put behind him.

The sleeping woman beside him had not only dredged up her past, but his as well. Plus, she was too beautiful, even with tear-stained cheeks, to close his eyes to. *I will watch over her and be the comfort she needs as long as I can,* he told himself.

When the glass with his drink was placed on his tray, he took it and sipped thoughtfully. He used his iPhone watch to send an email. It would send as soon as they arrived at the gate. In it, he told his driver to be prepared to drive to Mexico in the morning. He couldn't make all her problems go away, but he could certainly help her with some of them. And he could keep her safe in the process.

Chapter 86—Deke & Shaw
The Kindness of Strangers

Shaw lifted her head and for a moment had no idea where she was. She saw the safety placard tucked into a vinyl sleeve attached to the wall several feet in front of her, and she remembered.

Oh dear, she had spilled her guts, again. Sobbed out her story to another stranger. This time to a man who was as handsome as a Polo model, who had seductive debauchery dancing in his long-lashed blue eyes, and who was entirely too approachable for a woman with as much baggage as she carried around in her head.

As usual, she blamed it on the alcohol for making her purge on her poor unsuspecting seatmate. She turned her head slowly to the left and took in a steadying breath. Deep blue vibrant eyes under dark slashing brows met hers, full on. They roamed her face as if checking for signs of distress, and not finding any, his lips broke into a wide smile. He had such nice white teeth and beckoning, full generous lips. She had the odd thought that he was going to kiss her, but instead he murmured, "Nice nap?"

She smiled back. "Yes. I'm sorry. I tend to do this after a few drinks. Like a Kewpie doll, my string gets pulled and I purge until the brain drain makes my eyelids close . . . then I'm out. I don't hold liquor well, it relaxes me a bit too much," she said, then added, "maybe that's why I crave it." Then she laughed at herself.

With her head tilted and her eyes bright, it was sweet and musical. Endearing to the point of engaging a wild desire to spark through his veins. He thought to himself that he would empty his bank account to see her do more of that.

He grinned back at her, "It's my drug of choice too." Then

said, "We're landing soon, so if you need to . . ." he indicated with his head toward the restroom.

"Oh no, I'm fine. I'll be good until I get to National City. I usually get a motel room there."

He set his lips and gave her a stern look. "Not tonight. Tonight you're staying in a decent hotel."

"Well that would certainly be exceptional, only I can't afford that," she muttered.

"You let me worry about that."

She sat back in her seat, visibly moving away from him.

He quickly countered, "No, no. I don't mean that way. I won't be coming with you. My driver will take you to a nice hotel after dropping me off at my home in Thousand Oaks. He'll see you inside, then pick you up in the morning and take you wherever you want to go in Tijuana. Then when you're finished, he will drive you to a hotel close to the airport where you can get a shuttle Sunday morning."

"I can't let you do that." Her lips were firm, her eyes flashing.

"Yes, you can." He touched her lips with the tip of his index finger when she started to open her mouth to continue her protest. The velvety feel made his cock jerk.

"No buts . . . and no bus . . . and no dingy motel room. You need a break. And I'm going to see that you get it. You and your magic bullet thing there," he said as he waved a hand in the general direction of her purse, "deserve to enjoy a soak in a nice bathtub and to sleep in a nice bed during your only two nights off in three months. I insist. I can easily afford it, and you would make me very happy if you accepted my gift to you."

She looked up into his face. He seemed sincere. And somehow she knew he *could* easily afford all that he was offering. "Okay. No strings?" she asked, just to be certain.

He smiled. "No, no strings."

Chimes pinged overhead and drew their attention to the front of the plane. The announcement that they were preparing to land with all its relevant instructions began and then ended with the same sonorous voice they'd heard all evening. Passengers shifted in their seats, gathering their belongings and chattering nervously, as they still had to endure the landing, deplaning, and baggage handling carousels.

He was pleased beyond measure. And wasn't exactly sure why. He was giving up his driver for the day and likely spending two thousand dollars for her accommodations. But yes, he was extremely happy. And he didn't care why. Wasn't going to question it. It had been a long time since he had been this excited about anything. Pleased to the point of being giddy. He smiled and grabbed her hand, threaded his fingers through hers and prepared to ease her through the often precarious landing at LAX. He smiled over at her and she returned an impish grin.

He was beginning to envy his driver, as he would be spending the whole day in her company tomorrow. She made things . . . cheery. She was interesting and funny. She giggled and she laughed . . . and she cried. She was the most genuine person he'd met in a long time.

Chapter 87–Deke & Shaw
No Longer Strangers

He took her hand to help her out of her seat, and then refused to let it go. With his laptop case strapped high on his left shoulder, and his right hand firmly clasping hers, he led them expertly down the ramp and through the airport to the baggage claim where his driver would be keeping an eagle eye out for his suitcase.

"What does your case look like?" he asked.

"I don't have one. This is all I have," she said, indicating the small backpack she wore, hanging off her right shoulder.

"That's it?" he asked. The women he was used to traveling with usually had five or six suitcases; his wife had always had at least three along with two carry-ons.

Shaw patted her backpack. "This has my bathing suit, two changes of underwear, a shirt, toothbrush, toothpaste, sunscreen, and my book. There's nothing else I need."

He stopped and stared at her. Took in her features. Examined her skin, her lashes, her lips. No makeup to be seen. Her features were exotic and she appeared to be a natural beauty. With genuine surprise, he realized that there was absolutely no need for embellishment. The thought caused him to inhale deeply through his nostrils.

"No cosmetics?" he asked to confirm his latest discovery of the woman named Shaw.

"I can't afford them. But even if I could, I wouldn't wear them on a trip like this. I am trying to blend in, not stand out. It's safer that way."

He smiled and squeezed her hand. Smart woman. And not a vain thought channeling though her complicated quirky brain. For some reason, that pleased him very much.

He spotted Kurt by the carousel as he was lifting the

distinctive steel blue Rimowa aluminum case from the conveyer belt. He lifted his hand and waved. Kurt smiled back.

Not bothering to slide up the handle and use the wheels, Kurt carried the case easily by the grip on the side. The big man made the large German-engineered suitcase seem dwarf-sized. Deke was six feet-three, Kurt was six-eight and muscled like a pro wrestler. He wasn't about to tell Shaw that Kurt was his bodyguard as well as his driver. She didn't need to know the very real threat of kidnapping that loomed large for men with his kind of wealth, especially those who lived close to the Mexican border and frequently traveled to factories there.

Hand-in-hand, because he was loath to let her go for some deep-seated reason that he didn't fully understand, they left the terminal and made their way to short term limo parking. Feeling as if a tangible link had to be sustained, he kept hold of her, trying very hard to keep his touch amiable and protective, though his thumb was tempted to stoke the pad of her thumb in a light caress.

He didn't miss Kurt's questioning brow, mocking lips, or surprised looks as he led her to the line of private cars. This was definitely not normal behavior for him, he knew that, but he didn't care and Kurt could just suck back his juvenile all-knowing smiles.

"Oh my," Shaw said as the driver opened the back door of the Lincoln town car. She had never been inside a limo before and as she slid across the leather seat to make room for Deke, she sighed her appreciation. The car had to have been running on auxiliary power, as it was nice and cool inside. As soon as Deke was in and the door closed, Kurt got behind the wheel and exited the lot. He expertly maneuvered them through traffic while Deke pulled out his cell phone.

He was searching and swiping screens with expert fingers, his face shuttered in concentration until suddenly he smiled and leaned forward. "The Ayres Hotel, 1710 Millennial Avenue in Chula Vista, it's five miles from Tijuana. Drop me home first, then make sure she gets to her room. Your room's across the hall. Plan to stay with her until she's back at the airport and through TSA."

Kurt nodded in affirmation of his new duties and then Deke sat back. He sighed with satisfaction and then pressed a button on the console in front of him. A gray screen slid up between the back of Kurt's seat and their compartment. Things quieted substantially. Only the whispering sound of tires meeting pavement could be heard.

Deke was still on his phone, swiping up screens and punching in numbers. The sight of such capable long fingers doing such nimble work made her think of other things he might do well with them.

After a few minutes, he sat up and turned to face her. "I've booked you into a hotel for two nights. Kurt will stay there as well. He'll take you to Tijuana, to wherever you want to go tomorrow and then back to the hotel. Sunday morning he'll make sure you get to the airport in time to make your flight. And this time you won't be flying stand-by. You're booked first-class through to Salt Lake City."

Shaw blinked and stared. "Why are you doing this?" she whispered.

"Because I want to. And because I can."

She shook her head back and forth. "No. I cannot accept."

"What if I said it was because you are living a life that parallels mine so much that it terrifies me."

"What do you mean?" she asked, confusion evident on her face.

"You know that crying jag you had on the plane?"

"Yes?"

"I've been there. Many times."

She tilted her head and lifted a brow in question. "I don't understand."

"I too, am a spouse who is a half-widow, or in my case, a half-widower."

She gasped and gripped the sleeve of his suit coat, "No!"

"Sadly . . .yes." He heaved out a huge chest-deflating sigh. "I know what you've gone through, and what you continue to go through each and every day." He covered her hand with his.

"Your wife is ill?"

He nodded and met her eyes with his. The vital blue of his irises had darkened. "She was in an automobile accident almost two years ago. She's been in a comma ever since. She is unresponsive to any stimuli.

"You're right. By all rights, you and I should be have been widowed. At first I was buoyed by the knowledge that I hadn't lost her. But just like you, I have lost my spouse. Stephanie is not there on that bed that adjusts her every half hour. I didn't believe it at first, but now I truly believe that her spirit left her body at the accident scene, and that all I've done with each heartbreaking decision is to continue to keep her body going. Probably against everything she would have wanted."

Shaw doubled over and dropped her head into her hands and started weeping as if her heart was broken. It melted his. That this woman would cry for him like this broke him.

After several moments, she lifted her head, and with tears cascading down her face said, "That is so tragic. So very sad. My heart hurts for you, and for her." More tears joined to pool in her eyes and run down her cheeks.

He reached over and tugged her into his chest, then enveloped her in his arms. Together they held each other, her sobbing quietly, him allowing her tears to wet his shirt.

By the time they reached his house in Thousand Oaks and she watched in wonder as the ornate wrought iron gates parted in the middle, then slowly swung open, he had told her the story of his wife's accident. How Stephanie had been the first person to stop at a red light at a busy intersection, while the distracted driver on the phone in the car directly behind her had never even looked up to see that traffic had stopped. He had hit the back of

Stephanie's Audi A8 full force, sending it into the middle of the intersection where Stephanie had been hit broadside by a full-sized pickup truck barreling through on a green light. The truck driver had been unable to avoid hitting her.

All three drivers had died on the scene. But an E.M.T. running from his car on the opposite side of the road had been able to get Stephanie breathing again before she was officially pronounced dead. It had given Deke something to hope for when he had received the call. But now, nearly two years later, he knew it had only prolonged the inevitable. His wife was not in the shell that was her body. He now believed that her soul had left her body on impact and found its way to heaven while he had been in a business meeting. It had been his birthday.

Driving up the long paved road to the mansion that sat at the end of it, he apologized for drawing her into his sad story. She had taken both of his hands in hers and chastised him, saying that. "Don't be sorry for sharing your tragedy. I know firsthand that you can't deal with this kind of devastation alone. It helps to talk to others. It helps to lessen the guilt you feel even though you didn't cause the accident. What you are going through is like carrying the heaviest burden imaginable. You need someone to help share it. Trust me. I know."

He looked into her solemn face, now in shadow as the sun was down. "Who shares yours?" For some reason he was terrified that she might have found solace in another man's arms.

"My sister, my mother, the other teachers at work."

"I have none of those."

"No brothers or sisters, no mother or father either?"

He shook his head. "No brother. No sister. My mom died of breast cancer when I was in college. My father retired to Costa Rica. I see him once a year at New Year's."

"Your wife's family?"

"We do not speak often. They are not dealing well."

"Friends?"

"I do have friends, but they are all far away, most on the

East Coast, although one recently moved back to the area. But he has problems of his own. His wife died giving birth to twins. I fear if he and I got together, we'd be tempted to play Russian Roulette," he said with a sardonic smile.

"Then I will be the one you share with!" she stated with conviction. "After all, it makes sense. We are both in boats, forever rowing in circles with the bow in the water."

He laughed at her analogy. "That puts it succinctly."

She lifted her left hand and used it to turn his right one upside down on top of his thigh. Then she placed her left hand into it. "You hold my hand," she said as she pulled his other hand down and gripped it in hers, "and I'll hold yours, and we can encourage each other."

He smiled at her. "You live too far away."

She returned his smile with a wider one, "But I will come back—every ninety days!" She said that as if three months was of no consequence. He knew for him it would be an eternity.

He laughed, "For drugs!"

"And now to check on you as well."

He gripped her hands in his. "Yes, please come back to check on me. And to comfort me. I would like that."

The sedan stopped in the circular drive in front of a massive house with impressive carved double oak doors. "You are a beam of sunshine in an otherwise dreary life," he breathed as he kissed her on the forehead.

She felt the tingle of his lips as they touched her skin. Wild butterflies and jumping beans vied for space in her core.

With their hands still connected, he lifted both of hers and caressed her fingertips with his lips. "Stay safe on your journey, sweet Shaw. I don't imagine you have a cell phone?" He hadn't seen her check one during the flight, and she wore a watch—a sure sign she probably didn't even own one.

"No. It's an extravagance I can't afford."

"Well Kurt has one, and you can use it to call me. I want to know that you are safe after your 'drug deal' tomorrow," he said with a devilish grin.

She gave him quid pro quo, "I'll let you know when I've scored."

He pushed the console button and the divider screen lowered. "I'll go in through the garage, Kurt. Can you let me know when Ms. Marin is in her room at the hotel?"

Kurt reached up over the visor and pressed a button. "Yes sir."

Shaw watched as one of the four matching oak garage doors opened. Kurt got out and retrieved Deke's high tech suitcase from the trunk. Back at the airport she'd seen a strobe light flash on both sides of the case and a shrill beeping sound emit from it when Kurt had lifted it off the conveyer belt. It had escalated in pitch and the lights in intensity until he'd punched in a code on the top, which had instantly stopped the lights and the alarm. She knew it contained important stuff and wondered about the man sitting beside her.

Deke got out with his computer case on his shoulder and together he and Kurt walked to the edge of the opening where the security lights lit the stone pavers in a wide arc. They stood in the circle of light and talked for a few minutes, no doubt about her, she thought. What a nuisance she'd become to such a nice man.

Then with a wave, Deke went inside the house and the door closed on what appeared to be a vintage Jaguar. She had never personally met someone so obviously wealthy. And she was genuinely surprised by how nice he had been to her, someone with evidently far less means than those he normally associated with.

Kurt got back into the car and expertly maneuvered the limo around the curved drive and back down the driveway and though the open gates. She turned after they went through and watched as the gates closed behind them. How nice it must be to return home to such a grand house, she thought. But then she remembered that he was returning to it all alone. There was no expectant spouse, no running children to welcome him. His wealth hadn't guaranteed his happily-ever-after.

She thought of Matt, at home, probably passed out on the couch after too many beers, trying to dull the memory of the wonderful life they had once lived. Deke, Stephanie, Matt and herself, they were all sad sacks, the lot of them.

Chapter 88—Deke & Shaw
Divine Decadence

Shaw stood alongside Kurt, who was staying on the same floor in a room across the hall from her. He had given her his cell phone number and on the way up in the elevator he had called Deke to let him know they had arrived at the hotel and that he was walking her to her door. Then Kurt had disconnected the call.

She and Kurt agreed to leave at seven the next morning. It could take two hours to get across the border, and the earlier one got in line, the better, she reasoned.

She was a bit miffed that Deke hadn't wanted to talk to her, but then why would he? No doubt he was already in bed. He'd said he had an early morning meeting.

She used her card key to open the door to her room and waved to Kurt, saying, "Good night."

"Good night, Ms. Marin. I'll meet you at seven in the lobby."

"Call me Shaw. Only my students call me Mrs. Marin."

His eyebrows tented as if he was surprised that she was married. "Okaay," he said. And she had to wonder at his thoughts. Did his boss put other women up in posh hotels often? If so, maybe it was odd for one to be a married woman? She had a sense that Deke and Kurt were close, but that this was unusual behavior for Deke.

She closed the door behind her and leaned her back against it. Then slowly sank to the floor, her feet flopped out on the plush carpet in front of her.

She blinked and took in the room. She had boarded a plane, found herself in a first-class seat, next to a man who was hot, sexy, and disarmingly nice, then upon landing, was led to a chauffeur-driven car and taken to a luxury hotel. And she hadn't spent a dime. In fact, she still had her cocktail money wadded up in her change purse.

As she got to her feet, she allowed her backpack to slide off her arms and drop to the carpet. Then she walked around taking everything in. A more modern, well-appointed room would be hard to imagine. Everything was pristine and new, no faux countertops, but real marble vanities, real wood furniture. She touched a bolster on the buttery leather sofa, ran her finger down the soft velvet duvet on the king-sized bed made up with swatches in soothing shades of dark and light teals, and stared at her image in the mirror behind the bar. Oh this was just too much. She jumped when the phone rang.

It took three shrill rings for her to spot it on the nightstand. Then she leapt to answer it, as it was incredibly loud in the quiet room and she wanted to silence it quickly. It was such an offensive sound intruding into the serene setting that her first thought was to put a stop to it, not to question who could be calling. Then with the receiver in her hand, she questioned her actions as she slowly brought the receiver to her ear.

"Uh, hello?"

"It's just me, calling to see that you're safely in the room and making sure that everything is all right."

"This is over the top, Deke. You should not have spent this kind of money on me. One night is probably more than my monthly house payment."

"I wanted you to be comfortable and to feel cherished. I think it's been a long time since anyone has pampered you. And I can't think of anyone who deserves it more than you. The money means nothing to me Shaw, truly. I only care about you being comfortable . . . and safe."

Shaw went to pull the corner of the duvet down so she could sit on the bed and saw the little box of chocolates sitting atop the pillow.

"Oh my God, chocolates! For bedtime. How yummy!"

He laughed. "It'll go well with the splits of champagne

in the mini-fridge. I made sure they stocked it with some."

She hissed. "Oh no! I never even open a mini-fridge. There's decadent and then there's ridiculously stupid. Who pays those prices?"

"I do. And I did. You enjoy those bottles, there's only two. And I paid for them when I asked them to stock them, so you're not saving me any money by leaving them there."

"Do you do this for all the drug mules who sit beside you on airplanes?"

He laughed again, full and throaty. She could picture his head thrown back, giving himself into laughter. She liked that. Especially knowing that any kind of laughter must be foreign to him right now.

"I rarely have people sitting beside me that I don't know. And if I do, I don't talk to them unless I absolutely have to. You, you're different. You're delightful. Charming. Enchanting, really. It's very refreshing to meet someone who—"

"Cries," she filled in for him.

"Cares enough to do so," he admonished her.

"Everybody would cry if they lived my life."

"Ahhh, that's where you're wrong. They would give up. Probably walk away. But you haven't. And I would bet my Austin Healey you haven't cried since the week the accident happened."

Shaw lowered herself to the bed and crossed one leg over the other. "I am stunned."

"That I have an Austin Healey or that I'm right?"

"Both. How do you know this?" she whispered.

"I see me in you. We're walking hand-in-hand on a railroad track, each waiting for the train and not knowing when it will come, but knowing we're not going to make it back to the station in one piece."

"You certainly have a way of saying things."

"Well, now I'm saying take a nice hot bath, use the bath salts, they're already paid for too. Sip some champagne and savor a chocolate or two, or eat the whole box, then get some sleep. You have a long day ahead of you."

Shaw yawned, ending it with a long sigh. "Yeah, you're right. It's off to bed I go."

"Hey?" he whispered.

"What?"

"Don't use that vibrator in the tub, okay."

She guffawed like a tanked-up sailor. And he loved the sound.

"You shouldn't make me laugh like that. I almost choked on my chocolate. As to my, ahem, 'neck massager,' I'm actually too tired tonight. Maybe I'll be up to something *stimulating* tomorrow night."

He groaned but tried to keep it to himself as he pictured her splayed out on the bed, that silly little bullet vibrating between her fingers on her clit.

He needed to get off the phone while he could still talk. "Let's talk tomorrow when you get back to the hotel. Can I leave you my number?"

"Yeah, I'd like that. And as it happens, there is a very fine pen and some expensive looking notepaper right here by this fancy art deco phone."

He rattled off his phone number, and then made her repeat it. "Call me anytime," he murmured.

"Okay. Gotta go. I hear some bath salts calling my name." She mimicked Minnie Mouse calling out her name then disconnected.

She sat for a few minutes longer, staring at the elegant draperies with the tasseled swags, wondering *what's going on here?*

She wasn't sure. But as she got up to find the bathroom and fill the tub, she realized she was happy. Something she hadn't been in a very long time.

Chapter 89—Deke & Shaw
Queuing Up

The line in front of the Farmacia didn't seem as long as usual. But then she had gotten here a lot earlier because Kurt had driven her instead of her taking the bus. Plus, he had a special security lane at the border and they'd cleared customs in record time.

It was 9:25 and she had already worked her way up to fifth in line. She couldn't help but smile. At this rate, she could be back at the posh hotel and down by that beautiful pool she'd seen from her window when she'd opened the drapes this morning, by early afternoon.

Another person made it past the door and into the Farmacia Y Botanica, while a man exited with two boxes of Novolin NPH in his arms and a huge smile. Another happy customer who had just saved the equivalent of a month's rent.

Everyone shuffled up into the empty space. It was not even ten o'clock but she could feel the perspiration at her hairline, diluting the essence of that wonderful cucumber and coconut conditioner she'd found in a basket on the counter.

She looked behind her and off to the right. Kurt, never more than ten steps away from her, was on his phone. He looked up and smiled at her, reassessed the area around her, and went back to talking on his phone, never once taking his eyes from her. She felt a chill tingle up her spine. *What the?* She thought he was Deke's driver but his physique and demeanor spoke of other things, darker things. *What was the deal here?*

She turned back in time to see the line move up again. Yay! Third in line.

Deke was on the phone with Kurt, getting an update on

Shaw's progress. As anticipated, she would be back in plenty of time to enjoy the hotel's pool. And with any luck, he could wrap up his meeting by lunchtime and join her poolside.

So far the meeting had gone well. He'd done his homework and knew the modifications they needed forward and backward, knew the suppliers they'd need, and knew the budget down to the dollar. What he didn't know were the labor costs. He'd had several spreadsheets done on the manpower hours that would be required for up-fitting the plant, but all of the reports he'd read seemed optimistic to him. From his experience, things took longer than expected. And there were always delays. He needed this project to come in for the budgeted amount. The viability of this plant, and the jobs that went along with it, were at stake. He'd close the plant if he had to, but that was not the decision he wanted to make. He opened his bottom desk drawer and took out a bottle of Canadian Club and poured two fingers and enjoyed the bite as the whiskey slid down his throat. It was a middle of the road whiskey, one he could afford while in college. He'd never jumped to another brand, even though now he could afford any whiskey he wanted.

Renewed and ready for battle, he prepared to go back to the conference room. He wanted an American company to do the refabricating. He wanted all the subcontractors and workers legal, documented, and insured. And he wanted quality work done fast. Now he just had to go back inside and settle for nothing less. Only two companies met his requirements, and the president of the one he wanted for the job was sitting in his conference room. He had to convince him to lower his bid by making him see that if this job went as planned, there'd be many more projects down the road. As workdays went, this one was pivotal. He followed the Canadian Club with two Excedrin and two Mentos, ran his fingers through his hair and returned to the boardroom. The smile on his face was because of a sassy, dark-haired vixen that could be waiting poolside for him in a matter of hours.

Chapter 90—Deke & Shaw
Riding Shotgun

Kurt had to grin as he watched Shaw come out the door of the Farmacia, all smiles and hugging two boxes of Lantus, the *tiene insulin* that brought so many pharmaceutical refugees over the border.

She was like a six-year-old holding up a filled Easter basket—the champion of the hunt. He had to admire her for her spunk and her willingness to go the distance for her disabled husband. Deke had filled him in a little last night, but this morning on their way south, she had told him about her husband's tragic accident and the impact it had on their lives. She hadn't complained, just seemed to accept how things had turned out.

And when they had parked around the corner from their destination, she had thanked *him* for everything he was doing for her; despite knowing he was being paid to attend her until she was winging her way back to Utah.

He saw what his boss saw in her, could see why he'd be smitten. Understood why he'd step out of his closed-up world to be kind to her. She was classy, yet approachable, humble and grateful for anything you did for her, and in an uncanny way that he suspected she wasn't even aware of, she was sexier than all get out. In the words of Brooks and Dunn, "There ain't nothing 'bout you that don't do something for me." He was sure his boss felt the same way.

When she came up beside him, he took the boxes from her and led her through the alleyways and streets to the place he'd parked the limo. He tossed a roll of coins to the street-wise youth who was watching it for him, and used the key fob to open the passenger door for her, murmuring, "It's safer to sit up front until we get out of Mexico."

"That's fine with me," she smiled up at him, "I'm not

really back seat material anyway. This car is way too classy for me."

He shook his head, commenting to himself. *You're plenty classy for this car or any other.*

"Besides, I like riding shotgun," Shaw added.

"Well, there's more to see up front, that's for sure. C'mon let's blow this town!"

She laughed. "Yeah, there's a gorgeous swimming pool waiting for me back at the hotel."

He laughed. He'd give a week's pay to see her in a bikini. And he was pretty sure his boss had plans to do exactly that. He'd say Deke was a lucky bastard. But knowing his story and having seen his wife once, when Deke had rushed to her bedside when she'd had an infection, he knew that he was not lucky. If Deke was feeling compelled to spend a few hours in this adorable woman's company, he was all for it. The man deserved a little happiness. All he did was work and visit his wife in the convalescence center. Yeah, they were both married. But so what? They were both being denied everything that a marriage included. Except maybe the bills. He had to shake his head at the money they were both spending to keep their spouses alive.

"You hungry Kurt? I've got ten pesos burning in my pocket. My treat for tacos."

"You're on. But not until we get back to the good ole U.S.A. I know a place. Best tacos on earth. Their Marlin Taco is the bomb."

"Well, that sounds like it's worth waiting for. Lead the way!"

He smiled over at her. "If you like tacos, you're in a for a real treat."

She shook her backpack. "I've got the pesos and the Tums, bring 'em on."

He smiled, "You crack me up. Mind if I call Deke and see if he'd like to join us. He's a big fan of Tex-Mex."

"Gosh no!" She started digging into her backpack. "I

think I have a few more pesos in here."

He laughed. "I am pretty sure he's not going to let you pay, and although some places close to the border do take pesos, I think you're going to need dollars."

"Oh, I have plenty of dollary-doos. Tell him if he's not going to let me treat, then don't bother coming."

He pressed a button on his steering wheel and she heard the sound of a phone ringing and then she heard Deke answer. "Yes, Kurt. Everything all right?"

"Perfect. I have Shaw in the car with me and we're about ten minutes from the border. Our girl here wants to buy us some tacos so I'm heading to Mariscos. You free to meet us? But I have to warn you, she says not to bother coming if you aren't going to let her pay."

"I have two questions. What's your ETA? And what do you mean by *our* girl. I saw her first."

"You know she's listening . . ."

"She *knows* I saw her first."

Kurt chuckled and Shaw cracked up. "I love it when guys fight over me."

"I'm almost finished here. I'll see you on Main Street." The phone disconnected.

"Looks like it's three for lunch," Kurt said with a broad smile.

Shaw finished digging in her backpack and waved a wad of bills. "I've got $33. Think that'll be enough?"

"Like two times over."

"Good."

"But he's not going to let you pay."

"Bet me."

He gave her a sideways look. "I wouldn't bet against you about anything. Get your passport out and look alive. We're at the border."

Chapter 91—Deke & Shaw
Messy Tacos

When they pulled onto Main Street, Shaw was surprised to see Deke sitting casually on a bar stool at a high-top table under a blue canopy, right in the middle of the street. The canopy had wildly colorful lettering and was between two food trucks. Apparently, they would be dining al fresco in a parking lot.

She gave him a huge grin as she opened the door and got out, thwarting Kurt who was trying to get around the car to get to her door.

"Don't you look like you own the cosmos, relaxed on that throne," she called out to him, as she took in his white dress shirt open at the collar and sleeves rolled up to the elbows. "You look like you've been working hard though," she said as she strode up to him. "How'd your meeting go?"

He stood, unfolding his long body from the high-backed seat and then stooping to place a kiss on her cheek. "I have been working very hard," he murmured, "I actually broke a sweat closing a major deal."

And then when Kurt was within earshot, he looked over at him and said, "Thank you for bringing her back, safe and sound."

"No problem," Kurt said, both hands in his front pockets as he took in his boss's happy countenance. Then just to tweak him, he added, "It was truly my pleasure."

She ignored their posturing and turned to Kurt as she took in the vibrant food trucks with their loud lettering and busy menu boards. "So this is where one gets the best tacos on earth? And they're only $2.29? I can eat five for that price."

"Trust me, you can't eat five. Unless you're one of those champion food eaters, two will do you in," Kurt replied.

Deke put his arm around Shaw's shoulders and turned

her toward the line.

The gesture was not lost on Kurt. He smiled back, genuinely happy to see his boss having a good time. "You guys order, I'll hold the table."

Under the protective cover of his arm draped around her, Deke bent and whispered, "So the morning went well? You got what you needed?"

She smiled up at him and he had to blink at how stunning she looked. She wore the same black jeans she'd had on yesterday, but the dark teal blouse was different. It drew out the lively blue of her eyes. In the bright sunshine he could see that her long black lashes were all hers. She wore a tiny bit of gloss on her lips, but other than that, her skin looked fresh and natural. And so kissable.

He felt his cock twitch against the zipper of his pants. And drew air deep into his lungs to fight the urge to press his lips into her neck, behind her ear, and then back to her throat.

"This morning was superb! I got up before the alarm and watched the sun come up over the pool outside the window. Then I got dressed and packed my bag and went down for breakfast. Kurt was there waiting and after some oatmeal and fruit, we were off. And the line wasn't so bad. Less than two hours I think. It was a good day!"

"Well that's wonderful. What kind of tacos do you want?" he asked, "and surely only two not five?"

"Actually, let me try one first. Beef please. We forgot to ask Kurt, but I think he likes the Marlin type."

"Yes, he certainly does. Don't worry, I know what he wants."

When he stepped up to the window, Shaw was surprised to hear him order in Spanish. Such rapid Spanish, and so much of it, that she knew he'd said a lot more than was required to order the food.

The man who took the order laughed and then nodded his head toward her and then turned to the grill behind him to prepare their food.

"They'll bring it to the table," Deke said as he took her elbow and led her away from the window.

"Wait! I haven't paid."

"You can leave a tip on the table. I give them five hundred at the beginning of the year and they let me know when I've spent it."

"I was supposed to pay."

"Says who?"

"Me. And you knew it."

"But I didn't agree . . ."

"So that was what the 'my girl' conversation was all about. Distracting me."

He threw his head back and laughed. "No, that was just Kurt and I posturing, fighting for the honor of taking care of you," he said as he helped her slide into her chair. "You're just too adorable not to want to protect. And neither of us has much interaction with women these days."

Shaw looked over at Kurt who was checking messages on his phone. She knew why that statement was so with Deke, but she wondered why that was the case with Kurt as well.

After a few minutes, a server with three loaded baskets of food weaved through the crowded tables to bring them their lunch. They all made room on the table, pushing their drinks aside and moving the basket of chips and salsa that had appeared while Deke and Shaw were ordering the tacos.

After the first bite, the only sounds around the table were appreciative moans and groans and mutterings, "Mmm, so good," "This is wonderful," "Love this sauce," and then Shaw asked, "How'd you two ever find this place?"

"I go to Mexico every other week. Kurt and I found this place on the way back one day, and we've been coming here ever since."

Shaw looked over at Kurt. "How long have you worked for Deke?"

Kurt looked at Deke and smiled, "Too long. Way

too long."

"Eight years isn't it?" Deke asked.

"Nine tomorrow. You and I lost a whole year, what with you being on autopilot."

Deke grimaced. "Yeah." Then he straightened in his chair. "If you hadn't taken me where I needed to be each day, I would never have gotten through those early days."

Kurt chuckled. "I know your schedule better'n you do."

"Oh yeah? Well just where am I supposed to be next, hot shot?"

Kurt made a big show of pulling out an imaginary notebook and thumbing the pages. "Oh yeah, here it is." He looked over and winked at Shaw. "You're supposed to be spending the rest of the afternoon having cocktails at some posh hotel pool with a Ms. Marin, and then afterward, taking her to dinner at Italianissimo Trattoria."

Deke looked over at Shaw and quirked a brow, "Am I?"

She shrugged, "Well, if you can find a bathing suit . . ."

"Well that's no problem, he always has a fully packed gym bag in the car," Kurt supplied.

"Then that's the plan. I'll take you back to your hotel in the Jag and Kurt can take the town car and have the afternoon and evening off. In fact, maybe I'll get a room at the hotel and take you to the airport myself tomorrow morning. If that's okay with you? I don't want to interfere with any plans you two have already made," he added with a smirk aimed at Kurt.

She smiled over at him. "My plans are flexible, and yours sound better. I love Italian food."

"And I know better than to make any plans without clearing them with you first," Kurt said as he stood. And then added, "I'll get out of your hair now. Let me get your stuff from the car, Shaw. And I'll get your gym bag," he said to Deke. He threw a few dollars onto the table, "Thanks for the grub, Boss."

Shaw picked up the money and handed it back to him.

"You were right, I didn't get to pay. But I was told I could take care of the tip." She smiled up at him. "Thank you for everything Kurt. You made the day a real pleasure."

"At your service," he took her hand, plucked the bills from it, and then lifted it higher to kiss the back of it. "Anytime."

After he left, Deke looked over at her, the warmth in his smile genuine. "Do you always put men in your thrall so easily?"

She leaned forward, her elbow bent on the table, her chin in her hand. "Do you feel as if you're under my power?" she whispered.

He leaned forward and drew his finger down her charming little nose, then across her full bottom lip, and along her jaw to where her hand was propping up her head. His fingertips caressed the pad below her little finger, then his thumb massaged her wrist. He watched as goose bumps pebbled the flesh along the outside of her arm, and he answered her question in a husky voice. "Yes. Most definitely."

"Well that's a shame," she murmured, "as I prefer to be under someone else's power."

Deke drew in a shocked breath. *Surely she hadn't just said what he thought she'd said?*

He stared into her eyes as he tilted his head, trying to decipher her meaning. She boldly met his intent gaze, and then winked at him.

Dear God. Was she telling him . . . and if she were, how perfect would that be?

Her audacity amused him, and her coy smile as she looked up at him through her lashes sent heat through his body, making him hard and aroused on so many levels.

He stood abruptly and offered her his hand, "C'mon, it's time to get you poolside. And I for one, need to cool off."

She slipped her hand into his and he walked her to his car.

Chapter 92—Deke & Shaw
A Promise of More

Deke drove Shaw back to their hotel. Unbeknownst to her, he'd booked a room for himself using his iPhone while he sat between the food trucks waiting for them arrive from Tijuana.

Now, sitting in the seat beside her as he maneuvered through traffic, he looked over and asked, "So . . . have you done this before?"

"She looked over at him, her perfectly arched eyebrow raised in question, "Done what?"

"Flirted with a man, hinting at the promise of more?"

She faced front and sighed. "No. Not since the day I said I do."

"But some level of philandering, seducing, or dallying is implied here?" he asked. "Or am I reading this all wrong?"

She turned in her seat and faced him square on. He was driving so he only gave her a cursory glance, both brows raised in query before he turned back to observe traffic.

Before she said anything she'd regret, she clamped her lips together and turned back to face front as if pissed. As she stared out the front window she heard him chuckle.

"That's what I thought." He drew in a deep breath. "Don't be embarrassed. I suspect we're both on the same page. We're both at the age where it's normal for us to like sex. And we've each gone without for two years or more. It's natural that when we encounter an attractive member of the opposite sex, that it stirs something inside."

He looked at her and she turned to meet his stare. It was obvious that she didn't want this bluntly spelled out. But he did. There was too much at stake for him not to. After all, he had a law degree from Stanford.

"We can be adults about this. We can make a decision to

act on our urges, or ignore them." He snorted. "But I will have to admit that ignoring them at this point is going to be difficult. I find you extremely attractive and sexier than Shakira in her leopard's suit."

He looked over at her and quirked his lips. "You know, you look a lot like her, 'cept your hair's darker and you're a smidge taller. And you smell better."

"How do you know that?" Her whole face scrunched up with surprise.

"My good friend Kurt has a daughter with a scratch and sniff coloring book."

She laughed loud and long. It did his heart good. And affected another body part as well. One she'd been awakening with her smiles, her scent, and her sweet, sexy, trilling laugh since he'd met her. It was almost musical, and something in him responded to it every time he heard it.

"You didn't answer my question," he said.

"Which one was that?"

He faced her. "Is there a promise of more with us, do you think?"

She looked him straight in the eye while they waited at a stoplight. "There is no promise of anything."

Then she sent him a seductive wink. "But if it's okay with you, I'll keep my options open. Mostly because you look a little like a dark-haired version of Chris Hemsworth. *And*, I'm off-the-charts horny."

He threw his head back and laughed, a sound so full of merriment she had to join in. He reached over and took her hand in his and squeezed it. "It's nice to know you're keeping your options open, and that one of my fantasies involving you and that bullet might be a consideration in the future."

She turned her hand over and caressed his fingers with hers. "Thank you for taking such good care of me, Deke. You can't know how much I appreciate not being so alone in this mess that is my life now, if only for a day." She shot him a quick smile and waggled both brows, "I am so looking forward to spending time at that glitzy pool with Deke Hemsworth this afternoon."

"When we get there, I'll take care of the poolside pina coladas."

"Thank you."

"Anything to see you in a bathing suit, Shaw-kira."

They both laughed as he pulled into a space in the hotel's parking lot.

Chapter 93—Deke & Shaw
A Sinful Swim Suit

My God, this woman can rock a swimsuit, he thought as he watched her walk around the pool apron to where he'd already set up an area for them—two loungers with side tables, and an umbrella in a stand behind them ready to be unfurled when the late afternoon sun got to be too much.

He watched, forcing his jaw not to drop and his eyes not to bug out of their sockets as she showered off at the outside shower, turning to display first her splendid ass filling the skimpy scrap of material that was barely covering her sweet little cheeks. Then turning to let the stream of water run down her chest to the bandeau top that threatened to pop open from the swell of her breasts, filling the stretchy material to what he felt certain was its absolute limit.

When she walked around the pool to join him, he noticed several other men admiring the woman in the sexy two-piece, watching her breasts rebound with each step, despite the stretchy wide band wrapped around her holding them snug to her chest. They all watched as a gust of wind blew the pink ruffle sewn along the top edge, sending it fluttering like a banner, bringing everyone's attention to high, full mounds that jutted out and stood firm as if on a shelf.

Deke could not stop staring at the fuchsia and pink strip that encased what he was sure were firm to the touch globes with dark rosy nipples. As she drew closer, water droplets cascading around her navel traveled down to join the vee of material that barley covered her mons, drawing his attention to the tiny triangle of fabric that covered her sex.

It was a flesh colored piece of material that covered only the essentials and made one do a double take. From thirty-feet away, it appeared she was naked from the waist down—naked and shaven. His heart was beating like timpani drums. He went rock hard, tenting his own swimsuit instantly.

Her bikini was the sexiest swimsuit he had ever seen on a woman and he was momentarily gratified that it was a weekday afternoon so there were fewer men around to see her in it. But just as that thought crossed his mind, he watched as a group of men in business suits came out of the glass doors that lead down the steps and into the pool area. They all gaped as she walked the last ten feet to the little enclave he had set up. He could only imagine the view they were seeing as her body in that flesh-toned suit sashayed toward him. No doubt her perfect tight ass was doing the Left Right, Left Right, Ba Donk-A-Donk.

As she drew closer, he forced himself to look up, into her face. Her smile was full and sexy, the angle of her face tipped to the sun, her eyes glittering with unabashed delight. She knew damn well what she was doing to him. And she reveled in it. God this woman was the whole package—beautiful, smart, funny, and sexy as all get out. With her skin covered in droplets from the shower, her thick hair gathered in a knot of curls on top of her head, and her long legs in her heeled sandals looking smooth and shapely, she was every inch a goddess.

"You take my breath away," he said honestly, as he stood to welcome her.

She took him in, his muscular chest, the pecs covered in dark curls, his long athletic length, his trim board shorts with the large projection aiming at her . . . and her eyes went wide.

"You are doing quite the same to me," she half whispered, half croaked.

He smiled and took her hand to help her get seated. "Sorry. My body's a traitor in that department. I no longer bother trying to hide it. It is what it is. You are a very becoming woman. That suit . . . it almost seems as if there is no bottom to it."

She laughed. "It's the new rage to mis-match the top and bottom. I liked the top, it fit well, but I couldn't find a bottom in my size in this same style, only this color." She shrugged, "So, this is my suit this summer."

"Well, I'm sure you have left every man here wondering as his tongue dragged the ground."

She laughed. "You are so complimentary. I love that. You are good for me."

"I hope to be better, starting with a cool drink. What would you like?"

"That pina colada you promised?"

"Of course." He got the attention of the server at the bar and the man came over to get their drink order. He ordered a pina colada for each of them, and before the man stepped away, he handed him a hundred dollar bill and said, "Keep them coming."

"I am tempted to throw a towel over you," he growled as he reseated himself. "He couldn't keep his eyes off you."

"Oh no," she laughed. "It is way too hot for that." She reached down into the bag she had placed by her seat and pulled out a tube of sunscreen. Then she started spreading it over her legs.

He groaned. "You're killing me."

"I can't get burned. I can't even get tanned too much, so I'm glad we have an umbrella. It would not be good if I came home looking like I had a good time."

He frowned. His first thought was, why wouldn't Shaw's husband want his wife to have a good time? But then as he drank her in again, his eyes wandering over her gorgeous body, he knew. And he couldn't help commiserating with the man. *He* was jealous, and he wasn't her husband. He was only a friend at this point. A friend that might get lucky tonight.

For a few moments he allowed himself to be in her husband's place. How must he feel? He had to be insane with jealously. If the tables were turned, he sure would be. And for the first time he wondered how things were with them in bed. Was he able to satisfy her at all, or had he lost the ability to do that too?

He should feel badly, sitting next to the man's wife, as he watched her apply sunscreen and don a pair of ridiculously large sunglasses. But he didn't. He couldn't. He wanted her too much.

Chapter 94—Deke & Shaw
Back Story

Sitting on loungers, sipping drinks and watching the palm tree fronds rustle in the wind, he posed a question that had been bothering him since Shaw had explained her "drug" problem.

"So, you're a Utah resident, right?"

"Yeah. I've lived there about five years now."

"And as an educator, you're eligible for Utah's Public Employee Health Plan, right?"

"I am."

"So why haven't you opted for the Pharmacy Tourism Program, the Right to Shop Bill Representative Norm Thurston championed in 2018? You'd be able to get the drugs you need for mmm . . . Matt that way." He didn't want to say "your husband," as earlier today, he'd realized, that he didn't want her to have a husband. He didn't want her to be married to Matt, or for that matter, married period.

"The family plan health insurance has high deductibles. So Matt has always carried his own insurance. We were planning to add him to my plan when open enrollment came around this fall since he's no longer employed as a lineman and he's used up most of his union benefits. He has some life insurance and cancer coverage, but that's about it now. He wasn't very smart when it came to his job. He kept chasing the money. He moved from Texas to North Carolina where we met, then we moved to Utah for the job here. As a journeyman lineman who won a lot of competitions, he was in great demand. He was always getting better offers to go to other counties and I've had to fight him over his grass is greener syndrome for years because I wanted more stability. I wanted to have a few kids. But for this last move, I lost the battle because they also offered a signing bonus and he wanted to get a boat."

"So he's not eligible for the Tourism Program?"

"Well technically no, I could probably get the insulin through my part, but when the plan was first offered I checked it out and the only thing I thought would be different was that I would have had shorter lines to deal with as I'd have an actual appointment at the hospital in Mexico, and I'd be assured that the drugs were safer, and more regulated coming directly from the hospital.

"But the drugs I'd been getting for him come in a sealed box, the very same box I'd get at the hospital—the American version, made in China, with Spanish writing on the box. No one has been prosecuted for buying insulin the way I do and no one has reported any problems with the drugs. Besides, I like the way I do this. I get two days off every three months and I look forward to them. So much."

He was tempted to tell her that with a phone call he could have ten year's worth of insulin delivered right to her door in Utah. But then he'd never see her again now, would he?

"I will look forward to those days now, as well."

"This will not work Deke. You will tire of me soon enough. You are successful, highly intelligent, and wealthy. I'm none of those."

"You are beautiful and just as intelligent. What does it matter about money?"

"Trust me, Deke. It always matters. It matters a lot."

He had no answer to that, as he knew that it did. It truly did.

But as he studied her, her serene expression, her intelligent if cynical eyes, he knew that she was a force to be reckoned with. "Circumstances have changed your expectations. Look ahead and plan new ones for yourself."

"What? The best I can hope for is a grant to get my Masters. Then I'll have two more years of busting my ass, working by day and taking classes by night, and coming home to a drunk I don't recognize in my bed."

"Does he harm you?" his muscles tightened at the thought of her being harmed in any way.

She laughed out loud. "Harm me? He has nothing in him to harm me. No matter what he or I do, he cannot complete the act. Hell . . . he can't even get it started. The drugs make him unable to. And the copious amounts of alcohol doesn't help any."

"I'm sorry Shaw, so very sorry."

"Well . . . at least you know why I travel with a silver bullet on my two-day vacations."

"It shouldn't be that way," he said.

"Well, you should know, that no matter how much we wish it otherwise, life is simply what it is."

"How did you two meet?"

She drew in a deep breath and then let out a long sigh. She noted the waiter approaching with fresh drinks and she flashed him a huge smile. "Just in time, thank you," she said as she accepted the tall Solo cup with the umbrella speared pineapple and cherry floating on top.

The young man's eyes took in the scantily clad stunner who had just smiled so companionably at him and his appreciation was evident. Deke cleared his throat and sent him a meaningful scowl when he was handed his drink and sheepishly the man made his way back to the bar.

"We met when I was studying for my senior finals. The last tests before certification to teach. And since I had already accepted a teaching position, there was a lot of pressure to do well on it.

"My mom and dad were going out of town for a long weekend so I decided to study at their house. The apartment I shared with two roommates was always noisy. They liked their music and they liked it loud, and their phones were constantly ringing and dinging with incoming texts or emails. I knew I needed some peace and quiet in order to retain what I studied. So I packed a small bag and moved back to my old bedroom just as Mom and Dad were leaving.

"By Friday afternoon I felt pretty confident that I knew the material enough to pass with decent scores so I took a break and decided to work on my tan by their pool. It was a beautiful spring day and the sun was shining bright. The clear blue water of the pool beckoned and I answered the call. There was a tall fence around the pool, and since nobody was home I opted to start the summer with no tan lines.

"I was on one of the loungers and just dozing off when I heard a noise high up in a tree. I looked up to find a man hanging off the side of the tree at the corner of the yard. He was staring down at me, his eyes wide and his face sporting a huge grin. I was mortified. I grabbed my towel and ran inside the house.

"A few minutes later the doorbell rang. By then I had thrown on a t-shirt and some shorts so I answered it. It was *him*. He said he was sorry for staring, but that he just couldn't help it. He said, and I quote, 'I was thinking about all the things I'd do to you, if you were mine.' And I have to admit; I just kind of melted there in the foyer.

He was with the electric company and he had just fixed a wiring problem caused by the previous week's spring storm. Looking at him in his uniform with his tall rubber boots, his tool belt hanging off his hips and his muscles bulging from his rolled up shirt sleeves, I damned near swooned when he smiled and said, "Do you have dinner plans, bathing beauty?"

"And of course I didn't. He went home to shower and change and I did the same. He took me to what he said was his favorite restaurant. And I'm sure it must've been everyone else's, because when we got there, there was a huge line out the door. But he sidestepped everyone and we went in through a side door. We were greeted by the bartender who said, 'Yo, Matt. Your table's ready. Number 19.' Turns out, during his last two years in college Matt worked at that steakhouse. We had a real nice dinner and talked non-stop the whole time.

"When he took me home, I said I didn't feel right letting a

man I didn't know into my parent's house. He said he understood and said goodnight at the door. Then he kissed me until my knees buckled, set me inside and closed the door. Then yelled though it for me to lock it. Thirty minutes later I got a text that had a picture of his driver's license, his high school diploma, his undergrad degree, and six certifications by the electric company for classes completed, and his Holy Communion and Confirmation cards, with a note that said, "Now that you know me a little, and you have enough evidence on your phone to convict me, what would you say to me grilling some steaks on your dad's fancy grill tomorrow night?"

"Of course I said yes. I think I also told him I'd take two steaks out of the freezer. I might even have said I'd make potatoes au gratin and a salad."

Deke laughed, "Sounds like something you'd do."

"Well we had a great time on the patio. I even fixed margaritas, but he would only let me have one. He said he needed me sober and in no way desensitized for what he had in mind. In a rare moment of brutal honestly I may have told him that I had never reached orgasm with any man. He may have mentioned he was going to right that wrong."

Deke snorted, "I'm just guessing, but he was the one who brought the subject up, somewhere between grilling, eating, and maybe dancing on the patio? Or had he talked you into skinny dipping?"

"No skinny dipping. But we did slow dance to my dad's Johnny Mathis collection."

"Mmm. Of course."

"He had brought a bag in when he arrived, and I thought it was presumptuous that he had planned to stay the night, but he said it was his "jump" bag. His lineman tools. He said they went where he went in case he got called out. He said he didn't want to leave it in his car because it had a special phone in it. I didn't think much of it—until it accompanied us to the bedroom.

"We kissed like teenagers, making out and necking for

probably an hour or more, then he asked me if I trusted him. And I said yes.

"So he took off all my clothes, and using some ropes and carabineers he took from his bag he tied me to all four bed posts. I had wondered why he wanted to go to the guest room instead of to my room. Now I knew why. The guest room had a four-poster bed; mine had panels.

"He ravished me. Praised my body and planted kisses everywhere. He had me begging, I mean seriously begging. He could have done anything. At one point, he took out his cell phone and I said no. He couldn't take any pictures. He said, " I just want to take a picture of something to show you. Then I'll delete it right away. You have to see this.

"I think I said okay, I must've. He said he had never seen anything as beautiful as my swollen clit. He held his fingers on either side of it and snapped a picture and then showed it to me. I swear it was the size of a walnut, it was so engorged. I remember he smiled and laid the phone on the night table as he said, 'And now you're going to feel your first man-induced orgasm. I'm going to rock your world, baby.'

"And he did. Sometimes if I close my eyes and go there, I can still hear my scream. It echoed off the walls forever. I fell down a well and kept falling, over and over. I came and came and then he entered me and took me impossibly higher. He held himself back and when I came, he came too. It was amazing. Mind-blowing. He undid my restraints and I fell asleep in his arms.

"In the morning he woke me with soft dreamy lovemaking. He made a point of showing me the picture again and I watched him as he deleted it. I was falling hard. He was so honorable, and I had never had a man end lovemaking with so many kisses and soft caresses.

"Then my parents walked into the room, back from their trip a day early. Matt looked up at my father, after he had made sure I was covered up, and said, "Mr. Sheridan, allow me to introduce myself, I'm Matt Marin. I'm the man who's going to marry your daughter.

"And he did. We had four wonderful years before the accident. Most days I have a hard time reconciling the man I now live with to the man I married. And dear God, I miss the sex."

Deke said nothing; there wasn't much to say. She had painted an idyllic picture of romance. Four years of a love like that would be devastating to lose. He knew that. His marriage, though shorter, had been much the same. Interestingly enough, there had also been restraints and some photography involved with him and Stephanie.

There was silence for several minutes then she looked over at him. "How do you handle that part, the no sex part?"

He laughed. "I go to the gym, I work out. I run in the mornings. I work long hours. I try to ignore it. When I can't any longer, I use my fist in the shower."

He sighed deeply. "I probably shouldn't tell you this, but once I tried to . . .mmm, stimulate her. I thought if I could just get her to climax that I could wake her up, find something inside her to remember us." He groaned in frustration, and it was as desolate a sound as she'd ever heard.

"I'm guessing it didn't turn out well?"

"No. It was horrendous. She was unresponsive and— forgive me—dry. An orderly walked in on us just as I was realizing how futile an effort it was. I was on top of her, trying to force my way in."

"Oh no!"

"Oh no is right. The administrator informed me that this was not feudal England and that as my wife was not capable of giving her consent anymore, I was to abstain from anything sexual in the future or be denied access to her entirely. I was dutifully chastised, and have not so much as kissed anything other than her cheek since. It's as if she and I are both incarcerated . . . but on other sides of the fence.

"It was the single most humiliating moment of my life."

She snickered. "Mine was when I found out Matt hadn't deleted that picture after all. That he had texted it to himself. He shared it with all his lineman buddies at his bachelor's party."

"Oh Shaw, no!"

"Yes."

"What the hell possessed him to do that?"

"He says he was drunk. Says he was too damn proud of himself not to show off. He told me about it a year after the accident, when he got really angry at me when I couldn't give him a blow job. I had tried—for well over an hour. I just hadn't been able to get him hard. The medicines he was on prevented it. And the beer he drank morning, noon, and night, hadn't helped matters."

"A moment ago, he sounded so perfect."

She sighed. "Yeah. That's the part that's hard to reconcile. Where did the man I love go? I don't much like the one who's taken his place."

He reached over and took her hand in his. "We're a couple of sad sacks aren't we?"

"So tell me about Stephanie."

"You really want to continue this?"

"Might as well get it all out. We're purging."

"Stephanie was amazing. Kind, funny, sexy, very elegant, very classy. She was president of her sorority, so she had lots of friends. We had a huge wedding."

"Where did you go for your honeymoon?"

"Bermuda. Yours?"

"Aruba."

"Did you want children?"

"We did. In fact, she was going to go off birth control on my birthday. Her accident was on my birthday. She was on the way back from the bakery with my cake."

"No!" Shaw's hand clutched his while her other one went to her heart.

"Yes. I've had to live, knowing she all but died getting a cake for me. She was throwing me a surprise party that night.

"A few weeks after the accident I had to go see the wreck, get stuff from the glove box and trunk, and take the tags off before it was disposed of. I could still smell the cake, my favorite—Devil's Food with chocolate icing. Seeing all the dried blood, smelling the cake that was all over the back seat, I vomited on the ground beside her car. To this day, I can't stand the smell of chocolate cake. It flips my stomach instantly."

"Deke, I am so sorry. That is awful."

"We both have awful stories today, what's with that?"

She smiled over at him and reached out to grip his hand. "We're getting the bad stuff sorted out. Our back stories are such a big part of our lives that if we're going to move on and become good friends we have to be immersed in each others' history."

"Are we going to be good friends?" he asked.

Her eyes limpid in the sun, she looked directly at him, seeing down into his soul. "We are. We're going to be better than good friends. I think we're going to be lovers."

He stood then and took her hand to bring her up out of the lounger. "If that's the case, then let's immerse ourselves even more." He stooped and put his arms behind her knees and easily lifted her into the air. Then he walked her to the edge of the pool at the deep end and jumped in with her.

She sputtered coming up but then she laughed and he joined her. They spent an hour frolicking in the pool, him entwining his muscled hair-covered legs with her trim smooth-shaven ones, his arms held her to his chest and he felt the weight of her breasts caress his nipples. And then they kissed. His eyes met hers and the question she read in them was, are you ready for this? Her mischievous grin was the only answer he needed.

Hanging off the ladder in the deep end, his arm around her waist, securing her to him, he drew her chest to his, lowered his head, and took her mouth. His lips covered hers completely.

His tongue entered her mouth and tangled with her tongue. Tentatively at first, then with wholehearted abandon. Their tongues dueled, lips rubbing and molding, tongues thrusting and claiming, their breaths mingling, and laughter pealing when Deke, in an attempt to draw her closer, lost contact with the ladder and dunked them both.

When the sun started to sink over the roof of the hotel, bringing a cool stillness to the water, they decided to go inside. As they gathered their things, and Shaw picked up her book from a side table, Deke murmured, "You never got a chance to read your book while sitting at the pool."

"I read to escape. There was nothing I wanted to escape from today."

His blue grey eyes sparkled across the distance, drawing her dancing dark blue ones to meet his. The heat he could not hide from her shimmered between them. "Will you allow me to take you to dinner?"

She smiled. "Sure, but nothing fancy. I only have a pair of jeans and two t-shirts with me."

"We could remedy that . . ."

"You've already spent way too much on me."

"Okay. We'll go casual. Was lunch the Mexican fix you needed, or are you still in the mood for more?"

"Please sir, I want some more," she mimicked Oliver Twist.

He laughed and drew her under his arm. "Then more you shall have," he said, completing the dialogue for the scene.

They walked into the building with his arm draped over her shoulder. The moment the air conditioning met her wet, towel-draped body, she shivered. "Yikes, it's cold in here," she said as he ushered her into a waiting elevator.

"Get yourself a nice hot shower and I'll meet you in the lobby in an hour, okay?"

"Are you showering too?" she asked.

"Of course."

"Well, why waste water?"

His eyes went wide and he stared down into her face. After a few seconds of examining every minute feature, he asked in a husky voice, "Are you sure?"

"I am. This thing between us is unavoidable. Or don't you feel it?"

He snorted, "Oh, I feel it all right." And as the elevator climbed higher, he took her hand and placed it over his erection. "It's been present in one form or another since I picked up your little vibrator."

She laughed. "I thought I would die from embarrassment."

He laughed, then bent and kissed her on her neck, sending trills of pleasure to her core. His warm lips worked their way up her neck then along her jaw, finally reaching their destination and covering her smooth cool lips with his, causing her to shiver in an entirely different way. His tongue delved deep stroking alongside hers, and they were still kissing when the elevator doors opened with a soft ding. He ignored the open door as his hand cupped the side of her face and pulled her in closer, letting his tongue learn her depths and taste the sweetness of the rum lingering there. When the doors began to shut, he reached out and hit the button to open them again.

Taking her hand in his, he walked her out of the elevator and to her room. "Are you using birth control?" he asked softly.

She looked up into his face, stunned that she hadn't thought of that. "Actually, no. There's been no need, so I stopped."

"I have some condoms in my room." They were in front of her door now. "My room has a connecting door to yours. Open your side and I'll come through."

"Should I be offended by your confidence?"

He smiled. "No. You should be awed by it. It's the same confidence that's going to take you to heights you never knew existed."

"Oh, I like the sound of that."

"Then open your door to me . . ." he said as he leaned into her. His hand gripped her butt cheek and pulled her tight into his body. Then he shocked her by swatting her ass. Hard.

"Ohhhh . . ." she moaned. It was the moan every Dom lived for, and every sub, knowing this, knew just how to do it.

His eyes closed and his nostrils flared as he drew the sound of her moan in and let it reverberate through his head while his cock twitched.

"I thought so," he murmured. "Go get ready for me. Open the connecting door and be standing by the shower, waiting for me, naked."

She drew in a deep breath and was ready to protest, but held the words inside. She was often ashamed of the things Matt had introduced her to, making her needy by his dominant bent. But being submissive was now something she longed for. And this was what she wanted, wasn't it? What she spent her nights dreaming about.

She looked over at Deke, at his commanding physique, those I-know-you-better-than-you-know-yourself eyes, and his handsome face with those sensuous lips that she wanted to feel all over her body. She whispered, "Yes, Sir," and heard his indrawn hiss.

She put her key card in the slot and he pushed the door open. Then he pinched her ass and she nearly leapt into the room. He closed the door behind her, murmuring, "Two minutes, naked."

Chapter 95—Deke & Shaw
Ecstatic Relief

Deke stripped off his wet swimsuit and gave his fully erect penis two sharp, almost painful tugs. If he wasn't careful he was going to unman himself with this woman. What possessed him to tell her to get naked and wait for him? The stimulation of seeing that gorgeous woman totally naked for the first time was going to boil his blood and threaten to pump his semen out of his body like lava from a volcano. After spanking her and hearing her moan, all the ways he knew to slow things down were just going to drive him insane. What an ass he was.

Still, he'd promised her he'd take her to new heights. He had to deliver. He thought about jerking himself off to dull the edge, but he'd said two minutes so there wasn't enough time to do it and recover. He had to laugh at the thought of him leaning against the shower wall snoring while she was in the next room juggling multicolored bullet vibrators. No, better to be wound too tight, than to be unwound all the way.

He took a pair of faded jeans from his travel bag and pulled them on, deciding that going commando was called for in this situation. He tucked four condoms into his right front pocket. If they weren't enough he'd crawl back to his room for more.

He had to smile. Five times in one night was his personal limit. And that had been during his Stanford years while living the dorm life with his friends, and trying to survive one hellacious spring break. There had been so many horny girls at that last frat house party. He and his friends had done double duty trying to sample all of them. And he meant double duty—Chaz and Brent had double teamed two girls that night. Unfortunately, one of them had been Chaz's fiancé. And what she'd said she wanted after four Tequila Sunrises wasn't what she wanted to remember while becoming intimately familiar with the Toto logo on the toilet in the frat house bathroom the next morning.

Fun times, he said to himself with chagrin. He'd done the two-on-one thing a few times, but it had never really done it for him. Thinking of Shaw with another man, even one that was her husband made him see red. No, absolutely not. She was his. She didn't know it yet, but she belonged to him. He was damned sure Kurt was wondering what the hell was going on with him. He'd never seen him entertain a woman other than Stephanie. Certainly had never known him to arrange a hotel room for one.

He heard the lock on the connecting door disengage and it jolted him back to the present. He smiled. Then he frowned. He hadn't been with a woman in over two years. And he was married. Could he even do this? He ran a hand over his face. He did what he did during his Stanford days. He walked over to the mini-bar, took out a miniature bottle of Cutty's and drank it down in one swallow. Feeling the familiar burn kicked him into gear, high gear. The thought of Shaw's beautiful face did the rest.

In three strides he was at the connecting door. Finding the bedroom empty, he grinned. Good girl. She was waiting as she was told. Her obedience thrilled him to his core. He knew that when he stepped into the bathroom and saw her dutifully undressed and waiting patiently for him that he would be bowled over by not only her beauty, but by her submissive nature. He was pleased that his jeans were snug and that the tight zipper kept his desire from being too evident.

He walked into the en suite and around the corner and then he saw her. His breath escaped him as he took in her long auburn hair cascading over her shoulders and covering all but the dusky rose tips of full magnificent breasts. His eyes were drawn down to her trim waist, then to the thick thatch of dark curls covering her mons. It was trimmed to exaggerate the vee, as if pointing the way to paradise. It was all he could do not to drop to his knees and pay homage at her altar.

"Dear God, you are gorgeous."

She smiled, taking in his muscular chest with the light coating of dark hair fanning out over his broad pecs and then defining a where-the-beast-resides trail that disappeared into his jeans. The bulge there promised one hell of a show, but she knew it would be later, much later. From the look in his eyes, she could tell he had plans to savor her first. And she could not wait.

He spun an index finger in the air, "Turn around."

She did as she was told. Her fine ass was beautifully displayed, round and sporting just the slightest trace of his handprint from a few minutes ago. He walked over and caressed the mark with his palm then outlined it with his thumb. He splayed his hand over her right cheek, drew it back, and spanked it. Hard. She almost toppled forward, but he anticipated her losing her balance from the blow, and wrapped his arm around her waist. He grabbed her just as her feet left the floor. He steadied her by running a hand up to her left breast and cupping it. "Easy," he crooned, as if talking to a spooked horse, "just wanted a matching pair of my handprints on you."

"Mmm," she moaned, from both his words and his wandering hand as he kneaded her breast—cupping and squeezing and hefting the weight in his palm. She hissed as he pinched her nipple. When he began tugging on it, and twisting it, her knees buckled.

He caught her and turned her to face him. Then with long, sure fingers, he gripped both nipples and alternately pinched and tugged until they were hard nubs, swollen and darkened in color. She was gasping and he was lightheaded from the sounds she was making. And from the scent of her.

His nostrils flared from her arousal. He put his hand between her legs, slicked his middle finger along her wetness and thrust a finger deep inside. The moan she made caused his cock to engorge even more than it already had.

He leaned in to kiss her, running his tongue over her lips before breaching her mouth and letting her taste the scotch lingering on his tongue. It was a heady feeling when she sucked his tongue in for more. He ran his thumb over her clit, tapped it a few times with the edge of his thumb, and had to smile when she tried to ride his hand. He removed his finger from her body and his hand from her between her legs and she immediately protested, "Nooo."

"Yes," he whispered into her ear. "First we wash, then I acquaint my tongue with your body, then I fuck you until your eyes roll back in your head. But before all that I need you sideways and upside down on my lap."

"What?" she looked confused.

He reached into the shower and turned on the water.

"I'm going to spank you."

"W-why?"

He could see that it both frightened and intrigued her. "I didn't like the way you looked at my driver. I didn't like the way he looked at you. And I didn't like the way that cabana boy stared at your tits."

"It didn't mean anything."

"I know. I just didn't like it. You're mine. Now come over here and lie across my lap." He sat on the edge of the garden tub that was across the room from the walk-in shower and beckoned with his finger for her walk over to him.

She did. Slowly. Full of trepidation, but wondering if he held the key to the hidden pleasures she had long been seeking.

"Turn over on to my knees. I want your ass in the air, under my eyes so I can watch it bloom and go from white to red beneath my hand."

He took her hand and tugged her the last few inches, then helped her to lie face down across his jean-clad knees. Her hair fell to the floor as her head hung over the side. A rolled-up towel from the pile beside him was shoved under her mid-section. It raised her backside and allowed him access to her sex.

He placed one hand low on her back to steady her as he ran his other hand over her ass, admiring the smoothness of her skin, the tautness of her glute muscles, the flawless perfection of her creamy white skin.

"I'm going to spank your ass six times, three for each buttock. If it hurts too much, tell me to stop and I will. But if you ride it out, the sensations will be pleasurable because your blood will be rushing through you and your hormones will race to enhance the experience. I think you need this. I promise that the sensitivity of your skin tingling will heighten your pleasure.

"Try not to be too loud if you cry out. We don't want hotel security at the door. And remember, this is all about your pleasure. We're priming the pump. Getting your senses in sync to feel everything your body desires you to feel. Try to relax, don't tense up. Ready?"

He saw her head nod and he lifted his hand. And then he lowered it. Hard. Once on each cheek. She yelped.

He caressed the redness that appeared on her ass cheeks. "Two."

He raised his hand and swatted her again. A tad harder.

She opened her mouth to cry out but instead bit into the denim material of his jeans. She imbedded her teeth to hold back the yelp and he smiled at her impudence. "Three. Make sure you don't bite your lip."

He rubbed her backside again. Then lifted his hand and hit her bottom hard enough to displace her had his other hand not been there to hold her. She screamed out that time and ended with a vile curse. He chuckled. "Four."

He smoothed her skin again, and then reached down to cover her mouth with his hand. Then double-tapped her, once on each cheek, "Five and six," he counted. She bit into the pad of his thumb and he let her until after a few moments she slowly released it. "Son of a bitch that hurt!"

He chuckled as he rubbed his hand over her ass, then ran a finger along the crack down to her labial lips. He stroked her, feeling the moisture that had collected. "You're very, very wet. Are you sure you're not protesting too much? I think you liked that a lot more than you're letting on."

She whimpered. "You were right. I needed to feel the power and the heat of being spanked. I've been numb for so long. Now I feel alive."

He massaged her pink and warm skin, then led his fingers glide down to feel the wetness between her legs. "Oh, baby, you are drenched."

He entered two fingers and started soothing her. As he gave his hand free reign, he murmured, "So pretty." Where his fingers were massaging her, spreading and opening her for his gaze, she was slick and a pretty blushing pink. "Such a very good girl, and look how wet you are." She squirmed on his lap, trying to get more of the length of his fingers into her. But he just wanted to tease her rosy lips. The sounds of her moaning were causing his cock to throb.

The room was now filled with steam. He used his other hand to sooth her backside, feeling the heat of her warmed blood course through his hand. She groaned with pleasure as his hand circled over her ass, spreading her ass cheeks. The fingers of one hand continued to dip into her pussy, while one wet finger from the other hand grazed her crack. She moaned and wiggled. He circled her puckered opening and crooned to her, "You were so brave, so strong, and your ass, my God, it's the most cock stirring sight."

Her lifting to her toes to get more of his touch and her long, low keen threated to undo him. He lifted her to her feet, and then pulled her into his arms. He looked down into her tear stained cheeks. "I need to taste you, right now." He walked her over to the shower. "Reach in and turn it off."

She did as she was told and then he carried her into the bedroom and placed her on the bed. He could see that she was dazed by her experience but knew that she needed more, so much more. He gently lifted her by her ankles and drew her to the bottom of the bed. Her hair was fanned out on the duvet, her breasts high and heaving on her chest and her pussy glistening with moisture. "You are the most beautiful woman I have ever seen. And I am going to love giving you the tongue lashing you deserve right now."

He dropped to his knees and began kissing along the insides of her thighs before inching toward his target, her swollen lips and beckoning clit.

He lavished her pussy with long, sensual laps along her coated lips, trying to get her essence onto his tongue so he could taste her. His cock was engorged to the point of being painful, so he reached down and undid the zipper.

His tongue made quick jutting thrusts into her vagina and fast flicks around her clit, being careful not to touch it directly. Yet.

Lifting up off the bed with the duvet gripped in both hands at her sides, she tried to direct him there. Circling, and thrusting against his mouth, she cried out and begged him to give her the sublime pleasure her body was fighting for, that of his mouth on her clit. "Deke! Please, please, please . . . suck it."

He knew it had been so long since she'd had a man's lips on her here, and that she needed the release.

"Okay, sweetheart," he crooned. He lightly flicked his tongue and rimmed the quivering blooming bud, then caught it between his lips and gently sucked. Then sucked harder. And sent her off into another world. One that included galaxies exploding, stars bursting, and her body being turned inside out from an orgasm that careened her into a dark welcoming void.

As she came down, she registered him on the bed beside her, holding her to him and whispering soft, cajoling words. "Find your way back angel. That's right, come back to me, baby."

She smiled at him and his heart thudded in his chest.

"Hey pretty lady, welcome back."

"Wow. I think I found heaven."

"I wasn't sure you were coming back."

She reached up and stroked his cheek, "Thank you, Deke. I needed that. More than anything, I needed that. It's been so long."

They were lying side-by-side, enjoying the quiet and tangible feeling of something shifting in their world.

She sighed, "Friends can bring you food, take you out for drinks, pray for you, and encourage you when you're down. But they can't do that for you."

He took her hand in his and lifted it to his mouth and kissed it. "No one but me. Promise me, no one but me."

She turned to look him in the eyes, her own still glazed over from her escape to pleasure. "No one but you."

"Promise." It was a plea, one he was not ashamed to make. The overwhelming desire for this woman, not just to pleasure her, but to own her, was overtaking him.

"Do that again, and I promise I'll promise. I feel wonderful. Loose. As if freed from something holding me back."

He laughed and scooped her up into his arms in one easy, graceful movement. "I will do it again. But first we shower, then I fuck you, then after you promise to only be with me, I'll do anything you want."

"Then you'll feed me?"

He laughed again. "Yes, then I'll feed you."

He set her down by the shower, reached in and turned it on again and swatted her butt to force her inside.

"Yikes!" she yelled as the cold water hit her skin before warming up.

He laughed again. He couldn't remember laughing so much. Ever.

After washing her from her hair to her toes and lavishing her with kisses in between, he allowed her to do the same to him. Groans and moans bounced off the walls, their sounds of pleasure echoing back to them.

Deke turned off the water and filled his hands with the mass of her wet hair. "Your hair is so beautiful, so thick, so heavy. And so long you can wear it to cover yourself. With a deft hand he gathered it and wound it around his fist. He used the knot he had gathered at her nape to tilt her head back as he stared into her eyes. "I think I'm falling for you," he whispered as he released the hold he had on her hair and drew her head down so he could kiss her forehead, but not before he saw the shock registering in her eyes.

"No," she whispered and the harshness of her breath told him she might be willing to play, but that she wasn't expecting a relationship.

Unfortunately, he had already decided he would move mountains to own her.

"Why?" he whispered back.

"We're married."

He felt a flare of anger. "Our situations are unique. Neither of us has a true spouse."

"But we said true vows."

"So we can do this," he motioned with his hand to their wet, naked bodies, "but not if it means anything?"

"No, we can't do this." She breathed in deeply then sighed in defeat. There was a space of a few moments where neither spoke as they stared into each other's eyes. "But I'm going to anyway," she huffed out as if resigned to the illicit nature of their relationship. "There's no way I can stop now."

He nodded. He would take what he could get for now and argue with her later. His chin firmed with conviction. He'd get her to see things his way. He wasn't letting her go.

As if she read his mind, she whispered, her voice harsh from threatening tears. "It can't mean anything. He would kill me. Or you."

"Then we won't let him know."

He grabbed a bath sheet and wrapped it around her, then picked her up and carried her to the bed. He quickly dried her off, then stood with the towel and dried himself. He covered her body with his and began to taste every inch of her silky sweet skin, starting with her neck and working his way down.

When she had come twice more from his deft kisses, plunging fingers, and soft sucking lips, he straddled her chest and let his penis bounce off her lips. "Kiss the tip," he commanded as he opened a condom. Her eyes were closed, as she was still comatose with pleasure. He wasn't sure she'd heard him, and hissed when she did his bidding, and then groaned when she tried to suck the head into her mouth.

"Not yet. Maybe later. I really need to be inside you now."

He rolled the condom down, gripped his balls in hopes of sustaining his full-to-bursting erection, and eased himself down her body.

She was drenched from his saliva and the juices from her last orgasm and he slid easily to her opening. "Look at me," he said.

Her eyes gradually opened and met his. He watched her irises bloom as he entered her, heard her gasp as he thrust home. Then the frenzy began. He could not tell who was more possessed, him or her. But the rush to stroke, caress, and feel each other in their most intimate places was almost too much for his heart. The bed caved and rose and shook from his forceful thrusts.

Then her legs lifted and wrapped around his torso and he was lost. Connected in such an intimate way, feeling her vagina clasp him so tightly, he drove like a pile driver into her, rolling his hips to keep friction on her clit as he cautioned himself not to pummel her. But to give that blooming sensitive nub every sweet sensation it deserved.

Inserting his hand between their bodies, his thumb caressed her in tiny circles low on her mons. He felt her jerk, spasm in a most erratic way. It caused her to arch and press into him so intimately, so deeply that he felt giddy with the feeling as he felt her throb and come apart around his cock. He joined her on a journey to oblivion, pumping and pumping his semen into her until, sapped of all energy, he collapsed on top of her. He tented his elbows at her sides at the last second to keep from smothering her.

When he was able to roll over, he took her with him and she reclined on his chest. When her fingers began to toy with his nipple, he hissed and clasped his hand over hers. "Thank you. That was amazing. Like my vintage Harley, I feel as if I've been kick started back to life." He stroked her long hair, "Shaw, you make me feel like a man again."

She murmured something into his chest he couldn't decipher. "What was that?"

"More please sir?"

He chuckled. "First we shower, again. Then we dine on steak fajitas, then you get to pick one from Column A, and one from Column B. Then we sleep. Deal?"

She inched up onto his chest and leaned over to kiss him. "Deal, but I already know what I want. And sucking you off better be on the menu."

He moaned and reached down to lightly swat her backside. "Oh what a bad girl you are."

She winced, her bottom still slightly sore. "Ouch! No, I'm a good girl. And I'm going to show you just how good I can be."

"I think I've already had a taste of your badness. You were a naughty girl in that teeny tiny bathing suit, showing off your delectable charms to all those men, especially to that preppie bartender. He looked at you like he wanted to drink you in."

She sighed and flopped over onto her back, throwing one hand over her head and using the other to pull the sheet up to cover her. "I don't know why I need affirmation from men. But I do. I love when they ogle me. That double take they do before appreciation lights up their eyes makes me swoony."

"All women like to be admired. They do all manner of things to be noticed. We could cancel the national debt if women were willing to forego make up, hair and nail color, and all but practical clothing."

He leaned over her and pulled the sheet down, exposing

her breasts. "Do you actually want strange men looking at these gems, or do you just like teasing them?"

"Oh I don't think I could display myself, if that's what you're asking." She tried to tug the sheet back up to cover herself, but he wouldn't let her.

"You want to in your fantasies, but not in real life?" he asked with a curious tilt of his chin.

"I suppose. It might be because I feel as if my body is being wasted right now. You're only young once, you know."

"Ah," he said as he ran a finger down between her breasts. "Like owning the Mona Lisa but keeping it hidden in your closet."

"Exactly!"

He bent and took a nipple into his mouth and sucked. "Your body will not be wasted any longer. I will see to it."

His splayed hand ran down her belly, and then cupped her sex. "I promise not to waste a single bit of this luscious body. And on occasion, I promise you will catch me leering."

He got out of the bed, rounded to her side and easily picked her up. "I'm going to touch each inch, lick each dimple, suck on every one of your fingers and toes, devour your tits, eat your pussy, fuck your vagina, and maybe even your ass. Trust me, I'm not going to waste a single part of this body."

He carried her into the bathroom, stood her by the shower and turned it on. When he was satisfied with the temperature, he got in and pulled her after him. "But first, I'm going to wash you again. Then dry you. Then dress you. And after feeding you, I'm going to start all over again. By the time you get on that plane tomorrow, there won't be any part of your body I won't have owned. You are mine. And every ninety days, I will prove it. Over and over again."

Chapter 96—Deke & Shaw
Fajitas for Two

He drove the Jaguar to a restaurant where the Maître d' knew his name, and seated them in a cozy window nook that looked out at the hills surrounding the city. She stared at the blinking lights, miles away, while chowing down on fresh tortilla chips and the best pico de gallo she'd ever tasted, while he ordered wine and entrees for them.

"Hungry?" he asked as the server left to fill their order. His smile wide over her eager and avid interest in the food and the view of the hills beyond the city surprised him. How long had it been since he'd been this happy? So attracted and drawn to a woman like this?

His answer, if he were honest, was never. There'd been plenty of women in his life and many had been gorgeous and exciting, especially his wife, but none had been this fascinating, this genuine, this taken with his world in the way of an ingénue.

The women he'd known had been used to this and more. A dinner in a restaurant of this caliber would have been another night in the life of an entitled highbrow elitist. With Shaw, it was like watching the world open up and perform just for her. She loved every single thing in it. Even the corn chips had her entranced. She not only examined each one and then carefully scooped up the tomato, onion, and cilantro mixture, she savored each bite. Closing her eyes, breathing in the spicy scent, she thoughtfully chewed, and then licking the salt off her lips and fingers, she dove into the basket for another.

He sat there thinking that he could watch her eat for hours. But then thoughts of what that tongue circling her lips could do to his cock pulled him in another direction. Thankfully, their dinner arrived. When he saw her eyes flare at the massive pile of sautéed peppers and onions and strips of grilled steak, he had to laugh out loud.

"You look like a kid at Christmas."

"This is unbelievable." She leaned in and sniffed. "Oohh, it smells so delicious." She looked up at the server. "Thank you, thank you so much for bringing this. It looks scrumptious!"

The server's eyebrows rose at the sincere, unaffected praise. Then he smiled, bowed to her and said, "You are most welcome. Enjoy!"

Deke frowned. Then smiled. She had captured another man's heart. And doubled the young man's tip in the process.

He watched her dig in, her enthusiasm for the humble meal making him introspective, as he silently contemplated this amazing woman. He couldn't believe that he'd met her on a plane. On a random flight that he'd taken for years.

He had almost cancelled the trip when his C.F.O. had come down with the flu. Now, he praised the heavens that he had decided to go to the meeting without him. He looked over to the woman filling a fajita with meticulous care.

He needed this woman in his life. And she needed him— to make her life a little easier, if for nothing else.

"Hey, what are you waiting for?" she asked around a bite of a perfectly rolled tortilla. "These are the bomb! Better hurry before I eat them all."

He laughed. "You couldn't eat them all . . ."

"Try me." But then she frowned. "That would kill the rest of our plans for the evening though. I fear I would need a major siesta, and that would take up all our time together."

"Well, in the interest of my libido, I'd better help you with that, then."

He reached for the serving spoon. She swatted his hand away.

"No, no, no. I have mastered the exact proportions for the perfect fajita. Let me make you one." And then without waiting for his answer, she moved her plate aside, reached over and grabbed his plate and proceeded to fix his meal for him. No one had ever done that for him before. He stared, fascinated as she layered each morsel, added a precise amount of onion, peppers, then rice, a smattering of beans, and then applied toppings before folding a perfectly stuffed packet. "The secret is not to over or under do it," she said as she handed the plate back to him. "It has to be just right . . . and as the man said, 'Enjoy!'"

Her smile was infectious. He smiled back and thanked her. Then neither spoke until the serving plate was empty. It was the best meal he'd ever eaten. And he was sure, that even though the food was delicious, she was the reason.

On the way back to the hotel, she asked him to tell her about the area he had grown up in. Then listened as if captivated by his stories. She was a very good listener, he thought, as he pulled into a parking space in the hotel's garage. Most people would not have been interested in his high school years when wrestling was his life. She made the drive back to the hotel pleasant, and way shorter than it should have been.

They held hands in the elevator and she looked up at him and asked, "So . . . Column A and Column B? What are my choices? And there better be some oral in there or I'm going to call the sex police."

"Sex police?"

"Yeah, those people who arrest you if you don't do it right, or live up to your potential."

He laughed and kissed her fingers. Then lowered his voice and murmured. "Well since I've never been arrested, it's safe to assume, I've been doing it right?"

"So far. But we have to check out the part about your full potential. Are you able to kneel at the foot of the bed for half an hour or more?"

"Probably." He drew out the word. "But somehow, with you, I don't think that will be necessary."

"Are you able to hold a wet slippery body against a shower wall for as long as it takes to get the deed done?"

He stepped back and eyed her. "You weigh what? 120?"

"122, before fajitas and chips."

"I believe I can heft close to 200 pounds, if you do as you're supposed to and wrap your arms around my shoulders and ride my cock while I'm pummeling you, I believe I can hold you for at least an hour, maybe longer . . . or until you come, whichever is first."

"Hmm, all very acceptable answers. Buuttt, are you capable of reclining back, and taking a tongue lashing without trying to take over the action?"

"Do I get to watch?"

"Yes."

"Then I believe I can do that."

"Good. Then we have an agenda?"

"An agenda?"

"Aw come on, you're a big to-do business man, surely you know what an agenda is."

"A work plan?"

"We'll call it a play plan. Up against the door as soon as we get in the room. I come, you don't. Over to the leather sofa, where you recline and I do tongue and lip magic, and you get to come. A breather in the shower where all we do is wash each other. Some snuggle time on the sofa watching late night TV, then it's Businessman's Choice in bed before I fall asleep. My flight is at 8:45, so unless you wake with a woody at 5, we'll have to table any further items on the agenda until our meeting in October."

"Whew, it's a good thing I was taking notes," he said as the elevator door opened and they stepped into the carpeted hall. At her door, he took her room key from her and used it to open her door. As soon as the door closed behind them, he had her up against it, his lips on hers, his hips grinding into hers.

His lips went to her neck and he placed tiny kisses along her jaw as he unbuttoned and unzipped her jeans. "Next time you plan an up against the door, a skirt would be better."

He stripped her jeans down her legs and removed her

heeled sandals. He lifted each foot, held it in his hand and kissed each toe before placing it back on the carpet. Then he looked up, smiled at her sensible white microfiber panties and stripped them off. He had no doubt that they were the only pair she'd brought and that she just kept hand washing them and putting them back on.

He placed one quick kiss between her legs at the end of the very tiny triangle of curls she had allowed to remain there. He loved a well shaven pussy, as he didn't want to miss any of the slippery parts.

He stood, and while he looked into her beautiful expectant face, and admired the dark depths of her glossy, sapphire colored eyes, he undid his pants with his left hand. He began to finger her moist slit with his right. She had flooded his fingers before he managed to drop his pants.

He groaned and closed his eyes to absorb the sensation of shoving two long fingers inside her and finding her already this wet and ready.

The condom he'd fished from his wallet before dropping his pants to the floor was snatched from his fingers and he watched as she opened the packet with her teeth. Their eyes intensely focused on each other, she took the condom from the foil, stretched the elastic of his boxers out and down over his erection and rolled it on.

He hissed at her tentative touch. He had the feeling she wasn't a pro at this, so murmured to her to make sure she left some room at the tip.

"Oh yeah, right," she whispered back. And just the knowledge that she wasn't all that worldly, that she had chosen him from all the men she ran into on a daily basis to experience this with, sent precum coating the tip and more blood rushing to his penis, making it incredibly hard and rigid as she rolled the condom down to the root.

"My goodness, this almost seems too big."

"Words every man loves to hear. But it fit just fine earlier."

"Well don't keep me waiting."

He laughed and lifted her leg over his hip and then raised her into his arms. His penis easily found the opening it was seeking and he speared her with it. Both of them gasped, her at the total breach of his body claiming hers, and him at the sensation of having her slick velvet channel envelop him so completely.

His forehead to hers, they stilled to experience their bodies settling into the intimate embrace. And then he began to move. And didn't stop until she gripped his shoulders, cried out his name and shattered.

It was everything he could do not to come with her, but he had been given an agenda. And he would do everything he could to adhere to it. Even though every cell in his body protested.

Chapter 97—Deke & Shaw
Oblivion and Back

"You didn't come," she whimpered as he slowly lowered her legs to the floor.

"Not on the agenda, remember?"

"Oh yeah. Sorry. So, was I heavy?"

"Not that I noticed. My muscles are just strained from holding back the tsunami orgasm that's developing."

"Well, let's see if we can bring that bad boy to shore, shall we?"

She took his hand in hers and he stepped out of his pants and boxers. Then he stripped her shirt off while she unbuttoned his and let it fall to the floor. He ran his hand inside her bra and cupped her breast. They both groaned in the same second. Then she removed his hand and swatted. "Don't distract me."

She bent from the waist and took a hair tie from the purse that had dropped to the floor the moment the door had closed behind them. She expertly wound her hair into a ropy bun and then used the tie to secure it. Then she retook his hand and walked him over to the sofa. Before she knew what he was up to, he'd used his other hand to reach over to the center of her back and expertly pop the catch on her bra. She was all but naked when the straps fell off her shoulders.

She turned to look up at him and found his gaze on her ass. The self-satisfied grin he had on his face made her smile, until he used his open palm to swat her butt, hard enough the make her misstep.

She dragged him the last few feet to the middle of the sofa, then turned him to face her, and none-too-gently pushed against his broad chest so that he fell with a plop to the sofa, legs sprawled open in blatant invitation.

"Well we won't need this," she said as she knelt and

stripped off the condom, placing it gingerly on a coaster on the coffee table behind her. Then she turned back, leaned in, and without so much as a by your leave, covered the head of his penis with her mouth. Her tongue immediately began circling the tip. Her cheeks drew in and she sucked.

The groan that escaped his lips was all the reward she needed. She went to work applying skills Matt had insisted she master. Only this time, her efforts produced results. Deke's penis, already long and thick, pulsed with need as Shaw licked and sucked and took him to the back of her throat.

Deke hadn't had a woman's mouth on him for two years. And he doubted he'd ever had a more skilled woman kneeling between his legs.

He had forgotten how incredible it felt to have a blowjob. How thrilling it was to watch as Shaw used her mouth on him. The pleasure was immense, more than his brain or body could process. Despite wanting to hold off as long as possible to savor the marvelous sensations, he was quickly overwhelmed by it all, and he began to come. He tried to pull her off but she would have none of it. He felt her breathe deep and clear her throat to accept the surge that was coming. He didn't disappoint her. He flooded her tongue as his body spasmed and he was sent reeling into a glorious oblivion.

She continued to gently suck and clean him with her tongue long after he had returned to terra firma. Then she stood, smiled, and said, "I'll see you in the bedroom whenever you can make it there." And with that she sauntered, totally naked, into the adjoining room.

It took him a few minutes to recover and to take in the feeling of bliss that had overcome him. He was happy. Deliriously happy. He took the time to thoroughly relish the sensation of being wondrously content. He knew this was a moment that very few people ever truly had.

He asked forgiveness from his wife, who was in the deepest sleep imaginable in her private room at the nursing home. Then thanked his partner for having the flu, and the pilot who managed the turbulence on their flight with just the right amount of skill to cause both terror in the woman beside him, and uncommon compassion in him.

Then he got to his feet and went to join Shaw in the bedroom.

Chapter 98—Deke & Shaw
To Sleep, Perchance to Dream

From the doorway he saw her tucked into the king-sized bed, duvet under her chin, eyes closed as if already asleep.

He went to the bathroom, did the necessary ablutions, brushed his teeth with her toothbrush and stared at himself in the mirror. Was that a smile he saw on his face? Damn straight. He was a man who had just achieved the best orgasm of his life. And he was about to get into bed with the woman who had made it happen.

He went into the bedroom, stood for a moment to take in the beauty of the woman in the bed in front of him. Then he went and collected their clothing and shoes, her purse, and his wallet—with one condom left in it—which he planned on using in the morning before he drove her to the airport. He piled everything on a chair and walked around to the unoccupied side of the bed, placed the condom packet on the night table, and slid under the covers.

His hairy legs met her smooth ones and just the interaction of his thighs pressed against hers threatened to make him moan out loud. He bit his lip to stifle it, kissed the back of her neck and ran his nose over her sloppy bun. Then he closed his eyes and fell asleep.

Chapter 99—Deke & Shaw
Angel in the Morning

Shaw woke as the sun filtered into the room. Out of habit, she looked over at her alarm clock to check the time. There was no clock on the night table. And the night table wasn't rustic pine; it was some sleek contemporary cabinet, no doubt some exotic wood from a rainforest. It all came back to her. Last night, Column A, Column B, and a fierce orgasm that, along with her full day, had totally wiped her out. Her left hand under the pillow, her face turned to the right, covers to her chin, was her starting sleep position. She obviously hadn't moved all night. She stretched out her legs and felt someone else's rub alongside hers. Very muscular, very long, very hairy—very male.

"Good morning, Angel," a husky voice murmured. Deke. She couldn't help but smile. He sounded a bit like John Forsythe.

"Which angel am I? Natalie, Dylan, or Alex?"

"I'm partial to the original cast, so that would be Jaclyn Smith as Kelly."

"Ah, you like them smart and beautiful."

"I do," he whispered against her neck as he pulled her close and rubbed his erection between her ass cheeks.

She reached behind her and gripped his long hard length.

"Are you sorry you have to get up so early?"

"Yes, but I'll survive. I'd have chartered a plane for you rather than miss this." One hand was around her waist pulling her tight to his chest, the other moved up to caress her right breast and tug on the nipple.

She moaned as the tip of his tongue circled her ear, then his teeth nipped the lobe.

He released her and straddled the backs of her thighs, kneeling on the bed to put on the condom, and then he lifted her hips so she was on her knees with her elbows supporting her on her pillow.

His fingers slid between her legs and he smiled with what he found there. "You're drenched."

"Can't help it. You do things to me."

"Oh, I'm definitely going to do things to you. Get comfortable. This is going to take more time than it did last night. And, as it has to last a long time, I'm not going to be in any hurry."

He knelt behind her and placed the tip of his penis at her opening. He slid it up and down and around her opening until her reciprocal actions of leaning into him and trying to maneuver him to stroke the top of her slit, drew him inside her slick channel, as if their male and female parts were magnetic.

He held her hips in his hands and watched where they were connected until he was fully seated inside her. He stroked slowly at first, coming almost all the way out and then easing back in until her moans and backward ass heightened every sensation and drew him close to the edge. He tried to slow them down, but she would have no part of it. She reached behind her to caress his balls, and then circled his length with her fingers where they were joined to stroke his pummeling length. The intense friction threatened to unman him, so he pried her fingers away and forced them to her clit where he directed her to touch herself, while he drove into her again and again, the root of his penis disappearing into her with each penetration.

His left hand gripped her swaying breast as his thumb stroked the peak. Then with thumb and forefinger, he pinched and pulled on her nipple. She cried out and he quickly dropped his hand to her clit in time to feel the swollen nub throb and ripen between both their fingers. Her vagina started to quiver and began gripping him, milking him with her contractions and sending him into delirious insensibility as he joined her fall into a cosmic abyss. Vaguely, he heard himself shout out her name in long, protracted syllables, the sound absorbed into the vaulted ceiling.

After he had emptied himself into her, he fell to his side taking her with him. It was many minutes before either of them moved or said anything. Then he ran his fingers over her back and kissed her shoulders. "Stay the day. I'll schedule a flight for you."

"If I didn't have to be back this afternoon, I might take you up on it. But I have to get back. We have dinner at my in-laws. And anything deviating from my original itinerary would not be taken well. Matt is insanely jealous as it is."

"As well he should be, you are a fascinating and extremely beautiful woman. And to my chagrin, I find I am jealous of him."

"You should not be jealous of him, he has a miserable life, and I am hardly in it anymore. I am glad you think I am a beautiful woman, but now I am a woman whose time to play is over."

He turned her to face him and shifted his body so he could look down into her eyes. "You will come back, right?"

She smiled. "I have to come back."

"And if you didn't, would you still?"

"If I could and you wanted me to."

"Oh, I definitely want you to. I will be counting the days. Is there any way we can make them less than ninety?"

"I'm afraid not. The prescription is for three months. I've worked myself into a pattern with these trips. If I were to depart from the norm, he'd pick up on it."

"Well, then it's best to leave things as they are for now. And I will just have to be satisfied with your quarterly visits."

She stroked the stubble on his chin. "I promise you, on our quarterly visits, you will be *extremely* satisfied."

He grinned back at her. "Ditto."

"I need to start getting ready now," she scrunched up her face and flashed him a pouty look.

He mirrored the expression. "I know. You hop in the shower and I'll have some breakfast sent up."

She shoved the covers aside and moved to sit on the edge

of the bed. "Just oatmeal and toast for me. As you know, I don't do so well on these flights."

He took her hand in his. And his look of vexation was priceless. "I do know. If it weren't for your absolute terror, we may never have spoken, never touched, never connected. I wish I could be there for you, whenever you're frightened." The sincerity in his eyes touched her.

She didn't want this separation to end on a sad note, so she waved her hand as if encompassing the world. "Well, there's bound to be another lonely, desolate man on board I can grip with terror."

He gave her a stern look. "Your flight has already been upgraded. I will call to get you seated next to a woman with a toddler."

She turned and made an X with her forefingers. "No, no, don't do that, I'll be good. I swear."

He laughed then lowered his eyes to her breasts. Heavy and flushed from their lovemaking, they were captivating. He hadn't even begun to pay them the attention they deserved. His eyes dropped to her sparsely covered mons and to the tops of her thighs framing the dark vee.

"You are gorgeous. I am going to have a hard time getting any work done remembering you like this." His knuckles brushed the side of a firm breast.

She turned away from him and stood with her hand on one hip, the other holding her tousled hair up high, "If you order me a mimosa, I'll let you spank a cheek."

"Done."

She walked backward to his side of the bed where he was now sitting on the edge. "Hmmm, now which one?" He played Eeany Meany Miney Mo, passing his hand over each cheek before drawing back and swatting her on her right cheek hard enough to unbalance her. He caught her by the arm and drew her back onto his lap. Then flipped her over to admire his handiwork. He ran his hand over her backside watching as her right cheek bloomed and a semblance of his handprint appeared. "Charming," he said in a husky, appreciative undertone. "Utterly charming."

Then he caressed and slapped the other one, causing her to cry out and jump off his lap. He laughed. "Don't worry, I'll order two mimosas."

She gave him a cheeky smile, looked toward the clock, and ran for the bathroom. "I need to hurry!"

"Don't worry, I won't let you miss your flight. Much as I'd like to."

He got up to order room service and to pull on pants.

He had removed the condom and tied it off, leaving it on the bed. Now, on his way to the connecting door that led back to his suite he picked it up. Upon entering the ensuite, he flushed the condom, grabbed a towel from the rack and debated joining her in her shower. Knowing they didn't have time and remembering that he had no more condoms, he called room service, and then stepped into his own shower.

Chapter 100–Deke & Shaw
Saying Good-bye

They rode in silence, Deke preoccupied with the early morning traffic and the thought of losing this amazing woman. This woman he had fallen so hard for. And Shaw, wondering what to say. Was this a one-off thing? It didn't feel that way but still . . . . Since coupling this morning, no one had mentioned the future. And she knew from her college days, that once the sex was over, things changed. Most guys wanted to move on to the next challenge. She knew Deke's history; the tragic story of his wife was hard to get out of her mind sometimes. Maybe she had been the bridge he needed to move on, to start dating and begin a relationship he could sustain until his circumstances changed and he could remarry and start a family.

She looked over at him and if she had to define in one word the look on his face, it was determination. Was he determined to get around that snazzy yellow Beamer that was blocking him in his lane? Was he determined to get to work on time despite her causing this delay? Was he determined to get her to the airport and be rid of her? Was he determined to get back to his normal life of work and visitations to a wife who would never leave her bed?

"Are you okay?" she asked, dismayed that her voice sounded timid. She sounded scared and she hated that. She was not afraid that this man who had come to mean so much to her in such a short amount of time, was minutes from dropping her off at the curb and saying goodbye to her forever. Okay, maybe she was.

He glanced over at her. "I'm fine. My mind is just racing. It sometimes does that in the morning. I'm pretty much always terrified I'm going to drop the ball on something important. Sometimes it's hard being the man in charge of a big company."

Deep in the recesses of his mind, he thought, *I'm afraid I'm going to drop the ball on you and lose the thing that matters most now.*

"You never really told me what you do exactly. You said something about a family business and some meetings involving refurbishing a plant."

He sighed. "I didn't really want you to know about my business life. Not that it's so spectacular, mind you. It's just . . . kind of . . . related to . . . production." He sighed again. "Of drugs."

She gasped and her hand flew to her throat.

"Not those types of drugs. Pharmaceutical drugs." He drew in a deep breath. "My family's company makes many kinds of drugs. And one of them happens to be the generic of the exact same drug you bought yesterday to take back to your husband."

Her eyes went wide and stayed that way as she tried to process what he'd just told her.

In the quiet lull, the sound of tires on pavement and someone honking eight lanes over were the only background, until his deep sigh dominated.

"I wanted to tell you from the start. But then I didn't want our relationship to be defined by what I could do for you."

"Ooohhh, I see. You thought I'd use you for the purpose of getting drugs for my husband. That I'd be willing to trade favors for favors," she spat out.

He reached over and brought her hand down from where it gripped the material at her neck to the padded leather console between them. He firmly covered it with his. Gripping it tight as he momentarily closed his eyes.

"No. I didn't tell you because I knew if I offered to help, that I'd probably never see you again. The drugs were the only reason you had to keep returning here. I couldn't chance taking that away."

She saw the sincerity in his face and so she relaxed and let her head fall back against the headrest. Her throat hurt from holding back tears that threatened to run down her face. "Oh what a pair we are."

He gripped her hand even tighter. "I could make things easier for you," he whispered and his voice was harsh as if his own throat was compromised. "I could even arrange to have the drugs you need shipped to you. But then I would be out of the picture with regard to you. And I need you, Shaw. I haven't needed anyone in a long time. But then there you were, a damsel in distress, needing me. And I fell into your trap. Now I need you more than I need to breathe, eat, or work, which is pretty much all I've done since the accident."

She returned his grip on her fingers then removed her hand from his to lovingly stroke alongside each finger. "Nothing will change because of this. I will come back. And I will get the drugs the same way I always have."

"Will you?" he looked over at her and she could see how broken he had been with the fear that her answer would be different.

"Yes. The drugs are important. Matt must have them. But I am important too. I need the break this trip gives me. I will do everything the same on each trip, just as I have done so many times before. I will go to Tijuana to the same Pharmacia and get Matt's insulin, and then I will come back to a motel near the airport and sit by a pool. The following day I will return home. To do anything differently would be to cause suspicion at home and I do not want that.

"But now I have something I can hold in my heart when I am flying back home. When I am flying away from you I will have the promise that you will be here when I return, and as happy to see me as I will be to see you."

She looked over at him and smiled broadly, her smooth full lips showcasing perfect white teeth. Until she purposefully touched the tip of her tongue to the bow of her top lip and drew it slowly down to the center of her bottom lip.

He groaned as he took the final turn into the airport, then

lifted her hand to his lips and kissed the back of it. "No, I will be happier by far. You are the light in my life that was once extinguished—the light that makes me see in color again. Only this time that light is so bright and filled with so many beautiful colors that I can't stand the thought of going back and living in the darkness again. I need you, Shaw. I need you to give me something to live for again. Promise you won't forget me."

"How could I forget a man such as you? Do you not know how rare you are in a world of men interested in only one thing?"

He smiled, "Well I am very interested in that one thing . . ."

She laughed and the musical sound of her sheer delight as well as her gorgeous face lifted to carry her laughter out through the sunroof made his insides vibrate with a new vitality. With a jolt he realized that he wasn't falling for this woman. Falling in such a way that he doubted he could grab a handhold and stop the headlong tumble even if he wanted to. He had already fallen. He was past the point of no return and there were no handholds. In a little over thirty hours, he had met, wined, dined, bedded, and fallen in love with this woman.

He prayed he wasn't taking a solitary nosedive, that he wasn't the only one plummeting and spinning out of control in such a terrifying yet intensely delightful way.

"You can just drop me off at Departures."

"Not a chance," he said as he made the turn into short-term parking. "I'll see you to TSA."

"You don't have to do that."

"I know, but I want to."

"You'll be late for work."

"I am the boss so I can do as I please." He pulled the Jag into a parking space in the huge garage and put it in park. All around them were the mechanical sounds of cars starting and stopping, braking and screeching on the turns and horns insistently honking as early morning passengers lost their patience. All of this echoed throughout the walls of concrete canyons. The din filled the car until Deke closed the sunroof and turned off the engine.

He turned to her and wrapped his hand around the side of her face. He drew her to him and kissed her thoroughly, his tongue taking charge and capturing hers, a reminder of the ways he had possessed her in bed.

He lingered as long as he dared, knowing she had a flight to catch, and that this airport wasn't the most hospitable when it came to getting through security. He released her lips and leaned his forehead on hers, his eyes closed, savoring the moment.

Then he reached behind her seat and drew out a package that he placed in her lap. "I got you this."

She looked down at the box in her lap. A picture of the latest iPhone was on top. "I can't accept this, Deke. I can't afford a cell phone bill."

"It's paid up for two years. "

'No," she shook her head, pushing it toward her knees, balking at even the idea of it. "I can't have a phone. If he ever saw it or heard it, he'd know something was up. There is no way I could hide this from him. And you know as well as I do, that every affair gets found out because of cell phones."

"I thought of that. And I came up with a solution. Keep it at school, with the sound and vibration turned off. I know we won't be able to talk to each other, but at least we can leave each other texts and voicemails. Surely, you have a desk drawer or a locker you can keep it in?"

She thought for a moment. "That might work. I can leave it in my car in my emergency travel kit until I get to school tomorrow, then I can keep it in the locker where I keep my purse and coat."

"That would be perfect. You can check it going and coming and that way we can at least stay in touch, be involved in each other's lives. I want to know how you're doing. I want to be there for you if you have a problem.

"You spoil me."

"If I could, I would spoil you rotten," he whispered as he bent to kiss her lightly on her lips.

"It's already set up. I had Kurt put my contact information in as well as his. Your passcode is 1-0-1-9-1-8, the day we met. And it's already set to airplane mode for your flight. You can use the time on the plane to get familiar with all the features. I asked him to download a few apps I thought you'd like, some games and some music. There are wireless ear buds in a case in the box as well. All you need to learn before you land is how to send me a text to let me know you arrived alright, okay?"

He seemed so eager for her to like this gift. But she couldn't help her chagrin. "I haven't had a cell phone in years, we just used to use the one Matt's company gave him so he could be on call for them."

"It's not that hard. There are several informational videos you can watch once you sign in. And if by any chance you get seated next to a teenager, you can get some free expert advice."

She smiled and opened the box. "How did you even get this? I've been with you since yesterday afternoon."

"Kurt got it for me and put it in the car sometime during the night."

"He's handy to have around."

"Yes he is. He not only works for me, but he's also become a good friend."

She took the phone out of the box and turned it over in her hand. "It's beautiful," she breathed.

"No, you are beautiful. The phone is merely attractive," he said with a huge smile. He was glad that she was pleased with his gift.

He showed her how to turn it on and put in her password, and then explained all the app icons. He showed her how to place a call to him and how to text him.

A military jet took off overhead and the sound of its

high-pitched engines screaming brought them back to reality. She had to go.

"I'll just take the phone and leave the box with you. My bag is full with the medicine now so I'll just keep it in my pocket until I get to my car. Thank you. This is a thoughtful gift."

He waved his hand, "It's a gift for me more than for you. I need to hear from you occasionally. I need to know how things are going for you. I need to know you're all right." He kissed her again. "I need to know you aren't forgetting me."

She smiled up at him. "Not a chance."

"Well I'd better get you inside. You only have an hour and forty minutes to get to the gate."

"That should be plenty. At least this time I don't have to fly standby. I already have a reserved seat thanks to you!"

"Let me know the flight you want to take to come back to me, and I will arrange for your ticket."

"No, I can't do that. You have already spent too much on me."

"You will make it harder on me if I have to have someone search for the flight to upgrade it. Make this easier on me would you please?" He gave her a raised eyebrow and a doleful smile to plead his case.

She laughed as he took her hand and pulled her from the car, easily lifting her backpack strap to his shoulder.

"You would do that too, wouldn't you?"

"Yes. I have the connections so you have no choice. Help me out here and save me an hour on the phone with my travel agent."

"How will I explain having a booked flight to my sister? And business class to boot. She'll want to know how I'm paying for all that."

"Tell her you have a corporate benefactor and leave it at that. You are close, right? She's your best friend, and she cares about you?"

"Yes. But she would worry . . ."

"Just tell her not to. That you've got this part covered from now on. And that mum's the word with the rest of the family. Then make her pinky swear."

"Pinky swear?" she laughed. "How do know about that?"

"Kurt's daughter. I have to pinky swear with her when I slip her chocolates."

The automatic doors slid open for them and they walked to the check-in line. He waited with her as they watched people and whispered hilarious comments back and forth. Then he walked her to the TSA area, pulled her into a quiet corner and kissed her soundly, using a finessing tongue and demanding lips to imprint his possession, all the while willing her senses to remember him, compelling her to return to him.

"I will be thinking about you the whole time you're up in the air. So if things get bumpy just pretend I'm holding your hand. I'll be in my office imagining your hand in mine."

He bent to kiss her forehead. "Travel back to me. I couldn't stand it if you didn't."

"Three months will speed by."

"Not for me." He shook his head emphatically and she didn't doubt that he meant it.

She sighed and gave him an endearing crooked smile while placing her open palm on his cheek. "Not for me either," she said as she spun and dashed away, turning to wave as she walked backward to disappear into a meandering TSA line around the corner.

He stood, waiting to get another glimpse of her as the line shuffled forward, but was blocked by a team of high school athletes whose height and bulk obscured her from view.

His heart heavy with the loss of her presence and his thoughts filled with the misery of the drive ahead and the mundane tasks ahead of him today. He heaved a huge sigh and turned toward the door and the parking garage. How had that little imp worked her way into his heart so fast? He had to laugh out loud as he walked through the open automatic doors.

His memory had latched onto the moment he'd retrieved her tiny little bullet vibrator and to the look on her face when he'd dropped it in her lap. God, she was a breath of fresh air in a life that hadn't had a reprieve from tireless duty in what seemed like forever.

He was in his car, making the turn to queue up in front of the gate to leave the lot when his phone pinged.

He removed it from his jacket pocket and glanced at the screen as it flashed Shaw. *Made it through TSA in record time along with a college football team. I think they've adopted me. The quarterback said he'd teach me how to use this phone during the flight. Looked what I learned!* She followed the missive with a line of alternating purple and pink heart emojis.

Great. Four hours sitting next to a sports jock who was a hell of a lot closer to her age than he was. The horn tooting behind him took him out of his reverie. He dropped the phone on the seat beside him, hoping for a traffic tie up so he could reply and tell her she'd better be good, that she was his.

But who was he kidding, as much as he wished it so, she wasn't his. She was married to her husband, just as he was married to his wife.

Chapter 101—Deke & Shaw
Sad to be Back Home

The ping of her text woke Deke as he slept sprawled out on the five-cushioned section of the sofa in his study. His hand closed over the phone and brought it to his face before the ping tone had ended. Expertly, he opened the screen and smiled to see she had landed.

I'm in my car, ready to pay for parking and head home. A real nice guy named J'Quan sat beside me and taught me how to play Solitaire, Woody Puzzle, Mario Kart, and Word Scapes. Miraculously, as soon as I was seated a split of Prosecco was put in my hand. Thank you. The flight was good, no turbulence this time, so that was a relief. Although your stewardess friend kept plying me with your special vintage splits so I doubt I would have been bothered if the Captain had decided to do a few rolls, spins, and nosedives. We had lasagna and salad for dinner. J'Quan had four helpings in the time it took me to eat one. It was good, but not that good! Missing you already. The next few days will be busy so that will keep my mind from wandering and remembering our amazing weekend as I settle back into the daily grind. Take care. It was followed by a plane emoji and two champagne glasses toasting.

Deke smiled as his thumb scrolled so he could read the message again. Then he went to YouTube, found Willie Nelson's rendition of *When I Dream* and sent it her with instructions to tap on the microphone to hear the song. Then he downed the rest of his vodka tonic and walked through the house to the entrance hall, and to the large staircase that swept grandly to the upper floor and to his bedroom. He usually trotted up the white marble steps, but this time he felt as if he needed the assistance of the wrought iron banister rails to pull him to the top. He knew the next three months were going to drag by like an anvil being pulled by a snail.

It was several days before she texted back: *I don't know how to send a music video yet so I'm just texting the words to "Another Suitcase in Another Hall." So many vocalists have done this, but I think I like Sarah Brightman's take on this song the best. I especially think the third verse suits how I'm feeling right now.*

Call in three months time and I'll be fine,
I know well, maybe not that fine,
But I'll survive anyhow.

Over the next several days, he listened to the song on his phone, in his car, on his laptop, and at home while undressing for bed. When Alexa started recommending other songs by the same artist, he had to wonder at his obsession with it. He finally took "her" suggestions and listened to what Alexa recommended, simply because Shaw liked Sarah Brightman.

Then texts with pictures showing Halloween preparations well underway followed two weeks later, including a picture of her with her class in costume. She was in a sexy leopard suit, with face paint expertly applied. In her hand she was holding a long black, velvet tail; it was curled to the underside of her cheek. He had to laugh at the caption. *Shakira's got nothing on me.*

Chapter 102—Deke & Shaw
Christmas Break

Christmas was a busy time for Shaw as Matt had a slew of doctors' appointments before the end of the year. His attorney wanted to begin proceedings on the lawsuit against the truck driver's insurance company after the first of the year, and needed confirmations that Matt was not expected to get better in any capacity, no matter the treatment or time involved. That he was as good as he was going to get and that the likelihood was, that given time, would progressively get worse.

Neither was happy to pursue this tack, yeah, the money would be nice. But every single dream Matt had ever wanted to have money to fulfill could not happen now. The bass boat, the ski shack in Colorado, the river rafting excursions in West Virginia, paddle boarding in Hawaii, surfing in Thailand, going on safari in Africa . . . no matter his bank account, he couldn't do any of them.

Already hating doctors' appointments, the reasons behind these in particular made things worse. Shaw had to force, cajole, and drag him protesting to each one.

The downward spiral of another deep depression combined with the television flashing happy families celebrating the holidays made each morning in December progressively wretched for Matt, and in turn, Shaw.

Shaw: *I just got back from a doctor's appointment with Matt where they listed his clinical issues (six pages!) and in the summation gave his life expectancy as 58. We were both shocked when we saw that number in the report. That a panel of doctors thought 58 years was the most Matt could expect to live stunned us both. Matt and I both cried. His attorney said that was just the number the court needed to see and not to focus on that. But, I have to tell you. Matt is focusing on it. I don't expect him to be sober when I get home from a parent teacher's meeting tonight. Not that he is on any night.* A leopard emoji and a purple heart ended the missive.

Deke: *What discouraging news. Your attorney should have told you that these "panels of doctors" are paid well for their time and that they are expected to provide data that will help the case. I wish I could cheer you somehow. But honestly, the thought of you being with Matt until he's 58 or better is very disheartening to me as well. How I would love to kidnap you away from the miserable life you're stuck in. I would take you to a sunny tropical place where I could pamper you with massages and Mai Tais. And big O's. Very big O's. Hang in there, just two weeks until you're back in my arms again. I am strongly considering not letting you return this time. But I probably shouldn't be telling you that.* Images of a beach, a palm tree and a fancy cocktail followed.

Shaw: *It's Christmas vacation. I have to leave my phone here at school. I am very sad about that. I will miss my games. Just joking. I will miss hearing from you and knowing that you are missing me as much as I am missing you. I am wishing you a Merry Christmas and a Happy New Year now. You said you were going to spend some time surfing with friends, I think that's wonderful. And your annual visit to Costa Rica to visit your father over New Years will be a special time for you both, so please be happy. Do fun things and eat delicious food. But do not ogle other women. Leopards can be vicious when jealous.* It was followed by a two-second video of a snarling, long-toothed leopard.

It was an hour later when he saw her message as he had been playing racquetball at the gym. Noting the time, he knew she had left school by then, and that the phone was sitting on a shelf in her locker on mute. But he sent the message anyway.

Deke: *I love you.*

Chapter 103—Deke & Shaw
Reunion at LAX

Shaw stepped off the plane and dodged around everyone on the ramp who was pulling a suitcase. With just her light backpack she felt younger, more energetic, and surprisingly agile as she edged her way around the other business class passengers to become the first one into the terminal.

Her heart fell when she didn't see him in the circle of people waiting to greet the passengers. But just as she turned her head to the right, she felt an arm confidently wrap around her waist and pull her aside. She had one second to see the smiling eyes looking down at her before Deke's lips descended to hers.

As airport kisses went, this one was pretty epic. Deke held the side of her face with his other hand and ravished her lips, allowing his tongue in on the action. Then he peppered kisses alongside her jaw to her earlobe, where he breathed into the tiny whorl, "God, how I've missed you."

Her fingers threaded through his hair, marveling at the luxuriously thick strands that were longer than the last time her fingers had been embedded in them. She held his face to hers as well as she returned his kisses. "I missed you too, so much." More kisses followed until a rowdy sports team poured out of the plane and jostled them.

He slid the backpack straps off her shoulders. "We'd better get out of the way, we're going to trampled by athletes and their fans if we don't."

She laughed as he pulled her along. She was having a hard time keeping up with his long strides. "What's the hurry?"

He turned to face her, his eyebrows raised to his hairline. "What's the hurry? I've only got thirty hours. And I intend to make the most of them!"

She laughed again. "I was kind of hoping for something to eat. I gave my salmon croquettes to Jaiden." She made a yucky face. "I'm not into breaded salmon, so he ate his as well as mine. I ate the salad though, and his too, as he isn't into veggies."

"What's with you giving your food away all the time?" He seemed miffed about that, and was not pleased that she sat next to another man all evening, talking and sharing food.

She looked up just then and waved to a tall black man with long dreadlocks tied together at the nape of his neck. He was well over six feet and easily three hundred pounds. The man flashed a broad grin showing perfect white teeth and lifted a meaty hand to brandish a big thumb's up her way as he followed his teammates through the gate.

"That's Jaiden. He's a bottomless pit. He kept pulling food out of his carry on. I don't think he ever stopped eating the whole time we were in the air."

He laughed. Relieved he had no reason to be jealous of the man. He was definitely not her type. At least he didn't think so. "We'll order room service. Anything you want."

"Are we staying at the same place?"

"Yes, but in just one suite this time." He hesitated as he tried to read her expression. "If that's okay with you?"

"I like that you're saving money."

"Is that all you like about the arrangement? No thoughts of carnal pleasures with a gym fanatic since the day you left?" He flexed a muscle. "Pick any wall, countertop, shower ledge . . ."

"One track mind here?" she quipped.

He stopped and leaned down to whisper in her ear, "I have focused on little else except the moment that I can be inside you again. It's been so long that I simply can't wait until we're alone." He waggled his eyebrows at her, "But room service first, if you insist."

"Well okay then," she acceded. "But I wish you would stop spending so much money on me. A motel with a drive-thru close by would suit me just fine."

"Right now, pampering you is the only way I have of making your life easier and more fun. I want so much to make you happy." The earnestness in his voice conveyed his intentions as true and honorable.

"Just being here makes me happy."

He gripped her hand in his and as they exited through the automatic doors, he made a beeline for the car at the curb that Kurt was standing beside. Kurt waved a hand and smiled radiantly at her and she waved back with an excited hand. Noting Deke's scowl, she tempered it from a frantic wave to a queenly one. When the back door opened, she slid inside and Deke was right behind her. Kurt closed the door after them, briskly walked around the back of the car and within seconds they were on the road leading away from the airport.

"You guys are very efficient at this," she murmured in appreciation as he settled her backpack onto the floor.

He chuckled. "Done it hundreds of times. Usually with a lot more luggage though. You travel amazingly light."

"That's because I would still be waiting for a bus."

He gripped her hand in his, and brought it to his lips. "No more buses for you. When you're here, I'm going to be taking care of you."

"Oh yeah?" She pushed the button on the console to raise the screen between the front and back seats. "Then you can start taking care of me right now. I've never had limo sex, but there seems to be plenty of room . . ." she patted the wide expanse of leather seating beside her.

Then without another thought, she pulled her sweater off.

His eyes bugged wide. The red push-up bra made the most of her ample breasts.

"Victoria's Secret, from the Angel Collection. I have a few Christmas presents I bought with you in mind. You know I travel light, so they're very tiny."

He palmed a breast held within its satin cup, ran his

thumb inside to stroke her nipple, then reached behind her undo the clasp. "I hate to make quick work of your wrapping efforts, but I want to get my hands on my presents right now."

He drew the straps off her shoulders and set his lips, teeth, and tongue to work on her nipples. She didn't know whether closing the screen made the rear compartment soundproof, but she imagined it did. However, she had no choice. The sounds she made could not be silenced. He drove her to delightful, torturous heights. And the fact that they were cruising along one of the most traveled boulevards in the world completely slipped her mind when he stripped her jeans off and put his hand into her matching red stain panties.

While his long fingers stroked her, and then entered her, first one, then two, he watched her face as she came apart. Her eyes closed, and he could see the smooth skin of her eyelids contrasting with her dark full lashes, the perfect arch of her brows, and the light purple shadowing under her eyes. The latter bothered him, as she looked tired, but she was still a very beautiful woman.

He removed her panties and lifted her so she was kneeling in front of him, one knee between his legs, the other on the seat so that she was straddling one of his legs. She was close to coming, but he wanted more than to just stimulate her clit and spear her vagina, he wanted to touch the spot that would break down her soul, the place deep inside her core that would liquefy her in his arms. The elusive tangle of nerves that many men didn't know how to reach; so many women did not get to experience the ultimate fulfillment their bodies were capable of.

He stretched his long, expert fingers inside her, crooked the longest one in a come hither manner, and with his other hand pressed her lower back to force her forward to meet it. He stroked it with a hardly perceptible movement. And watched as she threw her head back, gasped, drew a hand to her throat, then splintered into the cosmos. He knew she owned the universe now as he took in every nuance of her beautiful face flushing and then relaxing while her essential nature liquefied and drenched his fingers. He felt he had accomplished something very meaningful, spiritual even, by bringing her to this place.

She arched back with an instinct to dislodge his hand, as the sensitivity in that region of her body was almost unbearable now, then she slumped into his chest. She felt his hand under her loose braid at the back of her neck massaging her. "That. Was. Amazing."

She felt him smile against her cheek.

"Did you mean it?" she asked.

"Mean what?"

"Your last text?"

He placed his forehead against hers and looked into her beautiful shining eyes. "Yes. Every word. I. Love. You."

Her broad smile lit up her face. Then as if shy, she whispered, "It's not love I feel for you, it's more than that. It's adoration. I want to kneel at your feet and worship you."

He threw his head back and laughed with great gusto. "Oh, I want that too," he exhaled out. Then he took her face in his hands and kissed her, mingling his tongue with hers until he heard the car intercom crackle. "Five minutes, sir."

Deke sighed. "We're almost at the hotel. We'd better get you decent." He reached to the floor for her panties, then over to the other side of the seat for her bra. "I like your new lingerie. And the gifts that were inside. Very much." He kissed her on the nose. Then took her hand and placed it over his erection. "And the idea of you kneeling and worshiping me is a very good one. Maybe we should implement it while we wait for room service to bring our dinner."

She ran her tongue over her bottom lip and gave him a wicked smile while he slid the straps of her bra up her arms and then reached behind her back to fasten it for her. Her fingers danced over the fly of his pants and he playfully slapped them away. "Patience. If I have to have it, so do you."

When she picked up the panties, he took them from

her and put them into his suit pocket. "Let's just get your jeans back on."

He helped her thread them onto her legs then she lifted her hips off the seat to get them up and zipped. They both felt the limo slow and then stop as it pulled up in front of the hotel. He marveled that she still looked so put together. But then she didn't wear makeup that would smear, and her hair was still held neatly in its intricate French braid. In his mind, braids always looked better when they were a little messy anyway. He had to smile to himself. Her lips though, they were those of a well-kissed woman. He would be proud to escort this stunning woman with the kiss-swollen lips through the posh hotel lobby, into the mirrored elevator, and up to the penthouse suite he had reserved for them

Chapter 104–Deke & Shaw
Pampering Foot Rubs

As she walked around admiring the room, running her fingertips over the sleek contemporary furniture, feeling the buttery softness on the back of an over-sized leather chair, touching the petals of a floribunda rose in an ostentatious floral arrangement, she murmured just loud enough for him to hear, "You really have to stop doing this, I only need a decent bed with clean sheets, a shower with some soap, and a clean potty."

He came to stand behind her, wrapped his arms around her waist and drew her into his chest. His lips kissed the side of her neck. "I know. I'm the one who needed to have the rest. I'm pretty spoiled you see. You're just along for the ride, so you're just going to have to suffer through it. Plush towels instead of thin scratchy ones, cushiony carpet instead of cracked tiles, hot rust-free water instead of tepid, water reeking of sulfur. You'll just have to put up with my odd penchant for comfort and cleanliness." He moved her braid aside and kissed along the nape of her neck. "I'm truly sorry I'm making you suffer like this."

She laughed and the musical sound of it made his blood warm. Her hand reached behind him and she stroked the top of his thigh. His cock jerked, and when her hand wandered to the placket covering his zipper and pressed, it grew to magnificent proportions. He groaned.

"You're the one who's going to suffer. I'm going to order dinner, take my time eating it, take a long hot bath, maybe polish my toenails, read my book, watch a little TV . . ."

He turned her to him and placed his hand on the side of her face. "Ah, I see . . . there *are* perks you will appreciate in this room. The room you were describing would not have had room service . . . probably no tub, no decent light to polish your nails or to read by . . . I think you need to thank me for my generosity." His hand went to his zipper and he slowly lowered it.

"You do have a point. I suppose I shouldn't question your generosity." Her tongue made a slow journey from the center of her top lip to the middle of her lower one.

He pulled his penis from the opening in his pants and tugged on it. "No, no you shouldn't," he whispered, his voice husky.

Her hand joined his, the tips of her fingers feeling the silky smooth texture of the skin stretched tight over the expanding shaft. Her thumb circled the tip and collected the moisture there. He watched as she brought the pad of her thumb to her lips and sucked it clean. He gasped at the sight of her tasting him. Then watched as she knelt and covered the tip of his penis with her mouth. His eyes closed tight and he threw his head back.

The animal noise he made, something between a roar and an anguished keening, reverberated through her and had her taking him deeper into her mouth, desperate to hear more sounds that he was pleased with her. She licked and sucked, wrapped her hand at the base and stroked, and then allowed her gentle tugs to become steadier and firmer, matching his cries and shouted curses. With his eyes closed to the ceiling, and the words, "Fuck, fuck, fuck!" being hissed through clenched teeth, his hand gripped her shoulder to steady himself, and he ejaculated to the back of her throat.

It felt as if copious amounts of heated cum slid down her throat as she tried to take it all down with his length still filling her mouth. She fought to swallow rather than gag and was grateful when he eased back and cleared the opening of her throat allowing her to catch her breath. She loved giving head, but the those last few seconds when a man was so centered around his instinctive need to procreate, he was mindless to the needs of the woman whose mouth was servicing him.

Deke's hand began to caress the crown of her head and she knew she could relax now, sit back on her heels and take a few deep breaths to regroup.

"That was so good, so good," he whispered. "Phenomenal good. God, I feel . . . well, spent." He laughed. "That's it, well spent. Definitely well spent."

He reached down and gripping her elbows, he pulled her up from the carpet. "Here, let's get you up from there."

He walked her to the sofa and helped her to recline on it. Then he removed her shoes and sat with her feet in his lap. He began massaging a small foot. When she started whimpering he smiled and said, "You are a beautiful woman. Even your feet are lovely. And your toenails are already expertly polished," he quipped. He was very pleased with the lovely sounds she was making and was bent on eliciting more from her.

He listened to her moans of pleasure with a smile on his face as he stroked each toe, tugged and massaged along the length and rubbed between, before moving on to the next toe. Over and over he did this. Then the whole foot was kneaded and plied with deft strokes and deep circling movements with his thumbs. He caressed her foot lightly between his large hands, and then finally bent to kiss along the arch before taking the other one in hand.

He tossed her the room service menu from the coffee table in front of the sofa. "Pick whatever you want, and select a bottle of wine as well."

She opened the fancy leather-bound book with the tassel and *Room Service* etched in gold on the front, and then closed it within the same second. "I already know what I want. A cheeseburger, fries, a small salad and a diet Pepsi. You choose the wine. I'm not so knowledgeable about wines."

He laughed. "You are a delight. Most women would want things I can't even pronounce and the most expensive wine on the list, regardless of its heritage. And you want something to drink with a straw." He shook his head.

"Well if that's the kind of woman you want, I'll have a Coeur a la Crème with Roasted Raspberry Sauce atop a Gateau

Basque for dessert."

He laughed with great gusto. "I would have thought you to be a cheesecake kind of girl."

"Well, that's basically what all that is. A cheesecake atop a cheesecake."

"How do you know this?"

"I collect cookbooks and I'm a passable cook. One of the ironies of my life now is that my husband can't smell or taste, so can't appreciate a single thing I make."

That changed the tone of the conversation. But it was useful information to know. This woman could cook. He loved the idea of her cooking for him. He called room service and placed their order, then worshipped the foot in his lap.

Chapter 105—Deke & Shaw
Traveling to Tijuana

Deke woke early with a satisfied grin on his face as he gently tugged the naked woman beside him closer. He liked this spooning position. Every part along her backside was touching a corresponding part of his front, and his hands had access to every part of her body. He inserted his leg between hers and with deft fingertips stroked the edges of her labial lips, smiling into her hair when they blossomed and opened for him.

"Mmm, who's knocking at my door?"

"The big bad wolf who wants to eat you all up."

"I believe you did that last night."

She felt him smile against her shoulder. "You make me want to investigate finding a soundproofed room."

"Was I loud?"

"Eh? I can't hear you. I think you blew out my eardrums."

She chuckled and turned over in his arms. "How does one learn all those interesting nuances you used on me?"

"Stanford. You may have heard it's an institution for higher learning."

She laughed out loud at that. "You must have had a virtual parade of women offering themselves up to enhance your technique, to help you continue your education. You're a pretty handsome guy," she said as she stroked her fingertip along his stubbled jaw.

"It was a pretty wild time. I am often amazed that I, along with my frat buddies, managed to graduate and earn our degrees."

"What is your degree?"

"I have an MBA."

"Ah, you so enjoy that *Master* moniker."

He rolled her over so that she was flat on the bed and he

rose over her as he nodded to the floor where the sashes of two bathrobes were coiled against the carpet. He had used them to tie her hands to a sheet he'd twisted and shoved under the mattress. "You didn't seem to object to being *mastered* last night."

She smiled up at him. "No, I certainly did not."

He kissed her nose and then pushed up and off of her. "Kurt will be downstairs waiting in less than an hour. We'd better get up and showered if you want to grab something to eat first. Unless you've changed your mind and will just accept the insulin I have in the trunk of my car."

She sat up in bed and ran her hair through her tumbling locks. "No. I'm a terrible liar. When Matt asks me how long I had to wait in line or how the traffic was at the border, I have to draw on the actual experience. If he knew . . ," she waved her hand between them, "well, it wouldn't be good."

"Would he hurt you?"

"He might, I'm not sure. But I don't want to find out. He's a different man now. Although he was always jealous of other men."

She got up out of bed, covering herself with the sheet and pulling it along behind her. As she passed Deke, making her way toward the en suite, he stepped on it and it fell away from her body to land on the carpet.

He reached out for her hand and tugged her into his embrace. Naked, they stood looking each other in the eyes. "If he ever hurt you—"

She covered his lips with her fingers. She didn't want to hear what he was about to say. "He's not going to hurt me. In all ways, I am likely stronger than him now. And I can certainly run faster."

"A man who abuses drugs and alcohol and is angry all the time can have a very short fuse."

"And that is why I try so very hard to appease him. And why I know I can never lie to him. So I must go to Tijuana today."

"I wish I could accompany you, but it is not safe for me. The insurgents know my face. I am at risk for being kidnapped by the cartels that need money. They have a list of businessmen whose wealth they covet and I have been told I am on that list."

"That's why you have a bodyguard."

"Yes. And why I don't go to Mexico anymore. It wouldn't be prudent. I hate that you insist on going. But I am somewhat mollified that Kurt is going to accompany you."

"Will you be here when I get back?"

He smiled down at her. "No. I will be downstairs at the pool procuring our pina coladas."

"Well now, there's a man who knows how to be helpful."

He laughed and swatted her on her butt. "Well the sooner you get there, the sooner you'll get back to me."

She turned and rubbed her cheek as she walked away from him. "Last time I had a handprint I had to hide, did I tell you that?"

He chuckled, "They don't last that long."

"Sitting on it all the way back to Utah must have imprinted it. I swear it was there when I took a bath at home that night."

"I will try to be more careful in the future."

"Oh, now where's the fun in that," she chided as she closed the door between them. Moments later he heard the shower running. He picked up his phone from the nightstand and called Kurt. "Switch to the Humvee. I'm going to tag along today. See if you can get another man to ride shotgun."

"You think that's wise?" Kurt asked.

"I'll stay in the truck. You stay with Shaw."

"Okay. I'm at the garage now. I'll change out vehicles."

"She's just in the shower."

"See you in thirty."

He ended the call and stood staring at the closed bathroom door. Why was that woman so stubborn? This trip to Tijuana was not at all necessary. He could easily provide her with the drugs she needed for her husband. But he had to smile at her lack of confidence in lying. It was refreshing to have someone like her in his life. Refreshing, invigorating . . . and until they returned from Tijuana, hopefully, death defying.

He wondered if she knew just how dangerous the city of Tijuana and its outlying territories had become in the last few months.

Chapter 106—Deke & Shaw
Bad Ass Bodyguards

As soon as she stepped out of the shower he stepped in, and twenty minutes later they were in the elevator and on their way down to the lobby. They stopped at the concierge's hospitality pantry and the concierge packed a tote with muffins, and some fruit and water bottles while they each fixed a thermo cup of coffee to their liking. He would never be able to get hers exactly right, he thought, as Shaw added and sipped several times before she got the sugar and cream just right—he was easy, he took his no-nonsense black.

"You look so different in a baseball cap, sweatshirt and jeans."

"That's the idea of going incognito. No one is supposed to recognize you."

"Is it so dangerous, really?"

"Yes, it is. Especially as this is a needless trip." He leaned in close and put his lips to her ear and whispered, "If I agree to let you pay me the exact amount the Pharmacia is going to charge you for the same medicine I have in my car, can we go back upstairs and stay in bed all day? I will ask you questions and coach you on lying."

She laughed and pushed against his chest. "I can't let you provide drugs for me. I have principles."

"Oh, but I can provide sex? Alcohol? Business class plane tickets? Just not lifesaving insulin?"

"Alright, I'm not so principled after all." She shot him an adorable pout that he wanted to kiss away.

Instead, he laughed as he led her from the lobby with his hand pressed to the small of her back.

He tipped the man who carried the tote with their breakfast items, as a rugged looking ginormous Humvee pulled to curb.

When Kurt jumped out of it and casually held open a door for her, instead of getting inside, she stepped back and stared. "Geasy Peasy!" Her eyes bulged wide at the sight of the military-styled all terrain vehicle. She looked over at Deke with both eyebrows arched high. He put out his hand to help lift her inside. "Geasy Peasy?"

"Kindergarten teacher, remember?"

He nodded in agreement.

"Will we need all this?" she asked, motioning to the weapons she could see that were attached around the inside perimeter.

"I hope not. But I want to assure our safe return."

"Where did this even come from?" her eyes were still agog at the enormity of the truck.

"My company leases it from a military outfitter. It comes in handy from time to time. Hop in, it's just a hybrid, not much more than a Jeep and a glorified tank . . . its saving grace is that it's bulletproof."

She allowed him to lift her up and she settled herself inside, amazed at how high up off the ground she was. And surprised that the seats were sturdy, yet still comfortable. As soon as they were both in, Kurt climbed up the side using a wheel well grip and slid in behind the massive steering wheel. They rumbled off down the circular drive, their mud-splattered incongruence noted by all the limo drivers standing beside pristine Cadillacs and Bentleys.

Shaw covered her ears until she was used to the uneven revving of the motor. It didn't sound as if the roar of the engine combined with the lack of insulation on the side panels and carpeting on the floor pans was going to provide for a very quiet ride. And indeed, it did not.

It was several minutes before she noticed that there was another man up front, to the right of the driver's seat and tucked into an alcove on a jump seat that was higher up than Kurt's. He appeared to have a 360 degree-view from a turret that was louvered steel and glass. She was told his name was Brad. Brad waved and went back to reading a map on his tablet. She and Deke were sunk low in comparison with hardly more than slits for windows. Deke could tell she was starting to get nervous.

"Here, eat a muffin. Unless you want to have a banana first."

"I think I'll just sip my coffee until this seems normal."

He laughed. "For L.A. anything is normal." He bit into his muffin. "Mmm, this is delicious, you should try it. You need to eat something. There's no telling how long you're going to be in line today."

She picked at her muffin and with a plastic knife ate half of a banana in dainty little slices. She was normally a voracious eater, so he knew she was upset about the extra security.

Three hours later, Shaw, accompanied by the baseball player/rock star version of Deke, made it through the line and into the store. Kurt was just outside the door, straddling the threshold, keeping his eyes trained on anything or anyone that could become a threat.

Brad was the first one to spot trouble. Both Kurt and Deke heard their ear buds crackle through a three-way communicator before Brad's voice came through. "Got a honcho taking a picture of the Hummer's license tag."

"Deke, who's it registered to?" this from Kurt.

"Scotchkiss and Simmons." Deke answered, knowing that didn't bode well. It was the name of the parent drug company he owned. That was bad enough, but the signature moniker for the well-known drug brand, was also broadcasting him as the owner and a much sought after victim for kidnapping.

"Every rebel in this country has a family member working for the California DMV," Brad said.

"Might be best to get back to the Humvee," Kurt added.

"Shit," was both men's response two seconds later. "From the look on this man's face, he just got wind of who you are,"

Brad stated, punctuated by a heartfelt sigh.

"Deke, stay inside with Shaw. Act normal but have your gun handy. I'll clear a path. Looks like this stoolie is signaling his mates. Four if I'm not mistaken."

Deke moved closer to Shaw, saw she had completed her transaction and when she turned to him with a wide grin, hefting two boxes, he spoke in Spanish to the clerk, requesting a bag with handles so they could buy a few souvenirs. He also asked her to throw in a box of Trojans. He thought they were getting low on protection, but the reality was, he needed to stall for a few more minutes. The clerk smiled at him and put both boxes in a large plastic-lined tote and then added the box of Trojans. He thanked her and Deke threw some bills on the counter. Then he gently turned Shaw toward the door.

He bent and whispered in her ear as they crossed the area that led to the door. "There's trouble outside. Stay here with me. Kurt and Brad are working to extract us."

He led her to the only window facing the street. He stood to the side with her tucked under his arm, both of them looking between the letters of the store's sign.

It was all over in a matter of seconds. During the height of the pandemonium, Deke took Shaw's hand in a firm grip and exited the store, telling her to run as soon as they cleared the casement. Brad appeared as if from nowhere, then Kurt. Both ran backward, brandishing MP5s, shielding Deke and Shaw until they were inside the Humvee. Kurt slammed the door after them before scrambling up the side and into the driver's seat. The engine, that had been left running with the doors locked, was gunned the second the transmission shifted. They fled, knocking over a stop sign and a moped in order to get behind cover of a building at the corner. Ten minutes later they were on the road that led to the United States border. Kurt jumped out to inform the U.S. Border Patrol of the incident and left money, supposedly for the damages, but they all knew it was a bribe to keep things hushed. They were escorted across the border, avoiding long queues that had assembled over the lunch hour.

Shaw had a short crying jag while Deke held her and rocked her as she sat sideways in his lap. It was decided that no one was hungry or in need of a rest stop so Kurt drove directly to the hotel.

Shaw sighed as if letting out all the air she had held for an hour, "I guess I'm going to have to lie about this anyway, since the truth is stranger than any story I could have made up."

She sighed out another resigned breath. "I'm going to sound as if I'm lying either way. Who's going to believe me if I tell them that the man I'm having an affair with was recognized by one of the cartel rebels, so he and three of his henchmen tried to kidnap him, so they could ransom his company for millions of dollars, but one of his bodyguard's managed to cut a man's jugular with a switchblade, kick another on the side of his knee and drop him screaming like a banshee, while the other bodyguard shoved a third bad guy's face into a brick wall and broke his nose and teeth in the process, then flipped the last one into a fountain, likely breaking his back before dropping a huge planter on his head. Seriously, I could never make this up."

He took her hand in his. "I'm sorry you had to see all that. But ever so grateful you're alive to tell whichever version you choose. But you and I know, that was your last trip to Tijuana."

She opened her mouth to protest. He silenced her with a firm finger under her chin, closing her mouth and sealing her lips.

"If you insist on going to Tijuana, I will call your husband and tell him why that should not happen again. Then you will have to lie or tell him the truth as to why I should be calling to tell him to forbid it."

Her lips clamped tightly together, turning white with her anger.

"I don't care how mad you get with me. You're not going back there."

"You are not the boss of me!"

He removed his finger and sat back in his seat. For now, content to remove his ear bud and communication device, his sunglasses and baseball cap. "Shoulda figured L.A. Dodgers wasn't the way to go," he muttered as he threw the cap to the floor.

She had to laugh at that.

He reached over and pulled her close, tucked her under his strong, protective arm. He knew she was shaken up, and that now probably wasn't the time to address Matt's need for drugs three months down the road.

"I'm sorry, I forgot. You are the master of me."

And that's all it took to get him hard and needy once again.

Chapter 107—Deke & Shaw
Rainy Days and Pizza at Wolfgang Puck

A rare rainstorm kept them from going to the pool when they got back to the hotel. Instead, Deke ordered a deli tray and some iced tea sent up and they sat at a table in front of a picture window watching the storm rage, wane, and then revert to a soft soothing drizzle.

He'd gently undressed her afterward, and together they lay in a locked embrace dozing to rhapsodies from the masters that Deke had on his playlist. It was a near perfect afternoon as they recouped from their terrifying misadventure. The only thing that got in the way of it being perfect was the unspoken thought that she'd be leaving in the morning and that there would be another ninety days before they could be like this again.

When his hands began caressing her back with barely there touches, she began placing small open-mouthed kisses along his pecs. They both moved into a slow rhythm of tender strokes with nimble fingers. Touching every place they could reach while still holding onto each other. They fanned the little fires erupting on their skin until their lazy lovemaking became a wild dance ending with a frenzied mating that left them both breathless.

"That was nice, really, really nice," she murmured into his chest.

"I forgot how the music can enflame one's passions," he chuckled with a nip to her shoulder. "We went from 30 miles per hour to 200 during that last movement."

"It was pretty intense."

"You're intense," he said, running a finger along her throat up to her chin to her ear, then circling and teasing her.

"I'm impressed you remembered a condom."

"If I hadn't thrown that box on the bed when we came in,

I probably wouldn't have. It was only because they were handy."

"Maybe I should go back on birth control so we won't have to use them . . ."

"How would you hide that?"

"They have something that works under the skin for several months at a time. I could check on it when I get back."

"I would like that."

"Since neither one of us has been with anyone else . . ." she let the words dangle, hoping for confirmation from him.

He kissed her on the lips then smiled. "I have not."

She smiled back at him, "And I have not."

"There's no reason not to then. I'll even pay for it."

"I think it's free at the clinic."

"Just make an appointment with a doctor. I'll put my charge card information on your phone and you can just use the Apple Pay feature."

"I can't let you do that."

"Why not. This benefits me more than it does you."

"How do you know I won't use it for other things . . ." she said as she ran a finger over his nipple, "like shoes or outfits."

"I don't care if you do."

"You are very trusting."

"One or both of us could have been kidnapped today. You spending my money is the least of my concerns. In fact, before you head back here next time, see if you can get some more of that sexy lingerie."

She smiled at him. "I have another set you haven't seen yet. And by the way, I need those red panties back."

"Not a chance," he whispered as he took her lips with his and began a seductive parlay with his tongue. "I'm keeping them."

He slid his body down until he was under the sheet, his shoulders between her thighs, and the hair on his head was grazing her belly. His lips and tongue began working their kaleidoscope magic to the music of Debussy's Clair de Lune.

Shaw had never felt so relaxed . . . so delightfully happy . . . so treasured.

At 7:00 Deke dragged her by her ankles to the end of the bed. "C'mon sleepy head, it's time to get dressed for dinner. We have reservations at 8 at Wolfgang's place."

"Can't we order in a pizza?" she moaned. "I don't want to get up."

"I'll admit, it's going to be hard to leave this love nest, but you've hardly eaten all day. And you can't have a heavy meal before flying, so this is it. I feed you now or you stay here."

She groaned again. "Why Wolfgang's?"

"Well, you did request it."

"Oh yeah, right." She lifted her hair off her neck and slid to the floor, sheets, comforter, pillow and all. She looked sexy as all get out. "Kinda think I'd settle for a drive thru Taco Bell instead . . ."

"Get your ass up. I'm taking you to dinner." He waved a piece of Godiva chocolate left by the turn down service under her nose. "Play your cards right, and you could be in for a to-die-for chocolate mousse."

"I died and went to heaven three times this afternoon. You're going to have to do better than a thin sliver of Belgian chocolate."

He laughed. "Okay . . . how about a bottle of Gloria Ferrer?"

That he remembered the champagne that was served on the flight where they had met warmed something in her heart. Majorly.

"Okay," she conceded, slowly getting up and taking the bed sheets with her toward the bathroom.

"I bet housecleaning is having a helluva time figuring out why the bed linens keep ending up in the en suite." He followed her until she closed the door in his face.

"No communal showers. I'm getting a bit tender," she called through the door.

He laughed and went into the kitchen to clean up with paper towels and Dawn soap. Then just ducked his head under the faucet to get rid of his comical bed head.

When he walked back into the bedroom, Shaw was standing by the closet debating about which of her two shirts to wear. She stood there in nothing but a satin lime green push-up bra with matching panties. She was stunning. With her dark hair flowing down her back and her lightly tanned skin, she was mesmerizing in a color that wouldn't suit most people. He couldn't help but gape. The woman stunned him and stopped him in his tracks all the time. He could not believe she was his. At least for tonight.

Once they were seated at a booth, Shaw surprised herself with how much Sweet Italian Fennel Sausage with roasted peppers, red onions, goat cheese, and wild oregano pizza pie she could scarf down, then she asked if she could sample his Wild and Domestic Mushroom pie, with caramelized garlic, thyme and Parmigiano Reggiano after having had a fair share of the Charcuterie Antipasto Board as an appetizer. Deke just sat back and watched as she had a food orgy.

"I hope when all that gets mixed up down there," he pointed to her tummy, "you don't have a culinary meltdown. The idea of you adding an Ultimate Dark Chocolate Brownie to all that makes me rethink not having separate rooms tonight."

She smiled a satisfied grin, "When I get home it's back to Kid's Meals at McDonald's and Ragu on pasta shells."

"Kid's meals?"

"Yeah, best deal out there. You get a burger or four chicken tenders, fries, milk or apple juice, and yogurt or apple slices for three bucks."

"Don't you have to prove you have a kid?"

"Nope, anybody can get a Kids Meal. I eat 'em all the time."

"Do you need money, Shaw? I hate the idea of you going without decent food."

"No, we're fine. It just doesn't pay to spend money on expensive ingredients when he can't taste anything anyway."

"But you can."

"He would feel worse I think, if I spent a lot of time preparing something that he used to love and then he had to watch me eat it, imagining how good it tasted. I just make sure he gets the right nutrients, mostly in canned or cardboard shakes."

"I wish your life was different."

"It is different. Every ninety days I get to taste good food again, and have good sex. And talk to someone who's not bitter or passed out drunk." She lifted her glass of champagne to him, "Life is good," she whispered.

But he knew that her life truly was not good. His mind searched for a solution. But there was none. She was tied to someone just as irretrievably as he was.

"You never replied to my text," he said.

She knew instantly what text he meant.

" I can't right now. Saying the words would make me . . . a bad woman . . . a bad wife. But I think them everyday."

He took his time letting his lips curl into a smile. "You've just earned yourself an exceptional spanking."

She jerked her head up and met his eyes. Her lips lifted into a smile, "Have I?"

"I think so."

"Well what are we waiting for?"

"Either dessert or the bill."

"I vote for the bill."

He laughed. "You never cease to surprise me. Not from the very first moment we met."

"Well, let's add this to the equation then. I do love you. So very much."

Mindless of the people around them enjoying very expensive but sublime food, and the waiters working to deliver it, he stood, walked over to her side of the booth, bent down and cupped her face with both hands. Then he gave her the longest most sensual kiss of her life. When he drew back, there was a fanfare of applause.

He knew the patrons were expecting him to drop to one knee. And if he wasn't already married, he would have.

Chapter 108—Deke & Shaw
Handprints to the Soul

"Look at this," she said, posing with a hand on her hip and flashing him her behind, showcasing a red handprint. It had happened at five in the morning when he'd had her on all fours in the middle of the bed, him over her and pumping into her for all he was worth. And something—he really couldn't name it—except to acknowledge it was primal, made him want to mark her.

"I'm going to have to keep boy shorts on until this disappears."

The thought of another man seeing her naked bottom had him inhaling deep through his nostrils and his hands fisting at his side. Even if that man was her husband.

"Do you often parade naked—around the house? He wanted to add "in front of *him*," meaning her husband, but stopped the words in time. He was not in the best of moods as she was about to get dressed and leave him.

"Well no. But I don't usually dress in the bathroom either. I'll have to remember to take panties into the bathroom when I shower. Don't worry about it. I'm sorry I said anything."

"It'll be gone by the time you get home."

She turned and rubbed the handprint. "I don't know, this is *pretty* well defined." Then she flashed him a cheeky grin. "As was the orgasm that accompanied it. Someday, you're going to have to explain to me why spanking me makes me come so damn hard."

He walked over and matched his hand to the print on her bottom. It covered a good portion of her right cheek. He met her eyes with his and then his mouth broke into a self-satisfied grin, "That was a fairly decent wallop. I'm sorry. But the short version in way of an explanation for your intensified pleasure is pain receptors."

"Well duh. I know it hurts. But why does it hurt so good?"

He sat on the edge of the bed and pulled her so she was standing between his knees.

"Pain is the strongest sensation imaginable. To be able to turn it into an erotic enhancement is quite the accomplishment for both the giver and the receiver. The more aroused the receiver is, the easier it is to convert the pain to pleasure. Nerve endings are stimulated to a great degree when pain is inflicted. Anytime your tissues are inflamed, you feel more, the stimulation goes into your core and you become aroused by your own body's natural flow of morphine-like endorphins. For a moment it's a give-into-it or a fight-it decision. If you let it happen, it's a high like no other when the serotonin comes into play. Pain is the strongest sensation you can feel, and your body and frame of mind determines whether it will be a good feeling or a bad one. The one administering the pain wields some of the power to help in your decision, pretty much instantly. And that is his high. Whether he chooses for you to go to bliss or to hell is in his to control. Whether he abates with your initial bloom, or becomes sadistic and goes for his pleasure instead of yours is under his control. A true Dom will always choose pleasure for his submissive over his own. It is in his nature to please and to bring forth pleasure, not genuine pain."

"How do you know all this?"

"It's my job to know. Pleasuring a woman is serious business. And I played at being a Dom for a while. I went to a few clubs, learned some things in my early twenties. But too much of it was depraved, and so many men were only into humiliating their subs, so I stopped. But I did love the spanking part, and I have found most women, if they are honest, love it too."

"Did Stephanie?"

"Yes. But not as much as you. She loved it because I loved it. You love it because you react to the stimuli honestly. You feel the pain, and you convert it to pleasure. You are exceptional. I have never enjoyed spanking anyone as much as I enjoy spanking you."

"Good to know," she whispered as she sank to her knees and took him into her mouth. They had come out of the shower and he had finished toweling off before he pulled her over to the bed to answer her questions. He knew she was tired, but they had both been loath to call it a night when they got back from Wolfgang's and had made love and talked late into the night. It was morning now and she would be gone soon, and he would be alone for another ninety days. They were making the most of their last moments together.

He said nothing, just threw his head back and closed his eyes to savor the sensations of her licking on him, sucking on him and fondling his balls.

She took him deep, sucked the tip hard, and used her hand to give him a blowjob she felt sure he'd remember for a long time. Maybe one he'd play out in his head while his hand worked his needy flesh when she was back in Utah. She hoped he would remember how she looked with her mouth around his cock, loving him and trying in her own way to bring him the ultimate pleasure, a pleasure that he gave to her . . . with *his* mouth, with *his* lips, and with his hard, open palm.

His words of encouragement, softly spoken and tender urged her on. When he came, she didn't waste any, swallowing and cleaning him with her tongue. He thanked her with his hand tangled in her hair, holding her close, and stroking her neck, her back, and her full breasts.

He urged her to get up off the floor and to sit in his lap. He kissed her on the forehead before pulling away and looking lovingly into her beautiful face. He loved that her lips were chapped because of him. And he loved how good she was when she was on her knees giving him everything a man could possibly desire. He held her for a long time, close to his chest. Neither saying anything. But both feeling the heavy weight of their time together ebbing away.

Finally, she pulled away and crawled off his lap and over the bed to get to the nightstand where she had an open bottle of water. She drank a good portion of what was left.

He picked up her phone from the dresser, the one he had given her and that she had become so familiar with. He used his thumb to scroll through screens and then to tap on a series of keys. "I sent you a sound text. Put your ear pods in and listen to it on take off. As you listen, remember what I was doing to you last time you heard that song."

"Do you know how hard it is leaving you like this?" She crawled back to him.

He took her hand in his and then placed it over his erection. "No. How hard is it?"

"Incredibly," she whispered and smiled hugely. "You just came. Does that never go down?"

"Not when you're around."

"Wish I could help with that, but I gotta go."

"I know. Get dressed. I'll call to have the car brought around."

"Aren't you driving me?" she asked as she stepped into her last pair of panties. He'd taken the other two and pocketed them, refusing to give them back.

"I don't have a car here remember? We took an Uber to dinner last night. Kurt took the Humvee back and swapped it out for the limo after he dropped us off yesterday. I told him to take the rest of the afternoon and the evening off."

"But now he has to work on a Sunday morning. That's a bummer," she huffed out.

"I don't believe he thinks of driving you around as work."

"Awww, he's sweet."

"Stop calling my bodyguard sweet."

By now she was dressed and sitting on a chair lacing her sneakers. Her face fell, her look sad and serious. "I'm sorry that's necessary."

He shrugged, "Hey, it's tax deductible and it gives Kurt

a job. And we've become good friends."

"I can see that. He seems lonely though."

"His wife left him for a big shot plastic surgeon and she plays ping pong with their daughter, Emily. He gets to see her, but not as much as he'd like."

He laughed and it was full bellied.

"What?"

"Last year he wanted to take Emily to a father daughter dance at school and she wouldn't let him, said they were taking her to see *The Nutcracker Suite* that night. I saw their names on the list of guests at a conference banquet my company was hosting for local physicians that very same night. I had them moved to my table and asked Kurt to come as my guest. Fifteen minutes into the meal, neither of them could take his constant non-blinking, condemning stare. She called the babysitter and told her to get Emily dressed for the dance, that her father would be picking her up shortly.

"She's been a little better about access since then. But honestly, I don't know what he saw in that woman to begin with. She is not a nice person."

"Social climbers rarely are. My friends always ask me why I'm content teaching Kindergarteners, knowing that I'm certified to teach the upper classes. I always tell them I am trying to make a difference in these children's lives and influence the way that they treat each other. I teach them to be kind, considerate, patient, polite, and unfailingly sympathetic to those who are hurt or sad, or just unable to keep up for whatever reason. Everyone is taught to help the last one in line, the one struggling to get a coat on, the one whose mom forgot to pack a lunch. I tell them that if they have more than they need to share it with others. I hope all of my students grow up to be nice people. It makes me happy, knowing I might be making their lives count for so much more."

He looped his duffle onto his shoulder and snagged her backpack from her. "Any child who's lucky enough to have you as a teacher is going to go places. This world needs more nice people like you."

He bent and kissed her on the lips.

"Thank you," she whispered as her eyes locked on his.

"I'm going to miss you," he said.

"Ditto."

His cell phone dinged. He took it out of his pocket and looked at it. Sighed. "Kurt's downstairs with the car."

"Well, I guess it's time to go. Again," she said.

He led her out of the suite and at the door, bent to put her backpack on the floor so he could close the door behind them.

"*Another Suitcase in Another Hall*," she whispered and pointed to the solitary bag sitting on the carpet along the long hall facing the elevator.

"*And When I Dream, I Dream of You*," he whispered in a husky voice.

They walked in silence down the long hallway.

When they got into the elevator, she said, "So when I come back next time, we don't go to Tijuana."

"Correct. I give you drugs and you give me sex *and* money."

"I hope they're not recording us."

He laughed at the thought of that and walked into her, pushing her back until she was against the rail, then he kissed her. He was still kissing her when the doors opened.

At the airport, he reminded her to check out the music he had texted her, borrowed her phone to load his charge card information, and set a reminder for her to get a doctor's appointment for birth control. Then told her once again, that he loved her. He stood solemnly and watched her go through TSA. Then he put his hands in his pockets and walked out of the airport. When he saw Kurt leaning on the car, he asked him to find a place where he could sit and watch her take off.

She closed her eyes and listened to Debussy while the plane taxied down the runway. Dutifully, she recalled him ducking under the covers and soon she was squirming with the memory of his tongue and lips. *Meditation* by Massenet followed and then she felt a hand on her shoulder and opened her eyes. The flight attendant smiled down at her, "I was told you might like a mimosa this morning."

She smiled back. She had missed the worst part of the flight, enjoying the music and the memory instead of shaking in her seat. And now this. Deke thought of everything. He took such good care of her.

"Yes, thank you. That would be perfect. Although orange juice tends to make me queasy while flying, can you just skip that part?"

The woman laughed. "Of course."

Chapter 109—Deke & Shaw
Long Dreary Winter

Shaw's text to Deke:

In my car, waiting in the long line to pay for parking. This will be a much sadder drive than it used to be. But as Matt keeps suggesting that since I don't need to have a prescription at the Pharmacia, we should try to find a way to buy six months worth at a time, I should be grateful. I do worry about what's going to happen when his settlement money comes sometime this summer and we can afford to buy a year or two's supply all at once. Spend thrift that he is, he says we'll be able to pay the price Wal-Mart wants for it and be done with all this traveling. But I shouldn't dwell on the future in negative terms. I'll just look forward to seeing you in the spring!

Deke's Reply:

So glad you're down and safe. Hopefully our future will not be full of "drug" problems. I miss you like crazy already. Rest up and have a good week. I hear on the news that you're in for some bad weather. Please take care to drive safely. I love you.

Shaw to Deke:

Matt made his way to the basement this week and saw the red and the lime green bras drying on top of the dryer and wanted to know where the matching panties were. He never goes to the basement because it's so much work getting down the stairs, so

I hadn't thought he'd see them. But I was quick with a reply and delivered it so well he didn't spot the lie! You'd be so proud of me. I told him I couldn't find matching panties in my size, and that I only needed the bras anyway. Adding that there was no sense spending money when I had plenty of other panties to wear. Then before he could think any more about it, I changed the subject and asked what he needed in the basement that couldn't wait until I got home. He said he was measuring for a slot car track. Seems he and his buddy, Jason, decided to go in together on a slot car track system they found on Ebay. Jason's wife said they couldn't have it in their house, so they're building a table and ramps for it in our basement. I can't believe he's going to venture up and down those steep steps just to play a stupid racecar game. Getting up and down those narrow wooden stairs in his condition is going to be a Herculean task for him. He says Jason has rigged up a strap like the movers use so he can carry him on his back. They need one more friend to turn this into a Three Stooges circus.

Deke to Shaw:

I'm all for guys having fun. I'm sure he doesn't get to do much that gives him pleasure these days. I used to play slot cars when I was a kid and it was a lot of fun. It's more fun with teams though, so maybe they will find a third wheel (feel free to substitute stooge).

Production on the factory retooling is going very well. I am pleased to say we are under budget, so I am patting myself on the back for that.

An old friend of Stephanie's came by last night. She happened to be visiting Stephanie at the same time I was last week and pigeonholed me for dinner. At my house. With her bringing the food. I wish I could have found a way to turn her down without hurting her feelings. She has a known agenda, as she is the last in her group of friends yet to marry. And the reason is obvious. She is constantly trying to tell people what they like and then insisting that they do when they say they don't. She showed up with a casserole dish, a bag salad, and a frozen cheesecake. I had to pretend I couldn't eat even though I was starving. How does one make a meatloaf rubbery? And did she really think I was going to let her hang around all night until the cheesecake defrosted? She was not happy when I shooed her out the door at eight. I try to be polite to all of Stephanie's friends, but Madeline makes it hard for me to practice good manners. I need her to stop coming by with unimaginative, and impalpable food. Any suggestions?

Have you had time to set up a doctor's appointment yet?

Shaw's reply to Deke:

Give her a nice big, thick cookbook, Williams Sonoma has a really hefty one, and tell her when she's done reading it, cover to cover, to make something from each section and then plan a dinner party. When you get the R.S.V.P. send regrets that your doctor has put you on a strict Paleo diet so unfortunately, you can't attend.

I called today. I got an appointment during spring break, as I can't take any time off from work right now. Skin to skin will have to be something we look forward to during our summer visit.

Deke to Shaw:

Stephanie has developed a lung infection. Her doctors are having a heck of a time finding an antibiotic to fight it. They're on the fourth course now. I can't sleep while all this is going on so I am spending hours at the gym running on the treadmill and lifting weights after work.

Kurt tells me you have a cold. Seems both of my girls are sick. He also tells me you send him funny puns. Why don't I get any of those? I could use something to make me laugh right about now.

Shaw's reply:

Yeah, one of my students gave it to me. And it's a doozy. I have to wear a mask everywhere I go. The skin of my hands is very dry from washing them forty times a day. I am living on chicken broth; tomorrow I am going to see if I can graduate to Pho. I am so sorry about Stephanie. I know this is hard on you. I hope they find the right drug to fight this infection. Don't overdo it in the gym. I like you just the way you are, you don't need massive muscles, you are already very well ripped. Here's one of my best puns, hope it makes you laugh:

Mahatma Gandhi, as you know, walked barefoot most of the time, which produced an impressive set of calluses on his feet. He also ate very little, which made him rather frail. With his odd diet, he suffered from bad breath. This made him . . . a super calloused fragile mystic hexed by halitosis.

.

Gotta go, young'uns marching in from recess. That is the only good thing about this cold, I get to stay inside with my runny nose, otherwise it might freeze and drop off. I love you. Always remember that. S.S.S.
Sexy, Sassy, Snotty.

Chapter 110—Deke & Shaw
A Badly Needed Winter Break

Kurt breathed out a huge sad sigh, "She's majorly stressed. It's testing time for her students, you know. Some of them she positively does not want back next year, so they have to pass and get accepted into first grade."

"How do you know all this?" Deke was obviously miffed that he didn't, but trying to act as if it was of no concern. Kurt knew better. It gave him cause to flash one of his rare smiles.

"She texts memes to me. Yesterday she sent me a YouTube video of a teacher mispronouncing kids' names. It was hilarious."

Deke couldn't help but raise his eyebrows to this. "I thought I was the boyfriend."

"She thinks you're too busy to look at this kind of stuff. Plus, she knows I have a kid in school, so sending puns back and forth is particularly apropos."

Deke looked up from his desk and shot him a questioning look. "So how do you think she'll react to this idea: I'm planning on having her at the house this weekend since we don't need to stay at a hotel close to the border."

He laughed. "She's going to be dumbfounded. She grew up in a single wide in North Carolina. Her parents worked their way up to a doublewide, but their lifelong dream was to have a stick-built house with a pool, that they finally got when they retired."

"Too much?"

"Definitely. But why not? It's a ton of empty space going to waste."

Kurt flipped through his Photos phone app. "Here, she sent me a picture of her childhood home."

Deke stood and walked around the desk and took the phone from him. It was a black and white photo of a stubby aluminum-clad house, underpinned with mismatched masonry cement blocks that had obviously been redeemed from another project. The front porch was up four wooden steps with a rail on one side. The front door wasn't visible as there was a storm door showing into the dark interior. The road in front of it was a rutted dirt path. A banana seat styled bike lay on its side in the sparse lawn. Deke pushed the appropriate places on the screen to send the picture to his phone.

Deke shook his head as he handed the phone back and asked, "Why is it she sends you this stuff instead of me?"

"Well, I've always been approachable to women."

"That's because they think you're gay."

"Better that than sleep with the wrong woman again and ruin another kid's life."

"There are good women out there."

Kurt gave a heartfelt sigh, "I think you found the last one."

Deke grinned. "Yeah, maybe I did."

There was silence for a heartbeat then Deke said, "It's four hours 'til we get Shaw, I'm going to visit Stephanie."

"Is she finally out of danger?"

"Yeah, the infection has cleared up but she's making this odd humming sound almost constantly now. After two years of nothing but silence, it's kind of eerie."

"Should I just pick Shaw up at the airport and meet you at the house then?"

"No way. Swing by and get me at eight, that should give us plenty of time."

Kurt gave Deke a crisp salute and left Deke's office.

When Shaw came off the plane at ten, she zeroed in on Deke first thing. Her grin could not have been wider. With her backpack secured on her shoulders, she leapt into his arms and wrapped her legs around his waist.

"Whoa Nelly," he exclaimed. "We have an audience, you know."

She smiled as she slowly lowered her jeans-clad legs to the floor. She kissed his lips with an urgent hunger. "I don't care. Let them be jealous."

He laughed. "Of which one of us?"

"Both. This weekend we are the luckiest people in the world."

"I think there is a song by that name."

She smiled up at him. "Barbara Streisand. People who need people . . . I need you Deke. Let's do that limo thing, okay?"

He laughed. "Actually, I thought we might spend the weekend at my house, if that's alright? It's incredibly close, no more than twenty five minutes."

She hesitated, and then whispered. "Stephanie's house?"

"No," he shook his head. "I couldn't stay in our old house, too many memories. I bought this one from a friend who moved to New York a few months after the accident."

"Well alright then. I assume you have a pool?" She said it so seriously, and with a highly quirked eyebrow that indicated a negative answer would most definitely quash his weekend plans.

He had to laugh at her tenacity. "Yes. It has a pool." He didn't tell her that it also had Roman statues, fountains, several hot tubs, secluded areas with opulent cabanas and even its own fully stocked swim up bar in the center. The only thing it didn't have was her, but he was going to remedy that tonight as he had arranged a catered dinner on the upper terrace where they could watch the colored fountains at each statue come on at midnight.

If there was ever a more dissimilar dwelling to the one he now carried a picture of on his phone, his pretentious mansion in one of the most prominent subdivisions of L.A., certainly qualified.

Chapter 111–Deke & Shaw
Putting on the Ritz

Shaw had seen Deke's house once before, when Kurt had dropped him off on the night they had met before taking her to the hotel. Walking inside and seeing the opulence, the hugeness, the myriad of rooms and levels . . . "This is not a house. You have your own hotel here."

She dropped her backpack onto the floor in the tiled foyer that was large enough to host a commencement party for her students and their families.

He laughed. "Sometimes it feels like that."

"Have you ever seen it all?"

He laughed again. "Yes, the day I made an offer I went through the whole place. It took a few hours. But I have to admit, in the two years since, I have only frequented my favorites."

"And they are?"

"My study, the kitchen, the gym, my bedroom, the solar, the game room and the theater room."

She huffed, "The theater room? And how many does that seat?" she asked with a touch of sarcasm in her voice, fully expecting him to say four or five.

"Thirty-two."

"Ye Gads. This is a city."

He took her hand in his, and pulled her through the main level salons to the backside of the house where the pool was all lit up.

"Holy Moly . . . this is like Disney Land."

He smiled and pulled her under his arm. "Let's get you settled. There's some champagne in a bucket at the table on the terrace that's set for dinner. Let's get you a glass then you can pick out your room."

"Pick out my room?"

"Yeah, there are fourteen to choose from."

"Can't I just stay in yours, with you?"

"I was hoping you'd say that."

He led her down the brick stairs to the lower level and to the table that was set for dinner. A waiter appeared out of nowhere and opened the champagne and poured them each a glass.

"To my SSS girl."

"I am no longer snotty," she said with defiance.

"Sexy, Sassy, S'naughty," he whispered as he clinked his glass with hers.

"So naughty I can do. Send all these guys away so I can show you."

"They'll all be gone once we're served. Let's get you upstairs. Put your bathing suit on. There are robes in the bathrooms and towels in the cabanas. After dinner, we'll laze about in the pool. How does that sound?"

"Too perfect to be true."

"No. That would be you."

He led her upstairs and left her in an opulent dressing room. With her simple, scarred backpack lying on a tufted bench she felt like a hobo crashing a ball. The closet reminded her of a salon she'd been in once in a very posh bridal shop. There were drawers, cabinets, and mirrors on every wall in a carpeted room that was curiously octagonal. Along one wall, there was an assortment of clothing. Each item was on a hanger in a clear bag with a label tag attached.

She walked over, tilted her head and read: Nordstrom Tropical Sun Dress Size 8 Petite; Neiman Marcus Persimmon Sweater Set Size 8 Petite; Lululemon Paisley Embossed Boot Leg Yoga Pants Size 8 Petite; Victoria's Secret Purple Passion Bandeau & Ruched Back Bottom Bikini Swimsuit Size 8 Petite; Victoria's Secret Mango Delight Strappy Monokini with Wraparound Cover-up Size 8 Petite; Neiman Marcus Pink Leather Jacket Size Medium Petite; John Vass Black Classic Dress Size 8 Petite, Johnny Was Silk Embroidered Kimono Top

Size Small; Johnny Was Coral Georgette Dress Size 8 Petite; Victoria's Secret Grey Rose Stretch Lace Top Size Small; VS Grey Rose Stretch Lacy Cami Size Small; VS Boyfriend Rolled Cuff Jean Blue Sky Angel Size 8; VS Siren Mid-rise Skinny Jean Ink Blue Denim Size 8 Petite. The clear garment bags went on and on, filing the bar along one wall. Was Deke's wife a Size 8 Petite?

She checked the drawers, opening one after the other to find all manner of lingerie—bras, panties, camis, slips, nighties, cropped tees, tank tees, sweaters, Sherpa sweatshirts, socks, stockings and short set pjs. Everything was in her exact size. After holding her hand to her mouth and turning around and around in wonder, she finally dropped to the velvet bench. Were these bought with her in mind?

The shoe carousel was filled with boxes too, but she was afraid to look at what was inside them. But 7M was on the end of each box. Her shoe size exactly.

She unzipped her backpack and dumped out her meager belongings. Everything would all fit in one of these drawers. She fished through the clothing for her red bathing suit with the flesh-colored bottom, then stripped and put it on. Then she found the plush robe on a padded hook and wrapped herself up in it. It was like being cocooned in a cloud.

It took her another minute to find where she had put her glass down. When she found it on a shelf in an alcove, she fortified herself with a big sip. Then tiptoeing across the thick carpeting, trying not to disturb the perfect pattern vacuuming had left, she found her way to the hallway where Deke was waiting to take her back downstairs.

"Do you ever get lost?"

He laughed. "I used to, but I've kind of figured it out. There's a central hall and everything kind of spreads out from there. If you get lost, there's a diagram by every phone. But basically all the entertainments are on the first level, the bedrooms are on the second level, servant's quarters are on the third, then there's an attic for storage running the length of the house on the top level. All the mechanicals are in the basement or on the roof, except for the pool, which has its own pump house and storage. The gardens have green houses, solars, mazes, and mudrooms all about the perimeter."

"Servants?"

"The house was made for a rather large extended family. But since it's just me, I don't have a full-time staff, just a housekeeper during the day, and occasionally a chef and servers as needed. Tonight I just hired a caterer."

"So after they leave, we'll be all alone?"

He smiled down at her. "All alone."

"We can hop on all fourteen beds?" her eyes lit with glee.

He laughed. "We can fuck on all fourteen beds if you like."

"Well that's challenging . . ."

"I might be up for it . . ."

She downed the rest of her champagne. "Well, let's go. I'm going to need some nourishment!"

He laughed and followed her down the grand staircase. "I'm going to need some Viagra," he muttered to himself. "But not the first five or six times!" he added, with a grin.

When she took off the robe to walk into the water he said, "Not that I'm complaining about the suit you're wearing, but didn't you want to wear one of the new ones?"

Standing down a few steps, in water up to her knees, she tilted her head up to him and raised an eyebrow in question. "The clothes in the closet are for me?"

"Who did you think they were for?"

"I thought they might be your wife's," she said, not able to keep the timorous tone from her voice.

"She's never lived here. Just last year I donated her clothing to a woman's shelter. Where she is now, he has no use for anything other than nightgowns. Even so, she's a size 12 and wouldn't be considered petite.

"And before you chastise me for spending money on you, I haven't spent a dime until you approve and decide to keep each selection. What you don't want, my personal shopper will return to inventory. But I wanted you to have some clothes here. I probably shouldn't tell you this, but every night since they were delivered, I've gone in there, fingered the different materials and imagined you in them."

"Aww Deke, that is so sweet. Thank you. I am the luckiest girl in the universe."

He walked down the steps to join her. "I wish you were. But your life is actually pretty shitty right now."

She laughed. "Pot calling kettle black here."

He moved a strand of hair from in front of her face and tucked it behind her ear. "When you're here, I'm deliriously happy. You make up for all the bad moments just by your smile."

She flashed him an extra wide smile and pushed him into the water, then followed him down laughing at his surprised spluttering. They played in the refreshing water, ate a fabulous dinner, talked and stared up at the stars, and after what she called *Reunion Sex*, they fell asleep in each other's arms.

On Sunday morning, when it was time to take Shaw to the airport, they had "starred," nine rooms. She said that, as any good kindergarten teacher would, she carried a little packet of stars in her purse to reward good behavior. In this case she had rewarded Deke's exceptionally good behavior with two stars on the door frames of eight rooms, the ninth she said, was only entitled to one as he had come within seconds of him entering her.

He had argued that it was all her fault as she had done some magically wonderful thing with her fingers to the area just behind his balls, causing him to spill his seed prematurely, but oh what an incredible orgasm that had been. It had left him drained and staring at the ceiling, spread-eagled on the bed for what seemed like an hour.

"What are you going to tell your housekeeper?" she asked as she stuffed her backpack full of the insulin packages he'd given her.

He frowned as he looked over at her, "Why do I have to tell her anything?"

"Well, after two years, only one bed to remake, now suddenly nine?"

"I don't have to explain things to anyone, least of all to a housekeeper I've never even met. You worry too much about what people think."

"Where I come from they can fire a school teacher for cussing. This type of behavior? They'd burn me at the stake. I don't suppose you ever have to worry about things like that?"

He laughed. "If I did, I never would have graduated from Stanford."

He walked over to where she was struggling to zip her bag and easily did it for her. Then he took her face in both of his hands, "If they fire you for misbehaving, I'll hire you," he said gruffly.

"Oh yeah, what position are you offering?"

"Any position you can dream up, but I'm particularly fond of the position you were in in bedroom number seven."

"Hmm, just like a housekeeper, you require me to be on my hands and knees."

"Well at least there are no harsh chemicals involved," he chided as he kissed her on the lips. "And I do offer fringe benefits . . ."

"Such as?"

"Fountains dancing in the moonlight, never ending flutes of champagne," he waved his hand in the direction of the backpack, "a medical plan with free drugs."

She put her fingertips against his lips, "Ah, ah, ah. I left money in your nightstand drawer."

He threw his head back and laughed, "It comes to this

then, being paid for my services."

She smiled, "I could never afford your services if they were for sale."

"Well fortunately for you, I make a nice living in an office so I can afford to service you for free."

"I was particularly fond of the way you serviced me on top of the pool bar yesterday afternoon."

He smiled. "Good thing I don't have any neighbors living close by. With your screams of ecstasy we would have had the cops at the door."

Deke's phone dinged. He took it out of his pants pocket and looked at the screen. "Kurt's here."

"It's gets harder and harder to leave you each time."

"I know. I'd like to tie you up and keep you here until your flight's long gone."

"I'd like you to tie me up . . ."

"Two of the bedrooms we have yet to get to have four-poster beds. I will endeavor to start with them when you return. Bring your little packet of stars, you're going to need them."

Again, he sat in his car in a field a mile away and watched as she flew back to Utah. To a husband she no longer knew, a house she spent more time cleaning than relaxing in, and a job that stymied her creativity and set unrealistic testing goals for her four and five-year-old students. He would have loved her to just stay here, live with him, and maybe give him a child or two she could tell all her wonderful stories to.

Chapter 112—Deke & Shaw
To Everything There is a Season

Shaw's text:

Arrived late, as we had to fly around a storm and come in from another direction. At least that's what I understand from the man sitting next to me. The Captain spoke so fast I couldn't understand him. The flight attendant said he was Egyptian. And of course, that sent us all into a tizzy. Safely down now. Sad I had to leave. I've never had so much fun. I love that I can be myself with you. And I love how special you make me feel.

Deke's reply:

I was wondering why it was taking so long for you to text. I hate that I can't be with you when you fly, as I know how it unnerves you so. It's a mistake having you fly business class. The odds of you having a man in the seat next to you rather than a woman are five to one. I am jealous of any man who gets to sit and talk with you for that length of time. I too, enjoyed this weekend tremendously. You'll never know how much you brighten my days. Sleep well my love, and have a good test week at school.

Shaw, two days later:

Matt fell down the basement stairs yesterday while I was at work. He hit his head on the steps multiple times and a few hours later one of his new slot track friends found him unresponsive. He died early this morning in the ICU. I had to go by the school on the way home from the hospital to get my phone, as I didn't have your number written down anywhere. I will be incommunicado for a while. Matt's parents have camped out here and are taking care of all the arrangements. I had no idea how many friends he had. It's overwhelming all the people who are traipsing in and out of the house. I am a real widow now.

Deke texts back right away:

Oh Shaw, I am so sorry. Do you need anything? You have my credit card information on your phone. You can charge up to $50,000 without me getting an alert for my approval. Please use it as you need it for any expenses that come up. I'll give you a few days, but then if I don't hear from you, I'm coming out there. Heal and come back to me.

She did not know what response she expected. But that one seemed pretty perfect.

Saturday night, after everyone left, including Matt's parents, Shaw walked around straightening up the house and putting away the food and the half-filled bottles of booze. Holding one up to the light and seeing very little in it, she poured the Kahlua into a glass with some ice, then added vodka. She plopped onto the sofa, exhausted. As she sipped, it occurred to her that she should call Deke before he showed up on her doorstep, as he had threatened.

She dragged herself up and went down to her car where she had left the phone Deke had given her. When she removed it from the console and turned it on, she had to laugh at how many texts there were. All concerned, all offering all kinds of assistance and encouragement, and all from the same man—as he was the only one who even knew she had a cell phone. Well... other than Kurt.

She read each one as she walked back inside the house and then pressed the call button as she sat back on the sofa and took a sip of her drink.

He answered after only one ring. She smiled that he was so eager.

"Hey," he whispered. "How are you?"

"I'm okay. Everyone just left. This is the first time I've been alone all week."

"I saw online that the funeral was today. How'd it go?"

"Okay I guess. As funerals go it was pretty typical. Everyone was very kind and said nice things about Matt. Then all his friends came back to the house with bottles of booze and drank themselves silly and sad."

"How are his parents doing?"

"They were pretty accepting. I think they've been bracing for this since the accident. They were very helpful. His dad cried a lot, but his mom pretty much held it together. I'm sure she'll be a basket case tonight though."

"And you? How about you?"

She shrugged, but then realizing he couldn't see her, she said. "I'm alright. The last few years have been hard. The depression was winning him over to the dark side, so I think he would have wanted it this way. It's just sad all around."

"I know. And I hate that for you."

She perked up, "There was this odd thing that happened today. It's actually kinda funny. I had a woman approach me at the reception who told me pointblank that him marrying me was the biggest mistake of his life, that he should never have left her for me. She waved a ring in front of my face and told me that he had proposed to her first. The ring she was flashing was the birthstone ring he'd taken off my finger when he proposed to me. I'd always wondered where it went. He said he didn't know where it was when I asked him about it. So apparently, he had proposed to *me* first."

Deke joined her in the chuckle. "That's pretty smarmy."

"Yeah, right? And it kinda makes me sad that he was two-timing me. I thought we were exclusive from the day we met. But you want to know the hardest part of being at the funeral reception?"

"What?"

"There were so many of his old co-workers there. Some who had been at his bachelor party . . ."

"Hmmm," he sighed, instantly making the connection. "The ones who had seen that picture."

"Yeah."

"I'll bet that was hard."

"Are you being punny?"

"I didn't say *they* were hard."

"It was just weird, wondering what they were thinking."

"Well, if it even crossed their minds, then they were thinking about *getting* hard," he said. "I would have been."

"It was just so weird to have all that going on when I was trying to be so polite and all."

"Funerals are a mixed bag as it is, sounds as if Matt's was more so."

"Yeah. But it's okay. And now it's over."

"When can I come see you?"

"I don't think that's a good idea right now. I'm going back to school tomorrow to finish up this week's testing. They have a sub, but I think the kids will respond to me better and get higher scores."

"Then what?"

"I think I'm going to organize the house and put it on the market."

"And move to L.A.?" he hinted.

She laughed. "You never know . . ." she said and he could hear the impish grin in her voice.

"I would welcome you with open arms, you know that don't you?"

"I know you would. "

There was silence on the line for a few seconds before she said, "There's so much to decide so quickly. And I'm probably not in the right state of mind to do any of it right now. But, I do know there's nothing for me here. We moved here for Matt's job, and then after the accident it wasn't possible to think about moving as he had so many doctors he had to see. But I've never really liked it here much. The only friends I have are the teachers at school. And it is howling, screaming, bitching cold here three quarters of the year, and I *hate* that."

"L.A. is always warm. Sunny. Never any snow . . ."

She laughed again.

"I don't know. My parents want me to move back home. I do miss it there. North Carolina is still home to me and I can get a teaching job there with no problem."

"That's even further away from me . . ."

"I know. Honestly, if it weren't for you, I'd probably be packing up tonight."

"Did your mom and dad come to the funeral?"

"No. Dad's not doing so well. He just had a hip replaced and the physical therapy is wearing him out. They said they were sorry they couldn't be here, but he just could not have flown so soon after the surgery."

"I want to see you, baby. Hold you, make sure you're okay."

"I'm all right. Or I will be. Give me some time to sort things out."

"Can I help with anything? Do you need any money?"

"No. I'll be okay. I have enough to get by on, especially if I sell the house. Two of the doctors that came to the funeral said that the legal issues related to the accident would be settled much faster now. Supposedly, the insurance boards have some guidelines they use for loss of income with regard to the death of a spouse that are more punitive and pretty much set in stone, whereas planning a future with lifelong treatment requires a lot more research and testing and is substantially harder to lock in. They said a settlement amount would probably be offered within a few months."

"I'm here if you need me and I want to help. I love you and I don't want to lose you. But I understand that you need some time."

"Thank you."

"Well, the nice thing is, we can talk on the phone now."

"Yes."

"The not nice thing, is there is no need for any more drug runs."

"I will still come see you. But I owe it to the man I married to mourn him for a while."

"For how long?"

"I don't know. This is all so new to me."

"Are you scared?"

"A little. I don't like being alone here. I think I'd feel better back home."

"Why don't you go for a visit?"

"I might. But I have to wait until the school year is over. It won't look good for my resume if I leave before the school year ends in June."

"Well, I'm here for you. And I can be there for you as well. You only have to say the word and I'll get on the next plane."

"I know. Thank you, Deke. Just talking to you makes things easier. Less daunting."

"You can call me anytime, you know that, right? Anytime."

"I'll remember that. Hey, I have to go. The house phone is ringing."

"I love you, Shaw."

"Ditto."

He would have liked to hear the words, he thought, as he closed the screen on his phone. But she had buried her husband today, so maybe she just couldn't manage to say them right now.

He walked over to the bar in his study and poured himself two fingers of bourbon. As the first sip burned on its way down he vowed he would not give her up. He'd give her time. But he would not give her up.

Chapter 113—Deke & Shaw
Planning a New Future

She made it through the week at school and when she came home on Friday night, she took a glass of wine in hand and walked in and out of each room. It didn't take long for her to decide that she definitely did not want to live in this house anymore.

She remembered she had a Lowe's card with a $15,000 limit that currently had a very low balance. The last thing charged to it had been the lumber for the slot car table that Matt's friends had carted off the day before the funeral.

During the week, Shaw had spoken to one of the curriculum administrators who was a part-time realtor. The woman was familiar with the house as she had been there for two baby showers. She said the house would sell quickly if she put in new flooring and countertops, upgraded the refrigerator and dishwasher, and "ungreened" the yard. Grass was on the way out, rock gardens and terraced gradients that climbed the hills on the sides of houses made a house like hers more desirable. She said the house would need to appeal to a young family, as it had three levels. And young, working people with children wanted a fresh new look and minimal yard work and upkeep.

So Friday night, she went to Lowe's and ordered flooring, countertops, and appliances. She took home paint swatches to run past her friend on Monday, and went on Home Advisor to check out landscapers.

Then she called Deke and told him her plans. He offered to come help paint. But she didn't think that wise, as she wasn't sure how to explain him to her neighbors—who had three children that attended her school.

He didn't want to accept her reasons for him not coming

to see her, or hers for not coming to see him, as he desperately needed to hold her close. To know she was safe. To confirm she was still his. But after listening to how excited she was about getting all these projects under way, and knowing that her selling the house would be a big step in securing her future with him, he agreed to give her the space she needed . . . for a little while.

Shaw worked on packing everything up and either giving things away to friends or taking the items to charity thrift shops. She allowed herself ten boxes of personal items, which turned out to be mostly treasured books. She figured she could get ten boxes in her car. No way was she hiring a mover or towing a trailer. She was determined to purge all but the things she truly cared about. Working in the evenings and on weekends she was doggedly transforming the so-so middle-class family home into a stunner that would bring a full price offer from the first prospective buyer to see it. She was sure of it.

She organized. She packed. She cleaned. She caulked. She painted. And she oversaw all the projects she had contracted out. Her goal was to have the house ready to list by the last day of school. And it was. The sign went up and the listing went online on the very first day of summer. By then she had given her notice and sent out resumes to schools in four North Carolina counties and two South Carolina counties. She did not tell Deke this, as she knew he was counting on her moving to L.A. And she had thought about it. Every single day she had thought about it.

She just didn't see how a relationship between them could work. It terrified her to think of moving to L.A., one of the most expensive areas in the country to live in, and then having everything fall apart after a few months.

Even though Stephanie was comatose and in an institution, she was still very much alive and a big part of Deke's life. He wouldn't be able to marry, maybe not even have someone live with him as long as she was alive. He was an important man. Many people were counting on him. And from a business perspective, he had to be respectable. She understood that. She just wasn't sure she could risk her heart and have things go kaflooey again.

She wanted someone to come home to, she wanted kids, and she even wanted a dog. Matt had been allergic to dog hair, cat hair, dander, feathers, dust mites, leaves and mold. He would not let her even consider having a pet, not even a goldfish.

At night, exhausted from cleaning out the basement, sorting out every whatnot in the cabinets and drawers, and scrubbing the windowsills and windows panes until they shone, she fell into bed. But then, during the night, she reached for Deke. Waking up and finding herself alone, she cried. Even though they were talking nearly every day, she missed him terribly.

Several times a week Kurt texted her and cheered her with corny puns. And her mom called, reassuring her, telling her that everything she was doing was leading her back home.

Chapter 114—Deke & Shaw
A Time for Every Purpose Under Heaven

When Shaw woke up on a rainy Monday in June, she had a feeling it was going to be a bad week. And it was. Not for her—for Deke.

Deke's text on Monday at 11:00am:

A problem at the plant produced forty cases of drugs without the tamperproof shield. The housekeeper's vacuum blew up in my closet ruining most of my clothes, and my Jag got a star in the windshield that developed into a crack the size of a Joshua Tree in no time flat and no glass company this side of the Mason-Dixon line has a replacement windshield. I feel like Joe Btfsplk's best friend.

Shaw:

Who's Joe Btfsplk? Seriously, a name with no vowels?

Deke:

He was a character in the comic strip Li'l Abner. He was depicted with a small, dark, rain cloud over his head. He brought disastrous misfortune to everyone around him. If he crossed your path, you were affected in a very bad way.

Shaw:

Li'l Abner? How old are you?

Deke

I'm thirty-six. The comic strip ran from 1934-1977. But it's iconic. It lives on for all generations.

Shaw:

I missed that one. I was a Betty Boop fan.

Kurt's text later that night:

Deke wanted me to tell you that Joe Btfsplk's curse continues. He lost his phone down an elevator shaft in the factory that's being revamped. He'll have a new one by morning, with the same number.

Ten minutes later, Kurt texted again:

He said to tell you not to worry about all the naked pictures he took of you. Everything was backed up to the "Cloud," so he still has them.

Do you want me to off him so I can be the new man in your life?

She had to laugh at their antics. It was so unusual to see a boss/friend relationship grow and flourish so well. It was comforting to her to know that should the need arise, Kurt would protect Deke with his life.

Deke's text Wednesday night at 10:

Stephanie died in her sleep last night. God I am so tired. Today there were people in and out of my house bringing me all manner of food. Don't they realize that I just need to be alone right now? That I'm not at all hungry? I am a widower now. And my house is full of women who want to rectify that as soon as possible. They were lining up at the gate with casserole dishes by noon. When I come out of this fog, please be there for me. The things I have to do now outnumber the hours there are in a day. I'm told all this busy work is designed to keep one's mind off the finality of losing someone you love. Don't let me lose you too. I'm sorry I'm such a wreck. I don't know how long it will take to process this. But please know you are foremost on my mind even though my thoughts are chaotic with organizing her funeral.

Kurt called her on Thursday just to check in with her. He told her that when Deke found out that Stephanie had died, he was furious with himself for not being there. He had been staying with a friend at his beach house in Malibu after the bad day he'd had on Monday. He had driven up after work on Tuesday and had likely been surfing when she died from a blood clot that lodged in her heart. He had missed the convalescent home's first four calls. The funeral was to be on Saturday. Kurt thought she should attend. She said it wouldn't be right. He said he was really worried about his boss, that just her presence would be uplifting for Deke. He ended by telling her to please think about it. She said she would and she did. All night long she thought about it.

In the morning, after much inner turmoil, she called the airline and booked an economy-class ticket. When it wasn't upgraded by the time she boarded, she knew Kurt hadn't mentioned her arrival to Deke.

In the receiving line, she watched as Deke looked blankly into the sea of faces as he shook hands and bent to hear words of sympathy. There were fifteen people flanking him. The man next to him she suspected was Deke's father, as there was an uncanny resemblance around the eyes, the same aquiline nose, and the same full head of hair, albeit the older man's was liberally streaked with gray.

Stephanie's family constituted the rest of the funeral party lined up to receive condolences. She knew from reading the memorial program and where people had been sitting, that their familial connection was to Stephanie and not to Deke.

When she stepped in front of Deke, she watched, as his eyes grew wide. His demeanor changed. She noted that even his father had picked up on it.

She gripped his hand in both of hers as tears filled her eyes. "I'm so sorry Deke. It's not your fault you weren't with her at the end. You know her spirit left her at the accident. Don't torture yourself like I've been doing. It's not our fault we weren't there; we've had to go on with our lives. It's what they would have wanted for us. Whatever you think you did wrong, she forgives you. Cherish the good memories; it's what she would want."

His face contorted as if stricken by what she was saying, but she saw a flicker of light enter his irises. Yet his practiced nod of appreciation was more automatic than personal as they were forced to part with the line moving forward. She looked back, but he was already dutifully acknowledging the next person and nodding to the words they were saying but that he was not hearing.

She couldn't stay for the reception. It hurt too much to see him like this. Unsmiling, shoulders slumped with grief, eyes blank with the terror of the finality of losing the woman he loved. When she walked out of the church's reception hall and down the steps, Kurt was waiting. She gave him a hug and he kissed her cheek.

"You going back now?"

"No, my flight isn't 'til tomorrow morning."

"He's going to need you, Shaw."

"He'll be fine. He just needs to get over the shock. Everything is a bit overwhelming at first. He'll settle."

"He won't be happy without you."

"I'm not sure either of us deserves to be happy right now. We just need to acclimate and then begin to move on."

"You two have something special."

"I think we both feel that we stole something and that we'll feel guilty if we keep it."

"Can I take you someplace?"

"Thank you, but I rented a car."

"If he asks, can I tell him where you're staying?"

"Sure. But I don't think he'll ask. I'm at The Hampton six miles from here. Room 319."

She stretched up on her tiptoes and managed to kiss his jaw. "Take care Hot Rod, and spend as much time as you can with Emily. Little girls need their daddies."

He squeezed her shoulders. "I will. You take care of you. And don't be surprised if you have a visitor at your door tonight."

"I don't want a visitor."

He grinned at her, "I don't believe you. But if that's true, don't open the door."

At one in the morning there was a knock on her door. When she asked who it was, the answer came back as simply, "It's me."

But she knew the gravely voice; would know it anywhere.

She unlocked the door and opened it wide. Deke stood there, still in his funeral suit, sans tie and rumpled. His jawline had developed a heavy shadow in the twelve hours since she'd last seen him. His eyes were bloodshot and his words slurred as he said, "I shouldna come but I need you. Can I come in?"

She stepped aside. "Of course." It surprised her how formal she sounded.

She was wearing a long silk nightgown held up with thin satin straps. As soon as the door closed behind him, he reached out and lifted the straps off her shoulders. The gown dropped and pooled onto the carpet at her feet.

One hand went around her back to pull her close. The other cupped a full breast. Her nipple pebbled from exposure to the air-conditioning and his thumb flicked over it. His mouth landed on hers, taking possession with a foraging tongue. Their moans mingled in the entryway before he lifted her into his arms and carried her to the bed.

She sobbed as he smothered her breasts with kisses then took each nipple into his mouth, laved it, then tugged until it was firm and hard and glistening.

Looking down at her chest, he murmured, "Your breasts are so beautiful. I dream about these." He brought them together and bestowed soft kisses all over them.

She smiled up at his adoring face. He had the lopsided smile of a drunk, but she didn't care. "You taste different, not like bourbon."

"Toasted Stephanie with friends tonight with scotch. She drank scothch, and not good scotha either—a leftover from her college days. It's already giving me a thick brain. Gonna have a head tomorra I fear."

She ran her fingers through his unkempt hair and brought his face down for a kiss. He was drunk, but he was adorable. And she wanted him so very much.

She helped him undress and felt for his wallet in his pants pocket. She was disappointed when she couldn't find a condom, but sloughed it off. *After all, who thought to carry a condom to their wife's funeral for God's sake?* She was kind of relieved that he hadn't thought he'd have a use for one.

Remembering all the times she had tried to get pregnant and failed, except for that one time she'd had the ectopic pregnancy and lost a fallopian tube, and along with it, fifty percent of her future chances, she threw caution to the wind and climbed onto his prone body. He might be inebriated, but his cock was jutting up proud and pointing to the ceiling when she took it in her hand and led it to the throbbing place inside her. She was so wet she accommodated his girth easier than she usually did at this angle. She looked down at his face and saw his huge grin.

"Ride 'em cowgirl. I'm too whipped to flip you and take charge, so have at it, my beauty. Ride your stud."

She would later recall how prophetic those words were. But for now, she took control and rode his cock as if it was a horn on a saddle. A mighty horn that entered and left her body with abandon. So fast and so hard, she feared if she stopped she'd hurt him. She felt her body begin to spasm at the same time he groaned her name, mumbled a few unintelligible words, and shot the essence of weeks of wanting her and not having her, into the deepest recess in her body.

Then, as if wanting her to keep his essence inside for as long as possible, he managed to flip her while keeping his cock in place. But then all consciousness left him, and he collapsed with his full weight on top of her.

She was able to inch her arms and legs wider to spread out his weight some so she could accommodate his dead weight without suffocating. His face was pressed into her neck and she could feel his steady breathing. She knew it might be hours before she could turn him so she just stroked his broad back and ran her fingers through the curls at the nape of his neck. And she whispered over and over again, that she loved him.

When her alarm went off at five, she was able to shove him over onto his back. He landed beside her, arms and legs akimbo, not having left the stupor of his slumber for a single second. Within minutes, vigorous snoring began. The guttural noises, the type that only those inebriated and in the deepest realms of slumber can make—with the walls seemingly absorbing the exhalations and expanding, before another round emanated and the walls contracted.

She had to laugh out loud. Not at all worried that she'd wake him. She had never heard such sounds coming from an inebriated man. And her husband could best anyone holding a beer can or a solo cup. She laughed again as she moved gingerly to the side of the bed and stretched out her back. Lord, that man was heavy.

She made her way to the bathroom; aware she had his cum dripping down her thigh. It was running down the side of her knee by the time she made it to the en suite. She turned on the shower and clipped her long hair on top of her head. As soon as the water was warm she stepped inside and began to wash the evidence of their lovemaking from her body.

She had to hurry if she was going to make her plane. She had already packed and arranged to take the hotel shuttle as she'd returned the rental when she got back from the funeral. But she needed to leave a note for Deke. She couldn't just leave without saying goodbye. She'd meant to tell him in person that she was moving back to North Carolina. But the funeral reception hadn't been the place to do that, and he'd been in no shape to process that information last night.

She was pretty sure it would be goodbye. The distance was just too great. He was free to do whatever he wanted now, after he grieved for his wife. And she knew that young beautiful women were already flocking around the new widower, preening for his attention and offering to be the type of woman he needed—sophisticated, cultured, smart, stunning, and adventurous in bed.

Statistically, she knew he'd likely be remarried within a year. Ensconced within a new growing family within two. The woman who had been a drug mule for her husband, whose vibrator he'd held in the palm of his hand upon their first meeting, would soon be long forgotten.

Toweling off, she mentally composed a note, pretty much encapsulating those two thoughts, and then with a towel around her she went over to the desk to write it. She dressed in the clothes she had laid out on the easy chair, slipped her bag of toiletries into her backpack, and zipped it shut. Looking around, she couldn't help but allow her gaze to fall on the gorgeous man sleeping in the bed, still rattling the walls. She had just applied lipstick, but leaned over anyway and kissed his cheek, leaving a kiss print for him to discover upon awakening.

Then she grabbed her purse, picked up her backpack, opened the door and left. She too, had to remember, that she had a new life ahead of her as well. Her grieving had been done over the years, as she watched her husband become pretty much the antithesis to the man he had been when she married him. And, remembering the lewd picture he had carried on his phone of her, she wondered if she had ever truly known him. Like she'd known Deke.

With Deke, there'd been some surprises. But she felt as if she truly knew him, down deep. Enough to know, that any woman who managed to land him would be beyond lucky, she'd be blessed.

The sun was just coming over the horizon when she boarded the shuttle, and as the tiny bus chugged its way through the traffic at the airport, she couldn't help feeling that she was leaving her heart behind.

Chapter 115—Deke & Shaw
Going Home

While Shaw was waiting for her flight to board, she finally remembered to turn her phone back on. She had received a text last night saying her agent had a full price cash offer on her house. All her hard work had paid off. It was bittersweet, but she was anxious to get home. She missed her mom and dad and could not wait to spend time on Sunset Beach.

She met with her agent as soon as she got back from L.A. and handed over the keys. She was so organized that all she had to do was load the ten boxes into her car and begin the drive home. Her agent was going to take care of everything else by overnight mail.

She had mapped out the route she would take on an Atlas and loaded her parents' address into the GPS on her phone.

Deke had called her twice since she had returned home, but it had gone to voice mail, because she had been busy packing and hadn't heard the phone ring. By the time she noticed the calls, it was too late to call him back. She worked until two a.m. making sure everything was ready, then having no place to sleep, and having already packed all the bedding besides, she decided to get a head start on traffic and locked up the house and left.

She was in Colorado by 7 a.m. By ten a.m. she was in need of a nap, so she pulled over to a rest area and dozed until her stomach reminded her that she hadn't eaten since the morning before. And that had been only a handful of mini-donuts and some coffee. She pulled into a Denny's, and as she sat waiting to order, she checked her phone. Deke had left another message. "Please call me. We need to talk."

She was afraid to call him back. She had a plan. She'd sold her house. She was moving back home. She knew he had the power to change all that—to talk her out of leaving. So she texted him: *I am driving. I'll call you tonight.*

She pulled into a motel in Kansas at nine, got a room and fell asleep on the bed without bothering to unmake it. At 1:40 she woke to get some water and realized it was too late to call Deke. She'd call him in the morning.

She punched in his number at eight o'clock and he answered on the first ring. "It's about time. I have been worried sick. Where are you?"

"Kansas."

"Kansas?"

"Yes. I'm driving home. The house sold for the asking price to a cash buyer so I left everything to the agent to handle and packed up and left. I need to go home Deke. I miss my parents. I need to see my mom. I need to see my beach. I need to eat grits and sausage gravy."

"What about me?"

"You need some time."

"I don't need time. I need you. Where do your parents live, exactly?"

"Calabash, North Carolina."

"That's close to Sunset Beach."

"Yes, six miles actually."

"I own a beach house with some of my fraternity brothers there. We have a reunion there each July. I wasn't planning on going this year, but I've just changed my mind. When I get there, can we spend some time together?"

"Sure. I'd like that."

"Okay. I'll text you the details. And Shaw?"

"Yes?"

"Don't make any permanent plans. I want you in my life."

She sighed. "Deke . . . we both need time to process things."

"I love you Shaw. I've already processed that. That's not going to change."

Her heart fluttered to hear the words. But still, L.A.? She didn't think she could do that. "I love you too, Deke. I just have so much to think about now."

"I know. Your life is your own now, for the first time in a long time. That's a big change for you."

"That's just it, and I kinda like it. It's a freedom I haven't had in . . . well, forever. And you . . . you're free to see other women openly now, don't you want to?"

"No. Not at all. There is no one I want to be with other than you."

"The thought of living in L.A. terrifies me."

"I don't have to live in California."

"You bought that big massive house . . ."

"As an investment. I buy and sell property all the time."

"You love that house."

"I love you more. Drive safely and have a good visit with your folks. Let's talk when I get there."

"You're gonna use sex to sway me."

"You bet your ass."

She laughed. "Okay. Text me the dates you'll be in North Carolina."

"I can be there tonight."

"Well then you'll beat me. I won't be there for a week."

"I hate that you're doing this cross country drive by yourself."

"I like it actually. It's giving me a lot of time to think."

"Okay, you think. About me . . . eating you, fucking you, kissing you senseless . . ."

"I already do."

"That's my girl. I'll see you in a few weeks, but I want to talk to you every day, okay?"

"Okay."

"Be safe. You are my world."

"Aww, that's sweet. 'Bye."

She hung up and went to shower. The drive ahead didn't

seem as long as it had. Deke was going to come see her in North Carolina. She marveled at the thought that he owned a share in a beach house that was so close to her hometown.

Four days later she pulled into her parents' driveway. Her mom came running out to see her, and her dad did a pretty good job keeping up with her using his walker. As she hugged them both, she looked around. This was home. God, it felt good to be here.

Chapter 116—Deke & Shaw
The Little Blue Cross

Shaw sat down on the closed toilet seat and stared at the stick. More specifically at the intersecting blue lines. She was pregnant. Her eyes bugged wide at the thought. She took a deep breath. And then she laughed.

She was pregnant. She was going to have a baby—Deke's baby. She let the feeling of euphoria wash over her. A baby. Her . . . pregnant. She didn't think it would happen after, well . . . not happening for so long.

She went looking for a padded envelope. Then she mailed the test to the address Deke had given her, to the house he'd be at in a few days. She'd wait to tell her parents. Deke had to be the first person she told.

She walked around in a daze, stopping and staring as each new thought occurred to her, smiling as she thought about buying things for a layette, and continually counting the months on her fingers to settle on the due date.

She wondered at Deke's reaction. Would he be happy about it? He'd been drunk at the time, and she, being the responsible party, had thrown caution to the wind. Would he want her to keep it? Regardless . . . she definitely would.

Three days later, on the date Deke said he'd arrive at the beach house, she got in her car and drove there. She'd already had three reconnaissance trips, scoping out the house—two from the street side and one from the beach side. It was an impressive beach house, one of the grandest on the beach for sure. She couldn't wait to see the inside.

The circular drive was full of high-end cars. Her six-year-old Honda SUV looked shabby in comparison when she pulled into the driveway. But she stepped out proudly, and walked up the tall flight of steps to the impressive front door and rang the bell. It took a minute before she heard steps, the door unlocking, then opening. Deke stood smiling at her. Behind him a beautiful blonde in only a towel stood behind him on the stairs calling out, "Who is it Deke?"

Shaw took one look at the gorgeous stunner who was trying to keep her big boobs covered by a beach towel, and her stomach churned. She knew from the past few days' experience that she had mere seconds to find a suitable place to upchuck. She spun around to run back down the steps but Deke managed to snag her arm and pull her back to face him. "Whoa. It's not what you think. Emma is my best friend's fiancé."

He managed to turn her to face him just as she lost control of her stomach contents. He was wearing a tropical shirt with big white gardenias splashed all over the front and tan linen shorts. She ruined both. Along with his leather sandals.

The woman laughed heartily. "Well that ends the mystery of who sent the pregnancy test!"

In that brief moment, she realized she hadn't put a return address on the envelope, and that this woman, who was thankfully someone else's fiancé, was going to become a good friend, and that Deke, covered in vomit, was the man she loved.

"Shaw, what the hell?" Then it dawned on him. Ever since that package had arrived two days ago with the positive test inside, the speculation of who was pregnant had the whole house of bachelors in an uproar. "*You* sent that pregnancy test? *You're* the one who's pregnant!"

Heedless of the remnants of Ritz crackers and her stomach bile all over him, he picked her up and swung her around. "We're going to have a baby!"

As far as reactions went—considering the circumstances—this one was pretty spectacular. After swinging her around in sheer jubilation, he lifted her into his arms and carried her into the house. "Clear the way, we're heading for a shower. Everybody this is Shaw."

There were people leaning over the catwalk, moving aside on the wide staircase, and ducking into rooms down the long hallway as Deke carried Shaw tight to his chest into what turned out to be his room.

Within moments he had stripped them both and led her into a walk-in shower big enough for six people. As the hot water caressed them both, he caressed her belly. "So it's true? You sent that package?"

"Yes. I forgot to add your name after I looked up the address on my phone. And I didn't include a return address because I was between homes."

He laughed. "Every man in here has been wondering if it was meant for him. Until you barfed all over me, it didn't occur to me that I could be the one it was intended for."

"Sorry. I was trying to give you a head's up in case you wanted to get back to L.A. before I showed up with the news."

"Why would you think I would do that?"

She shrugged. "I don't know. Most men aren't thrilled to hear they got someone they're not married to pregnant. And it was all my fault. I wanted you, even though I couldn't find a condom in your pants. I thought it unlikely I could conceive after trying to for years with no success."

"I couldn't be happier. Wait a minute."

He walked out of the shower, found the pocket in his soiled shorts and pulled out a small box. Then he returned to the shower and knelt at her feet, the water sluicing off her and hitting him in the chest. He flipped open the velvet case with his thumb. "Shaw Marin, will you marry me?"

She looked down at the man, who still had part of a Ritz cracker stuck to the side of his neck and smiled. "Yes."

He slid the ring onto her finger, and as she moved it around in the light marveling at the huge diamond in the impressive setting, he washed them both.

An hour later, reclining his head on his arm beside her on the bed, looking down at her beautiful face as she stared adoringly up at him, he asked if she had thought up any names for the baby yet.

"Twins run in my family. If we have twin boys we could name one Juan and one Amal. That way I only have to carry one picture around. 'Cause if you see Juan, you've seen Amal. "

He groaned. "Tell me you don't have a punny name for a girl."

"If it's a girl then you get to name her. 'Cause I'm sure she's going to be a daddy's girl."

"You got that right. Whatever we have and whatever we name it, I already love this baby." He patted her tummy.

"Is living in North Carolina going to be an option?" she asked.

"I've already picked out a place in Raleigh that would be perfect for a new headquarters, and there are a lot of abandoned factories just begging to be retooled in North Carolina."

"Then let's get married!"

"Name the date."

"Today, tomorrow?"

"That soon?"

"Changing your mind?"

"Not a chance."

"We both just lost our spouses, so let's not make a big deal about it. How would you feel about a wedding on the beach?"

"Any way I can call you mine works for me. Let me go make a few phone calls. Meanwhile, you get dressed so I can introduce you around. Properly this time, without the vomit and with my ring on your hand. You are going to love my crazy circle of friends and they are going to adore you."

Chapter 117—Rutger
An Unanswered Letter

He seldom drank. He just didn't think it was healthy in the long run. And he was all about health, sports, body image . . . always had been. Since cross-country running during high school, he'd pretty much been dedicated to making his body the best it could be. But tonight? Tonight he was going to drink.

He'd asked Kyle what they had on hand in the wine category, because despite evidence to the contrary for tequila, he truly thought hard liquor was a burden on the liver.

Kyle produced a bottle of Prosecco from the walk-in wine cooler that he swore would not give him a hangover, even if he drank the whole bottle. He said he'd had a case shipped from Italy around the holidays and had several leftover, adding that bottled for America, it had been a Gold Medal Award Winner at the San Francisco Wine Competition in 2016. Kyle knew he didn't drink very often so he knew he never drank inferior wine.

"It has a bouquet of peach and apple," Kyle said as he deftly opened the bottle with a fancy opener, "and finishes with a delicate rush of bubbles."

"Cut the crap, Kyle. You've sold me. Fill the cup." Rutger held out a blue Solo cup. Kyle grimaced.

"You're not going to drink this out of that." He reached behind him and pulled down a champagne flute from a high cabinet and began filling it. Then he handed it to Rutger.

Rutger took a sip, scrunched his nose and tilted his head back and forth. "Yeah, pretty decent. But this isn't going to be enough. Here fill this," he shoved the Solo cup back at him, "I'll refill from this."

Kyle turned and went into the utility room where he grabbed a champagne bucket from a shelf and then dipped it into the free standing icemaker they had around the corner. He capped the bottle with a Metrokane screw stopper and then shoved it into the ice.

"Refill from this. I will not let you lose those precious bubbles."

Rutger took the bucket with the bottle in it and tucked it under his arm. With his other hand he picked up the flute. "Fine, fine. Heaven forbid we let it go flat. I'll be in my room if anyone needs me. But they better not. I have an email to answer that I've been putting off for a week."

"Another offer for a product endorsement?"

"No. An offer from a woman who wants to sub for me."

"Substitute for you?"

"No. She fancies herself to be the perfect *submissive*. She's looking for a Dom."

"And you're drinking because you don't know how to say no?"

"No. I'm drinking because I'm thinking about saying yes."

Chapter 118—Rutger
Twitchy Palm

Rutger put the ice bucket on top of the dresser, using a hand towel as a coaster for the ebony wood. Then he took the glass of Prosecco to his nightstand, and plopped down on the bed, his back to the padded headboard. He pulled his laptop from his backpack and took the sleeve off. And after it was set up and running on his lap, he let out a long sigh.

Grabbing the glass he took a long swallow. Then looked at the glass, it was nearly empty. He cursed. He shouldn't have listened to Kyle. He was going to be refilling this puny glass over and over and over again. He finished the rest and put the empty glass on the night table.

Talking to himself he said, "Well, before I answer this Etty girl, I guess I'd better reread her emails." He used his thumb on the built-in mouse to pull up his email program and to click on the message thread from one Pauline O. Ethel Rossi.

Mr. Rummel:

They say that people find a way to live up to their name. I can tell you for a fact that for the last ten years I have found a way *not* to live up to mine. My name is Pauline O. Ethel Rossi. My mom tried once to change my last name to Roissy, but the judge was well read and wouldn't allow it.

If what I read about you in *Men's Health* is true, you know what I am referring to. But I'll spell it out anyway, in case you don't. Pauline Réage was the pen name of Anne Desclos who wrote *The Story of O*, which takes place in a private chateau in Roissy, France. She is probably the most famous submissive ever divined.

Of course, she's fictional, whereas I am not.

When I was sixteen, my mother gave me a copy of the infamous book that was an obsession with her, and told me to read it. Suffice it to say my life has been difficult since then, knowing my mother wished me humiliated, beaten, whipped, mutilated and with impossibly sore knees.

Of course I didn't live up to her expectations and bring home a Neanderthal who got pleasure from my pain and who would enjoy sharing me with his buddies in front of others. I fear I went the opposite way and became a good Catholic girl even though I was Episcopalian.

So for ten years, I ignored my first name and the O that stands for nothing, and went by Etty, short for Ethel (she also loved the *I love Lucy* show, but she didn't care for redheads).

I have been with a total of five men, none of them longer than eight months, despite one proposing. While they seemed perfectly content with the sex we were having, I was not. I have yet to achieve orgasm. And I'll bet by now that you know why.

Despite fighting it since I lost my virginity at seventeen, I find I am craving a man to control me in the bedroom. A man who will have power over me and my pleasure, even if it means tolerating a certain level of pain. Not much mind you. I want to submit to a man who will dominate me and train me for his pleasure as well as for mine. Of course, I have no idea how to do this.

I have been following you for years as you support several of the charities I support. I run marathons for Multiple Sclerosis, Girls on the Run, Optimist Club of Coronado, Cancer Survivors, Kids Run, and have even run the Boston Marathon twice since the bombing. So I am physically capable of being the submissive to a powerful Dom such as yourself, and an Ironman in the flesh.

So you probably think this is a bit forward of me. And yeah, it is. But everything I read on the subject says to choose someone you trust. I know no one living the lifestyle of D/s and I am afraid to go to a club and take my chances. And in case you're wondering about dear ol' Mom . . . she died last year about a month after I decided I might want to see about living up to my name. I never got to talk to her about it. I talked to a few people who showed up at her funeral that I had never met. It seems she was pretty popular with a few swing clubs in her day and had once subbed for a man named "Danny," who said she gave the best head he'd ever had—a truly strange thing to hear at your mother's funeral from a man who looked like Willie Nelson.

So . . . my dilemma, and forgive me for being so forward, but would you be interested in teaching me to be a submissive? If not for you, than for someone who trusts and admires you, and supports your work?

I am afraid. But I can't fight this anymore. And I don't have the money to go to a place like Roissy. If one even exists.

So . . . can I please call you Master Rutger at any time in the near future?

Pauline,
and owning it.

I Ξ

Rutger read the letter six times, noting on the last pass through that she had ended with the symbol for dominance and the symbol for passive/submissive. Not particularly well known unless you ran in those circles, or as she had said, read a lot.

He had read the letter every day this week, several

times on the days he had been traveling as it was saved on his phone. After four days she had sent her picture. Nothing lewd or suggestive as many had done. Hers was just a headshot, like something taken from a yearbook or passport. He'd actually copied that too, taking a photo with his phone so that he could enlarge it.

She was lovely. Truly lovely. Beguilingly fresh looking despite the nature of her letter. She had dark hair; it appeared to be long as she had it wrapped in a messy knot on top of her head with a pencil stuck through it. She was wearing dark framed glasses that gave her a bookish look, and he was reminded of the stereotypical librarian in the black pencil skirt and white blouse stripping everything off until all that was left were those studious looking black-framed glasses. Her smile was genuine and he couldn't help running his thumb over her bottom lip and being disappointed to feel only the glass screen of his phone. The more he looked at it, and focused on her clear perceptive eyes the more enchanted he became.

By day five, he got a hard on just looking at her picture. By day six, he was captivated by those lips and the promise of things to come if he accepted her offer.

It had been a week now. He had to do something. Answer her in some way, even if it was to say no or to hand her off to someone he trusted. Or leave her to her own devices and recommend a club.

Two hours later he left his room in search of another bottle of Casa Catelli. Kyle was in the kitchen mixing something up in a big ceramic bowl. It looked like he was making bread.

Rutger plopped the ice bucket on the counter saying, "I need some more of this."

"They sell it at Lowes you know," Kyle said as he wiped his hands on a towel hung at his waist and walked to the wine cooler.

"Yeah. But it won't be cold. Or free."

Kyle laughed. "You've been holed up in there a long time. Haven't you got that email answered yet?"

"Almost. Just need a little more courage before writing something and pressing send."

"You might want to switch to vodka."

"Even I know you don't switch ponies in the middle of the stream. I'll probably have a headache tomorrow as it is."

Kyle twisted the cork barehanded this time and it gave a loud healthy pop. "Suit yourself. But mind your head. Remember you're not used to this. Here, I'll help you out." He grabbed another flute from the high cabinet and filled it, then raised it to his lips.

"Mmm. I forgot how good this stuff is. You're not getting the last two bottles. So drink your courage and go tell the lady you'd love to spank her. Or hell, give me her email address and I'll spank her for you."

Rutger grabbed the open bottle from Kyle's hand and sneered at him. "You just pound your dough. I've got this." He took the bottle and returned to his room.

Kyle laughed after hearing his door slam. And turning back to his bowl of dough said *sotto voce*, "I think you have a twitchy palm my man, and you'd better find a nice fine ass to smack it against."

Chapter 119—Rutger
Questions

He sat up in bed, his shoulders hunched over his laptop, his fingers poised. Nothing. He had no idea what to say to this woman. He pushed the laptop off his lap onto the comforter and sat back against the headboard, throwing an arm over his eyes.

What did he *want* to say to her?

He moved his arm and stared at the ceiling fan as it went around and around. Fan . . . hmm. Was she just a fan? A groupie or something. He was famous, sort of. He was wealthy. Very. And he wasn't bad looking. A few times he'd jokingly been called Tatum, so he guessed that wasn't a bad thing.

But she didn't sound all swoony and adoring like most fans did. She seemed kind of down-to-Earth really. Could he hand her off? He knew a few guys who would love the opportunity to hook up with an eager sub. And she was a knock out. Very pretty, probably with an athletic bod due to running. Jake from his gym would hop on this in a New York minute. But just the thought of some other man touching her made his skin heat. Naw, Jake had a mean streak. He wasn't one to train a newbie. He liked it hard and rough and was known to leave bruises. John, his agent was into the lifestyle. Maybe he'd be interested. But then he remembered he was bi. She might not like that element. She had mentioned more than once that she wanted a man. And probably not multiples. At least not initially.

He threw his legs over the side of the bed and stood. Then paced. Running his hand alongside his jaw, he frowned as he tried to figure this dilemma out. He wished he knew more about this woman. That was it! He stopped pacing. Then turned to face his laptop and snapped his fingers. Yes, that was it! Answer her questions with some of his own.

He grabbed the laptop off the bed, sat on the edge, and

settled it on his lap. His fingers flew over the keys.

Etty (I don't feel I can call you Pauline at this time, knowing what it means to you),

That was quite a lot to unload. I am sorry about your mom. Both with her death and the issues you have that are now unresolved. I'm sure you've figured it out by now that it takes all kinds to spin this planet we're on, and that you shouldn't hold anyone's lifestyle choices against them.

I read *The Story of O* when I was in high school. It was kind of "must reading" for guys who were too busy with sports to have girl friends and needed inspiration for jacking off. I've never heard of anyone liking it so much that they named their kid after the writer and the main character though. A bold move considering your last name was already Rossi.

About your question . . . I must admit, I am grappling with the answer. Since you mentioned that *Men's Health* article, I'm assuming you read the blog article that garnered their attention and hence the interview. When I wrote *"The Perfect Submissive,"* it was years ago when I was just getting into it. And quite honestly, I was studying some humanities stuff at Stanford that was boring the crap out of me and so I often fantasized during lectures. I hadn't meant for it to be published but one of my ex-girlfriends found it and thought it would be good revenge for me dumping her. It kind of backfired on her and ended up boosting my stock and sending sales through the roof. I actually tried to turn down the *Men's health* interview but my CFO wouldn't let me. Said it was the best free advertising we could ever hope for. But my point is this, if you read the piece I wrote, then you know the perfect sub is the person you desire to please more than anything else. We don't have the foundation for that.

There is so much involved with D/s. Chemistry being major, trust being mandatory, and desire being necessary. Then there are personality issues. I like my women snarky, not meek and mild. I don't like to sense fear, it's a huge turn off for me. And then there are the limits. If you've done your research, then you know that there are so many things to go over before a relationship can even begin.

So here's what I suggest. Let's get to know each other. First through email, then if things go well, we can meet and see if we have those invisible qualities that are so important to a successful match.

I am currently unattached as I am training for an upcoming Ironman competition, and I have a bum foot right now. Please don't pass that on. If the media got a hold of that, they'd have a field day.

If this works for you, we can start with some basic questions:

Where do you live? From your email address it looks as if you're in California. San Francisco area? San Diego?

What do you do for a living?

What kind of time will you have available to establish a rapport?

And once we get going, if everything is simpatico, are you available to travel?

Most importantly, the origin of your name aside, why do you feel the submissive life is for you? Is the vanilla sex you've been having all that bad?

Let's start with that and see how things go.

FYI: I have homes in L.A., North Carolina, New York State, and Vermont. You already know what I do for a living. I own several sports companies and I promote and support athletic events. My time is flexible, although I do have meetings to attend and weekend sports events to attend all year long. I travel a lot. Both continentally and internationally. However, I am my own man, I know how to delegate, and I have very good executives and employees backing me up, so if I need time off, I take it.

Rutger
I☰

Love the symbol. Not everyone knows that in red with a black background, it's our flag.

So . . . if we set this up, are you willing to show up in a taxi and let me cut your bra off in front of the driver?
Her answer came a few minutes later.

Chapter 120—Etty
Answers

Etty vs. Pauline

I live in the Coronado area but it's really only a condo I park my stuff in. I don't even have houseplants, as I'm not here to water them. I travel a lot for my job. I work for a non-profit that my grandparents founded forty years ago. We arrange and promote sporting events such as half marathons, marathons, Walk 4 you-name-the-organization, dance and gymnastic competitions, highland-type games, summer camps for disadvantaged children, winter ski camps for disabled children and adults, cheerleading and computer camps, and special exercise event cruises.

We basically raise a lot of money, and then put it back where it's needed the most. To me, that's always the hardest part of the job. So many organizations are worthy and I want to help them all. I am on the board because of my family's legacy, but I prefer the organizational side. I have thirty employees who alternately love or hate me depending on my mood. I am hoping a kinky lifestyle will send me to work with a smile on my face more often. Oh, and about getting to work? I usually fly. I have a pilot's license and a Cirrus jet I keep at San Diego International. No frills and very small as I want to funnel as much money as possible to the charities. I am Simon Legree about administrative expenses, but California traffic is ludicrous. I have two competent assistants and I try very hard to delegate and not let everyone rely on me to get things done, so with a little advance planning, my time is my own.

So that answers your first four questions, now for the biggie:

Why do I feel like the life of a submissive would suit me? The sex I've had has not been satisfying. Though pleasurable, I always feel unfulfilled and empty when it's over. After a while, the men I've been with sense this and stop calling. They don't want to work this hard to achieve so little. I fear I might have given one very sweet aviation mechanic a complex. He asked me what he was doing wrong. When I told him it was my fault and that he should punish me with a paddling, he developed a stutter and suddenly remembered an engine he had to work on.

Orgasms are non-existent or of no consequence, even by my own hand. Although I think I got close to something significant last week envisioning myself naked and being spanked by a man who looked remarkably like you. But then the phone rang.

As I said before, I think I need to cede control and put the power with a man who knows what he's doing and who knows how to get the right response from different punishments. My doctor says there's no physical reason I can't achieve orgasm, I've got all the right parts.

There's one factor I have neglected to mention so far. I've darned near driven myself crazy trying to figure out where the hell this particular craving could have come from, but if I've analyzed it right, textbook-wise, I think I may be into humiliation. If you could enlighten me as to how one develops that twisted kink, I would truly appreciate it.

So . . . it should be obvious to you that I need to have a partner who knows what he's doing or I could be in for a whole world of hurt. I haven't been able to develop enough of a relationship with anyone to be able to ask for what I want. Nor have I been with anyone who would know how to give it to me. I think I need a specialist. Or in my case, an experienced Dominant.

I'm begging you (I understand that's what Dom's need).

To your last question: A resounding YES! And I have just the bra in mind—a white demi-cup that's all lace so I can spill right into your hands.

Chapter 121—Rutger
A Well-Laid Plan

Sweet Jesus. His eyes bugged wide on those last sentences. He couldn't help but imagine it. Her being into humiliation. Her on her knees begging. Him cutting off her bra and having her breasts tumble out while another man watched.

He had resisted Googling her and finding out more about her. But now he had to see what her public persona was all about, maybe see other photos of her. Get an idea of her body so he could be more accurate in his thoughts as to what those breasts might look like. Would she be petite and her breasts small with tiny pert nipples? Or would she be an Amazon with double Ds and nipples the size of half dollars? He was hoping for the former.

He minimized his email program and clicked on the Google tab. He searched for Pauline O. Rossi. The screen flickered and several links popped up. He chose the one for Wikipedia. A picture flashed on the screen and there she was, standing in front of a red and white jet in front of a hangar.

She was petite. With a headful of dark curls lifting in the wind. They looked soft. He wanted to run his fingers through the fiery strands. And then grip a handful and use it to pull her head back for his kiss. A pummeling kiss that she would feel down to her toes. His eyes looked lower to where her button-down white shirt was pulled tight across her chest. 38Cs if he wasn't mistaken. They *would* spill into his hands. And if she was a natural brunette, the nipples would be a dusky cinnamon color. His mouth watered. And there on the bed, leaning against the headboard with his legs stretched out in front of him, he reached under his laptop and gripped his erection.

Within seconds the computer was pushed aside and his shorts shoved down. He closed his eyes, fisted himself, and pictured Pauline on her knees playing with her breasts and tugging on the nipples he'd put clamps on, despite her crying out that they hurt. He knew they did. But he also knew it was what she needed. He imagined that he bent and pinched her clit, still swollen from the swats he'd landed on her pussy. She'd cry out, then shudder and come from a man-induced tidal wave wetting his fingers.

He groaned and visualized coming on her breasts. But in actuality, he ended up coming on his own chest. There, in bed by himself.

His laptop was humming when he looked up and saw that in his haste to get it out of the way his finger had touched the mouse pad and scrolled down. The scene had flipped to another picture of Pauline. This one was a headshot. A graduation picture with her in a cap and gown. The cap part of the mortarboard covered the crown of her head, but long chestnut curls fell to her shoulders on either side. She had rose-colored lips that were full and smiling. And eyes the color of wet emeralds. She looked Irish, not French as her first name would imply, or Italian as her last name would suggest. He could not wait to get her in front of him on her knees wearing nothing but that cap. Well . . . and the nipple clamps. And he wanted to taste the wetness that would come out of her when he bent her over his knee and spanked her until she came.

It was now two in the morning but he couldn't wait to message her and tell her that she was now his sub, and he was her Dom.

Your Dom says to come here and show me your pussy.

Her reply was instant: **Tell me where you are and I'll be on my way. I've already called to have them get my jet ready.**

He typed back the name and address of the Ocean Isle Beach airport along with his cell phone number, telling her to call him when she got there, that he would be there within ten minutes to pick her up.

He left the program open on the laptop in case she sent another message, but pushed it farther way so he could get some sleep. He had a lot to do in the morning. He had to go to Myrtle Beach to get some of the toys he'd need, and then he'd arrange a suite at one of the luxury resorts. The fully occupied *Cockpit* was no place to be when breaking in a new sub. He'd need a place where she could be uninhibited. No doubt the first time she submitted to him there would be tears. And if he had anything to say about it, there would also be screams from multiple orgasms.

At nine the next morning, six San Diego time time, she texted to his phone that she was next in line to taxi down the run way at SAN. She signed the text Etty.

It was late afternoon and he had just gotten back from buying some sex toys in Myrtle Beach when her text came in. He had already called a friend and used his connections to secure special accommodations for the night. He had also arranged for Sean to be the "taxi driver," from the beginning of the book, *The Story of O*.

When they got back from collecting her at the airport, he would introduce her to his friends at *The Cockpit*. She would be topless. Then the two of them would have a late lunch on the walled-in terrace on the ground level where she would remain topless for him. Then he would drive her to their penthouse suite in North Myrtle Beach for the night—topless all the way. It would unnerve her, but he knew that the side windows on Dev's Hummer were too dark for anyone to see through. Only he would be able to see her tits. He smiled. She would die of shame when men looked their way, thinking they were looking at her, when they were actually admiring Dev's Beast, with its spectacular custom paint job.

When they reached the hotel and valet parking, he would

allow her to button only two buttons on the tiny little shirt he'd bought for her at Adam & Eve. But only if she exchanged her panties for it. Those she would have to pull off from under the teeny tiny little black skirt he had also bought for her to wear. He would have bought her a pair of CFM heels, but he had no idea what her size was. He was probably not going to be looking at her feet anyway.

His bag had been packed since early this morning so he'd be ready to pick her up when she texted. And now she had. She was here. He couldn't remember ever being so excited for a first date. Of course, this was not your typical first date scenario. He texted back:

Your first order: You will answer to Pauline as long as you are my submissive. Your second order: Get ready to combust. You're going to be so shamed, so hot, you're going to burn for me.

Chapter 122—Rutger & Pauline
By the Book

By the time Sean pulled the car up to where she was waiting, she had already secured her plane on the tarmac and was literally walking around kicking the tires to check the pressure.

Rutger had left his walking boot in the trunk of the car, as he hadn't wanted her first impression of her Dom to be a man hobbling about. That was not the masterful image he wanted to convey.

Forcing the ache in his calf to abate and his leg to cooperate, he walked over to her and picked up her flight bag. As he bent to kiss her on the cheek he said, "Welcome to the beach, Beautiful." As his lips grazed her smooth cheek, he whispered close to her ear, "I am so looking forward to training you."

He was delighted to see her full-on blush.

He indicated the waiting car. "It's not a French taxi, but it will have to do," he said as Sean stepped out to take the bag from Rutger to put it in the trunk of Sean's Jaguar sedan. Sean returned to the driver's door without having said a word or been introduced to her.

Rutger took her by the elbow and walked her to the open back door, then indicated for her to slide onto the rear seat before closing the door. His foot ached but he braved the pain of walking around the car and sliding across the seat to join her. He was determined not to use the boot, now sitting beside her small case, when she got her first command from her Dom.

Her small hand rested on the smooth leather. He placed his hand over it and it disappeared under his, only her tiny pink fingernails peeked out through his long fingers. He looked over at her, smiled, and then nodded at Sean.

The car pulled away from the airport and headed down Beach Drive.

With the flick of his thumb against the side of a survival knife that he'd taken from his pocket, he ejected the blade. He touched the tip to a button on her white blouse. "I hope you're wearing that white lace bra."

"Of course," she said with a tentative smile. The smile disappeared when she saw Sean staring at her through the rear view mirror.

Rutger saw her eyes flare as she tilted her head to one side, processing what was about to happen. He saw the moment she realized how things were going to go, that this was for real. She took in a deep breath, her ample chest heaving and causing the knife that was resting on her shirt button to rise. She gave the tiniest nod of her head as she accepted was he was about to do.

He grinned. His little submissive was submitting. His heartbeat sped up and his muscles tightened. He felt his cock react. Just the thought of her accepting his terms made him dizzy with lust. He mentally jerked back to the moment. There would be time later to try to figure out how this little slip of a woman could make him weak and lightheaded so quickly.

For Rutger's part, he couldn't breathe; he was so taken with her. She stoically faced front, allowing him to slice the buttons off her pristine silk blouse then to use the tip of his knife to spread the shirt plackets revealing her gorgeous breasts held up in the most inviting way inside the lacy demi bra.

He carefully ran the tip under the elastic in the center and let the tension help to slice up through the binding, severing the lovely, sexy bra in half. He forced himself to breathe. With gentle fingers he pulled the cups away, revealing her sweet plump breasts. Round and full, with dusky tips, they were flawless bubbles that matched her frame perfectly.

He inhaled the scent of her—something spicy and exotic, but clean and uniquely hers. He picked out essences of gardenia and cloves, and knew he would recall this moment anytime he smelled either.

He slit each strap close to her shoulder and the bra,

hanging open, fell into her lap. Not moving his eyes from her breasts, he dropped it onto the floorboard.

He stared down at her, taking in the sight. Her tits were gorgeous. 34Bs if he wasn't mistaken, firm and perky, with what looked like the perfect weight, with dusky mauve areolas, the tips of which were getting hard and drawn in from the sudden exposure and the air-conditioning of the car. It hadn't been in the plan, but he lifted his hand to cup one, hefting it and then brushing his thumb over the peak. They both groaned. Actually, he thought Sean might have too.

He moved away and sat back on his seat.

She stared at the review mirror watching the driver as he forced his eyes back to the road, only to have them return over and over to drink her in. Rutger studied her as she looked at Sean, her nostrils flaring. He noticed that she seemed more concerned with having Sean's eyes on her than his. Yes, Sean's reaction to her bared breasts, not his, was the one that was unnerving her the most. His had been expected; she'd been prepared for it. But not for Sean's.

No one spoke as Sean drove through the light at 904, then down Sunset Boulevard to the circle that would lead up to the Sunset Beach Bridge and over to the island. When the sedan crested the bridge, he looked over at her and saw her admiring the view. No one could keep from admiring the peaceful waterway and the wending marshes with the graceful waterfowl settling in to feed among the rushes of spartina edging the tidal waters.

The high-rise bridge was not a stretch of road for a driver to be taking his eyes away from, but he noticed Sean ogling her tits between keeping his eyes on where they were going.

He had a few questions to ask her, and now was the best time. They'd be at *The Cockpit* soon.

"Do you have a safe word?"

"Zebra."

He raised his brows in question.

"Zebra Echo is part of my plane's call letters."

"Oh. And hard limits?"

She looked to the pocket where he had put his knife. "No cutting, no hot wax, no burning, no urine fountains, or fisting. Not crazy about suspension or being caged, but I'll try to be open-minded."

He smiled and made a fist, turning it this way and that for her to inspect it. "Sure?"

She snorted. "I'm sure I don't want something the size of a bowling ball in any of my orifices."

He laughed. "I agree to your hard limits. And if I'm even tempted with the soft ones, we'll discuss it. I'm not into caging or suspension but I do like to tie a submissive up and sometimes blindfold them. Any problems with those?"

"No. I've been held in a bind before, and I kinda liked it. And I've read that blindfolding intensifies every sensation."

He gripped her hand again and smiled. "It does. You'll soon see. Are you on birth control?"

"Yes."

"Close to your period?"

"Just had it."

"So we can forgo condoms? We're both clean?"

"I can go online if you need to see my latest health report. I haven't been with anyone in quite some time."

"Neither have I, having my foot in a boot has kept me out of circulation and left me . . . unmotivated in that department."

"Your last blog said you were in a celibate state while training for another Ironman."

"I am. Or I was until I got your emails last night. I'll get back to it, it's still a few weeks away. Mostly, I'm trying to strengthen my foot. I can go without the boot now for long stretches but my ankle is still weak, and I'm working the kinks out from the lack of using it. I need to get back on the track next week. Enough about me, today is all about you."

He turned in his seat and cupped her left breast. It felt heavy and full in his hand. He bent and kissed the tip. He heard her quick indrawn breath and smiled. He liked how responsive she was.

They turned left at the four-way intersection and Sean drove east toward *The Cockpit*. "The house where we're going to have a late lunch is one I own with nine of my best friends. We're all Stanford grads and went to college together. I would trust every one of them with my life. Now I want to trust them with you. I want you to meet them, topless." He gave her a moment to absorb this, watching carefully for her reaction. Her chest heaved slightly and she shivered, but she seemed to accept the idea, if not exactly pleased with it.

"Then we will dine on an outside terrace, just you and I. And after that, I will take you to a suite I've arranged for us in North Myrtle Beach where we'll spend the night together, to see if this works for us. Any objections, still up for this sexual adventure?"

She looked down at her chest. Then up to the mirror at Sean, then over at him. She was flushed with embarrassment. It was charming. And he was enchanted with her.

He gave her his best smile. "I think you're right. I suspect that you just might need a little shame and humiliation to get off. Can we work on that?"

She looked at his face, took every aspect in. She knew he was testing her. If she couldn't do this—give him complete control over her body, then she couldn't be submissive. Not to him or to anyone else.

She had to do this or she'd never know if this was what she truly wanted . . . needed. And it did excite her. In a very strange, yet thrilling way.

He was patiently waited her out. He knew how important it was for her to choose to do this. Anything he required, she'd have to agree to. If she didn't, she had come all this way for nothing.

She continued to take in every feature of his face as he looked back at her . . . patiently waiting. He could sense that she couldn't wait to please a man in this way. He was hoping she would decide he was the man who would get the honor to own and tame her.

"I want you to be proud of me. If showing all your friends my tits is what you want me to do, then I'll do it." She nodded and whispered, "Yes, I'll do it."

"Yes, sir," he commanded.

"Yes, sir," she said, in a small breathy voice.

"Good girl."

Those two words did more for her sexually than any others she had ever heard uttered. She felt her panties dampen. Felt her breath hitch.

He watched as her eyes glazed over. He felt a shudder go through himself in reaction. Sweet Lord, this was unreal. She was as true a submissive as he'd ever seen. She was perfect.

When they got to the beach house and Sean drove onto the circular drive, Rutger heard Pauline take a deep breath. She hoped she was ready for what was coming, that he wasn't rushing things. But for her to be initiated safely, it had to be among his friends, not among strangers.

As soon as Sean pulled up in front of the impressive cantilevered stone steps leading up to the house, put the car in park and turned off the ignition, Rutger reached for her. Taking her by the shoulders he turned her to face him. Then he took each nipple between his thumbs and forefingers and pinched. She hissed in sharply, and at first he thought he might have been too brutal with her. But then she groaned in the unmistakable way women had of letting you know, you'd given them pleasure.

Sean had remained seated behind the wheel. Now he lifted a hand and adjusted the rearview mirror. She raised her head and watched Sean's face as he took in her impossibly hard peaks. Rutger kept his eyes focused on hers as she stared at Sean. He broke their contact by ducking his head and taking her right nipple between his lips and sucking. The other nipple got the same treatment. She visibly melted into the seat, her shoulders relaxing, her body becoming pliant. She reached for him, but he couldn't allow her to touch him, not yet. Her grabbed both of her hands, held them up to his lips and kissed her fingertips. "You can't touch me, unless I allow it. This is about you. Being the object of my affection. And me wanting to show you off because I am proud of you. You do understand that right?"

"Yes," she whispered. The lazy haze in her eyes told him she was beginning to go under. She was turned on and ready to serve her master.

Taking a deep breath, he opened his door. Standing in the drive, he straightened his trousers, adjusting his cock in the process and walked around to her side and opened her door. He reached a hand down and smiled when she took it. Then he pulled her up and out of the car. She was still wearing her torn blouse; that he would allow. But her breasts, due to their ample size, were gloriously uncovered. Anyone driving by or looking out a window of one of the adjoining houses would be able to see how exposed she was. His cock strained against his zipper, slid off to the side and tented his pants in a very weird but obvious angle. If she had bothered to look in his direction, she would have seen he had an impressive hard on straining the material of his pants. But she wasn't looking down. Her shoulders were back, her head was held proud, her eyes focused solely on his, seeking his approval. Later she would bow in deference to her Dom. Right now she was projecting an arrogance he knew she wasn't feeling. She was perfect. He was very pleased with her. With a finger to her chin, he leaned in and kissed her. A quick meshing of their lips, signifying she was his.

Sean closed his door and faced her, taking all of her in, minutely examining her tits in the bright sunshine. She stood and let him.

Then Rutger tucked her arm in the crook of his, and led her slowly up each step to the front door. A sexual fog could make one clumsy. He would not leave her side now.

Sean got to the door before them and opened it. Then

angled his head to enjoy the view of her lightly jouncing breasts. Inside, the cool air drew her nipples in even tighter and Rutger couldn't remember ever being this turned on by a submissive's obedience.

He walked her through the foyer, commenting on the antique mirror on the wall that he'd brought back from Spain, and then up the flight of stairs to the first level where he could hear the guys gathered in the kitchen. Before he'd left to get her from the airport, he'd given them a quick run through so they all knew they'd be introduced to her before he took her out to the terrace for a quick bite. Then they would head out to the penthouse suite in North Myrtle Beach.

When they got to the top of the stairs and walked through the archway that opened to the expansive kitchen, he reached for her hand and gripped it. She was breathing hard and she was flushed, but didn't seem overly unnerved yet.

He pulled her forward and began introducing her. "This is Pauline. Pauline, these are my good friends."

Then one by one, he pulled her forward to meet each man. There were five men standing around the kitchen, all leaning against countertops and enjoying the view. The others weren't home right now, but five was plenty for a newbie's first topless scene. Each man stared at her, none able to take his eyes from her chest.

"Palo is our Italian world traveler."

Palo bowed, took her hand and kissed it. His eyes glued to her breasts, he said, "Ciao Bella."

To Rutger he murmured an aside, "Bellisimo, caro mio." His sarcastic way of saying life is hard my friend.

"Kyle, our resident chef who graciously fixed our meal for us."

Rutger heard her gasp as she recognized the world famous chef. He saw her hands jerk as if to lift them so she could cover herself. He subtly jerked on the one he was holding and she settled. Just to be sure, he reached behind her and captured her other hand. Then joined them together behind her back, both hands now held tightly by one of his. Pulling her arms behind her and down caused her back to arch and the effect was lost on no one. Her tits jutted out even further and they were now on display even more blatantly.

Kyle winked at her and said, "Welcome to our humble abode, beautiful lady."

He got a wry smile and a lifted eyebrow from her about the humble abode part.

"Dev, who's about to drop his drink," he pointed to a dark haired, dark-eyed man who looked like he could hold his own in a bar fight, "and Brent, who designed and help build this house. And you've already met Sean, who agreed to be our driver."

He dropped his hand from where he had been keeping hers prisoner behind her back, and wrapped an arm around her shoulders. "Gentlemen, if you'll excuse us. I promised her lunch before I take her to North Myrtle Beach where I intend to spank her ass."

She gasped and turned red from the tops of her breasts to the tips of her ears.

Rutger chuckled. "There are no secrets in this house. They all know why you're here. And there's no shame in it." He leaned down and whispered in her ear, "Unless that's what you want to experience . . ." he nipped her on her ear lobe.

She shivered and damned if his cock didn't jump at the sight of her flushed and eager. He knew she had to feel his hard length against her ass.

He led her outside and as they walked down the steps, she took in the ocean view, and seemed to relax as there was no one on the deck or in the yard to ogle her.

Once out on the terrace, he helped her to a seat facing the ocean then removed her ripped blouse. Now she was completely bare from the waist up. And it was a most marvelous view. Much better than the ocean, he thought. He took a seat beside her and within seconds Kyle carried out trays laden with slivers of marinated beef, and long strips of grilled vegetables. Rutger had asked Kyle to keep things light and for them to be high on the protein side.

After Kyle had set out the trays, and then blatantly ogled her until she burned with shame, he left them alone, closing the door leading back into the house and silencing the conversations going on within the house.

He heard her sigh with relief and he chuckled. He lifted her hand and kissed the center of her palm. "You did amazing. I am so proud of you. Every one of them is so jealous of me right now."

She looked over at him and grinned. "I was so nervous."

"It didn't show. That was, until you recognized Kyle."

"Oh my God, I adore him! I watch his show all the time."

Rutger raised his eyebrow to her. "There will be no adoring any other man. As long as you're my sub, you belong to me and you have eyes for no other. Do you understand?"

"Yes."

He quirked his brow, "Yes, what?"

"Yes, sir."

"That's better. Now are you hungry?"

"Starved!"

"Good." He stood and pulled out her chair and indicated for her to stand.

"What are you doing?"

He tossed the seat cushion onto the flagstone. "You're going to kneel beside me, and I'm going to feed you."

Chapter 123—Rutger & Pauline
"O" is not for Orange

"This is an amazing suite. It's got everything you could possibly need," she whispered in a reverent voice as she opened cabinets in the kitchen.

He opened a panel on a custom walnut cabinet that ran the width of the living room. Inside, on intricately engraved custom pegs set into a button-tucked velvet backing, were all manner of floggers, switches, feathers and whips. He ran his fingers over each "toy" moving down the length of the box. "Yes," he whispered in a husky voice, "everything you could possibly need."

He noted her look of shock and laughed. "Relax. These aren't mine. Although I do have an impressive collection myself, they're not here. Whereas you are."

"Whose place is this?"

He walked over to where she was and opened and closed the drawers around the island. Nodding with pleasure at what he saw inside.

"I called in a favor from a friend. It belongs to a local BDSM Club, they rent it out to their members."

"A very good friend I would say."

"We used to do some scenes together in my early days. And this is pay back for all the times I put on a demo at his club."

" You did a demo for a BDSM club?"

"Yeah. All the kink you could never imagine," he chuckled, yet there was no mirth in his laughter.

"I wonder at your candor. You seem disheartened by it all."

"I kind of am. I'm tired of investing so much of myself and walking away with nothing. Some of it's getting old, you get used to things and then get inured to them. And I get leery because most of the hangers-on have an agenda. And it's hard to go incognito in those clubs now. You found my email address pretty easily, from a fan-based blog?"

"No, a contact in the sports field. I was surprised that you answered, and then agreed to meet me."

"All you're looking to do is find out who you really are. I get that. I don't mind helping with those kinds of things. But then once you get what you want, you'll move on too."

"Maybe. You never know. Each time I thought about contacting you, I backed away. Each time I thought I could approach you, I held back. Yet, here we are. There's something serendipitous here."

"Why do you think that is?" His fingers strolled lightly up the soft skin on the inside of her arm. Then he slowly retraced the trail over and over again. He smiled when she shivered.

"My wicked side won out. Did I tell you I have a wicked side? A bad girl lives inside me who thinks about all the dirty things she wants to have done to her. And then I have a timid side. Owned by a good girl who thinks she should live in a convent and go to vespers three times a day to pray for the evil side."

"Mmmm. A convent. That poses some interesting scenarios. I've often thought of myself as having a priestly manner. A sub used to call me Father McGowan when she came."

"That's odd. Did you ever ask her why?"

"She wasn't my sub, I was just doing some scenes with her at the club. But I assume that was the name of her parish priest, either then or while she was growing up. She'd say, 'Oh, Father McGowan, we shouldn't . . .' but then dig her nails into my ass and suck my dick to the back of her throat. After I came, she'd always thank me for her penance. I heard she married a defrocked priest. So . . . your evil side finally won you over and you contacted me. Tell me about your good side."

"My good side wants a committed long lasting love

affair . . . honesty in that relationship, with a partner that's fun and challenging. Unfortunately, all the prospects for that kind of happy-ever-after haven't ever done anything for my libido. They don't make my body sing. So my bad side taunts me and says, "Get someone to own you, to control you, to possess you and make you theirs. A man who will punish you when you don't obey him, and one who will make you beg to get back into his good graces. Then you'll have something."

"So you're finally listening to the evil witch, hearing her out and giving her some space in your head?"

"Yes, I'm finally listening to her wayward ways." She threw her arms wide and turned in a circle. "And here I am."

"And what is she telling you?"

"She's telling me that I need to be open minded to being spanked, flogged, whipped, blindfolded, tied up, and gagged until I submit willingly to anything you desire. I figure until I give her a chance, I'll never find out which side of me is destined to be the victor."

He ran a thumb across her bottom lip. "I already know which side is going to win out." He looked into her eyes with such intensity, such protectiveness, such a look of desire and lust that she felt her stomach drop just like it always did in the elevator going to the roof of Rockefeller Center.

"Take off your clothes. This time I want you to show off your tits *and* your pussy. But just to me. And you will not complain when I keep you that way until I've looked my fill."

She felt her toes curl while her labia actually fluttered as moisture escaped. *Yes, she sighed. Yes!*

Her eyes blinked and she had a moment when she wasn't sure she would keep her footing. He noticed and reached for her.

"Oh, Baby. You are a she-devil incarnate. It's going to be fun bringing you to heel. Now, either get those clothes off in the next ten seconds or I'll tear them off and you'll have to walk out of here naked when we leave."

She quickly pulled off the top he'd allowed her to tie

in a knot at her belly, and then stripped her stretch jeans down, taking her panties with them. She toed her Go Walks off and stood before him naked.

He looked her up and down, his eyes missing nothing.

"Muss your hair."

She reached up and ran her fingers through her thick curls, pulling them out and away from her face.

He quirked a brow and looked pointedly at her pubes.

"Oh," she said, and scruffed up the thick thatch that made a dark vee between the tops of her thighs.

"That's an impressive forest you have there."

She flushed, her face and chest flaring in uneven red tones. "I didn't know how you might want it."

"Generally I like pussies bare. But yours intrigues me. We'll leave it natural, for now." He pointed to the island counter in the center of the kitchen. It was topped with a massive slab of black obsidian granite. Over it was a grid of lights that lit up the area below.

"Climb up there and spread your legs. Put your feet on the corners and your butt on the edge. Time for you to show me my new play toy."

On her way over to the counter and while climbing up onto a barstool to get herself up to the countertop, she had a moment of doubt. For some reason, she'd thought this would progress slower. Hell, he hadn't even kissed her yet. Weren't they supposed to make out and grope each other a little first?

As soon as she got up onto the cold island countertop, he turned on the overhead light. Not only did the area light up, but also she was front and center in the spotlight like a stripper on stage.

He stood with his hands on his hips and watched her as she positioned herself as instructed. Then he strolled over, stood between her splayed knees and looked down at her most intimate place. And Lord help her, she couldn't stop the wetness that pooled, and then trickled down the crack of her ass to wet the granite.

Not saying a word, he left her to go over to the sink. She turned her head and watched him as he washed his hands with meticulous care. Oh my. It was obvious that he intended to use them in some fashion. He walked back with a dishtowel, drying them. Then he folded the towel and draped it over her eyes. Her mind shifted to his perspective and she imagined how she must look to him right now. Naked and allowing a stranger unheard of liberties.

Using both hands, he gently tugged at her public hair, smoothed it back from her genitalia, and then thumbed it away from what it was he wanted to see.

"Here it is," he said as if uncovering something he'd been looking for for some time. "The jewel."

Then he began to tap lightly on her clit. Over and over again until she began to moan. He stopped at the sound then used his forefinger to move it back and forth as if studying it. Intimately. Another moan slipped out. And he stopped again. She bit her lower lip to stop herself from making any noise, and he chuckled.

A finger slid down her outer fold, parting it, though she was sure it had to have been gaping open anyway. As soon as his finger breeched her outer defenses to find the smooth inner fold she shuddered. She felt fingers from each hand pull back her slick petals to reveal the entrance to her vagina. She shivered and moaned. Then hurriedly dug her teeth into her lip again.

"So pretty. And so wet. You're excited about what I'm going to do to you here, aren't you?"

"Yes," she breathed.

"You like me looking at you like this, don't you?"

"Yes."

"Would you like it if I let other men look at you like this?"

There was silence for all of thirty seconds before she whispered, "Yes."

"I thought so. Maybe we'll do that one day. Today, I'm

going to tie you down and spank you. I'm going to spank your pussy."

She hissed.

"Do you know why I'm going to spank your pussy?"

She shook her head back and forth.

"Because you want to show it to other men. And it's mine. It belongs to me. You're going to have to beg me to let you show it off when the time comes. But I'll probably allow it, as this pussy of yours is too pretty not to share. But right now," he said as he slid a finger inside her and made her come up off the countertop, "right now, I'm going to play with it. Spank it. And eat it. Then I'm going to watch it flutter when you come for me."

He walked around the island thinking, no man is ever going to see this woman's pussy but me. Then he opened one of the drawers and removed four straps. He secured one to each wrist and wound it around a hook hidden on the underside of the counter. Then he did the same for her ankles, pulling them apart so her legs were spread wide.

He walked back to the living room area and grabbed three throw pillows. He shoved one under her ass to lift her butt high, another under the middle of her back to ease the strain of the hard granite. Then tucked one under her head, and while he was there, he bent and gave her their first kiss.

His lips moved over hers opening them to his tongue and then he drew swirls along each lip tasting her, before entering her mouth and devouring her. Her moan set the blood in his veins on fire. When she touched his tongue with hers, trying to draw it into her mouth, he followed it and traced her mouth, letting out a low moan himself.

Then he opened another drawer and removed a blindfold.

He removed the towel and tossed it toward the sink and looked down into her face. His eyes met hers. Then he pointedly looked down her body, letting her see where he was looking, Where his eyes were caressing her breasts and belly, examining her splayed womanhood, following the lines of her legs to her polished coral toenails. "Your body is gorgeous. Every inch." He bent and lightly kissed each nipple. It wasn't enough. She wanted more.

"Remember you have a safe word if anything becomes too much for you. I expect you to use it if you feel distressed in any way. I can learn your body and your mind over time, but this first time, I need you to stop me if anything is too much for you. Will you do that?"

She nodded and looked up at him, his eyes meeting hers until the blindfold was placed over her eyes and secured behind her head.

"You are mine," he whispered. "And I can do anything I want to you. And I want to do it all."

Using his thumbs and forefingers he pinched her taut nipples. They peaked like hard pebbles atop her round breasts. With her wrists attached to the sides of the countertop her breasts had flattened, leaving a valley between them. He kissed all along the area between them. The groan she let out threatened to unman him. He was hard behind the zipper in his pants. Harder than he'd been in a long time. In fact, he never thought he'd get this hard again. Sex had gotten old. Even with a new partner every night, he had gotten bored with it all.

But this tiny sprite of a woman with her perky firm tits and thickly covered mound, lying openly spread on a granite countertop displaying herself to him was turning him on like no other. He could feel the head of his penis engorge a few drops in preparation for fucking her.

But he had a long way to go before he allowed himself to sink inside her and spill into her. First, he would make her come by tugging on her nipples, lavishing her breasts, getting her mind to visualize herself as he saw her, and then sucking on that sweet little clitoris.

He moved to stand behind her head now, pinching and tugging on her nipples and drawing out the most exquisite sounds.

"There's a mirror on the wall a few feet in front of your pussy and I'm looking right between your legs now as you arch and open wider for me. I see you trying to close your knees and flex your thighs, trying to get something to rub against you. It's okay to lift up and squirm, but keep those knees wide. I want to see everything that pretty pink pussy is doing. And right now it's glistening with your sweet dew. Your lips are opening for me. I can see the entrance to your vagina. You want to show me your honey hole, don't you?"

"Yes."

"Tell me."

"I want to show you."

"Show me what? What do you want to show me?"

"My pussy."

"Say it all."

"I want to show you my pussy."

"I can see you flooding with moisture, your lips are fluttering, and your vagina is quivering. You are so naughty to show me your pussy like this, so very naughty. I'm a stranger to you, and we've only just met. But look at you. Knees wide, showing me everything. What a bad girl you are. Very, very bad. And oh, so very beautiful. He pinched her nipples and tugged on them even harder. She arched off the table and groaned.

He moved to her side and let his fingers drift down her torso. Then he used the pad of his middle finger to graze her clit on the way to her sex. He smoothed his finger over her drenched lips, reveling in the silky texture and slick coating. Wetting his finger with it, he slid it down and entered her. Her long, drawn out moan was his reward.

His finger explored her depths and then he used it and another to fuck her a few times. He moved into position at the end of the counter and placed his mouth on her. He kissed every area and then used his lips to draw her clit out. His tongue laved it, circled it, and lapped at it. His fingers went back to her breasts to pinch and tug on her nipples some more, and to bite lightly on the undersides of her breasts. She cried out in a low harsh moan.

He tugged harder. Thought about getting out his nipple clamps, but didn't want to take the time to leave her. His nostrils flared as he drew in her essence. He couldn't wait any longer; he situated himself between her legs again. Wrapped his lips around her clit and sucked. She lifted her ass up off the counter and tried to press herself into his mouth. He pulled her back by a hank of her pubic hair, and didn't let her. She keened with want.

"More, more, more," she hissed. "Please."

He smiled. And sucked a tad bit harder.

"More!" she screamed. "Pleeease!"

He gave her more. More tugging, more licking, more sucking. Then he drew her clit between his teeth and sucked hard.

Her whole body went spastic, unintelligible babble joined loud, "Ohhh, Ohh, Ohhhhhs." He stopped sucking and let his tongue feel her orgasm. Her first man-induced orgasm. He didn't know if her solo attempts had produced more than insignificant jerks and trembling. But this one sure had. He had felt her clit explode as if some entity was dying to come out of that tiny ball of pulsing flesh and high-five the world. The quivering of her nub slowed, and then it shrank considerably. Her thighs stopped quaking and her overall body trembling wound down. This was a woman who had come undone. By his tongue. He was elated. More than elated, ecstatic.

He stood and watched as the opening to her vagina convulsed one last time. A thick coating of cum sluiced out to coat her inner lips. He'd seen many women come over the years, too many to count. But this time, the sight sent him to his knees.

He caught himself using his elbows, and leaned in to lick her clean. Then couldn't stop and settled in to give her another. His tongue delved into every crevice, then his fingers joined in on the action, first one then two, and within minutes he sent her over the edge again.

She heard herself scream out as another climax washed over her, causing her raised thighs to tremble and her toes to curl around the edges of the countertop.

Chapter 124—Rutger & Pauline
Herr Gräfenberg

When her body stopped trembling, he walked around the counter and his hand captured hers as it gripped the strap. Her fingers were white from holding the strap so tightly. He gently loosened her fingers and released her hand from the restraint, rubbing it and meshing her fingers with his. Then he did the same for the other hand. He undid her feet, gave them a good rubbing, and then removed the blindfold.

He looked down at her face. Her riot of hair was framing her dewy face and her blue eyes were bright with a new kind of carnal knowledge. He was sure now that she had never possessed such a wondrous awakening of her body with another man.

He lifted himself onto the counter and climbed over her body, settling himself and covering her body with his.

"You were perfection in your submission. Absolutely magnificent." In this push-up position, he powerfully lowered himself in increments and took her lips, savoring each soft petal and laving them both with lingering swipes of his tongue. He tasted salt from the sweat on her upper lip and inserted his tongue into her mouth and fed the salty tang back to her. He kissed her for long minutes, lavishly learning her mouth and nipping at her lips, murmuring, "Perfection," and "I'm so very pleased with you."

Then he vaulted over the side, and lifted her into his arms. He carried her into the bedroom and placed her on the duvet while he stripped his clothes off.

She languidly turned her head and watched as he shed each item and she rewarded him with saucer eyes when his long, pulsing length was revealed.

"You are mighty impressive," she whispered, her voice raspy.

He smiled and winked. "The better to service you, my dear."

He left the room and returned with two cold bottles of water. He placed one on the nightstand and handed her the other. "Drink, you need to hydrate. You came like a raging river. You must be parched."

"Thank you." She drank a quarter of the bottle and placed it next to his on the night table.

"I've been looking at your pussy for a long time—"

She smiled over at him, "I know. My thighs are burning from the laser eyes you had on me."

He walked over to the bed and massaged one inner thigh and then the other while smiling back at her. He tangled his fingers in her pubic hair. "What I was going to say, is that something about your pronounced bush—your thick, full, sculpted triangle of stark dark hair reminded me of someone else's. At first I thought I was recollecting the youthful mound of Sophia Loren when she posed naked for a cheesy photographer before becoming famous. But then my mind filled in with the answer."

"What's the answer?" she asked as he drew tiny circles on her belly. Her nipples were responding to the air conditioning kicking in, and with one knee bent and her foot resting flat on the duvet, she looked comfortable in her skin. Different from his earlier perusals of her, when she'd been anxious and insecure. He'd done his best to allay her fears, but really, if her hot spot was humiliation, a fair amount of angst was paramount.

"I know you said you read the book *The Story of O*, but did you ever watch the movie?"

"No. My mom gave me a copy when I was a teenager, but I burned it on the stove."

"Well maybe you should have watched it." He looked pointedly at the vee between her legs. You look exactly like Corinne Clery down there."

"Exactly?"

"Well, in the movie there were only flashes of total nudity, and you never saw between her legs. But she was graced with a most generous bush, just like yours. And she trimmed it exactly as you do, unapologetically. I find it immensely arousing. Earthy, shameless, and intoxicating, just like Corinne's was and Sophia Loren's too, for that matter."

"I've always been self conscious about it. Felt there was too much going on down there."

"Don't be. I know men who would love for their wives or girlfriends to give up their sparse landing strips and go natural."

"I'll bet her breasts weren't small like mine."

"Yours are not small. More the high end of medium plump. They are perfect. The shape. The weight. The delectable nipples that are so responsive . . . But Corinne's *were* bigger . . . in fact; I imagine her breasts won her that part. She was a stunning woman. As are you."

"Was?"

"Well, the movie was done in the mid 70s. I imagine she's a bit long in the tooth now."

"Long in the tooth . . . do you know where that expression came from?"

"Mmm. Nope." From his smile, an outsider would have sworn he loved it when she went off on a tangent.

"Horses teeth continue to grow with age, so it became a common practice to examine their teeth to determine how old they were. Long in the tooth meant you might be getting a nag."

He climbed over her, covering the lower half of her body with his. "I love your mind. Almost as much as I love your body. But now it's time for you to submit to me and give me what *I* need. And that would be my cock inside you, fucking you." He caged her head with his arms.

She felt his erection brush against her thigh as he moved up her body. His eyes met hers and he took in her face as if studying her. When his eyes lingered on her mouth, and she felt him probing her, she trembled under him.

"You are beautiful, Pauline. Truly beautiful, you know that?"

"I have been told I'm merely attractive."

"You're much more than attractive. You're stunning. And I love that lower lip of yours, the way it pouts under the bow of your top lip. I can't wait to see those lips wrapped around my cock. But that's going have to wait as I need to fuck you right now. You know what the first part of my name means?"

"Rut?'

"Yes."

"Like a deer ruts?"

"Used like that it means a season when the stags fight for dominance to gain access to the doe for sexual activity. As a noun it can mean a furrow, a groove, or a channel. But as a verb, from its Latin origins as *rugitus* and Middle English to *rugire*, it means to roar.

"So as your dominant, I mean to gain access to your sweet sex, plow through your channel, and then roar like a lion when you clench my cock with your hot, tight pussy. And all you have to do is take me in and enjoy it.

"I think I can do that."

"Well, if you're not too overwhelmed by the most marvelous orgasm I'm going to bring to you first, you could remember to call out my name as you come."

He positioned the head of his cock at her opening. Feeling how slick she was, he drenched himself in her wetness.

"I would rather you make me come so hard I can't remember your name," she whispered through clenched teeth.

In one stroke he shoved inside her. She gasped and he groaned.

"I know I said I loved your mind, but God, I do love your body."

He closed his eyes and savored the moment of their joining. And then repeatedly made the headboard hit the wall so hard and so fast that it sounded as if someone was pounding into the wall using a jackhammer above her head.

When he slowed to grind against her, then used both hands to lift her ass to meet the root of his penis that was pressing just where she needed him, she arched her back, curled her toes into the mattress and keened, "Ruuuutttgerrr!"

Her flying over the edge sent him spiraling out of his universe, and taking one last plunge, he threw his head back as his jaw clenched and he roared, pulsing a hot stream of his seed inside her.

After many moments of complete and utter bliss when he didn't even know where he was, nonetheless his name, he collapsed, falling onto the bed beside her with a heavy, protracted sigh.

"You are O," he whispered. "And every story she inspired."

"I came," she whispered, the awe apparent in her voice. "With you inside me."

He turned on his side and rested his head on his fist, his arm bent at the elbow. "Sweetheart, you've come four times so far."

"Yes, but that orgasm came from inside me. My first vaginal orgasm," she sighed with dazed wonder.

He chuckled. "Was it more spectacular than the other three?"

"Oh yes. Sometimes I can give myself those, the clitoral ones. But they're tiny, only a second or two. Almost not worth the set up and stimulation time involved. Not quite as stupendous as you with your mouth, but that last one . . . I would die to have another one like that."

He rolled her onto her back and bit the side of her breast. "Well, fortunately for you, you won't have to do that."

He took her nipple into his mouth and laved it, circling the tip and then nipping at it. Then he jumped up and out of bed.

She looked up at him, questioning his sudden departure from her.

He extended his hand. "Come, let me bathe you. Then we will move on to phase two of your submissive training."

"Phase two?"

"Yes. That's when I spank your ass until it's red. And maybe, if you're a good girl, I'll flog you with the softest strands of brushed suede money can buy."

"What do I get if I'm a bad girl?"

"My cock in every opening you have."

"Bad girl doesn't sound so very bad . . ."

"Maybe I'll invite some of the bellhops we saw downstairs to come up and join me," he said with an evil grin as he tugged her up and gathered her into his arms.

"Uhh, okay. Good girl it is. Not ready for sharing."

He kissed her on the side of her neck. "Sweetheart, I'm pretty sure that I'm never going to be ready to share you with anyone."

His words, spoken in his deep, gravely, after-sex voice, caused her belly to flop in on itself and butterflies to flutter everywhere in her chest. Him being possessive about her was not something she had expected, and the thought made her nerves shimmer, sending gooseflesh along her arms. God, to have this man want to keep her for himself would be a dream come true. A dream she had lived with for a long, long, time.

"In one of your letters you asked me where you could have gotten this weird kink from. You might be surprised that most girls have it to some extent. The Latin word pudenda, the medical term for what's referred to as the female external genitalia, means shamed, or more accurately, "the whereof one ought to feel shame." It's believed that the word pussy derived from it. Women are predisposed to feel shame when exposing the area they have kept protected and hidden most of their lives. It's only been in the last hundred years or so that men have been allowed to look at a woman's labia. A man became acquainted with the area by touch. Any woman who would allow a man to examine her there was thought to be shameful, wanton, immoral . . . impious. Those feelings continue today, as little girls are encouraged by their mothers to be chaste, pure . . . virtuous.

"Then along comes a man who intrigues them, makes them hot and bothered, gives them tingling sensations down there. They have urges they want satisfied. But how can they and still remain pure?

"The only way is if the decision is taken from them. And that is the reason they like to be tied up or handcuffed. Because they believe themselves to be good girls, yet as hard as they work to deny it, they want to do the things that the bad girls are doing.

"And the only way they can justify that in their minds is if they're tied up or bound in some way so they have no choice. That way they can tell themselves: *I couldn't stop him; I couldn't get away; I had no choice but to let him have his way with me.* The fact that it's beyond their control, and in the hands of another, releases them of their guilt in the forbidden act, since they justify that they had no way to prevent it. They can rationalize that it's not their fault when they succumb to the bidding of a dominant man who ties them up and has his way with them, because the choice was taken from them by the act of him binding their hands . . . tying them down . . . muffling their voice . . . blindfolding them so they can't see the man who has dishonored them. Taking them against their will. When in actuality they get what they really want, without the guilt. Because their psyche said they couldn't have stopped it if had they wanted to."

"So I'm normal."

He laughed. "You are so not normal."

"But you said . . ."

He pulled her into his arms. "You have a legacy to live up to. And permission from your momma—carte blanche if you will—to relax and give yourself up to your needs and wants . . . to a Dom. A Dom you can trust to take care of you and protect you from harm. A Dom who will give you pleasure and take pleasure from you."

"Are you that Dom?"

"I *am* that Dom."

He pulled her from the bed then lifted her into his arms. On the way to the shower, he whispered in her ear, "The seat in the shower is the perfect place for me to see if I can find your Gräfenberg spot."

"Gräfenberg?"

"The man the G spot was named after."

"I've checked. I don't have one."

He threw his head back and laughed. "Silly girl. No woman can find her own. It's not possible to get a finger that high up inside you and crook it at the necessary angle, for the time it takes to stimulate it to ejaculation. That's why she needs a man had to find it."

"Well don't be disappointed if I'm defective. I'm pretty sure one's not up there."

"Bet me."

"What?"

"A blow job. You, naked, on your knees in front of that big picture window, facing the courtyard, taking me into your mouth while people at the swimming pool across the way watch. You'll wear a mask and I'll wear a balaclava so no one will be able to recognize us." He wasn't going to tell her that the suite, do to its nature and what it was designed for, had one way glass for that express purpose. Shame was her kink, and he was going to give it to her. But in a safe way, a way she would suffer no harm.

"Do I have to take that bet?"

"Forget the bet. You have to do anything I tell you to. I own you. You belong to me. I am your Dom and you are my sub. If you continue to do my bidding, I wouldn't be surprised if you earn your collar within the next few months."

"You want to keep me, and keep seeing me?"

"Well, not if you're defective and don't have a Gräfenberg spot," he said with a grin. "So let's take care of finding that little gem right now."

He sat her on the tiled ledge that went around the perimeter of the walk-in shower. Then knelt at her feet. "But first, we are way behind in the kissing department."

He took her lips with his and let his tongue wander. Then her hands slid behind his neck and pulled him closer and she joined in. He marveled at her talented tongue. He was going to find her G spot and win the bet, and then he was going to feel that amazing tongue do its magic on his cock.

Chapter 125—Dev & Gentry
Kitten Caboodle

Dev had just gotten back from the shooting range and was putting his gun in his gun safe when he saw it. A flash of silver.

He spun, gun in hand, just in time to see something dart out the bedroom door. He leapt into action and ran.

He caught up to the culprit at the landing. A big gray cat, traipsing a long white cord after it. He chased it down the steps, through the kitchen and out the open French doors to the upper terrace, calling out, "Hey, hey, hey!" and "Stop you piece of shit, stop!" pretty much all the way. So that by the time he'd cornered the cat on the lower terrace by the steps, where the elevator and outside shower were, he had most of the house's inhabitants behind him.

So there they were. A big ol' hairy cat and a big man pointing a gun. And a group of men staring, eyes wide, some with gaping mouths.

"You're not going to shoot that cat, are you?" Kyle asked.

"He's got my phone cord."

"Ah, so that's where all the electronic cords have been going," Chaz murmured.

"Still, no shooting the cat," Sean called out. "Put the gun down."

"Relax, I'm not going to shoot the cat," Dev said, his exasperation evident.

The cat, looking from one person to another, nonchalantly put its paw on the Hardi-plank siding and a small door opened. Then the cat disappeared behind the opening.

The men all stared, stunned. Only Brent, as the architect of the house, knew that it was a spring-latched door for access to the elevator emergency switches and breakers. Inside was an encapsulated crawl space that went under the steps, but for only a few feet on each side. The small access door was rarely noted by anyone except the exterminator.

Dev inched forward and used his gun to nudge the panel and reopen the door.

He bent and looked inside. "Aw shit!"

"What?" seven male voices said as one.

"Kittens, lots of 'em. And every electronic cord you can imagine chewed to smithereens."

"That's where the charger for my new iPhone went. And my Kindle," said Chaz.

"And my iPad," added Kyle.

"My FitBit," this from Rutger.

"My iWatch," called out Brent.

"My iMac Airbook," said Palo.

"Thank God I never got my electronics unpacked," said Alex who had only arrived two days ago.

It was their last day, and everyone was in the process of packing up. Except for Dev, who was going to stay for another week.

"Well, what do we do? We can't leave these cats here," said Sean.

"I'll shoot them," said Dev.

"You will not!" said Cam.

"Well, what do you suggest?" he snarled back at him.

There was silence for the space of a minute while everyone thought out and rejected solutions.

"We could put them in a tall box with a sign saying free kittens and leave them at the curb," said Dev.

"It's 87 degrees right now Dev, and it's only ten a.m.," said Chaz. "And I'm already late. I'm supposed to be following Mags home in an hour. You're going to be the only one left here to keep an eye on them."

"Yeah, I'm due at Amy's to help her with a cake at noon," said Kyle.

Cam snapped his fingers. "I remember seeing something on WECT about an animal recue group here in Brunswick County. I think it's called RACE or something like that."

Brent pulled out his iPhone and Googled to find the number for RACE cat rescue and read, "R.A.C.E. Rescue Animals Community Effort Incorporated, in Shallotte, North Carolina, number's 910-579-0407."

He dialed the number and explained the problem, then disconnected the call. "They're going to send someone, but not for an hour or two. Somebody's going to have to stay."

All heads turned to Dev.

"Aww, not me. I hate cats."

"You hate everything, Dev. Soften up some, why don't you?" said Cam.

"Besides, you're the one staying an extra week. The rest of us have to leave," said Palo. "That cat and her kittens can't stay here. And someone has to clean up all that cat shit."

"I am not cleaning up cat shit!"

Brent sighed, "Just take care of getting rid of the cats, I'll call the handyman and get him to tighten that latch and to hose out the area. Finder's keepers Dev. They're your cats now. All you have do is hand them off to the rescue people when they show up. "

"All right, all right. But leave me the number in case no one shows."

"I'll get them some milk," said Kyle.

"No! Don't feed them!" yelled Dev.

Chaz shook his head. "Dev, you're one hardhearted bastard, you know that? They're kittens for God's sake."

"I don't care. They shouldn't be here."

"Well they are. And I'm going to feed them," Kyle turned and went upstairs.

An hour later, everyone had left. Fifteen minutes after that, the doorbell rang.

Dev opened the door to a young woman wearing a

flannel shirt over a tank top, jeans and mucking boots, already coated with something brownish gray. His eyes followed the line of her boots, up her legs, to the flannel shirt then to the broad brimmed that had shielded her face from the bright sun. She had an abundance of springy chestnut curls framing her face, green flashing eyes, light coral colored lips, and copper freckles dusting her nose. He was slayed when she removed the hat.

She smiled broadly and said, "Got kittens?"

My God, she was lovely. Farm girl, girl-next-door, feeding chickens on a Hummel plate lovely. Dev just stood and stared.

She repeated herself. "I was told you had kittens?"

"Uh, yes," he said, finally snapping out of it. "Please, come in."

He opened the door wider and his eyes followed her as she came inside. Not so much her, but her jean-clad butt. And her legs in those tall black boots.

"Where are they?" she asked, turning and allowing her loose, unkempt French braid to move from her back to her shoulder.

"Uh, downstairs. I'll show you."

"Nice house," she said as he led her up the stairs and then through the kitchen.

"Thank you. You know, I'm not thinking straight right now. We have to go back downstairs. I should have just taken you around from the front of the house. Sorry."

"No problem. When did you find them?"

"Find what?"

"The cat and her kittens . . ." she looked at him with a frown. For the first time getting a weird vibe. Maybe he had been drinking?

"Oh! Just this morning. We called you right away." He opened the door to the terrace. "I was in my bedroom putting away my gun when I saw this flash of silver out of the corner of my eye and I ran after it."

Oh my, she thought. He has a gun. She quickly stepped through the door, knocking into him in her haste.

He caught her just as she stumbled over his foot and the doorsill.

He looked down and their eyes met.

"You weren't going to shoot the kittens were you?" she said after a long moment of her eyes taking in his. She'd heard of a lot worse things happening to cats, experienced the aftermath of many others.

"No, no. Of course not," he boldfaced lied. "I'd just come from the shooting range is all; the gun was in my hand. No! I would never do something like that."

"Good," she said as she stepped away. "I was worried there for a minute. Now where are they?"

"On the bottom level, by the elevator." He led her down one flight of steps, then around to another.

"Do you live here full-time?"

"No, just a few weeks a year."

"Is it rented out the rest of the time, maybe someone left them here?"

"Oh no, we don't rent the house out. It's only occupied for about half the year though."

"So the cat found a nice place to have her kittens, with no one to bother her."

"Well, until we got here two weeks ago."

"How long do you think she's been here?"

"No idea. But electronic cords went missing from the first day we arrived. We found them all today, under the steps, pretty chewed up, all of them."

She shook her head. "Squirrels, rodents, rabbits, and some cats crawl under cars and get into the engine compartments and chew on the wire coating. The companies use some kind of soy-based oil in the process of making the coating and animals eat it all the time. Maybe electronic cords are the same. I don't know. If the momma is feral, she's probably used to scavenging for food. Do you keep food in the house when you're not here?"

"Well, I actually own the house with nine other guys. *I* don't leave anything here. But they may. I think Kyle does. He's our resident chef. And they all leave booze and wine. And we have a freezer in the basement that's always stocked."

"I mean like chips, crackers, rice, pasta, cereal. Things in bags animals can chew through."

"No, I don't think so. Maybe?"

They were on the bottom level now. Dev pointed. "See that little door under the steps? They're in there. It has a spring latch and the cat apparently figured how to use it."

"Cats are incredibly smart animals. And very resourceful. She just needed a safe place to have her kittens. And with no food readily available, she must have seen your cords as a familiar food source. Hardly good for her though. Was she nursing, do you know?"

"How would I know that?"

"She'd be huge, her belly practically dragging on the ground."

"Well, she's pretty big. But also plenty fast, I had to run to catch her."

"If you managed to catch her, she was likely hampered by her belly. Let's see what you've got here."

She stooped and pulled the little door open. "Clever cat," she cooed in admiration.

The sound of her voice praising that dumb cat sent electric vibrations through Dev's body.

"The kittens look like they're three or four weeks old. They were probably born here, hard to tell for sure though, as the momma licks off the afterbirth from each."

Dev held back a gag. "Interesting." What he wanted to say was "*Ew.*"

"I'm Gentry, by the way."

"I'm Dev."

"There you are momma. Easy, easy, now. Oh, what a

sweet girl! You gonna come to me?" She made some kissing noises with her mouth.

Dev watched her, imaging her mouth in other places. Heat coiled in his groin and flashed through his body.

She tried again, getting down on her elbows, her butt in the air. "Hey, there pretty girl."

He had to turn from watching her. It was doing strange things to him.

She backed away from the door and stood. "Nope, not gonna come willingly. I count five kittens. How many did you see?"

He grimaced, "I didn't count them."

"Don't like cats?"

"I'm more familiar with the big cats." He wasn't going to tell her that he hunted them. It didn't seem as if a woman who worked for animal rescue would be impressed with that.

"You mean the golf courses at Ocean Ridge?"

"Yeah. Lions, Panthers, Tigers, Leopards." He went with it. No point in antagonizing her with his dislike of cats.

She brushed off her hands. "Well, I'm going to go get some food and try to lure the momma out. The kittens will be easy after that. I'll be back in a few minutes. I need to get a carrier and some kibble."

"Can I help?"

"Sure. Maybe you can find some bowls I can use? Put some water in one. I see you gave them milk, but they need water more than anything else right now. It's really hot in there."

"Of course. It would be my pleasure." He felt like a smarmy liar.

"Great."

It took half an hour to get the momma in the cage. By then Dev was smitten. He knew what most people thought of him. They thought he was a troublemaker, a mischievous practical joker, a smart man with deadly aim, but also a fun guy to be with. They knew he cared about his friends but had rare, short relationships with women. But for some reason, he wanted to get to know this woman. This woman whose name meant wellborn. This woman who loved animals. This woman who protected animals, while he hunted them down and killed them to make trophies out of them. He wondered how this would go—if he could even get her to go out on a date with him.

Chapter 126—Dev & Gentry and Palo & Trixie
An Unexpected Delay

Through the open French doors, Dev heard someone stomping around in the kitchen on the next level. He looked up and saw Palo leaning over the railing.

"What are you doing back?" Dev called up to him.

"I rear ended a woman."

"That's usually a good thing, no?"

Palo smirked. Gentry frowned and stomped off.

"Oops. Sorry," Dev murmured.

"I ran into her car. With mine, you dumbass."

"Oh, everybody okay?"

"Yeah. Her car got the worst of it and had to be towed. Mine's drivable but not looking pretty."

"Don't you have to be in Milan the day after tomorrow?"

"Yeah, but I missed my flight, so I'm not going to make the tour. I called and got someone to handle the first few days for me. Helluva morning."

"Geez, I'm sorry. How can I help?"

Palo looked at him oddly, tilting his head and drawing his brows together. "You're being nice, what's wrong?"

Gentry was back at her car, he could see her leaning inside, trying to adjust the carrier on the seat, so he whispered up to him. "I think I'm in love."

Palo hooted and then waved him off as if that was not at all possible.

Gentry came back just then, and Dev introduced her to Palo. Palo thanked her for coming out to help them with the kitten situation.

"I've got to meet this woman I hit and see if we can work things out without upping my business insurance in Italy. It's going to be far cheaper to pay her off than report it in the long run. She's getting an estimate now. I'm going to run to the bookstore. I can't get another flight until the day after tomorrow so I need another book to read to take my mind off this fiasco."

"Okay, I'll see you later."

"Hey, I had to give the woman this address, as my license has the one in Milan. She may call my cell first, or she might just come by here. I said I'd give her a check for the damages and for a rental car. Have her wait if I'm not back yet."

"Okay. What's her name?"

"Trixie. Trixie Sanderson."

"Got it."

Dev turned back to Gentry who was dabbing at a scratch on her arm. "Now for the kittens before she gets too hot in that car . . ."

"I'll be happy to help you."

"Thanks, that would be great."

"Can I get you something for that cut?"

"Yeah, you got some peroxide?"

"We have a big ol' first aid kit. I'll go get it."

He looked up at Palo, who was shaking his head and smiling.

While he got the kit, Gentry got all the kittens into a smaller carrier. He was disinfecting and bandaging her arm when she looked up at him and asked, "So your friend, he's just writing this girl Trixie a check, rather than letting his insurance pay for the damage to her car?"

"He lives in Italy, it's much easier this way."

"Are you guys, what, millionaires?"

He turned his head and was thoughtful for a moment, running through all the names of his friends. "Yeah, I think so. Cam's the only one who might not be. I don't know anything about his finances."

"So maybe, you can . . . uh, make a donation to R.A.C.E.? It's going to cost us money to spray or neuter the kittens, plus pay for their shots and food. And the momma may not be adoptable right away so we'll have her to take care of as well."

He laughed. "How much do want?"

She shrugged. "A thousand?"

"Hmmm."

"Too much? I always start high when someone asks. Don't want to leave money on the table."

He laughed again. "I'll tell you what, you go out to dinner with me and I'll write you a check for $5,000."

"What? That's crazy!"

"Crazy that I want you to go out with me, or crazy me thinking that you would?"

"Crazy you'd pay that much money. Of course I would! Now, I don't have to do anything for that right? This is just going to be dinner?"

"Well, you do have to eat," he said with a smile.

"Oh, I can do that. Sure. No problem. You have a deal!" She put her hand out for him to shake.

He laughed again and shook her hand, hesitant to let it go when they had finished. He couldn't remember a time when he'd laughed so much.

"I just have to take the cats back to the shelter, get them checked in and get cleaned up."

"Where do you want to go for dinner?"

"Oh, it's already costing you so much. Feel free to pick someplace cheap. I eat most anything, as long as it's vegetarian."

He chuckled. "Well, we'll work with that then. Where can I collect you?"

"I'll meet you. It'll be easier. Just text me where."

"How about you just come here since you know the way, and we'll go from here?"

"Okay. Say, six?"

"Perfect."

She handed him a card that had her name and phone number printed on it under the R.A.C.E No Kill banner.

He took the card and walked her and the kittens in their carrier to her car. Her hips wiggled enticingly when he had to get behind her on the stone path. He smiled. For the first time in a long time, he had something to look forward to that wasn't a drink in his hand.

A preview of *The Beach Boys of Sunset Beach—End of the Season*

Chapter 1—Sean & Sandy
His Secretary

Sean had been back from his annual reunion vacation since Monday. Now it was Friday evening, and Sandy had an unsettled feeling. Her boss had been looking at her a little oddly this week. A few times she caught him staring at her with his brows creased as if looking at a rare creature he'd never seen before.

She'd gone to the restroom several times to see if her makeup was smeared, or if a strand of hair had come out of its twist. Checked her blouse to see if it was buttoned properly, scanned her hose for runs. And then this morning, out of the blue, he'd asked her to work late tonight. That was odd because it was so rare, but not unheard of, in their four years of working together.

At five, her phone set chimed in her ear, and when she touched the sensor to answer the summons, she heard Sean say, "Sandy, are you free to take some dictation now?"

"Yes, Sir. I'll be right there."

She stood, straightened her black pencil skirt, checked to make sure her white silk blouse was properly tucked in, and ran a hand under her French twist to make sure it was still tidy. She kept a small tube of Vaseline in her middle desk drawer. She used a little to slick her lips. She often found herself biting her lower lip when she was around Sean, and keeping her lips moist kept her from doing that as much. She picked up her notebook and pen and walked the few feet to his office door, gave the cursory two quick taps and entered.

He was pacing back and forth when she walked into his office. That was unusual. She didn't know whether to sit or stand. He sensed it and motioned for her to take one of the two chairs in front of his desk.

She waited as she watched him return to his desk. But he didn't sit; he just stood, staring down.

This was so odd. It unnerved her. What could be wrong? She didn't know of anything business-wise. Was someone in his family ill?

She looked over at him; he was staring at her now. She forced her eyes to meet his. His eyes bored into hers as if looking for something hidden in them, and seemingly asking a hundred questions.

"I know we agreed two years ago that you would do some personal shopping for me from time to time when I lost my personal shopper at Nordstrom's. You told me then that you knew me better than a stranger would, and offered to take over those duties, and I offered to compensate you for the extra time involved."

"You didn't like the swim suit." She was crushed. She thought the boards shorts perfect for him, conservative in dark blue, yet with just the right touch of a tropical embellishment in the form of a white flowering hibiscus.

"No, the swim suit was fine. Perfect in fact." Still standing, he reached down and opened the long center drawer. "But when did I ask you to select my reading material?"

He took out a book and tossed it to the center of his desk.

As soon as she saw the quilted cover, she recognized it as the book she had been in the middle of reading. The book that she had been looking for, for over two weeks.

She felt her face flush while every other part of her body turned to ice. *Oh dear God. He had seen what she had been reading. Her go-to recreational reading—the smuttiest erotica about secretaries and bosses she could find.* She was mortified. Beyond mortified. Shamed, humiliated, and embarrassed in so many ways.

He gave her a few moments to absorb the enormity of this. Then said, "I don't know if it was intentional or not, but I found this in my suitcase."

Her mind flashed back to when she'd added the swimsuit to his already packed suitcase. The suitcase had been open on the sofa in his office waiting for her to add the items he had requested her to buy. She had already added the shorts and the new tropical beach shirts the previous day. She had purchased the swimsuit during her lunch break on the last day he was going to be at work before leaving on vacation. She had been reading her book at the park before returning to the office. And now she remembered that she had put the book in the shopping bag along with the swimsuit wrapped in tissue for the walk back to the office. She had put them both right into the suitcase, bag and all. She cringed at the memory.

That night and the following days she had looked everywhere for the book and had finally accepted the fact that she had left it on the park bench and bought another copy.

"You're fired."

"What?" Surely, he couldn't do that? Wasn't she entitled to read whatever she wanted on her own time?

"I said you're fired."

She just blinked. She had no idea what to say to that.

"Until Monday. When you can ask for you job back again."

"What?" she sounded like a parrot with a one-word vocabulary.

He walked around his desk, and leaned back against it, his feet crossing at the ankles. He looked professional and dominant in his Armani suit; wearing the tie she had bought him last Christmas. He always seemed in control, in command of everything. Even now, while firing her, he was resplendent and masterful.

"This weekend I plan on tying you up and giving you the longest tongue lashing you've ever had, and I want to make sure you know it's not a job requirement that you *submit* to it. Because this weekend, you have no job while we play at being boss and secretary. You will call me Sir, and I will call you Avery, the name of the secretary in your book. And you will do my bidding, and I will see to it that you come. Over. And over. And over again."

She looked him in the face, her eyes wide, her lips parted with surprise. She saw the heat in his eyes and felt wetness pool in her panties.

Was she dreaming? Had the man she fantasized about submitting to actually told her he wanted to tie her up . . . and lash her with his tongue?"

She bit her bottom lip. Realized what she was doing and soothed it with her tongue before pressing her lips together.

He drew in a long breath. She watched his nostrils flare. He knew. He knew she was wet for him. And he knew exactly what she wanted. What Avery had wanted. It was all in that book. *My God, he'd read her book.*

He walked back around to his desk, took out a piece of paper with typing on it, and placed it on her side of the desk in front of her. "You'll need to read this. If this is what you want, you'll need to sign it. If it's not, this conversation never happened and we'll go back to our normal business relationship Monday morning."

She was speechless. She had no idea what to say or what to ask.

He knew this. He pushed the paper closer to her. "Read," he instructed. "Then we'll see if you have any questions."

She took a deep breath, pulled the paper forward and began to read.

Read more about the Beach Boys of Sunset Beach in:

The Beach Boys of Sunset Beach—Another Reunion
Due out in 2021

Contact me at www.jacquelinedegroot.com for comments. Thank you for reading my latest book.

Jack DeGroot

About the Author

Jacqueline DeGroot and her husband, Bill, live in Sunset Beach. They spend their time being Nana and Poppy to their grandson, Cohen, and their granddaughter, Alanna. They love to go RVing when they're not working on projects around the house or entertaining guests.

2018 and 2019 were difficult years as Jack lost both her sister and her mother within months of each other. It was a real mind stopper for the book she had in progress, as her creative mind couldn't get back into it for some time. Thankful for her faith, her friends, and her family, who got her through everything, she's glad to be back writing.

The Kindred Spirit Mailbox and How it Came to Be

Once upon a time, there was a woman named Claudia who loved walking the tide line of Sunset Beach. She was young and beautiful and resembled a young Ava Gardner. She lived in Hope Mills, NC, which is near Fayetteville, and worked as a kindergarten teacher. She was single, but hopeful of finding a husband and having children one day. It was a great joy for her to be able to travel to the beach on weekends. She was an artist and a musician and a happy-go-lucky, free-spirited woman who loved nature and thought everyone a kind soul. She wore a Carnaby Street-styled hat to protect her head from the sun and had a canoe named *Moses* she hid in the marshes to use when she visited the beach. She was adventurous and was once known to have climbed the extremely tall crane left empty on weekends when workers were installing the huge rocks for the jetty at the Little River Inlet, a few hundred yards past the mailbox. She sat at the top of the crane and took panoramic pictures—one by one, for a 360 panoramic view. Frank Nesmith keeps the roll of pictures curled in a coil at the bottom of a tin bucket.

For many years Claudia had a daydream while walking the tideline—she saw a rural mailbox shimmering in a sandbar. She called the dream a "mirage," as she could never reach the mailbox stuck in the sand. It would disappear before she got to it. She continued to wonder why she saw the mailbox mirage. In her thirties, she gathered a mailbox mounted on a post, along with a posthole digger, and she trekked down to the beach to the east end of Sunset Beach toward Tubbs Inlet..

When she had difficulty getting the mailbox to remain embedded in the sand, she turned and there was Frank Nesmith. Another Kindred Spirit. A man who she would come to love and a man who would help her fulfill the purpose of her mirage—to secure Bird Island as the beautiful coastal reserve it is today, and will be, for future generations. It has since been moved to the west end of the island.

Emma's Slumgullion

A warm, beefy, tomato-based, medium pasta stew with depression–era roots, similar to Goulash but with more intense flavors. We always double the recipe as it freezes so well, and is a great gift to neighbors.

1 lb. ground chuck
1 Tbsp. butter
1 Tbsp. olive oil
1 yellow onion chopped
1 green bell pepper chopped
1 package fresh mushrooms coarsely chopped
1 15-oz. can stewed tomatoes
1 15-oz. can tomato sauce
1 8-oz. can tomato paste
2/3 cup tomato ketchup (don't be a snob and omit this, it's crucial)
3 tsp. minced garlic
1 tsp. dried oregano
½ tsp. chili powder
1 cup water
8 oz. corkscrew or medium elbow pasta
Salt and pepper to taste (approx. ¼ tsp. of each)
Shredded Parmesan cheese, optional

Use good quality Italian tomatoes such as Tuttorosso or Centa, and Heinz, Hunt's, or Delmonte ketchup.

In a large Dutch oven or stew pot, add olive oil and butter together. Sauté the onion and green pepper until the onions are opaque. Add the mushrooms, then add the ground chuck and cook until lightly browned. Add the stewed tomatoes, tomato sauce, tomato paste, ketchup, garlic, oregano, chili powder, water, and salt and pepper. Cover and simmer for 45 minutes. Stirring occasionally. Meanwhile cook the pasta to al dente stage and drain. When the 45 minutes is up, add the pasta to the pot and simmer 10 minutes more. Ladle into bowls. Add a scant amount of shredded Parmesan cheese if desired.

CPSIA information can be obtained
at www.ICGtesting.com
Printed in the USA
LVHW051625010623
748371LV00020B/472